PRAISE FOR THESE
New York Times
Bestselling Authors

Janet Dailey

"A master storyteller of romantic tales,
Dailey weaves all the 'musts' together to
create the perfect love story."
—*Leisure Magazine*

Barbara Delinsky

"When you care to read the very best,
the name of Barbara Delinsky should
come immediately to mind."
—*Rave Reviews*

Elizabeth Lowell

"For smoldering sensuality and exceptional
storytelling, Elizabeth Lowell is incomparable."
—*Romantic Times*

Janet Dailey has enjoyed unprecedented success as a romance writer. Since publishing her first novel, *No Quarter Asked,* in 1976, she has gone on to publish more than eighty-five novels, which have sold in ninety-eight countries and nineteen languages worldwide. In addition to her immense reader appeal, Janet treasures the fact that she was the first American author to be accepted by Harlequin. Between 1976 and 1984, she wrote sixty-nine novels at the rate of twenty-five pages per day! These days, her books frequently enjoy long runs on the *New York Times* bestseller list, making her one of the most popular female writers in America.

Barbara Delinsky was born and raised in suburban Boston. She worked as a researcher, photographer and reporter before turning to writing full-time in 1980. With more than fifty novels to her credit, she is truly one of the shining stars of contemporary romance fiction! This talented author has received numerous awards and honors, and her books have appeared on many bestseller lists. With over twelve million copies in print worldwide, Barbara's appeal is definitely universal.

Elizabeth Lowell is a *New York Times* bestseller with over four million copies of her books in print. One of romance's most versatile and successful authors, she has won countless awards. She has written several romance bestsellers as Elizabeth Lowell, and with her husband, Evan Maxwell, she has written mysteries as A.E. Maxwell and romantic suspense as Ann Maxwell.

Summer Lovers

Janet Dailey
Barbara Delinsky
Elizabeth Lowell

Harlequin Books

TORONTO • NEW YORK • LONDON
AMSTERDAM • PARIS • SYDNEY • HAMBURG
STOCKHOLM • ATHENS • TOKYO • MILAN
MADRID • WARSAW • BUDAPEST • AUCKLAND

HARLEQUIN BOOKS
225 Duncan Mill Road, Don Mills,
Ontario, Canada M3B 3K9

ISBN 0-373-83352-0

SUMMER LOVERS

The publisher acknowledges the copyright holders
of the individual works as follows:

STRANGE BEDFELLOW
Copyright © 1979 by Janet Dailey

FIRST, BEST AND ONLY
Copyright © 1986 by Barbara Delinsky

GRANITE MAN
Copyright © 1991 by Two of a Kind, Inc.

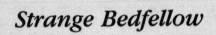

Strange Bedfellow

CHAPTER ONE

THE AIR WAS CLEAR and the moon over Rhode Island was new, but there was a tangle of cobwebs in her mind. Dina Chandler couldn't seem to think her way out of the confusion. She shut her ears to the voices quietly celebrating in other parts of the house and stared out the window.

A shudder passed through her. It couldn't have been from the night's chill, since the house was comfortably heated. Her blue eyes slid to her arms, crossed in front of her, hugging her middle. Perhaps it was the cold weight of the precious metal around her finger.

Dina turned from the window. Her restless gaze swept the library, noting all that was familiar. Interrupting the dark, richly paneled sides of the room was a wall of bookshelves, floor to ceiling. A myriad of deeply toned bindings formed rows of muted rainbows. A sofa covered in antique velvet faced the fireplace, flanked by two chairs upholstered in a complementing patterned fabric. In a corner of the room stood a mahogany desk, its top neat and orderly.

The door to the library opened and Dina turned. Her hair shimmered in the dim light, a paler gold than the ring on her finger. A pang of regret raced through her that her solitude had been broken, followed by a twinge of remorse that she had felt the need to be alone at this time.

Closing the door, Chet Stanton walked toward her, smiling despite the faintly puzzled gleam in his eyes.

"So this is where you've got to," he murmured, an unspoken question behind the indulgent tone.

"Yes," Dina nodded, unaware of the sigh in her voice, or how forced her smile looked.

As he came closer, her gaze made a detached inspection of him. Like hers, his coloring was fair, sandy blond hair falling rakishly across his forehead, always seeming to invite fingers to push it back in place. His eyes were a smoke blue as opposed to the brilliant shade of hers.

At thirty-six, he was twelve years her senior, a contemporary of Blake's, but there was a boyish air about him that was an integral part of his charm. In fact, it was with Blake that Dina had first met Chet. The cobwebs spun around that thought to block it out. Slim and supple, Chet was only a few inches taller than she was in her heels.

He stopped in front of her, his intent gaze studying her expressionless face. Dina was unconscious of how totally she masked her inner turmoil. As his hands settled lightly on her shoulders, she was passive under his touch.

"What are you doing in here?" Chet cocked his head slightly to the side, his gaze still probing.

"I was thinking."

"That's forbidden." His hands slid around her and Dina yielded to his undemanding embrace, uncrossing her arms to spread them across his chest.

Why not? His shoulder had become a familiar resting place for her head, used often in the last two and a half years. Her eyes closed at the feathery caress of his lips over her temple and cheek.

"You should be in the living room noisily celebrating with the others," he told her in mock reproof.

Dina laughed softly in her throat. "They're not 'noisily' celebrating. They don't 'noisily' do anything, whether it's rejoice or grieve."

"Perhaps not," he conceded. "But even a restrained celebration should have the engaged couple in attendance, namely you and me. Not just me alone."

"I know," she sighed.

His shoulder wasn't as comfortable as it had seemed. Dina turned out of his unresisting embrace, nerves stretching taut again as the niggling sense of unease and confusion wouldn't leave. Her troubled gaze searched the night's darkness beyond the windowpanes as if expecting to find the answer there.

With her back turned to him, she felt Chet resting his hands on either side of her neck, where the contracted cords were hard bands of tension.

"Relax, honey. You've let yourself get all strung up again." His supple fingers began working their magic, gently kneading the coiled muscles in her neck and shoulders.

"I can't help it." A frown puckered her forehead despite the pleasant manipulations of his hands. "I simply don't know if I'm doing the right thing."

"Of course you are."

"Am I?" A corner of her mouth lifted in a half smile, self-mocking and skeptical. "I don't know how I let you talk me into this engagement."

"Me? Talk *you* into it?" Chet laughed, his warm breath fanning the silver blond strands of her hair. "You make it sound as if I twisted your arm, and I'd never do that. You're much too beautiful to risk damaging."

"Flatterer!" But Dina felt old, old beyond her years.

"It got me you."

"And I know I agreed willingly to this engagement," she admitted.

"Willingly but hesitantly," added Chet, continuing the slow and relaxing massage of her shoulders and neck.

"I wasn't sure. And I still don't know if I'm sure."

"I didn't rush you into a decision. I gave you all the time you wanted because I understand why you felt you needed it," he reasoned. "And there won't be any marriage until you set the date. Our agreement is a little more than a trial engagement."

"I know." Her voice was flat. Dina didn't find the necessary reassurance in his words.

"Look—" Chet turned her to face him "—I was Blake's best friend."

Yes, Dina thought. He had been Blake's right arm; now he was hers. Always there, ready to support her decision, coaxing a smile when her spirits were low and the will to go on had faded.

"So I know what kind of man your husband was," he continued. "I'm not trying to take his place. As a matter of fact, I don't want to take his place any more than I want you to take his ring from your finger."

His remark drew her gaze to the intertwining gold band and diamond solitaire on the third finger of her left hand. The interlocking rings had been joined by a third, a diamond floret designed to complement the first pair. It was Chet's engagement ring to her.

He curved a finger under her chin to lift it. "All that I'm hoping is that with a little more patience and persistence I can carve some room in your heart to care for me."

"I do, Chet," Dina stated. "Without you, I don't know how I would have made it through those months when Blake was missing—when we didn't know if he was alive or dead. And when we were notified that he'd been kil—"

The rest of her words were silenced by his firm kiss. Then he gathered her into his arms to hold her close, molding her slenderly curved shape to his lean, muscular body.

His mouth was near her temple, moving against her silken hair as he spoke. "That's in the past. You have to forget it."

"I can't." There was a negative movement of her head against his. "I keep remembering the way I argued with Blake before he left on that South American trip," she sighed. "He wanted me to go to the airport with him, but I refused." Another sigh came from her lips, tinged with anger and regret. "Our quarrels were always over such petty things, things that seem so stupid now."

"The strong vying with the strong." Chet lifted his head to gaze at the rueful light in her eyes. "I'm partial to strong-minded women."

His teasing words provoked the smile he sought. "I suppose I have to admit to being that, don't I?"

A fire smoldered in his look, burning away the teasing light. "And I love you for being strong, Dina." His hand slid to the small of her back. "And I love you for being all woman."

Then his mouth was seeking hers again in a kiss that was warm and passionate. She submitted to his ardor, gradually responding in kind, reveling in the gentle caress of his hands that remained short of intimate. Chet never demanded more from her than she was willing to give. His understanding restraint endeared him to her, making her heart swell with quiet happiness.

When he lifted his head, Dina nestled into the crook of his arm, resting her cheek against his shoulder, smiling with tender pleasure. That lock of hair, the color of sun-bleached sand, was across his forehead. She gave in to the impulse to brush it back with the rest, knowing it would spring forward the instant it was done. Which it did.

"Feel better?" His fingers returned the caress by tracing the curve of her cheekbone.

"Mmm."

"What were you thinking about when I came in?"

Her hand slid to his shirt, smoothing the collar.

"I don't know. I guess I was wishing."

"Wishing what?"

Dina paused. She didn't know what she had been wishing. Finally she said, "That we hadn't told the others about our engagement, that we'd kept it to ourselves for a while. I wish we weren't having this engagement party."

"It's just family and friends. There's been no official announcement made," Chet reminded her.

"I know." She usually had no difficulty in expressing herself, but the uncertainty of her own thoughts made it impossible.

Something was bothering her, but she didn't know what it was. It wasn't as if she hadn't waited a proper time before deciding to marry again. It had been two and a half years since Blake had disappeared and a little more than a year since the South American authorities had notified her that they had found the plane wreckage and there had been no survivors.

And it wasn't as if she didn't love Chet, although not in the same tumultuous way she had loved Blake. This was a quieter and gentler emotion, and probably deeper.

"Darling—" his smile was infinitely patient "—we couldn't keep our engagement from our family and friends. They need time, too, to get adjusted to the idea that you soon won't be Mrs. Blake Chandler."

"That's true," Dina acknowledged. It was not an idea that could be implanted overnight.

The door to the library opened, and an older woman dressed in black was framed in its jamb. An indulgent smile curved her mouth as she spied the embracing pair. Dina stiffened for an instant in Chet's arms, then forced herself to relax.

"We've been wondering where the two of you had gone," the woman chided them. "It's time you came back to the party and received some of the toasts being made."

"We'll be there in a minute, Mother Chandler," Dina replied to the woman who was Blake's mother, her mother-in-law.

Norma Chandler was the epitome of a society matron, belonging to all the right garden clubs and fund-raising organizations for charity. Her role in life had always been the traditional one, centered around her home and family. With both husband and son dead, she clung to Dina as her family and to her home as security.

"If you don't, I'm afraid the party will move in here, and there's hardly enough room for them all." A hand touched the strands of pearls at her throat, the gesture indicating such a thing could never dare happen at one of her parties. The pearl-gray shade of her elegantly coiffed hair blended with the jewelery she wore.

"We'll be there in a minute, Mother Chandler," Chet added his promise to Dina's. With a nod the woman closed the door, and Chet glanced at Dina. "Do you suppose you'll be able to persuade her to wear something other than black to our wedding?"

"I doubt it." She moved out of his arms, a faintly cynical smile curving her lips. "Norma Chandler likes portraying the image of a tragic figure."

Within a few weeks after Dina's marriage to Blake, Kyle Chandler, his father, had died unexpectedly of a heart attack, and Norma Chandler had purchased an entire wardrobe of black. She had barely been out of mourning when they received news that Blake's plane was missing. Instantly Mrs. Chandler began dressing in black, not waiting for the notification that came a year ago declaring her son to be considered officially dead.

"She approves of our marriage. You know that, don't you?" Chet asked.

"Yes, she approves," Dina agreed, "for the sake of the company." And for the fact that there would only be one "widow" Chandler instead of two—but Dina didn't say that, knowing it would sound small and unkind when her mother-in-law had been almost smothering in her love toward her.

"Mother Chandler still doesn't believe you're capable of running the company after all this time," Chet concluded from her response. He shook his head wryly.

"I couldn't do it without you." Dina stated it as a fact, not an expression of gratitude.

"I'm with you." He curved an arm around her waist as she started for the door to leave the room. "So you won't have to worry about that."

As Chet reached forward to open the door for her, Dina was reminded of that frozen instant when Norma Chandler had opened the door seconds ago. She wondered if the same thought had crossed her mother-in-law's mind as it had her own. She had recalled the numerous times Mrs. Chandler had opened the library door to find Dina sitting on Blake's lap locked in one of his crushing and possessive embraces. This time it had been Chet's arms that held her instead of Blake's. She wondered if her mother-in-law was as aware of the vast differences between the two men as she was.

In the last months, after the uncertainty of Blake's fate had been settled and there had been time to reflect, Dina had tried to imagine what the last two and a half years might have been like if Blake had lived. Theirs had been such a brief, stormy marriage, carrying the portent of more years of the same, always with the possibility that one battle could have ended the union permanently.

Chet, on the other hand, was always predictable, and the time Dina spent with him was always pleasant. Under his supportive influence she had discovered skills and potentials she hadn't known she possessed. Her intelligence had been channeled into constructive fields and expanded to encompass more knowledge instead of being sharpened for warring exchanges with Blake.

Her personality had matured in a hurry, owing to the circumstances of Blake's disappearance. She had become a very confident and self-assured woman, and she gave all the credit for the change to Chet.

Some of her misgivings vanished as she walked out with Chet to rejoin the party in the main area of the house. There was no earthly reason not to enjoy the engagement party, none whatsoever.

The instant they returned to the spacious living room, they were engulfed by the sedate gathering of well-wishers. Each seemed to display a reverence for the antique furniture that abounded in the room, beautiful Victorian pieces enhanced by paintings and art objects. The atmosphere decreed formality and civil behavior.

"I see you found the two of them, Norma," Sam Lavecek announced belatedly. His voice had a tendency to boom, an abrasive sound that drew unnecessary attention to their absence from the party. "Off in some secluded corner, no doubt." He winked with faint suggestiveness at Dina. "Reminds me of the times you and Blake were always slipping away to cuddle in some corner." He glanced down at the brandy in his hand. "I miss that boy." It was an absent comment, his thoughts spoken aloud.

An awkward tension charged the moment. Chet, with his usual diplomacy, smoothed it over. "We all miss him, Sam," he asserted quietly, his arm curving protectively around Dina's shoulders.

"What?" Sam Lavecek's initial reaction was blankness, as if unaware that he said out loud what was on his mind. He flushed uncomfortably at the newly engaged pair. "Of course, we do, but it doesn't stop any of us from wishing you much happiness together," he insisted and lifted his glass, calling the others to a toast. "To Dina and Chet, and their future together."

Dina maintained her facade of smiling happiness, but it was an odd feeling to have the celebrants of their engagement party consist of Blake's family and friends. Without family herself, her parents having been killed in an automobile crash the year before she had met Blake, there had been no close relatives of her own to invite. What friends she had in Newport, she had met through Blake. Chet's family lived in Florida.

When Norma Chandler had asked to give them an engagement party, it had been a difficult offer to reject. Dina had chosen not to, finding it the easiest and quickest means to inform all of the Chandler relatives and friends of her decision to accept Chet's proposal. She wasn't blind to her mother-in-law's motives. Norma Chandler wished to remain close to her. All her instincts were maternal, and Dina was the only one left to mother.

But the engagement party had proved to be more of a trial than Dina had thought. The announcement had raised too much inner restlessness and vague doubts. None of the celebrants could see that. She was too well schooled in concealing her feelings. When the party ended at a suitable hour, no one was the wiser. Not even Chet suspected that she was still plagued by apprehensions when he kissed her good night. It was something Dina knew she would have to work out alone.

OVER THE WEEKEND, the news of their engagement had filtered into the main office of the Chandler hotel chain in Newport. Dina felt certain she had spent the bulk of the morning confirming the rumors that she was engaged to Chet.

She sincerely doubted that there was anyone in the building who had not stopped at her office to extend congratulations and questioning looks.

A mountain of work covered the massive walnut desk top—letters to be answered, reports to be read and memos to be issued. With her elbows on the desk top, Dina rested her forehead on her hands, rubbing the dull throb in its center. Her pale blond hair had grown to the point where it could be pulled to the nape of her neck in a neat bun, the style adding a few years to her relatively youthful appearance.

The clothing she wore to the office was chosen, too, with an eye to detracting from her youth. Today, it was a long-sleeved blouse of cream yellow with a wine-colored vest and skirt, attractive and stylish yet professional-looking.

The intercom buzzed and Dina lifted her head, reaching over to press the button. "Yes?"

"Harry Landers is here to see you, Mrs. Chandler," was the reply from her secretary, Amy Wentworth—about the only one of the executive staff younger than Dina was.

"Send him in."

Dina picked up her reading glasses, which were lying on a stack of papers she had been reading, and put them on. She could see to read without them, but invariably after hours of reading the eye strain became too much. Lately she had taken to wearing them almost constantly at the office to avoid the headaches that accompanied the strain, and subconsciously because they added a businesslike air to her appearance. There was a wry twist of her mouth as the doorknob to her office turned, an inner acknowledgement that she had been wrong in thinking everyone had been in to offer congratulations. Harry Landers hadn't, and the omission was about to be corrected. As the door opened, her mouth finished its curve into a polite smile of greeting.

"Good morning, Harry."

The tall and brawny white-haired man who entered smiled and returned the greeting. "Good morning, Mrs. Chandler." Only Chet used her Christian name at the office, and then only when they were alone. "I just heard the news that you and Chet are getting married. Congratulations," he offered predictably.

"Thank you," she nodded for what seemed like the hundredth time that morning.

There was no silent, unasked question in the look he gave her. "I'm truly glad for you, Mrs. Chandler. I know there are some people here who think you're somehow being unfaithful to Blake's memory by marrying again. Personally, I think it speaks well of your marriage to him."

"You do?" Her voice was briskly cool; she did not care for discussions about her private life, although her curiosity was rising by degrees as she tried to follow his logic.

"Yes—I mean, obviously your marriage to Blake was very satisfactory or you wouldn't want to enter the wedded state again," he reasoned.

"I see." Her smile was tight, lacking warmth. "Blake and I did have a good marriage." Whether they did, she couldn't say. It had been too brief. "And I know Chet and I will, too."

"When is the wedding?"

"We haven't set the date yet."

"Be sure to send me an invitation."

"We will." Dina's hopes for a quiet wedding and no reception were fast dissipating under the rush of requests to attend. An elopement was beginning to look inviting.

"At least you won't have to concern yourself with the company after you're married," Harry Landers observed with a benign smile.

"I beg your pardon?" Dina was instantly alert and on the defensive, no longer mouthing the polite words she had repeated all morning.

"After you're married, you can go back to being a simple housewife. Chet will make a good president," he replied.

Why the accent on "simple," Dina wondered bitterly. "My marriage to Chet will have no effect on the company. It will continue to be run jointly by both of us with myself as president," she stated, not wanting to remember that the work had been done by Blake alone. Rigid with anger, she turned to the papers on her desk. "I don't see the monthly report from the Florida hotel. Has it come in?"

"I don't believe so." Her abrupt change of subject warned the man he was treading on forbidden ground. His previous open expression became closed and officious.

"Frank Miller is the manager there, isn't he?"

"Yes."

"Call him and find out where the report is. I want it on my desk by four this afternoon even if he has to telex it," she ordered.

"I'll see to it right away, Mrs. Chandler."

When the door closed behind him, Dina rose from the overstuffed cushion on her swivel office chair and walked to the window. Afterquakes of resentment were still trembling through her. Almost since Blake's disappearance, she had run the company with Chet's help; but her competence to fill the position still wasn't recognized by some of the executive officers.

It hadn't been by design but through necessity that she had taken over. When Blake disappeared over South America, the company had been like a ship without a rudder, without guidance or direction. It had operated smoothly for a while, then it began to flounder helplessly.

The key members of the executive staff, those who might have been competent enough to take over, had resigned to take positions with more solid companies, like rats deserting a sinking ship. That was when Dina had been forced to step in, by virtue of the Chandler name.

It hadn't been easy. The odds were stacked against her because she was young and a woman and totally ignorant of the machinations of the company, not to say limited in experience. Exerting her authority had been the most difficult part. Most of the staff were old enough to be her parents; and some, like Harry Landers, were old enough to be her grandparents.

Dina had learned the hard way, by trial and many errors. The worries, the fears that she had about Blake, she had to keep to herself. Very early she discovered that the men who offered her a shoulder to cry on were also insistently offering their beds.

More and more in those early days, she began turning to Chet for his unselfish and undemanding support. Not once did he make a single overture toward her, not until several months after Blake's death had been confirmed. She trusted him implicitly and he had never given her a reason to doubt him.

But Harry Landers had just put a question in her mind—one Dina didn't like facing, but there seemed to be no eluding it.

Shaking her head, Dina walked back to her desk. She picked up the telephone receiver and hesitated, staring at the numbers on the dial. There was a quick knock on her office door, followed by the click of the latch as it was opened without waiting for her permission to enter. Replacing the receiver, Dina turned to the door as Chet appeared.

"You'll never guess what I just heard," he whispered with exaggerated secrecy.

"What is it?" Dina grew tense.

"Chet Stanton is going to marry Mrs. Chandler."

What she expected him to say, Dina had no idea. But at his answer she laughed with a mixture of amusement and relief, some of her tension fleeing.

"You've heard that rumor, too, have you?" she retorted.

"Are you kidding?" He grimaced in a boyish fashion that made her heart warm to him all the more. "I've been trying to get to my office since nine o'clock this morning and haven't made it yet. I keep getting stopped along the way."

"As bad as that?" Dina smiled.

"The hallway is a veritable gauntlet."

She knew the feeling. "We should have called everybody together this morning, made the announcement, then gone to work. It would have made a more productive morning."

"Hindsight, my love," he chided, walking over to kiss her lightly on the cheek.

"Yes," Dina agreed. She removed her glasses and made a show of concentrating on them as she placed them on the desk top. "Now that everyone knows, they're all waiting for me to hand in my resignation and name you as the successor to the Chandler throne." Without seeming to, she watched Chet's reaction closely.

"I hope you set them straight about that," he replied without hesitation. "We make an excellent team. And there certainly isn't any reason to break up a winning combination in the company just because we're getting married."

"That's what I thought," she agreed.

Taking her by the shoulders, Chet turned her to face him, tipping his head to one side in an inquiring manner. "Have I told you this morning how beautiful you are?"

"No." The edges of her mouth dimpled slightly as she answered him in the same serious tone that he had used. "But you can tell me now."

"You're very beautiful, darling."

With the slightest pressure, he drew her yielding shape to him. As his mouth lightly took possession of hers, the intercom buzzed. Dina moved out of his arms with a rueful smile of apology.

She pressed the button. "Yes, Amy?"

"Jacob Stone is on line one," came the reply.

"Thank you." Dina broke the connection and glanced at Chet with a resigned shrug of her shoulders.

"Jake Stone," he repeated. "That's the Chandler family attorney, isn't it?"

"Yes," she nodded, reaching for the telephone. "Probably some business to do with Blake's estate."

"That's my cue for an exit." And Chet started for the door.

"Dinner tonight at eight?" Dina questioned.

"Perfect," he agreed with a wink.

"Call Mother Chandler and tell her I've invited you." She picked up the telephone receiver, her finger hovering above the blinking button on line one.

"Consider it done."

Dina watched him leave. Just for a few minutes, Harry Landers had made her suspect that Chet might be marrying her to elevate his position in the company. But his instant and casual rejection of the suggestion of becoming president had erased that. Her trust in him was once again complete.

She pushed the button. "Hello, Mr. Stone. Dina Chandler speaking."

"Ah, Mrs. Chandler. How are you?" came the gravelly voice in answer.

"Just fine, thank you."

CHAPTER TWO

BY THE END of the week, the excitement generated by the news of their engagement had died down and work was able to settle into a routine again. The invisible pressure the news had evoked eased as well.

Yet on Saturday morning Dina wakened with the sun, unable to go back to sleep. Finally she stopped trying, arose and dressed in slacks and white blouse with a pullover sweater. The other members of the household, Blake's mother and their housekeeper, Deirdre, were still asleep.

Dina hurriedly tidied the room, unfolding the blue satin coverlet from the foot of the four-poster bed and smoothing it over the mattress. Deirdre was such a perfectionist that she would probably do it over again. Fluffing the satin pillow shams, Dina placed them at the head of the bed.

The clothes she had worn last night were lying on the blue and gold brocade cushion of the love seat. Dina hung them up in the large closet. The neck-scarf she folded and carried to its drawer.

Inside, the gilt edge of a picture frame gleamed amidst the lingerie and fashion accessories. It lay face down, concealing the photograph of Blake. Until Chet had given her an engagement ring, the picture had been on the bedside table. Now it was relegated to a dresser drawer, a photograph of the past that had nothing to do with the present. Dina closed the drawer and glanced around the room. Everything seemed to be in order.

After Blake's disappearance two and a half years ago, it had seemed senseless for both Dina and his mother to keep separate households, especially when the days began to stretch into weeks and months. In the end Dina had sublet the apartment she and Blake had in town to move to the suburbs with his mother.

She had thought it would ease her loneliness and provide an outlet for her inner fears, but it hadn't proved to be so. Dina had spent the bulk of her private time consoling Mother Chandler, as she called her mother-in-law, and had received little if any consolation in return.

Still, it was a suitable arrangement, a place to sleep and eat, with all the housekeeping and meals done by others. With most of her time and energy spent in keeping the company going, the arrangement had become a definite asset.

Now, as she tiptoed out of the house into the dawn, Dina wished for the privacy of her own home, where she could steal into the kitchen and fix an early morning breakfast without feeling she was invading someone else's turf. And Deirdre was jealously possessive about her kitchen.

Closing the door, she listened for the click of the lock. When she heard it, she turned to the steps leading to the driveway and the white Porsche parked there. Inside the house the telephone rang, loud in the silence of the pink morning.

Dina stopped and began rummaging through her oversize purse for the house key. It was seldom used since there was always someone to let her in. Before she found it, the phone had stopped ringing. She waited several seconds to see if it would start ringing again. Someone in the house must have answered it, Dina decided, or else the party must have decided to call later in the morning.

Skimming down the steps, she hurried to the Porsche, folding the top down before climbing in and starting the engine. With doughnuts and coffee in a Styrofoam container from a pastry shop, she drove through the quiet business streets.

There was a salty tang to the breeze ruffling her hair. Dina shook her head to let its cool fingers rake through the silken gold strands. Her blue eyes narrowed in decision as she turned the sports car away from the street that would take her to the office building and headed toward the solitude of an early morning ocean beach.

Sitting on a piece of driftwood, Dina watched the sun finish rising on Rhode Island Sound, the water shimmering and sparkling as the waves lapped the long strand of ocean beach. The city of Newport was located on the island of Rhode Island, from which the state derived its name.

The doughnut crumbs had been tossed to the seagulls, still swooping and soaring nearby in case she had missed one. It was peaceful and quiet. The nearest person was a surf fisherman, a stick figure distantly visible. It was one of those times when she thought of many things as she sat, but couldn't remember a single one when she rose to leave.

It was nine o'clock, the time she usually arrived at the office for a half-day's work, minimum. But Dina couldn't think of a single item that was pressing, except the one the family attorney had called about the first of the week.

Returning to her Porsche parked off the road near the beach, she drove to the nearest telephone booth and stopped. She rummaged through her purse for change and dialed the office number. It was answered on the second ring.

"Amy? This is Mrs. Chandler." She shut the door of the phone booth to close out the whine of the semitrailer going by. "I won't be in this morning, but there's some correspondence on the dictaphone I would like typed this morning.''

"I've already started it," her young secretary answered.

"Good. When you have it done, leave it on my desk. Then you can call it a day. All right?"

"Yes, thank you, Mrs. Chandler." Amy Wentworth was obviously delighted.

"See you Monday," Dina said, and hung up.

Back in the white sports car, she headed for the boat marina where Blake's sailboat was docked. She parked the car by the small shed that served as an office. A man sat in a chair out front.

Balanced was the better word, as the chair was tilted back, allowing only the two rear legs to support it. The man's arms were folded in front of him and a faded captain's hat was pulled over his face, permitting only a glimpse of his double chin and the graying stubble of beard.

Dina hopped out of the sports car, smiling at the man who hadn't changed in almost three years. "Good morning, Cap'n Tate."

She waited for his slow, drawling New England voice to return the greeting. He was a character and he enjoyed being one.

The chair came down with a thump as a large hand pushed the hat back on top of his head. Gray eyes stared at her blankly for a minute before recognition flickered in them.

"How do, Miz Chandler." He rose lumberingly to his feet, pulling his faded trousers up to cover his paunch. The end result was to accentuate it.

"It's been so long since I've seen you. How have you been?"

"Mighty fine, Miz Chandler, mighty fine." The owner of the marina smiled and succeeded in extending the smile to his jowled cheeks. "I s'pose you're here to get the *Starfish* cleaned out. Shore was sorry when your attorney told me you was goin' to rent it out."

"Yes, I know." Her smile faded slightly. Getting rid of the boat seemed to be like closing the final chapter about Blake in her life. "But it was pointless to keep the boat dry-docked here, unused."

"She's a damn fine boat," he insisted, puffing a bit as he stepped inside the shed door and reached for a key. "Never know, someday you might want it yourself."

Dina laughed, a little huskily. "You know I'm not a sailor, Cap'n Tate. I need a whole bottle of motion-sickness pills just to make it out of the harbor without getting seasick!"

"Then you sleep the whole time." He guffawed and started coughing. "I never will forget that time Blake came carrying you off the boat sound asleep. He told me aft'wards that you didn't wake up till the next morning.''

"If you will recall, that was the last time he even suggested I go sailing with him.'' She took the key he handed her, feeling a poignant rush of memories and trying to push them back.

"D'ya want some help movin' any of that stuff?'' he offered.

"No, thank you.'' She couldn't imagine the two of them in the small cabin, not with Cap'n Tate's protruding belly. "I can manage.''

"You just give me a holler if you need anything,'' he said nodding his grizzled head. "You know where she's docked.''

"I do.'' With a wave of her hand, Dina started down the long stretch of dock.

Masts, long, short and medium, stood in broken lines along the pier, sails furled, the hulls motionless in the quiet water. Her steps were directed by memory along the boards. Although she had rarely ever joined Blake after her first two disastrous attempts at sailing, Dina had often come to the marina to wait for his return. But Blake wouldn't be coming back anymore.

The bold letters of the name *Starfish* stood out clearly against the white hull. Dina paused, feeling the tightness in her throat. Then, scolding herself, she stepped aboard. The wooden deck was dull, no longer gleaming and polished as Blake had kept it.

It didn't do any good to tell herself she shouldn't have waited so long to do something about the boat. There had been so many other decisions to make and demands on her time. Plus there had been so many legal entanglements surrounding Blake's disappearance. Those had become knots at the notification of his death. Since his estate wasn't settled, the boat still couldn't be sold until the court decreed the dispensation of his property.

The *Starfish* had been dry-docked since his disappearance, everything aboard exactly the way he had left it after his last sail. Dina unlocked the cabin to go below. The time had come to pack away all his things. Jake Stone, the family attorney, had decided the boat should be leased, even if it couldn't be sold yet, to eliminate the maintenance costs and to keep it from deteriorating through lack of use.

It had occurred to Dina that she could have arranged for someone else to clear away his things and clean up the boat. That was what she planned to do when the attorney had phoned the first of the week to tell her he had received the court's permission to lease the boat. But she was here now and the task lay ahead of her.

Opening drawers and doors, she realized there was a great deal more aboard than she had supposed. The storehouse of canned goods in the cupboards would have brought a smile of delight to any gourmet, but Blake had always been very particular about his food and the way it was prepared. Sighing, Dina wondered how many of the cans were still good. What a waste it would be if she had to throw them all out.

Picking up a can, she quickly set it down. The first order was to get a general idea of what had to be done. She continued her methodical examination of the cabin's contents. The clean, if now musty, clothes brought a smile to her lips. It was funny how a person's memory of little things could dim over such a short time as a few years.

A glance at his clothes brought it all back. Blake had been very meticulous about his clothes, being always clean and well dressed. Even the several changes of denim Levi's kept aboard the boat were creased and pressed. A thin coating of dust couldn't hide the snow-white of his sneakers.

Both seemed something of an extreme, yet Dina couldn't remember a time when she had seen him dressed in a manner that could be described as carelessly casual. It made him sound a bit pompous, but the trait hadn't been at all abrasive.

Blake had been used to good things all his life—a beautiful home, excellent food, vintage wines and specially tailored clothes. Spoiled? With a trace of arrogance? Perhaps, Dina conceded. He had been something of a playboy when she had met him, with devastating charm when he wanted to turn it on. Brilliantly intelligent and almost dreadfully organized, he had been exciting and difficult to live with.

Not at all like Chet, she concluded again. But what was the point in comparing? What could be gained by holding up Blake's smooth sophistication to Chet's easygoing nature? With a shrug of confusion, she turned away from the clothes, shutting her mind to the unanswerable questions.

For the better part of the day she worked aboard the boat, first packing and carrying Blake's belongings to the Porsche, where she stuffed them in every conceivable corner of the small sports car. Then she began cleaning away the years of dust and salt spray, airing the mattresses and cushions, and polishing the interior woodwork.

Dirty and sweaty and physically exhausted, she returned the key to the crusty marina operator. Yet the laborious job had been cathartic, leaving her with an oddly refreshed feeling. Lately all her energy had been expended mentally. The hard work felt good even if her muscles would be stiff and sore tomorrow.

She was humming to herself as the white Porsche rounded the corner onto the street where she lived with her mother-in-law. Ahead was the Chandler home, an imposing brick structure that towered two and a half stories into the air. It was set back from the road by a formal lawn dotted with perfectly shaped trees and well-cut shrubs and a scattering of flower beds. The many windows and double entrance doors were a pristine shade of ivory. At the sight of the half dozen cars parked around the cul-de-sac of the driveway, Dina frowned and slowed the car, forced to park it some distance from the entrance.

There wasn't any dinner party she had forgotten, was there, she wondered to herself. The cars resembled those belonging to close family friends. One, the silver gray Cadillac, was Chet's. She glanced at her watch. He had said he would stop around seven for a drink before taking her out to dinner. It was barely five o'clock.

Her mouth formed a disgruntled line. She had hoped to soak in a tubful of scented bubbles for an hour, but obviously that luxury was going to be denied her. And why hadn't Mother Chandler mentioned she would be entertaining this evening? It wasn't like her.

Puzzled, Dina raised the convertible top of her sports car and rolled up the windows. This was not the time to transport all the items from the car into the house, so she climbed out of the car, her handbag slung over her shoulder, and locked the doors.

Happy voices were talking all over each other from the living room as she entered the house. The double doors of carved oak leading into the room were closed, concealing the owners of the voices. The foyer, with its richly grained oak woodwork complementing pale yellow walls, was empty. The wide staircase rising to the second floor beckoned, its gold carpeted treads like sunlight showing her the path, the carved oak balustrade catching the reflected color. She hesitated, then decided to go for a quick wash and change while her return was still unnoticed.

Only it wasn't unnoticed. As she started to cross the foyer for the stairs leading to the second floor and her bedroom, one of the double doors was surreptitiously opened. Her eyes widened as Chet slipped out, his handsome features strained and tense.

"Where have you been?" There was a hint of desperation in his voice.

If it weren't for the joyful tone of the voices in the other room, Dina might have guessed that some catastrophe had befallen them, judging by Chet's expression.

"At the marina," she answered.

"The marina?" he repeated in disbelief. Again there was that strangled tightness in his voice. "My God, I've been calling all over trying to find you. I never even considered the marina. What were you doing there, for heaven's sake?"

"The *Starfish*—the boat has been leased. I was getting it cleaned up."

The explanation was made while Dina tried to think what crisis could have arisen that Chet would have so urgently needed to contact her about.

"Of all the times—"

Dina broke into sharply. "What's going on?" His attitude was too confusing when she couldn't fathom the reason for it.

"Look, there's something I have to tell you." Chet moistened his lips nervously, his gray blue gaze darting over her face as if trying to judge something from her expression. "But I don't know how to say it."

"What is it?" she demanded impatiently. His tension was becoming contagious.

He took her by the shoulders, his expression deadly serious as he gazed intently into her eyes. Her muscles were becoming sore and they protested at the tightness of his hold.

"It's this..." he began earnestly.

But he got no further as a low, huskily pitched male voice interrupted. "Chet seems to think you're going to go into a state of shock when you find out I'm alive."

The floor rocked beneath her feet. Dina managed a half turn on her treacherously unsteady footing, magnetically drawn to the voice. The whole floor seemed to give way when she saw its owner, yet she remained upright, her collapsing muscles supported by Chet.

There was a dreamlike unreality to the moment.

Almost nightmarelike, since it seemed a cruel joke for someone to stand in the doorway of the living room masquerading as Blake, mimicking his voice.

She stared wordlessly at the tall figure framed by the living-room doors. There was much about the chiseled features that resembled Blake—the wide forehead, the carved cheek and jaw, the strong chin and classically straight nose.

Yet there were differences, too. The sun had burned this man's face a dusky tan, making it leathery and tough, giving a hardness to features that in Blake had been suavely handsome. The eyes were the same dark brown, but they wore a narrowed, hooded look as they seemed to pierce into the very marrow of her soul.

His hair was the same deep shade of umber brown, but its waving thickness was much longer than Blake had ever worn it, giving the impression of being rumpled instead of smoothly in place. As tall as Blake, this man's build was more muscled. Not that Blake had been a weakling by any means; it was just that this man seemed more developed without appearing heavier.

The differences registered with computer swiftness, her brain working while the rest of her was reeling from the similarities. The buzzing in her head continued nonstop, facts clicking into place.

But it wasn't her eyes that Dina trusted. What finally led her to a conclusion was Chet's peculiar behavior before this man appeared; his innate kindness, which would never have permitted a cruel joke like this to be played on her; and the something that he was going to tell before they were interrupted.

Blake was alive. And he was standing in the doorway. She swayed forward, but her feet wouldn't move. Chet's hands tightened in support and she turned her stunned gaze to him. The confirmation was there in his carefully watchful face.

"It's true," she breathed, neither a statement nor a question.

Chet nodded, a silent warning in his eyes. It was then that Dina felt the cold weight of his engagement ring around her finger, and the blood drained from her face. Her hands reached out to cling to Chet's arms, suddenly and desperately needing his support to remain upright.

"It seems Chet was right," that familiar, lazy voice drawled in an arid tone. "My return is more of a shock to you than I thought it would be," Blake observed. The angle of his head shifted slightly to the side to direct his next words over his shoulder without releasing Dina from his level gaze. "She needs some hot, sweet coffee, laced with a stiff shot of brandy."

"Exactly," Chet agreed, and curved a bracing arm around her waist. "Let's find you a place to sit down, Dina." Numbly she accepted his help, aware of his gaze flickering to Blake. "Seeing you standing in the doorway was bound to have been like seeing a ghost. I told you we were all convinced you were dead."

"Not me," Mother Chandler contradicted him, moving to stand beside her son. "I always knew somehow that he was still alive somewhere out there, despite what everyone said."

Fleetingly, Dina was aware of the blatant lie in her mother-in-law's assertion. The thought had barely formed when she realized there were others in the living room. She recognized the faces of close family friends, gathered to celebrate Blake's return. They had been watching the reunion between husband and wife—or rather, the lack of it.

In that paralyzing second, Dina realized she had not so much as touched Blake, let alone joyously fallen into his arms. Her one swaying attempt had been accidentally checked by Chet's steadying hold. It would seem staged and faked if she did so now.

Equally startling was the discovery that she would have to fake it because, although the man in front of her was obviously Blake Chandler, he did not seem like the same man she had married. She felt as if she were looking at a total stranger. He knew what she was thinking and feeling; she could see it in the coolness of his expression, aloof and chilling.

As she and Chet approached the doorway, Blake stepped to one side, giving them room. He smiled down at his mother, his expression revealing nothing to the others that might let them think he found her behavior unnatural under the circumstances.

"If you were so positive I was alive, mother, why are you wearing black?" he chided her.

Color rose in Norma Chandler's cheeks. "For your father, Blake," she responded, not at a loss for an explanation.

Everyone was still standing, watching, as Chet guided Dina to the empty cushions of the sofa. After she was seated, he automatically sat down beside her. Blake had followed them into the room.

Every nerve in Dina's body was aware of his presence, although she wasn't able to lift her gaze to him. Guilt burned inside her, gnawing away at any spontaneous reaction she might have had. It didn't help when Blake sat down in the armchair nearest her end of the couch.

The housekeeper appeared, setting a china cup and saucer on the glass-topped table in front of the sofa. "Here's your coffee, just the way Mr. Blake ordered it."

"Thank you, Deirdre," she murmured. She reached for the china cup filled with steaming dark liquid, but her hands were shaking like aspen leaves and she couldn't hold on to it.

Out of the corner of her eye, she caught a suggestion of movement from Blake, as if he was about to lean forward to help her. Chet's hand was already there, lifting the cup to carry it to her lips. It was purely an automatic reaction on Chet's part. He had become used to doing things for her in the past two and a half years, just as Dina had become used to having him do them.

Instinctively, she knew he hadn't told Blake of their engagement and she doubted if anyone else had. But Chet's solicitous concern was telling its own story. And behind that facade of lazy interest, Blake was absorbing every damning detail. Without knowing it, Chet was making matters worse.

The hot and sweetly potent liquid Dina sipped eased the constriction strangling her voice, and she found the strength to raise her hesitant gaze to Blake's.

"How..." she began self-consciously. "I mean when...."

"I walked out of the jungle two weeks ago." He anticipated her question and answered it.

"Two weeks ago?" That was before she had agreed to marry Chet. "Why didn't you let...someone know?"

"It was difficult to convince the authorities that I was who I claimed to be. They, too, believed I was dead." There was a slashing line to his mouth, a cynical smile. "It must have been easier for Lazarus back in the Biblical days to return from the dead."

"Are you positive I can't fix you a drink, Mr. Blake?" the house-keeper inquired. "A martini?"

"Nothing, thank you."

Dina frowned. In the past Blake had always drunk two, if not three martinis before dinner. She had not been wrong. There were more than just surface changes in him during the last two and a half years. Uncon-sciously she covered her hand with her right, hiding not only the wedding rings Blake had given her, but Chet's engagement ring, as well.

"The instant they believed Blake's story," his mother inserted to carry on his explanation, "he caught the first plane out to come home." She beamed at him like the adoring and doting mother that she was.

"You should have phoned." Dina couldn't help saying it. Forewarned, she might have been better prepared for the new Blake Chandler.

"I did."

Simultaneously as he spoke, Dina remembered the telephone ringing in the dawn hour as she had left the house. Seconds. She had missed knowing about his return by seconds.

"I'd switched off my extension," Norma Chandler said, "and Deidre was wearing her earplugs. Did you hear it, Dina?"

"No. No, I'd already left," answered Dina.

"When Blake didn't get any answer here," Chet continued the story, "he called me."

"Chet was as stunned as you were, Dina," Blake smiled, but Dina suspected that she was the only one who noticed the lack of amusement in his voice. She knew her gaze wavered under the keenness of his.

"I came over right away to let you and Mrs. Chandler know," Chet finished.

"Where were you, Dina?" Sam Lavecek grumped. He was Blake's godfather and a very old friend of both Blake's mother and father. Over the years he had become something of a Dutch uncle to Blake, later extending the relationship to Dina. "Chet has been half out of his mind worrying about where you were all day. Played hooky from the office, did you?"

"I was at the marina," she answered, and turned to Blake. "The *Starfish* has been leased to a couple, and they plan to sail it to Florida for the winter. I spent the day cleaning it up and moving out all of your things.''

"What a pity, boy!'' Sam Lavecek sympathized, slapping the arm of his chair. "You always did love going out on that boat. Now, the very day you come home, it's being turned over to someone else.''

"It's only a boat, Sam.'' There was an enigmatic darkness to his eyes that made his true thoughts impossible to see.

To Dina, in her supersensitive state, he seemed to be implying something else. Perhaps he didn't object to his boat being loaned to someone else—as long as it wasn't his wife. Her apprehension mounted.

"You're right!'' the older man agreed with another emphatic slap of his hand on the armchair. "It's only a boat. And what's that compared to having you back? It's a miracle! A miracle!''

The statement brought a surfeit of questions for Blake to answer about the crash and the events that followed. Dina listened to his narrative. Each word that came from his mouth made him seem more and more a stranger.

The small chartered plane had developed engine trouble and had crashed in the teeming jungle. When Blake had come to, the other four people aboard were dead and he was trapped in the twisted wreckage with a broken leg and a few broken ribs. There had been a deep gash on his forehead, still seeping blood, and other cuts and bruises. Dina's gaze found the scar that had made a permanent crease in his forehead.

Blake didn't go into too much detail about how he had got out of the plane the following day, but Dina had a vivid imagination and pictured the agony he must have endured fighting his way out with his injuries, letting the wreckage become a coffin for the mangled lifeless bodies of the others. Not knowing when or if he would be rescued, Blake had been forced to set his own leg.

That was something Dina could not visualize him doing. In the past, when there was anything that required professional skill or experience, Blake had always hired someone to do it. So for him to set his own broken bone, regardless of the dire circumstances, seemed completely out of character, something the man she had known would never have done.

When the emergency supply of rations from the plane had run out, Blake had foraged for his food, his diet consisting of fruits and whatever wild animals he could trap, catch or kill. And this was supposed to be the same Blake Chandler who had considered the killing of wild game a disgusting sport and who dined on gourmet cuisine.

Blake, who despised flies and mosquitoes, told of the insects that swarmed in the jungle, flying, crawling, biting, stinging, until he no longer noticed them. The heat and humidity of the jungle rotted his shoes and clothes, forcing him to improvise articles of clothing from the skins of the animals he had killed. Blake, the meticulous dresser, always presenting such a well-groomed appearance....

As he began his tale of the more than two-year-long walk out of the jungle, Dina discovered the crux of the difference. Blake had left Rhode Island a civilized man and had come back part primitive. She stared at him with seeing eyes.

Leaning back in his chair, he looked indolent and relaxed, yet Dina knew his muscles were like coiled springs, always ready to react with the swiftness of a predatory animal. His senses, his nerves were alert to everything going on around him. Nothing escaped the notice of that hooded dark gaze. From the lurking depths of those hard brown eyes, Blake seemed to be viewing them all with cynical amusement, as if he found the so-called dangers and problems of their civilized world laughable when compared to the battle of survival he had fought and won.

"There's something I don't understand," Sam Lavecek commented, frowning when Blake had completed his basically sketchy narrative. "Why did the authorities tell us you were dead after they'd found the wreckage? Surely they must have discovered there was a body missing," he added bluntly.

"I don't imagine they did," Blake answered in a calm, matter-of-fact tone.

"Did you bury their bodies, Blake?" his mother asked. "Is that why they didn't find them?"

"No, mother, I didn't." The cynical amusement that Dina suspected he felt was there, glittering through the brown shutters of the indulgent look he gave his mother. "It would have taken a bulldozer to carve out a grave in that tangled mess of brush, trees and roots. I had no choice but to leave them in the plane. Unfortunately, the jungle is filled with scavengers."

Dina blanched. He sounded so cold and insensitive! Blake had been a passionately vital and volatile man, quick to fly into a temper and quick to love.

What had he become? How much would the savagery in his life in the last two and a half years influence his future? Would his determination become ruthlessness? Would his innate leadership become tyranny? Would his compassion for others become contempt? Would his love turn to lust? Was he a virile man or a male animal? He was her husband, and Dina shuddered at what the answers to those questions might be.

Distantly she heard the housekeeper enter the room to inquire, "What time would you like dinner served this evening, Mrs. Chandler?"

There was hesitation before Norma Chandler replied, "In about an hour, Deirdre. That will be all right for everyone, won't it?" and received a murmur of agreement.

From the sofa cushions beside her, Chet expanded on his agreement to remark, "That will give you ample time to freshen up before dinner, won't it, Dina?"

She clutched at the lifeline he had unknowingly tossed her. "Yes, it will." She wanted desperately to be alone for a few minutes to sort through her jumbled thoughts, terribly afraid she was overreacting. Rising, she addressed her words to everyone. "Please excuse me. I won't be long."

Dina had the disquieting sensation of Blake's eyes following her as she walked from the room. But he made no attempt to stop her, nor offer to come with her to share a few minutes alone, much to her relief.

CHAPTER THREE

THE BRIEF SHOWER had washed away the last lingering traces of unreality. Wrapping the sash to her royal blue terry-cloth robe around her middle, Dina walked through the open doorway of the private bath to her bedroom. She moved to the clothes closet at the far corner of the room to choose what she would wear for dinner, all the while trying to assure herself that she was making mountains out of molehills where Blake was concerned.

There was a click, and then movement in her peripheral vision. She turned as the door opened and Blake walked in. Her mouth opened to order out the intruder, then closed. He was her husband. How could she order him out of her bedroom?

His gaze swept the room, located her, and stopped, fixing her with a stare like a predator would his prey. Her fingers clasped the folds of her robe at the throat, her palms moistening with nervous perspiration. Dina was conscious of the implied intimacy of the room and her own nakedness beneath the terry-cloth material. Blood pounded in her head like a thousand jungle drums signaling danger. Vulnerable, she was wary of him.

The brand-new tan suit and tie he wore gave him a cultured look, but she wasn't taken in by the thin veneer of refinement. It didn't conceal the latent power of that muscled physique, nor soften the rough edges of his sun-hardened features. Blake closed the door, not releasing her from his pinning gaze, and searing alarm halted her breath.

"I've come through hell to get back to you, Dina, yet you can't seem to walk across a room to meet me." The accusation was made in a smooth, low tone rife with sardonic amusement.

His words prodded her into movement. Too much time had elapsed since his return for her to rush into his arms. Her steps were stiff, her back rigid as she approached him. She was cautious of him and it showed. Even if she wanted to, she doubted if she could batter down the wall of reserve she had erected. Stopping in front of him, she searched her mind for welcoming words that she could issue sincerely.

"I'm glad you came back safely," were the ones she could offer that had the ring of truth.

Blake waited...for her kiss. The muscles in her stomach contracted sharply with the realization. After a second's hesitation, she forced herself on tiptoe to bring her lips against his mouth in a cool kiss. His large hands spanned the back of her waist, their imprint burning through the material onto her naked flesh. His light touch didn't seem at all familiar. It was almost alien.

At her first attempt to end the kiss, his arms became a vise, fingers raking into her silver gold hair to force her lips to his. Her slender curves were pressed against the hard contours of his body. Her heartbeat skittered madly, then accelerated in alarm.

The hungry demand of his bruising mouth asked more than Dina could give to a man who seemed more of a stranger than her husband. She struggled to free herself of his iron hold and was surprised when Blake let her twist away.

Her breathing was rapid and uneven as she avoided his eyes. "I have to get dressed." She pretended that was her reason for rejecting his embrace. "The others are waiting downstairs."

Those fathomless brown eyes were boring holes into her. Dina could feel them even as she turned away to retrace her steps to the closet and her much-needed clothes. Her knees felt watery.

"You mean Chet is waiting," Blake corrected her with deadly softness.

Her blood ran cold. "Of course. Isn't Chet there with the others?" She feigned ignorance of his meaning and immediately regretted not taking advantage of the opening he had given her to tell him about Chet.

"I've had two and a half years of forced celibacy, Dina. How about you?" The dry contempt in his question spun her around, blue fires of indignation flashing in her eyes, but Blake didn't give her a chance to defend her honor. "How long was it after I disappeared before Chet moved in?"

"He did not move in!" she flashed.

With the swiftness of a swooping hawk, he seized her left hand. His savage grip almost crushed the slender bones of her fingers into a pulp, drawing a gasp of pain from her.

"Figuratively speaking!" His mouth was a thin, cruel line as he lifted her hand. "Or don't you call it moving in when another man's ring joins the ones I put on your finger? Did you think I wouldn't see it?" he blazed. "Did you think I wouldn't notice the looks the two of you were exchanging and the way all the others watched the three of us?" He released her hand in a violent gesture of disgust. Dina nursed the pain-numbed fingers, cradling them in her right hand. "And neither of you had the guts to tell me!"

"Neither of us really had a chance," she responded defensively, her temper flaring from the flame of his. "It isn't an announcement one wants to make in front of others. What was I supposed to say when I saw you standing in the doorway, a husband I thought was dead? 'Darling, I'm so glad you're alive. Oh, by the way, I'm engaged to another man.' Please credit me for having a bit more delicacy than that!"

He gave her a long, hard look. His anger was so tightly controlled that it almost frightened her. It was like looking at a capped volcano, knowing that inside it was erupting, and wondering when the lid would blow.

"This is some homecoming," Blake declared in a contemptuous breath. "A wife who wishes I were still in the grave!"

"I don't wish that," she denied.

"This engagement—" he began, bitter sarcasm coating his words.

"The way you say it makes it sound like something sordid," Dina protested, "and it isn't. Chet and I have been engaged for barely more than a week. At the time that he proposed to me, I thought you were dead and I was free to accept."

"Now you know differently. I'm alive. You're my wife, not my widow. You're still married to me." The way he said it, in such cold, concise tones, made it sound like a life sentence.

Dina was trembling and she didn't know why. "I'm aware of that, Blake." Her voice was taut to keep out the tremors. "But this isn't the time to discuss the situation. Your mother is waiting dinner and I still have to get dressed."

For a few harrowing seconds, she thought he was going to argue. "Yes," he agreed slowly, "this isn't the time."

She heard the door being yanked open and flinched as it was slammed shut. If this was a new beginning for their marriage, it was off to a rotten start. They had argued before Blake had disappeared, and now war had nearly been declared on his return. Dina shuddered and walked to the closet again.

Her arrival downstairs coincided with Deirdre's announcement that dinner would be served. Blake was there to escort her into the formal dining room. A chandelier of cut crystal and polished brass hung above the table, glittering down on the Irish linen tablecloth set with the best of his mother's silver and china. An elaborate floral arrangement sat in the center of the buffet, not too near the table so its scent would not interfere with the aroma of the food. Blake was being warmly welcomed home, by everyone but her, and Dina was painfully conscious of the fact.

As they all took their chairs around the Danish styled dining table, the tension in the air was almost electrical. Yet Dina seemed to be the only one who noticed it. Blake sat at the head of the table, the place of honor, with his mother at the opposite end and Chet seated on her right. Dina sat on Blake's left.

Ever since she had come down, Blake had possessively kept her at his side, as if showing everyone that she was his and effectively separating her from Chet. On the surface, he seemed all smiles, at times giving her glimpses of his former devastating charm. But there was still anger smoldering in his brown eyes whenever his gaze was directed to her.

When everyone was seated, the housekeeper came in carrying a tureen of soup. "I fixed your favorite, Mr. Blake," she announced, a beaming smile on her square-jawed face. "Cream of asparagus."

"Bless you, Deirdre." He smiled broadly. "Now that's the way to welcome a man home!"

The sharp side of his double-edged remark sliced at Dina. She paled at the censure, but otherwise retained a firm hold on her poise.

The meal was an epicurean's delight, from the soup to the lobster thermidor to the ambrosia of fresh fruit. Blake made all the right comments and compliments, but Dina noticed he didn't seem to savor the taste of the various dishes the way she remembered he had in the past. She had the impression that dining had been reduced to the simple matter of eating. Food was food however it was prepared, and man needed food to live.

Coffee was served in the living room so Deirdre could clear away the dishes. Again Dina was kept at Blake's elbow. Chet was on the far side of the room. As she glanced his way, he looked up, smoke blue eyes meeting the clear blue of hers. He murmured a quick excuse to the older woman who had him cornered—a Mrs. Burnside, an old school friend of Norma Chandler—and made his way toward her.

Through the cover of her lashes, Dina dared a glance at Blake and saw the faint narrowing of his gaze as Chet approached. The smile on Chet's face was strained when he stopped in front of them. Dina guessed he was trying to find a way to tell Blake of their engagement and she wished there was a way to let him know that Blake was aware of it.

"It seems like old times, Blake," Chet began, forcing a camaraderie into his voice, "coming over to your house for dinner and seeing you and...." His gaze slid nervously to Dina.

"Chet," Blake interrupted calmly, "Dina has told me about your engagement."

The room grew so quiet Dina was certain a feather could have been heard dropping on the carpet. All eyes were focused on the trio, as if a brilliant spotlight were shining on them. She discovered that, like everyone else, she was holding her breath. After the savage anger Blake had displayed upstairs, she wasn't sure what might happen next.

"I'm glad you know. I...." Chet lowered his gaze searching for words.

Blake filled in the moment's pause. "I want you to know I don't bear any ill feelings. You've always been a good friend and I'd like it to continue that way." Dina started to sigh with relief. "After all, what are friends for?"

No one except Dina seemed to pay any attention to the last caustic comment. Chet was too busy shaking the hand Blake offered in friendship. The others were murmuring among themselves about the moment for which they had been waiting all day.

"Naturally the engagement is broken," Blake joked with a smile that contrasted with the sharply serious light in his eyes.

"Naturally," Chet agreed with an answering smile.

And Dina felt a rush of anger that she could be tossed aside so readily without protest. For that matter, she hadn't even been consulted about her wishes.

Immediately she berated herself. It was what she wanted. Blake was alive and she was married to him. She didn't want to divorce him to marry Chet, so why was she fussing? A simple matter of ego, she decided.

After the confrontation over the engagement, the party became anticlimactic. There was a steady trickle of departures among the guests. One minute Dina was wishing Mrs. Burnside goodbye and the next she was alone in the foyer with Blake, his eyes watching her in that steady, measured way she found so unnerving.

"That's the last of them," he announced.

Dina glanced around. "Where's your mother?"

"In the living room helping Deirdre clean up."

"I'll give them a hand." She started to turn away.

But Blake caught her arm. "There's no need." He released it as quickly as he had captured it. "They can handle it by themselves."

Dina didn't protest. The day had been unconscionably long and she felt enervated from the physical and mental stress she had experienced. What she really wanted was a long night of hard, dreamless sleep. She started for the stairs, half aware that Blake was following.

"You didn't return Chet's ring," he reminded her in a flat tone.

Raising her left hand, she glanced at the flowerlike circlet of diamonds. "No, I...must have forgotten." She was too tired at this point to care about such a small detail.

When she started to lower her hand, Blake seized it and stripped the ring from her finger before she could react to stop him. He gave it a careless toss onto the polished mahogany table standing against the foyer wall.

"You can't leave valuable things lying around!" Dina instantly retrieved it, clutching it in her hand as she frowned at him—Blake, who insisted there was a place for everything and everything in its place.

"Valuable to whom?" he questioned with cool arrogance.

Her fingers tightened around the ring. "I'll keep it in my room until I can give it back to him." She waited for him to challenge her decision. When he didn't, she walked to the stairs.

"He'll be over tomorrow," Blake stated, speaking from directly behind her. "You can give it to him then."

"What time is he coming?" Dina climbed the stairs knowing she was loath to return the ring when Blake was around, but he seemed to be leaving her little option.

"At ten for Sunday brunch."

At the head of the stairs, Dina turned. Her bedroom was the first door on the right. She walked to it only to have Blake's arm reach around her to open the door. She stopped abruptly as he pushed it open, her look bewildered.

"What are you doing?" She frowned.

"I'm going to bed." An eyebrow flickered upward as he eyed her coolly. "Where did you think I was going to sleep?"

She looked away, her gaze darting madly around. She was thrown into a trembling state of confusion by his taunting question. "I didn't think about it," she faltered. "I guess I've become used to sleeping alone."

His hand was at the small of her back, firmly directing her into the room. "Surely you don't expect that to continue?"

"I...." Oh, God, yes she did, Dina realized with a frozen start. "I think it might be better...for a while." She stopped in the center of the room and turned to face him as he closed the door.

"You do?" Inscrutable brown eyes met her wavering look, his leathery, carved features expressionless.

"Yes, I do."

Her nerves were leaping around as erratically as jumping beans, not helped by the palpitating beat of her heart. She watched with growing apprehension as Blake peeled off his suit jacket and tie and began unbuttoning his shirt.

She tried to reason with him, her voice quivering. "Blake, it's been two and a half years."

"Tell me about it," he inserted dryly.

Her throat tightened to make her voice small. "I don't know you anymore. You're a stranger to me."

"That can be changed."

"You aren't trying to understand, Blake." Dina fought to keep control of herself. "I can't just hop into bed with—"

"Your husband?" he finished the sentence, and gave her a searing look. "Who else would you choose?"

The shirt was coming off, exposing a naked chest and shoulder tanned the same dusky shade as his face. The result heightened Dina's impression of a primitive male, powerful and dangerous, sinewy muscles rippling in the artificial light.

Her senses catapulted in alarm as she felt the force of his earthly, pagan attraction. In an attempt to break the black magic of its spell, she turned away, walking stiffly to her dresser to place Chet's ring in her jewel case.

"No one. That isn't what I meant." She remained at the dresser, her hands flattened on its top, knuckles showing white. He came up behind her and she lifted her gaze. In the dressing-table mirror her wary eyes saw his reflection join with hers. "You've become hard, Blake, a cynic," she said accusingly. "I can imagine what you've gone through...."

"Can you?" There was a faint curl of his lip. "Can you imagine how many nights I held onto my sanity by clinging to the vision of a blue-eyed woman with corn-silk hair?" His fingers twined themselves through the loose strands of her pale gold hair and Dina closed her eyes at the savage note in his voice. "Roughly nine hundred and twenty-two nights. And when I finally see her again, she's clinging to the arm of my best friend. Is it any wonder that I'm hard, bitter, when I've been waiting all this time for her lips to kiss away the gnawing memory of those hours? Did you even miss me, Dina?" With a handful of hair as leverage, he twisted her around to face him. "Did you grieve?"

Her eyes smarted with tears she refused to shed at the tugging pain in her scalp. "When you first disappeared, Blake, I was nearly beside myself with fear. But your mother was even more distraught—losing her husband, then possibly you. I had to spend most of my time comforting her. Then the company started to fall apart at the seams and Chet insisted I had to take over or it would fail. So I was plunged headfirst into another world. During the day I was too busy to think about myself, and at night there was your mother depending on me to be her strength. The only moments I had alone were in this room. And I took sleeping pills so I would get enough rest to be able to get through another day. To be truthful, Blake, I didn't have time to grieve."

He was unmoved by her words, his dark eyes flat and cold. "But you had time for Chet," he accused her with icy calm.

Dina winced as the point of his arrow found its target. "It began very innocently. He was your closest friend so it was natural that he kept in touch with your mother and me. Later, there was the company connection. He was always there, bolstering me, encouraging me, and offering me a shoulder to lean on the odd moments that I needed it, without mauling me in return,'' she explained, refusing to sound guilty. "It grew from there after you were reported killed. I needed him.''

"And I need you—now." He drew her inside the steel circle of his hands, flattening her against his chest.

The hard feel of his naked flesh beneath her hands rocked her senses. The warmth of his breath wafted over her averted face, the musky scent of him enveloping her. She pushed at his arms, straining to break out of his hold.

"You haven't listened to a word I've said!" she stormed angrily, inwardly battling against his physical arousal of her senses. "You've changed. I've changed. We need time to adjust!"

"Adjust to what?" Blake snapped. "The differences between a man and a woman? Those are differences we could discover and compensate for very quickly." The zipper of her dress was instantly undone.

"Stop it!" She struggled to keep him from sliding the dress off her shoulders. "You're making me feel like an animal!"

"You are. We both are animals, species Homosapiens." The words were issued in a cold, insensitive tone. "Put on this earth to sleep, eat and breed, to live and die. I learned in the jungle that that's the essence of our existence."

Hysterical laughter gurgled in her throat. "Oh, my God." Dina choked on the sound. "That sounds like 'You Tarzan, me Jane!'"

"Eliminate the trappings of society and the pretty words and that's what it comes down to in the end."

"No, our minds are more fully developed. We have feelings, emotions," she protested. "We...."

The dress was stripped away despite her efforts.

"Shut up!" He growled the order against her mouth and smothered the sounds when she refused to obey.

Leaning and twisting backward, Dina tried to escape the domination of his kiss, but his hands used the attempt to mold her lower body more fully to his length, her hipbones crushed by oak-solid thighs. The silk of her slip was a second skin, concealing and revealing while callused fingers moved roughly around in exploration.

Cruelly, Blake ravaged the softness of her lips. Dina thought her neck would snap under his driving force. Beneath her straining hands she felt the flexing of his muscles, smooth like hammered steel, latent in their sensuality. He was devouring her strength by degrees, slowly and steadily wearing her down. Doubling her fingers, she began hammering at him with her fists, puny blows that had little effect.

The effort seemed to use up the reserves of her strength. Within seconds, a blackness swam in front of her eyes and a dizzying weakness spread through her limbs. Her fingers dug into his shoulders and she clung to him to keep from falling into the yawning abyss that seemed to be opening in front of her.

As her resistance ebbed into nothingness, so did the brutality of his assault. The terrible bruising pressure of his mouth eased, permitting Dina to straighten her neck. Gradually she began to surface from the waves of semiconsciousness, enough to become aware of his loosened hold.

With a determined effort, she broke out of his arms. Gasping in air in panicked breaths, she backed away from him, her knees quivering. Blake swayed toward her, then stopped. A second later she realized why, as her retreat was stopped short by a wall. A cornered animal, she stared at the man who held her at bay. A stranger who was her husband.

She lifted her head, summoning all her pride to beg, "Don't do this, Blake."

Slow, silent strides carried him to her and she didn't attempt to flee. There was no mercy in his eyes and she would not submit to the ignominy of cowering. Her resistance became passive as he undressed, her eyes tightly closed.

"Are you choosing to portray the martyred wife submitting to the bestiality of her husband?" Blake taunted. "This display of frigidity is a farce. My memory wasn't damaged. I remember, too well, what a passionate lover you are."

Dina paled as she remembered, too. A flicker of the old searing fire licked through her veins as he drew her to him and her bare curves came in contact with his nude body. The tiny flame couldn't catch hold, not when the hands fanning it were callused and rough instead of the smooth, manicured hands that had once brought it to a full blaze.

"Don't destroy our marriage," she whispered, trying not to see the curling, sun-bleached hairs forming a pale cloud against the burnished bronze of his chest. "I want to love you again, Blake."

With a muffled imprecation, he buried his face in her hair. "Damn you! Why didn't you say that when I came home?" he muttered thickly in a rasping sound that suggested pain. "Why did you have to wait until now?"

"Would it have mattered?" Dina caught back a sob.

"It might have then." Effortlessly he swung her off her feet into his arms, his jaw set in a ruthless line. "I couldn't care less now. You're mine and I mean to have you."

The overhead light was switched off, throwing the room into darkness. As if guided by animal instinct, Blake carried her to the bed. Without bothering to pull down the covers, he laid her on the bed and towered beside it.

"Blake." There was an unspoken plea in the way she spoke his name, a last attempt to make him understand her unwillingness.

"No," he answered, and the mattress sagged under his weight. "Don't ask me to wait." His low voice was commanding near her ear, his breath stirring her hair. "It's been too long."

And we both have changed, Dina thought, stiffening at the moist touch of his mouth along her neck. *Can't you see the differences, Blake? Physical as well as mental. Haven't you noticed I'm wearing my hair longer?* As his hand slid over her ribs, to cup her breast, she remembered when the roundness had filled it. Now, with maturity, it overflowed.

But Blake seemed intent on discovering the ripeness of her female form, ignoring comparisons. His caressing hands roamed over her with intimate familiarity and she felt her body responding, reluctantly at first. A series of long, drugging kisses soon made her mind blank to all but the demands of her flesh.

Her senses took over, reigning supreme. She gloried in the taste of his lips probing the sensual hollows of her mouth and the brush of the soft, curling hairs on his chest hardening her nipples into erotic pebbles.

The rapidly increasing throb of her pulse was in tempo with the pagan beat of his, building to a climax. And the heady male scent of him, heightened by perspiration and his rising body heat, served to stimulate all her senses until she was filled with nothing but him.

For a time she glimpsed heights she had thought she would never see again. Blake sought all the places that brought her the most pleasure, waiting until she moaned his name in final surrender.

CHAPTER FOUR

DINA LAY IN BED, the covers pulled up to her neck, but she knew the blankets couldn't warm the chill. Her passion spent, she felt cold and empty inside as she stared upward into the darkness of the room. A tear was frozen on an eyelash.

Physically her desires had been satisfied by Blake's skilled knowledge, but she had not been lifted to the rapturous heights of a spiritual union. That only happened when there was love involved. Tonight it had been merely a mutual satisfaction of sexual desires. And that special something that had been missing eliminated the warm afterglow Dina had previously known.

Blake was beside her, their bodies not touching. An arm was flung on the pillow above his head. She could hear the steady sound of his breathing, but doubted that he was asleep. Her sideways glance sought his carved profile in the dim light. There seemed to be a grim line to his mouth, as if he was experiencing the same reaction.

As if feeling her look and hearing her question, he said in a low, flat voice, "There's one argument you didn't make, Dina. If you had, it might have prevented this disillusionment."

"What is it?" she asked in a tight, throbbing voice, longing to know what it was so she could keep this from happening again.

"The real thing can't match two and a half years of expectations."

No, she agreed silently, *not when there are no words of love exchanged, no mating of our hearts nor coming together of our souls.* It had been an act of lust, born out of anger and frustration.

"Passion never can, Blake," she murmured.

He tossed aside the blanket draped across his waist and swung his feet to the floor. Her head turned on the pillow to stare at him in the darkness.

"Where are you going?" she asked softly. Something told her that if Blake would hold her in his arms, the aching void inside her might close.

There was a faint sheen to his sun-browned skin in the shadowy light. She could make out the breadth of his shoulders and the back muscles tapering to his waist. His steps were soundless, silent animal strides.

"Another unfortunate discovery I've made since returning to civilization is that the mattresses are too soft." He spoke in a low voice, a biting, cynical tone. "I'm used to firm beds. That's what comes from spending too many nights sleeping in trees and on hard ground."

She lost him in the darkness and propped herself up on an elbow, keeping the covers tightly around her. "Where are you going?"

"To find a spare blanket and a hard floor." There was the click of the door being opened. "You have part of your wish, Dina," he added caustically. "The bed is yours. You can sleep alone."

As the door closed, a convulsive shudder ran through her. She turned her face into the pillow, curling her body into a tight ball of pain. With eyes squeezed shut, she lay there, aching for the forgetfulness of sleep.

A HAND GENTLY but persistently shook her shoulder. "Mrs. Blake? Wake up, please." Dina stirred, lashes fluttering as she tried to figure out whether or not she was imagining the voice. "Wake up, Mrs. Blake!"

But she wasn't imagining the hand on her arm. Her head throbbed dully as she opened her eyes and rolled over, dragging the covers with her. Her sleepy gaze focused on the agitated expression of the housekeeper hovering above her.

Dina became conscious of several things at once: the rumpled pillow beside her where Blake had lain so briefly, her own naked state beneath the covers, and the clothes scattered around the room—hers and Blake's. *My God, the room is a mess,* she thought.

"What is it, Deirdre?" she questioned, trying to maintain a measure of composure despite the surge of embarrassment.

The older woman bit her lip as if uncertain how to reply. "It's Mr. Blake."

The anxious look on the housekeeper's face brought an instant reaction as Dina propped herself up on her elbows, concern chasing away the remnants of sleep. "Blake? What's wrong? Has something happened to him?"

"No, it's...it's just that he's sleeping downstairs—on the floor in the library." A dull red was creeping up her neck into her cheeks. "And he isn't wearing any...any pajamas."

Dina swallowed back a smile, her relief lost in amusement. Poor Deirdre Schneider, she thought, never married in her life nor seriously close to it and probably shocked to her prim core when she found Blake sleeping in the library in the altogether.

"I see," she nodded, and tried to keep her face straight.

"Mr. Stanton will be arriving in just more than an hour." The woman was trying desperately to avoid looking at the bareness of Dina's shoulders. "I thought you should be the one to...to wake up Mr. Blake."

"I will," said Dina, and started to rise, then decided against adding to the housekeeper's embarrassment. "Would you hand me my robe at the foot of the bed, Deirdre?"

After handing the robe to her, the housekeeper turned discreetly away while Dina slipped into it. "Mrs. Chandler had a few things sent over yesterday for Mr. Blake," she informed Dina. "There are pajamas and a robe. I put them in the empty closet."

"I'll take them to him." Dina finished tying the sash of her robe. "And, Deirdre, tomorrow I think you'd better make arrangements with Mrs. Chandler to purchase a bed with a very firm mattress, one that's as hard as a rock."

"I will," Deirdre promised as if taking an oath. "Sorry to have awakened you, Mrs. Blake."

"That's quite all right, Deirdre," Dina answered, smiling.

With a brief self-conscious nod, the housekeeper left the room. Dina put on her slippers and walked to the small closet Deirdre had indicated. It was used mostly for storage. Amid the few boxes and garment bags hung three shirts and a brown suit. On the two inside door hooks were the pajamas and matching dressing robe in a muted shade of cranberry silk. Leaving the pajamas, Dina took the robe.

Downstairs, her hand hesitated on the knob of the library door. Tension hammered in her temples and her stomach was twisted into knots. Steeling herself to ignore the attack of nervousness, she opened the door quietly and walked in. Her gaze was directed first to the floor and its open area around the fireplace.

"Deirdre sent in the reserves, I see," Blake's male voice mocked from the side of the room.

Dina turned in its direction and saw him standing near the solid wall of shelves filled with books. A dark green blanket was wrapped around his waist, his naked torso gleaming in that deep shade of tan. Fingers had combed his thick brown hair into a semblance of order, a suggestion of unruliness remaining. Dina's pulse fluctuated in alarm, her head lifted as if scenting danger. He looked like a primitive native, proud, noble and savage.

"Did you hear her come in?" She realized it was a foolish question after she had asked it. Those long months in the jungle had to have sharpened his senses, making them more acute.

"Yes, but I decided it was wiser to pretend I was still asleep rather than shock her sensibilities," he admitted with cynical derision. "I thought she would scamper up the stairs to inform you or my mother of my lewd behavior."

Behind his veiled look Dina felt the dark intensity of his gaze scanning her face—searching for something, but she didn't know what. It made her uncomfortable and she wished she had dressed before coming down.

"I brought you a robe." She held it out to him aware of the faint trembling that wasn't yet visible.

"No doubt at Deirdre's suggestion. She must have been more shocked than I thought." But Blake made no move toward it, forcing Dina to walk to him.

"Deirdre isn't accustomed to finding naked men sleeping on the library floor," she said, defending the housekeeper's reaction and discovering a similar one in herself as Blake reached down to unwrap the blanket from around his waist. Self-consciously she averted her eyes, her color mounting as if it were a stranger undressing in front of her instead of her husband.

There was a rustle of silk, then, "It's safe to look now," Blake taunted, his mouth curving in ungentle mockery.

She flashed him an angry look for drawing attention to her sudden burst of modesty and turned away. The vein in her neck pulsed with a nervousness that she wasn't able to control. His hand touched her shoulder and she flinched from the searing contact.

"For God's sake, Dina, I'm not going to rape you!" he cursed beneath his breath. "Dammit, can't I even touch my wife?"

Her blue eyes were wide and wary as she looked over her shoulder at his fiercely burning gaze. "I don't feel like your wife, Blake," she said tightly. "I don't feel as if I'm married to you."

Immediately the fires were banked in his eyes, that freezing control that was so unlike him coming into play. "You are married to me," he stated, and walked by her to the door. Opening it, he called, "Deirdre! Bring some coffee into the library for my wife and myself." With emphasis on "wife."

"Chet is coming and I still have to dress." Dina reminded him, objecting to spending more minutes alone with him.

"He isn't due for an hour," Blake said, dismissing her protest, and walked to the leather-covered sofa, pausing beside its end table to lift the lid of the ceramic cigarette box. "Cigarette?" He flicked a questioning glance in her direction.

"No, I don't smoke. Remember?" she said with a faintly taunting arch to her voice.

"You might have acquired the habit during my absence," he shrugged.

"I didn't."

Brisk footsteps in the foyer signaled the housekeeper's approach. Seconds later she entered the library with a coffee service and two china cups on the tray she carried. A pink tint was still rouging her cheeks as Deirdre steadfastly avoided looking directly at Blake.

"Where would you like the tray?" she asked Dina.

"The table by the sofa will be fine."

Blake carried the ceramic table lighter to the cigarette in his mouth and snapped the flame to its tip. Smoke spiraled upward and he squinted his eyes against it. Despite his show of disinterest, Dina knew he was aware of the housekeeper's every movement. After setting the tray on the table at the opposite end of the sofa from where Blake stood, Deirdre straightened up erectly.

"Will there be anything else?" Again her query was directed to Dina.

It was Blake who answered. "That will be all," he said, exhaling a thin trail of smoke. "And close the door on your way out, Deirdre."

"Yes, sir." Two red flags dotted her cheeks.

As Deirdre made a hasty exit, firmly closing the door, Blake walked to the tray. Lifting the coffee pot, he filled the two cups and offered one to Dina.

"Black, as I remember, with no sugar," he said in a tone that baited.

"Yes, thank you." Dina refused to bite as she took the cup and saucer from his hand.

Scalding steam rose from the brown liquid and Blake let his cup sit. He studied the glowing tip of his cigarette and the gossamer-thin white smoke rising upward. A wry smile crooked his mouth.

"I'd forgotten how good a cigarette can taste first thing in the morning," he mused.

Dina felt as edgy as a cat with its tail caught in a vise. She couldn't help retorting, "I thought you hadn't forgotten anything."

"Not the important things, I haven't," Blake replied, levelly meeting her irritated glance.

With a broken sigh, she wandered to the library window overlooking the expansive front lawn of the house and the cul-de-sac of its driveway. She was caught by the memory of the last time she had stared out the window in troubled silence. Oddly, it seemed an eternity ago instead of the short time that it was.

"What are you thinking about?" Blake was close, only a scant few feet behind her.

"I was merely remembering the last time I stood at this window." She sipped at the hot coffee.

"When was that?" He seemed only idly curious.

Dina felt his gaze roaming her shapely length as surely as if he touched her, and stiffened to answer bluntly, "The night of my engagement party to Chet."

"Forget about him." The command was crisp and impatient, as Dina guessed it would be.

"It isn't that easy to turn back the clock," she muttered tightly.

The cup nearly slipped from her fingers as she felt the rasping brush of his fingers against her hair. Her throat constricted, shutting off her voice and her breath.

"Have I told you I like your hair this length?" His low voice was a husky caress running down her spine.

He lifted aside the molten gold of her hair, pushing it away from her neck. The warmth of his breath against her skin warned her an instant before she glimpsed the waving darkness of his hair in her side vision.

His unerring mouth sought and found the ultrasensitive and vulnerable spot at the base of her neck. Her heart felt as though it had been knocked sideways, and Blake took full advantage of her Achilles' heel. She felt boneless as her head tipped down and to the side to give him freer access.

The cup rattled in its saucer, but she managed to hold on to it. His arms wound around her waist to mold her back to his muscular length. For a magic second she was transported back to another time. Then a roughened hand slid under the overlapping fold of her robe to encircle the swell of her breast, a callused finger teasing its nipple, and the arms felt suddenly strange.

"Blake, no!" Weakly she tugged at his wrist, no match for his strength.

She gasped as his sensual mouth moved upward to her ear, and desire licked through her veins at the darting probe of his tongue. An all-pervading weakness went through her limbs. It was a dizzying sensation, wild drums pounding in her ears.

"Do you remember the way we used to make love in the mornings?" Blake murmured against her temple.

"Yes," she moaned, the memory all too vivid.

The cup disappeared from her hand, carried away by a fluid movement of Blake's hand. It took only the slightest pressure to turn her around. She was drawn to his side, a muscular, silk-covered thigh insinuating itself between her legs as she was arched against him. She lifted her head, subconsciously braced for the punishment of his rough kisses. Her fingers curled into his shoulders for support.

There was the tantalizing touch of his lips against hers. "After last night, I thought I had you out of my system," he said against them, "but I want you more than before."

A half sob came from her throat at the absence of any mention of love. In the next second she didn't care, as his mouth closed over hers with sweet pressure. There was no plundering demand, only a persuasive exhorting to respond.

Her lips parted willingly, succumbing to the rapturous mastery of his exploration. The dream world of sensation seemed almost enough. She slid her fingers through the springing thickness of his hair, the scent of him earthy and clean.

As if tired of bending his head to reach her lips, Blake tightened his arm around her waist to lift her straight up, bringing her to eye level. It was another indication of his increased strength, that he should carry her weight so effortlessly. At the moment, Dina was oblivious to this example of his change.

His mouth blazed a moist trail downward to explore the pulsing vein in her neck. "Did Chet ever make you feel like this?" An attempt to exorcise the memory of Chet's kisses from her mind? Had it been motivated by nothing more than that? She pushed out of his hold, staring at him with wounded pride.

"Did he?" Blake repeated, a faintly ragged edge to his breathing.

"You'll never know," she answered in a choked voice. "Maybe he made me feel better."

He took a threatening step toward her, his features dark with rage. There was nowhere for Dina to retreat. She had to stand her ground, despite its indefensibility. Just then there was a knock at the door. Blake halted, casting an angry glance at the door.

"Who is it?" he demanded.

The door opened and Chet walked in. "I'm a bit early, but Deirdre said you were in here having coffee. She's going to bring me a cup." He stopped, as if sensing the heaviness in the atmosphere. "I didn't think you'd mind if I joined you." But it was something of a question.

"Of course not." Dina was quick to use him as a buffer.

"Come in, Chet," Blake continued the invitation. "Speak of the devil, Dina and I were just talking about you."

"Something good, I hope," Chet joked stiffly.

"Yes." Blake's dark gaze swung to Dina, a considering grimness in their depths. "Yes, it was." But he didn't explain what it had been.

She started breathing again, her hand sliding up to her throat. She became conscious of her partially clothed state and used it as an excuse to leave.

"If you two don't mind, I'll leave you to have coffee alone," she said.

"I hope you aren't going on my account," Chet said, frowning.

"No," Dina assured him quickly, avoiding Blake's mocking look. "I was going upstairs anyway to dress before Deirdre serves brunch. I'll be down shortly."

As Dina left, she met Deirdre bringing the extra cup for Chet. The housekeeper's composure was under admirable control now and she was her usual calm-faced self.

Once she was dressed, Dina slipped Chet's ring into the pocket of her dirndl skirt. At some point during the day she hoped to have the chance to return it to him while they were alone. But it was late afternoon before the opportunity presented itself.

THE PRESS HAD LEARNED of Blake's return and the house was in a state of siege for the greater part of the day. Either the doorbell or the telephone seemed to be ringing constantly. Blake had to grant interviews to obtain any peace, but his answers were concise, without elaboration, downplaying his ordeal. As his wife, Dina was forced to be at his side, while Chet adopted the role of press secretary and spokesman for the Chandler company.

Finally, at four o'clock, the siege seemed to be over and a blessed quietness began to settle over the house. Norma Chandler, who had insisted that coffee and sweets be served to all those who had come, was busy helping Deirdre clear away the mess.

The ringing of the telephone signaled a last interview for Blake, one conducted over the phone. Dina had started helping the other two women clean up. When she noticed Chet slip away to the library, she excused herself, knowing she might not have another chance to speak him alone.

As she stepped inside the library, she saw him pouring whiskey from a crystal decanter over ice cubes in a squat glass. The engagement ring seemed to be burning a circle in her pocket.

"Would you pour me a sherry, Chet?" She quietly closed the door, shutting out Blake's voice coming from the living room.

Chet's sandy blond head lifted, his surprised look vanishing into a smile when he saw her. "Of course." He reached for another glass and a different decanter. Pouring, he remarked, "It's been quite a hectic day."

"Yes, it has." Dina walked over to take the sherry glass from his hand.

Ice clinked as Chet lifted his glass to take a quick swallow of whiskey. "A reporter that I know from one of the local papers called and got me out of bed this morning. He'd gotten wind that there was a shake-up in the Chandler hotel chain and he wanted to know what it was. I pleaded ignorance. But that's why I rushed over here so early, to warn Blake that the onslaught was coming. I knew it was only a matter of time before they found out."

"Yes." She nodded in agreement, glad there had been no announcement of their engagement in the newspaper or the reporters would have turned Blake's return into a circus.

"Blake really knows how to handle himself with the press," Chet stated with undisguised admiration.

"Yes, he does." Dina sipped at her drink.

"And it will make good publicity for the hotels," he added.

"Yes." She was beginning to feel like a puppet whose string was being pulled to nod agreement to everything Chet said—when it really wasn't what she wanted to talk about at all.

"I imagine somebody in the company let it slip about Blake." He stared thoughtfully at the amber liquid in his glass. "I called around to all the major officers yesterday to let them know he was back. That's probably how the word got out."

"Probably," Dina agreed, and promptly took the initiative to lead into her own subject. "Chet, I've been wanting to see you today, alone—" she reached in her pocket to take out the circlet of diamonds "—to return this to you."

He took it from her outstretched hand, looking boyishly uncomfortable. His thumb rubbed it between his fingers as he stared at it, not meeting the sapphire brightness of her gaze.

"I don't want you to get the idea that I was deserting you yesterday." His voice was uncertain, almost apologetic. "But I know how you felt about Blake and I didn't want to stand in the way of your happiness."

With the explanation given for the way he had so readily abandoned their engagement, Chet lifted his head to gaze at her earnestly, a troubled shade of clouded blue in his eyes. Affection rushed through Dina at his unselfishness, sacrificing his wants for hers.

"I understand, Chet."

Relief glimmered in his smile. "You must really be glad to have him back."

"I...." She started to repeat the positive assertion she had been making all day, ready to recite the words automatically, but she stopped herself. Among other things, Chet was her best friend, as well as Blake's. With him she could speak her mind. "He's changed, Chet."

He hesitated for a second before answering, as if her response had caught him off guard and he wanted to word his reply carefully.

"Considering all Blake has been through, it's bound to have left a mark on him," he offered.

"I know, but...." She sighed, agitated and frustrated, because she couldn't find the words to explain exactly what she meant.

"Hey, come on now," Chet cajoled, setting his glass down and grasping her gently by the shoulders, his head bent down to peer into her apprehensive face. "When two people care as much about each other as you and Blake do, they're bound to work out their differences. It just can't happen overnight," he reasoned. "Now come on. What do you say? Let's have a little smile. You know it's true that nothing is ever as bad as it seems."

Mountains and molehills. Reluctantly almost, her lips curved at his coaxing words. His steadying influence was having its effect on her again.

"That's my girl!" he grinned.

"Oh, Chet," Dina declared with a laughing sigh, and wrapped her arms lightly around him, taking care not to spill her drink. She hugged him fondly. "What would I do without you?" She drew her head back to gaze at him.

"I hope neither of us has to find out," he remarked, and affectionately kissed the top of her nose.

The knob turned and the library door was pushed open by Blake. At the sight of Dina in Chet's arms he froze, and the same paralysis gripped her. She paled as she saw his lips thin into an angry line.

But the violence of his emotion wasn't detectable in his voice as he remarked casually, "Is this a private party or can anyone join?"

His question broke the chains holding Dina motionless. She withdrew her arms from around Chet to hold her sherry glass in both hands. Chet turned to greet him, insensitive to the heightening tension in the air.

"Now that you're here, Blake, we can drink a toast to the last of the newspaper reporters," he announced in a celebrating tone, not displaying any self-consciousness about the scene Blake had interrupted.

"For a while anyway," Blake agreed, his gaze swinging to Dina. "What are you drinking?"

"Sherry." There would be no explosion now, Dina realized. Blake would wait until they were alone.

"I'll have the same."

It was late that evening before Chet left. Each dragging minute in the interim honed Dina's nerves to a razor-thin edge. By the time he had left, she could no longer stand the suspense of waiting for the confrontation with Blake.

With the revving of Chet's car coming from the driveway, Dina paused in the foyer to challenge Blake. "Aren't you going to say it?"

He didn't pretend an ignorance of her question, his gaze hard and unrelenting. "Stay away from Chet."

All the blame for the innocent encounter was placed on her, and she reacted with indignant outrage. "And what about Chet?"

"I know Chet well enough to be assured he isn't going to trespass, unless encouraged, on my territory."

"So I'm supposed to avoid him, is that it?" she flashed.

"Whatever relationship you had with him in my absence is finished," Blake declared in a frigid tone. "From now on he's simply an acquaintance of mine. That's all he is to you."

"That's impossible!" She derided his suggestion that she could dismiss Chet from her life with a snap of her fingers. "I can't forget all he's meant to me that easily."

A pair of iron clamps dug into the soft flesh of her arms and she was jerked to him, the breath knocked out of her by the hard contact with the solid wall of his chest. Her lips were crushed by the angry fire of his kiss, a kiss that seared his brand of possession on her and burned away any memory of another's mouth.

Dina was released from his punishing embrace with equal force. Shaken and unnerved, she retreated a step. With the back of her hand she tried to rub away the fiery imprint of his mouth.

"You—" she began with impotent rage.

"Don't push me, Dina!" Blake warned.

They glared at each other in thundering silence. Dina had no idea how long the battle of wills would have continued if his mother hadn't entered the foyer seconds later. Each donned a mask to conceal their personal conflict from her eyes.

"Deirdre just told me you'd asked her to bring some blankets to the library, Blake." Norma Chandler was wearing a frown. "You aren't going to sleep there again tonight, are you?"

"Yes, I am, mother," he responded decisively.

"But it's so uncivilized," she protested.

"Perhaps," Blake conceded, for an instant meeting Dina's look. "It's also infinitely preferable to not sleeping."

"I suppose so." His mother sighed her reluctant agreement. "Good night, dear."

"Good night, mother," he returned, and coldly arched an eyebrow at Dina. "Good night."

CHAPTER FIVE

THE LIBRARY DOOR stood open when Dina came down the stairs the next morning. She smoothed a nervous hand over her cream linen skirt and walked to the dining room where breakfast coffee and juice were already on the table. But there was no sign of Blake. Dina helped herself to juice and coffee and sat down.

"Isn't Blake having breakfast this morning?" she questioned the housekeeper when she appeared.

"No, ma'am," Deirdre replied. "He's already left. He said he was meeting Jake Stone for breakfast and going to the office from there. Didn't he tell you?"

"Yes, I believe he did," Dina lied, and forced a smile. "I must have forgotten."

"Mrs. Chandler was most upset about it," the woman remarked with a knowing nod.

Dina frowned. "Because Blake is meeting the attorney?"

"No, because he's going into the office. Mrs. Chandler thought he should wait a few days. I mean, he just came back and all, and right away he's going to work," Deirdre explained.

"He's probably anxious to see how everything is." There was a smug feeling of satisfaction that he would find the entire operation running smoothly knowing that a great deal of the credit was hers.

"What will you have this morning, Mrs. Blake? Shall I fix you an omelet?"

"I think I'll just have juice and coffee, Deirdre, thank you." She wanted to be at the office when Blake arrived to be able to see his face when he realized how capably she had managed in his absence.

"As you wish," the housekeeper sniffed in disapproval.

The morning traffic seemed heavier than usual and Dina chafed at the delay it caused. Still she arrived at the office building well within her usual time. As she stepped out of the elevator onto the floor the company occupied, she was relieved that Chet had already notified the various executive personnel of Blake's return and that she was spared that task. She would have time to go over her notes on the departmental meeting this afternoon and have much of the Monday morning routine handled before Blake arrived.

She breezed down the corridor to her office, keeping her pace brisk while she nodded greetings and returned good mornings to the various employees along the way. She didn't want to stop and chat with anyone and use up her precious time. She felt very buoyant as she entered the office of her private secretary.

"Good morning, Amy," she said cheerfully.

"Good morning, Mrs. Chandler." The young woman beamed back a smile. "You're in good spirits this morning."

"Yes, I am," Dina agreed. Her secretary was going through the morning mail and she walked to her desk to see if there was anything of importance she should know about before Blake arrived.

"Your good spirits wouldn't have anything to do with Mr. Chandler's coming back, would they?" Amy Wentworth inquired with a knowing twinkle. Dina wasn't obliged to make a comment as her secretary continued, "All of us here are so happy he's back safely."

"So am I, Amy," Dina nodded, and glanced over the girl's shoulder for a glimpse at the mail. "Anything special in the mail this morning?"

"Not so far," her secretary replied, returning her attention to the stack of letters.

"Any calls?"

"Only one. Mr. Van Patten called."

"Did he leave a message?" Dina asked, her quick perusal of the mail completed.

"Oh, no," Amy hastened to explain. "Mr. Chandler took the call."

"Mr. Chandler?" she repeated. "Do you mean Blake is already here?"

"Yes, he's in the office." Amy motioned towards Dina's private office. "I'm sure he won't mind if you go right on in, Mrs. Chandler."

For several seconds Dina was too stunned to speak. It was *her* office, her pride protested. And *her* secretary was grandly giving her permission to enter it. Blake had moved in and managed to convey the impression that she had moved out.

Her blue eyes darkened with rage. Turning on her heel, she walked to the private office. She didn't bother to knock, simply pushing the door open and walking in. Blake was seated behind the massive walnut desk— *her* desk! He glanced up when she entered. The arrogantly inquiring lift of his eyebrow lit the fuse of her temper.

"What are you doing here?" she demanded.

"I was about to ask you the same question," countered Blake with infuriating calm.

"It happens to be *my* office and that's *my* secretary outside!" Dina retorted. Her flashing eyes saw the papers in his hands and she recognized the notes as those she had been going to go over for the departmental meeting that afternoon. "And those are *my* notes!"

He leaned back in the swivel chair, viewing her tirade with little emotion. "I was under the impression that all of this—" he waved his hand in an encompassing gesture "—belonged to the company."

"I happen to be in charge of the company," she reminded him.

"You *were* in charge of the company," Blake corrected her. "I'm taking over now."

She was trembling violently now, her anger almost uncontrollable. She fought to keep her voice low and not reveal how thoroughly he had aroused her.

"You're taking over," she repeated. "Just like that!" She snapped her fingers.

"Your job is done." Blake shrugged and fingered the papers on the desk. "And excellently, from all that I've seen this morning."

It was the compliment she had sought, but not delivered the way she had intended it to be. Therefore it brought no satisfaction; the thunder was stolen from her glory.

"And what am I supposed to do?" she demanded.

"Go home. Go back to being my wife." His sun-roughened features wore a frown, as if not understanding why she was so upset.

"And do what?" challenged Dina. "Twiddle my thumbs all day until you come home? Deirdre does all the cooking and the cleaning. It's your mother's house, Blake. There's nothing for me to do there."

"Then start looking for an apartment for us. Or better yet, a house of our own," he suggested. "That's what you wanted before, a place of our own that you could decorate the way you wanted it."

A part of her wanted it still, but it wasn't the motivating force in her life. "That was before, Blake," she argued. "I've changed. If we did have a house and the decorating was all done the way I wanted it, what would I do then? Sit around and admire my handiwork? No, I enjoy my work here. It's demanding and fulfilling."

He was sitting in the chair, watching her with narrowed eyes. "What you're saying is you enjoy the power that goes along with it."

"I enjoy the power," Dina admitted without hesitation, a hint of defiance in the tightness of her voice. "I enjoy the challenge and the responsibility, too. Men don't have a monopoly on those feelings."

"What are you suggesting, Dina? That we reverse our roles and I become the house husband? That I find the house, do all the decorating, cleaning and entertaining?"

"No, I'm not suggesting that." Confusion was tearing at her. She didn't know what the solution was.

"Perhaps you'd like me to take another flight to South America and this time not bother to come back?"

"No, I wouldn't—and stop twisting my words!"

Hot tears flooded her eyes, all the emotional turmoil inside her becoming too much to control. She turned sharply away, blinking frantically at the tears, trying to force them back before Blake saw them.

There was a warning squeak of the swivel chair as Blake rose and approached her. Her lungs were bursting, but she was afraid to take a breath for fear it would sound like a sob.

"Is this the way you handle a business disagreement?" he lashed out in impatient accusation.

Aware that he towered beside her, Dina kept her face averted so he wouldn't see the watery blue of her eyes. "I don't know what you mean," she lied.

His thumb and fingers clamped on her chin and twisted it around so he could see her face. "Do you usually indulge in a female display of tears when you don't get your own way?"

The wall of tears was so solid that Dina could barely see his face. "No," she retorted pushing at the hand that held her chin. "Do you always attack on a personal level whenever someone doesn't agree with you wholeheartedly?"

She heard his long impatient sigh, then his fingers curved to the back of her neck, forcing her head against his chest. An arm encircled her to draw her close. His embrace was strong and warm, but Dina made herself remain indifferent to Blake's attempt to comfort her. She felt the pressure of his chin resting atop her head.

"Would you mind telling me what the hell I'm supposed to do about this?" Blake muttered.

She wiped at the tears with shaking fingers and sniffed, "I don't know."

"Here." He reached inside his suit jacket to hand her his handkerchief. There was a light rap on the door and Blake stiffened. "Who is it?" he snapped, but the door was already opening.

Self-consciously Dina tried to twist out of his arms, but they tightened around her as if closing ranks to protect her. She submitted to their hold, her back to the door.

"Sorry," she heard Chet apologize with a trace of chagrin. "I guess I've gotten used to walking in unannounced."

He must have made a move to leave because Blake said, "It's all right. Come on in, Chet." Unhurriedly he withdrew his arms from around

Dina. "You'll have to excuse Dina. She still gets emotional once in a while about my return," he said to explain away her tears and the handkerchief she was using to busily wipe away their traces.

"That's understandable," said Chet, "I came in to let you know everyone's here. They're waiting in the meeting room."

His statement lifted Dina's head with a start. "Meeting?" She picked up on the word and frowned. "There isn't any meeting scheduled on my agenda this morning."

"I called it," Blake announced smoothly, his bland gaze meeting her sharp look. Then he shifted his attention to Chet in a dismissing fashion. "Tell them I'll be there in a few minutes."

"I will." And Chet left.

At the click of the closing door, Dina turned roundly on Blake, her anger returning. "You weren't going to tell me about the meeting, were you?" she accused him.

Blake walked to the desk and began shuffling through the papers on top of it. "Initially, no. I didn't see the need to tell you."

"You didn't see the need?" Dina sputtered at his arrogantly dismissive statement.

"To be truthful, Dina—" he turned to look at her, his bluntly chiseled features seeming to be carved out of teakwood "—it didn't occur to me that you would come into the office today."

"Why ever not?" She stared at him in confusion and disbelief.

"I assumed you would be glad, if not grateful, to relinquish charge of the company to me. I thought you saw yourself as a stopgap president and would relish being free of the burdens of responsibility. I thought you would be happy to resume the role of a homemaker."

"You obviously don't know me very well," Dina retorted.

"So I'm beginning to discover," Blake responded grimly.

"What now?" she challenged him.

"No man likes to compete with his wife for a job, and I have no intention of doing so with you," he stated.

"Why not?" Dina argued. "If I'm equally competent—"

"But you are not," Blake interrupted, his eyes turning into dark chips of ironstone.

"I am." Surely she had proven that.

He ignored the assertion. "In the first place, our age difference alone gives me fourteen more years of experience in the business than you. Secondly, my father put me to work as a busboy when I was fifteen. Later I was a porter, a desk clerk, a cook, a manager. Compared to mine, your qualifications are negligible."

His logic deflated her balloon of pride. He made her seem like a fool, a child protesting because a toy was taken away. Dina had learned how to disguise her feelings and she used the skill to her advantage.

"You're probably quite right," she said stiffly. "I'd forgotten how much of a figurehead I was. Chet did the actual running of the company."

"Don't be ridiculous!" Blake dismissed the statement with a contemptuous jeer. "Chet is incapable of making an important decision."

Her eyes widened at the accusation. "How can you say that? He's been so loyal to you all these years, your best friend."

The lashing flick of his gaze laughed at her reference to Chet's loyalty, reminding her of Chet's engagement to her, but he made no mention of it when he spoke. "Just because he's been my friend doesn't mean I'm blind to his faults."

Although puzzled, Dina didn't pursue the topic. It was dangerous ground, likely to turn the conversation to a more personal level. At the moment, she wanted to keep it on business.

"None of that really matters. It still all comes down to the same basic thing—I'm out and you're in."

Blake raked a hand through his hair, rumpling it into attractive disorder. "What am I supposed to do, Dina?" he demanded impatiently.

"That's up to you," she shrugged, feigning cold indifference while every part of her rebelled at the emptiness entering her life. "If you don't object to my borrowing *your* secretary, a letter formally tendering my resignation will be on *your* desk when you return from your meeting."

"No, I don't object." But Blake bristled at her cutting sarcasm. As she turned on her heel to leave, he covered the distance between them with long strides, grabbing at her elbow to spin her around. "What do you expect me to do?" His eyes were a blaze of anger.

"I don't know—"

He cut across her words. "Do you want me to offer you a position in the administration? Is that it?"

Excited hope leaped into her expression. After Blake had put it into words, she realized that that was exactly what she wanted—to still have a part in running the company, to be involved in its operation.

"Dammit, I can't do it, Dina!" Blake snapped.

Crushed, she demanded in a thin voice, "Why?"

"I can't go around sweeping people out of office so you can take their place. Disregarding the fact that it smacks of nepotism, it implies that I don't approve of the people you hired to fill key positions. The logical deduction from that would be that I believed you'd done an inadequate job of running the company in my absence." His expression was hard and grim. "It's going to be several years before I can make any changes without them reflecting badly on you."

"That settles it, then, doesn't it?" Her chin quivered, belying the challenge in her voice.

His teeth were gritted, a muscle leaping along his jaw. "If you weren't my wife..." he began, about to offer another explanation of why his hands were tied in this matter.

"That's easily remedied, Blake," Dina flashed, and pulled her arm free before his grip could tighten. She didn't expect it to last long, but he made no attempt to recapture her.

"That's where you're wrong." He clipped out the words with biting precision.

Inwardly quaking under his piercing look, Dina turned away rather than admit his power to intimidate her. "It's immaterial anyway," she said with a small degree of composure. "My resignation will be on your desk within an hour." She walked to the door.

"Dina." The stern command of his voice stopped her from leaving.

She didn't remove her hand from the doorknob or turn to face him. "What?"

"Maybe I can keep you on in an advisory capacity." The stiffness of his words took away from the conciliatory gesture.

"I don't want any favors! And certainly not from the great Blake Chandler!" Dina flared, and yanked open the door.

It closed on a savage rush of expletives. When Dina turned away from the door, she looked into the curious and widened gaze of the secretary, Amy Wentworth. Dina silently acknowledged that the walls of the private office were thick, but she doubted if they were thick enough to deafen the sound of voices raised in argument. She wondered how much of the aftereffect of her quarrel with Blake was apparent in her face. She strained to appear composed and in command of herself as she walked to Amy's desk.

"Put aside whatever you're doing, Amy," she ordered, trying to ignore the widening look she received.

"But...." The young secretary glanced hesitantly toward the inner office Dina had just left, as if uncertain whether she was to obey Dina or Blake.

Dina didn't give her a chance to put her thoughts into words. "I want you to type a letter of resignation—for me. You know the standard form of these things. Just keep it simple and direct. Effective immediately."

"Yes, Mrs. Chandler," Amy murmured, and immediately removed the dustcover from her electric typewriter.

The connecting office door was pulled open and Dina glanced over her shoulder to see Blake stride through. She could tell he had himself under rigid control, but it was like seeing a predatory animal restrained in chains. The minute the shackles were removed, he would pounce on his prey and tear it apart. And she was his prey.

Yet, even knowing she was being stalked, she was mesmerized by the dangerous look in his gaze. She waited motionless as he walked toward her, the force of his dark vitality vibrating over her nerve ends, making them tingle in sharp awareness.

"Dina, I..." Blake never got the rest of his sentence out.

Chet entered the room through the door to the outer corridor. "Oh, I see you're on your way," he concluded at the sight of Blake. "I was just coming to see how much longer you'd be." His gaze switched its attention to Dina and became a troubled blue as he noticed the white lines of stress on her face.

"Yes, I'm on my way," Blake agreed crisply, and looked back at Dina. "I want you to attend the meeting, Dina." The veiled harshness in his gaze dared her to defy him.

But Dina felt safe in the company of others. "No. It's better for everyone to realize that you're in charge now and not confuse them by having a former head of the company present." She saw his mouth thin at her response and turned away in a gesture of dismissal.

"Dina has a good point," Chet offered in agreement, but a darting look from Blake made him vacillate. "Of course, unless you think it's wiser to—"

"Let's go," Blake snapped.

In a silent storm, he swept from the room, drawing Chet into his wake and leaving Dina feeling drained and colorless. Her nerves seemed to be delicate filaments, capable of snapping at the slightest pressure. When the letter of resignation was typed, her hand trembled as she affixed her signature to it.

"Put it on Mr. Chandler's desk," she ordered, and returned it to Amy.

"It was nice working for you, Mrs. Chandler," the young secretary offered as Dina turned to go, the words spoken in all sincerity.

"Thank you, Amy." Dina smiled mistily, then hurried from the room.

Leaving the building, she walked to her car. She knew there was no way she could return to the house and listen to Mother Chandler's happy conversation about Blake's return. With the top down on the white sports car, she removed the scarf from her hair and tucked it in the glove compartment.

With no destination in mind, she climbed into the car and drove, the wind whipping at her hair, which glittered like liquid sunlight in the morning air. Around and through the back streets, the main streets, the side streets of the city of Newport she went.

Half the time she was too blinded by tears to know where she was. She didn't notice the row of palatial mansions on Bellevue Avenue, or the crowds gathered on the wharf for the trial of the America Cup races.

She didn't know who she was, what she was, or why she was. Since Blake's return, she was no longer Dina Chandler. She was once again Mrs. Blake Chandler, lost in her husband's identity. She was no longer a businesswoman, nor did she feel like a housewife, since she had no home and a stranger for a husband. As to the reason why, she was in total confusion.

It was sheer luck that she glanced at the dashboard and noticed the gasoline gauge was hovering at the empty mark. Practicality forced her out of the bewildering whirlpool of questions. They stayed away until she was parked in a gas station and waiting in the building where her tank was being filled.

Then they returned with pounding force and Dina reeled under the power of them. Her restlessly searching gaze accidentally spied the telephone inside the building. She walked blindly to the phone and, from long habit, dialed the number of the one person who had already seen her through so much emotional turmoil.

The impersonal voice of an operator answered and Dina requested in an unsteady voice, "Chet Stanton, please."

"Who is calling, please?"

Dina hesitated a fraction of a second before answering, "A friend."

There was a moment when Dina thought the operator was going to demand a more specific answer than that, then she heard the call being put through. "Chet Stanton speaking," his familiar voice came on the line.

"Chet, this is Dina," she rushed.

"Oh." He sounded surprised and guarded. "Hello."

She guessed at the cause for the way he responded. "Are you alone?"

"No."

Which meant that Blake must be in his office. Dina wasn't certain how she knew it was Blake and not someone else, but she was positive of it.

"Chet, I have to talk to you. I have to see you," she declared in a burst of despair. Glancing at her wristwatch, she didn't give him a chance to reply. "Can you meet me for lunch?"

She heard the deep breath he took before he answered, "I'm sorry, I'm afraid I've already made plans for lunch."

"I have to see you," she repeated. "What about later?"

"It's been a long time since I've seen you." Chet began to enter into the spirit of the thing, however uncertainly. "Why don't we get together for a drink? Say, around five-thirty?"

It was so long to wait, she thought desperately, but realized it was the best he could offer. "Very well," she agreed, and named the first cocktail lounge that came to mind.

"I'll meet you there," Chet promised.

"And, Chet—" Dina hesitated "—please don't say anything to Blake about meeting me. I don't want him to know. He wouldn't understand."

There was a long pause before he finally said, "No, I won't. See you then."

After hanging up the receiver, Dina turned and saw the gas station attendant eyeing her curiously, yet with a measure of concern. She opened the pocketbook slung over her shoulder and started to pay for the gasoline.

"Are you all right, miss?" he questioned.

She glimpsed her faded reflection in the large plate-glass window of the station and understood his reason for asking. Her hair was windblown, and in riotous disorder. Tears had streaked the mascara from her lashes to make smutty lines around her eyes. She looked like a lost and wayward urchin despite the expensive clothes she wore.

"I'm fine," she lied.

In the car, she took a tissue from her bag and wiped the dark smudges from beneath her eyes. A brush put her tangled mass of silky gold hair into a semblance of order before it was covered by the scarf she had discarded.

"You have to get hold of yourself," she scolded her reflection in the rearview mirror.

Turning the key in the ignition, she started the powerful motor of the little car and drove away, wondering what she was going to do with herself for the rest of the day.

CHAPTER SIX

TYPICALLY, THE LOUNGE was dimly lit. Overhead lighting was practically nonexistent and the miniature mock lanterns with their small candle flames flickering inside the glass chimneys provided little more. The dark wood paneling of the walls offered no relief, nor did the heavily beamed low ceiling.

Tucked away in an obscure corner of the lounge, Dina had a total view of the room and the entrance door. A drink was in front of her, untouched, the ice melting. Five more minutes, her watch indicated, but it already seemed an interminable wait.

An hour earlier she had phoned Mother Chandler to tell her she would be late without explaining why or where she was. Blake would be angry, she realized. Let *him*, was her inward response. The consequences of her meeting with Chet she would think about later.

Brilliant sunlight flashed into the room as the door was opened. Dina glanced up, holding her breath and hoping that this time it might be Chet. But a glimpse of the tall figure that entered the lounge paralyzed her lungs. Her heart stopped beating, then skyrocketed in alarm.

Just inside the lounge, Blake paused, letting his eyes adjust to the gloom. There was nowhere Dina could run without drawing his attention. She tried to make herself small, hoping he wouldn't see her in this dim corner of the room. Dina felt rather than saw his gaze fasten on her seconds before his purposeful strides carried him to her table.

When he stopped beside her, Dina couldn't look up. Her teeth were so tightly clenched they hurt. She curled her hands around the drink she hadn't touched since it had been set before her. Despite the simmering resentment she felt, there was a sense of inevitability, too. Blake didn't speak, waiting for Dina to acknowledge him first.

"Imagine meeting you here," she offered in a bitter tone of mock surprise, not letting her gaze lift from the glass cupped in her hands. "Small world, isn't it?"

"It's quite a coincidence," he agreed.

There was a bright glitter in her blue eyes when she finally looked at him. His craggy features were in the shadows, making his expression impossible to see. The disturbing male vitality of his presence began to make itself felt despite her attempt to ignore it.

"How did you know I was here?" she demanded, knowing there was only one answer he could give.

And Blake gave it. "Chet told me."

"Why?" The broken word came out unknowingly, directed at the absent friend who had betrayed her trust.

"Because I asked him."

"He promised he wouldn't tell you!" Her voice was choked, overcome by the discovery that she was lost and completely alone in her confusion.

"So I gathered," Blake offered dryly.

Dina averted her gaze to breathe shakily. "Why did he have to tell you?"

"I am your husband, Dina, despite the way you try to forget it. That gives me the right to at least know where you are."

His voice was as smooth as polished steel, outwardly calm and firm. Her gaze noticed his large hands clenched into fists at his side, revealing the control he was exercising over his anger. He was filled with a white rage that his wife should arrange to meet another man. Dina was frightened, but it was fear that prompted the bravado to challenge him.

"You were in Chet's office when I called, weren't you?" she said accusingly.

"Yes, and I could tell by the guilty look on his face that he was talking to you. After that, it didn't take much to find out what was going on."

"Who did you think I would turn to? I needed him." Dina changed it to present tense. "I need Chet."

Like the sudden uncoiling of a spring, Blake leaned down, spreading his hands across the tabletop, arms rigid. In the flickering candlelight his features resembled a carved teakwood mask of some pagan god, harsh and ruthless and dangerously compelling.

"When are you going to get it through that blind little brain of yours that you've never needed him?" he demanded.

Her heart was pounding out a message of fear. "I don't know you," she breathed in panic. "You're a stranger. You frighten me, Blake."

"That makes two of us, because I'm scared as hell of myself!" He straightened abruptly, issuing an impatient, "Let's get out of here before I do something I'll regret."

Throwing caution away, Dina protested, "I don't want to go anywhere with you."

"I'm aware of that!" His hand clamped a hold on her arm to haul her to her feet, overpowering her weak resistance. Once she was upright, his fingers remained clamped around her arm to keep her pressed to his side. "Is the drink paid for?" Blake reminded her of the untouched contents of the glass on the table.

As always when she came in physical contact with him, she seemed to lose the ability to think coherently. His muscular body was like living steel and the softness of her shape had to yield. Everything was suddenly reduced to an elemental level. Not until Blake had put the question to her a second time did Dina take in what he had asked.

She managed a trembling, "No, it isn't."

Releasing her, Blake took a money clip from his pocket and peeled off a bill, tossing it on the table. Then the steel band of his arm circled her waist to guide her out of the lounge, oblivious to the curious stares.

In towering silence he walked her to the white Porsche, its top still down. He opened the door and pushed her behind the wheel. Then, slamming the door shut, he leaned on the frame, an unrelenting grimness to his mouth.

"My car is going to be glued to your bumper, following you every inch of the way. So don't take any detours on the route home, Dina," he warned.

Before Dina could make any kind of retort, he walked to his car parked in the next row of the lot. Starting the car, she gunned the motor as if she were accelerating for a race, a puny gesture of impotent defiance.

True to his word, his car was a large shadow behind hers every block of the way, an ominous presence she couldn't shake even if she had tried—which she didn't. Stopping in the driveway of his mother's house—their house—Dina hurried from her car, anxious to get inside where the other inhabitants could offer her a degree of safety from him.

Halfway to the door Blake caught up with her, a hand firmly clasping her elbow to slow her down.

"This little episode isn't over yet," he stated in an undertone. "We'll talk about it later."

Dina swallowed the impulse to challenge him. It was better to keep silent with safety so near. Together they entered the house, both concealing the state of war between them.

Mother Chandler appeared in the living-room doorway, wearing an attractive black chiffon dress. Her elegantly coiffed silver hair was freshly styled, thanks to an afternoon's appointment at her favorite salon. She smiled brightly at the pair of them, unaware of the tension crackling between them.

"You're both home—how wonderful!" she exclaimed, assuming her cultured tone. "I was about to suggest to Deirdre that perhaps she should delay dinner for an hour. I'm so glad it won't be necessary. I know how much you detest overcooked meat, Blake.''

"You always did like your beef very rare, didn't you, Blake?'' Dina followed up on the comment, her gaze glittering at his face with diamond sharpness. "I have always considered your desire for raw flesh as a barbaric tendency.''

"It seems you were right, doesn't it?'' he countered.

Mother Chandler seemed impervious to the barbed exchange as she waved them imperiously into the living room. "Come along. Let's have a sherry and you can tell me about your first day back at the office, Blake.'' She rattled on, covering their tight-lipped silence.

IT WAS AN ORDEAL getting through dinner and making the necessary small talk to hide the fact that there was anything wrong. It was even worse after dinner when the three of them sat around with their coffee in the living room. Each tick of the clock was like the swing of a pendulum, bringing nearer the moment when Blake's threatened discussion would take place.

The telephone rang and the housekeeper answered it in the other room. She appeared in the living room seconds later to announce, "It's for you, Mr. Blake. A Mr. Carl Landstrom.''

"I'll take it in the library, Deirdre,'' he responded.

Dina waited several seconds after the library door had closed before turning to Mother Chandler. "It's a business call.'' Carl Landstrom was head of the accounting department and Dina knew that his innate courtesy would not allow him to call after office hours unless it was something important. "Blake is probably going to be on the phone for a while,'' she explained, a fact she was going to use to make her escape and avoid his private talk. "Would you explain to him that I'm very tired and have gone on to bed?''

"Of course, dear.'' The older woman smiled, then sighed with rich contentment. "It's good to have him back, isn't it?''

It was a rhetorical question, and Dina didn't offer a reply as she bent to kiss the relatively smooth cheek of her mother-in-law. "Good night, Mother Chandler.''

"Good night.''

Upstairs, Dina undressed and took a quick shower. Toweling herself dry, she wrapped the terry-cloth robe around her and removed the shower cap from her head, shaking her hair loose. She wanted to be in bed with the lights off before Blake was off the telephone. With luck he wouldn't bother to disturb her. She knew she was merely postponing the discussion, but for the moment that was enough.

Her nightgown was lying neatly at the foot of the bed as she entered the bedroom that adjoined the private bath, her hairbrush in hand. A few brisk strokes to unsnarl the damp curls at the ends of her hair was all that she needed to do for the night, she decided, and sat on the edge of the bed to do it.

The mattress didn't give beneath her weight. It seemed as solid as the seat of a wooden chair. Dina was motionless as she assembled the knowledge and realized that the new mattress and box springs she had ordered for Blake had arrived and hers had been removed.

She sprang from the bed as if discovering a bed of hot coals beneath it. No, her heart cried, she couldn't sleep with him—not after that last humiliating experience; not with his anger simmering so close to the surface because of today.

The door opened and Blake walked in, and the one thing in the forefront of her mind burst out in panic. "I'm not going to sleep with you!" she cried.

A brow flicked upward. "At the moment, sleep is the furthest thing from my mind."

"Why are you here?" She was too numbed to think beyond the previous moment.

"To finish our discussion." Blake walked to the chair against the wall and motioned toward the matching one. "Sit down."

"No," Dina refused, too agitated to stay in one place even though he sat down with seemingly relaxed composure while she paced restlessly.

"I want to know why you were meeting Chet." His hooded gaze watched her intently, like an animal watching its trapped prey expend its nervous energy before moving in for the kill.

"It was perfectly innocent," she began in self-defense, then abruptly changed her tactics. "It's really none of your business."

"If it was as perfectly innocent as you claim," Blake said, deliberately using her words, "then there's no reason not to tell me."

"What you can't seem to understand, or refuse to understand, is that I need Chet," she flashed. "I need his comfort and understanding, his gentleness. I certainly don't receive that from you!"

"If you'd open your eyes once, you'd see you're not receiving it from him, either," Blake retorted.

"Don't I?" Her sarcastic response was riddled with disbelief.

"Chet doesn't comfort. He merely mouths the words you want to hear. He's incapable of original thought."

"I would hate to have you for a friend, Blake," she declared tightly, "if this is the way you regard friends when they aren't around, cutting them into little pieces."

"I've known Chet a great deal longer than you have. He can't survive unless he's basking in the reflected glory of someone else. When I disappeared, he transferred his allegiance to you, because you represented strength. He's a parasite, Dina, for all his charm," Blake continued his cold dissection. "He lived on your strength. He persuaded you to take charge of the company because he knew he was incapable of leading a child, let alone a major corporation."

"You don't know what you're saying," Dina breathed, walking away from his harsh explanation.

"The next time you're with him, take a good look at him, Dina," he ordered. "And I hope you have the perception to see that you've been supporting him through all this, not the other way around."

"No!" She shook her head in vigorous denial.

"I should have stayed away for a couple more months. Maybe by then the rose-colored spectacles would have come off and you would have found out how heavily he leans on you."

Pausing in her restless pacing, Dina pressed her hands over her ears to shut out his hateful words. "How can you say those things about Chet and still call him your friend?"

"I know his flaws. He's my friend in spite of them," Blake responded evenly. "Yet you were going to marry him without acknowledging that he had any."

"Yes. Yes, I was going to marry him!" Dina cried, pulling her hands away from her ears and turning to confront him.

"Only when I came back, he dropped you so fast it made your head swim. Admit it." Blake sat unmoving in the chair.

"He wanted me to be happy," she argued defensively.

"No," he denied. "My return meant you were on the way out of power and I was in. Chet was securing his position. There was nothing chivalrous in his reason for breaking the engagement. He wasn't sacrificing anything, only insuring it."

"So why did you hound him into admitting he was meeting me today?" challenged Dina.

"I didn't hound him. He was almost relieved to tell me."

"You have an answer for everything, don't you?" She refused to admit that anything Blake was saying made any sense. She fought to keep that feeling of antagonism; without it, she was defenseless against him. "It's been like this ever since you came back," she complained, uttering her thoughts aloud.

"I knew when everyone discovered I was alive, it was going to be a shock. But I thought it would be a pleasant shock," Blake sighed with wry humor. "In your case, I was wrong. It was a plain shock and you haven't recovered from it yet."

Dina heard the underlying bitterness in his tone and felt guilty. She tried to explain. "How did you think I would feel? I'd become my own person. Suddenly you were back and trying to absorb me again in your personality, swallow me up whole."

"How did you think I would react when you've challenged me every minute since I've returned?" His retaliation was instant, his temper ignited by her defensive anger, but he immediately brought it under control. "It seems we've stumbled onto the heart of our problem. Let's see if we can't have a civilized discussion and work it out."

"Civilized!" Dina laughed bitterly. "You don't know the meaning of the word. You spent too much time in the jungle. You aren't even civilized about the way you make love!"

Black fires blazed in his eyes. The muscles along his jaw went white from his effort to keep control. "And you go for the jugular vein every time!" he snarled, rising from the chair in one fluid move.

Dina's heart leaped into her throat. She had aroused a beast she couldn't control. She took a step backward, then turned and darted for the door. But Blake intercepted her, spinning her around, his arms circling her, crushing her to his length.

His touch sizzled through her like an electric shock, immobilizing her. She offered not an ounce of resistance as his mouth covered hers in a long, punishing kiss. She seemed without life or breath, except what he gave her in anger.

Anger needs fuel to keep it burning, and Dina gave him none. Gradually the brutal pressure eased and his head lifted a fraction of an inch. She opened her eyes and gazed breathlessly into the brilliant darkness of his. The warm moistness of his breath was caressing her parted lips.

His hand stroked the spun gold of her hair, brushing it away from her cheek. "Why do you always bring out the worst in me?" he questioned huskily.

"Because I won't let you dominate me the way you do everyone else," Dina whispered. She could feel the involuntary trembling of his muscular body and the beginnings of the same passionate tremors in her own.

"Does it give you a feeling of power—" he kissed her cheek "—to know that—" his mouth teased the curling tips of her lashes "—you can make me lose control?" He returned to tantalize the curving outline of her lips. "You are the only one who could ever make me forget reason."

"Am I?" Dina breathed skeptically, because he seemed in complete control at the moment and she was the one losing her grip.

"I had a lot of time to think while I was trying to fight my way out of that tropical hell. I kept remembering all our violent quarrels that got started over the damnedst things. I kept telling myself that if I ever made it back, they were going to be a thing of the past. Yet within hours after I saw you, we were at each other's throats."

"I know," she nodded.

As if believing her movement was an attempt to escape his lips, Blake captured her chin to hold her head still. With languorous slowness, his mouth took possession of hers. The kiss was like a slow-burning flame that kept growing hotter and hotter.

Its heat melted Dina against his length, so hard and very male. Her throbbing pulse sounded loudly in her ears as the flames coursed through her body.

Before she succumbed completely to the weakness of her physical desire, she twisted away from his mouth. She knew what he wanted, and what she wanted, but she had to deny it.

"It won't work, Blake." Her throat worked convulsively, hating the words even as she said them. "Not after the last time."

"The last time...." He pursued her lips, his mouth hovering a feather's width from them, and she trembled weakly, lacking the strength to turn away. "I hated you for becoming engaged to Chet, even believing I was dead. And I hated myself for not having the control to stop when you asked me not to make love to you. This time it's different."

"It's no good." But the hands that had slipped inside her robe and were caressing her skin with such arousing thoroughness felt very good.

For an instant Dina didn't think Blake was going to pay any attention to her protest, and she wasn't sure that she wanted him to take note of it. Then she felt the tensing of his muscles as he slowly became motionless.

He continued to hold her in his arms as if considering whether to concede to her wishes or to overpower her resistance, something he could easily accomplish in her present half-willing state.

A split second later he was setting her away from him, as if removing himself from temptation. "If that's what you want, I'll wait," he conceded grimly.

"I...." In a way, it wasn't what she wanted; and Dina almost said so, but checked herself. "I need time."

"You've got it," Blake agreed, his control superb, an impenetrable mask concealing his emotions. "Only don't make me wait too long before you come to a decision."

"I won't." Dina wasn't even certain what decision there was to make. What were her choices?

His raking look made her aware of the terry robe hanging loosely open, exposing the cleavage of her breasts. She drew the folds together to conceal the naked form Blake knew so well. He turned away, running his fingers through the wayward thickness of his dark hair.

"Go to bed, Dina," he said with a hint of weariness. "I have some calls to make."

Her gaze swung to the bed and the quilted spread that concealed the rock-hard mattress. "The new box spring and mattress that I had Deirdre order for you came today, and she put it in here. I'll...I'll sleep in the guest room."

"No." Blake slashed her a look over his shoulder. "You will sleep with me, if you do nothing else."

Dina didn't make the obvious protest regarding the intimacy of such an arrangement and its frustrations, but offered instead, "That bed is like lying on granite."

There was a wryly mocking twist of his mouth. "To use an old cliché, Dina, you've made your bed, now you have to lie in it."

"I won't," she declared with a stubborn tilt of her chin.

"Am I asking too much to want my wife to sleep beside me?" He gave Dina a long, level look that she couldn't hold.

Averting her head, she closed her eyes to murmur softly "No, it isn't too much."

The next sound she heard was the opening of the door. She turned as Blake left the room. She stared at the closed door that shut her inside, wondering if she hadn't made a mistake by giving in to his request.

Walking over to the bed, she pressed a hand on the quilt to test its firmness. Under her full weight it gave barely an inch. It was going to be quite a difference from the soft mattress she usually slept on, but then her bed partner was a completely different man from the urbane man she had married. Dina wondered which she would get used to first—the hard bed or the hard man?

Nightgowned, with the robe lying at the foot of the bed, she crawled beneath the covers. The unyielding mattress wouldn't mold to her shape, so she had to attempt to adjust her curves to it, without much success. Sleep naturally became elusive as she kept shifting positions on the hard surface trying to find one that was comfortable.

Almost two hours later she was still awake, but she closed her eyes to feign sleep when she heard Blake open the door. It was difficult to regulate her breathing as she listened to his quiet preparations. Keeping to the far side of the bed, she stayed motionless when he climbed in to lie beside her, not touching but close enough for her to feel his body heat.

Blake shifted a few times, then settled into one position. Within a few minutes she heard him breathing deeply in sleep. Sighing, she guessed she was still hours away from it.

CHAPTER SEVEN

A HAND WAS MAKING rubbing strokes along her upper arm, pleasantly soothing caresses. Then fingers tightened to shake her gently.

"Come on, Dina, wake up!" a voice ordered.

"Mmm." The negative sound vibrated from her throat as she snuggled deeper into her pillow.

Only it wasn't a pillow. There was a steady thud beneath her head, and the pillow that wasn't a pillow moved up and down in a regular rhythm. No, it wasn't a pillow. She was nestled in the crook of Blake's arm, her head resting on his chest. She could feel the curling sun-bleached hairs on his chest tickling her cheek and nose.

Sometime in the night she had forsaken the hardness of the mattress to cuddle up to the warm hardness of his body. Her eyelids snapped open at the familiarity sleep had induced. Dina would have moved away from him, but the arm around her tightened to hold her there for another few seconds.

A callused finger tipped her chin upward, forcing her to look at him, and her heart skipped a beat at the lazy warmth in the craggy male face.

"I'd forgotten what it was like to sleep with an octopus," Blake murmured. "Arms and legs all over the place!"

Heat assailed Dina at the intimacy of her position. Sleep had dulled her reflexes. When his thumb touched her lips to trace their outline, Dina was too slow in trying to elude it. As the first teasing brush made itself felt, she lost the desire to escape it. Rough skin lightly explored every contour of her mouth before his thumb probed her lips apart to find the white barrier of her teeth.

It became very difficult to breathe under the erotically stimulating caress, especially when his gaze was absorbing every detail of his action with disturbing interest. Situated as she was, with a hand resting on the hard muscles of his chest, afraid to move, Dina felt and heard the quickening beat of his pulse. Hers was racing no less slowly.

The muffled groan of arousal that came from his throat sent the blood rocketing through her heart. The arm around her rib cage tightened to draw her up. His mouth renewed the exploration his thumb had only begun. With a mastery that left her shattered, Blake parted her lips, his tongue seeking out hers to ignite the fires of passion.

In the crush of his embrace, it was impossible for Dina to ignore the fact that Blake was naked beneath the covers. It was just as impossible to be unaware that her nightgown was twisted up around her hips. It was a discovery his roughly caressing hands soon made.

As his hands slid beneath it, his fingers catching the material to lift it higher, Dina made a weak attempt to stop him. It seemed the minute her own hands came in contact with the living bronze of his muscled arms, they forgot their intention.

More of her bare skin came in contact with his hard flesh. The delicious havoc it created with her senses only made Dina want to feel more of him. Willingly she slipped her arms from the armholes as Blake lifted it over her head. His mouth was absent from her lips for only that second. The instant the nightgown was tossed aside, he was back kissing her with a demanding passion that she eagerly returned.

Blake shifted, rolling Dina onto her back, the punishing hardness of the mattress beneath her. His sun-bronzed torso was above her, an elbow on the mattress offering him support. His warm, male smell filled her senses, drugging her mind. When he dragged his mouth away from hers, she curved a hand around his neck to bring it back. Blake resisted effortlessly, the burning darkness of his gaze glittering with satisfaction at her aroused state.

At sometime the covers had been kicked aside. As his hand began a slow, intimate exploration of her breasts, waist and hips, Blake watched it, his eyes drinking in the shapely perfection of her female form. The blatant sensuality of the look unnerved Dina to the point that she couldn't permit it to continue. Again came the feeling that it was a stranger's eyes looking at her, not those of her husband.

Gasping back a sob, she tried to roll away from him and reached the protective cover of the sheets and blankets. Blake thwarted the attempt, forcing her back, his weight crushing her to the unyielding mattress that had already bruised her muscles and bones.

"No, Dina, I want to look at you," Blake insisted in a voice husky with desire. "I imagined you like this so many times, lying naked in the bed beside me, your body soft and eager to have me make love to you. Don't blame me for wanting to savor this moment. This time no screech of a jungle bird is going to chase away this image. You are mine, Dina, mine."

The last word was uttered with possessive emphasis as his head descended to stake its first claim, his mouth seeking her lips, kissing them until passion overrode her brief attempt at resistance. A languorous desire consumed her as he extended his lovemaking to more than just her lips. She quivered with fervent longing at the slow descent of his mouth to her breasts, favoring each of them in turn to the erotic stimulations of his tongue.

Under his sensuous skill, Dina forgot the strangeness of his arms and the hardness of the rocklike mattress beneath her. She forgot all but the dizzying climb to the heights of gratification and the dazzling view from the peak. They descended slowly, not finding their breath until they reached the lower altitudes of reality.

Dina lay enclosed in his arms, her head resting on his chest as it had when she had awakened. This time there was a film of perspiration coating his hard muscles and dampening the thick, wiry hairs beneath her head. Dina closed her eyes, aware that she had come very close to discovering her love for Blake again, its light glittered in the far recesses of her heart.

Blake's mouth moved against her hair. "I had forgotten what an almost insatiably passionate little wench you are." His murmured comment suddenly brought the experience down to a purely physical level. What had bordered on an act of love, became lust. "I enjoyed it. Correction, I enjoyed you," he added, which partially brought the light back to her heart.

Crimsoning, Dina rolled out of his arms, an action he didn't attempt to prevent. The movement immediately caused a wince of pain. Every bone and fiber in her body was an aching reminder of the night she had spent in the hard-rock bed.

"How can you stand to sleep in this bed?" Dina was anxious to change the subject, unwilling to speak of the passion they had just shared. "It's awful."

"You'll get used to it." When Blake spoke, Dina realized he had slid out of bed with barely a sound while she had been discovering her aches and pains. Her gaze swung to him as he stepped into the bottoms of his silk pajamas and pulled them on. Feeling her eyes watching him, Blake glanced around. There was a laughing glint in his dark eyes as he said, "It's a concession to Deirdre and her Victorian modesty this morning."

Dina smiled. Even that hurt. "What time is it?"

"Seven," he answered somewhat absently, and rubbed the stubble of beard on his chin.

"That late?"

Her pains deserted her for an instant and she started to rise, intent only on the thought that she would be late getting to the office unless she hurried. Then she remembered she no longer had any reason to go to the office and sank back to the mattress, tiredness and irritation sweeping over her.

"Why am I getting up?" she questioned herself aloud. "It took me so long to get to sleep last night. Why didn't you just let me keep right on sleeping?" Then he wouldn't have made love to her and she wouldn't be experiencing all this confusion and uncertainty, about herself and him.

"You'd be late to work," was Blake's even response.

"Have you forgotten?" Bitterness coated her tongue. "I've been replaced. I'm a lady of leisure now."

"Are you?" He gave her a bland look. "Your boss doesn't think so."

"What boss? You?" Dina breathed out with a scornful laugh. "You're only my husband."

"Does that mean you're turning it down?"

"What? Will you quit talking in riddles?"

"Maybe if you hadn't been so proud and stubborn yesterday morning and attended the meeting as I asked you to, you'd know what I'm talking about."

She pressed a hand against her forehead, tension and sleeplessness pounding between her eyes. "I didn't attend the meeting, so perhaps you could explain."

"We're starting a whole new advertising campaign to upgrade the image of the Chandler Hotel chain," he explained. "We can't possibly compete with the bigger chains on a nationwide basis, especially when most of our hotels are located in resort areas, not necessarily heavily populated ones. We're going to use that fact to our advantage. From now on, when people think of resort hotels, it's going to be synonymous with Chandler Hotels."

"It's a sound idea," Dina conceded. "But what does that have to do with me?"

"You're going to be in charge of the campaign."

"What?" Blake's calm announcement brought her upright, wary disbelief and skepticism in the look she gave him. "Is this some kind of a cruel joke?"

There was an arrogant arch to one dark eyebrow. "Hardly." He walked around the bed to where she stood. "I put the proposal to the rest of the staff yesterday, along with the recommendation that you handle it."

"Is this a token gesture? Something for me to do to keep me quiet?" She couldn't accept that there wasn't an ulterior motive behind the offer. It might mean admitting something else.

"I admit that picking you as my choice to head the campaign was influenced by the tantrum you threw in the office yesterday morning when you discovered I was taking over." His gaze was steady, not yielding an inch in guilt. "But you can be sure, Dina, that I wouldn't have suggested your name to the others if I didn't believe you could handle the job. You can put whatever interpretation you like on that."

Dina believed him. His candor was too forthright to be doubted, especially when he acknowledged the argument they had had earlier. It surprised her that he had relented to this extent, putting her in charge of something that could ultimately be so important to the company. True, she would be working for him, but she would be making decisions on her own, too.

"Why didn't you tell me about this last night?" She frowned. "Your decision had already been made. You just said a moment ago that you told the staff yesterday. Why did you wait until now to tell me?"

Blake studied her thoughtfully. "I was going to tell you last night after we'd had our talk, but circumstances altered my decision and I decided to wait."

"What circumstances?" Dina persisted, not following his reasoning.

"To be perfectly honest, I thought if you knew about it last night you might have been prompted to make love to me out of gratitude," Blake replied without a flicker of emotion appearing in his impassive expression.

There was an explosion of red before her eyes. "You thought I'd be so grateful that I'd...." Anger robbed her of speech.

"It was a possibility."

Dina was so blind with indignant rage that she couldn't see straight, but it didn't affect her aim as her opened palm connected with the hard contour of his cheek. As the white mark turned scarlet, Blake walked into the bathroom. Trembling with the violence of her aroused temper, Dina watched him go.

When her anger dissipated, she was left with a niggling question. If he hadn't made that degrading remark, would she still be angry with him? Or would this have been the first step towards reestablishing the foundation of their marriage, with Blake recognizing that she had the talent and skill to be more than a simple housewife? Hindsight could not provide the answer.

At the breakfast table, their conversation was frigidly civil.

"Please pass the juice."

"May I have the marmalade?"

That fragile mood of shy affection they had woken up to that morning was gone, broken by the doubting of each other's motives.

When both had finished breakfast, Blake set his cup down. "You may ride to the office with me this morning," he announced.

"I would prefer to take my own car."

"It's impractical for both of us to drive."

"If you had to work late, I would be without a way home," Dina protested.

"*If* that should arise, you may have the car and *I'll* take a taxi home," he stated, his demeanor cold and arrogant.

Dina was infuriatingly aware that Blake would have an argument for every excuse she could offer. "Very well, I'll ride with you." She gave in with ill grace.

The morning crush of Newport traffic seemed heavier than normal, the distance to the office greater, the time passing slower, and the polar atmosphere between them colder than ever.

Feeling like a puppy dog on a leash, Dina followed Blake from the parking lot to his office. There she sat down, adopting a business air to listen to specific suggestions that had been offered by Blake and the staff for the campaign. It was a far-reaching plan, extending to redecorating some hotels to meet with their new resort image.

At that one, Dina couldn't help commenting caustically, "I'm surprised I'm not limited to that task. Decorating is woman's work, isn't it?"

The thrust of his frigid gaze pierced her like a cold knife. "Do you want to discuss this program intelligently? Or do you want to bring our personal difficulties into it? Because if you do, I'll find someone else for the job."

Her pride wanted to tell him to find that person, but common sense insisted she would ultimately be the loser if she did. The project promised to be a challenge, and Dina had come to enjoy that. Her pride was a bitter thing to swallow, but she managed to get it down.

"Sorry. That remark just slipped out." She shrugged. "Go on."

There was a second's pause as Blake weighed her words before continuing. When he had concluded, he gave her a copy of the notes from the staff meeting and a tentative budget.

Dina glanced over them, then asked, "Where am I to work?"

"I'll take you to your new office."

She followed him out of the office and walked beside him down the long corridor until they came to the end. Blake opened the last door.

"Here it is."

The metal desk, chair and shelves seemed to fill up the room. Three offices this size could have fit into Blake's office, Dina realized. And that wasn't all. It was cut off from the other staff offices, at the end of the hall, isolated. She could die in there and nobody would know, she thought to herself.

Blake saw the fire smoldering in her blue eyes "This is the only office that was available on such short notice," he explained.

"Is it?" she retorted grimly.

"Yes—" he clipped out the word challengingly "—unless you think I should have moved one of the executive staff out of his or her office to make room for you."

Dina knew that would have been illogical and chaotic, with records being shifted and their exact location possibly unknown for several days. Still, she resented the size and location of her new office, regardless of how much she accepted the practicality of its choice. But she didn't complain. She didn't have to, since Blake knew how she felt.

She looked at the bare desk top and said, "There's no telephone?"

"Arrangements have already been made to have one installed today."

"Fine." She walked briskly into the room, aware of Blake still standing in the doorway.

"If you have any questions—" he began in a cool tone.

Dina interrupted, "I doubt if I will." The banked fires of her anger glittered in the clear blue of her eyes.

His gaze narrowed, his expression hardening. "You can be replaced, Dina."

"Permanently?" she drawled in a taunting kitten-purr voice.

For an instant she thought he might do away with her violently, but instead he exhibited that iron control and pivoted to walk away. There was a tearing in her heart as he left. Dina wondered if she was deliberately antagonizing him or merely reacting to his attempted domination of her.

Pushing the unanswerable question aside, she set to work, taking an inventory of the supplies on hand and calculating what she would need. After obtaining the required items from the supply room, she began making a list of information she would need before drawing up a plan of action for the advertising campaign.

At the sound of footsteps approaching the end of the hallway, she glanced up from her growing list. She had left the door to her office open to lessen the claustrophobic sensation, and she watched the doorway, curious as to who would be coming and for what reason.

Chet appeared, pausing in the doorway, a twinkle in his gray blue eyes, an arm behind his back. "Hello there," he smiled.

"Are you lost or slumming?" Dina questioned with a wry curve to her lips.

He chuckled and admitted, "I was beginning to think I was going to have to stop and ask directions before I found you."

"It's certain I'm not going to be bothered with people stopping by to chat on their way someplace else. This is the end of the line," she declared with a rueful glance around the tiny office. "Which brings me to the next obvious question."

"What am I doing here?" Chet asked it for her. "When I heard you were exiled to the far reaches of the office building, I decided you might like a cup of hot coffee." The arm that had been behind his back moved to the front to reveal the two Styrofoam cups of coffee he was juggling in one hand. "At least, I hope it's hot. After that long walk, it might be cold."

"Hot or lukewarm, it sounds terrific." Dina straightened away from the desk to relax against the rigid back of her chair. "I shall love you forever for thinking of it."

She had tossed out the remark without considering what she was saying, but she was reminded of it as a discomfited look flashed across Chet's face.

"I guess that brings me to the second reason why I'm here." He lowered his head as he walked into the room, not quite able to meet her gaze.

"You mean about not meeting me yesterday and sending Blake in your place," Dina guessed, accurately as it turned out.

"Yes, well—" Chet set the two cups on the desk top "—I'm sorry about that. I know you didn't want me to tell Blake and I wouldn't have, either, except that he was in my office when you called and he guessed who I was talking to."

"So he said," she murmured, not really wanting to talk about it in view of the discussion she had with Blake last night regarding Chet.

"Blake didn't lay down the law and forbid me to go or anything like that, Dina."

"He didn't?" she breathed skeptically.

"No. He asked if you sounded upset," Chet explained. "When I said that you did, he admitted that the two of you were having a few differences and he thought it was best that I didn't become involved in it. He didn't want me to be put in the position of having to take sides when both of you are my friends."

Friends? Dina thought. Just a few days ago, Chet had been her fiancé, not her friend. But he looked so pathetically sorry for having let her down yesterday that she simply couldn't heap more guilt on his bowed head.

Instead she gave him the easy way out. "Blake was right, it isn't fair to put you in the middle of our disagreements. If I hadn't been so upset I would have realized it. Anyway, it doesn't matter now." She shrugged.

"It all worked out for the best." That was a white lie, since it almost had, until their blowup that morning.

"I knew it would." The smile he gave her was tinged with relief. "Although I wasn't surprised to hear Blake admit that the two of you had got off to a rocky start." He removed the plastic lid from the cup and handed the cup to her.

"Why do you say that?" she asked.

"The two of you were always testing each other to see which was the stronger. It looks like you still are."

"Which one of us is the stronger? In your opinion," Dina qualified her question.

"Oh, I don't know." His laughter was accompanied by a dubious shake of his head. "A feeling of loyalty to my own sex makes me want to say Blake, but I have a hunch I would be underestimating you."

In other words, Dina realized, Chet was not taking sides. He was going to wait until there was a clear-cut winner. In the meantime he was keeping his options open, buttering up both of them.

The minute the last thought occurred to her, Dina knew it had been influenced by Blake's comment that Chet was always beside the one in power. But she immediately squashed the thought as small and not deserving of someone as loyal as Chet.

"You're a born diplomat, Chet." She lifted the coffee cup in a toast. "No wonder you're such an asset to this company."

"I try to be," he admitted modestly, and touched the side of his cup to hers. "Here's to the new campaign."

The coffee was only medium hot and Dina took a big sip of it. Chet's reference to the new project made her glance at the papers, notes and lists spread over her desk.

"It's going to be quite a formidable project." She took a deep breath, aware of the magnitude of the image change for the Chandler Hotel chain. "But I can feel it's right and that it will be very successful."

"That's the third reason I'm here."

Her startled gaze flew to his face, her blue eyes rounded and bright with inquiry. "Why?"

Had she made Blake so angry that he was already taking her off the campaign? Oh, why hadn't she held her tongue, she thought, angered by the way she had kept pushing him.

"Blake wants me to work with you on it," Chet announced.

Her relief that Blake hadn't replaced her didn't last long. "Doesn't he think I'm capable of handling it by myself?" Her temper flared at the implied doubt of her ability.

"You wouldn't be here if he didn't believe you could," he said placatingly. "But after all, you said it yourself. It's going to be a formidable project and you're going to need some help. I've been nominated to be your help. Besides, Blake knows how well we worked together as a team while he was gone."

Dina counted to ten, forcing herself to see the logic of Chet's explanation. But she wasn't sure that she liked the idea. There was still the possibility that Blake had appointed Chet as her watchdog and he would go running to Blake the instant she made a mistake.

She was doing it again, she realized with a desperate kind of anger. She was not only questioning Blake's motives, but making accusations against Chet's character, as well. Damn Blake, she thought, for putting doubts about Chet in her mind.

Chet took a long swig of his coffee, then set it aside. "Where shall we begin?"

"I've been making some lists," Dina readjusted her attention to the project at hand.

She went over the lists with Chet, discussing various points with him. Although Dina was still skeptical of Blake's motives in having Chet assist her, she accepted it at face value until she could prove otherwise. An hour later, Chet left her small office with a formidable list of his own to carry out.

The bulk of the day Dina spent getting the project organized. In itself, that was no easy task. At five o'clock, she was going over the master list again, making notes in the margins while various ideas were still fresh in her mind.

"Are you ready?" Blake's voice snapped from the open doorway.

Her head jerked up at the sound. The lenses of her glasses blurred his image, deceptively softening the toughness of his features. For an instant, Dina almost smiled a welcome, then the sharpness of his demanding question echoed in her mind. Recovering from that momentary rush of pleasure, Dina bent her head over the papers once again.

"I will only be a few more minutes." She adjusted the glasses on the bridge of her nose.

Blake walked in, his dislike at being kept waiting charging the air with tension. He sat in the straight-backed chair in front of her desk. Dina was conscious of his scrutiny, both of her and her work.

"Since when did you wear glasses?" he accused.

She touched a finger to a bow, realizing he had never seen her wearing them. "I began wearing them about a year ago."

"Do you need them?"

"What a ridiculous question!" she snapped. "Of course, I need them."

"It isn't so ridiculous," Blake contradicted with dry sarcasm. "They enhance the image of a crisp, professional career woman who has turned her back on domestic pursuits."

It was a deliberately baiting comment. Dina chose not to rise to the tempting lure. "With all the reading and close work I have had to do, it became too much of a strain on my eyes. After too many headaches, I put my vanity aside and began wearing glasses to read. They have nothing to do with my image," she lied, since the choice of frame styles had been made with that in mind.

"Then you do admit to having an image," he taunted her coldly.

It was no use. She simply couldn't concentrate on what she was doing. It took all of her attention to engage in this battle of words with him. Removing her glasses, she slipped them into their leather case. Dina set her notes aside and cleared the top of her desk.

"You haven't answered my question," Blake prompted in a dangerously quiet voice when she rose to get her coat.

"I hadn't realized your comment was a question." She took her purse from the lower desk drawer, unconsciously letting it slam shut to vent some of her tightly controlled anger.

"Is that how you see yourself, Dina, as a career woman whose life is centered around her work, with no time for a husband?" This time Blake phrased it as a question. The office was so small that when he stood up, he was blocking her path.

"That is hardly true." She faced him, her nerves quivering with his closeness.

"No?" An eyebrow lifted in challenging disbelief.

"Have you forgotten?" It was bravado that mocked him. "I was going to marry Chet, so I must have felt there was room for a husband in my life."

"I am your husband," Blake stated.

"I don't know you." Dina looked anywhere but into those inscrutable dark eyes.

"You knew me well enough this morning, in the most intimate sense of the word that a wife can 'know' her husband," Blake reminded her deliberately.

"This morning was a mistake." She brushed past him to escape into the hallway, but he caught her arm to half turn her around.

"Why was it a mistake?" he demanded.

"Because I let myself listen to all your talk about long, lonely nights and I started feeling sorry for you, that's why," Dina lied angrily, because she was still confused by her willingness to let him make love to her this morning when he still remained so much of a stranger to her in many ways.

His mouth thinned into a cruel line, all savage and proud. "Compassion is the last thing I want from you!" he snarled.

"Then stop asking me to pick up the threads of our life. The pattern has changed. I don't know you. The Blake Chandler that spent two and a half years in a jungle is a stranger to me. You may have had to live like an animal, but don't ask me to become your mate. I am more than just an object to satisfy your lust." The words streamed out, flooding over each other in their rush to escape. With each one, his features grew harder and harder until there was nothing gentle or warm left in them.

Blake gave her a push towards the door. "Let's go before you goad me into proving that you're right," he snapped.

Aware that she had nearly wakened a sleeping tiger whose appetites were ravenous, Dina quietly obeyed him. All during the ride back to his mother's house she kept silent, not doing anything to draw attention to herself. Blake ignored her, not a single glance straying to her. The cold war had briefly exploded into a heated battle, but once again the atmosphere was frigid.

Within minutes of entering the house, Blake disappeared into the library. Dina found herself alone in the living room with her mother-in-law, listening to the latest gossip Norma Chandler had picked up at the afternoon's meeting of the garden club

"Of course, everyone was buzzing with the news about Blake," the woman concluded with a beaming smile. "They wanted to know every single detail of his adventure in the jungle. I thought they were never going to let me leave. Finally I had to insist that I come home to be here when you and Blake arrived."

Dina was certain that Norma Chandler had been the center of attention. No doubt, the woman had reveled in it, even if the spotlight had been a reflection of her son's.

"It was a thoughtful gesture to be waiting at the door when Blake came home from the office," she murmured, knowing some appreciation should be expressed. It was expected.

"I only wish he had waited a few more days before returning to the office," sighed Norma Chandler. "After all he's been through, he was entitled to rest for a few days."

Unspoken was the fact that it would have given her a chance to dote on him, coddle him like a little boy again. But the chance had been denied her and Norma Chandler was protesting. Dina wasn't sure if she was being blamed for Blake's decision to return to work so quickly. In case she was, she decided to set the record straight.

"It wasn't my idea that he had to come back right away. Blake has some bold, new plans for the company. I think he was eager to get back to work so he could put them into operation," Dina explained.

"I am sure you are right, but he isn't giving us much time to enjoy the fact that he is back. There I go," Norma Chandler scolded herself. "I'm complaining when I should be counting my blessings. It's just that I can't help wondering how much longer I'll have him."

"That's a peculiar thing to say," Dina frowned.

"You will probably be moving out soon—into a place of your own, won't you? Then I'll only be able to see him on weekends," she pointed out.

"We have discussed the possibility of getting a place of our own," Dina admitted, choosing her words carefully as she recalled their argument the previous morning. "But I don't think it will happen in the near future. We both will probably be too busy to do much looking. Naturally we don't want to move into just any place," she lied.

It wasn't that Dina had become so career-oriented that she didn't long for a home of her own as she had led Blake to believe. At the moment, she was relieved to live in the Chandler home where his mother and the housekeeper could serve as buffers. She wasn't ready yet to share a home solely with the stranger who was her husband. Maybe she never would be.

"I won't pretend that I'm not glad to hear you say that." Her mother-in-law smiled broadly at the statement. "You know how much I have enjoyed having you live here, Dina. Now that Blake is back, my happiness has been doubled. There is something about having a man around the house that makes it seem more like a home."

"Yes," Dina agreed, if not wholeheartedly.

"I don't like to pry." There was a hesitancy in the woman's voice and expression. "But I have the feeling that there is a bit of tension between you and Blake. If I am wrong, you just say so or tell me to mind my own business. I don't want to become an interfering mother-in-law, but—" Her voice trailed off in the expectancy of a response from Dina.

It was Dina's turn to hesitate. She doubted if Mother Chandler would understand, but she felt a need to confide her fears in someone.

"There is a tension between us," she admitted cautiously. "It's just that Blake has changed. And I have changed. We aren't the same people we were two and a half years ago."

"It's Chet, isn't it?" Norma Chandler drew her own conclusions, hardly listening to what Dina had said. "I know that Blake behaved in front of the others as if he understood and forgave, but it bothered him, didn't it?''

"To a certain extent, yes." But not to the degree that her mother-in-law was implying.

"It is only natural that he'd be upset to find his wife engaged to his best friend, but he'll come around. In a few years, you'll be laughing about it."

"Probably," Dina nodded, but she couldn't help wondering if they would be together in a few years. For that matter, she wondered if they would be together in a few months.

The housekeeper entered the living room. "Dinner is ready whenever you wish," she announced.

"Now is fine, Deirdre," Norma Chandler stated. "Blake is in the library. Would you please tell him?"

Dinner that evening was an awkward meal, one that was made more awkward because Norma Chandler seemed determined to convince Blake how very properly Dina had behaved during his absence. Dina knew it was an outgrowth of their conversation and there was simply no way she could intervene. Blake seemed indifferent to the praise his mother heaped on Dina, which only prompted Norma Chandler to pile more on.

It was a relief to escape to the privacy of the bedroom after coffee had been served. The tension of the day and the evening had tightened her muscles into taut bands. The sight of the bed and the thought of sleeping beside Blake another night increased the tension. She was the captive of a crazy confusion, torn between dreading the idea of Blake making love to her again and looking forward to the possibility.

Dina walked from the bedroom into the private bath that adjoined it. She filled the porcelain tub with hot water and added a liberal amount of scented bubble bath. From her bedroom closet, she brought her robe and hung it on a door hook. Shedding her clothes, Dina stepped into the tub and submerged herself up to her neck in the steamy mound of bubbles.

Lying back in the tub, she let the warm water soak away the tension, and slowly relaxed in the soothing bath. The lavender fragrance of the bubbles wafted through the air, a balm to her senses. The water cooled and Dina added more hot, losing track of time in her watery cocoon.

The bedroom door opened and closed. Dina heard it, but she wasn't unduly concerned that Blake had come to the room. The bathroom door was closed. She expected him to respect the desire for privacy it implied.

When the bathroom door was opened anyway, Dina sat up straight in a burst of indignation. The sound of sloshing water drew Blake's gaze. Minus his suit jacket and tie, he had unbuttoned the front of his shirt down to his stomach, exposing a disturbing amount of hard muscled flesh and dark chest hairs.

"Sorry, I didn't know you were in here," he apologized insincerely.

The bubbles had been slowly dissipating during her long soak. Only a few bits of foam remained around the uplifting curve of her breasts. The fact did not escape Blake's attention. It kept him from leaving.

Self-consciously Dina grabbed for a handcloth, holding it in front of her. "Now that you've discovered I'm in here, get out."

"I thought you might want me to wash your back, or wouldn't you consider that civilized behavior?" Blake mocked.

"I don't need my back washed, thank you." Dina wasn't sure why she had bothered with the washcloth. It was becoming wet and very clingy. "Please leave," she requested stiffly. "I'm finished with my bath and I'd like to get out of the tub."

"I'm not stopping you. The sooner you are out, the sooner I can take my shower." Blake turned and walked into the bedroom, closing the door behind him.

Not trusting him, Dina quickly rinsed away the bubbles that were drying on her skin and stepped out of the tub. After rubbing herself down with the towel, she slipped into her robe and zipped it to the throat. Another few minutes were spent tidying the bathroom.

When she entered the bedroom, her senses were heightened to a fever pitch. Blake was sitting on the love seat, smoking a cigarette, his posture seemingly indolent. His hooded gaze swept over her.

"It's all yours." Dina waved a hand toward the bathroom.

Blake stubbed out his cigarette and uncoiled his length from the love seat. "Thank you." His response was cool and tauntingly lacking in gratitude.

Dina suppressed a shudder at his freezing politeness and wondered whether their heated exchanges were preferable to this. As he crossed the room, she walked to the closet. At the door, she stopped to glance at him.

It suddenly became imperative that she make him understand that she was not going to let him persuade her to make love, not until she was able to sort out her true feelings for him. She wanted to end this sensation that she was married to a stranger before they shared any further intimacies.

"Blake, I have no intention—" Dina began.

"Neither have I," he cut in sharply and paused at the doorway to the bathroom to pin her with his gaze. His mouth slanted in a cruel line. "I won't be exercising my husbandly rights with you. Didn't you think I was capable of phrasing it politely?" Blake mocked the sudden paleness of her complexion. "Perhaps if I had promised not to rape you, it would have been more in keeping with your image of me, wouldn't it?"

Dina turned away from his caustic challenge. "As long as we understand each other," she murmured stiffly.

"Just so there isn't any mistake. I won't touch you again until you come to me. And you will come to me, Dina." There was something almost threatening in the savagely controlled tone he used.

The closing of the bathroom door left Dina shaken. She changed out of her robe into her nightgown without being aware of her actions. She heard the shower running in the bathroom and tried not to visualize Blake standing beneath its spray, all sun-browned flesh, naked and hard, as paganly virile as a jungle god.

Shaking away the heady image, she walked to the bed and folded down the satin coverlet. Dina was between the silk sheets when Blake came out of the bathroom, a towel wrapped around his waist. He didn't glance her way as he switched off the light and walked around to the opposite side of the bed, unerringly finding his way in the dark. The mattress didn't give beneath his weight, but she was aware of him. The sheets seemed to transmit the heat from his nude body.

A tidal wave of longing threatened to swamp her. Dina closed her eyes tightly. Blake was fully aware of what he was doing to her. He had a motive for everything he did. She didn't believe that he was denying himself the possession of her out of respect, any more than she believed he had assigned Chet to help on the new project purely because she needed competent help. He wanted to undermine her trust in Chet. She vowed he wouldn't succeed.

But the aspersions Blake had made against Chet's character haunted her over the next two weeks. Again and again she cursed in silent protest at the seeds of doubt Blake had planted in her mind. The cold war between herself and Blake neither accelerated in those two weeks, nor was there even a hint of a thaw.

A knock at the opened door brought her out of her gloomy reverie. She had been staring out the dusty pane of the solitary window in her small office. She turned, slipping her reading glasses to a perch on top of her head.

"Hello, Chet." She stiffened at the sight of him and tried to relax, but she had become too self-conscious lately in his company, not feeling the same freedom and trust she had once found with him.

"I've finally got all the interior and exterior photographs of the hotels that you wanted." He indicated the stack of folders he was carrying with both hands. "I thought we should go over them together. Are you too busy to do it now?"

"No, bring them in." Dina began moving the papers from her desk. "Just give me a second to make some room."

Before the actual advertising campaign could begin, there was a lot of groundwork to be done. The most time-consuming part was improving the physical appearance of the hotels.

"I've already looked through them," Chet told her.

"Good," Dina nodded, and began to scan them herself.

The line of her mouth kept growing grimmer and grimmer. By the time she reached the bottom of the stack of photographs, she realized she had underestimated the amount of time and money it would take to superficially redo the hotels.

"It's worse than I thought," she sighed.

"Yes, I know," Chet agreed, matching her expression.

"Let's take the hotels one by one and make notes." She sighed. "The one thing we want to keep in mind is that each hotel should be different, its decor indigenous to its location. We don't want a vacationer to think that if he's been in one Chandler Hotel, he's been in them all."

"That's right."

"Okay, let's start out with the one in Florida." Dina gazed at the photographs. "I think it has to be the most challenging. I didn't realize it looked so sterile."

She flipped her glasses into place on her nose and reached for her note pad. "Here we'll take advantage of the tropical environment. Heavy on wicker furniture, light and airy colors, no carpeting, cool tile floors, and lots of potted plants and greenery. Something like the decor in our Hawaiian hotel would be good, but without the Polynesian accent."

"What about the exterior?"

Dina thought of the budget and winced. "I hope we can get by with some landscaping. I don't want to do a major face lift unless there's no other way."

Down the list of hotels and their photographs they went. The one in Maine would be done with a nautical flavor. The one in Mexico would have a lazy siesta look, complete with mock overhead fans turning leisurely from the ceiling. The founding hotel in Newport already had an elegant yachting atmosphere, which would now be stressed. The themes varied with each hotel, depending on its location.

When the last photograph had been examined and set aside, Dina looked at the copious collection of notes and sighed at the dollar signs they meant. She remembered her spiteful comment to Blake about the interior decorating to be done, remarking that it was woman's work. Well, there was a mountain of it here, one that she doubted Blake would have the patience to tackle.

90 STRANGE BEDFELLOW

"Now what?" Chet questioned.

"Now—" Dina took a deep breath "—now we need to have these notes transferred into sketches."

"Do you want me to start contacting some decorating firms?"

"I suppose so. With the scope of the work that needs to be done, I'm just wondering how we should handle it." She nibbled thoughtfully at her lower lip. "Something, either major or minor, has to be done at each of the hotels."

"In the past we've always used firms within the area of the hotels, in the same city when we could," Chet reminded her.

"Yes, I know." Dina slid the pencil through the platinum gold hair above her ear. "I checked the records last week to get an idea of the possible costs and noticed that in the past we'd always used local firms. Before, it had proved to be both economical and good business to trade with a company in the same area as one of our hotels."

"But, since virtually all the hotels are involved, it might not be practical because of all the traveling that would have to be done," he observed. "That cost could eat into whatever savings we might realize by using a local decorator."

"I'm afraid you're right," she agreed with a rueful nod. "We might be better off with a major firm capable of doing all the work. In the long run it might prove to be the more economical choice."

"I tell you what—" Chet leaned forward, his blue gray eyes bright with suggestion "—first let's get these notes typed up. Then why don't I contact two major companies to give us estimates on the work? To get a comparison, I can pick a half dozen hotels that are fairly close to here and obtain bids from local firms. I can use the hotel in Maine, the one here in Newport, naturally, the one in the Poconos—I can check the list."

"That might work," she agreed, turning the idea over in her mind and liking it. It had been a half-formed thought in her own mind, but when Chet had spoken it aloud, it had solidified. "Excellent suggestion, Chet."

"I'll get started on it right away." He began gathering up the notes and the photographs from her desk. "We don't want to waste time."

"Before you go, there's something else I've been thinking about that I wanted to talk over with you to get your opinion," Dina said to detain him.

"What's that?" Chet sat back down.

"To keep this continuity of every hotel being individual, I think we should carry it into the restaurants," she explained.

"But we're doing that." He frowned. "There are going to be decor changes in the restaurants and lounges, too. We just went over them."

"No, I was thinking of extending the idea to the food."

"Do you mean changing the menus?"

"Not completely. We would have to keep the standard items like steaks, et cetera, but add some regional specialities, as well. We do it already along the coast with the seafood."

"I see what you're saying." Chet nodded. "In the Poconos, for instance, we could add some Pennsylvania Dutch foods. We could even carry it down to little touches, like serving genuine johnnycake made out of white cornmeal with the dinner rolls here in Newport."

"Exactly," Dina nodded.

"I'll contact the restaurant managers of all the hotels. Those that aren't already doing this can send us a list of three or four speciality dishes they can add to their menus," he suggested.

"Yes, do that. We can initiate this change right away by simply adding a flyer to the menus until new ones can be printed."

"Consider it done, Dina." He started to rise, then paused. "Is that all?"

"For now, anyway," she laughed.

"I'll be talking to you. And I'll have my secretary send you a copy of these notes," he promised, and gathered the stack of notes and photographs into his arms.

As Chet walked out of the office, the smile left Dina's face and was replaced by a wary frown. She stared at the open doorway, feeling those uneasy suspicions rearing their ugly heads. Then with a firm shake of her head she dismissed them and turned back to the papers she had been working on.

CHAPTER EIGHT

BENT OVER HER DESK, Dina was concentrating on the proposals from the selected advertising agencies. Absently she stroked the eraser tip of her pencil through her hair. Intent on the papers, she didn't hear the footsteps in the hallway or notice the tall figure darkening her open doorway.

"Are you planning to work late?"

The sound of Blake's voice jerked her head up. He stood there, so lithely powerful, so magnetically attractive. The darkness of his tan seemed to have faded little, its bronze hue accentuated by the white turtleneck sweater. Through half-closed lids he looked at her, creating the impression of lazy and friendly interest, yet his expression seemed masked.

As always when he caught her unaware, her pulse accelerated. An odd tightness gripped her throat, leaving her with a breathless sensation. For an instant the room seemed to spin crazily.

It was at moments like these that Dina wanted to let the powerful attraction she felt simply carry her away. But that was too easy and too dangerous. It wouldn't solve any of the differences that had grown in the years they were apart.

His question finally registered. She managed to tear her gaze away from his ever watchful eyes to glance at her wristwatch, surprised to see it was a few minutes before six o'clock.

Then she noticed the silence in the rest of the building. There were no muffled voices coming in from the hallway, no clackety-clack of typewriters. Nearly everyone had left for the day, except herself and Blake.

"I hadn't realized it was so late," she offered in answer to his question. "I just have to clear these things away and I'll be ready to leave."

As she stacked the proposals one on top of the other, preparatory to slipping them into their folder, Blake wandered into the room. He suddenly seemed to fill every square inch of it. Within herself, Dina was conscious of the sensuous disturbance his presence caused.

"How is the campaign progressing?" he inquired, his gaze flicking to the papers in her hand.

Dina had to search for the chilling antagonism that would keep him at a distance. "Hasn't Chet been keeping you informed?"

"No. Was he supposed to?" There was a baiting quality to the blandness of his voice.

"I presumed he would," she retorted, opening a desk drawer to put the folder away.

"If you didn't tell him to keep me up to date, Chet won't," said Blake, hooking a leg over the desk corner to sit on its edge. "He only does what he's told."

The desk drawer was slammed shut. "Will you stop that!" Dina glared at him.

"Stop what?" Blake returned with seeming ignorance.

"Stop making remarks like that about Chet!" The antagonism was there; she no longer had to search for it.

Blake made an indifferent shrug. "Whatever you say."

Impatiently she swept the remaining papers and pens into the middle drawer of her desk, leaving the top neat and orderly. Setting her bag on top, she pushed her chair up to the desk. Her sweater was lying on the back of the chair near where Blake stood.

"Hand me my sweater, please." Frigid politeness crept into her voice.

Glancing around, Blake slipped it off the chair back and held it out to her as she walked around the desk to the front. "How are you and Chet getting along?"

"The same as always—very well." Dina gave him a cool look and started to reach for the sweater. "Did you expect it to be different?" It was spoken as a challenge, faintly haughty. A light flashed in her mind and she forgot about the sweater. "You did expect it to change, didn't you?" she accused.

"I don't know what you're talking about."

"That's why you told Chet to give me a hand. I thought it was because you didn't think I could handle the job, but that wasn't it at all, was it?" Her anger was growing with each dawning thought.

Completely in control, Blake refused to react. "You tell me."

"You planted all those doubts in my mind about Chet, then made me work with him, hoping I would become poisoned against him. That's what this was all about, wasn't it?" Dina was incensed at the way Blake had attempted to manipulate her thinking.

"I admit that after our little talk about Chet, I hoped the blinkers would come off and you would see him as he really is." There wasn't a trace of regret in his expression or his voice that his motive had been uncovered.

"That is the lowest, dirtiest thing I've ever heard!" she hissed.

Trembling with rage, she was completely unaware of her hand lashing out to strike him until it was caught in a vise grip short of its target. She gasped in pain as he twisted her arm to force her closer. He had straightened from the desk to stand before her, the sweater cast aside on the desk top.

"The last time you slapped me, I let you get away with it because I might have deserved it. But not this time," Blake told her flatly. "Not when I'm telling the truth."

"But it isn't the truth!" Dina flared, undaunted by his implied threat. "Not one word you've said against Chet is true. It's all lies. None of it is true!"

That darkly piercing look was back in his eyes as they scanned her upturned face. "You know it's true, don't you?" he breathed in a low, satisfied voice. "You've started to see it for yourself—that's why you're so angry."

"No, it isn't true," she denied. "I haven't seen it."

"You have. Why don't you admit it?" Blake insisted with grim patience.

"No," Dina continued to resist and strained to break free of his hold. "And I'm not going to stay here and listen to you tear Chet down anymore."

He increased the pressure of his grip and issued a taut denial. "I am not trying to make him appear less of a man. I'm trying to make you see him the way he is and not the way you've imagined him to be. Why can't you understand that what I'm saying is not a personal attack on him?"

Suddenly, unexpectedly, she did understand and she believed him. The discovery took the heat out of her anger. Dina stopped fighting him and stood quietly.

"All right," she admitted.

"All right what?" Blake lowered his gaze to her mouth, watching her lips as they formed the answering words.

"I have noticed a few things," Dina admitted further.

"Such as?"

"The way he takes a suggestion and elaborates on it until you're almost convinced the idea was his in the first place."

"He's done that?"

"Yes. Today, when I mentioned an idea I had about adding regional dishes to the restaurant menus." She wished Blake would stop watching her talk. It was unsettling, heightening her senses. "He's already contacting the restaurant managers to see about starting it."

"Chet is very good at organizing and carrying out a suggestion," Blake agreed. "What else?"

"I don't know. A lot of little things." The compliment Blake had given Chet prompted Dina to mention another conversation that had bothered her. "When I didn't take a stand today about having a local or a major decorating firm redo the hotels, Chet didn't either. He suggested getting comparison bids from both and avoided offering a concrete opinion. In the last two weeks, I honestly can't remember Chet making a decision or offering a proposal of his own."

Looking back, she realized that his proposal of marriage had been an outgrowth of a conversation about whether she would marry again or not. When she had conceded the possibility, Chet had asked if it would be someone like Blake she would choose. Her negative answer had then led to Chet's suggesting himself, after first testing out his ground.

That was hardly the mark of the strong, dependable man she had believed him to be. His reliability was limited to the times when someone else told him what to do.

Lost in her thoughts, Dina was unaware of the silence that had fallen between them until Blake spoke. "I have another equally selfish reason for wanting Chet to work with you on this project." His fingers were lightly stroking the inside of her wrist, a caressing motion that was disturbing.

A tingling warmth spread up her arm, her nerves fluttering in awareness of how close she stood to him. "What is it?" There was a breathless catch to her voice. She looked into his eyes, nearly overcome by the sensation that she could willingly drown in the dark pools.

"Because I know that eventually this project is going to entail a good deal of traveling and I wanted to make certain it wasn't my wife who went on these trips."

"I see." She couldn't think of anything else to say.

"You might as well know this, Dina," he said. "You and I are never going to be separated for any reason."

The ruthlessly determined note underlying his statement made her shiver. There was a sense of being trapped, a feeling that his wishes were inescapable. Whatever Blake wanted, he got. But not from her, her pride protested—not unless it was her own decision to agree.

With a degree of reluctance, she withdrew from his touch, turning to the desk to pick up her sweater and handbag. "I'm ready to leave now," she said, aware of the conflicting magnetic currents between them, alternately pulling and repelling.

Blake didn't make a move to leave. He just stood there looking at her, making her feel more uncomfortable and unsure of her own wants and needs.

"Sooner or later you're going to have to make a decision," he told her.

"I know. Sooner or later," she echoed softly.

"Why are you waiting? What is holding you back?" he questioned. "It isn't Chet anymore, so what's left?"

"I don't know." Dina shook her head uncertainly.

Needing to move, she started for the door. With that animal silence she was beginning to associate with him, Blake came up behind her, his hands sliding over her shoulders. The mere touch of him stopped her in her tracks.

"Decide now," Blake ordered in a low murmur.

The silvery gold length of her hair was secured in a bun low on the back of her head. She felt the warm stirring of his breath on the exposed skin of her neck, sensitive and vulnerable. The sensuous pressure of his lips exploring that special pleasure point sent a delicious tremor through her.

His hands slid down to her forearms, crossing them in front of her as he molded her shoulders, waist and hips to the hard contours of his body. Dina felt as pliable as putty, willing to be shaped into anything he wanted. Primitive passions scorched through her veins.

She struggled out of the emotional upheaval going on within her to protest, "Blake, I can't!"

"You want to." His mouth moved to her ear, his teeth nibbling at its lobe. "You know you do."

"I don't know anything," she breathed raggedly.

"Then feel," Blake instructed.

That was the problem. She felt too much and it blocked out her thinking processes. She didn't want to make a decision in the heat of an embrace. And certainly not in this inferno that was consuming her now.

"Blake, no!" She swallowed and pushed his hands from around her waist.

She took a step away from his tempting embrace and stopped, shaking and weak with desire. Her head was lowered, her chin tucked into her throat. She felt his gaze boring into her shoulders.

"Blake, no!" He mimicked her words with a biting inflection. "That's always your answer. How much longer are you going to keep giving it?"

"Until I'm absolutely sure that I know what I'm doing," Dina answered.

"And how long will that be?" Blake was striving for control. It was evident in the clipped patience of his tone.

"I don't know," she sighed. "I just know it's easy to surrender to passion now and not so easy to face tomorrow."

"Then you're a hell of a lot stronger than I am, Dina," he snapped, "because I don't give a damn about tomorrow!" He slipped a hand under her elbow. Her first thought was that he intended to ignore her uncertainties and kiss her into submission, something that would not be too difficult to do. Instead his hand pushed her forward. "Let's go," he muttered.

His long, ground-eating strides made it impossible for Dina to keep up with him without half running. The rigid set of his jaw kept her from drawing attention to herself or her plight. He didn't slow down until he reached the parking lot, where she struggled to catch her breath as they walked to the car.

Without looking directly at her, Blake unlocked the passenger door and held it open for her, slamming it shut when she was safely inside. Walking around the car, he unlocked his own door and slid behind the wheel. He put the key in the ignition, but didn't start the car.

Resting his hands on the steering wheel, he stared straight ahead for several long seconds, a forbiddingly hard line to his mouth. Dina grew increasingly uneasy at the silence and felt pinned when his dark gaze finally swung to her. It wasn't a pleasant sensation.

"The first day I was back," Blake said, "you claimed we needed time to get to know each other again—that we had to become adjusted to each other again. You felt we should talk."

"I'm surprised you remember," she remarked, and could have bitten off her tongue for issuing such caustic words.

"Believe me, I remember everything you've said," he returned with dry weariness, his attention shifting to the windshield in front of him. Dina shifted uncomfortably in her seat, but remained silent. "The point is, Dina, that we aren't getting to know each other again. We aren't talking. The only place we spend any time together alone is in the bedroom. And we both know there isn't any communication taking place there, physical or otherwise."

"So what are you suggesting? That we should communicate on a physical level and work on from there?" Dina questioned stiffly, her pulse quickening in a reaction that did not reject the idea.

"No, that isn't what I'm suggesting—" there was a cynical twist to his mouth "—although I know you're convinced that my instincts have become purely primitive."

A slight flush warmed her cheeks. "Then what are you suggesting?"

"That we spend more time together, as you wanted."

"That's a bit difficult with both of us working."

"Neither of us works on the weekend," Blake reminded her.

"You're forgetting we live in your mother's house." And Mother Chandler had still not got over her son's miraculous return. She still hovered around him every possible moment she could.

"No, I'm not," Blake returned calmly. "The key word is alone—no friends, no relatives, just you and I. I realize that can't be accomplished in my mother's home. That's why I've decided we'll spend the weekend at Block Island so we can have the time alone together that you claim we need."

"Block Island." Dina repeated the name of the resort island located roughly fourteen miles off the Rhode Island coast.

"That's what I said. Any objections?" He turned his head to look at her, a challenging glitter in his dark eyes.

"None." How could there be when he had cornered her with her own words?

"There is one thing more, Dina." Blake continued to study her, aware of her reluctant agreement—although why it was reluctant, Dina didn't know.

"What's that?" She was almost afraid to ask.

"I want this clearly understood before we go. If you haven't made up your mind about us by Sunday night, I'm not waiting any longer." At the sight of her paling complexion, he smiled without humor. "And I don't care whether you consider that a threat or a promise."

"You can't make a deadline like that," she protested.

"Can't I?" Blake had already turned away to start the car, ignoring her now that he had stated his intentions.

"All you're doing is turning this weekend into a farce," Dina retorted.

"Call it what you like," Blake said indifferently. "Just be sure to pack a suitcase and bring it to the office with you Friday morning. We'll catch the ferry to Block Island after work."

AS THE FERRY LEFT the protected waters of Narragansett Bay for the open waters of the Atlantic heading for the porkchop-shaped island off-shore, Dina stared sightlessly at the Brenton Reef Light Tower. She and Blake had barely exchanged five words with each other since leaving the office, and the silence was growing thicker.

She knew the reason her lips were so tightly closed. Blake's Sunday night ultimatum had made her feel as if he was pointing a gun at her head. So how could she look forward to the weekend ahead of them?

He had already foreordained the outcome, so what was the purpose? She should have refused to come. Why hadn't she?

Pressing a hand to her forehead, she tried to rub away the dull throb. The pills she had taken to stave off the sea sickness were working, but they clouded her thinking processes. At least she had been spared the embarrassment of being sick all over the place, even if she did feel slightly drugged.

Sighing, she glanced at Blake standing a few yards away talking to a fellow passenger. Their attention was on the low-hanging, dull gray clouds overhead. There was nothing menacing about them, but they added to the gloom Dina felt.

The two were obviously discussing the weather, because Dina overheard the man remark, "I hope you're right that it's going to be sunny and clear at the island. I don't know anything about ocean currents and how they affect the weather. All I know is that I want to get a weekend of fishing in."

Blake's prediction of good weather on Block Island proved correct. They were within sight of their destination when the clouds began to thin, permitting glimpses of blue sky and a sinking yellow sun. When the ferry docked at the Old Harbor landing, there were only patches of clouds in the sky.

But the silence between Dina and Blake didn't break. Despite that, she felt her spirits lift as they drove off the ferry onto the island, named after Adrian Block, the first European to explore it. The island's atmosphere was refreshing and Dina understood why it had been a fashionable health spa in the Gay Nineties.

She became absorbed in the scenery as Blake drove across the island to the picturesque resort village of New Harbor stretched along the banks of the Great Salt Pond. It had once been an inland lake, but a man-made channel now linked it to the ocean, providing a spacious harbor for both pleasure craft and commercial fishing boats.

Much of the previous tension returned when Blake parked in front of a hotel. It seemed different somehow to share a hotel room. Just why, Dina couldn't say, since they'd been sharing a bedroom almost ever since Blake had returned. She felt self-conscious walking beside him into the lobby.

Blake glanced down at her, his gaze inspecting the discomfited look on her face. "How are you feeling?"

"Fine," Dina rushed out the answer.

"No leftover nausea from the ferry trip?"

"None. Actually I never felt I was going to be sick. Except for a slight headache, I'm fine," she insisted. "Either the pills are getting stronger or I'm finally outgrowing my sea sickness."

"Good." His smile was somewhat grim. "Excuse me. I'll go check on our reservation."

As he walked to the desk to register, she lingered near a rack of postcards, pretending an interest in their colorful pictures. There was a curling sensation in her stomach when she saw the porter take their bags. Blake walked toward her and she immediately picked a card from the rack, ostensibly to study it more closely.

"Where you planning to send a postcard to someone?" The cynically amused query didn't help her fluttering stomach.

"No." She quickly returned it to the rack. "I was just looking at the picture."

"Tomorrow we'll take a look at the real thing."

Dina had to glance at the postcard. She had been so conscious of Blake she hadn't noticed what the subject of the card had been. Now she saw it was a lighthouse.

"It looks interesting," she offered, just to be saying something.

"Yes," Blake agreed dryly, as if aware that she hadn't previously known what it was. "Shall we go to our rooms?"

"Rooms?" In the plural, her eyes asked.

"Yes, two," he answered. Dina was surprised by the gentle, almost tender expression of patience that crossed his usually hard features. "We have adjoining bedrooms. I intend to give this weekend every chance of proving whatever it is that you feel needs proving, Dina."

There didn't seem to be any response she could make. Strangely, this seemed more of a concession than all the nights when Blake had shared her bed without forcing an intimacy—perhaps because he was granting her the privacy to think without his presence to disturb or influence her.

When he handed her one of the keys in his hand, she managed a quiet, "Thank you."

"When a man is desperate, he'll try anything," Blake returned cryptically, but Dina thought she caught a glimmer of humor in his dark eyes. It made him seem more human.

They walked to their rooms in silence, but it was no longer as strained as it had been. Blake hesitated outside his door, catching her eye for an instant before he turned the key in his lock and walked in.

Entering her room, Dina noticed her suitcase lying on the luggage rack and walked over to it, intending to unpack. Instead, she paused at the interior door that connected the two bedrooms. Blake was on the other side of it. Unconsciously she reached for the doorknob. It refused to turn; the door was locked. Regret conflicted with relief as she walked back to her suitcase and unpacked.

An hour later she had showered and was dressed in a wheat-colored shirtwaist dress that was elegantly casual. Blake hadn't said whether he would meet her at the restaurant for dinner or go down with her. She debated whether she should wait in the room or go to the restaurant, then decided to wait and she sat down on the bed.

Instantly a smile curved her lips. The mattress was blissfully soft, sinking beneath her weight like feather down. It was going to be a wonderful change from Blake's rock-firm mattress at the house.

Just then there was a knock at her door and Dina rose to answer it, the smile lingering on her lips. Blake stood outside, his eyes warming to a dark brown at her expression.

"You look pleased at something," he commented.

"My bed," Dina explained, a pair of dimples etching grooves in her cheeks. "It's soft."

His chuckle of understanding was soft, almost silent—a disarming sight and sound. Her heart skipped a beat, then refused to return to an even tempo.

"Shall we go to dinner?"

It was more of a statement than a question as Blake held out his hand for hers. Self-consciously she let her fingers be engulfed in his hand, but he continued to block the doorway, not permitting her to step out. His hold on her hand shifted, raising the inside of her wrist to his mouth.

"Have I told you how very beautiful you are?" he murmured.

"Blake, please," Dina protested, her lashes fluttering down at the heady touch of his warm lips against the sensitive area of her wrist.

"It's simply a compliment," he interrupted with a wry smile as he brought her hand away. "All you have to do is say 'thank you.'"

"Thank you," she repeated in a tight little voice, more disturbed than she cared to acknowledge by the effect he had on her.

"That's better." Blake moved to the side, leading her out of the room and reaching behind her to close the hotel-room door.

Fresh seafood was the natural selection to make from the menu. Once that decision had been made, Dina sat in the chair opposite from Blake. Inside she was a bundle of twisted nerves, but she forced herself to be still.

Without the steady chatter of Mother Chandler to lead a table conversation, she couldn't think of anything to say. It seemed an indication of how far she and Blake had grown apart. Her tongue was tied into knots.

"I'm going to have to make a trip to the bookstore soon," Blake commented with seeming idleness. "I have a lot of reading to catch up on."

"Yes, I suppose you do." Dina wanted to cry at how stilted her response had been.

But Blake either didn't notice it or deliberately ignored it. "It sounds a little crazy, I know, but reading was one of the things I really missed. More than good meals and clean clothes. I never considered it a necessity before."

"I doubt if I have, either," she admitted, forgetting her self-consciousness at his provocative comment.

"Any new titles you'd like to recommend?"

Dina hesitated, then suggested, *Roots*.

Before she realized what was happening, she found herself becoming engrossed in a discussion of new books that had been published in Blake's absence, and titles they had both read in the past. From reading, their conversation drifted to movies and Broadway shows. It seemed a natural progression to tell him about things she had done while he was gone, decisions she had been forced to make, such as subletting their apartment and sorting their furnishings.

When Blake later signaled their waiter for the check, Dina was astounded to discover that it was after ten o'clock and there had not been one awkward moment between them, not a single remark that had been in any way argumentative. She hadn't thought it was possible. She wondered if Blake had noticed it, but was afraid to ask. She didn't want to risk breaking whatever kind of temporary truce they had established.

They both seemed to be in a reflective mood as they retraced their way to their rooms. Dina was conscious of his hand lightly resting on the back of her waist, a faintly possessive air to his guiding touch, but she didn't object to it in the least.

"Do you know what this reminds me of?" Blake questioned her when they paused in front of her door.

"What?" Dina looked up, curious and thoughtful.

"All those times I used to walk you to the door of your sorority house and kiss you good night in a dark corner of the building." He glanced around the hallway, "Of course, here there aren't any dark corners." His gaze returned to her face. "But I *am* going to kiss you good night."

His head bent and Dina lifted hers to meet him halfway. The kiss was searingly light and questing, both seeking answers to unknown questions. Each seemed to realize that it would take only the slightest provocation to deepen the embrace to one of passion. Yet neither made it, merely testing the temperature of the water without becoming submerged in it.

With obvious reluctance they both withdrew from the embrace, gazing silently at each other. Blake took a step back, a closed look stealing over his face.

"Do you have your key?" he asked.

"Yes." Dina unfastened her clutch purse and took it out.

He hesitated a fraction of a second. "Good night, Dina." He moved toward his own door.

"Good night, Blake," she murmured, and entered her hotel room alone.

CHAPTER NINE

DINA DIDN'T SLEEP WELL that night. The irony of it was that it was because the mattress was too soft. She was wakened from her fitful dozing by a knock on the door and stumbled groggily across the room to answer it.

"Who is it?" She leaned tiredly against the door, her hand resting on the locked night latch.

"Blake," was the answer. "Are you ready for breakfast?"

Dina groaned. It couldn't possibly be morning already.

"Are you all right?" His tone was low and piercing.

"Fine," she mumbled, adding silently, *I just need some sleep.*

The doorknob rattled as he attempted to open it. "Unlock the door, Dina," he ordered.

She was too tired to think of a reason to refuse and too tired to argue if she had one. Slipping off the night chain, she unlocked the latch and stepped aside as Blake pushed the door open. Concern was written all over his expression, but she didn't notice.

"I don't want breakfast," Dina was already turning to make her way back to the bed. "You go ahead without me."

Blake's arm went around her to turn her back. He pushed the tangle of corn-silk hair behind her ear and held it there, his hand cupping the side of her head and tipping it up. His strength was a glorious thing and Dina willingly let him support her weight, too weary to stand on her own.

"What's the matter, Dina? You look exhausted." Blake was frowning.

"I am," she sighed. "My beautifully soft bed was too soft. I barely slept all night."

He laughed softly. "Why didn't you take a pillow and blanket off the bed and sleep on the floor? Or was that too uncivilized for you?" He mocked her in a gently teasing voice.

"I suppose that's what you did?" Dina lifted her tired lashes to glance at him. He looked disgustingly refreshed and rested.

"Yes," he nodded.

"And probably slept like a baby," she added enviously.

"I didn't sleep all that well," Blake denied.

"Why not?" Dina slid her arms around his hard, warm body and rested her head against his shoulder, closing her eyes.

"I haven't liked sleeping alone since I met you."

His provocative statement sailed over her sleepy head. Dina was only aware of how very right it felt to be in his arms, so comfortable and so warm. She snuggled closer.

"Why don't you just hold me for a while and let me sleep?" she suggested in a sleepy murmur.

"I don't think so." The arm that had been around her withdrew to press a hand against her rib cage just below her breast to push her away. "If I hold you much longer, I won't be thinking about sleep," Blake stated, a half smile curving one corner of his mouth. "Why don't you shower and dress? I'll go get some coffee to help you wake up before we go to breakfast."

Dina didn't have a chance to agree or disagree. One minute she was in his arms and the next he was walking to the door, leaving her swaying there unsteadily. The closing of the door goaded her into movement. She looked longingly at the bed, but knew it was no use. Even if she could go back to sleep, Blake would be back shortly to waken her. Following his suggestion, she walked to the bathroom.

It was shortly after midmorning by the time Blake and Dina finished their breakfast and started out on a leisurely tour of the island, dotted with freshwater ponds. It was not the first visit for either of them, but it had been several years since their last.

There was little noticeable change on the island, with the possible exception that a few more trees had been planted by property owners. The young saplings looked forlorn in a landscape that was remarkably devoid of trees. Early settlers had long ago cut down the native ones for lumber to build their homes. Reforestation was a new and slow process.

Stone fences crisscrossed the rolling terrain. The rocks had been deposited on the island by glaciers from the Ice Age and stacked, probably long ago by slave labor, to erect property boundaries of early farms. They were a picturesque touch on the island, called by an early Italian navigator God's Little Isle.

On the southeastern shore Blake parked the car on Mohegan Bluffs. The picture-postcard lighthouse sat on the point of the bluffs, the rustic house and tower looking out to sea. Its navigational beacon was one of the most powerful on the New England coastline.

The salty breeze off the ocean was cool. Dina zipped the coral windbreaker up to her neck while Blake locked the car. Screeching seagulls soared overhead as they walked together past the lighthouse to the steep path leading down the headland to the beach.

A fisherman stood knee-deep in the surf, casting a fly line into the whitecaps. He nodded a friendly acknowledgment to them as they strolled by. Blake's arm was around Dina's shoulders, keeping her close to his side. She stepped over a piece of driftwood and turned her gaze up to his face. His features were relaxed with a look of contentment about them.

"Why are we getting along so well?" she mused, more to herself than to him.

"Maybe it's because we've stopped looking at each other," Blake suggested.

"What?" A bewildered frown creased her forehead, confusion darkening the blue of her eyes.

"It does sound a bit strange, doesn't it?" A faint smile touched his mouth when he glanced at her, then he directed his gaze ahead of them, a contemplative look about his expression. "What I think I mean is that we've stopped trying to see the flaws in each other, the differences. We've started looking outward together."

"Do you suppose that's it?" Dina, too, shifted her gaze to the beach in front of them.

"Why bother to analyze the reason?" he countered. "Why not just enjoy it?"

"That's true." She scuffed a canvas toe against a stone. "Except that I like to know the why of things."

"So I remember," Blake murmured dryly. "Like the time I gave you your engagement ring and you wanted to know what made me decide to propose to you."

Dina laughed. "And you said it was because I would make such a beautiful ornament in your home." The laughter died as she gave him a guarded look. "Is that the way you regard women? As ornaments?"

There was a hint of exasperation in his impatient glance. "You should know me better than that, Dina."

She was silent for several paces. "That's the problem, I guess—I'm not certain anymore how well I know you. You always seemed so cultured. Now—" she lifted her hand in a searching gesture "—you are so...earthy."

"I suppose I learned that the basics of life are more important. The rest is just window dressing. Fundamentally I don't believe I've changed."

"Perhaps I was so busy looking for the window dressing that I didn't recognize you," she wondered aloud.

"Perhaps," Blake conceded. He flashed her a quick smile. "How did we get started on such a serious discussion?"

His lightning switch from a pensive mood to one that was lightly teasing was infectious. Dina responded immediately, "I don't know. You started it."

"No, I didn't. You did," he corrected her in the same light vein, "when you questioned why we weren't arguing."

"You didn't have to answer me, so therefore it's all your fault," she shrugged.

"Logic like that could only come from a woman," Blake declared with an amused shake of his head.

"Are you making disparaging remarks against my sex again?" she demanded in mock anger.

"I'm just stating facts," he insisted.

Dina gave him a sideways push with her shoulder. Knocked off balance, his arm slipped from around her and he had to take a step to one side to recover. Their aimless pace had taken them closer to the water's edge than either had realized, and when Blake took that step, his foot—shoe, sock and trouser cuff landed in salt water—Dina gasped in a laugh at the one wet foot.

"So you think it's funny, do you?" He took a playfully threatening step toward her.

Unconsciously she began to retreat. "Honestly, Blake, I'm sorry." She was trying hard not to laugh, but it bubbled in her voice. "I didn't know. I didn't mean to push you in the water, honestly."

Blake continued to approach her. "Let's see if it's so funny when you get wet."

"Blake, no!" Dina kept backing up, swallowing the laughter as she negatively shook the silver gold mane of her hair.

The wicked glint in his eye warned her that words would not appease him. Turning, she ran, sprinting for the rock bluff at a safer distance from the lapping ocean waves. Blake chased her, his long strides eating up her short lead. Any moment he would overtake her, Dina knew, and she spared a laughing glance over her shoulder.

A piece of driftwood in her path tripped her and sent her sprawling headlong onto the beach. Her outstretched arms broke most of her fall. Unharmed, she rolled onto her back, out of breath but still trying not to laugh, as Blake dropped to his knees beside her.

"Are you all right?" he asked, half smiling and half concerned.

"Fine," she managed to gasp.

Sitting on his heels, Blake watched silently as she caught her breath. But as her breathing slowed, her heartbeat increased. An exciting tension was leaping between them, quivering over her nerve ends in lightning stimulation.

Blake moved forward as if to assist her to her feet, but as he moved closer, arms bracing him above her, her lips parted, glistening moistly. Dina lifted her hands to his chest as if to resist him, but instead they slid around his neck, pulling him down.

Fire ignited at the hard pressure of his mouth, hungry and demanding. It spread through her veins, her bones melting under the intense heat. The weight of his body crushed her to the rocky sand. It was an exquisite pain. No part of her was immune to the fire Blake was arousing so thoroughly.

Reeling under the torrid assault of his desire, she knew she had lost control. She made no attempt to regain it, willing to let his lips dominate hers for as long as he chose. With each breath, she drew in the intoxicating scent of him, warm and magic, a fuel for the fire that consumed her.

Never had Dina felt so alive. Every corner of her heart was filled with love, overflowing and spilling out like a volcano. Any differences were burned away by the fiery embrace that transcended physical limits.

"Hey, mister?" She heard a child's voice when previously she had only been able to hear the pagan rhythms of their matching heartbeats. "Hey, mister!" This time the voice was more insistent and Blake dragged his mouth from hers to roll onto his side. "Have you seen my puppy?"

A young boy of six stood beside them, knees dirty, a baseball cap on his light brown hair, staring at them innocently. Dina could feel Blake gathering the control to answer him.

"No, son, I haven't." His reply was tight and brief to conceal the raggedness of his breathing.

"He's white and black with a red collar," the boy explained.

"Sorry, we haven't seen him," Blake repeated patiently.

"If you do, would you bring him back to me?"

"Sure."

"Thanks." And he trotted off, disappearing around a jutting promontory on the beach.

Blake stared in the direction the boy had taken. "A few more seconds and it could have been embarrassing," he remarked grimly. "Come on." Rolling to his feet, he caught at Dina's hand to pull her along with him.

"Where are we going?" There was a faint pink to her cheeks.

"Back to the hotel."

"Why?"

"You're forgetting," he answered accusingly, flashing her a look that still had the smoldering light of desire. "I have a wet shoe, sock and pant leg."

Slightly subdued, Dina offered, "I'm sorry about that."

"I'm not." His finger touched her lips, tracing their outline, warm and still throbbing from his possession of them. "If that's what I get for a wet foot, I can't help wondering what would happen if I'd been drenched from head to toe." She breathed in sharply, wanting to tell him he didn't have to wait to find out, but she simply couldn't say the words. Blake didn't wait for her to speak, removing his fingers from her lips to encircle her hand. "Let's go, shall we?"

Dina nodded in silent agreement.

The magic moment lay between them on their return trip to the hotel, the irrevocable change it had made unspoken. But it was there in the looks they exchanged, in the things they didn't say and in the way they avoided physical contact with each other. They each seemed to know how combustible a touch could be and were not ready to start a false fire.

Neither of them was willing to acknowledge the change in the relationship. At the same time, they couldn't go back to the cold hostility that had preceded the visit to the island. They each played a waiting game.

After a late lunch in the hotel restaurant, they entered the lobby. Blake stopped short and turned to Dina. "We're checking out and going home," he announced.

"It's only Saturday," she protested.

"Yes. I know," he agreed with a hint of impatience. "But I'm not looking forward to spending another night here."

Dina hesitated, uncertain of his meaning. Finally she acknowledged him. "The beds aren't very comfortable."

His mouth twisted wryly. "Yes, they're too soft."

"Do we have time to catch the ferry?"

"If you don't waste too much time packing, we do," he told her.

"I won't," she promised.

"I'll check out while you get started," said Blake.

During the ferry crossing neither mentioned the abrupt change of plans that had them returning early. They talked around it as if unwilling to delve too deeply into the reason. When the ferry docked in Newport they stopped talking altogether, both absorbed in their own thoughts.

It was several seconds before Dina noticed that Blake had missed a corner. "You were supposed to turn at that last block," she reminded him.

"We aren't going back to the house right away," he said.

Dina waited for him to tell her their destination. When he didn't, she asked, "Where are we going?"

"There's something I want to show you," was all he answered.

After several more blocks, he turned onto a tree-shaded street, branches arching overhead, nearly touching. He slowed the car down, seeming to read the house numbers as he drove down the street. Dina's curiosity grew with each second of his continued silence. Finally he turned into a driveway and stopped the car, switching off the engine.

Dina glanced at the large white house surrounded by a green lawn with lots of trees and flowering shrubs. She didn't recognize the place.

"Who lives here?" she asked.

Blake was already opening his car door and stepping outside. "You'll see."

She flashed him a look of irritation as he came around to open her door. He was carrying all this mystery business just a little too far. But she said nothing and walked ahead of him along the winding sidewalk to the front door.

There was a jingle of metal behind her and she turned. Blake was taking a set of keys from his pocket. Selecting one, he stepped ahead of her and inserted it in the front-door lock. Suspicion glittered in her eyes.

Pushing the door open, he motioned to her. "Go on in."

Her gaze swerved to the opened door as she moved forward to cross the threshold. On her right, carved oak posts ran from floor to ceiling to partition the mock entryway from the spacious living room beyond. Although the room was sparsely furnished, the items that were there Dina recognized as furniture stored from their apartment.

"What is this supposed to mean?" Unable to look at him, she thought she already knew the answer, and his high-handedness made her tremble with anger.

"Do you like it?" Blake ignored her question to ask one of his own.

"Am I to presume you bought this house without consulting me?" she demanded accusingly in a low, shaking voice, barely able to control her ire.

"As I recall, you were too busy to be bothered with looking for a place for us to live or furnishing it," he reminded her in an expressionless tone. "But to answer your question—no, I haven't signed any documents to purchase this house."

"If that's true, what is all our furniture doing here?" Her hand waved jerkily to the sofa and chairs.

"I obtained permission from the owner to have it brought in to see how it would fit in the rooms and to give the decorator an idea of what still has to be done."

Dina turned on him roundly, her eyes flashing fire. "In other words, you're presenting me with an accomplished fact! It doesn't matter what

I want! You've decided on this house and if I don't like it, that's just too bad, isn't it?''

"Your opinion does matter.'' A muscle was twitching along his jaw, the only outward sign that he felt the lashing of her words. ''That's why I brought you here.''

There was a skeptical lift of her chin, disbelief glittering in her eyes despite his smooth denial. ''Why now? Why not before? All this furniture wasn't just brought here and arranged overnight.''

"No, it wasn't,'' Blake agreed.

"Then why now?'' Dina repeated her demand.

"Because I had the impression you were ready to start looking for a place we might share together.''

His narrowed gaze was piercing, impaling her on its point until she wanted to squirm under his sharp scrutiny. She averted her attention to the room, unable to admit that it might have been more than an impression.

"Was I wrong, Dina?'' Blake questioned.

She didn't want to answer that question—not yet, not until she had more time to think about it. She didn't want to be manipulated into a commitment.

"Since I'm here, you might as well show me through the rest of the house,'' she said with forced indifference.

Blake hesitated, as if to pursue the answer to his question, then gestured with his hand. ''The dining room and kitchen are this way,'' he directed.

As Dina toured the house, she realized it was everything they had ever talked about in a home of their own. Spacious without being too large, with ample room for entertaining, a study for Blake where he could work undisturbed in the evenings, a large patio in back, and plenty of closets.

"Since you're working, I thought we could arrange to have a maid to come in and do the housework,'' Blake explained as they walked down the hallway from the master bedroom to the main living area of the house.

"Yes,'' Dina agreed absently. At the open doorway of one of the two empty rooms, she paused to look inside again. The spare bedrooms were smaller than the master bedroom, but still adequately large.

"There is one thing I haven't asked you.'' Blake stopped beside her.

"What's that?'' She turned to meet his gaze.

"I haven't asked how you felt about having children.''

Slightly flustered, Dina looked back to the empty room, visualizing it not as a guest bedroom but as a children's room. ''We've talked about it before." They had discussed having two children, possibly three, she remembered.

"That was several years ago," Blake pointed out, "before you became a career woman."

"Working women raise children." She hedged, avoiding a direct answer and speaking in generalities instead.

"And there are some working women who prefer not to have children," he added. "I'm asking what you prefer, Dina."

He seemed to silently demand that she look at him. Reluctantly she let her gaze swing back to him, but she was unable to look any higher than his mouth. There were no soft curves to it; it was strong and firm and masculine. Dina had the impulse to raise her fingertips to it and trace the strength of its outline.

"I would like to have children, yes." Her reply was soft, almost inaudible.

"Do you have any objections to my being their father?" There was a husky quality to his voice.

The movement of his mouth when he spoke broke the spell and Dina looked away, her heart pulsing erratically. She didn't make a response. She couldn't seem to speak. Something was blocking her voice.

"Do you?" Blake repeated. When she remained silent, his fingers turned her chin to force her to look at him. "Was I mistaken this afternoon on the beach?" His steady gaze didn't waver as he looked deeply into her eyes, seemingly into her very soul. "Did you give me your answer, or was it a fleeting surrender to passion?"

"I don't know." Dina wanted to look away, but she couldn't. Her mind was reeling from his touch, incapable of coherent thought. "I...I can't think."

"Just this once, don't think," Blake requested. "Tell me what you're feeling."

His hands slipped to her shoulders, tightening for a fraction of a second as if he wanted to shake the answer out of her, but they relaxed to simply hold her. Dina stared into the bluntly chiseled features, leather-tanned, and those compelling dark eyes. This was Blake, a man, her husband, and not quite the stranger she had thought him to be.

She swayed toward him and he gathered her into his arms, prepared to meet her more than halfway. Her lips parted under the plundering force of his mouth, taking the prize she so readily surrendered to him. As if it had never been away, her soft shape molded itself to the hard contours of his body.

His roaming hands caressed and shaped her ever closer to his solidly muscled flesh. Their combined body heat melted them together, fusing them with the glorious fire of their love. His driving male need made Dina aware of the empty aching in the pit of her stomach, which only he could satisfy.

Soon the torrid embrace was not enough. It was unable to meet the insatiable needs of their desires. Bending slightly, Blake curved an arm under her knees to lift her bodily and carry her to the master bedroom and the bare mattress of their old marriage bed.

As he laid her on the bed, the twining arms around his neck pulled him down to join her. Nothing existed for either of them but each other—not the past and not the future, only the moment, eternally suspended in time.

The initial storm of their passion was quickly spent. When Blake came to her a second time, their lovemaking was slow and languorous. Each touch, each kiss, each intimate caress was enjoyed and prolonged, savored and cherished.

The beauty of it brought tears to Dina's eyes, jewel-bright and awesomely happy. Blake kissed them away, gently, adoringly. Never had it been like this between them, as near to perfection as mere mortals can get.

Blake curved her to his side, locking his arms around her. Dina sighed in rapturous contentment and snuggled closer, not wanting to move, never wanting to move. Here was where she belonged, where she would always belong.

CHAPTER TEN

BLAKE STROKED HER HAIR, absently trailing his fingers through the silken ends, watching the fairness of its color glisten in the light. Her eyes were closed in supreme contentment.

"Would you say it now, Dina?" His huskily caressing voice rumbled from deep within his chest.

"Say what?" she questioned in equal softness, not sure words could express anything close to what she was feeling.

"Welcome home, darling." He supplied the words he wanted to hear.

Tipping back her head, she looked up to his face, love bringing a dazzling brilliance to the blue of her eyes. "Welcome home, darling." She repeated the words in a voice that trembled with the depth of her meaning.

A strangled moan of a torment ending came from his throat as he lifted her the few inches necessary to plant a hard, possessive kiss on her lips. Then his trembling fingers moved over her lips as if to apologize for hurting them.

"I've been waiting so long to hear that." There was a sad, almost wistful curve to his strong mouth. "Now, it doesn't seem nearly as important."

"A thousand times I've wondered if it might not have been different if I'd known you were alive before I saw you at the house," Dina whispered, her heart aching at the time together they had lost. "I thought it was someone's twisted idea of a joke."

"I should have made more of an effort to get hold of you or have the authorities reach you before I came back," Blake insisted. "I knew it would be a shock. Chet tried to convince me to let him break the news to you, but I didn't listen, not even when my own mother was so stunned that she didn't believe it was me. I was expecting too much not to think you would react the same way. In the end I went to my mother, but I tried to make you come to me."

"It wasn't just shock," she explained. "It was guilt, because I'd become engaged to Chet. And there you were, my husband. I wanted to run to you, but I couldn't. Then suddenly, you seemed so different—a stranger, someone I didn't know. It was window dressing," Dina sighed.

"Subconsciously I didn't want to admit there'd been any changes in either of us," he murmured with a rueful smile. "I wanted everything to be the way it was, as if I'd never been gone."

"Still, everything might have been different if I hadn't been engaged to Chet." Dina turned to rest her head again on his bronzed chest and listen to the strong rhythm of his heartbeat.

"It might have made us less wary of each other, but we still would have had to adjust to our growth as human beings. It would have been painful under any circumstances," he insisted.

"Yes, but Chet—" Dina started to argue.

Blake interrupted. "He was never a threat to our relationship. Even if I hadn't come back, I'm convinced you would never have married him. You might have drifted along with the engagement for a year, but you're much too intelligent not to eventually have seen that it wouldn't work."

She relaxed, suddenly knowing he was right, and the last little doubt vanished. Smiling, she slid her hand over his flat, muscular stomach, as smooth and hard as polished bronze.

"Weren't you just a little bit jealous of Chet?" The question was half teasing and half serious.

"No, I was never jealous of him," he chuckled, and tugged at a lock of hair.

"Never?" Dina was almost disappointed.

"Never," Blake repeated in an absolutely positive tone. "There were times, though, when I was envious."

"Why?"

"Because you were so natural with him, so warm and friendly, trusting him, relying on him, and turning to him when you were confused. I wanted it to be me," he explained. "A man's instinct to protect is as strong as the maternal instinct in a woman. That's why I was envious of Chet—because you wouldn't look to me for security."

"I feel very secure now." Dina hugged him. "I love you, Blake. I've never stopped loving you."

"That's what I really wanted to hear." His arms tightened around her, crushing her ribs. "Welcome home was just a substitute for I love you."

"I love you," she repeated. "You don't have to prompt me into saying that. I shall keep saying it until you get sick of it."

"Never, my love." He shook his head.

There was a long silence as they reveled inwardly at the rediscovery of their love and the eloquently simple words that expressed so much.

"I hate to bring up something so mundane," Dina whispered, "but where are we going to sleep tonight?"

"I don't even want to go to sleep," said Blake.

"Aren't you tired?" Her sleepless night on the soft mattress was beginning to catch up with her, aided by the dreamy contentment of his embrace.

"Exhausted," he admitted with a smile in his voice. "But I'm afraid if I go to sleep, I'll wake up and find none of this has happened. Or worse, that I'm still in the jungle."

"If you are, I'm going to be there with you," she declared, and poked a finger in his chest. "You Tarzan, me Jane." Blake chuckled and kissed her hair. "Seriously, Blake, are we going back to the house tonight?"

"Not if the storage boxes in the garage have any blankets in them. Do they?" he questioned.

"Did you take everything out that I had in storage?"

"Every single solitary thing," he confirmed.

"Then there are blankets in the boxes in the garage," she promised. "As a matter of fact, there's everything there needed to set up house-keeping."

"Is that what you'd like to do?" Blake asked. "Stay here tonight?"

"I thought you'd already decided we were."

"I'm asking if that's what you want to do," he explained patiently.

"I must remember that and mark it on the calendar," Dina murmured. "Blake asked me what I wanted to do instead of telling me what I was going to do."

"All right, troublemaker," he laughed. "You know what I'm really asking."

"You want to know whether I like the house?" Dina guessed, propping herself up on an elbow beside him.

"Do you?"

"Yes. As a matter of fact, I love it," she smiled. "It's everything we ever said we wanted in a house."

"Good. That's what I thought, too. Monday morning I'll have the agent draw up the papers for us to sign. In the meantime, I don't think he'll mind if we start unpacking the boxes in the garage."

"What if he sells it to somebody else?"

"He won't. I put earnest money down to hold it until you saw it and, I hoped, approved of my choice."

"Were you so positive I'd like it?"

"As positive as I was that you'd love me again," Blake answered.

"Conceited!" Dina teased. "It would serve you right if I hadn't liked it."

"But you do, and now you can take over the decorating of it."

"It might end up looking like a hotel," she warned.

"It better not," he laughed, and pulled her into his arms.

THERE WAS A SCATTERING of snowflakes outside her office window, falling from pearl gray clouds. A serenely joyful light was in Dina's eyes as she smiled at the telephone receiver she held to her ear.

"Thank you, I'll tell him," she promised. "Merry Christmas."

Hanging up, she let her attention return to the papers on her desk while absently humming a Christmas carol. The interoffice line buzzed and she picked up the telephone again.

She had barely identified herself when Blake ordered crisply, "I want you in my office immediately."

"What's it about?"

"We'll discuss it when you get here."

An eyebrow arched at his sharpness. "Very well," Dina agreed calmly. "Give me about fifteen minutes."

"I said now," he snapped.

"You're forgetting it takes that long to walk from my little cubbyhole to your office," she reminded him dryly.

"Now, Dina!" And the connection was broken.

Breathing in deeply, she stared at the dead phone before finally replacing it on its cradle. She took a few precious seconds to put her desk into some kind of order, then walked into the corridor, closing her office door as she left.

Her statement of fifteen minutes was an exaggeration. Eight minutes later, Amy Wentworth glanced up from her typewriter and motioned her into Blake's office with a greeting wave of her hand. Dina knocked once on the connecting door and opened it to walk in.

Blake sat behind his desk leaning back in his chair when Dina entered. The bluntly male features still retained much of his tropical tan, but they were drawn into coldly harsh lines to match the temperature outdoors. Anger glittered in his dark eyes and Dina had no idea why.

"You wanted to see me, Blake?" She walked to his desk, smiling warmly at her husband, but it didn't thaw his expression. "Am I being called on the carpet about something?"

"You're damned right you are!" He reached forward to shove a paper across his desk toward her, his glittering and watchful gaze never leaving her face for an instant. "What's this all about?"

Dina reached for the paper and glanced over it. "This is the revised budget request," she answered, frowning as she recognized it. "Where did you get it?"

"From Chet," Blake snapped.

Her mouth became a straight line of grim exasperation. "He wasn't supposed to give it to you. I wanted to go over it with you when I submitted it."

"He didn't give it to me, I took it. And you can go over it with me now," he ordered. "This is the—what—third or fourth budget revision?"

"The third." Dina was determined not to match his biting tone. "And if you'd told me why you wanted to speak to me, I could have brought some supporting papers."

"I'm not interested in supporting papers, I want an explanation. What's the cause for the increase this time? And don't tell me it's inflation."

"It's a combination of things," she began. "We had to change advertising agencies for the campaign because the original firm wasn't able to produce due to some internal problem. That meant an increase in the cost."

"You should have checked more thoroughly into the first company," he rebuked her.

"Their difficulties occurred after we'd signed a contract with them," she replied sharply to his criticism.

There was disbelief in his look, but he didn't pursue that aspect. "What else?"

"We had to revise the cost figures on revamping the hotels. The—"

"I knew it," he declared through clenched teeth. "The redecorating costs for the hotels have escalated every time you've submitted a budget. Are you redecorating them or rebuilding?"

The slow-burning fuse of her temper was lit. "There are times when I'm not so positive myself," she said, simmering. "Have you seen that hotel in Florida? It looks like a hospital. We've tried landscaping and painting, but it needs a whole new facade."

"Why don't you just arrange to tear it down and build a new one?" he flashed.

"That's the best suggestion I've heard yet!" she retorted. "Why don't you bring that up to the expansion department?"

"At the rate you're going, it might be the most economical decision!" With controlled violence, Blake pushed out of his chair, standing behind the desk to glance at her. "I should have known this would happen. You put a woman in charge and give her a free hand, and right away she thinks it means she has a blank check!"

Hot tears burned her eyes. "If that's what you think—" pain strangled her voice "—why don't you take over? I never asked for the job in the first place! If you think a man can do so much better, go ahead!"

"And don't think I couldn't!"

"The great Blake Chandler. Oh, I'm sure you could do a much better job," Dina issued sarcastically, and turned away, hugging her arms in front of her in a mixture of disgust and hurt. "I don't know what ever made me think I'd want your baby."

"I don't know, either!" Blake snarled behind her. "It's a lucky thing you have a choice, isn't it?"

"That's the whole point! I don't have a choice anymore," she cried bitterly.

Her sentence hung in the air for a long, heavy second before Blake broke the silence with a low demand. "What did you say?"

"Didn't I tell you?" She tossed the question over her shoulder, her chin quivering with the forced attempt at lightness. "I'm going to have a baby."

In the next second his hands were on her shoulders to gently turn her around. Dina kept her chin lowered, still angry and hurt by his barbed attack.

"Are you sure?" he asked quietly.

"Yes, I'm sure." She closed her eyes to try to force back the tears. "Doctor Cosgrove called me a few minutes ago to confirm the test results."

"Why didn't you tell me?" His tension was exhaled with the question.

"How could I when you've been yelling at me for the past five minutes?" Her eyes flared open to glare at him.

His fingers lightly touched her cheek before he cupped it in his hand. "I was, wasn't I?" There was a rueful twist to his mouth.

"Yes, you were." But her assertion didn't carry any sting of anger.

"I lost my perspective for a moment, the order of importance. I could lose everything I have and it wouldn't matter as long as I didn't lose you."

The glow radiating from his face was warm and powerful and Dina basked in the love light. That serene joy she had known before their argument returned with doubled strength.

"No, it doesn't matter as long as I have you," she agreed, and turned her lips to his hand to press a kiss into his open palm.

His head lowered, his mouth claiming hers in a sweetly fierce kiss that rocked her senses. She clung to him, reveling in the possessive embrace that gathered her close to his male length. A wild, glorious melody raced through her veins, its tune timeless, the universal song of love.

She was breathless when the kiss ended, and the sensation remained as Blake buried his face in the silver gold hair, his mouth trailing a blazing fire to the sensitive skin of her neck. She felt the tremors vibrating through his muscular form and knew she disturbed him as sensually as he disturbed her.

When he finally lifted his head, there was a disarming smile softening his roughly carved features. His hands moved to tangle his fingers in her hair and hold her face up for his gaze to explore. Dina knew this was a moment she would treasure forever in her heart.

"We're really going to have a baby?" There was a faintly marveling look in his eyes as Blake turned the statement into a near question.

"Yes," Dina nodded.

"Are you all right?" he frowned.

"I'm fine." She smiled. With a sighing shake of her head, she asked, "Why do we argue so much, Blake?"

"It's our nature, I guess." He smiled wryly in return. "We'd better get used to the fact, because we'll probably do it the rest of our lives."

"Always testing to find out which of us is stronger." Dina recalled Chet's explanation for their constant quarrels.

"Don't worry, honey, I'll let you be stronger once in a while," he promised.

"Blake!" She started to protest indignantly at his superior remark.

"Can you imagine what our children are going to be like?" he laughed. "Pigheaded, argumentative little rebels, more than likely."

"More than likely," Dina agreed, "And we'll love every battling moment of raising them."

"The same as every battling moment you and I have together." He kissed her lightly and gazed into her eyes. "When's the baby due?"

"July."

"The new campaign will be in full swing by then. I can just see you directing operations from the maternity ward," Blake chuckled.

"You mean that I still have the job?" Dina arched a mocking brow at him.

"Of course," he returned with an arrogant smile. "Aren't you glad you have an understanding boss who will let you set your own hours or work at home, if that's convenient?"

"I'm very lucky." She slid her arms around his neck, rising on tiptoes. "Lucky in more than one way."

"Dina." Blake spoke her name in an aching murmur against her lips.

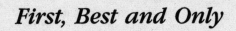

First, Best and Only

INSTINCT TOLD MARNI LANGE that it was wrong, but she'd long ago learned not to blindly trust her instincts. For that very reason she'd surrounded herself with the best, the brightest, the most capable vice-presidents, directors and miscellaneous other personnel to manage those ventures in which she'd invested. Now her staff was telling her something, and though she disagreed, she had to listen.

"It's a spectacular idea, Marni," Edgar Welles was saying, sitting forward with his arms on the leather conference table and his fingers interlaced. His bald head gleamed under the Tiffany lamps. "There's no doubt about it. The exposure will be marvelous."

"As vice-president of public relations, you'd be expected to say that," Marni returned dryly.

"But I agree," chimed in Anne Underwood, "and I'm the editor in chief of this new baby. I think you'd be perfect for the premier cover of *Class*. You've got the looks and the status. If we're aiming at the successful woman over thirty, you epitomize her."

"I'm barely thirty-one, and I'm not a model," Marni argued.

Cynthia Cummings, Anne's art director, joined the fray. "You may not be a model, but you do have the looks."

"I'm too short. I'm only five-five."

"And this will be a waist-up shot, so your height is irrelevant," Cynthia went on, undaunted. "You've got classic features, a flawless complexion, thick auburn hair. You're a natural for something like this. We wouldn't be suggesting you do it if that weren't true."

Anne shifted in her seat to more fully face Marni, who had opted to sit among her staff rather than in the high-backed chair at the head of the long table. "Cynthia's right. We have pretty high stakes in this, too. You may be putting up the money, but those of us at the magazine have our reputations on the line. We've already poured thousands of hours into the conception and realization of *Class*. Do you think we'd risk everything with a cover we didn't think was absolutely outstanding?"

"I'm sure you wouldn't," Marni answered quietly, then looked at Edgar. "But won't it be awfully...presumptuous...my appearing in vivid color on every newsstand in the country?"

Edgar smiled affectionately. He'd been working with Marni since she'd taken over the presidency of the Lange Corporation three years before. Personally, he'd been glad when her father had stepped down, retaining the more titular position of chairman of the board. Marni was easier to work with any day. "You've always worked hard and avoided the limelight. It's about time you sampled it."

"I don't like the limelight, Edgar. You know that."

"I know you prefer being in the background, yes. But this is something else, something new. Lange may not be a novice at publishing, but we've never dealt with fashion before. *Class* is an adventure for the publications division. It's an adventure for *all* of us. You want it to be a success, don't you?" It was a rhetorical question, needing no answer. "It's not as though you're going to give speech after speech in front of crowds of stockholders or face the harsh floodlights of the media."

"I'd almost prefer that. This seems somehow arrogant."

"You have a right to arrogance," broke in Steve O'Brien. Steve headed the publications division of the corporation, and he'd been a staunch supporter both of Marni and of *Class* from the start. "In three years you've nearly doubled our annual profit margin. *Three years.* It's remarkable."

Marni shrugged. She couldn't dispute the figures, yet she was modest about flaunting them. "It's really been more than three years, Steve. I've been working under Dad since I graduated from business school. That adds another four years to the total. He gave me a pretty free hand to do what I wanted."

"Doesn't matter," Steve said with a dismissive wave of his hand. "Three, five, seven years—you've done wonders. You've got every right to have your picture on the cover of *Class.*"

"One session in a photographer's studio," Edgar coaxed before Marni could argue further. "That's all we ask. One session. Simple and painless."

She grimaced. "Painless? I *hate* being photographed."

"But you're photogenic," came the argument from Dan Sobel, *Class*'s creative director. He was a good-looking man, no doubt photogenic himself, Marni mused, though she felt no more physical attraction for him than she did for either Edgar or Steve. "You've got so much more going for you than some of the people who've been on magazine covers. Hell, look what Scavullo did with Martha Mitchell!"

Marni rolled her eyes. "Thanks."

"You know what I mean. And don't tell me *she* had any more right to be on a cover than you do."

Marni couldn't answer that one. "Okay," she said, waving her hand. "Aside from my other arguments, we're not talking Scavullo or Avedon here. We're talking Webster." She eyed Anne. "You're still convinced he's the right one?"

"Absolutely," Anne answered with a determined nod. "I've shown you his covers. We've pored over them ourselves—" her gaze swept momentarily toward Cynthia and Dan "—and compared them to other cover work. As far as I'm concerned, even if Scavullo or Avedon had been available I'd have picked Webster. He brings a freshness, a vitality to his covers. This is a man who loves women, loves working with them, loves making them look great. He has a definite way with models, and with his camera."

Marni's "Hmmph" went unnoticed as Dan spoke up in support of Anne's claim.

"We're lucky to get him, Marni. He hasn't been willing to work on a regular basis for one magazine before."

"Then why is he now?"

"Because he likes the concept of the magazine, for one thing. He's forty himself. He can identify with it."

"Just because a man reaches the age of forty doesn't mean that he tires of nubile young girls," Marni pointed out. "We all have friends whose husbands grab for their *Vogues* and *Bazaars* as soon as they arrive."

Dan agreed. "Yes, and I'm not saying that Webster's given up on nineteen-year-old models. But I think he understands the need for a publication like ours. From what he said, he often deals with celebrities who are totally insecure about the issue of age. They want him to make them look twenty-one. He wants to make them look damned good at whatever age they are. He claims that some of the most beautiful women he's photographed in the last few years have been in their mid-forties."

"Wonderful man," Anne said, beaming brightly.

Marni sent an amused smile in her direction. Anne was in her mid-forties and extremely attractive.

Dan continued. "I think there's more, though, at least as to why Webster is willing to work with us. When a man reaches the age of forty, he tends to take stock of his life and think about where's he's going. Brian Webster has been phenomenally successful in the past ten years, but he's done it the hard way. He didn't have a mentor, so to speak, or a sponsor. He didn't have an 'in' at any one magazine or another. He's built his reputation purely on merit, by showing his stuff and relying on its quality to draw in work. And it has. He calls his own shots, and even aside from his fashion work gets more than enough commissions for portraits of celebrities to keep him busy. But he may just be ready to consolidate his interests. Theoretically, through *Class*, his name could become as much a household word as Scavullo or Avedon. If we're successful, and *he's* successful, he could work less and do better financially than before. Besides, his first book of photographs is due out next summer. The work for it is done and that particular pressure's off. I think we lucked out and hit him at exactly the right time."

"And he's agreed to stick with us for a while?" Marni asked, then glanced from one face to another. "It was the general consensus that we have a consistent look from one issue to the next."

"We're preparing a contract," Steve put in. "Twelve issues, with options to expand on that. He says he'll sign."

Marni pressed her lips together and nodded. Her argument wasn't really with the choice of Webster as a photographer; it was with the choice of that first cover face. "Okay. So Webster's our man." Her eyes narrowed as she looked around the group again. "And since I have faith in you all and trust that you're a little more objective on the matter of this cover than I am, it looks like I'll be your guinea pig. What's the schedule?" She gave a crooked grin. "Do I have time for plastic surgery first? I could take off five pounds while I'm recuperating."

"Don't you dare!" Anne chided. "On either score." She sat back. "Once Webster's signed the contract, we'll set up an appointment. It should be within the next two weeks."

Marni took in a loud breath and studied the ceiling. "Take your time. Please."

IT WAS ACTUALLY CLOSER to three weeks before the photographer's contract had been signed and delivered and Marni was due to be photographed. She wasn't looking forward to it. That same tiny voice in the back of her mind kept screaming in protest, but the wheels were in motion. And she did trust that Edgar, Anne and company knew what they were doing.

That didn't keep her from breaking two fingernails within days of the session, or feeling that her almost shoulder-length hair had been cut a fraction of an inch too short, or watching in dire frustration while a tiny pimple worked its way to the surface of her "flawless" skin at one temple.

Mercifully, she didn't have to worry about what to wear. Marjorie Semple, the fashion director for *Class*, was taking care of that. All Marni had to do was to show up bright and early on the prescribed morning and put herself into the hands of the hairstylist, the makeup artist, the dresser, numerous other assistants and, of course, Brian Webster. Unfortunately, Edgar, Steve, Anne, Dan, Cynthia, Marjorie and a handful of others from the magazine were also planning to attend the session.

"Do you *all* have to be there?" Marni asked nervously when she spoke with Anne the day before the scheduled shoot.

"Most of us do. At least the first time. Webster knows what kind of feeling we want in this picture, but I think our presence will be a reminder to him of the investment we have in this."

"He's a professional. He knows what he's being paid for. I thought you had faith in him."

"I do," Anne responded with confidence. "Maybe what I'm trying to say is that it's good PR for us to be there."

"It may be good PR, but it's not doing anything for my peace of mind. It'll be bad enough with all of Webster's people there. With all of *you* there, I'll feel like I'm a public spectacle. My God," she muttered under her breath, "I don't know how I let myself be talked into this."

"You let yourself be talked into it because you know it's going to be a smashing success. The session itself will be a piece of cake after all the agonizing you've done about it. You've been photographed before, Marni. I've seen those shots. They were marvelous."

"A standard black-and-white publicity photo is one thing. This is different."

"It's easier. All you have to do is *be* there. Everything else will be taken care of."

They'd been through this all before, and Marni had too many other things that needed her attention to rehash old arguments. "Okay, Anne. But please. Keep the *Class* staff presence at a minimum. Edgar was going to take me to the studio, but I think I'll tell him to stay here. Steve can take me—*Class* is his special project. The last thing I need is a corporative audience."

As it happened, Steve couldn't take her, since he was flying in from meetings in Atlanta and would have to join the session when it was already underway. So Edgar swung by in the company limousine and picked her up at her Fifth Avenue co-op that Tuesday morning. She was wearing a silk blouse of a pale lavender that coordinated with the deeper lavender shade of her pencil-slim wool skirt and its matching long, oversized jacket. Over the lot she wore a chic wool topcoat that reached mid-calf and was suitably protective against the cold February air.

In a moment's impulsiveness, she'd considered showing up at the session in jeans, a sweatshirt and sneakers, with her hair unwashed and her face perfectly naked. After all, she'd never been "made over" before. But she hadn't been able to do it. For one thing, she had every intention of going to the office directly from the shoot, hence her choice of clothes. For another, she believed she had an image to uphold. Wearing jeans and a sweatshirt, as she so often did at home alone on weekends, she looked young and vulnerable. But she was thirty-one and the president of her family's corporation. Confidence had to radiate from her, as well as sophistication and maturity. True, Webster's hairstylist would probably rewash her hair and then do his own thing with it. The makeup artist would remove even those faint traces of makeup she'd applied that morning. But at least she'd walk into the studio and meet those artists for the first time looking like the successful, over-thirty businesswoman she was supposed to be.

The crosstown traffic was heavy, and the drive to the studio took longer than she'd expected. Edgar, God bless him, had his briefcase open and was reviewing spread sheets aloud. Not that it was necessary. She'd already been over the figures in question, and even if she hadn't, she was a staunch believer in the delegation of authority, as Edgar well knew. But she sensed he was trying to get her mind off the upcoming session, and though his ploy did little to salve her unease, she was grateful for the effort.

The limousine pulled to the curb outside a large, seemingly abandoned warehouse by the river on the west side of Manhattan. Dubious, Marni studied the building through the darkened window of the car.

"This is it," Edgar said. He tucked his papers inside his briefcase, then snapped it shut. "It doesn't look like much, but Brian Webster's been producing great things inside it for years." He climbed from the limousine, then put out a hand to help her.

Moments later they were walking past piles of packing crates toward a large freight elevator, which carried them up. Marni didn't waste time wondering what was on the second, third and fourth floors. She was too busy trying to imagine the scene on the fifth, which, according to the button Edgar had pressed, was where they were headed.

The door slid open. A brightly lit reception area spread before them, its white walls decorated with a modest, if well-chosen, sampling of the photographer's work. The receptionist, an exquisite young woman with raven-black hair, amber eyes and a surprisingly shy smile, immediately came forward from behind her desk and extended her hand.

"Ms. Lange? I'm Angie. I hope you found us all right."

Marni shook her hand, but simply nodded, slightly awed by the young woman's raw beauty. Because of it, she was that little bit more unsettled than she might have been if Webster's receptionist had been middle-aged and frumpy. Not only was Angie tall, but she wore a black wool minidress with a high-collared, long-sleeved fuchsia blouse layered underneath, fuchsia tights and a matching belt double-looped around her slender waist. She was a model, or a would-be model, Marni realized, and it seemed far more fitting that she should be there than Marni herself.

Angie didn't seem at all disturbed by the silence. "I think just about everyone else is here. If you'll come this way..."

Marni and Edgar followed her to a door, then through it into what was very obviously the studio. It was a huge room, as brightly lit as the reception area had been. Its central focus was a seamless expanse of white wall, curving from the ceiling to the floor without a break. Numerous lights, reflecting panels and other paraphernalia were scattered around the area, and at the center was a tripod and camera.

Marni absorbed all of this in a moment, for that was all the time she was given. Anne was quickly at her side, introducing her to Webster's chief assistant and to the others who'd be aiding in one way or another. Marni was beginning to feel very much like a fish in a bowl when Anne said, "Brian will be back in a minute. Angie's gone to call him down."

"Down?"

"He lives upstairs. When he saw that everything was set up here, he went back to make a few phone calls." Her gaze skipped past Marni, and she smiled. "There he is now. Come. I'll introduce you."

Marni turned obediently, but at the sight of the tall, dark-haired man approaching, her pulse tripped. A face from the past...yet vaguely different; she had to be imagining. But she was frozen to the spot, staring in disbelief as he drew nearer. Webster was a common name...it wouldn't be him, not *him*. But he was looking at her, too, and his eyes said she wasn't mistaken. Those blue eyes...she could never mistake those eyes!

Her breath was caught in her throat, and her heart began to hammer at her chest as though it were caught, trapped, locked in a place it didn't want to be. Which was exactly the way she felt herself. "Oh, no," she whispered in dismay.

Anne felt both her momentary paralysis and the ensuing trembling. "It's okay," she murmured soothingly by Marni's ear. "He may be gorgeous, but he's a nice guy to boot."

Marni barely heard her. She stared, stunned and shaken, as Brian Webster approached. His eyes were on her, as they'd been from the moment she'd turned and caught sight of him, but they held none of the shock Marni's did. He'd known, she realized. Of course. He'd known. There was only one Lange Corporation, and only one Marni Lange to go with it. But Webster? It was a common name, as was Brian. Not that it would have made a difference. Around her house he'd been referred to as "that wild kid" or simply "him." As for Marni, she'd never even known his first name. He'd been "Web" to her.

"Brian," Anne was saying brightly, "this is Marni."

He'd stopped two feet away, taking in the look in Marni's eyes, the ashen hue of her skin, her frozen stance. "I know," he said softly, his voice barely carrying over the animated chatter of the others in the room. "We've met before."

"You've met...but I don't understand." Anne turned confused eyes on Marni. "You didn't say..." Her words trailed off. She'd never seen a human being turn into a shadow before, but that was exactly what seemed to be happening. "Marni?" she asked worriedly. "Are you all right?"

It was Web who answered, his eyes still glued to Marni's. "I think she needs a minute alone." He took her arm gently, adding to Anne, "We'll be back soon. Coffee and doughnuts are on the way, so that should keep everyone satisfied until we're ready." His fingers tightened fractionally, and he led Marni back across the floor. She wasn't sure if he was afraid she'd make a scene and resist, or if he simply sensed she needed the support. As it was, she could do nothing but go along with him. Her mind was in too great a turmoil to allow for any other action.

The din of the studio died the minute Web closed the door behind them. They were in a bright hall off which no less than half a dozen doors led, but it was to the open spiral staircase that he guided her, then up through another door and into the large living room that was obviously his own. Natural light poured through skylights to give the simply but elegantly furnished room an aura of cheer, but none of that cheer seeped into Marni, who was encased in a crowding prison of memory.

He led her to a chrome-framed, cushioned chair, eased her down, then turned and headed for the bar.

Marni watched him go. He moved with the same fluidity, the same stealthy grace he'd possessed years before when she'd known him. He seemed taller, though perhaps he'd just filled out in maturity. His legs were lean and long as they'd been then, though they were sheathed in clean, stylishly stitched, button-fly jeans rather than the faded, worn denim he had once sported. The muscle-hugging T-shirt had been replaced with a more reputable chambray shirt, rolled to the elbows and open at the neck. His shoulders seemed broader, his hair definitely shorter and darker.

He'd aged well.

"I know it's a little early in the day to imbibe," he said, giving a brittle smile as he returned to her, "but I think you ought to drink this." He placed a wineglass in her shaky fingers, then watched while she took a healthy swallow of the pale amber liquid. Her eyes didn't leave his, not while she drank, nor when he crossed to the nearby sofa and sat down.

He propped his elbows on his outspread thighs and dangled his hands between his knees. "You didn't know," he stated in a very quiet voice.

Marni took another swallow of wine, then slowly shook her head.

He was grateful to see that she'd stopped shaking, and could only hope that a little more wine would restore the color to her cheeks. He sympathized with her, could understand what she was feeling. He'd been living with the same feelings for the past three months, ever since he'd first been approached by *Class*. And those feelings had only intensified when he'd learned that the editorial staff had decided to use the chief executive officer on its first cover.

He'd had the advantage that Marni hadn't, and still he was stunned seeing her, being with her after all that had happened fourteen years before.

"I'm sorry," he said, meaning it. "I thought for sure that you'd have been involved on some level when the decision was made to hire me."

"I was," Marni heard herself say. Her voice was distant, weak, and it didn't sound at all like her own. She took a deep, unsteady breath and went on, trying to sound more like the executive she was. "I've been involved with every major decision involving *Class*, including the one to hire you. But I never knew your name was Brian, and even if I had I probably would never have guessed *the* Brian Webster to be you."

His half smile was chilly. "I've come a ways since we knew each other."

"That's two of us," she murmured somberly. She looked down at her glass, looked back at Web, then finally took another swallow. Afterward she clutched the stem of the wineglass with both hands and frowned at her whitened knuckles. "I had bad vibes about this from the start. Right from the start."

"About hiring me?"

"About posing for the cover. I argued with my people for a good long time, but I've always been one to delegate authority. In the end I told myself that they were specialists and had to know what they were doing. I couldn't possibly have known who you were, but I was *still* reluctant to do it. I shouldn't have agreed." She punctuated her words with one harsh nod, then another. "I should have stuck to my guns."

There was a lengthy silence in the room. As long as Marni was thinking of business, as long as she wasn't looking at Web, she felt better. Maybe the wine had helped. Tipping her head back, she drained the glass.

"I think they're right," Web said softly.

Her head shot up and, in that instant, the fact of his identity hit her squarely in the face again. The bright blotches that had risen on her cheeks faded quickly. "You can't be serious," she whispered tremulously.

"I am." He leaned back and threw one long arm across the back of the sofa. His forearm was tanned, corded, lightly furred with hair. "You're right for the cover, Marni. I've spent a lot of time going over the concept of the magazine with your staff, and you're right for the cover. You've got the looks. You've always had the looks, only they're better now. More mature. And God knows you've got the position to back them up."

His voice took on a harder edge at the end. Marni thought she heard sarcasm in it, and she bolted to her feet.

It was a mistake. She swayed, whether from the wine or the lingering shock of seeing Web after all these years, she didn't know. But that was irrelevant; before she could utter a protest, she found herself back in the chair with her head pressed between her knees.

Web was on his haunches before her. "Deep breaths. Just relax." His large hand chafed her neck, urging the flow of blood back to her head. But the flood that came to Marni was of memories—memories of a gentler touch, of ecstasy, then of grief, utter and total. Seared by pain she hadn't known in years, she threw his hand off and pressed herself back in the chair, clutching its arms with strained fingers.

"Don't touch me," she seethed, eyes wide and wild.

Web felt as though she'd struck him, yet she looked as though she'd been struck herself. As he watched, she seemed to crumble. Her chest caved in, her shoulders hunched, and she curled her arms protectively around her stomach. She was shaking again, and it looked like she might cry. She blinked once, twice, took a slow breath, then forcibly straightened her body. Only then did she look at him again.

"You knew. I didn't, but you did. Why did you agree to this?"

"To work for *Class*? Because I think it's an idea whose time has come."

"But you had to have learned pretty quickly who the publisher was. Why did you go ahead?"

"If your father had still been at the helm, I might not have. I wouldn't have worked for him. I knew he'd been kicked upstairs, and I'd been told you ran everything, but I wasn't sure how involved he still was. For a while there I waited to get that thank-you-but-no-thank-you call, and if it had been from him I would have said the words before he did."

"He only comes in for quarterly meetings," she said, defending her father against the bitterness in Web's tone. "He isn't interested in the details of the business anymore. And even if he'd heard your name, I doubt he'd have said anything."

Web gave a harsh laugh. "Don't tell me he's forgiven and forgotten."

"Not by a long shot," she muttered, then added pointedly, "None of us has. But he wouldn't have associated that...that Web we once knew with Brian Webster the photographer any more than I did." Her renewed disbelief mixed with confusion. "But *you* knew, and still you went ahead. Why?"

He shrugged, but it was a studied act. "I told you, the idea was good. I felt it might be the right move for my career."

"I don't recall your being ambitious."

A muscle in his jaw flexed. "I've changed."

He'd spoken in a deep voice that held cynicism, yes, but a certain sadness, even regret as well. All of it worked its painful way through Marni's system. When she spoke, her voice was little more than a whisper. "But when you found out you'd be photographing me, didn't you have second thoughts?"

"Oh, yes."

"And still you agreed to it. *Why?*"

It took him longer to answer, because he wanted to give her the truth. He felt he owed her that much. "Curiosity," he said at last.

She shook her head, unable to believe him. If he'd said "revenge" or "arrogance" or "sadism," she might have bought it, but he wouldn't have said any of those. He'd always been a charmer.

She couldn't take her eyes from his, and the longer she looked the more mired in memory she became. "This isn't going to work," she finally said in a low, shaky voice.

Web stood, feeling nearly as stiff as she looked. One part of him agreed with her, that part swamped with pain and guilt. The other part was the one that had grown over the years, that had come to accept things that couldn't be changed. He was a professional now. He had a name, a reputation and a contract. "You can't back out, Marni," he forced himself to say. "There's an entire crew out there waiting to go to work."

She eyed him defensively. "I don't care about the crew. I'll pay for the services they would have given today, and for yours. We can find another model for this cover."

"On such short notice? Not likely. And you've got a production deadline to meet."

"We're way ahead, and if necessary we'll change the schedule. I can't do this."

His eyes hardened. He wasn't sure why—yes, he'd had personal reservations when the idea had first been presented to him—but he was determined to photograph her. Oh, he'd been curious all right, curious as to what she'd be like, what she'd look like fourteen years later. He hadn't expected to feel something for her, and those feelings were so confused that he couldn't quickly sort them out. But they were there. And he *was* going to photograph her.

He wondered if it was the challenge of it, or sheer pride on his part, or even the desire for a small measure of vengeance. Marni Lange's family had treated him like scum once upon a time. He was damned if one of them, least of all Marni, would ever do it again.

"Why can't you do it?" he asked coolly.

She stared at him, amazed that he'd even have to ask. "I didn't know you'd be the photographer."

"That shouldn't bother you. You smiled plenty for me once upon a time."

She flinched, then caught herself. "That was a world away, Web."

"Brian. I'm called Brian now...or Mr. Webster."

"I look at you and I see Web. That's why I can't go through with this."

"Funny," he said, scratching the back of his head, another studied act, "I thought you'd be above emotionalism at this point in your life." His hand dropped to his side. "You're a powerful woman, Marni. A powerful businesswoman. You must be used to pressure, to acting under it. I'd have thought you'd be able to rise to the occasion."

He was goading her, and she knew it. "I'm a human being."

He mouthed an exaggerated "ahhhhh."

"What do you want from me?" she cried, and something in her voice tore at him quite against his will.

His gaze dropped from her drained face to her neck, her breasts, her waist, her hips. He remembered. Oh, yes, he remembered. Sweet memories made bitter by a senseless accident and the vicious indictment of a family in mourning.

But that was in the past. The present was a studio, a production crew and equipment waiting, and a magazine cover to be shot.

"I want to take your picture," he said very quietly. "I want you to pull yourself together, walk out into that studio and act like the publisher of this magazine we're trying to get off the ground. I want you to put yourself into the hands of my staff, then sit in front of my camera and work with me." His voice had grown harder again, though he barely noticed. Despite his mental preparation for this day, he was as raw, emotionally, as Marni was.

He dragged in a breath, and his jaw was tight. "I want to see if this time you'll have the guts to stand on your own two feet and see something through."

Marni's head snapped back, and her eyes widened, then grew moist. As she'd done before, though, she blinked once, then again, and the tears were gone. "You are a bastard," she whispered as she pushed herself to her feet.

"From birth," he said without pride. "But I never told you that, did I?"

"You never told me much. I don't think I realized it until now. What we had was...was..." Unable to find the right words when her thoughts were whirling, she simply closed her mouth, turned and left the room. She walked very slowly down the winding staircase, taking one step at a time, gathering her composure. He'd issued a challenge, and she was determined to meet it. He wanted a picture; he'd get a picture. She *was* the publisher of this magazine, and, yes, she was a powerful businesswoman. Web had decimated her once before. She was not going to let it happen again.

By the time she reentered the studio, she was concentrating on business, her sole source of salvation. Anne rushed to her side and studied her closely. "Are you okay?"

"I'm fine," she said.

"God, I'm sorry, Marni. I didn't realize that you knew him."

"Neither did I."

"Are you over the shock?"

"The shock, yes."

"But he's not your favorite person. You don't know how *awful* I feel. Here we've been shoving him at you—"

"But you were right, Anne. He's a superb photographer, and he's the right man for *Class*. My personal feelings are irrelevant. This is pure business." Her chin was tipped up, but Anne couldn't miss the pinched look around her mouth.

"But you didn't want to be on the cover to begin with, and now you've got to cope with Brian."

"Brian won't bother me." It was Web who would...if she let him. She simply wouldn't allow it. That was that! "I think we'd better get going. I've got piles of things waiting for me at the office."

Anne gave her a last skeptical once-over before turning and gesturing to Webster's assistant.

In the hour that followed, Marni was shuttled from side room to side room. She submitted to having her hair completely done, all the while concentrating on the meeting she would set up the next day with the management of her computer division. She watched her face as it was cleaned, then skillfully made up, but her thoughts were on a newly risen distribution problem in the medical supplies section. She let herself be stripped, then dressed, but her mind was on the possibility of luring one particularly brilliant competitor to head Lange's market research department. As a result, she was as oblivious to the vividly patterned silk skirt and blouse, to the onyx necklace, bracelet and earrings put on her as she was to the fact that the finished product was positively breathtaking.

The audience in the main room was oblivious to no such thing. The minute she stepped from the dressing room she was met by a series of "ooohs" and "ahhhs," immediately followed by a cacophony of chatter.

But she was insulated. In the time it had taken for Webster's people to make her camera-ready, she'd built a wall around herself. She was barely aware of being led to a high, backless stool set in the center of the seamless expanse of curving white wall. She was barely aware of the man who continued to poke at her hair, or the one who lightly brushed powder on her neck, throat and the narrow V between her breasts, or the woman who smoothed her skirt into gentle folds around her legs and adjusted the neckline of her blouse.

She was aware of Web, though, the minute he came to stand before her with his legs planted apart and his eyes scrutinizing what she'd become. She felt her heart beat faster, so she conjured the image of that particularly brilliant competitor she wanted to head the market research division.

She'd met the man several times, yet now his image kept fading. She blinked, swallowed and tried again, this time thinking of the upcoming stockholders' meeting and the issues to be dealt with. But the issues slipped from mind. Something about rewriting bylaws...hostile takeover attempts...

Web turned to issue orders to his assistants, and she let out the breath she hadn't realized she'd been holding. A quartz floodlight was set here, another there. Reflectors were placed appropriately. A smaller spotlight was put farther to one side, another to the back, several more brought down from overhead. Web moved around her, studying her from every angle, consulting his light meter at each one.

She felt like a yo-yo, spinning to the end of its rope when he looked at her, recoiling in relief when he looked away. She didn't want to think ahead to when he'd be behind his camera focusing solely on her, for it filled her with dread. So she closed her eyes and thought yoga thoughts, blank mind, deep steady breaths, relaxation.

She'd never been all that good at yoga.

She put herself into a field of wildflowers glowing in the springtime sun. But the sun was too hot, and the wildflowers began doing something to her sinuses, not to mention her stomach. And there was a noise that should have been appropriate but somehow was grating. The chirping of birds, the trickle of a nearby stream... No, the sounds of a gentle piano...a lilting love song...

Her eyes riveted to Web, who approached her barehanded. "That music," she breathed. "Is it necessary?"

He spoke as softly as she had. "I thought it might relax you, put you in the mood."

"You've got to be kidding."

"Actually, I wasn't. If it bothers you—"

"It does. I don't like it."

"Would you like something else?"

"Silence would be fine."

"I need to be put in the mood, too."

"Then put on something else," she whispered plaintively, and breathed a sigh of relief when he walked to the side to talk with one of his assistants, who promptly headed off in the other direction. Marni barely had time to register the spectators gathered in haphazard clusters beyond camera range, sipping coffee, munching doughnuts and talking among themselves as they observed the proceedings, when Web returned. He stood very close and regarded her gently. She felt the muscles around her heart constrict.

He put his hands on her shoulders and tightened his fingers when she would have leaned back out of his grasp. "I want you to relax," he ordered very softly, his face inches above hers. He began to slowly knead the tension from her shoulders. "If we're going to get anything out of this, you've got to relax."

The background music stopped abruptly. "I can't relax when you're touching me," she whispered.

"You'll have to get used to that. I'll have to touch you, to turn you here or there where I want you."

"You can tell me what to do. You don't have to do it for me."

His hands kept up their kneading, though her muscles refused to respond. "I enjoy touching you. You're a very beautiful woman."

She closed her eyes. "Please, no. Don't play your games with me."

"I'm not playing games. I'm very serious."

"I can't take it." Just then the music began again, this time to a more popular, faster beat. Her eyes flew open. "Oh, God, you're not going to have me *move*, are you?"

He had to smile at the sheer terror in her eyes. "Would it be so awful?"

Her expression was mutinous. "I won't do that, Web. I'm not a model, or a dancer, or an exhibitionist, and I *refuse* to make an utter fool out of myself in front of all these people."

He was still smiling. At the age of thirty-one, she was more beautiful than he'd ever imagined she'd be. Though he had no right to, he felt a certain pride in her. "Take it easy, Marni. I won't make you dance. Or move. We'll just both flow with the music. How does that sound?"

It sounded awful, and his smile was upsetting her all the more. "I'm not really up for flowing."

"What are you up for?"

Her eyes widened on his face in search of smugness, but there was none. Nor had there been suggestiveness in his tone, which maintained the same soft and gentle lilt. He was trying to be understanding of her and of the situation they'd found themselves in, she realized. She also realized that there were tiny crow's-feet at either corner of his eyes and smile lines by his mouth, and that his skin had the rougher texture maturity gave a man. A thicker beard, though recently shaven, left a virile shadow around his mouth and along his jaw.

His hands on her shoulders had stopped moving. She averted her gaze to the floor. "I'm not up for much right about now, but I guess we'd better get on with this."

"A bit of pain...a blaze of glory?"

She jerked her eyes back to his, and quite helplessly they flooded. "How *could* you?" she whispered brokenly.

He leaned forward and pressed his lips to her damp brow, then murmured against her skin, for her ears alone, "I want you to remember, Marni. I want you to think about what we had. That first time on the shore, the other times in the woods and on my narrow little cot."

Too weak to pull away from him, and further hamstrung by the people watching, she simply closed her eyes and struggled to regain her self-control. Web drew back and brushed a tear from the corner of her eye.

"Remember it, Marni," he whispered gently. "Remember how good it was, how soft and warm and exciting. Pretend we're back there now, that we're lovers stealing away from the real world, keeping secrets only the two of us share. Pretend that there's danger, that what we're doing is slightly illicit, but that we're very, very sure of ourselves."

"But the rest—"

"Remember the good part, babe. Remember it when you look at me now. I want confidence from you. I want defiance and promise and success, and that special kind of feminine spirit that captivated me from the start. You've got it in you. Let me see it."

He stepped back then and, without another word, went to his camera.

Stunned and more confused than ever, Marni stared after him. Brushes dabbed at her cheeks and glossed her lips; fingers plucked at her hair. She wanted to push them away, because they intruded on her thoughts. But she had no more power to lift a hand than she had to get up and walk from the room as that tiny voice of instinct told her to do.

It began then. With his legs braced apart and his eyes alternating between the camera lens and her, Web gave soft commands to the lighting crew. Then, "Let's get a few straightforward shots first. Look here, Marni."

She'd been looking at him all along, watching as he peered through the lens, then stepped to the side holding the remote cord to the shutter. She felt wooden. "I don't know what to do. Am I supposed to...smile?"

"Just relax. Do whatever you want. Tip your head up...a little to the left...atta girl." Click.

Marni made no attempt to smile. She didn't want to smile. What she wanted to do was cry, but she couldn't do that.

"Run your tongue over your lips." Click. "Good. Again."

Click. Click. "Shake your head...that's the way...like the ocean breeze... warm summer's night..."

Marni stared at the camera in agony, wanting to remember as he was urging but simultaneously fighting the pain.

He left the camera and came to her, shifting her on the stool, repositioning her legs, her arms, her shoulders, her head, all the time murmuring soft words of encouragement that backfired in her mind. He returned to the camera, tripped the lens twice, then lifted the tripod and moved the entire apparatus forward.

"Okay, Marni," he said, his voice modulated so that it just reached her, "now I want you to turn your face away from me. That's it. Just your head. Now close your eyes and remember what I told you. Think sand and stars and a beautiful full moon. Let the music help you." The words of a trendy pop ballad were shimmering through the room. "That's it. Now, very slowly, turn back toward me...open your eyes...a smug little smile..."

Marni struggled. She turned her head as he'd said. She thought of sand—she and Web lying on it—and stars and a beautiful full moon—she and Web lying beneath them—and she very slowly turned back toward him. But when she opened her eyes, they were filled with tears, and she couldn't muster even the smallest smile.

Web didn't take a shot. Patiently, he straightened, then put out a hand when Anne started toward Marni. She retreated, and Web moved forward. "Not exactly what I was looking for," he said on a wistfully teasing note.

"I'm sorry." She blinked once, twice, then she was in control again. The music had picked up, and she caught sight of feet tapping, knees bending, bodies rocking rhythmically on the sidelines. "I feel awkward."

"It's okay. We'll try again." He gestured for his aides to touch her up, then returned to stand by his camera with the remote cord in his hand. "Okay, Marni. Let your head fall back. That's it. Now concentrate on relaxing your shoulders. Riiiiight. Now bring your head back up real quick and look the camera in the eye. Good. That's my girl! Better." He advanced the film once, then again, and a third time. What he was capturing was better than what had come before, he knew, but it was nowhere near the look, the feeling he wanted.

He could have her hair fixed, or her clothes, or her makeup. He could shift her this way or that, could put her in any number of poses. But he couldn't take the pain from her eyes.

He'd told her to remember the good and the beautiful, because that was what he wanted to do himself. But she couldn't separate the good from all that had come after and, with sorrow on her face and pain in her eyes, he couldn't either.

So he took a different tack, a more businesslike one he felt would be more palatable to her. He talked to her, still softly, but of the magazine now, of the image they all wanted for it, of the success it was going to be. He posed her, coaxed her, took several shots, then frowned. He took the stool away, replaced one lens with another his assistant handed him and exposed nearly a roll of film with her standing—straight, then with her weight balanced on one hip, with her hands folded before her, one hand on her hip, one hand on each, the two clasped behind her head. When her legs began to visibly tremble, he set her back on the stool.

He changed lights, bathing the background in green, then yellow, then pale blue. He switched to a hand-held camera so that he could more freely move around, changing lenses and the angle of his shots, building a momentum in the hopes of distracting Marni from the thoughts that brought tears to her eyes every time he was on the verge of getting something good.

For Marni it was trial by fire, and she knew she was failing miserably. When Web, infuriatingly solicitous, approached her between a series of shots, she put the blame on the self-consciousness she felt, then on the heat of the lights, then on the crick in her neck. One hour became two, then three. When she began to wilt, she was whisked off for a change of clothes and a glass of orange juice, but the remedial treatment was akin to a finger in the dike. She ached from the inside out, and it was all she could do to keep from crumbling.

The coffee grew cold, the doughnuts stale. The bystanders watched with growing restlessness, no longer tapping their feet to the music but looking more somber with each passing minute. There were conferences—between Edgar, Anne, Marni and Web, between Dan, Edgar and Web, between Cynthia, Anne and Marni.

Nothing helped.

As a final resort, when they were well into the fourth hour of the shot, Web turned on a small fan to stir Marni's hair from behind. He showed her how to stand, showed her how to slowly sway her body and gently swing her arms, told her to lower her chin and look directly at him.

She followed his instructions to the letter, in truth so exhausted that she was dipping into a reserve of sheer grit. She couldn't take much more, she knew. She *wouldn't* take much more. Wasn't she the one in command here? Wasn't she the employer of every last person in the room?

While she ran the gamut of indignant thought, Web stood back and studied her, and for the first time in hours he felt he might have something special. Moving that way, with her hair billowing softly, she was the girl he remembered from that summer in Maine. She was direct and honest, serious but free, and she exuded the aura of power that came from success.

He caught his breath, then quickly raised his camera and prepared to shoot. "That's it. Oh, sunshine, that's it...."

Her movement stopped abruptly. *Sunshine.* It was what he'd always called her at the height of passion, when she would whisper that she loved him and would have to settle for an endearment in place of a returned vow.

It was the final straw. No longer able to stem the tears she'd fought so valiantly, she covered her face with her hands and, heedless of all around her, began to weep softly.

MARNI LANGE WAS on top of the world. Seventeen and eager to live life to its fullest, she'd just graduated from high school and would be entering Wellesley College in the fall. As they did every June, her parents, brother and sister and herself had come to their summer home in Camden, Maine, to sun and sail, barbecue and party to their hearts' content.

Ethan, her older brother by eight years, had looked forward to this particular summer as the first he'd be spending as a working man on vacation. Having graduated from business school, he'd spent the past eight months as a vice-president of the Lange Corporation, which had been formed by their father, Jonathan, some thirty years before. Privileged by being the son of the founder, president and chairman of the board of the corporation, Ethan was, like his father, conducting what work he had to do during the summer months from Camden.

Tanya, Marni's older sister by two years, had looked forward to the summer as a well-earned vacation from college, which she was attending only because her parents had insisted on it. If she'd had her way she'd be traveling the world, dallying with every good-looking man in sight. College men bored her nearly as much as her classes did, she'd discovered quickly. She needed an older man, she bluntly claimed, a man with experience and savvy and style.

Marni felt light-years away from her sister, and always had. They were as different as night and day in looks, personality and aspirations. While Tanya was intent on having a good time until the day she reeled in the oil baron who would free her from her parents and assure her of the good life forever, Marni was quieter, serious about commitment yet fun-loving. She wanted to get an education, then perhaps go out to work for a while, and the major requirement she had for a husband was that he adore her.

A husband was the last thing on her mind that summer, though. She was young. She'd dated aplenty, partying gaily within society's elite circles, but she'd never formed a relationship she would have called deep. Too many of the young men she'd known seemed shallow, unable to discuss world news or the stock market or the latest nonfiction best-seller. She wanted to grow, to meet interesting people, to broaden her existence before she thought of settling down.

The summer began as it always did, with reunion parties among the families whose sumptuous homes, closed all winter, were now buzzing with life. Marni enjoyed seeing friends she hadn't seen since the summer before, and she felt that much more buoyant with both her high school degree and her college acceptance letter lying on the desk in her room back at the Langes' Long Island estate.

After the reunions came the real fun—days of yachting along the Maine coast, hours sunning on the beach or hanging out on the town green or cruising the narrow roads in late-model cars whose almost obscene luxury was fully taken for granted by the young people in question.

Marni had her own group of friends, as did Tanya, but for very obvious reasons both groups tagged along with Ethan and his friends whenever possible. Ethan never put up much of a fight...for equally obvious reasons. Though his own tastes ran toward shapely brunettes a year or two older than Tanya, he knew that several of his group preferred the even younger blood of Marni's friends.

It was because of the latter, or perhaps because Ethan was feeling restless about something he couldn't understand, that this particular summer he made a new friend. His last name was Webster, but the world knew him simply as Web—at least, the world that came into contact with the Camden Inn and Resort where he was employed alternately as lifeguard, bellboy and handyman.

Ethan had been using the pool when he struck up that first conversation with Web, whom he discovered to be far more interesting than any of the friends he was with. Web was twenty-six, footloose and fancy-free, something which, for all his social and material status, Ethan had never been. While Ethan had jetted from high-class hotel to high-class hotel abroad, Web had traveled the world on freighters, passenger liners or any other vehicle on which he could find employment. While Ethan, under his father's vigilant eye, had met and hobnobbed with the luminaries of the world, Web had read about them in the quiet of whatever small room he was renting at the time.

Web was as educated as he and perhaps even brighter, Ethan decided early on in their friendship, and the luxury of Web's life was that he was beholden to no one. Ethan envied and admired it to the extent that he found himself spending more and more time with Web.

It was inevitable that Marni should meet him, nearly as inevitable that she should be taken with him from the first. He was mature. He was good-looking. He was carefree and adventurous, yet soft-spoken and thoughtful. Given the diverse and oftentimes risky things he'd experienced in life, there was an excitement about him that Marni had never found in another human being. He was free. He was his own man.

He was also a roamer. She knew that well before she fell in love with him, but that didn't stop it from happening. Puppy love, Ethan had called it, infatuation. But Marni knew differently.

After her introduction to Web, she was forever on Ethan's tail. At first she tried to be subtle. She'd just come for a swim, she told Web minutes before she dived into the resort pool, leaving the two men behind to talk. But she wore her best bikini and made sure that the lounge chair she stretched out on in the sun was well within Web's range of vision.

She tagged along with Ethan when he and Web went out boating, claiming that she had nothing to do at home and was bored. She sandwiched herself into the back of Ethan's two-seater sports car when he and Web drove to Bar Harbor on Web's day off, professing that she needed a day off too from the monotony of Camden. She sat intently, with her chin in her palm, while the two played chess in Web's small room at the rear of the Inn, insisting that she'd never learn the game unless she could observe two masters at it.

Ethan and Web did other things, wilder things—racing the wind on the beach at two in the morning on the back of Web's motorcycle, playing pool and drinking themselves silly at a local tavern, diving by moonlight to steal lobsters from traps not far from shore, then boiling them in a pot over a fire on the sand. Marni wasn't allowed to join them at such times, but she knew where they went and what they did, and it added to her fascination for Web...as did the fact that Jonathan and Adele Lange thoroughly disapproved of him.

Marni had never been perverse or rebellious where her parents were concerned. She'd enjoyed her share of mischief when she'd been younger, and still took delight in the occasional scheme that drew arched brows and pursed lips from her parents. But Web drew far more than that.

"Who *is* he?" her mother would ask when Ethan announced that he was meeting with Web yet again. "Where does he come from?"

"Lots of places," Ethan would answer, indulging in his own adult prerogative for independence.

Jonathan Lange agreed wholeheartedly with his wife. "But you don't know anything about the man, Ethan. For all you know, he's been on the wrong side of the law at some point in his, uh, illustrious career."

"Maybe," Ethan would say with a grin. "But he happens to know a hell of a lot about a hell of a lot. He's an extension of my education...like night school. Look at it that way."

The elder Langes never did, and Web's existence continued to be viewed as something distasteful. He was never invited to the Lange home, and he became the scapegoat for any and all differences of opinion the Langes had with their son. Starry-eyed, Marni didn't believe a word her parents said in their attempts to discredit Web. If anything, their dislike of him added an element of danger, of challenge, to her own attempts to catch his eye.

She liked looking at him—at his deeply tanned face, which sported the bluest of eyes; his brown hair, which had been kissed golden by the sun; his knowing and experienced hands. His body was solid and muscular, and his fluid, lean-hipped walk spoke of self-assurance. She knew he liked looking at her, too, for she'd find him staring at her from time to time, those blue eyes alight with desire. At least she thought it was desire. She never really knew, because he didn't follow up on it. Oh, he touched her—held her hand to help her from the car, bodily lifted her from the boat to the dock, stopped in his rounds of the pool to add a smidgen of suntan lotion to a spot she'd missed on her back—but he never let his touch wander, as increasingly she wished he would.

Frustration became a mainstay in her existence. She dressed her prettiest when she knew she'd see Web, made sure her long auburn hair was clean and shiny, painted her toenails and fingernails in hopes of looking older. But, for whatever his reasons, Web kept his distance, and short of physically attacking the man, Marni didn't know what more she could do.

Then came a day when Ethan was ill. Web was off duty, and the two had planned to go mountain climbing, but Ethan had been sick to his stomach all night and could barely lift his head come morning. Marni, who'd spent the previous two days pestering Ethan to take her along, was sitting on his bed at seven o'clock.

"I'll go in your place," she announced, leaning conspiratorially close. Her parents were still in bed at the other end of the house.

"You will not," Ethan managed to say through dry lips. He closed his eyes and moaned. "God, do I feel awful."

"I'm going, Ethan. Web has been looking forward to this—I heard him talking. There's no reason in the world why he has to either cancel or go alone."

"For Pete's sake, Marni, don't be absurd."

"There's nothing absurd about my going mountain climbing."

"With Web there is. You'll slow him down."

"I won't. I've got more energy than you do even when you're well. I've got youth on my side."

"Exactly. And you think Web's going to *want* you along? You're seventeen and absolutely drooling for him. Come on, sweetheart. Be realistic. We both know why you want to go, and it's got nothing to do with the clean, fresh air." He rolled to his side, tucked his knees up and moaned again.

Marni knew he was indulgent when it came to her attraction for Web.

He humored her, never quite taking her seriously. So, she mused, fair was fair... "Okay, then. I'll go over to his place and explain that you can't go."

"Call him."

She was already on her feet. "I'll go over. *He* can be the one to make the decision." And she left.

Web was more than surprised to find Marni on his doorstep at the very moment Ethan should have been. He was also slightly wary. "You're trying to trick me into something, Marni Lange," he accused, with only a half smile to take the edge off his voice.

"I'm not, Web. I like the outdoors, and I've climbed mountains before."

"When?" he shot back.

"When I was at camp."

"How long ago?"

"Four...five years."

"Ahhh. Those must have been quite some mountains you twelve-year-old girls climbed."

"They were mountains, no less than the one you and Ethan were planning to climb."

"Hmmph.... Do your parents know you're here?"

"What's that got to do with anything?"

"Do they know?"

"They know I won't be home till late." She paused, then at Web's arched brow added more sheepishly, "I told them I was driving with a couple of friends down to Old Orchard. They won't worry. I'm a big girl."

"That's right," he said, very slowly dropping his gaze along the lines of her body. It was the first time he'd looked at her that way, and Marni felt a ripple of excitement surge through her because there was a special spark that was never in his eyes when Ethan was around. It was the spark that kept her spirits up when he went on to drawl, "You're a big girl, all right. Seventeen years old."

When she would have argued—like the seventeen-year-old she was—she controlled herself. "My age doesn't have anything to do with my coming today or not," she said with what she hoped was quiet reserve. "I'd really like to go mountain climbing, and since you'd planned to do it anyway, I didn't see any harm in asking to join you. Ethan would have been here if he hadn't been sick." She turned and took a step away from his door. "Then again, maybe you'd rather wait till he's better."

She was halfway down the hall when he called her back, and she was careful to look properly subdued when he grabbed his things from just inside the door, shut it behind him, then collared her with his hand and propelled them both off.

It was the most beautiful day Marni had ever spent. Web drove her car—he smilingly claimed that he didn't trust her experience, or lack of it, at the wheel—and they reached the appointed mountain by ten. It wasn't a huge mountain, though it was indeed higher and steeper than any Marni had ever climbed. She held her own, though, taking Web's offered hand over tough spots for the sake of the delicious contact more than physical necessity.

The day had started out chilly but warmed as they went, and they slowly peeled off layers of clothing and stuffed them in their backpacks. By the time they stopped for lunch, Marni was grateful for the rest. She'd brought along the food Cook had packed for Ethan and had made one addition of her own—a bottle of wine pilfered quite remorselessly from the huge stock in the Langes' cellar.

"Nice touch," Web mused, skillfully uncorking the wine and pouring them each a paper cup full. "Maybe not too wise, though. A little of this and we're apt to have a tough time of it on the way back down."

"There's beer if you prefer," Marni pointed out gently. "Ethan had it already chilled, so evidently he wasn't worried about its effects."

"No, no. Wine's fine." He sipped it, then cocked his head. "It suits you. I can't imagine your drinking beer."

"Why not?"

He propped himself on an elbow and crossed his legs at the ankle. Then he looked at her, studying her intently. Finally, he reached for a thick ham sandwich. "You're more delicate than beer," he said, his eyes focusing nowhere in particular.

"If that's a compliment, I thank you," she said, making great efforts— and succeeding overall—to hide her glee. She helped herself to a sandwich and leaned back against a tree. "This is nice. Very quiet. Peaceful."

"You like peaceful places?"

"Not all the time," she mused softly, staring off into the woods. "I like activity, things happening, but this is the best kind of break." And the best kind of company, she might have added if she'd dared. She didn't dare.

"Are you looking forward to going to Wellesley?"

Her bright eyes found his. "Oh, yes. It was my first choice. I was deferred for early admission—I guess my board scores weren't as high as they might have been—and if I hadn't gotten in I suppose I would have gone somewhere else and been perfectly happy. But I'm glad it never came down to that."

Web asked her what she wanted to study, and she told him. He asked what schools her friends were going to, and she told him. He asked what she wanted to do with her future, and she told him—up to a point. She didn't say that she wanted a husband and kids and a house in Connecticut because she'd simply taken that all for granted, and it somehow seemed inappropriate to say to Web. He wasn't the house-in-Connecticut type. At this precise moment, being with him as she'd dreamed of being so often, she wasn't either.

They talked more as they ate. Web was curious about her life, and she eagerly answered his questions. She asked some of her own about the jobs he'd had and their accompanying adventures, and with minor coaxing he regaled her with tales, some tall, some not. They worked steadily through the bottle of wine, and by the time it was done and every bit of their lunch had been demolished, they were both feeling rather lazy.

"See? What did I tell you?" Web teased. He lay on his back with his head pillowed on his arms. Marni was in a similar position not far from him. He tipped his head and warmed her with his blue eyes. "We might never get down from this place."

Her heart was fluttering. "We haven't reached the top yet."

"We will. It's just a little way more, and the trip down is faster and easier. Only thing is—" he paused to bend one knee up "—I'm not sure I want to move."

"There's no rush," she said softly.

"No," he mused thoughtfully. His eyes held hers for a long time before he spoke in a deep, very quiet, subtly warning voice. "Don't look at me that way, Marni."

"What way?" she breathed.

"*That* way. I'm only human."

She didn't know if he was pleased or angry. "I'm sorry. I didn't mean—"

"Of course you didn't mean. You're seventeen. How are you supposed to know what happens when you look at a man that way?"

"What way?"

"With your heart on your sleeve."

"Oh." She looked away. She hadn't realized she'd been so transparent, and she was sure she'd made Web uncomfortable. "I'm sorry," she murmured.

Neither of them said anything for a minute, and Marni stared blindly at a nearby bush.

"Ah, hell," Web growled suddenly, and grabbed her arm. "Come over here. I want you smiling, not all misty-eyed."

"I wasn't misty-eyed," she argued, but she made no argument when he pulled her head to the crook of his shoulder. "It's just that...maybe Ethan was right. I am a pest. You didn't want me along today. I'm only seventeen."

"You were the one who pointed out that your age was irrelevant to your going mountain climbing."

"It is. But..." Her cheeks grew red, and she couldn't finish. It seemed she was only making things worse.

He brushed a lock of hair from her hot cheek and tucked it behind her ear. The action brought his forearm close to her face. Marni closed her eyes, breathed in the warm male scent of his skin, knew she was halfway to heaven and was about to be tossed back down.

"I think it's about time we talk about this, Marni," he said, continuing to gently stroke her hair. "You're seventeen and I'm twenty-six. We have a definite problem here."

"I'm the one with the problem," she began, but Web was suddenly on his elbow leaning over her.

"Is that what you think...that you're the only one?"

Her gaze was unsteady, faintly hopeful. "Am I wrong?"

"Very."

She held her breath.

"You're a beautiful woman," he murmured as his eyes moved from one of her features to the next.

"I'm a girl," she whispered.

"That's what I keep trying to tell myself, but my body doesn't seem to want to believe it. I've tried, Marni. For the past month I've tried to keep my hands off. It was dangerous to come here today."

Marni reached heaven by leaps and bounds. Her body began to relax against his, and she grew aware of his firm lines, his strength. "You didn't do it single-handedly."

"But I'm older. I should know better."

"Are there rules that come with age?"

"There's common sense. And my common sense tells me that I shouldn't be lying here with you curled against me this way."

"You were the one who pulled me over," she pointed out.

"And you're not protesting."

She couldn't possibly protest when she was floating on a cloud of bliss. "Would you like me to?"

"Damn right I would. One of us should show some measure of sanity."

"There's nothing insane about this," she murmured, distracted because she'd let her hand glide over his chest. She could feel every muscle, every crinkling hair beneath his T-shirt, even the small dot of his nipple beneath her palm.

"No?" he asked. Abruptly he flipped over and was on top of her. His blue eyes grilled hers heatedly, and his voice was hoarse. "Y'know, Marni, I'm not one of your little high school friends, or even one of the college guys I'm sure you've dated." He took both of her hands and anchored them by her shoulders. Though his forearms took some of his weight, the boldness of his body imprinted itself on hers. "I've had women. Lots of them. If one of them were here instead of you, we wouldn't be playing around. We'd be stark naked and we'd be making love already."

Marni didn't know where she found the strength to speak. His words—the experience and maturity and adventure they embodied—set her on fire. Her blood was boiling, and her bones were melting. "Is that what we're doing...playing?"

He shifted his lower body in apt answer to her question, then arched a brow at the flare of color in her cheeks. "You don't want to play, do you? You want it all."

She was breathing faster. "I just want you to kiss me," she managed to whisper. The blatancy of his masculinity was reducing her to mush.

"Just a kiss?" he murmured throatily. "Okay, Marni Lange, let's see how you kiss."

She held her breath as he lowered his head, then felt the touch of his mouth on hers for the first time. His lips were hot, and she drew back, scalded, only to find that his heat was tempting, incendiary where the rest of her body was concerned. So she didn't pull back when he touched her a second time, and her lips quickly parted beneath the urging of his.

He tasted and caressed, then drank with unslaked thirst. Marni responded on instinct, kissing him back, feeding on his hunger, willingly offering the inside of her mouth and her tongue when he sought them out.

His breathing was as unsteady as hers when he drew back and looked at her again. "You don't kiss like a seventeen-year-old."

She gave a timid smile. She'd never before received or responded to a kiss like that, but she didn't want Web to know how inexperienced she really was. "I run in fast circles."

"Is that so?" His mouth devoured her smile in a second mind-bending kiss, and he released one of her hands and framed her throat, slowly drawing his palm down until the fullness of her breast throbbed beneath it. "God, Marni, you're lovely," he rasped. "Lovely and strong and fresh..."

Her hands were in his hair, sifting through its thickness as she held him close. "Kiss me again," she pleaded.

"I may be damned for this," he murmured under his breath, "but I want it, too." So he kissed her many, many more times, and he touched her breasts and her belly and her thighs. When his hand closed over the spot where he wanted most to be, she arched convulsively.

"Tell me, Marni," he panted next to her ear, "I need to know. Have you done this before?"

She knew he'd stop if she told him the truth, and one part of her ached so badly she was tempted to lie. But she wasn't irresponsible. Nor could she play the role of the conniving female. He'd know, one way or the other. "No," she finally whispered, but with obvious regret.

Web held himself still, suspended above her for a moment, then gave a loud groan and rolled away.

She was up on her elbow in an instant. "Web? It doesn't matter. I want to. Most of my friends—"

"I don't give a damn about most of your friends," he growled, throwing an arm over his eyes. "You're seventeen, the kid sister of a man who's become my good friend. I can't do it."

"Don't you want to?"

He lifted his arm and stared at her, then grabbed her hand and drew it down to cover the faded fly of his jeans. The fabric was strained. He pressed her hand against his fullness, then groaned again and rolled abruptly to his side away from her.

Her question had been answered quite eloquently. Marni felt the knot of frustration in her belly, but she'd also felt his. "Can I...can I do something?" she whispered, wanting to satisfy him almost as much as she wanted to be satisfied herself.

"Oh, you can do something," was his muffled reply, "but it'd only shock you and I don't think you're ready for that."

She leaned over him. "I'm ready, Web. I want to do it."

Glaring, he rolled back to face her, but his glare faded when he saw the sincerity of her expression. His eyes grew soft, his features compassionate. He raised a hand to gently stroke the side of her face. "If you really want to do something," he murmured, "you can help me clean up here, then race me to the top of this hill and down. By the time we're back at the bottom, we should both be in control. Either that," he added with a wry smile, "or too tired to do anything about it."

It was his smile and the ensuing swelling of her heart that first told Marni she was in love. Over the next week she pined, because Web made sure that they weren't alone again. He looked at her though, and she could see that he wasn't immune to her. He went out of his way not to touch her and, much as she craved those knowing hands on her again, she didn't push him for fear she'd come across as being exactly what she was—a seventeen-year-old girl with hots that were nearly out of control. She knew that in time she could get through to Web. He felt something for her, something strong. But time was her enemy. The summer was half over, and though she wanted it to last forever, it wouldn't.

She was right on the button when it came to Web and his feelings for her. He wasn't immune, not by a long shot. He told himself it was crazy, that he'd never before craved untried flesh, but there was something more that attracted him to her, something that the women he'd had, the women he continued to have, didn't possess.

So when a group of Ethan's friends and their dates gathered for a party at someone's boat house, Web quite helplessly dragged Marni to a hidden spot and kissed her willing lips until they were swollen.

"What was that for?" she asked. Her arms were around his neck, and she was on tiptoe, her back pressed to the weathered board of the house.

"Are you protesting?" he teased, knowing she'd returned the kiss with a fever.

"No way. Just curious. You've gone out of your way to avoid me." She didn't quite pout, but her accusation was clear.

He insinuated his body more snugly against hers. "I've tried. Again... still. It's not working." He framed her face with his hands, burying his fingers in her hair. "I want you, Marni. I lie in bed at night remembering that day on the mountain and how good you felt under me, and I tell myself that it's nonsense, but the chemistry's there, damn it."

"I know," she agreed in an awed whisper.

"So what are we going to do about it?"

She shrugged, then drew her hands from his shoulders to lightly caress the strong cords of his neck. "You can make love to me if you want."

"Is it what you want?" His soberness compelled her to meet his gaze.

She blinked, her only show of timidity. "I've wanted it for days now. I feel so...empty when I think of you. I get this ache...way down low..."

"Your parents would kill you. And me."

"There are different kinds of killing. Right now I'm dying because I want you, and I'm afraid you still think of me as a little kid who's playing with fire. I may only be seventeen, but I've been with enough men to know when I find one who's different."

He could have substituted his own age for hers and repeated the statement. He didn't understand it, but it was the truth, and it went beyond raw chemistry. Marni had a kind of depth he'd never found in a woman before. He'd watched her participate in conversations with Ethan and his friends, holding her own both intellectually and emotionally. She was sophisticated beyond her years, perhaps not physically, but he felt that urgency in her now.

"I'm serious about your parents," he finally said. "They dislike me as it is. If I up and seduce their little girl—"

"You're not seducing me. It's a mutual thing." Made bold by the emotions she felt when she was in this man's arms, she slid her hand between their bodies and gently caressed the hard evidence of his sex. "I've never done this to another man, never touched another man this way," she whispered. "And I'm not afraid, because when I do this to you—" she rotated her palm and felt him shudder and arch into it "—I feel it inside me, too. Please, Web. Make love to me."

Her nearness, the untutored but instinctively perfect motion of her hand, was making it hard for him to breathe. "Can you get out later?" he managed in a choked whisper.

"Tonight? I think so."

He set her back, leaving his fingers digging into her shoulders. "Think about it until then, and if you still feel the same way, come to me. I'll be on the beach behind the Wayward Pines at two o'clock. You know the one."

She nodded, unable to say a word as the weight of what she was about to agree to settled on her shoulders. He left her then to return to the group. She went straight home and sat in the darkness of her room, giving herself every reason why she should undress and go to sleep for the night but knowing that she'd never sleep, that her body tingled all over, that her craving was becoming obsessive, and that she loved Web.

It didn't seem to matter that he was a roamer, that he'd be gone at the end of the summer, that he couldn't offer her any kind of future. The fact was that she loved him and that she wanted him to be the first man to know, to teach her the secrets of her body.

Wearing nothing but a T-shirt, cutoffs and sandals, she stole out of the house at one-forty-five and ran all the way to the beach. It was an isolated strip just beyond an aging house whose owner visited rarely. As its name suggested, tall pines loomed uncharacteristically close to the shore, giving it a sheltered feeling, a precious one.

Web was propped against the tallest of the pines, and her heart began to thud when he straightened. Out of breath, and now breathless for other reasons, she stopped, then advanced more slowly.

"I wasn't sure you'd come," he said softly, his eyes never leaving hers as he held out his hand.

"I had to," was all she said, ignoring his hand and throwing her arms around his neck. His own circled her, lifting her clear off her feet, and he held her tightly as he buried his face in her hair.

Then he set her down and loosened his grip. "Are you sure? Are you sure this is what you want?"

In answer, she reached for the hem of her T-shirt and drew it over her head. She hadn't worn a bra. Her pert breasts gleamed in the pale moonlight. Less confidently, she reached for one of his hands and put it on her swelling flesh. "Please, Web. Touch me. Teach me."

He didn't need any further encouragement. He dipped his head and took her lips while his hands explored the curves of her breasts, palms kneading in circles, fingers moving inexorably toward the tight nubs that puckered for him.

She cried out at the sweet torment he created, and reached for him, needing to touch him, to know him as he was coming to know her. He held her off only long enough for him to whip his own T-shirt over his head, then he hauled her against him and embraced her with arms that trembled.

"Oh, Web!" she gasped when their flesh came together.

"Feels nice, doesn't it?" His voice held no smugness, only the same awe hers had held. She was running her hands over his back, pressing small kisses to his throat. "Easy, Marni," he whispered hoarsely. "Let's just take it slow this first time."

"I don't think I can," she cried. "I feel...I feel..."

He smiled. His own hands had already covered her back and were dipping into the meager space at the back of her shorts. "I know." He dragged in a shuddering breath, then said more thickly, "Let's get these off." He was on his knees then, unsnapping and unzipping her shorts, tugging them down. She hadn't worn panties. He sucked in his breath. "Marni!"

Her legs were visibly shaking, and she was clutching his sinewed shoulders for support. "Please don't think I'm awful, Web. I just want you so badly!"

He pressed his face to her naked stomach, then spread kisses even lower. "Not any more so than I want you," he whispered. Then he was on his feet, tugging at the snaps of his jeans, pushing the denim and his briefs down and off.

Seconds later they were tumbling onto the sand, their greedy bodies straining to feel more of the other's, hands equally as rapacious. Marni was inflamed by his size, his strength, the manly scent that mixed with that of the pines and the salty sea air to make her drunk. She felt more open than she'd ever been in her life, but more protected.

And more loved. Web didn't say the words, but his hands gave her a message as they touched her. They were hungry and restless, but ever gentle as they stimulated her, leaving no inch of her body untouched. Her breasts, her back, her belly, thighs and bottom—nothing escaped him, nor did she want it to. If she'd ever thought she'd feel shy at exposing herself this way to a man, the desire, the love she felt ruled that out. There was a rightness to Web's liberty, a rightness to the feel of his lips on her body, to the feel of his weight settling between her thighs.

Her fingers dug into the lean flesh of his hips, urging him down, crying wordlessly for him to make her his. She felt his fingers between her legs, and she arched against him as he stroked her.

"Marni...Marni," he whispered as one finger ventured even deeper. "Oh, sunshine, you're so ready for me...how did I ever deserve this..."

"Please...now...I need you..." When he pulled back, she whimpered, "Web?"

"It's okay." He was reaching behind him. "I need to protect you." He took a small foil packet from the pocket of his jeans and within minutes was back, looming over her, finding that hot, enfolding place between her splayed thighs.

He poised himself, then stroked her cheeks with his thumbs. "Kiss me, sunshine," he commanded deeply.

She did, and she felt him begin to enter her. It was the most wonderful, most frustrating experience yet. She thrust her hips upward, not quite re-alizing that it was her own inner body that resisted him.

He was breathing heavily, his lips against hers. "Sweet...so sweet. A bit of pain...a blaze of glory..." Then he surged forward, forcefully rupturing the membrane that gave proof of her virginity but was no more.

She cried out at the sharp pain, but it eased almost immediately.

"Okay?" he asked, panting as she was, holding himself still inside her while her torn flesh accommodated itself to him. It was all he could do not to climax there and then. She was so tight, so sleek, so hot and new and all his.

"Okay," she whispered tightly.

"Just relax," he crooned. He ducked his head and teased the tip of her nipple with his tongue. "I'm inside you now," he breathed, warm against that knotted bud. "Let's go for the glory."

She couldn't say a word then, for he withdrew partway, gently returned, withdrew a little more, returned with growing ardor, withdrew nearly completely, returned with a slam, and the feel of him inside her, stroking that dark, hidden part was so astonishing, so electric that she could only clutch his shoulders and hang on.

Nothing else mattered at that moment but Web. Marni wasn't thinking of her parents and how furious they'd be, of her brother and how shocked he'd be, of her friends and how envious they'd be. She wasn't thinking of the past or the future, simply the present.

"I love you," she cried over and over again. His presence had become part and parcel of her being. Without fear, she raised her hips to his rhythm, and rather than discomfort she felt an excitement that grew and grew until she was sure she'd simply explode.

"Ahhh, sunshine...so good...that's it...oh, God!"

His body was slick above hers, their flesh slapping together in time with the waves on the shore. Then that sound too fell aside, and all awareness was suspended as first Marni, then Web, strained and cried out, one body, then the next, breaking into fierce orgasmic shudders.

It was a long time before either of them spoke, a long time before the spasms slowed and their gasps quieted to a more controlled breathing.

Web slid to her side and drew her tightly into his arms. "You are something, Marni Lange," he whispered against her damp forehead.

"Web...Web...unbelievable!"

He gave a deep, satisfied, purely male laugh. "I think I'd have to agree with you."

She nestled her head more snugly against his breast. "Then I...I did okay?"

"You did more than okay. You did *super*."

She smiled. "Thank you." She raised her head so that she could see those blue, blue eyes she adored. At night, in the moonlight, they were a beacon. "Thank you, Web," she said more softly. "I wanted you to be the first. It was very special...very, very special." She wanted to say again that she loved him, but he hadn't returned the words, and she didn't want to put him on the spot. She was grateful for what she felt, for what he'd made her feel, for what he'd given her. For the time being it was more than enough.

They rested in each other's arms for a while, listening to the sounds of the sea until those became too tempting to resist. So they raced into the water, laughing, playing, finally making love again there in the waves, wrapped up enough in each other not to care whether the rest of the world saw or heard or knew.

In the two weeks that followed, they were slightly more cautious. Unable to stay away from each other, they timed their rendezvous with care, meeting at odd hours and in odd places where they could forget the rest of the world existed and could live those brief times solely for each other and themselves. Marni was wildly happy and passionately in love; that justified her actions. She found Web to be intelligent and worldly, exquisitely sensitive and tender when she was in his arms. Web only knew that there was something special about her, something bright and luminous. She was a free spirit, forthright and fresh. She was a ray of sunshine in his life.

Marni's parents suspected that something was going on, but Marni always had a ready excuse to give them when they asked where she was going or where she'd been, and she was careful never to mention Web's name. Ethan knew what was happening and, though he worried, he adored Marni and was fond enough of Web to trust that he was in control of things. Tanya was jealous, plainly and simply. She'd been stringing along another of Ethan's friends for most of the summer, but when—inevitably, through one of Marni's friends—she got wind of Marni's involvement with Web, she suddenly realized what she'd overlooked and sought to remedy the situation. Web wasn't interested, which only irked her all the more, and at the time Marni made no attempt to reason with her sister.

It was shortsighted on her part, but then none of them ever dreamed that the summer would end prematurely and tragically.

With a week left before Labor Day, Web and Ethan set out in search of an evening's adventure in the university town of Orono. Marni had wanted to come along, but Ethan had been adamant. He claimed that their parents had been questioning him about her relationship with Web, and that the best way to mollify them would be for him to take off with Web while she spent the evening home for a change. She'd still protested, whereupon Ethan had conned Web into taking the motorcycle. It only sat two; there was no room for her.

For months and months after that, Marni would go over the what ifs again and again. What if she hadn't pestered and the two had taken Ethan's car as they'd originally planned? What if she'd made noise enough to make them cancel the trip? What if her parents hadn't been suspicious of her relationship with Web? What if there hadn't been anything to be suspicious of? But all the what ifs in the world—and there were even more she grappled with—couldn't change the facts.

It had begun to rain shortly after eleven. The road had been dark. Two cars had collided at a blind intersection. The motorcycle had skidded wildly in their wake. Ethan had been thrown, had hit a tree and had been killed instantly.

3

"OKAY," WEB SIGHED, straightening. "That's it for today."

Anne rushed to him, her eyes on Marni's hunched form. "But you haven't got what you want," she argued in quiet concern.

"I know that and you know that, but Marni's in no shape to give us anything else right now." He handed his camera to an assistant, then raked a hand through his hair. "I'm not sure I am either," he said. In truth he was disgusted with himself. Sunshine. How could he have slipped that way? He hadn't planned to do it; the endearment had just come out. But then, it appeared he'd handled Marni wrong from the start.

Dismayed murmurs filtered through the room, but Web ignored them to approach the stool where Marni sat. He put an arm around her shoulder and bent his head close, using his body as a shield between her and any onlookers. "I'm sorry, Marni. That was my fault. It wasn't intentional, believe me."

She was crying silently, whitened fingers pressed to her downcast face.

"Why don't you go on in and change. We'll make a stab at this another day."

She shook her head, but said nothing. Web crooked his finger at Anne, then, when she neared, tossed his head in the direction of the dressing room and left the two women alone.

"Come on, Marni," Anne said softly. It was her arm around Marni's shoulders now, and she was gently urging her to her feet.

"I've spoiled everything," Marni whispered, "and made a fool of myself in the process."

"You certainly have not," Anne insisted as they started slowly toward the dressing room. "We all knew you weren't wild about doing this. So you've shown us that you're human, and that there are some kinds of pressure you just can't take."

"We'll have to get someone else for the cover."

"Let's talk about that when you've calmed down."

Anne stayed with her while she changed into her own clothes. She was blotting at the moistness below her eyes when a knock came at the door. Anne answered it, then stepped outside, and Web came in, closing the door behind him.

"Are you okay?" he asked, leaning against the door. Though he barred her escape, he made no move to come closer.

She nodded.

"Maybe you were right," he said. "Maybe there are too many people around. You felt awkward. I should have insisted they leave."

She stared at him for a minute. "That was only part of the problem."

He returned her stare with one of his own. "I know."

"I told you I couldn't do this."

"We'll give it another try."

"No. I'm not going through it again."

He blinked. "It'll be easier next time. Fewer people. And I'll know what not to do."

Marni shook her head. "I'm not going through it again."

"Because it brought back memories?"

"Exactly."

"Memories you don't want."

"Memories that bring pain."

"But if you don't face them, they'll haunt you forever."

"They haven't haunted me before today."

He didn't believe her. She probably didn't dwell on those memories any more than he did, but he knew there were moments, fleeting moments when memory clawed at his gut. He couldn't believe she was callous enough not to have similar experiences. "Maybe you've repressed them."

"Maybe so. But I can't change the past."

"Neither can I. But there are still things that gnaw at me from time to time."

Marni held up a hand. "I don't want to get into this. I can't. Not now. Besides, I have to get into the office. I've already wasted enough time on this fiasco."

Web took a step closer. His voice was calm, too calm, his expression hard. "This is what I do for a living, Marni. I'm successful at it, and I'm respected. Don't you ever, ever call it a fiasco."

Too late she realized that she'd hit a sore spot. Her voice softened. "I'm sorry. I didn't mean it that way. I respect what you are and what you do, too, or else we'd never be paying you the kind of money we are. The fiasco was in using me for a model, particularly given what you and I had...what we had once." She looked away to find her purse, then, head bent, moved toward the door.

"I'm taking you to dinner tonight," Web announced quietly.

Her head shot up. "Oh, no. That would be rubbing salt in the wound."

"Maybe it would be cleansing it, getting the infection out. It's been festering, Marni. For fourteen years it's been festering. Maybe neither of us was aware of it. Maybe we never would have been if we hadn't run into each other today. But it's there, and I don't know about you, but I won't be able to put it out of my mind until we've talked. If we're going to work together—"

"We're not! That's what I keep trying to tell you! We tried today and failed, so it's done. Over. We'll get another model for the cover, and I can go back to what I do best."

"Burying your head in the sand?"

"I do *not* bury my head in the sand." Her eyes were flashing, but his were no less so, and the set of his jaw spoke of freshly stirred emotion.

"No? Fourteen years ago you said you loved me. Then I lay there after the accident, and you didn't visit me once, not once, Marni!" His teeth were gritted. "Two months I was in that hospital. *Two months*, and not a call, not a card, nothing."

Marni felt her eyes well anew with tears. "I can't talk about this," she whispered. "I can't handle it now."

"Tonight then."

She passed him and reached for the door, but he pressed a firm hand against it. "Please," she begged. "I have to go."

"Eight-thirty tonight. I'll pick you up at your place."

"No."

"I'll be there, Marni." He let his hand drop, and she opened the door. "Eight-thirty."

She shook her head, but said nothing more as she made good her escape. Unfortunately, Edgar and Steve, Anne, Cynthia, Dan and Marjorie were waiting for her. When they all started talking at once, she held up a hand.

"I'm going to the office." She looked at the crew from *Class*. "Go through your files, put your heads together and come up with several other suggestions for a cover face. Not necessarily a model, maybe someone in the business world. We'll meet about it tomorrow morning." She turned her attention to Edgar and Steve, but she was already moving away. "I'm taking the limousine. Are you coming?"

Without argument, they both hurried after her.

Web watched them go, a small smile on his lips. She could command when she wanted to, he mused, and she was quite a sight to behold. Five feet five inches of auburn-haired beauty, all fired up and decisive. She'd change her mind, of course, at least about doing the cover shot. He'd *make* her change her mind...if for no other reason than to prove to himself that, at last, he had what it took.

EIGHT-THIRTY THAT NIGHT found Marni sitting stiffly in her living room, her hands clenched in her lap. She jumped when the phone rang, wondering if Web had changed his mind. But it was the security guard calling from downstairs to announce that Brian Webster had indeed arrived.

She'd debated how to handle him and had known somehow that the proper way would *not* be to refuse to see him. She had more dignity than that, and more respect for Web professionally. Besides, he'd thrown an accusation at her earlier that day, and she simply had to answer it.

With a deep breath, she instructed the guard to send him up.

By the time the doorbell rang, her palms were damp. She rubbed them together, then blotted them on her skirt. It was the same skirt she'd worn that morning, the same jacket, the same blouse. She wanted Web to know that this was nothing more than an extension of her business day. Perhaps she wanted to remind herself of it. The prospect of having dinner with him was a little less painful that way.

What she hadn't expected was to open the door and find him wearing a stylish navy topcoat, between whose open lapels his dark suit, crisp white shirt and tie were clearly visible. He looked every bit as businesslike as she wanted to feel, but he threw her off-balance.

"May I come in?" he asked when she'd been unable to find her tongue.

"Uh, yes." She stood back dumbly. "Please do." She closed the door behind him.

"You seem surprised." Amused, he glanced down at himself. "Am I that shocking?"

"I, uh, I just didn't expect...I've never seen you in..."

"You didn't expect me to show up in a T-shirt and jeans, did you?"

"No, I...it's just..."

"Fourteen years, Marni. We all grow up at one point or another."

She didn't want to *touch* that one. "Can I...can I take your coat? Would you like a drink?" She hadn't planned to offer him any such thing, but then she didn't know quite *what* she'd planned. She couldn't just launch into an argument, not with him looking so...so urbane.

He shrugged out of the topcoat and set it on a nearby chair. "That would be nice. Bourbon and water, if you've got it," he said quietly, then watched her approach the bar at the far end of the room. She was still a little shaky, but he'd expected that. Hell, he was shaky, too, though he tried his best to hide it. "This is a beautiful place you've got." He admired the white French provincial decor, the original artwork on the walls. Everything was spotless and bright. "Have you been here long?"

"Three years," she said without turning. She was trying to pour the bourbon without splashing it all over the place. Her hands weren't terribly steady.

"Where were you before that?" he asked conversationally.

"I had another place. It was smaller. When I took over from...took over the presidency of the corporation, I realized I'd need a larger place for entertaining."

"Do you do much?"

She returned with his drink, her full concentration on keeping the glass steady. "Much?"

"Entertaining." He accepted the drink and sat back.

"Enough."

"Do you enjoy it?"

She took a seat across from him, half wishing she'd fixed a hefty something for herself but loath to trust her legs a second time. "Sometimes."

He eyed her over the rim of his glass. "You must be very skilled at it...upbringing and all." He took a drink.

"I suppose you could say that. My family's always done its share of entertaining."

He nodded, threw his arm over the back of the sofa and looked around the room again. It was a diversionary measure. He wasn't quite sure what to say. Marni was uncomfortable. He wanted her to relax, but he wasn't sure how to achieve that. In the end, he realized that his best shot was with the truth.

"I wasn't sure you'd be here tonight. I was half worried that you'd find something else to do—a late meeting or a business dinner or a date."

She looked at her hands, tautly entwined in her lap, and spoke softly, honestly. "I haven't been good for much today, business or otherwise."

"But you went back to the office after you left the studio."

"For all the good it did me." She hadn't accomplished a thing, at least nothing that wouldn't have to be reexamined tomorrow. She'd been thoroughly distracted. She'd read contracts, talked on the phone, sat through a meeting, but for the life of her she couldn't remember what any of it had been about. She raised her eyes quickly, unable to hide the urgency she felt. "I want you to know something, Web. That time you were in the hospital...it wasn't that I wasn't thinking about you. I just...couldn't get away. I called the hospital to find out how you were, but I...I couldn't get there." Her eyes were growing misty again. It was the last thing Web wanted.

"I didn't come here to talk about that, Marni. I'm sorry I exploded that way this morning—"

"But you meant it. You're still angry—"

"Not this minute. And I really *didn't* come here to talk about it."

"You said we had to talk things out."

"We will. In time."

In time? In *future time*? "But we haven't got any time." She looked away, and her voice dropped. "We never really did. It seemed to run out barely before it had begun."

"We've got time. I spoke with Anne this afternoon. She agrees with me that you're still the best one for this cover. You said yourself that we're well ahead of the production schedule."

A spurt of anger brought Marni's gaze back to his. "I told you, it's done. I will not pose for that cover. You and Anne can conspire all you want, but I'm still the publisher of this magazine, and as such I have the final say. I'm not a child anymore, Web. I'm thirty-one now, not seventeen."

He sat forward and spoke gently. "I know that, Marni."

"I won't be told what's good for me and what isn't."

"Seems to me you could *never* be told that. In your own quiet way, you were headstrong even back then."

She caught her breath and bowed her head. "Not really."

"I don't believe you," was his quiet rejoinder. When she simply shrugged, he realized that she wasn't ready to go into that. In many respects, he wasn't either. He took another drink, then turned the glass slowly in his hands. "Look, Marni. I don't think either of us wants to rehash the past just yet. What I'd like—the real reason I'm here now—is for us to get to know each other. We've both changed in fourteen years. In addition to other things, we were friends once upon a time. I don't know about you, but I'm curious to know what my friend's been doing, what her life is like now."

"To what end?" There was a thread of desperation in her voice.

"To make it easier for us to shoot this picture, for one thing." When she opened her mouth to protest, he held up a hand and spoke more quickly. "I know. You're not doing it. But the reason you're not is that working with me stirs up a storm of memories. If we can get to know each other as adults—"

"You were an adult fourteen years ago. I was a child—"

"I was a man and you were a woman," he corrected, "but we were both pretty immature about some things."

She couldn't believe what he was saying. "You weren't immature," she argued. "You were experienced and worldly. You'd lived far more than I ever had."

"There's living, and there's living. But that's not the point. The point is that we've both changed. We've grown up. If we spend a little time together now, we can replace those memories with new ones...." He stopped talking when he saw that she'd shrunk back into her seat. Was that dread in her eyes? He didn't want it to be. God, he didn't want that! He sat forward pleadingly. "Don't you see, Marni? You were shocked seeing me today because the last thing we shared involved pain for both of us. Sure, fourteen years have passed, but we haven't seen or spoken with each other in all that time. It's only natural that seeing each other would bring back all those other things. But it doesn't have to be like that. Not if we put something between those memories and us."

"I'm not sure I know what you're suggesting," she said in a tone that suggested she did.

"All I want," he went on with a sigh, "is to put the past aside for the time being. Hell, maybe it's a matter of pride for me. Maybe I want to show you what I've become. Is that so bad? Fourteen years ago, I was nothing. I wandered, I played. I never had more than a hundred bucks to my name at a given time. You had so much, at least in my eyes, and I'm not talking money now. You had a fine home, a family and social status."

Marni listened to his words, but it was his tone and his expression that reached her. He was sincere, almost beseechful. There was pain in his eyes, and an intense need. He'd never been quite that way with her fourteen years before, but she suddenly couldn't seem to separate the feelings she'd had for him then from the ache in her heart now. It occurred to her that the ache had begun when she'd first set eyes on him that morning. She'd attributed it to the pain of memory, and it was probably ninety-nine percent that, but there was something more, and she couldn't ignore it. Fourteen years ago she'd loved him. She didn't love him now, but there was still that...feeling. And those blue, blue eyes shimmering into her, captivating her, magnetizing her.

"I want to show you my world, Marni. I'm proud of it, and I want you to be proud, too. You may have thought differently, but my life was deeply affected by that summer in Camden." For a minute the blue eyes grew moist, but they cleared so quickly that Marni wondered if she'd imagined it. "Give me a chance, Marni. We'll start with dinner tonight. I won't pressure you for anything. I never did, did I?"

She didn't have to ponder that one. If anyone had done the pressuring— at least on the sexual level—it had been her. "No," she answered softly.

"And I won't do it now. You have my word on it. You also have my word that if anything gets too tough for you, I'll bring you back here and leave you alone. You *also* have my word that if, in the end, you decide you really can't do that cover, I'll abide by your decision. Fair?"

Fair? He was being so reasonable that she couldn't possibly argue. What wasn't fair was that he wore his suit so well, that his hair looked so thick and vibrant, that his features had matured with such dignity. But that wasn't his fault. Beauty was in the eye of the beholder.

She gave a rueful half smile and slowly nodded. "Fair."

He held her gaze a moment longer, as though he almost couldn't believe that she'd agreed, but his inner relief was such that he suddenly felt a hundred pounds lighter. He pushed back his cuff and glanced at the thin gold watch on his wrist.

"We've got reservations for five minutes ago. If I can use your phone, I'll let the maître d' know we're on our way."

She nodded and glanced toward the kitchen. When he rose and headed that way, she moved toward the small half bath off the living room. She suddenly wished she'd showered, done over her hair and makeup and changed into something fresher. Web was so obviously newly showered and shaved. She should have done more. But it was too late for that now, so the best she could do was to powder the faint shine from her nose and forehead, add a smidgen more blusher to her cheeks and touch up her lipstick.

Web was waiting when she emerged. He'd already put on his topcoat and was holding the coat she'd left ready and waiting nearby. It, too, was the same she'd worn that morning, but that decision she didn't regret. To wear silver fox with Web, even in spite of his own debonair appearance, seemed a little heavy-handed.

He helped her on with the coat, waited while she got her purse, then lightly took her elbow and escorted her to the door. They rode the elevator in a silence that was broken at last by Marni's self-conscious laugh. "You're very tall. I never wore high heels in Camden, but they don't seem to make a difference." She darted him a shy glance, but quickly returned her gaze to the patterned carpet.

He felt vaguely self-conscious, too. "I never wore shoes with laces in Camden. They add a little."

She nodded and said nothing more. The elevator door purred open. Web guided her through the plush lobby, then the enclosed foyer and finally to the street. He discreetly pressed a bill into the doorman's hand in exchange for the keys to his car, then showed Marni to the small black BMW parked at the curb. Before she could reach for it, he opened the door. "Buckle up," was all he said before he locked her in and circled the car to the driver's side.

The restaurant he'd chosen was a quiet but elegant one. The maître d' seemed not in the least piqued by their tardiness, greeting Web with a warm handshake and offering a similarly warm welcome to Marni when Web introduced them, before showing them to their table.

Web deftly ordered a wine. Then, when Marni had decided what she wanted to eat, he gave both her choice and his own to the waiter. Watching him handle himself, she decided he was as smooth in this urban setting as he'd been by the sea. He had always exuded a kind of confidence, and she assumed it would extend to whatever activity he was involved in. But seeing him here, comfortable in a milieu that should have been hers more than his, took some getting used to. It forced her to see him in a different light. She struggled to do that.

"Have you been here before?" he asked softly.

"For a business dinner once or twice. The food's excellent, don't you think?"

"I'm counting on it," he said with a grin. "So...tell me about Marni Lange and the Lange Corporation."

She shook her head. Somewhere along the line, she realized he was right. They'd been...friends once, and she *was* curious as to what he'd done in the past years. "You first. Tell me about Brian Webster the photographer."

"What would you like to know?"

"How you got started. I never knew you had an interest in photography."

"I didn't. At least, not when I knew you. But the year after that was a difficult one for me." His brow furrowed. "I took a good look at myself and didn't like what I saw."

She found herself defending him instinctively. "But you were an adventurer. You did lots of different things, and did them well."

"I was young, without roots or a future," he contradicted her gently. "For the first time I stopped to think about what I'd be like, what I'd be doing five, ten, fifteen years down the road, and I came up with a big fat zip."

"So you decided to be a photographer, just like that?" She was skeptical, though if that had been the case it would be a remarkable success story.

"Actually, I decided to write about what I'd been doing. There's always a market for adventure books. I envisioned myself traveling the world, doing all kinds of interesting things—reenacting ancient voyages across oceans, scaling previously unscaled mountain peaks, crossing the Sahara with two camels and canteens of water..."

"Did you do any of those things?"

"Nope."

"Then...you wrote about things you'd already done?"

"Nope." When she frowned, he explained. "I couldn't write for beans. I tried, Lord how I tried. I sat for hours and hours with blank paper in front of me, finally scribbling something down, then crossing it out and crumbling the sheet into a ball." He arched a brow in self-mockery. "I got pretty good at hitting the wastebasket on the first try."

A small smile touched her lips. "Oh."

"But—" he held up a finger "—it wasn't a total waste. Y'see, I'd pictured my articles in something like *National Geographic*, and of course there were going to be gorgeous photographs accompanying the text, and who better to take them than me, since I was there—actually I was in New Mexico at the time, on an archaeological dig."

"Had you ever used a camera before?"

"No, but that didn't stop me. It was an adventure in and of itself. I bought a used camera, got a few books, read up on what I had to do, and...click. Literally and figuratively."

He stopped talking and sat back. Marni felt as though she'd been left dangling. "And...?"

"And what?"

"What happened? Did you sell those first pictures?"

"Not to *National Geographic*."

"But you did sell them?"

"Uh-huh."

Again she waited. He was smiling, but he made no attempt to go on. She remembered that he'd been that way fourteen years ago, too. When she'd asked him about the things he'd done, there'd been a quiet smugness to him. He'd held things back until she'd specifically asked, and when his stories came out they were like a well-earned prize. In his way he'd manipulated her, forcing her to show her cards. Perhaps he was manipulating her now. But she didn't care. Hadn't he been the one to say that they should get to know each other?

"Okay," she said. "You photographed a dig in New Mexico and sold the pictures to a magazine. But photographing a dig is a far cry from photographing some of the world's most famous personalities. How did it happen? How did you switch from photographing arrowheads, or whatever, to photographing *head* heads?"

He chuckled. "Poetically put, if I don't say so myself. You should be the writer, Marni. You could write. I could photograph."

"I've already got a full-time job, thank you. Come on, Web. When did you get your first break?"

Just then the wine steward arrived with an ice bucket. He uncorked the wine, poured a taste for Web, then at Web's nod filled both of their glasses.

Web's thoughts weren't on the wine, but on the fact that he was thoroughly enjoying himself. The Marni sitting across from him now was so like the Marni he'd known fourteen years before that he couldn't help but smile in wonder. She was curious. She'd always been curious. She couldn't help herself, and he'd been counting on that. Personalities didn't change. Time and circumstances modified them, perhaps, but they never fully changed.

"Web...?" she prodded. "How did it happen?"

"Actually it was on that same trip. The dig I was working at was being used as the backdrop for a movie. Given the way I always had with people—" he winked, and she should have been angry but instead felt a delicious curling in her stomach "—I got myself into the middle of the movie set and started snapping away."

"Don't tell me that those first shots sold?"

"I won't. They were awful. I mean, they had potential. I liked the expressions I caught, the emotions, and I found photographing people much more exciting than photographing arrowheads or whatever. Technically I had a lot to learn, though, so I signed on with a photographer in L.A. After six months, I went out on my own."

"Six months? That's all? It takes years for most photographers to develop sufficient skill to do what you do and do it right."

"I didn't have years. I felt I'd already wasted too many, and I needed to earn money. There's that small matter of having a roof over your head and food enough to keep your body going, not to mention the larger matter of equipment and a studio. I started modestly, shooting outside mostly, working my buns off, turning every cent I could back into better equipment. I used what I'd learned apprenticing as a base, and picked up more as I went along. I read. I talked with other photographers. I studied the work of the masters and pored through magazine after magazine to see what the market wanted and needed. I did portfolios for models and actors and actresses, and things seemed to mushroom from there."

"Did you have a long-range goal?"

"New York. Cover work. Independence, within limits."

"Then you've made it," she declared, unaware of the pride that lit her eyes. Web wasn't unaware of it though, and it gave him unbelievable pleasure.

"I suppose you could say that," he returned softly. "There's always more I want to do, and the field keeps pace with changes in fashion. The real challenge is in making my work different from the others. I want my pictures to have a unique look and feel. I guess I need that more than anything—knowing I'll have left an indelible mark behind."

"Are you going somewhere?" she teased.

There was sadness in his smile. "We're all mortal. I think about that a lot. At the rate I'm going, my work will be just about all I do leave behind."

"You never married." It was a statement, offered softly, with a hint of timidness.

"I've been too busy.... What about you?"

"The same."

The waiter chose that moment to appear with their food, and they lapsed into silence for a time as they ate.

"Funny," Web said at last, "I'd really pictured you with a husband and kids and a big, beautiful home in the country."

She gave a sad laugh. "So had I."

"Dreams gone awry, or simply deferred?"

She pondered that for a minute. "I really don't know. I've been so caught up with running the business that it seems there isn't time for much else."

"You must do things for fun."

"I do...now and again." She stopped pushing the Parisienne potatoes around her plate and put down her fork. "What about you? Are you still working as hard as you did at first?"

"I'm working as hard, but the focus is different. I can concentrate on the creative end and leave the rest to assistants. I have specialists for my finish work, and even though I'm more often than not at their shoulders, approving everything before it leaves the studio, I do have more free time. I try to take weekends completely off."

"What do you do then?"

He shrugged. "Mostly I go to Vermont. I have a small place there. In the winter I ski. In the summer I swim."

"Sounds heavenly," she said, meaning it.

"Don't you still go to Camden?"

She straightened, and the look of pleasure faded from her face. "My parents still do. It's an institution with them. Me, well, I don't enjoy it the way I used to. Sometimes staying here in New York for the summer is a vacation in itself." She gave a dry laugh. "Everyone else is gone. It's quieter."

"You always did like peace and quiet," he said, remembering that day so long ago when they'd gone mountain climbing.

Marni remembered, too. Her gaze grew momentarily lost in his, lost in the memory of that happy, carefree time. It was with great effort that she finally looked away. She took a deep breath. "Anyway, I try to take an extra day or two when I'm off somewhere on business—you know, relax in a different place to shake off the tension."

"Alone?"

"Usually."

"Then there's no special man?"

"No."

"You must date?"

"Not unless I'm inspired, and I'm rarely inspired." Just then her eye was caught by a couple very clearly approaching their table. Following her gaze, Web turned around. He pushed his chair back, stood and extended his hand to the man.

"How are you, Frank?"

The newcomer added a gentle shoulder slap to the handshake. "Not bad."

Web enclosed the woman's hand in his, then leaned forward and kissed her cheek. "Maggie, you're looking wonderful. Frank, Maggie, I'd like you to meet Marni Lange. Marni, these are the Kozols."

Marni barely had time to shake hands with each before Frank was studying her, tapping his lip. "Marni Lange...of the Lange Corporation?"

She cast a skittish glance at Web, then nodded.

"I knew your father once upon a time," Frank went on. "Gee, I haven't seen him in years."

"He's retired now," she offered gracefully, though mention of her father in Web's presence made her uneasy.

"Is he well? And your mother?"

"They're both fine, thank you."

Maggie had come around the table to more easily chat with her. "Frank was with Eastern Engineering then, though he went out on his own ten years ago." She looked over to find her husband engrossed in an animated discussion with Web, and she smiled indulgently. "You'll have to excuse him. I know it's rude for us to barge in on your dinner this way, but he's so fond of Brian that he simply had to stop in and say hello."

Marni smiled. "It's perfectly all right. Have you known...Brian long?"

"Several years. Our daughter is—was—a model. When she first went to Brian to be photographed, she was pretty confused. He was wonderful. I really think that if it hadn't been for him, she would have ended up in a sorry state. She's married now and just had her first child." Maggie beamed. "The baby's a jewel."

"Boy...girl?" Out of the corner of her eye, Marni saw Web standing with one hand in his trousers pocket. He looked thoroughly in command, totally at ease and very handsome. She realized that she was proud to be with him.

"A boy. Christopher James. He's absolutely precious."

Marni retrained her focus on Maggie. "And you're enjoying him. Do they live close by?"

"In Washington. We've been down several times—"

"Come on, sweetheart," Frank cut in. "The car's waiting, and these folks don't need us taking any more of their time."

Maggie turned briefly back to Marni. "It was lovely meeting you." Then she gave Web a kiss and let her husband guide her off.

"Sorry about that," Web murmured, sitting down again. He pulled his chair closer to the table.

"Don't apologize." It was the first time she'd ever met any friends of Web's. "They seemed lovely. Maggie was mentioning her daughter. They're both in your debt, I take it."

He shrugged. "She was a sweet kid who was lost in the rat race of modeling. Maggie and Frank say that she was 'confused,' and she was, but she was also on drugs and she was practically anorexic."

"Isn't that true of lots of models?"

"Mmm, but it was particularly sad with Sara. She had a good home. Her folks are loaded. I'm not sure she even wanted to model in the first place, but she had the looks and the style, and she somehow got snagged. If she hadn't gotten out when she did, she'd probably be dead by now."

Marni winced. "What did you do for her?"

He grew more thoughtful. "Talked, mostly. I took the pictures and made sure they were stupendous. Then I tried to convince her that she'd hit the top and ought to retire."

"And just like that she did?"

"Not...exactly. I showed her my morgue book."

"Morgue book?"

"Mmm. I keep files on everyone I've photographed, with a follow-up on each. I have a special folder—pictures of people who made it big, then plummeted. When I'm feeling sorry for myself about one thing or another, I take it out, and it makes me grateful for what I've got. I don't show it to many people, but it gave Sara something to think about. She came back to see me often after that, and I finally convinced her to see a psychiatrist. Maggie and Frank are terrific, but Sara was their daughter, and the thought that she'd actually need a psychiatrist disturbed them."

"But it worked."

"It helped. Mostly what helped was meeting her husband. He's a rock, a lawyer with the Justice Department, and he's crazy about her. He supported her completely when she decided to go back to school to get the degree she missed out on when she began modeling." He cleared his throat meaningfully. "I think the baby has interrupted that now, but Sara knows she can go back whenever she's ready."

"That's a lovely story," Marni said with a smile. "I'll bet you have lots of others about people you've photographed." She propped her elbow on the table and set her chin in her palm. "Tell me some."

For the next hour, he did just that. There was a modesty to him, and she had to coax him on from time to time, but when he got going his tales fascinated her every bit as much as those he'd told fourteen years before had done. The years evaporated. She listened, enthralled, thinking how exciting his life was and how he was fully in control of it.

By the time they'd finished their second cup of coffee, they'd fallen silent and were simply looking at each other. Their communication continued, but on a different level, one in which Marni was too engrossed to analyze.

"Just like old times," Web said quietly.

She nodded and smiled almost shyly. "I could sit listening to you for hours. You were always so different from other people. You had such a wealth of experience to draw on. You still do."

"You've got experience of your own—"

"But not as exciting. Or maybe I just take it for granted. Do you ever do that?"

"I wish I could. If I start taking things for granted, I'll stop growing, and if that happens I'll never make it the way I want to."

"That means a lot to you…making it." So different from how he'd been, she mused. Then again, perhaps he'd only defined success differently fourteen years ago.

"Everyone wants success. Don't you? Isn't that why you pour so much of yourself into the business?"

She didn't answer him immediately. Her feelings were torn. Yes, she wanted to be successful as president of the Lange Corporation, but for reasons she didn't want to think about, much less discuss. "I guess," she said finally.

"You don't sound sure."

She forced herself to perk up. "I'm sure."

"But there was something else you were thinking about just now. What was it, Marni?"

She smiled and shook her head. "Nothing. It was really nothing. I think I'm just tired. It's been a long day."

"And a trying one."

"Yes," she whispered.

Not wanting to push her too far, Web didn't argue. He'd done most of the talking during dinner, and though there were still many things he wanted to know about Marni, many things he wanted to discuss with her, he felt relatively satisfied with what he'd accomplished. He'd wanted to tell her about his work, and he had. He'd wanted to give her a glimpse of the man he was now, and he had. He'd wanted to give her something to think about besides the past, and he had. He was determined to make her trust him again. Tonight had simply been the first down payment on that particular mortgage. There would be time enough in the future to make more headway, he mused as he dug into his pocket to settle the bill. There would be time. He'd make time. He wasn't sure what he wanted in the long run from Marni, but he did know that their relationship had been left suspended fourteen years ago, and that it needed to be settled one way or another.

They hit the cold night air the instant they left the restaurant. Marni bundled her coat around her more snugly, and when Web drew her back into the shelter of the doorway and threw his arm around her shoulder while they waited for the car, she didn't resist. He was large, warm and strong. He'd always been large, warm and strong.

For an instant she closed her eyes and pretended that that summer hadn't ended as it had. It was a sweet, sweet dream, and her senses filled to brimming with the taste, the touch, the smell of him. She loved Web. Her body tingled from his closeness. They were on their way to a secret rendezvous where he'd make the rest of the world disappear and lift her onto a plane of sheer bliss.

"Here we go," he murmured softly.

She began to tremble.

"Marni?"

Web was squeezing her shoulder. She snapped her eyes open and stared.

"The car. It's here."

Stunned, she let herself be guided into the front seat. By the time she realized what had happened, the neon lights of the city were flickering through the windshield as they passed, camouflaging her embarrassment.

Web said nothing. He drove skillfully and at a comfortable pace. When they arrived at her building, he left his keys with the doorman and rode the elevator with her to her door. There he took her own keys, released the lock, then stood back while she deactivated the burglar alarm.

With the door partially open, she raised her eyes to his. "Thank you, Web. I've...this was nice."

"I thought so." He smiled so gently that her heart turned over. "You're really something to be with."

"I'm not. You carried most of the evening."

He winked. "I was inspired."

Her limbs turned to jelly and did nothing by way of solidifying when he put a light hand on her shoulder. His expression grew more serious, almost troubled.

"Marni, about that cover—"

"Shhhh." She put an impulsive finger on his lips to stem the words, then wished she hadn't because the texture of his mouth, its warmth, was like fire. She snatched her hand away and dropped her gaze to his tie. It was textured, too, but of silk, and its smooth-flowing stripes of navy, gray and mauve were serene, soothing. "Please," she whispered. "Let's not argue about that again."

"I still want to do it. Don't you think it would be easier for you now?"

"I...I don't know."

"Will you think about it at least? We couldn't try it again until early next week anyway. Maybe by then you'll be feeling more comfortable."

She dipped her head lower. "I don't know."

"Marni?"

She squeezed her eyes shut, knowing she should slip through her door and lock it tight, but was unable to move. When he curved one long forefinger under her chin and tipped it up, she resisted. He simply applied more pressure until at last she met his gaze.

"It's still there," he whispered. "You know that, don't you?"

Eyes large and frightened, she nodded.

"Do we have to fight it?"

"I'm not ready." She was whispering, too, not out of choice, but because she couldn't seem to produce anything louder. Her heart was pounding, its beat reverberating through her limbs. "I don't know if I'm...ready for this. I suffered so...last time..."

He was stroking her cheek with the back of his hand, a hand that had once known every inch of her in the most intimate detail. His blue eyes were clouded. "I suffered, too. You don't know. I suffered, too, Marni. Do you think I want to go through that again?"

She swallowed hard, then shook her head.

"I wouldn't suggest something I felt would hurt either of us."

"What *are* you suggesting?"

"Friday night. See me Friday night. There's a party I have to go to, make a quick appearance at. I'd like you to come with me, then we can take off and do something—dinner, a movie, a ride through the park, I don't care what, but I have to see you again."

"Something's screwed up here. I was always the one to do the chasing."

"Because I was arrogant and cocksure, and so caught up in playing the role of the carefree bachelor that I didn't know any better." His thumb skated lightly over her lips. "I'm tired of playing, Marni. I'm too old for that now. I want to see you again. I *have* to see you again.... How about it? Friday night?"

"I can't promise you anything about the picture."

"Friday night. No business, just fun. Please?"

If fourteen years ago anyone had told Marni that Web would be pleading with her to see him, she would never have believed it. If thirteen years ago, ten years ago, five or even one year ago anyone had told Marni that she'd *be* seeing him again, she would never have believed it.

"Yes," she said softly, knowing that there was no other choice she could possibly make. Web did something to her. He'd *always* done something to her. He made her feel things she'd never felt with another man. Shock, pain, shimmering physical awareness...she was alive. That, in itself, was a precious gift.

4

THE PARTY WAS unbelievably raucous. Pop music throbbed through the air at ear-splitting decibels, aided and abetted by the glare of brightly colored floodlights and the sea of bodies contorting every which way in a tempest of unleashed energy.

The host was a rock video producer whom Web had met several months before through a mutual subject of their respective lenses. The guest list ran the gamut from actors to singers to musicians to technicians.

Marni could barely distinguish one garishly lit face, one outrageously garbed body from another, and she would have felt lost had it not been for the umbilical cord of Web's arm. He introduced her to those he knew and joined her in greeting others he was meeting for the first time. Marni couldn't say that it was the most intellectually stimulating group she'd ever encountered, but then her own mind could barely function amid the pulsating hubbub of activity.

In hindsight, though, it was an educational hour that she spent with Web at the party. She learned that he was well-known, well-liked and held slightly in awe. She learned that he didn't play kissy-and-huggy-and-isn't-this-a-*super*-party, but maintained his dignity while appearing fully congenial and at ease. She learned that he disliked indiscriminate drinking and avoided the coke corner like the plague, that he hated Twisted Sister, abided Prince, admired Springsteen, and that he was not much more of a dancer than she was.

"I think I'm getting a migraine," he finally yelled at her over the din. "Come on. Let's get out of here." He tugged her by the hand, leading her first for their coats, then out the door. Once in the lobby, where the music was little more than a dull vibration, he leaned back against the wall. Their coats were slung over his shoulder. He hadn't released her hand once. "Sorry about that," he said, tipping his head sideways against the stucco wall to look at her. "I hadn't realized it'd be so wild. Well, maybe I had, but I promised Malcolm I'd come. Are you still with me?"

She, too, was braced against the wall, savoring their escape. She gave his hand a squeeze and smiled. "A little wilted, but I'm still here."

"I want you to know that these aren't really my friends. I mean, Malcolm is, and I know enough of the others, but I don't usually hang around with them in my free time. Even if I did it'd be one at a time and in a quieter setting, but I really do have other, more reputable friends.... What are you laughing at?"

"You. You were so confident back there, but all of a sudden you're like a little boy, all nervous and apologetic." She punctuated her words with a chiding headshake, but she was grinning. "I'm not your mother, Web. And I'm not here to stand in judgment on your friends and acquaintances."

"I know, but...why is it I suspect that your friends are a little more...dignified?"

She grimaced. "Maybe because I'm the staid president of a staid corporation."

"Hey, I'm not knocking it.... What *are* your friends like?"

"Oh...diverse. Quieter, I guess." She paused pensively. "It's strange. When I think back to being a teenager, to the group I was with then, I remember irreverent parties and a general law-unto-ourselves attitude."

"You were never really that way."

"No, but I was on the fringe of it. When I think of what those same people, even the most rebellious ones, are doing now, I have to laugh. They're conventional, establishment all the way. Oh, they like a good time, and by and large they've got plenty of money to spend on one, but they seem to have outgrown that wildness they so prided themselves on."

"You say 'they.' You don't identify with them?"

She plucked at the folds of the chic overblouse she'd worn with her stirrup pants. "It wasn't that I outgrew it. I was shocked into leaving it behind. Somehow I lost a taste for it after...after..."

"After Ethan died," he finished for her in a sober voice. When she didn't reply, he took her coat from his shoulder. "Come on," he said gently. "Let's take a walk."

Without raising her head, she slipped her arms into the sleeves of the coat and buttoned it up, then let Web take her hand and lead her into the February night. The party had been in SoHo at the lower end of Manhattan. They'd taxied there, but a slow walk back uptown was what they both needed.

"You still miss him, don't you?" Web asked.

The air was cold, numbing her just enough to enable her to talk of Ethan. "I adored him. There were eight years between us, and it wasn't as though we were close in the sense of baring our souls to each other. But we shared a special something. Yes, I miss him."

Web wrapped his arm around her shoulders and drew her close as they walked. "He would have been president of Lange, wouldn't he?"

"Yes."

"You took over in his place."

"My parents needed someone."

"What about your sister...Tanya?"

Marni's laugh was brittle. "Tanya is hopeless. She ran in the opposite direction when she thought she might have to do something with the business. Not that Dad would have asked her. Maybe it was because he *didn't* ask her that she was so negative about it. She never did get her degree. She flunked out of two different colleges and finally gave up on the whole thing."

"What is she doing now?"

"Oh, she's here in New York. She's been through two husbands and is looking around for a third. She's got alimony enough to keep her living in style, so she spends her days shopping and her nights partying."

"Not *your* cup of tea."

"Not...quite."

"Were you ever close, you and Tanya?"

"Not really. We fought all the time as kids, you know, bickered like all siblings do. When I read things about sibling placement, about how the middle child is supposed to be the mediator, I have to laugh. Tanya was the *instigator*. It's like she felt lost between Ethan and me, and had to go out of her way to exert herself. I was some kind of threat to her—don't ask me why. She's prettier, more outgoing. And she can dance." They both chuckled. "But she always seemed to think that I had something she didn't, or that I was going to get something better than what she did."

"She was two years older than you?"

"Mmmm."

"Maybe she resented your arrival. If Ethan was seven when she was born, and she was the first girl, she was probably pampered for those first two years of her life. Your birth upset the applecart."

Marni sighed. "Whatever, it didn't—doesn't—make for a comfortable relationship. We see each other at family events, and run into each other accidentally from time to time, but we rarely talk on the phone and we never go out of our way to spend time together. It's sad, when you think of it." She looked up at Web. "You must think it's pathetic...being an only child and all."

"I wasn't an only child."

Her eyes widened. "No? But I thought...you never mentioned any family, and I always assumed you didn't have any!"

His lips twitched. "Just hatched from a shell and took off, eh?"

"You know what I mean. What *do* you have, Web? Tell me."

"I have a brother. Actually a half brother. He's four years younger than me."

"Do you ever see him?"

"We work together. He's my business manager, or agent, or financial advisor, or whatever you want to call it. Lee Fitzgerald. He was there Tuesday morning...but you don't remember much of that, do you?"

She eyed him shamefacedly. "I wasn't exactly at my best Tuesday morning."

"You wouldn't have had any way of knowing he was my brother. We don't look at all alike. But he's a nice guy, and very capable."

Marni was remembering what Web had said that Tuesday morning, in a moment of anger, about his being a bastard. "The name Webster?"

"Was my mother's maiden name."

"Did you ever know your father?"

"Nope. It was a one-night stand. He was married."

"Do you ever...wonder about him?"

He caressed her shoulder through the thickness of her coat as though he needed that small reassurance of her presence. Though his tone was light, devoid of bitterness, almost factual, Marni suspected that he regretted the circumstances of his conception.

"I wouldn't be human if I didn't. I used to do it a lot when I was a kid— wonder who he was, what he looked like, where he lived, whether he'd like me. I can almost empathize with Tanya. I spent all those years wandering, traveling, never staying in one place long. Maybe I didn't want to learn that he wasn't looking for me. As long as I kept moving, I had that illusion that he might be looking but, of course, couldn't find me. Pretty dumb, huh? He doesn't even know I exist."

Marni's heart ached for him. "Your mother never told him?"

"My mother never *saw* him, not after that one night. She knew his name, but he was a salesman from somewhere or other. She didn't know where. And she knew he was married, so she didn't bother. She married my stepfather when I was two. He wasn't a bad sort as stepfathers go."

They turned onto Fifth Avenue, walking comfortably in step with each other. "Is your mother still living?"

"She died several years ago."

"I'm sorry, Web," Marni said, feeling all the more guilty about the times she'd resented her own parents. At least they were alive. If she had a problem, she had somewhere to run. "Do you still wonder about your father?"

"Nah. I reached a point when settling down meant more than running away from the fact that he didn't know about me. I decided I wanted to do something, be something. I'm proud of what I've become."

"You should be," she said softly, holding his gaze for a minute, until the intensity of its soul-reach made her look away.

They walked silently for a few blocks, their way lit frequently by storefront lights or the headlights of cars whipping through the city night. The sound of motors, revving, slowing, filled the air, along with the occasional honk of a horn or the squeal of brakes or the whir of tires.

"What about you, Marni? I know what you've become, but what would you have done if...things had been different. I knew you wanted a college degree, but you hadn't said much more than that. Had you always wanted to join the corporation?"

"I hadn't thought that far. Business, a career—they were the last things on my mind—" her voice lowered "—until Ethan died. I grew up pretty fast then."

"Why? I mean, you were only seventeen."

"Ethan had already started working, and I knew he was being groomed to take over Dad's place one day. It wasn't like I wanted the presidency per se, but my father needed someone, and it seemed right that I should give it a try."

"Did you go to Wellesley after all?"

"Mmmm. I did pretty lousy my first term. I was still pretty upset. But after that I was able to settle down. I got my M.B.A. at Columbia, and joined the corporation from there."

"Are you sorry? Do you ever wish you were doing something else?"

"I wish Ethan were here to be president, but given that he's not, I really can't complain. I do have an aptitude for business. I think I'm good at what I do. There's challenge to the work, and a sense of power because the corporation is profitable and I'm free to venture into new things."

"Like *Class*."

"Like *Class*."

They turned from Fifth Avenue onto a side street that was darker and more deserted. Marni couldn't remember the last time she'd walked through the city like this at night. She'd always been too intent on getting from one place to another, via cab or car or limousine, to think of walking. Yet, now it was calming, therapeutic, really quite nice. Of course, it helped that Web was with her. Talking with him was easy. He made her think about things—like Ethan—and doing so brought less pain than she'd have expected. Ethan was gone; she couldn't bring him back. But Web was here.

He'd never take the place of her brother; for that matter, she couldn't even *think* of Web as a brother. It wasn't a brother she wanted anyway. She wasn't sure just what she did want from Web—she hadn't thought that far. But his presence had an odd kind of continuity to it. Tonight, even Tuesday night when he'd taken her to dinner, she'd felt an inner excitement she hadn't experienced since she'd been seventeen years old. She felt good being with him—proud of what he was, how he looked, how he looked at *her*—and she felt infinitely safe, protected with his arm around her and his sturdy body so close.

Just then, a muffled cry came from the dark alleyway they'd just passed. They stopped and looked at each other, and their eyes grew wider when the sound came again. Suddenly Web was moving, pressing Marni into the alcove of a storefront. "Play dead," he whispered, then turned and ran back toward the alley. He'd barely reached its mouth when a body barreled into him, sending him sprawling, but only for an instant. Acting reflexively, he was on his feet and after the man, who was surprisingly smaller and slower than he.

But smaller and slower was one thing. When he dragged the nameless fugitive to the ground nearly halfway down the block, he found that he was no match for the shiny switchblade that connected with his left hand. Shards of pain splintered through him, and he recoiled, clutching his hand. He had no aspirations to be a hero or a martyr. Letting the man go, he ran back to where he'd left Marni. She was gone.

"Maaaarni!" he yelled, terrified for the first time.

"In here, Web! The alley!"

He swore, then dashed into the alley, skidding to a halt and coming down on his haunches beside her. She was supporting a young woman who was gasping for air.

"It's all right," Marni was saying softly but tightly. "It's all right. He's gone."

"Did he rape her?" Web asked Marni. He could see that the woman's clothes were torn.

She shook her head. "Our passing must have scared him off. He took her wallet. That's about it."

Web put a hand on the woman's quivering arm. "I'm going to get the police. Stay with Marni until I get back."

Her answering nod was nearly imperceptible amid her trembling, but Marni doubted she could have moved if she'd wanted to.

Web dashed back to the street, wondering where the traffic was when he wanted it. He ran to the corner of Fifth Avenue, intent on hailing some help. Cars whizzed by without pausing. The cabs were all occupied, so they didn't bother to stop. And there wasn't a policeman or a cruiser in sight. Spotting a pay phone, he dug into his pocket for a quarter, quickly called in the alarm, then raced back to the alley.

Marni was where he'd left her, still cradling the woman. Frightened, she looked up at him. "He must have hurt her. She has blood on her sleeve, but I don't know where it's coming from."

"It's mine," Web said, crouching down again. He was feeling a little dizzy. Both of his hands were covered with blood, one from holding the other. Tugging the scarf from around his neck, he wound it tightly around his left hand.

"My God, Web!" Marni whispered. Her heart, racing already, began to slam against her ribs. "What *happened*?"

"He had a knife. Lucky he used it on me, not her."

"But your hand—"

"It'll be all right."

The woman in Marni's arms began to cry. "I'm sorry...it's my fault. I shouldn't have...been walking alone...."

Marni smoothed matted strands of hair from the young woman's cheeks. She couldn't have been more than twenty-two or twenty-three, was thin and not terribly attractive. Yes, she should have known better, but that was water over the dam. "Shhhh. It's all right. The police will be here soon." She raised questioning eyes to Web, who nodded. Then she worriedly eyed his hand.

"It's okay," he assured her softly. He turned to the woman who'd been assaulted. "What's your name, honey?"

"Denise...Denise LaVecque."

"You're going to be just fine, Denise. The police will be along shortly." As though on cue, a distant siren grew louder. "They're going to want to know everything you can remember about the man who attacked you."

"I...I can't remember much. It was dark. He just...jumped out..."

"Anything you can remember will be a help to them."

The siren neared. It hit Marni that Denise wasn't the only one in for a long night. "They'll want to know everything you remember, too," she told Web.

He closed his eyes for a minute, frowning. His hand was beginning to throb. He wasn't sure if his wool scarf had been the best thing to wrap around it, but he'd needed to hide its condition from Marni—and from himself, if the truth were told. "I know."

Marni's hand on his cheek brought his eyes back open. "Are you really okay?" she whispered tremulously.

He gave a wan smile and nodded.

The siren rounded the corner and died at the same time a glaring flash of blue and white intruded on the darkness of the alley. It was a welcome intrusion.

The next few minutes passed by in a whir for Marni. A second police car joined the first, with four of New York's finest offering their slightly belated aid, asking question after question, searching the alley for anything Denise's assailant may have dropped, finally bundling Denise off in one car, Web and Marni in another. Marni wasn't sure what their plans were for Denise, but she was vocal in her insistence that Web be taken to a hospital before he answered any further questions.

The drive there was a largely silent one. Marni held Web's good hand tightly, worriedly glancing at him from time to time.

"It's just a cut," he murmured when he intercepted one such glance, but his head was lying back against the seat and the night could hide neither his pallor nor the blood seeping through the thickness of his scarf.

"My hero," was her retort, but it was more gentle than chiding, more admiring than censorious. She suspected that he'd acted on sheer instinct in chasing after the man who'd attacked Denise, and in a city notorious for its avoidance of involvement in such situations she deeply respected what Web had done. Of course, tangling with a switchblade hadn't been too swift....

The nurse at the emergency room desk immediately took Web to a cubicle, but when she suggested that Marni might want to wait outside, Marni firmly shook her head. She continued to hold Web's hand tightly, releasing it only to help him out of his coat and to roll up his sleeve. He sat on the examining table with his legs hanging down one side; she sat with her legs hanging down the other, her elbow hooked with his, her eyes over her shoulder focusing past him to his left hand, which a doctor was carefully unwrapping.

She didn't move from where she sat. Her arm tightened periodically around Web's as the doctor cleaned the knife wound, then examined it to see the extent of the damage. When Web winced, so did she. When he grunted at a particularly painful probe, she moaned.

"You okay?" he asked her at one point. The doctor had just announced that the tendon in his baby finger had been severed and that it would take a while to heal, what with stitches and all.

"I'm okay," she told Web. "You're the one who's sweating."

He grinned peakedly. "It hurts like hell."

Feeling utterly helpless, she turned on the doctor. "He's in pain. Can't you help—"

"Marni," Web interrupted, "it's only my hand."

"But the pain's probably shooting up your arm, and don't you tell me it isn't!" She felt it herself, through her hand, her arm, her entire body. Again she accosted the doctor. "Aren't you going to anesthetize him or something?"

The doctor gave her an understanding smile. "Just his hand. Right now." He took the needle that the nurse assisting him had suddenly produced, and Marni did look away then, but only until Web rubbed his cheek against her hair.

"You can open your eyes now," he said softly, a hint of amusement in his tone. "It's all done."

What was done was the anesthetizing. The gash, which cut through his baby finger and continued across his palm, was as angry-looking as ever.

"You may think this is funny, Brian Webster," she scolded in a hoarse whisper, "but I don't. Who knows what filthy germs were on that knife, or how you're going to handle a camera with one hand immobilized."

"Do you think I'm not worried about those same things?" he asked gently.

"No need to worry, Mr. Webster," the doctor interjected. "I'll give you a shot to counter whatever may have been on the knife, and as for your work, it's just your pinkie that will be in a splint. Between your thumb and the first two fingers of that left hand, you should be able to manage your camera. Maybe a little awkwardly at first, but you'll adapt."

"See?" Web said to Marni. "I'll adapt."

Marni didn't reply. She felt guilty for having badgered him, but she was worried and upset, and she'd had to let off the tension somehow. Turning her gaze back to his wound, which the doctor was beginning to stitch, she slid her free arm over Web's shoulder. He reached up, grasped her hand and wove his fingers through hers.

"Does it hurt?" she whispered.

He, too, was closely following the doctor's work, but he managed to shake his head. "Don't feel a thing."

"I'm glad one of us doesn't," she quipped dryly, and he chuckled.

Millimeter by millimeter the doctor closed the gash. Once, riding a wave of momentary fatigue, Marni pressed her face to the crook of Web's neck. He tipped his head to hold her there, finding intense comfort in the closeness.

When the repair work was done, the doctor splinted the finger and bandaged the hand. He gave Web the shot he'd promised, plus a small envelope with painkillers that he claimed Web might need as soon as the local anesthetic wore off. Marni would have liked nothing more than to take him home at that point, but the police were waiting just beyond the cubicle to take them to the station.

"Can't this be done tomorrow?" Marni asked softly. "I think he should be resting."

Web squeezed her hand. "It's okay. If we go now, we'll get it over with. The sooner the better, before the numbness wears off. Besides, I'm not sure I want to spend my Saturday poring through mug shots."

She would have argued further, but she realized he had a point. "You'll tell me if you start feeling lousy?"

"I think you'll know," he returned, arching one dark brow. She hadn't let go of him for a minute, and he loved it. Barely five minutes had gone by when she hadn't looked at his face for signs of discomfort or asked how he felt, and he loved it. He'd never been the object of such concern in his life. And he loved it.

He didn't love wading through page after page of mug shots in search of the man he'd seen and chased, but the police were insistent, and he knew it was necessary. He particularly didn't love it when the wee hours of the morning approached and they were still at it, he and Marni. His hand was beginning to ache again, and as the minutes passed, his head was, too. He knew that Marni had to be totally exhausted, and while he wanted to send her home, he also needed her by his side.

"Nothing," he said wearily when the last of the books were closed. "I'm sorry, but I don't think the man I saw tonight is here."

The officer who had been working with them rose from his perch on the corner of the desk and took the book from Web. "Hit and run. They're the damnedest ones to catch. May have been wearing a wig, or have shaved off a mustache. May not have any previous record, if you can believe that."

Marni, for one, was ready to believe anything the man said, if only to secure her and Web's release. Not only was she tired, but the events of the night had begun to take an emotional toll. She was feeling distinctly shaky.

"Is there anything else we have to do now?" she asked fearfully.

"Nope. I've got your statements, and I know where to reach you if we come up with anything."

Web was slipping his coat on. He didn't bother to put his left arm into the sleeve. It wasn't worth the effort. "Do you think you will?"

"Nope."

Web sighed. "Well, if you need us..."

The officer nodded, then stood aside, and Web and Marni wound their way through the maze of desks, doorways and stairs to the clear, cold air outside. They headed straight for a waiting taxi.

"I'd better get you home," he murmured, opening the door for Marni. As she slid in, she leaned forward and gave the cabbie Web's address. Web didn't realize what she'd done until they pulled up outside his riverfront building, at which point he was dismayed. "I can't send you home alone in a cab," he protested. "Not after what happened tonight."

Some of her spunk had returned. "I have no intention of going home alone, *especially* after what happened tonight. Come on, big guy." She was shoving him out the door. "We could both use a drink."

He was paying the cabbie when she climbed out herself. She was the one to put her arm around his waist and urge him into the building. "This is not...what...I'd planned," he growled, disgusted when he looked back on an evening that was supposed to have been so pleasant. "I never should have taken you to that party. If we hadn't gone, we wouldn't have been walking down that street—"

"And that poor girl would have been raped." Marni pressed the elevator button. The door slid open instantly, and she tugged him inside. "What ifs aren't any good—I learned that a long time ago. The facts are that we did go to the party, that we were walking down that street, that we managed to deter a vicious crime, that your hand is all cut up and that we're both bleary-eyed right about now." The elevator began its ascent. "I'm exhausted, but I'm afraid to close my eyes because I'll see either that dark alleyway, that girl, or your poor hand.... How is it?"

"It's there."

"You wouldn't take one of the painkillers while we were at the police station. Will you take one now?"

"A couple of aspirin'll do the trick."

He ferreted his keys from his pocket and had them waiting when the elevator opened. Moments later they'd passed through the studio, climbed the spiral staircase and were in his living room. He went straight to the bar, tipped a bottle into each of two glasses without thought to either ice or water, took a long drink from his glass, then handed the other to Marni.

"Come. Sit with me." He moved to the sofa, kicked off his loafers and sank down, stretching out his legs and leaning his head back.

"Where's the aspirin?" Marni asked softly.

"Medicine chest. Down the hall, through the bedroom to the bathroom."

She found her way easily, so intent on getting something into Web that she saw nothing of the rest of his apartment but the inside of the medicine chest above the sink. When she returned, he downed the aspirin with another drink from his glass. She sat facing him on the sofa, her elbow braced on the sofa back.

"You look awful," she whispered.

He didn't open his eyes. "I've felt better."

"Maybe you should lie down."

"I am." He was sprawled backward, his lean body molded to the cushions.

"In bed. Wouldn't you be more comfortable there?"

"Soon."

Very gently, she lifted his injured hand and put it in her lap. She wanted to soothe him, to do something to help, but she wasn't sure what would be best. She began to lightly stroke his forearm, and when he didn't complain she continued.

He smirked. "Some night."

"It certainly was an adventure. You were always into them. This is the first one I've taken part in."

"I think I'm getting too old for this. I'm getting too old for lots of things. I should be up in Vermont. It's quieter there."

"Why aren't you? I thought you went up every weekend."

He opened one eye and looked at her. "I wanted to be with you. I didn't think you'd go up there with me." When she said nothing, he closed his eye and returned his head to its original position. "Anyway, I often wait till Saturday morning to drive up. If there's something doing here on a Friday night."

"You can't drive tomorrow! Well, you can, I suppose, but your hand will be sore—"

"Forget my hand." He made a guttural sound. "The way I feel now, I don't think I'm going to be able to drag myself out of bed before noon, and by then it'd be pretty late to get going."

"You'll go next weekend. It'll still be there."

"Mmmm." He lay still for several minutes, then drained his drink in a single swallow.

Marni set her own glass firmly on the coffee table. She took his empty one, put it beside hers, then gently slid her hand under his neck. "Come on, Web," she urged softly. "Let me get you to bed."

Very slowly and with some effort he pushed himself up, then stood. His hand was hurting, his whole arm was hurting. For that matter, his entire body felt sore. The aftermath of tension, he told himself. He *was* getting old.

Marni led him directly to the bed. The king-sized mattress sat on a platform of dark wood that matched a modern highboy and a second, lower chest of drawers. A plush navy carpet covered the floor. Two chairs of the same contemporary style as those in the living room sat kitty-cornered on one side of the room, between them a low table covered with magazines. Large silk-screen prints hung on the walls, contemporary, almost abstract in style, carrying through the navy, brown and white scheme of the room.

Clear-cut and masculine, like Web, Marni mused as she unbuttoned his shirt and eased it from his shoulders. As soon as it was gone, he turned and whipped the quilt back with his good arm, then stretched out full-length on the bed and threw that same arm across his eyes.

Marni stood where she was with his shirt clutched in her hands and her eyes glued to his bare chest. He was every bit as beautiful as he'd been fourteen years ago, though different in a way that made her heart beat faster than it ever had then. His shoulders were fuller, his skin more weathered. The hair that covered his chest was thicker, more pervasive, even more virile, if that were possible.

Anything was possible, she thought, including the fact that she was as physically attracted to him now as she'd been fourteen years before. Biological magnetism was an amazing thing. Web had been her first, but there'd been others. None of them had turned her on in quite the same way, with quite the intensity Web did.

None of them had stirred feelings of tenderness and caring that Web did either, and he was hurting now, she reminded herself with a jolt. Pushing all other thought aside, she dropped his shirt onto the foot of the bed and came to sit beside him. She unsnapped his jeans and was about to lower the zipper when his arm left his eyes and his hand stilled hers.

"I was...just trying to make you more comfortable," she explained, feeling the sudden flare of those blue eyes on her. "Wouldn't it be better without the jeans?"

"No. I'm fine as I am." Most importantly, he didn't want her to see his leg. She'd had as rough a night as he had, and he didn't feel she was ready to view those particular scars. They were old and well-faded, true, but the memories they'd evoke would be harsh.

Trusting that she wouldn't undress him further, he returned his arm to his eyes and gave a rueful laugh. "Y'know, since I saw you last Tuesday morning, I've been dreaming of having you again. Making love to you...here in my bed. Now here you are and I feel so awful that I don't think I could do a thing even if you were willing."

His words hung in the air, unresolved. Marni couldn't get herself to give the answer she knew Web wanted to hear. There was no doubt in her mind that on the physical level she was willing. Emotionally, well, that was another story. Much as she'd opened up to him since their reunion, much as she'd been able to talk of Ethan more easily than she had in the past, there were still thoughts that she couldn't ignore, raw feelings going back to that summer. Illogical perhaps, but logical ones as well. She knew from experience that one time with Web wouldn't be enough. He'd been an addiction that summer in Maine. She wasn't sure that if she gave in to him, to herself, it would be any different now. And the question would be where they went from there.

"I don't think the time's right for either of us," she said in a near-whisper. "You're right. You're feeling awful. And I feel a little like I've been flattened by a steamroller." She reached for the second pillow and carefully worked it under his bandaged hand. Then she rose from the bed. "I'll just sit over here—"

He raised his arm and looked at her. "You won't leave, will you?"

"No, I won't leave."

"Then why don't you lie down, too. The bed's big enough for both of us."

She wasn't sure she trusted herself that far. "In a little bit," she said, but paused before she sank into the chair. "Can I get you anything?"

Eyes closed, he shook his head. "I think I'll just rest..."

When his voice trailed off, she settled into the chair, studying him for a long time until a reflexive twitch of his good hand told her he was asleep. Soon after, her own eyelids drooped, then shut.

Ninety minutes later she came to feeling disoriented and stiff. The first problem was solved when she blinked, looked around the room, then saw Web lying exactly as he had been. The second was solved when she switched off the light, stretched out on the empty half of the bed, drew the quilt over them both and promptly fell asleep.

She awoke several times during the night when Web shifted and groaned. Once she felt his head and found it cool, and when he didn't wake up she lay down again. Her deepest sleep came just before dawn. When next she opened her eyes, the skylit room was bright. The same disorientation possessed her for a minute, but it vanished the minute she turned her head and saw Web.

He was still sleeping. His hair was mussed, and his beard was a dark shadow on his face. But it was his brow, corrugated even in sleep, that drew her gaze. He'd had an uncomfortable night. Silently, she slipped from beneath the sheet and padded to the bathroom for aspirin and water.

He was stirring when she returned, so she sat close by his side, raised him enough to push the aspirin into his mouth and give him a drink, then very gently set his head back down.

"Thanks," he murmured, coming to full awareness. He hadn't been disoriented, since this was his home. Finding Marni sitting beside him, well, that was something else.

"You're welcome. How does it feel...or shouldn't I ask?"

"You shouldn't ask," he drawled, then stretched, twisting his torso. When he settled back, his eyes were on her. "Actually, it's not bad. The discomfort's localized now. It was worse when I was sleeping, because I couldn't pinpoint it and it seemed to be all over." He raised the hand in question and glared at the white gauze. "Helluva big bandage. I'll have to get rid of some of this stuff."

"Don't you dare! If it was put on, it was put on for a reason."

"How am I gonna shower?"

"Hold your hand up in the air out of the spray...or forget the shower and take a bath."

"I never take baths."

She shrugged. "Then take a shower with your hand in the air, and be grateful it's your left hand. If it had been your right, you'd be in *big* trouble."

He ran his palm over the stubble on his jaw. "You've got a point there." His gaze skittered hesitantly to hers. "I must look like something the cat dragged in."

She couldn't have disagreed with him more. He looked a little rough, but all man, every sinewy, stubbly, hairy inch. "You look fine, no, wonderful, given the circumstances." Her voice softened even more. "I've never seen you in the morning this way. We...we never spent a full night together."

He smiled in regret, his voice as soft as hers. "So now we've done it, and we haven't even *done* it." He raised his good hand and skimmed a finger over her lips, back and forth, whisper-light. "Do you know, I haven't even kissed you? Lord, I've wanted to, but I didn't know if you wanted it, and it seemed more important to talk."

Marni felt her insides melting. "Fourteen years ago it was the other way around."

"We're older now. Maybe we've got our priorities straight.... But I still want to kiss you." He was stroking her cheek ever so gently, and she'd begun to tremble. "Will you let me?"

"You always had the bluest eyes," she whispered, mesmerized by them, drowning in them. "I could never deny you when you looked at me that way."

"What way?"

"Like you wanted me. Like you knew that maybe it wasn't the smartest thing, but you wanted me anyway. Like there was something about *me* that you wanted, just me."

"There is." He slid his fingers into her hair and urged her head down. "There is, Marni. You're...very...special...." The last was whispered against her lips, the sound vanishing into her mouth, which had opened, and waited, but was waiting no more.

It started gently, a tender reacquaintance, kisses whispered from one mouth to the other in a slow, renewing exchange. For Marni it was a homecoming; there was something about the taste of Web, the texture of his lips, the instinctive way he pleased her that erased the years that had passed. For Web the homecoming was no less true; there was something about the softness of Marni's lips, the way they clung to his, the way her honeyed freshness poured warmly into him that made him forget everything that had come between this and their last kiss.

Familiarly their lips touched and sipped and danced. As it had always done, though, desire soon began to clamor, and whispered kisses were no longer enough. Web's mouth grew more forceful, Marni's demanded in return, and it was fire, hot, sweet fire surging through their veins, singeing all threads of caution.

Eyes closed under the force of sensation, Marni took everything he offered and gave as much in return. His mouth slanted openly against hers, hungrily devouring it. Her mouth fought fiercely for his, possessing it in turn. He ran his tongue along the line of her teeth and beyond; she caressed it with her own, then drew it in deeper. And while his hand wound restlessly through her hair, her own spread feverishly across his chest.

"C'mere," he growled, and swiftly rolled her over him until she was on her back and he was above her. Her neck rested in the crook of his elbow, and it was that elbow that propped him up so he could touch her as she'd done him.

Even had their mouths not come together again, she wouldn't have said a word in protest, because the fire was too hot, the sweetness too sweet to deprive herself of this little bit of heaven. Web had always been this for her, a flame licking at her nerve ends, spreading a molten desire within her that water couldn't begin to quench.

He cupped her breast through the knit of her overblouse, molding it to his palm, kneading and circling until at last his fingers homed in on the tight nub at its crest. Her flesh swelled, and she arched up, seeking even closer contact with the instrument of such bliss. She'd been starving for years; now she couldn't get enough. It was sheer relief when he impatiently tugged the overblouse from her hips.

"Lift up, sweet...there...I need...to touch you, Marni!"

She helped him, because she needed the very same thing, and she was tossing the blouse aside even as Web unhooked her bra and tore it away. Then he was lying half over her again, his large hand greedily rediscovering her blossoming flesh, and she was moaning in delight, straining for more, bunching the damp skin of his back in hands that clenched and unclenched, shifted, then clenched again.

She was in a frenzy. The tight knot in her belly was growing, inflamed not only by his thorough exploration of her nakedness but by the hardness of his sex pressing boldly against her thigh. When he slid down, she dug her fingers into his hair, holding on for dear life as his mouth opened over her breast, his tongue bathed it, his teeth closed around one distended nipple and tugged a path to her womb.

"Web!" she cried. "Oh, God, I need...I need..."

He slid back up, and her hand lowered instinctively to him, cupping him, caressing him until even that wasn't enough. His hand tangled with hers then, clutching at the tab of his zipper, tugging it down. He took her fingers and led them inside his briefs. He was trembling as badly as she was, and his voice shook with urgency.

"Touch me...touch me, sunshine..."

This time the pet name was so perfectly placed, so very right that it was stimulation in and of itself. She touched him, stroked him, pleasured him until he gave a hoarse cry of even greater need. Then he was tugging at her pants, freeing her hips for his invasion.

What happened then was something neither Marni nor Web had expected. She felt his tumescence press against the nest of curls at the apex of her thighs, and it was so intense, so electric that she recoiled and, in a burst of emotion, began to cry.

"Web...oh..." she sobbed, tears streaking down her cheeks and into the hairs of his chest. "Web...I...I..."

She couldn't say anything else. Her crying prevented it. He held her head tightly to his chest with his left arm and ran his good hand over and around her naked back, knowing that he could easily be inside her but ignoring that fact because, at the moment, her emotional state was far more important.

"It's okay. Shhhhh. Shhhhh."

"I want," she gulped, "want you...so badly, but...but..."

"Shhhhh. It's okay."

She wiped the tears from her eyes, but they kept flowing. She felt frustrated and embarrassed and confused. So she simply gave herself up to the outpouring of whatever it was and waited until at last the tears slowed before trying to speak again.

"I'm sorry...I didn't mean to do that...I don't know what happened..."

"Something's bothering you," he said softly, patiently. "Something snapped."

"But it's awful...what I did. A woman has no right to do that to...to a man."

"I know you want me, so you're suffering, too."

She raised wide, tear-filled eyes to his. "Let me help you." Her hand started back down. "Let me do it, Web—"

He flattened her body against his, trapping her hand. "No. I don't want that."

"But you'll be uncomfortable—"

"The discomfort is more in my mind than my body." Her tears had instantly cooled his ardor. He allowed a small space between them. "Feel. You'll see. Go on."

She did as he told her and discovered that he was no longer hard. Her eyes widened all the more, and she suddenly grappled with her pants, tugging them up. "You *don't* want me..."

He gave a short laugh and rolled his eyes to the ceiling. "I'm damned if I do and damned if I don't." His gaze fell to catch hers. "Of course I want you, sunshine. You are my sunshine, y'know. You're bright and warm, the source of an incredible energy, but only when you're sure of yourself, when you're happy. Something happened just now. I don't know exactly what it was, but it's pushed that physical drive into the background for the time being."

Marni wasn't sure what to think. She nervously matted the hair on his chest with the flat of her finger. "It used to be that nothing could push that physical drive into the background."

"We're older. Life is more complex than it used to be. When I was twenty-six, sex was a sheer necessity. It was a physical outlet, sure, but it was also a means of communicating things that either I didn't understand or didn't see or didn't want to say." His arm was beginning to throb. Shifting himself back against the pillow, he drew Marni against him, cradling her with his right arm, letting his left rest limply on the sheet.

"If I was still twenty-six, I'd have made love to you regardless of your tears just now. I wouldn't have had the strength to stop, the control. But I'm not twenty-six. I'm forty. I have the control now, and the strength." He paused for a minute, but there was more he wanted to say. "I haven't been a monk all these years, Marni. For a while I was with any and every woman who turned me on. Then I realized that the turn-on was purely physical, and it wasn't enough. Maybe I've mellowed. I've become picky. I think...I think that when we do make love, you and I, it'll be an incredibly new and wonderful experience."

To her horror, Marni began to cry again. "Why do you...do you *say* things like that, Web? Why are...are you so incredibly understanding?"

He hugged her tighter. "It hurts me when you cry, sunshine. Please, tell me what's bothering you. Tell me what happened back there."

"Oh, God," she cried, then sniffled, "I wish I knew. I was so high, so unbelievably high, and then it was like...like this door opened somewhere in the back of my mind, and in a lightning-quick instant I felt burned to a crisp, and frightened and nervous and guilty..."

He held her face back. "Guilty?"

She looked at him blankly, her lashes spiked with tears when she blinked. "Did I say that?" she whispered, puzzled.

"Very clearly. What did you mean?"

"I don't know. Maybe...maybe it's that we haven't been together long..."

"Maybe," he returned, but skeptically. "You've been with other men since that summer, haven't you?"

She nodded. "But it's been a long time for me and...maybe it was too easy and that bothered me."

"You've always been honest with me, Marni," he chided softly. "Tell me. These are modern times, and you're a fully grown, experienced woman. If you met a guy and felt something really unique with him, and if he felt the same, and the two of you wanted desperately to make love, would you hold out on principle?" When she didn't answer, he coaxed gently, "Would you?"

"No," she whispered.

"But you do feel guilty now. Why, sunshine? Why guilty?"

"Maybe it was too fast. And your hand..."

"My hand wasn't hurting just then. Loving you blotted everything out. I wasn't complaining, or moaning. Come on, Marni. Why guilty?"

Her gaze darted blindly about the room. She frowned, swallowed hard, then began to breathe raggedly. "I guess...I guess that...maybe I felt that...well, we'd made love so much during that summer, and it was so good and right, and then...and then..." Her eyes were wide when she raised them to his. Fresh tears pooled on her lower lids but refused to over-flow. "And then the accident happened and Ethan was killed and you were in the hospital and my parents...forbade me to...see you..."

Web closed his eyes. An intense inner pain brought a soft moan to his lips, and he slipped both arms around her. "Lord, what they've done... what they've done..."

He held her for a long time without saying a word, because only then did he realize the enormity of the hurdle he faced.

5

WEB HAD MUCH to consider. He understood now that there was a link in Marni's mind between their lovemaking of fourteen years ago and Ethan's death. He understood that, though she may not have been aware of it at the time, some small part of her had felt guilty about their affair, and Ethan's death must have seemed to her a form of punishment. And he understood that her parents had done nothing to convince her it wasn't so.

Much to consider...so much to consider. He held Marni tightly, wanting desperately to protect her, to take away the pain. She was such a strong woman, yet still fragile. He tried to decide what to do, what to say. In the end he wasn't any more ready to discuss this newly revealed legacy of that summer in Maine than she was.

"Marni?" he murmured against her hair. He ran his hand soothingly over her naked back, then kissed her forehead. "Sweetheart?"

Marni, too, had been stunned by what she'd said. But rather than think of it, she'd closed her eyes and let the solid warmth of Web's body calm her. She took a last, faintly erratic breath. "Hmmm?"

"Are you any good at brewing coffee?"

She knew what he was doing and was grateful. A faint smile formed against his chest, and she opened her eyes. "Not bad."

"Think you could do it while I use the bathroom? I'm feeling a little muzzy right about now."

His voice did sound muzzy, so she took pity on him. Reaching for her discarded blouse, she dragged it over her breasts as she sat up. "I think I could handle that."

He was looking at the blouse, then at the hands that clutched it to her. "Hey, what's this?" he asked very softly, gently. When he met her gaze, his blue eyes were infinitely tender. "You never used to cover up with me."

Embarrassed, she looked away. "That was fourteen years ago," she whispered.

"And you don't think that what we have now is as close?"

"It isn't that..."

He lightly curled his fingers over her slender shoulders. "What is it, sunshine? Please, tell me."

Her eyes remained downcast. "I...I'm older...I look different now."

"But I saw you a few minutes ago. I touched you and tasted you, and you were beautiful."

"That was in the heat of passion."

"And you're afraid I'll look at you now and see a thirty-one-year-old body and not be turned on?"

She shrugged. "Time does things."

"To me, too. Don't you think I'm aware that my body is older? I'm forty, not twenty-six. Do you think I'm not that little bit nervous that you'll see all the changes?"

Her gaze shot to him. "But I saw you last night, and not in passion, and you're body's better than ever!"

"So is yours, Marni," he whispered. Very slowly he eased the knit fabric from her hands and drew it away. His eyes took on a special light as they gently caressed her bare curves. "Your skin is beautiful. Your breasts are perfect."

"They're not as high as they used to be."

"They're fuller, more womanly." He didn't touch her, but his heart was thumping as he captured her gaze. "If I wanted a seventeen-year-old now, I'd have one. But I don't want that, Marni. I want a mature woman. I want you." Very gently he pulled her forward and pressed a warm kiss to each of her breasts in turn. She sucked in a sharp breath, and her nipples puckered instantly. "And if you don't get out of here this minute, mature woman," he growled only half in jest, "I'm going to have you." He shot a disparaging glance at the front of his jeans, then a more sheepish one back at her.

"Oh, Web," Marni breathed. She threw herself forward and gave him a final hug. "You always know the right thing to say."

He wanted to say that he didn't, but the words wouldn't come out because he'd closed his eyes and was caught up enjoying the silken feel of her against him. Only when the pressure in his loins increased uncomfortably did he force a hoarse warning. "Marni...that coffee?"

"Right away," she whispered, jumping up and running for the door, then returning, cheeks ablaze, for her bra and blouse before dashing for the kitchen.

Not only did she brew a pot of rich coffee, but by the time Web joined her she'd scrambled eggs, toasted English muffins and sliced fresh oranges for their breakfast.

"So you can cook," he teased. He remembered her telling him, during those days in Camden, that Cook had allowed no interference in the kitchen.

Marni put milk in his coffee, just as he'd had it that night when they'd been at the restaurant, and set the mug beside him. Then she joined him at the island counter. "I may not be a threat to Julia Child, but I've learned something. Post-graduate work, if you will."

He sipped the strong brew and smiled in appreciation. "An A for coffee." He took a forkful of the eggs, chewed appreciatively, then smacked his lips together. "An A for scrambled eggs. Very moist and light."

She laughed. "Don't grade the muffins or the orange. I really can't take much credit for either."

"Still, you didn't burn the muffins."

"You have a good toaster."

"And the orange is sliced with precision."

"You have a sharp knife, and I have a tidy personality." Amused, she was watching him eat. "You'll choke if you don't slow down."

"I'm suddenly starved. You should be, too. We didn't get around to having dinner last night."

Marni ate half of her eggs, then offered the rest to Web, who devoured them and one of her muffins as though his last meal had been days ago. When he was done, he sat back and studied her. "What now?" he asked softly.

"You're still hungry?"

"What now...for us? Will you stay a while?"

She'd been debating that one the whole time she'd been making breakfast. "I...think I'd better head home. A lot has happened. Too quickly. I need a little time."

He nodded. More than anything he wished she'd stay, but he understood her need for time alone to think. He could only hope it would be to his benefit.

She began to clean up the kitchen. "Will you be okay...your hand, and all?"

"I'll be fine.... Marni, what say we try for that picture again on Tuesday? If you can manage it with your schedule, I can make all the other arrangements."

She finished rinsing the frying pan, then reached for the dish towel. "Do you really think you'll be up for it?"

"I've got another shoot set for Monday. It has to go on, no matter what. I'll be up for it.... But that's not the real question here." Not wanting to put undue pressure on her, he remained where he was at the island. "Are you willing to give it another try?"

Her head was bowed. "You really think it's the cover we need?"

"I do. But more than that, I *want* to do it. You have no idea how much it means to me to photograph you and put your face out there for the world to see. I'm proud of you, Marni. Some men might want to keep you all to themselves, and I do in a lot of respects, but I'm a photographer, and you happen to mean more to me than any other subject I've ever photo-graphed. I want you to be on the premier cover of *Class* because I feel you belong there, and because I feel that I'm the only one who can see and capture on film the beauty you are, inside and out." When she simply stood with her back to him, saying nothing, he grew more beseechful. "I know that may sound arrogant, but it's the way I feel. Give me a chance, Marni. Don't deny me this one pleasure."

"It's not only your eyes that get to me, Brian Webster," she muttered under her breath, "it's your tone of voice. How can you prey on my *vulnerability* this way?"

He knew then that he'd won. Rising, he crossed to the sink and gave her waist a warm squeeze. "Because I know that it's right, Marni. It's right all the way."

MARNI STILL HAD her doubts. She left him soon after that and returned to her apartment. She had errands to run that afternoon—food shopping, a manicure, stockings to buy—and she would have put them all off in a minute if she'd felt it wise to stay longer with Web. But she did need to be alone, and she did need to think. At least, that was what she told herself. Then she did everything possible to avoid being alone, to avoid thinking.

She dallied in the supermarket, spent an extra hour talking with the woman whose manicure followed hers, and whom she'd come to know for that reason, then browsed through every department of Bloomingdale's before reaching the hosiery counter. When she finished her shopping, she returned home in time to put her purchases away, then shower and dress for the cocktail party she'd been invited to. It was a business-related affair, and when she got there she threw herself into it, so much so that when she finally got home she was exhausted and went right to bed.

When she woke up the next morning, though, Web was first and foremost on her mind. She thought back to the same hour the day before, remembering being on his bed, on the verge of making love with him. Her body throbbed at the memory. She took a long shower, but it didn't seem to help. Without considering the whys and wherefores, she picked up the phone and dialed his number.

"Webster, here," was the curt answer.

She hesitated, then ventured cautiously, "Web?"

He paused, then let out a smiling sigh. "Marni. How are you, sunshine?"

"I'm okay.... Am I disturbing you?"

"Not on your life."

"You sounded distracted."

"I was sitting here feeling sorry for myself. Just about to drag out the old morgue book."

"Why feeling sorry for yourself?"

"Because I'm here and you're there, and because my hand hurts and I'm wondering how in hell I'm going to manage tomorrow."

"It's still really bad?"

"Nah. It's a little sore, but self-pity always makes things seem worse."

She grinned. "Then, by all means, drag out the old morgue book."

"I won't have to, now that you've called.... I tried you last night."

She'd been wondering about that, worrying ... hoping. "I had to go to a cocktail party. It was a business thing. Pretty dry." In hindsight that was exactly what it had been, though she'd convinced herself otherwise at the time. No, not really dry, but certainly not as exciting as it might have been had Web been there.

"I sat here alone all night thinking of you," he said without remorse.

"That's not fair."

"I'll say it's not. You're out there munching on scrumptious little hors d'oeuvres while I dig into the peanut butter jar—"

"It's not fair that you're making me feel guilty," she corrected him, but she was grinning. If he'd spent last night with a gorgeous model, she'd have been jealous as hell.

He feigned resignation with an exaggerated sigh. "No need to feel guilty. I'm used to peanut butter—"

"Web..." she warned teasingly.

"Okay. But I really did miss you. I do miss you. Yesterday at this time we were having breakfast together."

"I know." There was a wistfulness to her tone.

"Hey, I could pick you up in an hour and we could go for brunch."

"No, Web. I have work to do. I promised myself I'd stay in all day and get it done."

"Work? On the weekend?"

She knew he was mocking her, but she didn't mind. "I always bring a briefcase home with me. Things get so hectic at the office sometimes that I need quiet time to reread proposals and reports."

"I wouldn't keep you more than an hour, hour and a half at most."

"I...I'd better not."

"You still need time to think."

"Yes."

He spoke more softly. "That I can accept.... We're on for Tuesday, aren't we?"

"I'll have to work it out with my secretary when I go in tomorrow, but I don't think I have anything that can't be shifted around."

"I've already called Anne. She'll have Marjorie get some clothes ready, but I said that I wanted as few people there for the actual shoot as possible.

That'll go for my staff, too, and you can leave Edgar and Steve behind at the office."

"I will. Thank you."

He paused, his tone lightening. "Can I call you tomorrow night, just to make sure you don't get cold feet and back out on me at the last minute?"

"I won't back out once all the arrangements are made."

"Can I call you anyway?"

She smiled softly. "I'd like that."

"Good." He hated to let her go. Her voice alone warmed him, not to mention the visual picture he'd formed of her auburn hair framing her face, her cheeks bright and pink, her lips soft, the tips of her breasts peaking through a nightgown, or a robe, or a blouse—it didn't matter which, the effect was the same. "Well," he began, then cleared his throat, "take care, Marni."

"I will." She hated to let him go. His voice alone thrilled her, not to mention the visual picture she'd formed of his dark hair brushing rakishly over his brow, his lean, shadowed cheeks, his firm lips, the raw musculature of his torso. She took an unsteady breath. "Are you sure you can manage everything with your hand?" If he'd said that he was having trouble, she would have rushed to his aid in a minute.

He was tempted to say he was having trouble, but he'd never been one to lie. "I'm sure.... Bye-bye, sweetheart."

"Bye, Web."

MARNI WOULD INDEED HAVE TRIED to back out on the photo session had it not been for the arrangements that had been made. Through all of Sunday, while she tried to concentrate first on the Sunday *Times*, then on her work, she found herself thinking of her relationship with Web. She was no longer seventeen and in that limbo between high school, college and the real world. She was old enough to have serious thoughts about the future, and she knew that with each additional minute she spent with Web those thoughts would grow more and more serious.

Though she wasn't sure exactly what he wanted, she knew from what he'd said that he envisioned some kind of future relationship with her. But there were problems—actually just one, but it was awesome. Her family.

It was this that weighed heavily on her when she arrived at Web's studio Tuesday morning. As he'd promised, Web had called the evening before. He'd been gentle and encouraging, so that when she'd hung up the phone she'd felt surprisingly calm about posing again. Then her mother had called.

"Marni, darling, why didn't you tell me! I had no idea what had happened until Tanya called a little while ago!"

Icy fingers tripped up Marni's spine. What did her mother know? She hadn't sounded angry.... What could *Tanya* know...or was it Marni's own guilty conscience at work? "What is it, Mother? What are you talking about?"

"That little business you witnessed on Friday night. Evidently there was a tiny notice in the paper yesterday. I missed it completely, and if it hadn't been for Tanya—"

Marni was momentarily stunned. She hadn't expected any of that episode to reach the press, much less with her name printed...and, she assumed, Web's. She moistened her lips, unsure as to how much more her mother knew. All she could say was a slightly cryptic, "Tanya reads the paper?"

"Actually it was Sue Beacham—you know, Tanya's friend whose husband is a state senator? They say he's planning to run for Congress, and he'll probably make it. He has more connections than God. Of course, Jim Heuer had the connections and it didn't help. He didn't get Ed Donahue's support, so he lost most of the liberal vote. I guess you can never tell about those things."

Marni took a breath for patience. Her mother tended to run on at the mouth, particularly when it came to name-dropping. "What was it that Sue saw?"

"There was a little article about how you and that photographer were instrumental in interrupting a rape."

"It wasn't a rape," Marni countered very quietly. "It was a mugging."

"But it could have been a rape if you hadn't come along, at least that was what the paper said. I'd already thrown it out, but Tanya had the article and read it to me."

Marni forced herself to relax. It appeared that Adele Lange hadn't made the connection between Brian Webster, the photographer, and the notorious Web. "It was really nothing, Mother. We happened to be walking down the street and heard the woman's cries. By the time we got to her, her assailant was already on his way."

"But this photographer you were with—it said he was injured."

"Just his hand. He's fine."

"Who is he, Marni? You never mentioned you were seeing a photographer, and such a renowned one, at least that's what Tanya says. She says that he's right up there with the best, and I'm sure I've seen his work but I've probably repressed the name. Webster." Her voice hardened. "I don't even like to say it."

Marni's momentary reprieve was snatched away. It didn't matter that her mother hadn't actually connected the two. What mattered was that the ill will lingered.

"Are you seeing him regularly?" Adele asked when Marni remained quiet.

"He's doing the cover work for the new magazine. There were some things we had to work out."

"Do you think you *will* be seeing him? Socially, that is? A photographer." Marni could picture her mother pursing her lips. "I think you should remember that a man in a field like his is involved with many, many women, and glamorous ones at that. You'll have to be careful."

The "many, many women" Marni's mother mentioned went along with the stereotype. Marni felt no threat on that score. Indeed, it was the least of her worries.

"Mother," she sighed, "you're getting a little ahead of yourself."

"It doesn't hurt to go into things with both eyes open."

"I've *got* both eyes open."

"All right, all right, darling. You needn't get riled up. I only called because I was concerned. I know incidents like that aren't uncommon, but witnessing it on the street can be a traumatic experience for a woman."

"It was traumatic for the victim. I'm okay."

"Are you sure? You sound tired."

"After a full day at the office, I am tired."

"Well, I guess you have a right to that. I'll let you rest, darling. Talk with you soon?"

"Uh-huh." Marni had hung up then, but she'd spent a good part of the night brooding, so she was tired and unsettled when Web came to greet her at the reception area of the studio. His smile was warm and pleasure-filled, relaxing her somewhat, but he was quick to see that something was amiss.

"Nervous?" he asked her as he guided her into the studio.

"A little."

"It'll be easier this time."

"I hope so."

"Is...everything all right?"

"Everything's fine."

"Why won't you look at me?"

She did then. "Better?"

He shook his head. "Smile for me."

She did then. "Better?"

He gestured noncommittally, but she was looking beyond him again, so he didn't speak. "See? It's almost quiet here."

Indeed it was. Anne, who appeared to be the only one present from *Class*, waved to her from the other side of the room, where she was in conference with the makeup artist. Marni recognized the hairstylist and, more vaguely, several of Web's assistants.

"Lee?" Web called out. A man turned from the group and, smiling, approached. "Lee, I'd like you to meet Marni. Formally. Marni, my brother, Lee."

Marni's smile was more genuine as she shook Lee's warm hand. He was pleasant-looking, though nowhere near as handsome or tall as Web. Wearing a suit, minus its tie, he was more conservatively dressed than the other men in the room, but his easy way made up for the difference. Marni liked him instantly.

"I'm pleased to meet you, Lee. Web's had only good things to say about you."

Lee shot Web a conspiratorial glance. "I'd have to say the same about you. I've heard about nothing else for the past week." He held up his hand. "Not that he's telling everyone, mind you, but—" he winked "—I think the old man needs an outlet."

Marni wondered just how much Lee knew, then realized that it didn't matter. He was Web's brother. The physical resemblance may have been negligible, but there was something deeper, an intangible quality the two men shared. She knew she'd trust Lee every bit as much as she trusted Web. Of course, trust wasn't really the problem....

"Enough," Web was saying with a smile. "We'd better get things rolling here."

Marni barely had time to squeeze Lee's arm before Web was steering her off toward the changing rooms. Once again she was "done over," this time more aware of what was happening. She asked questions—how the hairstylist managed such a smooth sweep from her crown, what the makeup artist had done for her eyes to make them seem so far apart—but she was simply making conversation, perhaps in her way apologizing for having spoiled these people's efforts the week before. And diverting her mind from the worry that set in each time she looked at Web.

If the villain of the previous Tuesday had been the shock and pain of memory, now it was guilt. Marni saw Web's face, so open and encouraging, then the horror-filled ones of her parents when they learned she was seeing him again. She heard his voice, so gentle in instruction, then the harsh, bitter words of her family when they knew she was associating with the enemy.

Web tried different poses from the week before, used softer background music. He tried different lights and different cameras—the latter mostly on his tripod, which he could more easily manage, but in the end holding the camera in his hand with his splinted pinkie sticking straight out.

Halfway through the session, he called a break, shooing everyone else away after Marni had been given a cool drink.

"What do you think?" she asked hesitantly. The face she made suggested that she had doubts of her own but needed the reassurance. "Any better than last week?"

"Better than that, but still not what I want. It's a little matter of... this...spot." With his forefinger, he lightly stroked the soft skin between her brows. "No amount of makeup is going to hide the creases when you frown."

"But I thought I was smiling, or doing whatever it was you asked me to do."

"You were. But those little creases creep in there anyway. When I ask for a tiny smile, the overall effect is one of pleading. When I ask for a broad smile, you look like you're in pain. When I ask you to wet your lips and leave them parted, you look like you're holding your breath."

"I am," she argued, throwing up a hand in frustration. "I'm no good at this. I told you, Web. This isn't my thing."

She was leaning against the arm of a director's chair. He stood close by, looking down at her. "It can't be the crowd, because there's no crowd today. It can't be the music, or the posing. And it can't be shock. Not anymore.... You're worried about something. That's what the creases tell me."

"I'm worried that I'll never be able to give you what you want, that you won't get your picture and you'll be disappointed and angry."

"Angry? Never. Disappointed? Definitely. But I'm not giving up yet. I'm going to get this picture, Marni. One way or another, I'm going to get it."

He spoke with such conviction, and went back to work with such determination, that Marni began to suspect he'd have her at it every day for a month, if that's what it took. She did her best to concentrate on relaxing her facial muscles, but found it nearly impossible. She'd get rid of the creases, but then her mouth would be wrong, or the angle of her head, or her shoulders.

The session ended not in a burst of tears as it had last time, but in sighs of fatigue from both her and Web. "Okay," he said resignedly as he handed his camera to one of his assistants, "we'll take a look at what we've got. There may be something." He ran his fingers through his hair. "God only knows I've exposed enough film."

Marni whirled around and stalked off toward the dressing room.

"Marni!" he called out, but she didn't stop. So he loped after her, enclosing them in the privacy of the small room. "What was that about? You walked out of there like I'd insulted you."

"You did." She removed the chunky beads from around her neck and put them on a nearby table. Two oversized bracelets soon followed.

"You're disgusted with me. You never have to go through this with nor-mal models. 'God only knows I've exposed enough film.' Did you have to say that, in that tone, for everyone in the room to hear?"

"It was a simple comment."

"It was an indictment."

"Then it was as much an indictment of me as it was of you. I'm the pho-tographer! Half of my supposed skill is in drawing the mood and the look from a model!"

She was swiftly unbuttoning her blouse, heedless of Web's presence. "I'm the model. A rank amateur. You're the renowned photographer. If anyone's at fault, we both know who it is."

"Then you're angry at yourself, but don't lay that trip on me!"

"See? You agree!" She'd thrown the blouse aside and was fumbling with the waistband of her skirt. Her voice shook as she released the button and tugged down the zipper. "Well, I'm sorry if I've upset your normal pattern of success, but don't say I didn't warn you. Right from the beginning I knew this was a mad scheme. You need a *model*, an *experienced* model." She stumbled out of the skirt, threw it on top of the blouse, then grabbed for her own clothes and began to pull them on. "I can't be what you want, Web, no matter how much you want to think otherwise. I am what I am. I do what I do, and I do it well, and if there's baggage I carry—like little creases between my eyes—I can't help it." She'd stepped into her wool dress, but left it unbuttoned. Suddenly drained from her outburst, she lifted a hand to rub at those creases.

Web remained quiet. He'd reached the end of his own spurt of temper minutes ago and was simply waiting for her to calm down enough to listen to what he had to say. When she sighed and slumped into a nearby chair, he slowly approached and squatted beside her.

"Firstly, I'm not angry at you. If anything I'm angry at me, because there's something I'm missing and I don't know how to get at it. Secondly, I'm not really angry, just tired." He flexed his unbound fingers. "My left hand is stiff because I'm not used to working this way." He put his hand down on her knee. "Thirdly, and most importantly, it *is* you I want. I'm not looking for something you're not. I'm not trying to make you into someone else. You're such a unique and wonderful person Marni—it's *that* that I'm trying to capture on film.... Look at me," he said softly, drawing her hand from her face. "You're right. It is much easier photographing a 'normal model,' but only because there isn't half the depth, because I can put there what I want. Creating a mood, a look, is one thing. Bringing out feeling, *in-dividual* feeling is another. Don't you see? That's what's going to make this issue of *Class* stand out on the shelves. Not only are you beautiful to look at, but you'll have all those other qualities shining out from you. The potential reader of *Class* will say to herself, 'Hmmm, this looks interesting.'"

Marni was eyeing him steadily. Her expression had softened, taking on a glimmer of helplessness. He brushed the backs of his fingers against her cheek, thinking how badly he wanted to reach her, to soothe her.

"But what happened this morning," he went on in a whisper-soft tone, "what we've been arguing about in here is really secondary. You've got something on your mind that you haven't been able to shake. Share it with me, Marni. If nothing more, talking about it will make you feel better. Maybe I can help."

She only wished it were so. How could she say that she was falling in love with him again, but that her parents would never accept it? That they hated him, that she'd spent the last fourteen years of her life trying to make up for Ethan's death by being what he might have been if he'd lived, and that she didn't know if she had the strength to shatter her parents' illusion?

"Oh, Web," she sighed, slipping her arms over his shoulders and leaning forward to rest her cheek against his. "Life is so complicated."

He stroked her hair. "It doesn't have to be."

"But it is. Sometimes I wish I could turn the clock back to when I was seventeen and stop it there. Ethan would be alive, and you and I would be carrying on without a care in the world."

"We had cares. There was the problem of where to go so that we could be alone to love each other. And there was the problem of your parents, and what would happen if they found out about us."

Marni's arms tightened around him, and she rubbed her cheek against his jaw, welcoming the faint roughness that branded him man and so very different from her. She loved the smell of him, the feel of him. If only she could blot out the rest of the world...

"It's still a problem, isn't it, Marni?" She went very still, so he continued in the same gentle tone. "I'm no psychologist, but I've spent a lot of time thinking the past week, especially the past few days, about us and the future. Your parents despised me for what I was, and wasn't, and for what I'd done. They'd be a definite roadblock for us, wouldn't they?"

Just then a knock sounded at the door. Web twisted around and snapped, "Yes?"

The door opened, and a slightly timid Anne peered in. Uncomfortably, she looked from Web to Marni. "I'm sorry. I didn't mean to interrupt. I just wanted to know if there was anything I could do to help."

"No. Not just now," Marni said. "You can go back to the office. I'll be along later."

"I'll take a look at the contact sheets as soon as possible and let you know what I think," Web added quietly.

Anne nodded, then shut the door, at which point Web turned back to Marni.

She was gnawing on her lower lip. "Did you know that there was an article in the newspaper about the incident last Friday night?" she asked.

His jaw hardened. "Oh, yes. I got several calls from friends congratulating me on my heroism. Of all the things I'd like to be congratulated on, that isn't one. I could kick myself for not instructing the cops to leave our names off any report they might hand to the press. Neither of us needs that kind of publicity." He frowned. "You didn't mention the article when I spoke with you last night."

"I didn't know about it."

"Then...?"

"My mother called right after you did."

He blinked slowly, lifted his chin, then lowered it. He might have been saying, "Ahhhhhh, that explains it."

"If you can believe it, my sister Tanya brought it to her attention." Marni's voice took on a mildly hysterical note. "Neither of them made the connection, Web. Neither one of them associated Brian Webster, the photographer, with you."

"But you thought at first they might have," he surmised gently, "and it scared the living daylights out of you."

Apologetically Marni nodded, then slid forward in the chair and buried her face against his throat. Her thighs braced his waist, but there was nothing remotely sexual about the pose. "Hold me, Web. Just hold me... please?"

She sighed when he folded his arms around her, knowing in that instant that this would be all she needed in life if only the rest of humanity could fade away.

"Do you love me, Marni?" he asked hoarsely.

"I think I do," she whispered in dismay.

"And I love you. Don't you think that's a start?"

She raised her head. "You love me?"

"Uh-huh."

"When did you... You didn't before..."

He knew she was referring to that summer in Maine. "No, I didn't before. I was too young. You were too young. I didn't know where I was going, and the concept of love was beyond me."

"But when...?"

"Last weekend. After you left me, I realized that I didn't want anyone but you pushing aspirin down my throat."

She pinched his ribs, but she wasn't smiling. "Don't tease me."

"I'm not. No one's ever taken care of me before. I've always wanted to

206

First, Best and OnlyFirst, Best and Only

be strong and in command. But somehow being myself with you, being able to say that I'm tired or that I hurt, seemed right. Not that I want to do it all the time—I'm not a hypochondriac. But I want to be able to take care of you like you did me. TLC, and for the first time, the L means something."

Marni lowered her head and pressed closer to him, feeling the strong beat of his heart as though it and her own were all that existed. "I do love you, Web. The second time around it feels even stronger. If only...if only we could forget about everything else."

"We can."

"It's not possible."

"It is, for a little while, if we want."

She raised questioning eyes to his urgent ones.

"Come to Vermont with me this weekend. Just the two of us, alone and uninterrupted. We can talk everything out then and decide what to do, but most importantly we can be with each other. I think we need it. I think we deserve it.... What do you say?"

She sighed, feeling simultaneously hopeless and incredibly light-headed. "I say that it's crazy.... The whole thing's crazy, because the problems aren't going to go away...but how can I refuse?" A slow grin spread over her face, soon matched by his. He hugged her again, then kissed her. It was a sweet kiss, deep in emotion rather than physicality. When it ended, she clung to him for a long time. "I feel a little like I'm seventeen again and we've just arranged an illicit rendezvous. There's something exciting about stealing away, knowing my parents would be furious if they knew, but doing it all the same."

He took her face in his hands and spoke seriously. "We're adults now. Independent, consenting adults. In the end, it doesn't matter what your parents think, Marni."

Theoretically speaking, he was right, she knew. Idealistically she couldn't have agreed with him more. Practically speaking, though, it was a dream. But then, Web hadn't grown up in her house, with her parents. He hadn't gone into her family's business. He hadn't been in her shoes when Ethan had died, and he wasn't in her shoes now. "Later," she whispered. "We'll discuss it later. Right now, let's just be happy..."

MARNI WAS HAPPY. She blocked out all thoughts except one—that she loved Web and he loved her. And she was *very* happy. Business took her to Richmond on Wednesday morning, but she called Web that night, and he was at the airport to meet her when she returned on Thursday evening. Her suitcase had been emptied and repacked, and was waiting by her door when he came to pick her up late Friday afternoon.

"I hope you know I've shocked everyone at the office," she quipped, shrugging into her down jacket. "They've never known me to leave work so early."

He arched a brow. "Did you tell them where you were going?"

"Are you kidding? And spoil the sense of intrigue?"

Web was more practical. It wasn't that he wanted any interruptions during the weekend, but neither did he want the police out searching for her. "What if there's an emergency? What if someone needs to reach you and can't? Shouldn't you leave my number with someone?"

"Actually, I did. Just the number. With my administrative assistant. If anyone wants me that badly, they'll know to contact her. She'll be able to tell from the area code that I'm in Vermont, but that's about it."

Web was satisfied. He felt no fondness for her parents, but regardless of her age, they might worry if she seemed to have disappeared from the face of the earth. He knew that *he*'d be sick with worry if he tried to reach her and no one knew where she was.

"Good girl," was all he said before grabbing her suitcase and leading her to the waiting car.

The drive north was progressively relaxing. The tension of the day-to-day world, embodied by the congestion of traffic, thinned out and faded. Marni's excitement grew. Her eyes brightened, her cheeks took on a natural rosy glow. She had only to look to her left and see Web for her heart to feel lighter and lighter until she felt she was floating as weightlessly as those few snowflakes that drifted through the cold Vermont night air.

Web suggested that they stop for supplies at the village market near his house, so that they wouldn't have to go out again if the weather got bad. Marni was in full agreement.

"So where is your place?" she asked when they'd left the market behind. "I see houses and lots of condominium complexes—"

"They're sprouting up everywhere. Vacation resort areas, they're called. You buy your own place, then get the use of a central facility that usually includes a clubhouse, a restaurant or two, a pool, sometimes a lake or even a small ski slope. Not exactly my style, and I'm not thrilled with all the development. Pretty soon the place will be overrun with people. Fortunately where I am is off the beaten track."

"Where *are* you?"

He grinned and squeezed her knee. "Coming soon, sunshine. Be patient. Coming soon."

Not long after, he turned off the main road onto a smaller dirt one. The car jogged along, climbing steadily until at last they reached a clearing.

Marni caught her breath. "It's a log cabin," she cried in delight. "And you're on your own mountain!"

"Not completely on my own, but the nearest neighbor is a good twenty-minute trek through the trees." He pulled into the shelter of an oversized carport on the far side of the house.

"This is great! What a change from the city!"

"That's why I like it." He turned off the engine and opened his door. "Come on. It'll be cold inside, but the heat'll come up pretty quickly."

"Heat? That *has* to be from an old Franklin stove."

He chuckled. "I'm afraid I'm more pampered than that. It's baseboard heating. But I do have a huge stone fireplace...if that makes you feel better."

"Oh, yes," she breathed, then quickly climbed from the car and tugged her coat around her. The air was dry, with a sharp nip to it. Snow continued to fall, but it was light, enchanting rather than threatening. Marni wondered if anything could threaten her at that moment. She felt bold and excited and happy.

She looked at Web and beamed. She was in love, and in this place, so far from the city, she felt free.

6

To Marni's amazement, what had appeared to be a log cabin was, from within, like no log cabin she'd ever imagined. Soon after Web had bought the place, he'd had it gutted and enlarged. Rich barnboard from ceiling to floor sealed in the insulation he'd added. The furniture was likewise of barnboard, but plushly cushioned in shades of hunter green and cocoa. Though there was a hall leading to the addition that housed Web's bedroom and a small den, all Marni saw at first was the large living area, with the kitchen and dining area at its far end. Oh, yes, there was a huge stone fireplace. But rather than being set into a wall as she'd pictured, it was a three-hundred-and-sixty-degree one with steel supports that would cast its warm glow over the entire room.

Like the apartment above Web's studio, there was a sparseness to the decor, a cleanness of line, though it was very clearly country rather than city, and decidedly cozy.

After Marni had admired everything with unbounded enthusiasm, she helped Web stow the food they'd bought. Then he opened a bottle of wine, poured them each a glass and led her to the living area, where he set to work building a fire. The kindling caught and burned, and the dried logs were beginning to flame when he came to sit beside her on the sofa, opening an arm in an invitation she accepted instantly.

"I'm so happy I'm here with you," she whispered, rubbing her cheek against the wool of his sweater as she snuggled close to him.

He tightened his arm and pressed a slow kiss to her forehead. "So am I. This has always been my private refuge. Now it's *our* private refuge, and nothing could seem righter."

She tipped her head back. "Righter? Is that a word?"

"It is now," he murmured, then lowered his head and took her lips in a slow, deep, savoring kiss that left Marni reeling. Dizzily she set her wine on the floor and shifted, with Web's eager help, onto his lap, coiling her arms around his neck, closing her eyes in delight as she brushed her cheek against his jaw.

"I love you," she whispered, "love you so much, Web."

He set his own wine down and framed her face with his hands. His mouth breezed over each of her features before renewing acquaintance with her mouth. A deep, moist kiss, a shift in the angle of his head, a second deep, moist kiss. The exchange of breath in pleasured sighs. The evocative play of tongues, tips touching, circling, sliding along each other's length.

Marni hadn't had more than a sip of her wine, but she was high on love, high on freedom. She was breathing shallowly, with her head resting on his shoulder, when he began to caress her. She held her breath, concentrating on the intensity of sensation radiating from his touch. He spread his large hands around her waist, moved them up over her ribs and around to her back in slow, sensitizing strokes.

"I love you, sunshine," he whispered hoarsely, deeply affected by her sweet scent, her softness and warmth, her pliance, her emotional commitment. He brought his hands forward and inched them upward, covering her breasts, kneading them gently as she sighed against his neck.

Everything was in slow motion, unreal but exquisitely real. He caressed her breasts while she stroked the hair at his nape. He stroked her nipples while she caressed his back. They kissed again, and it was an exchange of silent vows, so deep and heartfelt that Marni nearly cried at its beauty.

"I was going to give you time," Web whispered roughly. His body was taut with a need he couldn't have hidden if he tried. "I was going to give you time...I hadn't intended an instant seduction."

"Neither had I," she breathed no less roughly. Her eyes held the urgency transmitted by the rest of her body. "I'm so pleased just to be here with you...but I want you...want to make love to you."

As much as her words inflamed him, he couldn't forget the last time they'd tried. "Are you sure? No doubts? Or guilt?"

She was shaking her head, very sure. "Not here. Not now." She pulled at his sweater. "Take this off. I want to touch you."

He whipped the sweater over his head, and she started working at the buttons of his shirt. When they were released, she spread the fabric wide, gave a soft sigh of relief and splayed her fingers over his hair-covered chest.

"You're so beautiful," she whispered in awe. Her hands moved slowly, exploring the sinewed swells of him, delving to the tight muscles of his middle before rising again and seeking the flat nipples nested amid whirls of soft, dark hair. She rubbed their tips until they stood hard, and didn't take her eyes from her work until Web forced her head up and hungrily captured her mouth.

His kiss left her breathless, and forehead to forehead they panted until at length he reached for the hem of her sweater and slowly drew it up and over her head. Slowly, too, he released one button, then the next, and in an instant's clear thought Marni reflected on the leisure of their approach. Fourteen years ago, when they'd come together for the first time, it had been in a fevered rush of arms and legs and bodies. Last Saturday the fever had been similar, as though they'd had to consummate their union before either of them had had time to think.

This time was different. They were in love. They were alone, in the cocoon of a cabin whose solid walls, whose surrounding forest warded off any and every enemy. This time there was a beauty in discovering and appreciating every inch of skin, every swell, every sensual conduit. This time it was heaven from the start.

Entranced, Marni watched as Web pushed her blouse aside. He unhooked her bra and gently peeled it from her breasts, then with a soft moan he very slowly traced her fullness, with first his fingertips, then the flat of his fingers, then his palm. She was swelling helplessly toward him, biting her lip to keep from crying out, when he finally took the full weight of her swollen flesh and molded his hands to it. His thumbs brushed over her nipples. Already taut, they puckered all the more, and she had to press her thighs together to still what was too quickly becoming a raging inferno.

Web didn't miss the movement. "Here..." He raised her for an instant, brought her leg around so that she straddled him, and settled her snugly against his crotch. With that momentary comfort, he returned his attention to her breasts.

"Web...Web..." she breathed. Her arms were looped loosely around his neck, her forehead hot against his shoulder. He was stroking her nipples again, and the action sent live currents through her body to her womb. Helplessly, reflexively, she began to slowly undulate her hips. "What you do to me—it's so...powerful...."

"It's what I feel for you, what you feel for me that makes it so good."

She was shaking her head in amazement. "I used to think it was good back then...because we do have this instant attraction...but I can't *believe* what...I'm feeling now."

"Then feel, sunshine." He slipped his hands to her shoulders and pushed her blouse completely off, then her bra. "I want you to feel this..." He cupped her breasts and brought them to his chest, rubbing nipple to nipple until she wasn't the only one to moan. "And this..." He sought her lips and kissed her hotly, while his fingers found the snap of her jeans, lowered the zipper and slid inside.

He was touching her then, opening her, stroking deeper and deeper until she was moving against his hand, taking tiny, gasping breaths, instinctively stretching her thighs apart in a need for more.

Her control was slipping, but she didn't want it to. She wanted the beauty to last forever, no, longer. Putting a shaky hand around Web's wrist, she begged him, "Please...I want to touch you, too...I need to..."

"But I want you to come," he said in a hushed whisper by her ear.

"This way, later. The first time—now—I want you inside. Please...take off your pants, Web..."

His fingers stopped their sweet torment and slowly, reluctantly, withdrew. He didn't move to take off his clothes until he'd kissed her so thoroughly that she thought she'd disintegrate there and then. But she didn't, and he shifted her from his lap, sat forward to rid himself of his shirt, then stood and peeled off the rest of his clothes. For a moment, just before lowering his jeans, he suddenly wished he hadn't been as adept at building that fire and that it was still pitch-black in the room. The last thing he wanted was to spoil the mood by having Marni see his scars. But they were there; he couldn't erase them, and if she loved him...

Marni sat watching, enthralled as more and more of his flesh was revealed. It was a long minute before she even saw his leg, so fascinated had she been with what else was now bare. But inevitably her gaze fastened on the multiple lines, some jagged, others straight, that formed a frightening pattern along the length of his right thigh.

"Web?" She caught her breath and, eyes filling with tears, looked up at him. "You didn't tell me... I didn't know...."

Quickly he knelt by her side and took both of her hands tightly in his. "Forget them, sweetheart. They're part of the past, and the past has no place here and now."

"But so many—"

"And all healed. No pain. No limp. Forget them. They don't matter." When she remained doubtful, he began to whisper kisses over her face. "Forget them," he breathed against her eyelids, then her lips. "Just love me...I need that more than anything..."

More than anything, that was what Marni needed, too. So she forgot. She pushed all thought of his scars and what had caused them from her mind. He was right. The past had no place here and now, and she refused to let it infringe on her present happiness. There would be a time to discuss scars she assured herself dazedly, but that time wasn't now, when the tender kisses he was raining over her face and throat, when the intimate sweep of his hands on her breasts was making clear thought an impossibility.

Her already simmering blood began to boil when he stood and reached for her hands to draw her up. She resisted, instead flattening her palms on his abdomen, moving them around and down. Gently, wonderingly, she encircled him and began a rhythmic stroking.

If he'd had any qualms about her reaction to his forty-year-old body, or fears that the sight of his leg would dull her desire, they were put soundly to rest by her worshipful ministration. He was digging his fingers into her shoulders by the time she leaned and pressed soft, wet kisses to his navel. Her hands, holding him, were between her breasts. Tucking in her chin, she slid her lips lower.

He was suddenly forcing her chin up, a pained smile on his face. "You don't play fair," he managed tightly. "I'm not made of stone."

"But I want you to—"

"This way, later," he whispered, repeating her earlier words. "For now, though, you were right..." When he reached for her hands this time, she stood, then with his help took off the rest of her clothes. They looked at each other, drenched in the pale orange glow of the fire. Then they came together, bare bodies touching for the first time in fourteen years, and it was so strangely new yet familiar, so stunningly electric yet right, that once again tears filled Marni's eyes and this time trickled down her cheeks.

Web felt them against his chest, and his arms tightened convulsively around her. "Oh, no..."

"Just joy, Web," she said as she laughed, then sniffled. "Tears of joy." She had her arms wrapped around his neck and held on while he lowered them both to the woven rug before the fire. Bracing himself on his elbows, he traced the curve of her lips with the tip of his tongue. She tried to capture him, but he eluded her, so she raised her head and tried again. Soon he was thrusting his tongue into her welcoming mouth, thrusting and retreating only to thrust again when she whimpered in protest at the momentary loss.

She welcomed the feel of his large body over hers. She felt sheltered, protected, increasingly aroused by everything masculine about him. Her hands skated over the corded swells of his back, glided to his waist and spread over his firm buttocks. She arched up to the hand he'd slipped between their bodies and offered him her breasts, her belly, the smoldering spot between her legs.

They touched and caressed, whispered soft words of love, of pleasure, of urging as their mutual need grew. It was as if nothing in the world could touch them but each other, as if that touch was life-giving and life-sustaining to the extent that their beings were defined by it. Web's lips gave form and substance to each of Marni's features, as his hands did to her every feminine curve. Her mouth gave shape and purpose to his, as her hands did to his every masculine line.

Finally, locked in each other's gaze, they merged fully. Web filled her last empty place, bowed his back and pressed even more deeply until he touched the entrance to her womb.

"I love you," he mouthed, unable to produce further sound.

The best she could do was to brokenly mouth the words back. Her breath seemed caught in her throat, trapped by the intensity of the moment. She'd never felt as much of a person, as much of a woman as she did now, with Web's masculinity surrounding her, filling her, completing her. Fourteen years ago they'd made love, and it had been breathtaking, too, but so different. Now she was old enough to understand and appreciate the full value of what she and Web shared. The extraordinary pleasure was emotional as well as physical, a total commitment on both of their parts to that precious quality of togetherness.

Web felt it, too. As he held himself still, buried deep inside Marni, he knew that he'd never before felt the same pleasure, the same satisfaction with another woman. The pleasure, the satisfaction, encompassed not only his body but his mind and heart as well, and the look of wonder on Marni's face told him the feeling was shared.

Slowly he began to move, all the while watching her. Waves of bliss flowed over her features as he thrust gently, then with increasing speed and force as she moved in tempo beneath him. The act he'd carried through so many times before seemed to have taken on an entirely new and incredible intimacy that added fuel to the flame in his combustive body.

Harder and deeper he plunged, his ardor matched by her increasing abandon. Before long they were both lost in a world of glorious sensation, a world that grew suddenly brilliant, then blinding. Marni caught her breath, arched up and was suspended for a long moment before shattering into paroxysms of mindless delight. The air left her lungs in choked spurts, but she was beyond noticing, as was Web, whose own body tensed, then jerked, then shuddered.

Only when the spasms had ended and his limbs grew suddenly weak did he collapse over her with a drawn-out moan. "Marni...my God! I've never...*never*..." He buried his face in the damp tendrils of hair at her neck and whispered, "I love you...so much..."

Marni was as limp and weak, but nothing could have kept the broad smile from her face. Words seemed inadequate, so she simply draped her arms over his shoulders, closed her eyes...and smiled on.

It was some time later before either of them moved, and then it was Web, sliding to her side, bringing her along to face him. He brushed the wayward fall of hair from her cheeks and let his hand lightly caress her earlobe.

"You give so much, so much," he whispered. "I almost feel as though I don't deserve it."

She pressed her fingers to his lips, then stroked them gently. "I could say the same to you."

He smiled crookedly. "So why don't you?"

"Because you know how I feel."

"Tell me anyway. My ego needs boosting, since the rest of me is totally deflated."

She grinned, but the grin mellowed into a tender smile as she spoke. "You're warm and compassionate, incredibly intelligent and sensitive. And you're sexy as hell."

"Not right now."

"Yes, right now." She raked the hair from his brow and let her fingers tangle in its thickness. "Naked and sweaty and positively gorgeous, you'd bring out the animal in me—" she gave a rueful chuckle "—if I had the strength."

"S'okay," he murmured, rolling to his back and drawing her against him, "a soft, purring kitten is all I can handle right about now. You exhaust me, sunshine, inside and out."

"The feeling's mutual, Brian Webster," she sighed, but it was a happy sigh, in keeping with the moment.

They lay quietly for a time, listening to the beat of each other's heart, the lazy cadence of their breathing, the crackling of the fire behind them.

"It's funny, hearing you call me that," he mused, rubbing his chin against her hair. "Brian. It sounds so formal."

"Not formal, just...strange. I keep trying to picture your mother calling you that when you were a little boy. 'Brian! Come in the house this minute, Brian!' When did they start calling you Web?"

"My mother never did, or my stepfather, for that matter. But the kids in school—you know how kids are, trying to act tough calling each other by their last names, then when they're a little older finding nicknames that fit. Web just seemed to fit. By the time I'd graduated from high school, I really thought of myself as Web."

"Did you consciously decide to revert to Brian when you got into photography?"

"It was more a practical thing at that point. I had to sign my name to legal forms—model releases, magazine contracts, that kind of thing. People started calling me Brian." He gave a one-shouldered shrug. "So Brian I became. Again."

"We'll call our son Brian."

He jerked his head up and stared at her. "Our son?"

She put her fingers back on his lips. "Shhh. Don't say another word. This is a dream weekend, and I'm going to say whatever I feel like saying without even thinking of 'why' or 'if' or 'how.' I intend to give due consideration to every impulse that crosses my mind, and the impulse on my mind at this particular moment is what we'll name our son. Brian. I do like it."

Once over the initial shock of Marni's blithe reference to "our son," Web found that he liked her impulsiveness. He grinned. "You're a nut. Has anyone ever told you that?"

"No. No one. I'm not usually prone to nuttiness. You do something to my mind, Web. Or maybe log cabins do something to me. Or mountains."

He propped himself on an elbow and smiled down at her. "Tell me more. What other impulses would you like to give due consideration to?"

"Dinner. I'm starved. Maybe *that*'s why I'm momentarily prone to nuttiness. I didn't eat lunch so I could leave the office that much earlier, and I can't remember breakfast, it was that long ago. I think I'm running on fumes."

Web nuzzled her neck. "I love these fumes. Mmmm, do I love these fumes."

Light-headed and laughing, Marni clung to him until, with a final nip at her neck, he hauled himself to his feet and gave her a hand up. He cleared his throat. "Dinner. I think I could use it, too." He ran his eyes the length of her flushed and slender body. "Did you bring a robe?"

"Uh-huh."

"Think you could get it?"

"Uh-huh."

"...Well?"

She hadn't moved. Her eyes were on his leanly muscled frame. "Have *you* got one?"

"Uh-huh."

"Think you could get it?"

"Uh-huh."

"...Well?"

Their gazes met then, and they both began to smile. If they'd been back in New York, they'd probably have made love again there and then, lest they lose the opportunity. But they were in Vermont, with the luxury of an entire weekend before them. There was something to be said for patience, and anticipation.

With a decidedly male growl, Web dragged her to his side and started off toward the bedroom, where he'd left their bags. Moments later, dressed in terry velour robes that were coincidentally similar in every respect but color—Web's was wine, Marni's white—they set to the very pleasant task of making dinner together. When Web opted out of chores such as slicing tomatoes and mushrooms for a salad, claiming that he was hampered by his injured hand, Marni mischievously remarked that his injured hand hadn't hampered his amorous endeavors. When Marni opted out of putting a match to the pilot light of the stove, claiming that she didn't like to play with fire, Web simply arched a devilish brow in silent contradiction.

They ate by the fire, finishing the wine they'd barely sipped earlier.

Then, leaving their dishes on the floor nearby, they made sweet, slow love again. This time each touched and tasted the spots that had been denied earlier; this time they both reached independent peaks before their bodies finally joined. The lack of urgency that resulted made the coming together and the leisurely climb and culmination all the more meaningful. Though their bodies would give out in time, they knew, their emotional desire was never-ending.

After talking, then listening to soft music for a while as they gazed into the fire, they finally retired to Web's big bed. When they fell asleep in each other's arms, they felt as satisfied as if they'd made love yet again.

Saturday was a sterling day, one to be remembered by them both for a long time to come. They slept late, awoke to make love, then devoured a hearty brunch in the kitchen. Though the snow had stopped sometime during the night, the fresh inch or two on top of the existing crust gave a crispness, a cleanness to the hilly woodlands surrounding the cabin.

Bundled warmly against the cold, they took a long walk in the early afternoon. It didn't matter that Marni couldn't begin to make out a path; Web knew the woods by heart, and she trusted him completely.

"So beautiful..." Her breath was a tiny cloud, evaporating in the dry air as she looked around her. Tall pines towered above, their limbs made all the more regal by the snowy epaulets they wore. Underfoot the white carpet was patterned, not only by the footprints behind them and the tracks of birds and other small forest creatures, but by the swish of low-hanging branches in the gentle breeze and the fall of powdery clumps from branches. The silence was so reverent across the mountainside that she felt intrusive even when she murmured in awe, "Don't you wish you had a camera?"

It had been a totally innocent question, an unpremeditated one. Realizing the joke in it, Marni grinned up at Web. "That was really dumb. You *do* have a camera...camera*s*. I'd have thought you'd be out here taking pictures of everything."

He smiled back at her, thoroughly relaxed. "It's too peaceful."

"But it's beautiful!"

"A large part of that beauty is being here with you."

She gave a playful tug at the arm hers was wrapped around. "Flattery, flattery—"

"But I'm serious. Look around you now and try to imagine that you were alone, that we didn't have each other, that you were here on the mountain running away from some horrible threat or personal crisis.... How would you feel?"

"Cold."

"Y'see? People see things differently depending on where they're coming from. Right now I'm exactly where I want to be. I don't think I've ever felt as happy or content in my life. So you're right, this scene is absolutely beautiful."

Standing on tiptoe, she kissed his cheek, then tightened her arm through his. "Do you ever photograph up here?"

He shrugged. "I don't have a camera up here."

"You're kidding."

"Nope. This is my getaway. I knew from the first that if I allowed myself to bring a camera here, it wouldn't be a true escape."

"But you love photography, don't you?"

"I love my work, but photography in and of itself has never become an obsession with me. I've met some colleagues, both men and women, whose cameras are like dog tags around their necks. It gives them their identity. I've never wanted that. The camera is the tool of my trade, much like a calculator or computer is for an accountant, or a hammer is for a carpenter. Have you ever seen a carpenter go away for the weekend with his tool belt strapped around his waist just in case he sees a nail sticking out on someone's house or on the back wall of a restaurant?"

Marni grinned. "No, I guess I haven't.... Why are you looking at me that way?"

"You just look so pretty, all bundled up and rosy-cheeked. You look as happy and content as I feel. I almost wish I did have a camera, but I'm not sure I could begin to capture what you are. Some things are better left as very special images in the mind." He grew even more pensive.

"What is it?" she asked softly.

"Impulse time. Can I do it, too?"

"Sure. What's your impulse?"

"To photograph you out here in the woods. In the summer. Stark naked."

She quivered in excitement. "That's a naughty impulse."

"But that's not all." His blue eyes were glowing. "I'd like to photograph you in bed right after we've made love. You're all rosy-cheeked then too, and naked, but bundled up in love."

She draped her arms over his shoulders. "Mmmm. I like that one."

"But that's not all."

"There's more?"

"Uh-huh." His arms circled her waist. "I'd like to photograph you in bed right after we've made love. You're naked and rosy and wrapped in love. And you're pregnant. You're breasts are fuller, with tiny veins running over them, and your belly is round, the skin stretched tightly, protectively over our child."

Marni sucked in her breath and buried her face against the fleece lining of his collar. "That's...beautiful, Web."

"But that's not all."

She gave a plaintive moan. "I'm not sure I can take much more of this. My legs feel like water."

"Then I'll support you." True to his words, he tightened his arms around her. "I'd like to photograph you with our child at your breast. It could be a little Brian, or a little girl named Sunshine or Bliss or Liberty—"

She looked sharply up in mock rebuke. "You wouldn't."

"Wouldn't photograph you breast-feeding our child? You bet your sweet—"

"Wouldn't name the poor thing Sunshine or Bliss or Liberty. Do you have any idea what she'd go through, saddled with any one of those names?"

"Then you choose the name. Anything your heart desires."

Marni thought for a minute. "I kind of like Alana, or Arielle, or Amber—no, not Amber. It doesn't go well with Webster."

"You're partial to *A*'s?"

She tipped up her chin. "Nope. Just haven't gotten to the *B*'s yet."

She never did get to the *B*'s because he hugged her, and she was momentarily robbed of breath. When he released her long enough to loop his arm through hers again and start them along the path once more, he was thinking of things besides children. "We could keep your place if you'd like. Mine above the studio wouldn't be as appropriate for the entertaining you have to do."

"I don't know about that. It might spice things up. If we were really doing something big, we could use the studio itself, or rent space at a restaurant. I think I'd like the idea of knowing you'd be there whenever I came home from work."

"Would you have to travel much?"

"I could cut it down."

"I'd feel lonely when you were away."

"Maybe you could come." Her eyes lit up. "I mean, if I knew far enough in advance so that you could rearrange your schedule, we could take care of my business and have a vacation for ourselves."

"With Brian or Arielle or whoever?"

"By ourselves. Two adults doing adult things. We'd leave the baby with a sitter.... Uh-oh, that could be one drawback about living above your studio. You wouldn't get much work done with a squalling baby nearby."

"Are you kidding? I'd love it! I mean, we would hire someone to take care of the baby, and no baby of ours is going to be squalling all the time. I'd be able to see him or her during breaks or when the sitter was passing through the studio going out for walks. I'd be proud as punch to show off my child. And I'd be right there in case of any problem or emergency."

"But you shoot on location sometimes."

"Less and less in the last year or so, and I've reached the stage where I could cut it out entirely if I wanted to. Just think of it. It'd be an ideal situation." His cheeks were ruddy, and his blue eyes sparkled.

"You really mean that, don't you?"

"You bet. I never knew my own father. I want to know my children and have them know me."

"Child*ren?* Oh, boy, how many are we having?"

"Two, maybe three. More if you'd like, but I'd hate to think of your being torn between your work and a whole brood of kids. I'm told that working mothers suffer a certain amount of guilt even with one child."

He was right, but she couldn't resist teasing him. "Who told you that?"

He shrugged. "I read."

"What?"

"Oh...lots of things."

She couldn't contain a grin. His cheeks were a dead giveaway, suddenly redder in a way that couldn't be from the cold. "Women's magazines?"

"Hell, my photographs are in them. Okay, sometimes one article or another catches my eye."

"And how long have you been reading about working mothers?"

"One article, Marni, that's it. It was—I don't know—maybe six or seven months ago."

"Did you know then that you wanted to have kids?"

"I've known for a long time, and when I read the article it was simply to satisfy an abstract curiosity." Smoothly, and with good humor, he took the offensive. "And you should be grateful that I *do* read. I'm thinking of you, sweet. Anything I've learned will make things easier for you."

"I'm not worried," she hummed, with a smile on her face.

They continued to walk, neither of them bothered by the cold air, if even aware of it. They were wrapped up in their world of dreams, a warm world where the sun was shining brightly. They talked of what they'd do in their leisure time, where they'd travel for vacations, what their children might be when they grew up.

The mood continued when they returned to the cabin. Marni sat on a barrel in the carport watching Web split logs for the fire. He sat on a stool in the kitchen watching her prepare a chicken-and-broccoli casserole. They sat by the fire talking of politics, the economy and foreign affairs, dreaming on, kissing, making love. Arms and legs entwined, they slept deeply that night—a good thing, because Sunday morning they awoke with the knowledge that before the day was through they'd be back in the real world facing those problems neither of them had been willing to discuss before.

Web lay in bed, staring at the ceiling. Marni was in a nearly identical position by his side. They'd been awake for a while, though neither had spoken. A thick quilt covered them, suddenly more necessary than it had seemed all weekend, for now they were thinking of an aspect of the future that was chilling to them both.

"What are we going to do about your parents, Marni?" Web asked. He'd contemplated approaching the topic gradually, but now he saw no point in beating around the bush.

She didn't twist her head in surprise, or even blink. "I don't know."

"What will they say if you announce that we're getting married?"

"Married. Funny...we haven't used that word before."

He tipped his head to look at her. "It was taken for granted, wasn't it?"

She met his gaze and spoke softly. "Yes."

"And you want it, don't you?"

"Yes."

"So—" his gaze drifted away "—what will they say?"

"They'll hit the roof."

He nodded, then swallowed. "How will you feel about that?"

"Pretty sick."

"It bothers you what they think?"

"Of course it does. They're my parents."

"You're not a child. You're old enough to make your own decisions."

"I know that, and I do make my own decisions every day of the week. This, well, this is a little tougher."

"Many adults have differences with their parents."

"But there are emotional issues here, very strong emotional issues."

"They blame me for Ethan's death."

"They blame you for everything that happened that summer."

"But mostly for Ethan's death." He sat up abruptly and turned to her, feelings he'd held in for years suddenly splintering outward. "Don't they know it was an accident? Those two cars collided and began spinning all over the road. There was no possible way I could have steered clear. Hell, we were wearing helmets, but a motorcycle didn't have any more of a chance against either of those monsters than Ethan's neck had against that tree."

Marni was lying stiffly, determined to say it all now. "It was your motorcycle. They felt that if Ethan had been with anyone else he would have been in a car and survived."

Frustrated, Web thrust his fingers through his hair. "I didn't force Ethan to come with me. For that matter, I didn't force Ethan to become my friend."

"But you were friends. My parents blame that on you, too."

"They saw their son as wasting his time with a no-good bum like me. Well, they were wrong, damn it! They were wrong! My friendship with Ethan was good for *both* of us. Ethan got a helluva lot more from me than he was getting from those other guys he hung around with, and I got more from him than you could ever believe. My, God! He was my friend! Do you think I wasn't crushed by his death?"

Tears glistened on his lower lids. Marni saw them and couldn't look away. She wanted to hold him, to comfort him, but at the moment there was a strange distance between them. She was a Lange. She was one of *them*.

"Y'know, Marni," he began in a deep voice that shook, "I lay in that hospital room bleeding on the inside long after they'd stitched me up on the outside. I hurt in ways no drug could ease. Yes, I felt guilty. It was my motorcycle, and I was driving, and if I'd been going a little faster or a little slower we would have missed that accident and been safe.... I called your father from the hospital. Did you know that?"

Eyes glued to his, she swallowed. "No."

"Well, I did. The day after the accident, when I'd been out from under the anesthetic long enough to be able to lift the phone. It was painful, lifting that phone. I had three cracked ribs, and my thigh was shattered into so many pieces that it had taken five hours of surgery to make some order out of it—and that's not counting the two operations that followed. But nothing, *nothing* I felt physically could begin to compare with the pain your father inflicted on me. He didn't ask how I was, didn't stop to think that I was hurting or that I was torn up by the knowledge that Ethan had died and I was alive. No, all he asked was whether I was satisfied, whether I was pleased I'd destroyed a life that would have been so much more meaningful, so much more productive than mine had ever been or could be."

An anger rose in Marni, so great that she could no longer bear the thought of presenting her parents' side of the story. She sat up and moved to Web, her own eyes flooding as she curled her hands around his neck. "He had no right to say that! It *wasn't* your fault! I told him that over and over again, but he wouldn't listen to me. I was an irresponsible seventeen-year-old who'd been stupid to have been involved with you, he said. That showed how much *I* knew."

Web dragged in a long, shaky breath. He was looking at her, but not actually seeing her. His vision was on the past. "I cried. I lay there holding the phone and cried. The nurse finally came in and took it out of my hand, but I kept on crying until I was so tired and in so much pain that I just couldn't cry anymore."

She brushed at the moisture in the corners of his eyes, though his face was blurred to her gaze. "I'm so sorry, Web," she whispered. "So sorry. He was wrong, and cruel. There was nothing you could have done to prevent that accident. It wasn't your fault!"

"But I felt guilty. I still do."

"What about me?" she cried. "If it hadn't been for me—for my pestering the two of you to take me along—you would have been in Ethan's car as you'd originally planned. Don't you think that's haunted me all these years? I tried to tell that to my father, too, because it hurt so much when he put the full blame on you, but he wouldn't listen. All he could think of was that Ethan, his only son and primary heir, was gone. And my mother seconded everything he said, especially when he forbade me to see you again."

"What about Tanya? Didn't she come to your defense?"

"Tanya, who'd been itching for you from the first moment she knew we were involved with each other? No, Tanya didn't come to my defense. She told my mother everything she knew, about the times I'd said I was out with friends but was actually out with you. She was legitimately upset about Ethan, I have to say that much for her. But she did nothing to help me through what was a double devastation. She sided with my parents all the way."

Marni hung her head. Tears stained her cheeks, and her hands clutched Web's shoulders for the solace that his muscled strength could offer. "I wanted to go to you, Web." Her voice was small and riddled with pain. "I kept thinking of you in that hospital, even when we returned to Long Island for the funeral. I wanted to go back to Maine to see you, because I needed to know you were okay and I needed your comfort. You'd meant so much to me that summer. I'd been in love with you, and I felt that you might be the only one to help me get over Ethan's death."

"But they wouldn't let you come."

"They said that if I made any move to contact you, they'd disinherit me. That if I tried to see you, they'd know that they'd failed as parents."

He smoothed her hair back around her ears, then said softly, "I waited. I was hoping you'd come, or call, because I thought maybe you could make me feel a little better about what had happened. I was in that godforsaken small-town hospital for two months—"

"How could I go against them?" she cried, trying desperately to justify what she'd done. "Regardless of how wrong they were about you, they were grief-stricken over Ethan. It wasn't the threat of being disinherited that bothered me. It wasn't a matter of money. But they'd given me everything for seventeen years. You'd given me other things, but for barely two months." She took a quick breath. "You said that you thought I was headstrong in my way even then, but I wasn't really, Web. I couldn't stand up for something I wanted. I'd already disappointed my parents. I couldn't do it again. They were going through too rough a time. Dad was never the same after the accident."

Web's expression had softened, and his voice was tinged with regret. "None of us were. That accident was the turning point in my life." His words hung, heavy and profound, in the air for a minute. Then he turned, propped the pillows against the headboard and settled Marni against him as he leaned back. "My leg kept getting infected and wouldn't heal, so I was transferred to a place in Boston. The specialist my stepfather found opened the whole thing up and practically started from scratch again, and between that and a second, less extensive operation, I was hospitalized for another six weeks. I had lots of time to think. Lots of time.

"Ethan and I, I realized, each represented half of an ideal world. He had financial stability, but though many of the things he had told me about in those hours we spent together sounded wonderful, they didn't come free. I had freedom and a sense of adventure, but without roots or money I was limited as to what I could do in life. As I lay there, I thought a lot about my father and about why I'd been running, and it was then I realized I wanted something more in life. Your parents thought I was dirt, and I felt like it after the accident. But I didn't want to be dirt. I wanted to be *someone*, not just a jock moving from job to job and place to place." He stroked her arm as though needing to reassure himself that he'd found a measure of personal stability at last.

"What happened to Ethan made me think about my own mortality," he went on in a solemn voice. "If I'd died then and there, no one—well, other than my immediate family—would have missed me, and it was questionable as to whether they'd really miss me, since I'd never been around all that much." He took a deep breath. "So I hooked onto that dig in New Mexico. It was the first time I'd ever done something with an eye toward the future. By the time I realized I'd never make it as a writer, my pictures were selling. I was on my way. I don't think anything could have stopped me from pushing ahead full steam at that point."

Marni, who'd been listening quietly, raised her face to his. "You've done Ethan proud. He gave you the motivation, and you worked your way up from scratch to become very successful."

Web was studying her tenderly. "And what about you? You've done much of what you have for him, too, haven't you?"

"For him...and my parents." She rushed on before he could argue. "I grieved so long after the accident, for both Ethan and you, and the sadness and guilt I felt were getting me nowhere. I decided that the only way I could redeem myself was to make my parents proud of me. Yes, I've tried to fill Ethan's shoes. I'm sure I haven't done it in the same way he would have, but I do think I've filled a certain void for my parents. After Ethan's death, Dad began to lose interest in the business. My decision to enter it was like a shot in the arm for him. Of course shots wear off after a while, and he eased away from the corporation earlier than he might have, but by then I was trained and ready to take over."

"You felt you were making up to your parents for having played a small part in Ethan's death."

Her whispered "Yes" was barely audible, but a shudder passed through Web, and he held her tightly to him.

"We've both suffered. We paid the fine for what we'd done, or thought we'd done, but the suffering isn't over if your parents are going to stand between us." They'd come full stride. "What are we going to do about them, Marni?"

"I don't know," she murmured, teeth gritted against the helplessness that assailed her. "I don't know."

"We'll have to tell them. We'll have to present ourselves and our best arguments to them—"

"Not 'we.' It'd never work that way, Web. They'd never listen. Worse, they'd kick you out of the house. It'd be better if I spoke with them first. I could break it to them gently."

"God, it's like we've committed some kind of crime."

"In their minds we have. What I've done will be tantamount to treason in their minds."

"They'll just have to change their way of thinking."

"That's easier said than done."

"What other choice will they have? They can't very well kick their own grown-up daughter out of the house. And then there's the matter of the corporation presidency. Your father may be chairman of the board, but no board worth its salt is going to evict its president simply because she falls in love with someone her father doesn't like. You've done a good job, Marni. You're invaluable to the corporation."

"Not invaluable. Certainly not indispensable. But I'm not really worried about anything happening at work. Dad wouldn't go *that* far. What I fear most is what will happen at home. Ethan's death left a gaping hole. Every time the family got together, we were aware of his absence. If Mom and Dad push us away because of my relationship with you, the unit will be that much weaker. If they could only reconcile themselves to gaining a son, rather than losing a daughter..."

"Reconcile. A powerful word."

Marni was deep in thought. "Mmmm.... What if I break it to them gently? Mother hasn't made the connection between you and that other Web. Apparently neither has Dad, since he didn't make a peep over the plans to use you as cover photographer for *Class*. What if I were to tell them that we were dating, that I was seeing the photographer and that we were pretty serious about each other?"

"They'd want to meet me. One look and they'd know."

"We could stall them. After all, I'm busy, and so are you, which would make it hard to arrange a meeting. In the meantime I could tell them all about Brian Webster, show them examples of your work and snow them with lists of your credits. I could create a picture in their minds of everything you are and everything you mean to me."

"And they won't ask about my background?" He knew very well they would.

"I could fudge it, be as vague as I like. Then, when they've got this super image in their minds, when they're as favorably inclined as possible, I could tell them the rest."

He raised her chin with his forefinger. "A super image can shatter with a few short words. What if, in spite of the advance hype, they go off the deep end?"

His eyes were a mirror of hers. Marni saw there the same trepidation, the same worry that was making her insides knot. "Then I'll have to make a choice," she said at last.

The trepidation, the worry were transferred to his voice, which came out in a tremulous whisper. Once before Marni had had a choice to make, and she'd made it in favor of her family. Web felt that his very life was on the line. "What will you choose?" he asked in a raw whisper.

Neither her eyes, lost in his, nor her voice faltered. "You're my future, Web. I'm grateful for everything they've given me, and I do love them, but you're my future. The love I feel for you is so strong that there's really no choice at all."

Web closed his eyes. His sigh fanned her brow, and his arms tightened convulsively around her. "Oh, baby..." He said nothing more but held her, rocking her, savoring the moment, the joy, the intense relief he felt.

Inevitably, though, the ramifications of what she'd said loomed before him. "It's going to be hard. You'll be upset."

"Yes. It's sad that I have to risk alienating them by telling them that I'm—"

"—marrying the guy who killed their son."

Her head shot up, eyes flashing in anger. "You *didn't* kill Ethan. Don't ever say that again!"

He felt compelled to prepare her. "They'll say it."

"And they'll be wrong again. They may have used you for a scapegoat that summer, they may be doing it still, and I suppose it's only natural that parents try to find someone to blame, some reason to explain a tragedy like that. But, damn it, you've been their scapegoat long enough!"

"You're apt to take over that role, if it comes down to an estrangement."

"Oh, Web, Web, let's not assume the worst until we come to it...please?"

THEY LEFT THE DISCUSSION on that pleading note, but the rest of the day was nowhere near as carefree as the day before had been. They breakfasted, walked again through the woods, packed their bags and closed up the house, all the while struggling to elude the dark cloud hovering overhead.

An atmosphere of apprehension filled the car during the drive back to the city. Web clutched her hand during most of the trip, knowing the dread she was feeling and in turn being swamped by helplessness and frustration. At the door of her apartment, he hugged her with a kind of desperation.

"I'm so afraid of losing you, sunshine...so afraid. I was a fool fourteen years ago for not realizing what I had, but I'm not a fool anymore. I'm going to fight, Marni. I'm going to fight, if it's the last thing I do!"

Those words, and the love behind them, were to be a much-needed source of strength for Marni in the days to come.

7

MARNI HAD HAD every intention on Monday of calling her mother about the wonderful weekend she'd had with Brian Webster, but she didn't seem to find the time. When, as prearranged, Web came to take her to dinner that night, she explained that something had come up in the computer division, demanding her attention for most of the day. She'd had little more than a moment here or there to think of making the call.

On Tuesday it was a problem with the proposed deal in Richmond, one she thought she'd ironed out when she'd gone down there the week before. On Wednesday it was a lawsuit, filed against the corporation's publishing division by one of its authors.

"You're hedging," Web accused when he saw her that night.

"I'm not! These things came up, and I need a free mind when I call her."

"Things are always coming up. It's the nature of your work. You can put off that call forever, but it's not going to solve our problem."

"Speaking of problems, what are we going to do about the cover of *Class*?" She knew the second batch of pictures had been better than the first, but that Web was still not fully satisfied.

"You're changing the subject."

"Maybe, but it is a problem, and we both do have a deadline on that one."

"We've got a deadline on both, if you look at it one way. The longer you put off breaking the news about us to your parents, the longer it'll be before we can get married."

"I know," she whispered, looking down at the fingernail she was picking. "I know."

Web knew she was torn, that she loved him and wanted to marry him, but that she was terrified of what her parents' reaction was going to be. He sympathized, but only to a point.

"I'll make a deal with you," he sighed. "I'll study all the proofs and decide what to do about them, if you call your mother.... Sound fair?"

"Of course it's fair," she snapped. He was right. She was only prolonging the inevitable. "I'll call her tomorrow."

SHE DID BETTER than that. Fearful that she'd lose her nerve when the time came, she called her mother that night and invited her to lunch. It was over coffee and trifle, the latter barely touched on her plate, that Marni broached the subject.

"Mother, do you remember that photographer I was with that night we witnessed the assault?"

Adele Lange, a slender woman with a surprisingly sweet tooth, was relishing every small forkful of wine-soaked sponge cake, fruit, nuts and whipped cream that made up the trifle. She held her fork suspended. "Of course I remember." She smiled. "He's the famous one everyone knows about but me."

Marni forced her own smile as she launched into the speech she'd mentally rehearsed so many times. "Well, we've been dating. I think it's getting serious."

Adele stared at her, then set down her fork. "But I thought you said it was a business thing."

"It started out that way, but it's evolved into something more." So far, the truth. Marni kept her chin up.

"Marni! It's been—how long—a week since that incident? How many times could you have seen this man to know that it's getting serious?"

"I'm thirty-one, Mom. I know."

"Does he? Remember what I told you about photographers?"

"You're hung up on the stereotype. You've never met Brian."

"Then tell me. What's he like?" Slowly Adele returned to her trifle, but she was clearly distracted.

"He's tall, dark and handsome, for starters."

"Aren't they all?"

"No. Some are squat and wiry-haired—"

"And wear heavy gold jewelry, have their eyes on every attractive woman in sight and can't make it through a sentence without a 'darling' or 'sweetie' or 'babe.'"

Marni grinned. "Brian doesn't use any of those words. He doesn't wear any jewelry except a watch, which is slim and unobtrusive, and he may have the same appreciation that any other man his age has for a beautiful woman, but he's never looked at another woman the way he looks at me." Nicely put, Marni thought, almost poetic. She'd have to remember that one.

"How old is he?"

"Forty."

"And he's never married?"

"No."

"That's something strange to think about. Why hasn't he married? A man who's got looks and a name for himself...maybe he's queer."

If Marni had had a mouthful of coffee, she would have choked on it. It was all she could do to keep a straight face. "Would he be interested in me if he was?"

Adele's lips twitched downward in disdain. "Maybe he goes both ways."

"He doesn't. Take my word for it."

"And you take his word that he doesn't have an ex-wife or two to support?"

"He's never been married," Marni stated unequivocally, then took a sip of her coffee. She knew her mother. The questions were just beginning. She only wished they would all be as amusing.

"Where does he come from?"

"Pennsylvania, originally."

Adele took another tiny forkful of trifle. "What about his parents?"

"His mother is dead. His father is an insurance broker." She'd anticipated the question and had thought about the answer she'd give. To say "stepfather" would only be to invite questions. Web had never known his biological father, hence Marni felt justified in responding as she did.

Adele was chewing and swallowing each bit of information along with the trifle. "How long has he been a photographer?"

"He's been at it since his mid-twenties."

"I assume, given the reputation Tanya claims he has, that he earns a good living."

"What kind of a question is that, Mother?"

"It's a mother's kind of question."

"I'm an independent adult. I earn a more than comfortable salary for myself. Why should it matter what W—what Brian earns?" The sudden skip of her heart hadn't been caused by her indignation. She'd nearly slipped. Brian was a safe name; Web was not. She'd have to be more careful.

Adele scolded her gently. "Don't get upset, darling. For the first time in your adult life, you've told me that you're serious about a man. Your father and I have waited a long time for this. It's only natural that we be concerned about whether he's right for you. Realistically speaking, you're a wealthy woman. We wouldn't want to think that some man was interested in you for your money."

Farcical. That was what it was, and Marni couldn't help but laugh. "No, Brian is *not* interested in my money. Not that it matters, but he's far from being a pauper. He has an extremely lucrative career, he owns the building that houses his studio and his apartment and he's got a weekend home on acres of woodland in Vermont." She hesitated, wondering just how much to say, then decided to throw caution aside. "We were there last weekend. It's beautiful."

Adele's eyes widened fractionally, and she pursed her lips, but said nothing about Marni's having spent the weekend with her photographer. Marni was, after all, thirty-one, and these were modern times. It was too much to expect that her daughter was still a virgin. "Vermont. A little...backwoodsy, isn't it?"

Marni rolled her eyes. "Vermont has become the vacation place of most of New York, or hadn't you noticed? Some of the finest and wealthiest have second homes there. Times have changed, Mother. It doesn't have to be Camden, or South Hampton, or Newport anymore."

"I know that, darling," Adele said gruffly. She scowled at what was left of her dessert, then abandoned it in favor of her coffee.

"I want you to be *pleased*," Marni said softly. "Brian is a wonderful man. He's interesting and fun to be with, he's serious about his work and he respects mine, and he treats me like I'm the best thing that's ever happened to him."

"I am pleased. I just want to make sure you know what you're doing before you get in over your head."

Marni might have said that she was already in over her head, but it wouldn't have served her purpose. "I know what I'm doing," she said with quiet conviction. "I'm happy. That's the most important thing...don't you think?"

"Of course, dear. Of course.... So, when will we be able to meet this photographer of yours?"

"Soon."

"When?"

"When I get up the courage to bring him out."

"Courage? Why would you need courage?"

"Because you and Dad can be intimidating in the best of circumstances. I'm not sure I'm ready to inflict you on Brian yet." Her words had been offered in a teasing tone and accompanied by a gentle smile. Adele was totally unaware of the deeper sentiment behind them.

"Very funny, Marni. We don't bite you know."

"You could send Brian running if you grill him the way you've grilled me. No man likes to have his background, his social standing and his financial status probed."

"Social standing. We haven't even gotten into that."

"No need. He's well-liked and respected, he's the good friend of many well-placed people and he chews with his mouth closed."

"That's a relief," was Adele's sardonic retort. "I wouldn't want to think you were going with some crude oaf."

"Brian can hold his own with any crowd. He'll charm your friends to tears."

"Well, *your father and I* would like to meet him before we introduce him to our friends. Why don't you bring him out to the house on Sunday?"

Marni shook her head. "We're not up to a showing just yet."

"If you're so afraid that we'll scare the man off, maybe you're not so sure about him yourself."

"Oh, I'm sure. But it's still a little early for introductions," she explained with impeccable nonchalance. "When the time's right, I'll let you know."

"YOU WOULD HAVE BEEN proud of me, Web," Marni declared when she arrived at the studio that night. Web had kissed her thoroughly. She was feeling heavenly. "I was cool and relaxed, I followed the script perfectly and I didn't lie once."

"How did she take it?"

"Hesitantly, at first. She asked questions, just as I'd expected." She told him some of them, and they shared a chuckle over the one about money. "I planted the bug in her ear. If I know my mother, she's already on the phone trying to find out whatever she can about you." A sudden frown crossed her brow. Web picked up on it instantly.

"Don't worry. There's nothing she could learn that will connect me with who I was fourteen years ago. Lee is about the only one who knows anything about what I did during those years, and even if someone called him, which they wouldn't, he'd be tight-lipped as hell."

"He must think my parents are awful."

"Not awful. Just...prejudiced."

"Mmmm. I guess that says it." Her eyes clouded. "It remains to be seen whether they're vengeful as well."

"Don't even think it," Web soothed. "Not yet. We've got more pressing things to consider."

"More pressing?" she asked, worried. But Web was grinning, drawing her snugly against him. "Ahhh. More pressing..."

His lips closed over hers then, and soon he was leading her to the bedroom, where he proceeded to set her priorities straight. It was what she needed, what they both needed—a reaffirmation of all they meant to each other. Passion was a ready spark between them, had always been a ready spark between them, but it was love that dominated the interplay of mouths and hands and bodies, and it was love that transported them to an exquisite corner of paradise.

MARNI'S FATHER DROPPED BY her office on Friday morning. She was surprised to see him, because there wasn't a board meeting scheduled and he rarely came in for anything else. But deep down inside she'd been awaiting some form of contact.

They talked of incidental things relating to the corporation, and Marni indulged him patiently. In his own good time, Jonathan Lange broached the topic that had brought him by. His thick brows were low over his eyes.

"Your mother tells me that you have a special man...this photographer...Brian Webster?"

"Uh-huh." Her pulse rate had sped up, but she kept her eyes and her voice steady and forcefully relaxed her hands in her lap.

"I know your mother has some reservations," he went on in his most businesslike tone, "and I hope you take them seriously. People today get married, then divorced, married, then divorced. Your sister is a perfect example."

"I'm not Tanya," Marni stated quietly.

"Exactly. You're the president of this corporation. I hope you keep that in mind when you go about choosing a husband."

She had to struggle to contain a surge of irritation. "I know who I am, Dad, and I think I have a pretty good grasp of what's expected of me."

"Just so you do. This fellow's a photographer, and big-name photographers often live in the fast lane. I wouldn't want you—or him—to do anything to embarrass us."

Embarrassment had never been among Marni's many worries. "I think you're jumping the gun," she said slowly. "In the first place, you've adopted the same stereotype Mom has. There's nothing fast about Brian. He lives quietly, and his face hasn't been plastered all over the papers, with or without women." Web had assured her of that. All she'd needed was for her mother or Tanya to do a little sleuthing and come up with a picture that would identify Web instantly. "Furthermore, I don't believe I said anything to Mom about marriage."

Jonathan's frown was one of reproof. "Then you'd move in with the man, without a thought to your image?"

"Come on, Dad. These are enlightened times. No one cares if two adults choose to live together."

"Is that what *you* choose?"

"No! I've never even considered it."

"But you haven't talked marriage with this photographer?"

That one was harder to fudge. She bought a minute's time. "His name is Brian. You can call him Brian."

"All right. Brian. Have you talked marriage with Brian?"

She held his gaze. "I think we'd both be amenable to the idea."

"Then it *is* serious."

"Yes."

"We'll have to meet him. That's all there is to it."

Marni bit her lower lip, then let it slide from beneath her teeth. "You know, Dad, I am a big girl. Technically, I don't need your approval. You may hate him, but that wouldn't change my feelings for him."

Jonathan's gaze sharpened. "If he's as wonderful as you say, why would we hate him?"

"Different people see things differently. You and Mom aren't keen on his profession to begin with."

"That's true. But we'd still like to meet him, and soon, if you're as serious as you say about him."

"Okay, soon. You will meet him soon."

THERE WAS SOON, and there was soon. Marni had no intention of running out to Long Island that Sunday as her mother had originally suggested. Not only did she have more subtle PR to do, but she and Web were going back to Vermont for the weekend, and not for the world would she have altered their plans.

They had a relaxed, quiet, loving weekend and returned to New York refreshed and anticipating the next step in Marni's plan. On Monday she sent her parents tear sheets of the best of Web's work. Each piece was identified as to where it had appeared; it was an impressive collection of credits. She also sent along copies of blurbs and articles praising Web's work.

On Monday night she and Web took in a movie. On Tuesday they went out to dinner. On Wednesday morning she called her mother as a follow-up to the package she'd sent. Yes, Adele had received it, and, yes, it was an impressive lot. Yes, Marni was planning to bring him out to the house, but, no, it couldn't be this week because they were both swamped with work.

Marni and Web spent a quiet Wednesday night at her place, then a similarly quiet Thursday night at his. After the full days they put in at their respective jobs, they found these private times to be most precious.

Friday night, though, they had a party to attend. It was given by the most recently named vice-president at Lange, Heather Connolly, whom Marni had personally recruited from another company four years before.

Had the party been an official corporate function, Marni might have thought twice about bringing Web along. She felt she was progressing well with her parents and wouldn't have done anything to jeopardize her plan. But the party was a personal one, a gathering of the Connollys' friends. Marni was looking forward to it; it was the first time she would be introducing Web to any of her own friends.

They had fun dressing up, Web in a dark, well-tailored suit, Marni in a black sequined cocktail dress. It was a miracle they noticed anyone else at the party, so captivated were they by each other's appearance. But they did manage to circulate, talking easily with Heather and Fred's friends, their spouses and dates.

At ten o'clock, though, the unthinkable happened. A couple arrived: the man a tennis partner of Fred's, the woman none other than Marni's sister, Tanya.

Marni was the first to see them. She and Web were chatting with another couple when they entered the room. Her heart began to pound, and she stiffened instantly. Instinctively she reached for Web's arm and dug in her fingers. He took one look at her ashen face, followed her gaze and stared.

"Tanya?" he whispered in disbelief. It had been fourteen years, but he would have recognized her even had Marni's reaction not been a solid clue. Clearing his throat, he turned smoothly back to the couple. "Would you excuse us? Marni's sister has just come. We hadn't expected to see her." Without awaiting more than nods from the two, he guided Marni toward the back of the room, ostensibly to circle the crowd toward Tanya.

Marni's whisper was as frantic as she felt. "What are we *going to do*? She'll recognize you! She's *sure* to recognize you, and she's trouble! Oh, God, Web, what do we do?"

He positioned himself so that his large body was a buffer between Marni and the rest of the crowd, then curved his fingers around her arms. "Take it easy. Just relax. There's not much we can do, Marni. If we try to slip out without being seen, our disappearance will cause an even greater stir. Tanya's not dumb. She'll put two and two together, and if she's the troublemaker you say, she'll run right back to your parents. The damage will be done anyway." He paused. "The best thing, the *only* thing we can do is to walk confidently up and say hello."

Marni's eyes were wide with dismay. "But she'll *recognize* you."

"Probably."

"But...that'll be awful!"

"It'll just bring things to a head a little sooner."

"Web, I don't want this...I don't want this!"

He slipped to her side, put his arm around her shoulder and spoke very gently. "Let's get it over with. The sooner the better. Take a deep breath...atta girl...now smile."

She tried, but the best she could muster was a feeble twist of her lips.

Web gave a tight smile of his own. "That'll have to do." He took his own deep breath. "Let's go."

Tanya and her date were talking with Heather and Fred when they approached. "Marni," Heather exclaimed, "look who's here! I never dreamed Tony would be bringing Tanya. Do you and Brian know Tony? Tony Holt, Marni Lange and Brian Webster."

Marni forced a smile in Tanya's direction. "Hi, Tanya." She clutched Web's arm. "I don't think you know Brian."

Tanya hadn't taken her eyes from Web since she'd turned at their approach. Her face, too, had paled, and there was a hint of shock in her eyes, but otherwise her expression was socially perfect. She extended a formal hand. "Brian...Webster, is it?"

If she'd put special emphasis on his last name, only Marni and Web were aware of it. Two things were instantly clear—first, that she did *indeed* know Brian and, second, that she was momentarily going along with the game.

Web took her hand in his own firm one. "It's a pleasure to meet you, Tanya."

"My pleasure entirely," was Tanya's silky response. The underlying innuendo was, again, obvious only to Web and Marni.

Web shook hands with Tony Holt, who, it turned out, was a plastic surgeon very familiar with his photographic work. Reluctantly, since he'd rather have been helping Marni, Web was drawn into conversation with the man. Heather and Fred moved off. Tanya seized Marni's arm. "We'll be in the powder room, Tony." She winked at her date. "Be right back."

Before Marni could think of a plausible excuse, she was being firmly led around the crowd and up the stairs to the second floor of the townhouse. Tanya said nothing until she'd found a bathroom and closed its door firmly behind them. Then she turned on Marni, hands on hips, eyes wide in fury.

"How could you! How could you *think* to do something like this to us! When I talked with Mom the other day, she told me you were serious about this Brian Webster. She didn't make the connection. *None* of us made the connection."

Marni refused to be intimidated. "The connection's unimportant."

"Unimportant? Have you lost your marbles?" Tanya raised a rigid finger and pointed to the door. "That man killed our brother, and you don't think the connection's important?"

"Brian did not...kill...Ethan," Marni stated through gritted teeth, her own fury quickly rising to match her sister's. "That accident was carefully documented by the police. Brian was in no way at fault."

Tanya sliced the air with her hand. "It doesn't matter what the police said. He was a bad influence on Ethan. If he hadn't come along that summer, Ethan would still be alive. Your *own brother*. How could you insult his memory by doing this?"

"Ethan liked and respected Web," Marni countered angrily. Quite unconsciously she'd reverted to calling Brian Web, but even if she'd thought about it, she'd have realized that there was no longer any need for pretense. "If he'd survived the accident, he'd have been the first one to say that Web wasn't at fault. And given the age that I am now, he'd have been the first to bless my relationship with Web."

"So you're desperate, is that it? You're thirty-one and single, and *that* man is your only hope?"

"Yes, that man is my only hope, but not because I'm thirty-one. I happen to love him. He fills needs I never realized I had."

"Very touching. Is that what you're going to say to Mom and Dad when they finally learn the truth? And when were you planning to tell them anyway? They're going to be thrilled, absolutely thrilled."

"Do you think I don't know that? Do you think I've been evasive simply to amuse myself? I'm finding no pleasure in this, Tanya, and the worst of it is that you people are making me feel guilty when I've got nothing to feel guilty about. I'd planned to tell Mom and Dad when the time was right. I was hoping that they'd form an image of what Brian Webster is like today, to somehow counter the image they've held of him all these years."

"You're dreaming, little sister—"

"Don't call me little sister," Marni said in a warning tone. "We're both adults now. It doesn't seem to me...." She closed her mouth abruptly. She'd been about to say that Tanya hadn't done anything with her life that would give her the right, or authority, to look down on Marni, but she realized that insults would get her nowhere. Yes, Tanya would go to their parents with what she'd learned, and maybe Marni *was* dreaming, but there was always that chance, that slim chance Tanya could be an ally.

Marni took a deep breath and raised both hands in a truce. "What I could use, Tanya, is your help. It's going to be very difficult for Mom and Dad, because I know they share your feelings that Web was responsible for Ethan's death. They're older, and Ethan was their child. I was hoping you could see things more objectively."

Tanya's eyes flashed. "You are *not* going to marry that man."

"And it matters that much to you who I marry?" Marni asked softly.

"You can marry anyone you please as long as it's not him."

Marni looked down at her hands and chose her words with care. "Fourteen years ago, you wanted Web for yourself. Could that be coloring your opinion?"

"Of course not. I didn't want him for myself. I knew what kind of a person he was from the start."

Marni bit back a retort concerning both Tanya's erstwhile interest in Web and the character of her two ex-husbands. "Do you know what kind of a person he is now?" she asked quietly.

"It doesn't matter. When I look at him I can only remember what he did. Mom and Dad are going to do the same."

"But think. He has a good career. He's successful and well-liked. He doesn't have the slightest blemish on his record. Can you still stand there and claim he's a killer?"

Before Tanya could answer, a light knock came at the door, then Web's voice calling, "Marni?" Marni quickly opened the door. Web looked from one sister to the other, finally settling a more gentle gaze on Marni. "Is everything okay here?"

"No, it's not," Tanya answered in a huff. "If you had any sense, you'd get out of my sister's life once and for all."

Marni turned to her with a final plea. "Tanya, I could really use your help—"

"When hell freezes over. I wouldn't—"

"That's enough," Web interrupted with quiet determination. His voice softened, and he reached for Marni's hand. "We've got to run, Marni. I've already explained to Heather that I have to be up early tomorrow. She understands."

With all hope that Tanya might aid her dashed, Marni didn't look at her sister again. She took Web's hand and let him lead her down the stairs and quietly out of the townhouse. She leaned heavily against him as they began to walk. Yes, Web had to be up early tomorrow. So did she. They were heading for Vermont, where she wouldn't be able to hear her phone when it began to jangle angrily.

8

MARNI'S PARENTS weren't put off by the fact that she wasn't home to answer her phone. They quickly called her administrative assistant, who gave them Web's Vermont number.

It was shortly after two in the afternoon. Marni and Web had left New York early, had stopped at their usual market for food and were just finishing lunch. When the phone rang, they looked up in surprise, then at each other in alarm. In all the time they'd spent at the cabin, the phone hadn't rung once.

"Don't answer it," Marni warned. Neither of them had moved yet.

"It may not be them."

The phone rang a second time. "It is. We both know it is."

"It may be a legitimate emergency. What if one of them is sick?" He began to rise from his seat. The only phone was in the den.

Marni clutched his wrist, her eyes filled with trepidation. "Let it ring," she begged.

"They'll only keep trying. I won't have the weekend spoiled. If we let it ring, we'll keep wondering. But if we answer it, at least we'll know one way or another."

"The weekend will be spoiled anyway.... Web!"

He was on his way toward the den. She ran after him.

He lifted the receiver and spoke calmly. "Hello?"

A slightly gruff voice came from the other end of the line. "Marni Lange, please."

"Who's calling?"

"...Her father."

As if Web hadn't known. He would have recognized that voice in any timbre. He'd last heard it when he'd been lying, distraught, in a hospital room.

"Mr. Lange—" Web began, not knowing what he was going to say, only knowing that he wanted to deflect from Marni the brunt of what was very obviously anger. He was curtly interrupted.

"My daughter, please."

Marni was at Web's elbow, trying to take the phone from him, but he resisted. "If this is something that concerns—"

"I'd like to *speak to my daughter!*"

Hearing her father's shout, Marni tugged harder on the phone. "Web, please..."

He held up his free hand to her, even as he spoke calmly into the receiver. "If you're angry, Mr. Lange, you're angry at me. Perhaps you ought to tell me what's on your mind."

"Are you going to put my daughter on the line?"

"Not yet."

Jonathan Lange hung up the phone.

Web heard the definitive click and took the phone from his ear, whereupon Marni snatched it to hers. "Dad? Hello? Dad?" She scowled at the receiver, then slammed it down. "Damn it, Web. You should have let me talk! What good does it do if he's hung up? Now nothing's accomplished!"

"Something is. Your father knows that I have no intention of letting you face this alone. You faced it alone fourteen years ago. I like to think I'm more of a man now."

"Then it's a macho thing?" she cried. "You're trying to show him who wears the pants around here?"

"Don't be absurd, Marni! Our relationship has been one of equals from the start. I simply want your father to know that we're standing together, that if he thinks he can browbeat you, he'll be browbeating both of us. And I don't take to being browbeaten."

"Then you'll shut every door as soon as it's opened. He *called. You* were the one who insisted on answering the phone. Now you've hung up on him—"

"He hung up on me!"

"Same difference—"

"No, it's not," Web argued angrily. "*He* shut the door. I was perfectly willing to talk."

"But he wouldn't talk with you, so now he's not talking with either of us."

"He'll call back. If he went to the effort of getting this number, he won't give up so easily."

"Then I'll answer it next time."

"And he'll bully you mercilessly. You've got to be firm with him, Marni! You've got to let him know that you're not a child who can be pushed around!"

"I'm *not* a child, and I don't like your suggestion that I am."

"I didn't suggest—"

"You don't trust me! You think I'm going to crumble. You think that I'll submit to every demand he makes. I told you I wouldn't, Web! I *told* you that my choice was made!"

"But you're torn, because you don't want to hurt them. Well, what about me? Don't I have a right to stand in my own defense? If he's going to call me a killer, it's my *right* to tell him where to get off!"

"But that won't accomplish anything!" she screamed, then caught her breath and held it. The silence was deafening, coming on the heels of their heated exchange. "Oh, God," she whimpered at last. She clutched his shoulders, then threw her arms around his neck and clung to him tightly. "Oh, God, he's doing it already. He's putting a wedge between us. Do you see what's happening? Do you see it, Web?"

His own arms circled her slowly, then closed in. Eyes squeezed shut, he buried his face in her hair. "I see, sweetheart. I see, and it makes me sick. If we start fighting about this, we'll never make it. And if *we* don't, *I* won't."

"Me neither," she managed shakily. "I love you so much, Web. It tears me up that you have to go through this, when you've already paid such a high price for something that wasn't your fault."

He rubbed soothing circles over her back. "That's neither here nor there at this point. I'm more than willing to go through hell if it means I'll get you in the end." His voice grew hoarse. "I don't know how I could have yelled at you that way. You're not responsible for the situation any more than I am."

The phone rang again. A jolt passed from one body to the other. Marni raised her face and looked questioningly at Web, who held her gaze for a minute before stepping back and nodding toward the phone.

Marni lifted the receiver. "Hello?"

"Marni!" It was her mother. "Thank goodness it's you this time! Your father is ready to—"

Cutting her off, Jonathan came on the line. "What do you think you're doing, Marni?" he demanded harshly. "Do you know who that man is?"

She felt surprisingly calm. Anticipation had prepared her well. With the moment at hand, she was almost relieved. "I certainly do. He's the man I'm going to marry." She reached for Web's hand and held it to her middle.

"Over my dead body!" came the retort. "Do you have any idea what this has done to your mother and me? You were very cagey, telling us everything about this Brian Webster of yours but his real identity. If Tanya hadn't called—"

"Everything I told you was the truth."

"Don't interrupt me, Marni. You may be the president of the corporation, but in this house you're still the baby."

"I am not still in that house, and I am *not* still the baby! I'm a grown woman, Dad. Isn't it about time you accepted that?"

"I had, until you pulled this little stunt. Are you out of your mind? Do you have any *idea* how I feel about this?"

Marni took a deep breath in a bid for calm. She had to be able to think clearly and project conviction. A glance at Web gave her strength a boost. "Yes, I think I do. I also think that you're wrong. But I won't be able to convince you of it over the phone."

"Damned right you won't. I'd suggest you get *that* man to drive you right back down here. He can drop you at the door and then leave. I won't have him in this house."

"Listen to yourself, Dad. You sound irrational. The facts are that Web and I are here in Vermont for the weekend, and that when we do come by to see you, we'll be together. Now, you can shut the door on us both, but that would be very sad, because I am your daughter and I do love you."

"I'm beginning to doubt that, young lady."

It was a low blow, and one she didn't deserve after all she'd done for her parents' sake in the past fourteen years. Clenching her jaw against the anger that flared, she went on slowly and clearly. "We'll be heading back to New York tomorrow afternoon. We'll stop by at the house sometime around seven. We can talk this all out then."

"Do *not* bring *him*."

"He'll be with me, and if you refuse to see me, we'll be married by the end of the week. Think about it, Dad. I'll see you tomorrow." Without awaiting his answer, she quietly put down the phone.

Web sucked in a deep breath, then let it out in a stunned whoosh. "You are quick, lady. I never would have dreamed up that particular threat, but you've practically guaranteed that he'll see us."

"Practically," she said without pride. Then she muttered, "He *is* a bastard."

Web drew her against him. "Shhhh. He's your father, and you love him."

"For that, yes, but as a person..."

"Shhhh. The door's open. Let's let it go at that."

THE DOOR WAS INDEED OPEN when Marni and Web arrived Sunday evening at the handsome estate where she'd grown up. Fourteen years before, Web would have been taken aback by the splendor of the long, tree-lined drive and the majesty of the huge Georgian colonial mansion. Now he could admire it without awe or envy.

They were greeted in the front hall by Duncan, Cook's husband, who'd served as handyman, chauffeur and butler for the Langes for as long as Marni could remember. "Miss Marni, it's good to see you. You're looking fine."

"Thank you, Duncan," she said quietly. "I'd like you to meet my fiancé, Mr. Webster."

"How are you, Duncan?" Web extended his hand. He, like Marni, was unpretentious when it came to hired help. He'd always treated the most lowly of his own assistants as important members of the crew. Whereas Marni was softhearted and compassionate, Web was understanding as only one who'd once been "hired help" himself could be.

Duncan pumped his hand, clearly pleased with the offering. "Just fine, Mr. Webster. And my congratulations to you both. I had no idea we'd be having a wedding coming up here soon."

Marni cleared her throat and threw what might have been an amused glance at Web had she not been utterly incapable of amusement at that moment. "We, uh, we haven't made final plans." She paused. "My parents are expecting me, I think."

"That's right," Duncan returned with the faintest hint of tension. "They're in the library. They suggested you join them there."

The library. Warm and intimate in some homes, formal and forbidding in this one. It had been the scene of many a reprimand in Marni's youth, and that knowledge did nothing to curb her anxiety now. There were differences of course. She was no longer in her youth, and Web was with her...

Head held high, she led the way through the large front hall and down a long hallway to the room at the very end. The door was open, but the symbolism was deceptive. Marni knew what she would find even before she entered the room and nodded to her parents.

Jonathan Lange was sitting in one corner of the studded leather sofa. His legs were crossed at the knees, and one arm was thrown over the back of the sofa while the other hand held his customary glass of Scotch. He was wearing a suit, customary as well; he always wore a suit when discussing serious business.

Adele Lange sat on the sofa not far from him. She wore a simple dress, nursed an aperitif and looked eminently poised.

"Thank you for seeing us," Marni began with what she hoped was corresponding poise. "I think you remember Brian."

Neither of the Langes looked at him. "Sit down," Jonathan said stiffly, tossing his head toward one of two leather chairs opposite the sofa. That particular symbolism did have meaning, Marni mused. The two chairs were well separated by a marble coffee table.

Marni took the seat near her father, leaving the one closer to her mother for Web. She sat back, folded her hands in her lap and spoke softly. "Brian and I are planning to get married. We'd like your support."

"Why?" Jonathan asked baldly.

"Because we feel that what we're doing is right and we'd like you to share our happiness."

"Why now? It's been fourteen years since you were first involved. Fourteen years is a long time for an engagement. Why the sudden rush to marry?"

Marni was confused. "We haven't been seeing each other all that time. I hadn't seen him since the day of the accident until three weeks ago when I went to his studio to be photographed."

"But you've carried a torch for him all these years."

"No! After the accident you forbade me to see him, so I didn't. I forced myself to forget about him, to put what we had down to a seventeen-year-old's infatuation, just as you said. It wasn't a matter of carrying a torch, and I never dreamed he'd be the photographer when I stepped foot in that studio—"

"I *was* wondering about that, too," Jonathan interrupted scornfully. "You were in favor of this magazine thing from the start—" his eyes narrowed "—and then to suddenly come up with the photographer who just happened to be the man you'd imagined yourself in love with—"

"It wasn't that way at all!"

Web, who'd been sitting quietly, spoke for the first time. "Marni's right. She had no idea I was—"

"I'm not talking to you," Jonathan cut in, his eyes still on Marni.

Web wasn't about to be bullied. "Well, I'm talking to you, and if you have *anything* to say to me, you can look me in the eye."

Marni put out a hand. "Web, please..." she whispered.

He softened his tone, but that was his only concession. His eyes were sharply focused on Marni's father. "I have pictures from that first photo session, one after the other showing the shock on Marni's face. She knew nothing of the past identity of Brian Webster the photographer. No one does except your family and mine."

Though Jonathan still refused to look at him, Adele did. Instinctively Web met her gaze. "Marni hadn't been pining away for me any more than I'd been pining away for her. In hindsight I can see that she was special even back then. But it's the woman I know today whom I've fallen in love with. And it's the man I am today whom I think you should try to understand."

"There's not much to understand," Adele returned. Her voice wasn't quite as cold as her husband's had been, but it was far from encouraging. "We firmly believe that had it not been for you our son would be alive today. Can you honestly expect us to let our daughter marry you, knowing that every time we look at you we'll remember what you did?"

Web sat back. "Okay, let's get into that. Exactly what *did* I do?"

"You were recklessly driving that motorcycle," Jonathan snapped, eyes flying to Web's for the first time.

Web felt a small victory in that he'd been acknowledged as a person at last. "Is that what the police said after the investigation?"

"Ethan would never have *been* on a motorcycle had it not been for you."

"I didn't force him to get on it. He wasn't some raw kid of fourteen. He was a man of twenty-five."

"You were a bad influence that entire summer!"

"That's what you assumed, since I was only an employee at the Inn. Did Ethan ever tell you what we did together? Did he tell you that we spent hours talking politics, or philosophy, or psychology? Or that we discussed books we'd both read, or that we played chess? I loved playing chess with Ethan. I beat him three times out of four, but he took it with a grin and came back for another game more determined than ever to win. There was nothing irresponsible about what we did, and I was probably a better influence on him than the spoiled and self-centered characters he would have been with otherwise. You really should have been proud of him. He chose to be with me because the time we spent together was intellectually productive."

Marni wanted to applaud, but her fingers were too tightly intertwined to move.

Jonathan wasn't about to applaud either. Choosing to ignore what Web had said, he turned his attention back to Marni. "What were you intending with the song and dance you've been doing for the past two weeks? Did you hope to pull the wool over our eyes? Did you think we were that foolish?"

"I had hoped that you'd see Brian as he is today. Aside from his profession, which you're unfairly biased against, he's everything I'd have thought you'd want in the man I decided to marry." She turned to her mother. "What did you find out? I'm sure you made calls."

"I did," Adele sniffed. "It appears he's fooled the rest of the world, but we know him as he is."

Marni scowled. "You don't know him at all. You may have met him in passing once or twice that summer, but you never spent any time talking with him, and you certainly never invited him to the house. Don't you think it's about time you faced the fact that Ethan's death just *happened*?"

"You wouldn't say that if you were a mother, Marni. You'd be angry and grief-stricken, just like we were, like we are."

"For God's sake, it's been fourteen years!"

"Have *you* forgotten?" Adele cried.

Marni sagged in her seat. "Of course not. I adored Ethan. I'll never forget him. And I've never forgotten the sense of injustice, the anger I felt that those two cars had to collide right in Web's path. But you can't live your life feeding on anger and grief. Ethan would never have wanted it. Have you ever stopped to consider that? Web was his friend. Whether you like it or not, he was. He suffered in that accident, both physically and emotionally." She suddenly sat forward and rounded on her father. "Your response when Web called you from the hospital was *inexcusable*! How could you have done something like that? He's a human being, for God's sake, a human being!" She took a quick breath and sat straighter. "Web mourned Ethan just as we did, and he suffered through his share of guilt, though God only knows he had nothing to feel guilty for. But that's all in the past now. There's nothing any of us can do to bring Ethan back, and I refuse to live my life any longer trying to make up to you for his loss!"

"What are you talking about, girl?" Jonathan snarled.

"Marni," Web began, "you don't have to—"

"I do, Web. It's about time the entire truth came out." She faced her parents, looking from one to the other. "I felt guilty because I'd loved both Ethan and Web. Ethan was dead. Web was as good as dead to me because you never let up on the fact that he was to blame, and if he was to blame, *I* was to blame, too." She focused on her father. "Do you think I wasn't aware that you'd been grooming Ethan for the corporation presidency? And that you practically lost interest in the business after he died? Why do you think I buckled down and whipped through Wellesley, then Columbia? Didn't it ever occur to you that I was trying to be what Ethan would have been? That I felt I could somehow make things easier for you if I joined the corporation myself?" She tempered her tone, though her voice was shaky. "I'm not saying that I'd had my heart set on something else, or that I'm unhappy being where I am, but I think you should both know that what I did I did for you, even more than for me."

"Then you were a fool," was Jonathan's curt response.

"Maybe so, but I don't regret it for a minute. I did make things easier for you. You won't admit it, any more than you'll admit that I've done a good job. You never did that, Dad. Do you realize?" Her eyes had grown moist and her knuckles were white as she gripped the arms of the chair. "I tried so hard, and you promoted me and gave me more and more responsibility until finally I became president. But not once, *not once* did you tell me you were proud of me. Not once did you actually praise my work—"

Her voice cracked, and she stopped talking. She was unaware that Web had risen from his seat to stand behind hers until she felt his comforting touch on her shoulder. Her hands left the arms of the chair and found his instantly.

Jonathan's expression was as tight as ever, though his voice was quieter. "I assumed that actions spoke louder than words."

"Well, they don't! I beat my tail to the ground trying to win your approval, but I failed, I failed. And now I'm tired." Her voice reflected it.

"I'm tried of trying to please someone else. I'm thirty-one years old, and it's about time I see to *my* best interests. I have every intention of continuing on as Lange's president, and I'll continue to do the best job I can, but for me now, and for Web. I'm going to marry him, and we're going to have children, and if you can't find it in your hearts to forgive, or at least forget, then I guess you'll miss out on the happiness. It's your choice. I've already made mine."

There was a moment's heavy silence in the room before Jonathan spoke in a grim voice. "I guess there's not much more to say, then, is there." It wasn't a question but a dismissal. Pushing himself from the sofa, he turned his back on them and walked toward the window.

Web addressed Adele. "There's one last thing I'd like to say," he ventured quietly. "I'd like you to consider what would have happened if Marni—or Tanya—had had Ethan for a passenger when her car crashed, killing him but only injuring her. Would you have ostracized one of your daughters from the family? Would you have held a permanent grudge? You know, that's happened in families, where two members were in an accident, one killed and the other survived. I don't know how those families reacted. Regardless of guilt or innocence, it's a tragic situation.

"Ethan and I were innocent victims of that accident fourteen years ago. Once those cars started spinning all over the road, the motorcycle didn't have a chance in hell of escaping them. If I had been the son of one of your oldest and dearest friends, would you still feel the way you do now?"

"You are *not* the son of one of our oldest and dearest friends," Jonathan said without turning. "And I thank God for it!"

MARNI AND WEB left then. They'd said what they'd come to say and had heard what they'd suspected they'd hear. They felt disappointed and saddened, hurt and angry.

"That's it, Web," Marni stated grimly as they began the drive into the city. "We know how they feel, and they're not going to change. I think we should get married, and as soon as possible."

Web kept his eyes on the road, his hands on the wheel. "Let's not do anything impulsively," he said quietly.

Her gaze flew to his face in dismay. "Impulsively? I thought marriage was what we both wanted! Weren't you the one who said that the longer we put off telling my parents the truth, the longer it would be before we got married? I thought *you* were the one who wanted to get married soon!"

"I do." His voice was even, and he didn't blink. "But we're both upset right now. It's not the ideal situation in which to be starting a marriage."

"Then what do we do? Wait forever in the hope that they'll do an about-face? They won't, Web!"

"I know. I know." He was trying to sort out his thoughts, to find some miraculous solution to their problem. "But if we rush into something, they'll be all the more perverse."

"I can't believe you're saying this! You were the one who felt so strongly that we were adults and didn't need their permission!"

He held the car steady in the right-hand lane. "We don't. And we are adults. But they're your parents, and you do love them. It'd still be nice if they came around. This all has to be a shock to them. Two days, Marni, that's all they've had."

"It wouldn't matter if it were two months!"

"It might. We presented our arguments tonight, and they were logical. I think your mother was listening, even if your father tried hard not to. Don't you think we owe them a little time to mull it over? They may never come fully around to our way of thinking, but it's possible they might decide to accept what they can't change."

Marni didn't know what to think, particularly about Web's sudden reluctance to get married. "Do you really think that could happen?" Her skepticism was nearly palpable.

"I don't know," he said with a sigh. "But I do think it's worth the wait. To rush and get married now will accomplish nothing more than throwing our relationship in their faces."

"It would accomplish much more. We'd be *married!* Or doesn't that mean as much to you as it does to me?"

"You're upset, Marni, or you wouldn't be saying that—"

"And why shouldn't we throw our relationship in their faces? We're in love. We want to get married. We asked for their support, and they refused it. They couldn't have been more blunt. I don't understand you, Web," she pleaded. "Why are you suddenly having reservations?"

He glanced at her then and saw the fear on her face. Reaching for her hand, he found it cold and stiff, so he enclosed it in his own, warmer hand and brought it to his thigh. "I'm not having reservations, sweetheart," he said gently. "Not about what I feel for you, or about getting married, or about doing all those things we've been dreaming about. If you know me at all, you know how much they mean to me. It's just that I'm trying to understand your parents, to think of what they must be feeling."

She would have tugged her hand away had he not held it firmly. "How can you be so generous after everything they've done to you?"

"Generosity has nothing to do with it," he barked. "It's selfishness from the word go."

"I don't understand."

Unable to concentrate on the road, he pulled over onto its shoulder and killed the engine. Then he turned to her and pressed her hand to his heart.

"It's for *us*, Marni," he stated forcefully. "You're right. They've done a hell of a lot to me—and to you, too—and for that they don't deserve an ounce of compassion. I'd like to ignore them, to pretend they don't exist, and in the end that may be just what we'll have to do. In the meantime, though, I refuse to let them dictate any of our actions, and that includes when we'll be getting married." His voice gentled, but it maintained its urgency, and his gaze pierced Marni's through the dark of night.

"Don't you see? Our rushing to get married just because of what happened tonight would be a kind of shotgun wedding in reverse. I won't have that! We'll plan our wedding, maybe for a month or two from now, and we'll do it right. I want you wearing a beautiful gown, and I want flowers all over the place, and I want our friends there to witness the day that means so much to us. I will *not* sneak off and elope behind someone's back. I won't have our marriage tainted in any way!"

Through her upset, Marni felt a glimmer of relief. She'd begun to think that Web would put off their marriage indefinitely. A month or two she could live with. And he did have a point; the only purpose of rushing to get married in three days would be to spite her parents. "In a month or two they'll still be resisting," she warned, but less caustically.

"True, but at least we'll know that we've given them every possible chance. If we've done our best, and still they refuse to open up their minds, we'll have nothing to regret in the future." He raised her hand to his lips and gently kissed her palm. "I want it to be as perfect as it can be, sweetheart. Everything open and aboveboard. We owe that to ourselves, don't you think?"

9

DURING THE DAY following the scene with Marni's parents, Web convinced himself that he'd been right in what he'd said to Marni. Deep in his heart he suspected that her parents would never accept their marriage, and he regretted it only in terms of Marni's happiness. He had cause to think of his own, though, when he received a call from a friend on Tuesday morning.

Cole Hammond wrote for New York's most notorious gossip sheet parading as a newspaper. The two men had met in a social context soon after Web had arrived in New York, and though Web had no love for Cole's publication, he'd come to respect the man himself. When Cole asked if he could meet with Web to discuss something important, Web promptly invited him over.

"I received an anonymous call today," Cole began soon after Web had tossed him a can of beer. They were in Web's living room. The studio was still being cleaned up from the morning's shoot. "It was from a woman. She claimed that she had a sensational story about you. Something to do with an accident in Maine fourteen years ago?"

Web had had an odd premonition from the moment he'd heard Cole's voice on the phone, which was the main reason he'd had him come right over. "Yes," he agreed warily. "There was an accident."

"This woman said that you were responsible for a man's death. Any truth to it?"

Curbing his anger against "this woman" and her allegations, Web looked his friend in the eye. "No."

"She gave me dates and facts. It was a rainy night, very late, and you were speeding along on a motorcycle with a fellow named Ethan Lange on the back."

"Not speeding. But go on."

"You skidded and collided with a car. Lange was thrown and killed."

"...Is that it?"

"She said you'd been drinking that night and that you had no business being on the road."

"What else?"

Cole shrugged. "That's it. I thought I'd run it by you before I did anything more with it."

"I'm glad you have, for your sake more than mine." Web's entire body was rigid with barely leashed fury. "If you're hoping to get a story out of this, I'd think twice. In the first place, she had the facts wrong. In the second place, the police report will bear that out. And in the third place, if you print something like this, you'll have a hefty lawsuit on your hands. I will not stand by and let you—"

"Hold on, pal," Cole interrupted gently, raising a hand, palm out. "I'd never print a thing without getting the facts straight, which is why I'm here. I know you don't trust the paper, but this is *me*. We've talked about situations like this many times. If the facts don't merit a story, there won't *be* a story." He sat back. "So. Why don't you tell me what happened that night?"

Web took a deep breath and forced himself to calm down. Very slowly and distinctly, he outlined the facts of the accident. By the time he was done, he was back on the edge of fury. "You're being used, Cole. I don't know who the caller was, but I've got a damned good idea.... Is this off the record now, just between us?"

"We're friends. Of course it is."

Web trusted him. He also knew that nothing he was about to say wouldn't come out eventually, and that if Cole chose to print it, friend or no, Web would have even greater grounds for a lawsuit. He knew that Cole knew it, too.

"I'm engaged to marry Marni Lange. It was her brother who died that night. Her parents have always blamed me for the accident, regardless of the facts or the police report. Needless to say, they're totally against our marriage. I suspect that it was her sister who called you, and that her major purpose was vengeance."

Cole ingested the possibility thoughtfully. "It's not a unique motive."

"You should be livid."

The other shrugged. "One out of four may be done for vengeance, but even then there's often a story that will sell."

"Well, there isn't one here. It's history. It may be tragic, but it's not spectacular. Hey, go ahead and check out my story. Get that police report. You can even interview the drivers of the other two cars. They were the first ones to say that there wasn't anything I could have done, that both of them had passed me on the road right before the accident, and that I wasn't weaving around or driving recklessly. The bartender at the tavern we'd been to said we'd been stone sober when we'd left. The first car skidded. The second one collided with it and started spinning. I braked, but the road was wet. I might even have been able to steer clear if one of those cars hadn't careened into me." He took a quick breath, then sagged. "It's all there in black and white. An old story. Not worth fiddling with."

"If you were a nobody, I'd agree with you." When Web bolted forward, he held up his hand again. "Listen, what you say makes sense. I'm just doing my job."

"Your job sucks. This isn't *news*, for God's sake!"

"I agree."

"Do you trust me?"

"I always have."

"Do you believe that what I've told you is the truth?"

Cole paused. "Yes, I believe you."

"Then...you'll forget you got that call?"

Another pause, then a nod. "I will." And a sly grin. "But will you?"

"Not on your life! Someone's going to answer for it!"

"Watch what you do," Cole teased. "You may give me a story yet. Though come to think of it, you've got my news editor wrapped around your little finger. I'm not sure she could bear to print anything adverse about you."

Web's answering grin was thin and dry. "If it'd sell, she'd do it.... Give her a kiss for me, will you?"

"My pleasure."

MARNI'S GUESS AS TO WHO the caller had been matched Web's, and her anger was as volatile as his had initially been. Fortunately he'd had time to calm down.

"Tanya! That bitch! How could she *dare* try to pull something like this?"

Web put his arm around her and spoke gently. "Maybe she's trying to score points with your parents."

"She's starting at zero, so it won't get her very far," Marni scoffed, then her voice rose. "Maybe my parents put her up to it!"

"Nah. I don't think so, and you shouldn't either, sweetheart. They wouldn't sink that low, would they? I mean, voicing their disapproval to us is one thing, dirty tricks another. And besides, if the whole story came out, particularly the part about our relationship, they'd be as embarrassed as anyone. They wouldn't knowingly hurt themselves."

"I'm not sure 'knowingly' has anything to do with it. They seem to be incapable of rational thought. That's the problem." She pulled away from Web and reached for the phone. "I'm calling Tanya."

His hand settled over hers, preventing further movement. "No. Don't do it."

"She may contact another paper. For that matter, how do we know she hasn't already?"

"Because Cole's is the sleaziest. It's the only one that would have considered touching the story. I'm sure she knew that."

Marni marveled at Web's composure. "Aren't you angry?"

"This morning I would have willingly rung Tanya's neck if I'd seen her. But that wouldn't accomplish anything. It's over, Marni. Cole won't write any story, and confronting Tanya will only make her more determined to do something else."

"What else could she do?" Marni asked with a hysterical laugh.

As IT HAPPENED, it wasn't Tanya, but Marni's father who had something else in mind. The first Marni got wind of it was in a phone call she received on Wednesday afternoon from one of the corporation's directors. He was an old family friend, which eased Marni's indignation somewhat when he suggested that her father was disturbed about her relationship with Brian Webster, and that he hoped she wasn't making a mistake. She calmly assured him that she wasn't, and that no possible harm could come to the corporation from her marriage to Web.

The second call, though, wasn't as excusable. It came on Thursday morning and was from another of the directors. This one was not a family friend and therefore, theoretically, had no cause to question her private life. Livid, she hung up the phone after talking with him, then stewed at her desk for a time, trying to decide on the best course of action. Indeed, action was called for. If her father was planning to undermine her authority by individually calling each member of the board, she wasn't about to take it sitting down.

She promptly instructed her administrative assistant to summon the board members for a meeting the following morning.

"Your father, too?" Web asked incredulously when she called him to tell him what had happened.

"Yes, my father, too. You were right. Everything should be open and aboveboard. He can hear what I'm going to say along with everyone else."

"What *are* you going to say?"

Her voice dropped for the first time. "I'm not sure." With the next breath, her belligerency resurfaced. "But I'm taking the offensive. Dad's obviously been planting seeds of doubt about me. The only thing I can do is nip it in the bud." She paused, knowing that for all the conviction she might project, she'd called Web because she desperately needed his support.

He didn't let her down. "I agree, sweetheart. I think you've made the right decision. One thing I've learned from talking with you about the corporation is that you haven't gotten where you are by sitting back and waiting for things to happen. You're doing the right thing, Marni. I know it."

She sighed. "I hope so. If Dad has an argument with what I say, he can voice it before the board. Maybe *they* can talk some sense into him."

"Will they?" Web asked very softly. "Will they stand up for you instead of him? How strong is his hold over them?"

"I'll know soon enough, won't I?" she asked sadly.

MARNI STAYED LATE at the office, working with her administrative assistant and secretary to gather, copy and assemble for distribution an armada of facts, figures and reports.

She spent the night with Web at his place, but a pall hung over them, one they couldn't begin to shake. They both sensed that the outcome of Marni's meeting would be telling in terms of her future with the corporation. While on the one hand it was absurd to think that she'd be ousted simply because she married Web, on the other hand neither of them had dreamed Jonathan Lange would do what he already had.

"And if it happens, sweetheart?" Web asked. They were lying quietly curled against each other in bed. Sleep eluded them completely. "What if they side with your father? What will you do then?"

She'd thought about that. "My choice has been made, Web. I told you that. I love you. Our future together is the most important thing to me."

"But you love your work—"

"And I have no intention of giving it up. If the board goes against me, I'll submit my resignation and look for another position. Corporate executives often jump around. We keep the headhunters in business."

"Would you be happy anywhere else but at Lange?"

She smiled up at him, very sure about what she was going to say. "If it meant that I could have both you and my own peace of mind, I'd be happy. Yes, I'd be happy."

AT TEN O'CLOCK the following morning, Marni entered the boardroom. She'd chosen to wear a sedate white wool suit with a navy blouse and accessories. Her hair was perfect, as was her makeup. She knew that no one in the room could fault her appearance. She represented Lange well.

Twelve of the fourteen members of the board were present, talking quietly among themselves until she took her seat at one end of the long table. Her father was at the other. He stood stiffly, and the room was suddenly quiet.

"I will formally call this meeting to order, but since my daughter was the one who organized it, and since I am myself in the dark as to its purpose, I will turn it over to her."

Ignoring both his glower and his very obvious impatience, Marni stood. She rested her hands lightly on the alternating stacks of papers that had been set there for her by her assistant. "Thank you all for coming," she said with quiet confidence, looking from one face to the next, making eye contact wherever possible. "I appreciate the fact that many of you have had to cancel other appointments on such short notice, but I felt the urgency was called for." Pausing, she lifted the first pile of papers from the stack, divided it and sent one half down each side of the table. "Please help yourselves. These are advance copies of our latest production figures, division by division, subsidiary by subsidiary. I don't expect you to read through them now, but I think when you do you'll see that the last quarter was the most productive one Lange has had to date. We're growing, ladies and gentlemen, and we're healthy."

She went to the next pile of papers and passed them around in like fashion. "These are proposals for projects we hope to launch within the next few months. Again, read them at your leisure. I believe that you'll find them exciting, and that you'll see the potential profit in each." She waited until the last of the papers had been distributed, using the time to bolster herself for the tougher part to come. When she had the attention of all those present once more, she went on quietly.

"It is important to me that the board knows of everything that is happening at Lange, and since I'm its president, and as such more visible than our other employees, I want you to be informed and up-to-date on what is happening to me personally." As she spoke her gaze skipped from one member to the next, though she studiously avoided her father's face. He would either intimidate or infuriate her, she feared, and in any case would jeopardize her composure.

"At some point within the next two months, I'll be getting married. My fiancé's name is Brian Webster. Perhaps some of you have heard of him. If not, you'll read about him in the papers I've given you. He's been chosen as the cover photographer for *Class*, the new magazine our publishing division will be putting out. Let me say now that, although Mr. Webster and I knew each other many years ago, the decision to hire him was made first and foremost by the publishing division. At the time I didn't realize that the man I knew so long ago was the same photographer New York has gone wild for. We met, and I realized who he was only after the contracts had been signed and he'd begun to work for us."

There were several nods of understanding from various members of the group, so she went on. "The fact of my marriage will in no way interfere with the quality of work I do for Lange. I believe you all know of my dedication to the corporation. Mr. Webster certainly knows of it. My father built this business from scratch, and I take great pride in seeing that it grows and prospers." She dared a glance at her father then. He was sitting straight, his eyes hard, his lips compressed into a thin line. She quickly averted her gaze to more sympathetic members of the group.

"You may be asking yourself why I felt it so important to call you here simply to tell you of my engagement. I did it because I wanted to assure you that I intend to continue as president of Lange. But there was another reason as well. There is," she said slowly, "a very important matter concerning Brian Webster and my family that some of you may already know about, but which I wanted all of you to hear about first hand. There is apt to be speculation, and perhaps some ill will, but I'm counting on you all to keep that in perspective."

She lifted her hand from the last pile of papers and sent them around the table. "Fourteen years ago Brian Webster and my brother Ethan were good friends. Brian was the one driving the motorcycle on the night Ethan was killed."

Barely a murmur surfaced among those present, which more than anything told Marni that her father had been busier than she'd thought. The knowledge made her all the more determined to thwart his efforts to discredit both her and Web.

"What you have before you are copies of the police report from that night. You'll learn that Mr. Webster was found entirely without fault in the accident. I've also included excerpts from articles about Brian and his work. They were gathered by the publishing division when it cast its vote for him as the *Class* photographer. I don't think any of us can fault either his qualifications or his character."

She took a deep breath and squared her shoulders. "There are some who will claim that Brian was responsible for Ethan's death, and that I am therefore acting irresponsibly by thinking of marrying him. Once you've read what I've given you, I feel confident that you'll agree with me that this is not the case. In no way could Brian Webster embarrass this corporation, or me, and in no way could he adversely affect the job I plan to do as your continuing president."

She looked down, moistened her lips, then raised her chin high. "Are there any questions I might answer? If any of you have doubts as to my moral standing, I'd appreciate your airing them now." Her gaze passed from one director to another. There were shrugs, several headshakes, several frighteningly bland expressions. And then there was her father.

With both hands on the edge of the table, he pushed himself to his feet. "I have questions, and doubts, but you've already heard them."

"That's right. I have. I'd like to know if any of the other members of the board share your opinion. If a majority of the others agree with you, I'll submit my resignation as of now and seek a position elsewhere."

That statement did cause a minor stir, but it consisted of gasps and grunts, the swiveling of heads and a shifting in seats, so that in the end Marni wasn't sure whether the group was in her favor or against. Her gaze encompassed all those who would sit in judgment on her.

"I truly believe that what we have here is a difference of opinion between my father and myself." She purposely didn't include mention of her mother or Tanya. "It should have remained private, and would have, had it not been for calls that were made to several of you that I know of, perhaps all of you—which is why I've asked you here today. It's not your place to decide who I should or shouldn't marry, but since it is in your power to decide whether or not I remain as president of this corporation, I felt that my interests, and Brian's, should be represented.

"As it is, someone tried to plant a story in one of the local papers." She was staring at her father then and was oblivious to the other eyes that widened in dismay. "It would have been a scandal based on nothing but sleazy headlines. Fortunately, Brian is well enough respected in this community that the writer who received the anonymous tip very quickly dismissed it as soon as he heard the truth. Now—" her eyes circled the room again "—do any of you have questions I can answer before I leave?"

Emma Landry spoke up, smiling. "When's the wedding?"

Marni smiled in return. She knew she had one ally. "We haven't set the date yet."

"Will we all be invited?" asked Geoffrey Gould.

"Every one of you," she said, seeking out her father's gaze and holding it for a minute before returning her attention to the group. There were several stern faces among them, several more meek. All she could do was to pray she'd presented her case well.

"If there are no further questions," she said, taking a breath, "I'll leave you to vote on whether I'll be staying on as president. If you say 'yes,' I'll take it as a vote of confidence in what I've done at Lange during the past seven years. If you say 'no,' I'll accept it with regret and move on." Her voice lowered and was for the first time less steady as she looked at her father a final time. "I'll be at my mother's awaiting your decision."

That, too, had been a studied decision. Marni had felt that it would be a show, albeit false, of some support from her family. But she did want to tell Adele what she'd done. If she failed with this group, her mother would witness firsthand her pain. If she succeeded, it would be a perfect opportunity to try to swing Adele to her way of thinking.

Marni had no idea that Web was a full step ahead of her.

"I APPRECIATE your seeing me, Mrs. Lange," Web said after he was shown into the solarium at the back of the house. "I would have called beforehand, but I didn't want to be turned down on the phone. I know that your husband is in the city at a meeting of the board of directors."

"That's right," Adele said quietly. She was sitting in a high-backed wicker chair, with her elbows on its broad arms and her hands resting in her lap.

"You're probably wondering why I'm here, and, to tell you the truth—" he rubbed the tense muscles at the back of his neck "—part of me is, too. It was obvious at our last meeting that you agree with your husband in your opinion of me, and I'm not sure I could change it if I wanted to." He sighed and sat forward, propping his elbows on his thighs. He studied his hands, which hung between his knees, then frowned.

"Perhaps this is a sexist thing to say, but I thought I might appeal to your softer side. All women have a softer side. I know Marni does. Right about now it's not showing, because she's addressing the board of directors, and I'm sure she's making as businesslike a pitch as she can for their under- standing. But the softer side's there, not very far from the surface. Marni loves me. She's aching because she loves you both, too, and it hurts her that she's had to make a choice between us."

"She chose you," Adele stated evenly. "I'd think you would be pleased."

He looked up. "Pleased, yes. I'm pleased, and relieved, because I don't think I could make it through a future without her. But I don't feel a sense of victory, if that's what you're suggesting. There's no victory when a fam- ily is torn apart, particularly one that has already suffered its share of loss."

Adele arched a brow. "Do *you* know about loss, Mr. Webster?"

"No. At least, not as you know it. One can't lose things one has never had. I never had a father. Did you know that?"

"No. No, I didn't."

"There's a lot you don't know about me. I'd like to tell you, if I may."

Adele paused, then nodded. Though she maintained an outer sem- blance of arrogance, there was a hint of curiosity in her eyes. Web wasn't about to pass that up.

"I never knew my father. He and my mother didn't marry. When I was two my mother married another man, a good man, a hard worker. I'm afraid I didn't make things terribly easy for him. For reasons I didn't un- derstand at the time, I was restless. I hated school, but I loved to learn. I spent my nights reading everything I could get my hands on, but during the days I felt compelled to move around. Instead of going to college, I took odd jobs where I could find them. I traveled the world, literally, work- ing my way from one place to the next.

"Then I met Ethan. We shared a mutual respect. Through him, I realized I had to settle down, that I wouldn't get anywhere if I didn't focus in on one thing and try to be good at it. I was a jack of all trades, master of none. And I was tired of it."

He gazed at his thumbnail, pressed it with his other thumb. "Maybe I'd simply reached an age where it was time to grow up. After Ethan died, I did a lot of thinking. There were many unresolved feelings I had, about my father and about myself. I don't know who my father is, so those feelings will remain unresolved to a point. But fourteen years ago I realized that I couldn't let them affect my life, that I didn't really need to be running around to escape that lack of identity. That if I stayed in one place and built a life, a reputation for myself, I could make up for it."

He raised his eyes to Adele's intent ones and wondered if she realized the extent of her involvement with his story. "I think I have. But there's more I want, and it involves Marni." He sat up in the chair. "I adore that woman, Mrs. Lange. You have no idea how much. I want to marry her, and we want children."

"You've already told us that," Adele pointed out, but the edge was gone from her voice.

"Yes, but I'm not sure if you realize how much Marni wants our family to encompass you and your husband. Do you want her to be happy, Mrs. Lange?"

"Of course. I'm her mother. What mother wouldn't want that for her daughter?"

"I don't know," he said slowly. "That's what I'm trying to understand."

"Are you accusing me of being blind to what Marni needs, when she sat here herself last Sunday night and announced that she'd go ahead with her plans regardless of what we said or did?"

He kept his tone gentle. "I'm not accusing you of anything. What I'm suggesting is that maybe you don't fully understand Marni's needs. I'm not sure I did myself until I heard what she said to you the other night. She badly wants your approval. You're right, she and I will go ahead and get married even if you continue to hold out. We'll have our home and our children, and we'll be happy. But there will always be a tiny part of Marni that will feel the loss of her parents, and it will be such a premature and unnecessary loss that it will be all the sadder." He paused. "How will *you* feel about such a loss? You lost your son through a tragedy none of us could control. This one would be a tragedy of your own making."

"Ethan would have been alive if it hadn't been—"

"Do you honestly believe that? *Honestly?* Am I a killer, Mrs. Lange? Look at me and tell me if you think I am truly a killer."

Scowling, she shifted in her seat. "Well, not in the sense of a hardened criminal..."

"Not in any sense. I think in your heart you agree. Otherwise you never would have let me talk with you today."

"My husband's out. That's why I'm talking with you today."

"Then he's the one who dictates your opinion?"

"We've been married for nearly forty years, Mr. Webster. I respect what my husband feels strongly about."

"Even when he's wrong?"

"I...I owe him my loyalty."

"But what about the loyalty you owe your children? You had a choice when it came to picking your husband. Your children had no choice about being born. You gave them life and brought them into this world. They had no say in the matter. Marni didn't *choose* you to be her mother, any more than she chose to be Ethan's sister. And she didn't choose to have him killed in that accident, yet she's spent the past fourteen years trying to make up to you for it. Don't you owe her some kind of loyalty for that?"

"Now you're asking me to make a choice between my daughter and my husband."

"No. I'm simply asking you to decide for yourself whether Marni's marrying me would be so terrible, and if you decide that it wouldn't be, that you try to convince your husband of it. We're not asking for an open-armed welcome. We'll very happily settle for peaceful coexistence. You don't have to love me, Mrs. Lange, but if you love your daughter you'll respect the fact that *she* loves me."

"Web!"

Both heads in the room riveted toward its door, where Marni was standing in a state of utter confusion. Web came instantly to his feet.

"What are you doing here?" she asked, her brows knitting as she looked from him to her mother and back.

"We were just talking." He approached her quickly, ran his hands along her arms and spoke very softly. "How did it go?"

"I don't know. I left before they took a vote. Then I needed a little time to myself, so I took the roundabout way getting here." Apprehension was written all over her face. "There's been no word?"

Web hesitated, then shook his head.

Adele frowned. "A vote? What vote?"

"As to whether I should remain as president. I tendered my resignation, pending the board's decision."

Adele, too, was on her feet then. "You didn't! What a foolish thing to do, Marni! You've been a fine president! You can't be replaced!"

"Oh, I can. No one's indispensable."

"But we always intended that the presidency should remain in the family!"

"Maybe Tanya should give it a try," Marni suggested dryly, only to be answered by an atypical and distinctly unladylike snort from her mother.

"Tanya! That's quite amusing." Her head shot up. "Jonathan! When did *you* get here?"

Web had seen the man approach, but Marni, with her back to the door, had had no such warning. Turning abruptly, her heart in her throat, she faced the tired and stern face of her father.

AT ONE TIME Marni might have run to Jonathan Lange. Too much had passed between them in recent days, though, and she grew rigid as he approached. Web dropped his hands to his sides but stayed close, offering his silent support as they both waited to hear what her father had to say.

The older man ran a hand through his thinning gray hair, then glanced at his wife. "I could use a drink."

"Duncan? Duncan!" Adele's voice rang out, and the butler promptly appeared. "Mr. Lange will have his usual. I'll have mine with water." She turned to Marni and Web, her brows raised. When they both shook their heads, she nodded to Duncan. "That will be all."

Jonathan walked past them, deeper into the solarium. He stopped before one glass expanse, thrust his hands in his pockets and, stiff-backed, stood with his feet apart as he gazed at the late March landscape.

Marni stared after him. She knew he had news, but whether it was good or bad she had no idea. In that instant she realized how very much she did want to stay on as president of Lange.

Adele looked from Marni to her husband, then back.

Web, standing close behind Marni, put his hands lightly at her waist. "Do you want to sit down?" he asked softly.

She shook her head, but her eyes didn't leave her father's rigid back. "Dad? What happened?"

Jonathan didn't answer immediately. He raised a hand and scratched his neck, then returned the hand to his pocket. Duncan entered the solarium, offered Adele her drink from a small silver tray, then crossed the room to offer Jonathan his. Only when the butler had left did Jonathan turn. He held the drink in both hands, watching his thumbs as they brushed against the condensation beginning to form on the side of the glass.

"I didn't know she'd done that, Marni," he began solemnly. "I had no idea Tanya had called that reporter—"

"What reporter?" Adele interrupted fearfully. "What has Tanya done?"

There was sadness, almost defeat in the expression Jonathan turned on his wife. "Tanya tried to plant a story in the newspaper about the accident and Webster's role in it."

Adele clutched her glass to her chest. "Tanya did *that?*"

Jonathan's gaze met Marni's. "I have no proof that it was Tanya, but no one else would have had cause except perhaps your mother and I. But I never would have condoned something like that. I'll have a thing or two to say to your sister when I call her later."

Marni couldn't move. Her heart was pounding as she waited, waited. "It's not important. What happened at the meeting? Was a vote taken?"

He took a drink. The ice rattled as he lowered his glass. "Yes."

"And...?"

Jonathan studied the ice, but it was Marni who felt its chill. "You'll be staying on as president of Lange. There was an easy majority in your favor."

Marni closed her eyes in a moment's prayerful thanks. Web's hands tightened on her waist when she swayed. It was his support, and the warmth of his body reaching out to her, that gave her the strength to open her eyes and address her father again.

"And you, Dad? How did you vote?"

Jonathan cleared his throat. "I exercised my right to abstain."

It was better than a flat-out "no," but it left major questions unanswered. "May I ask why?"

He tipped his head fractionally in a gesture of acquiescence. "I felt that I was too emotionally involved to make a rational decision."

"Then you do question my ability as president?"

He cleared his throat again. As before, it brought him an extra few seconds to formulate his response. "No. I simply question my own ability to see the truth one way or the other."

Such a simple statement, Marni mused, yet it was a powerful concession. Up to that point, Jonathan had refused to see anything but what he wanted to see. The fact that he could admit his view might be jaded was a major victory.

Web felt the release of tension in Marni's body. He, too, had immediately understood the significance of Jonathan's statement, and he shared her relief and that small sense of triumph, even hope. Lowering his head, he murmured, "Perhaps we should leave your parents alone now. I think both you and your father have been through enough today."

She knew he was right. It was a matter of quitting while she was ahead. If she stayed and forced her father to say more, she might well push him into a corner. He was a proud man. For the present it was enough to leave with the hope that one day he might actually join her in *her* corner.

Mutely she nodded. Under Web's guiding hand, she left the solarium and walked back through the house to the front door. Only when she reached it did she realize that her mother had come along.

"Darling..." Adele began. Her hand clutched the doorknob, and she seemed unsure of herself. Marni had turned, surprised and slightly wary. "I...I'm pleased things worked out for you with the board."

"So am I," Marni answered quietly. "I never really wanted to leave Lange."

Adele's voice was a whisper. "I know that." She gave an awkward smile, reached up as if to stroke Marni's hair, but drew her hand back short of physical contact. "Perhaps...perhaps we can get together for lunch one day next week?"

Marni wasn't about to look a gift horse in the mouth. She was pleased, and touched. "I'd like that, Mom. Will you call?"

Adele nodded, her eyes suspiciously moist. She did touch Marni then, wrapping an arm around her waist and pressing a cheek to hers in a quick hug. "You'd better leave now," she whispered. "Drive safely."

Marni, too, felt the emotion of the moment. She nodded and smiled through her own mist of tears, then let Web guide her out the door and down the front steps to their cars.

"I DON'T BELIEVE THESE!" Marni exclaimed in delight. She was sitting cross-legged on Web's bed, wearing nothing but the stack of photographs he'd so nonchalantly tossed into her lap moments before. "They're incredible!"

He came to sit behind her, fitting his larger body to hers so that he could look over her shoulder at the pictures he'd taken three days before. "They're *you*. Exactly what I wanted for the premier cover of *Class*."

Astonished, Marni flipped from one shot to the next. "They're all so good, Web! How are you ever going to decide which one to use? For that matter, how did you ever get so many perfect ones?"

He nipped at her bare shoulder, then soothed the spot with his chin. "I had a super model. That's all there is to it. As for which one to use, I've got my personal preference, but your people will have some say in that." He curled one long arm around hers and extracted a print from the pile. "I sent a duplicate of this one to your parents yesterday."

She met his gaze at her shoulder. "You didn't."

"I did. It's beautiful, don't you think? Every parent should have a picture like this of his daughter."

"But...isn't that a little heavy-handed? I mean, Mom and I have just begun to talk things through." Two weeks had passed since the board meeting, and she'd met with her mother as many times during that stretch.

"You said yourself that she's softening up. And if anything will speed up the process, this will. Look at it, Marni. Look at your expression here. It's so...*you*. The determined set of chin, the little bit of mischief at the mouth, the tilt of the eyebrows with just a hint of indignation, and the eyes, ah, the eyes..."

"Filled with love," she whispered, but she wasn't looking at the picture. Her own eyes were reflected in Web's, and the love flowing between them was awesome.

Web caught his breath, then haphazardly scattered the pictures from Marni's lap and turned her so she was straddling his legs. His fingers delved into her hair, and he held her face steady. "I love you, sunshine. Ohhh, do I love you." When she smiled, he ran his tongue over the curve. Then he caught her lower lip between his own lips and sipped at it.

Marni was floating wild and free, with Web as her anchor, the only one she'd ever truly need. She slipped her arms around his neck and tangled her fingers in the hair at his nape, fighting for his lips, then his tongue, then the very air he breathed.

"Where did you ever...get that passion?" he gasped. His hands had begun a questing journey over the planes and swells of her soft body.

"From you, my dear man," she breathed, greedily bunching her fingers over the twisting muscles of his back. "You taught me...fourteen years ago...and I haven't been the same since...ahhh, Web..." He'd found her breasts and was taunting them mercilessly. "Will it always...be this way?"

"Always." He rolled her nipples between his thumb and forefinger and was rewarded by her gasp.

"Promise?" She spread her hand over his flat middle and let it follow the tapering line of dark hair to that point where it flared.

"Sunshine...mmmmmmm...ah, yesss..." What little thought her artful stroking left him was centered in his fingers, which found the tiny nub of pleasure between her legs and began to caress it as artfully. "Ahhhh, sweet...so moist, soft..."

They were both breathing shallowly, and Marni's body had begun to quiver in tune with his.

"C'mere," he ordered. Cupping her bottom, he drew her forward, capturing her mouth and swallowing her rapturous moan as he entered her.

Knees braced on either side of his hips, she moved in rhythm with him. Her breasts rubbed against his with each forward surge, and their mouths mated hungrily. They rose together on passion's ladder, reaching the very highest rung before Web held her back.

"Watch," he whispered. He lowered his gaze to the point of their joining, then, when her head too was bowed, he slowly withdrew, as slowly filled her again, then repeated the movement.

It was too much for Marni. She cried his name once, then threw back her head and closed her eyes tight upon the waves of pulsing sensation that poured through her.

Web held himself buried deep inside her, hoping to savor each one of her spasms, but their very strength was his undoing. Without so much as another thrust, he gave a throaty moan and exploded. Arms trembling, he clutched her tightly to him. She was his anchor in far more than the storm of passion. He could only thank God that she was his.

ON A BRIGHT, SUNNY MORNING in early June, Marni and Web were married. The ceremony was held beneath the trees in the backyard of the Langes' Long Island estate and was followed by a lavish lawn luncheon for the two hundred invited guests.

Marni's mother was radiant, exuding the air of confidence that was her social trademark. Marni's father was gracious, if stoical, accepting congratulations with the formality that was his professional trademark.

Marni was in seventh heaven. Her mother had been the one to insist that the wedding be held there, and she'd personally orchestrated every step of the affair. While her father hadn't once vocally blessed the marriage, Marni had seen the tears in his eyes in those poignant moments when he'd led her down the rose-strewn aisle and to the altar, then given her away. She'd whispered a soft "I love you" to him as she'd kissed him, but after that her eyes had been only for Web.

"I now pronounce you man and wife," the minister had said, and she'd gone into Web's arms with a sense of joy, of fulfillment and promise that had once only been a dream.

In the years to come, they'd have their home, their careers and their children. Most important, though, they'd have each other. Their ties went back to when they'd both been young. They'd weathered personal storms along the way, but they'd emerged as better people, and their love was supreme.

Granite Man

One

Forcing herself to let out the breath she had been holding, Mariah MacKenzie fumbled with the brass door knocker, failed to hang on to it, and curled her trembling fingers into a fist.

Fifteen years is a long time. I should have telephoned. What if my brother doesn't remember me? What if he throws me off the ranch? Where will I go then?

Using her knuckles, Mariah rapped lightly on the door frame of the ranch house. The sound echoed like thunder, but there was no response. She lifted her hand again. This time she managed to hold on to the horseshoe-shaped knocker long enough to deliver several staccato raps.

"Keep your shirt on! I'm coming!"

The voice was deep, impatient, unmistakably masculine. Mariah's heartbeat doubled even as she nervously took a backward step away from the door. A few instants later she was glad she had retreated.

The man who appeared filled the doorway. Literally. Mariah started to say her brother's name, only to find that her mouth was too dry to speak. She retreated again, unable to think, unable to breathe.

Cash McQueen frowned as he stared down at the slender girl who was backing away from him so quickly he was afraid she would fall off the porch. That would be a pity. It had been years since he had seen such an appealing female. Long legs, elegant breasts, big golden eyes, tousled hair that was the color of bittersweet chocolate, and an aura of vulnerability that slid past his hard-earned defenses.

"Can I help you?" Cash asked, trying to soften the edges of his deep voice. There was nothing he could do to gentle the rest of his appearance. He was big and he was strong and no amount of smiling could change those facts. Women usually didn't mind, but this one looked on the edge of bolting.

"My car b-boiled," Mariah said, the only thing she could think of.

"The whole thing?"

Cash's gentle voice and wry question drew a hesitant smile from Mariah. She stopped inching backward and shook her head. "Just the part that held water."

A smile changed Cash's face from forbidding to handsome. He walked out of the house and onto the front porch. Clenching her hands together, Mariah looked up at the big man who must be her brother. He had unruly, thick hair that was a gleaming chestnut brown where it wasn't streaked pale gold by the sun. He was muscular rather than soft. He looked like a man who was accustomed to using his body for hard physical work. His eyebrows were wickedly arched, darker than his hair, and his eyes were—

"The wrong color."

"I beg your pardon?" Cash asked, frowning.

Mariah flushed, realizing that she had spoken aloud.

"I'm—that is—I thought this was the Rocking M," she managed to stammer.

"It is."

All other emotions gave way to dismay as Mariah understood that the unthinkable had happened: the MacKenzie ranch had been sold to strangers.

Of the many possibilities she had imagined, this had not been among them. All her plans for coming back to the lost home of her dreams, all her half-formed hopes of pursuing a lost mine over the landscape of her ancestors, all her anticipation of being reunited with the older brother whose love had been the bright core of her childhood; all that was gone. And there was nothing to take its place except a new understanding of just how alone she was.

"Are you all right?" Cash asked, concerned by her sudden pallor, wanting to fold her into his arms and give her comfort.

Comfort? he asked himself sardonically. *Well, that too, I suppose. God, but that is one sexy woman looking like she is about to faint at my feet.*

A big, callused hand closed around Mariah's upper arm, both steadying her and making her tremble. She looked up—way up—into eyes that were a dark, smoky blue, yet as clear as a mountain lake in twilight. And, like a lake, the luminous surface concealed depths of shadow.

"Sit down, honey. You look a little pale around the edges," Cash said, urging her toward the old-fashioned porch swing. He seated her with a restrained strength that allowed no opposition. "I'll get you some water. Unless you'd like something with more kick?"

"No. I'm fine," Mariah said, but she made no move to stand up again. Her legs wouldn't have cooperated. Without thinking, she wrapped her fingers around a powerful, hairy wrist. "Did Luke MacKenzie—did the former owner leave a forwarding address?"

"Last time I checked, Luke was still the owner of the Rocking M, along with Tennessee Blackthorn."

Relief swept through Mariah. She smiled with blinding brilliance. "Are you Mr. Blackthorn?"

"No, I'm Cash McQueen," he said, smiling in return, wondering what she would do if he sat next to her and pulled her into his lap. "Sure you don't want some water or brandy?"

"I don't understand. Do you work here?"

"No. I'm visiting my sister, Luke's wife."

"Luke is married?"

Until Cash's eyes narrowed, Mariah didn't realize how dismayed she sounded. He looked at her with cool speculation in his eyes, a coolness that made her realize just how warm he had been before.

"Is Luke's marriage some kind of problem for you?" Cash asked.

Dark blue eyes watched Mariah with a curiosity that was suddenly more predatory than sensual. She knew beyond a doubt that any threat to his sister's marriage would be taken head-on by the big man who was watching her the way a hawk watched a careless field mouse.

"No problem," Mariah said faintly, fighting the tears that came from nowhere to strangle her voice. She felt her uncertain self-control fragmenting and was too tired to care. "I should have guessed he would be married by now."

"Who are you?"

The question was as blunt as the rock hammer hanging from a loop on Cash's wide leather belt. The cold steel tool looked softer than his narrowed eyes. The almost overwhelming sense of being close to hard, barely restrained masculinity increased the more Mariah looked at Cash—wide, muscular shoulders, flat waist, lean hips, long legs whose power was hinted at with each supple shift of his weight. Cash was violently male, yet his hand on her arm had been gentle. Keeping that in mind, she tried to smile up at him as she explained why she was no threat to his sister's marriage.

"I'm Mariah MacKenzie. Luke's sister." Still trying to smile, Mariah held out her hand as she said, "Pleased to meet you, Mr. McQueen."

"Cash." The answer was automatic, as was his taking of Mariah's hand. "You're Luke's *sister*?"

Even as Cash asked the question, his senses registered the soft, cool

skin of Mariah's hand, the silken smoothness of her wrist when his grip
shifted, and the racing of her pulse beneath his fingertips. Hardly able
to believe what he had heard, he looked again into Mariah's eyes. Only
then did he realize that he had been so struck by her sexual appeal that
he had overlooked her resemblance to Luke. He, too, had tawny topaz
eyes and hair so brown it was almost black.

But Mariah's resemblance to her brother ended there. All five feet,
eight inches of her was very definitely female. Beneath the worn jeans
and faded college T-shirt were the kinds of curves that made a man's
hands feel both empty and hungry to be filled. Cash remembered the
smooth resilience of her arm when he had steadied her, and then he
remembered the warmth beneath the soft skin.

"What in hell brings you back to the Rocking M after all these
years?"

There was no way for Mariah to explain to Cash her inchoate longings
for a lost home, a lost family, a lost childhood. Each time she opened
her mouth to try, no words came.

"I just wanted to—to see my brother," she said finally.

Cash glanced at his wrist. His new black metal watch told the time
around the globe, was guaranteed to work up to a hundred and eighty
feet underwater and in temperatures down to forty below zero. It was
his third such watch in less than a year. So far, it was still telling time.
But then, he hadn't been out prospecting yet. The repeated shock of rock
hammer or pickax on granite had done in the other watches. That, and
panning for gold in the Rocking M's icy mountain creeks.

"Luke won't be in from the north range until dinner, and probably
not even then," Cash said. "Carla is in Cortez shopping with Logan.
They aren't due back until late tomorrow, which means that unless the
Blackthorns get in early from Boulder, there won't be anyone to cook
dinner except me. That's why I don't expect Luke back. Neither one of
us would walk across a room to eat the other's cooking."

Mariah tried to sort out the spate of names and information, but had
little success. In the end she hung on to the only words that mattered:
Luke wouldn't be back for several hours. After waiting and hoping and
dreaming for so many years, the hours she had left to wait seemed like
an eternity. She was tired, discouraged and so sad that it was all she
could do not to put her head on Cash's strong shoulder and cry. Her
feelings were irrational, but then so was her whole hopeful journey back
to the landscape of her childhood and her dreams.

*It will be all right. Everything will work out fine. All I have to do is
hang on and wait just a little longer. Luke will be here and he'll remember me and I'll remember him and everything will be all right.*

Despite the familiar litany of reassurance Mariah spoke in the silence of her mind, the tears that had been making her throat raspy began to burn behind her eyelids. Knowing it was foolish, unable to help herself, she looked out across the ranch yard to MacKenzie Ridge and fought not to cry.

"Until then, someone had better go take a look at your car," Cash continued. "How far back down the road did it quit?"

He had to repeat the question twice before Mariah's wide golden eyes focused on him.

"I don't know."

The huskiness of Mariah's voice told Cash that she was fighting tears. A nearly tangible sadness was reflected in her tawny eyes, a sadness that was underlined by the vulnerable line of her mouth.

Yet even as sympathy stirred strongly inside Cash, bitter experience told him that the chances were slim and none that Mariah was one-tenth as vulnerable as she looked sitting on the porch swing, her fingers interlaced too tightly in her lap. Helpless women always found some strong, willing, stupid man to take care of them.

Someone like Cash McQueen.

Mariah looked up at Cash, her eyes wide with unshed tears and an unconscious appeal for understanding.

"I guess I'll wait here until..." Mariah's voice faded at the sudden hardening of Cash's expression.

"Don't you think your time would be better spent trying to fix your car?" Cash asked. "Or were you planning on letting the nearest man take care of it for you?"

The brusque tone of Cash's voice made Mariah flinch. She searched his eyes but saw none of the warmth that had been there before she had told him who she was.

"I hadn't thought about it," she admitted. "I didn't think about anything but getting here."

Cash grunted. "Well, you're here."

His tone made it clear that he was less than delighted by her presence. Fighting tears and a feeling of being set adrift, Mariah told herself that it was silly to let a stranger's disapproval upset her. She looked out toward the barn, blinked rapidly, and finally focused on the building. Its silhouette triggered childhood memories, Luke playing hide-and-seek with her, catching her and lifting her laughing and squirming over his head.

"Yes, I'm here," Mariah said huskily.

"And your car isn't."

"No." She banished the last of the memories and faced the big man who was watching her without pleasure. "I'll need something to carry water."

"There's a plastic water can in the barn."

"Is there a car I could drive?"

Cash shook his head.

Mariah thought of the long walk she had just made and was on the edge of suggesting that she wait for her brother's return before she tried to cope with her car. Cash's coolly appraising look put an end to that idea. She had received that look too many times from her stepfather, a man who took pleasure only in her failures.

"Good thing I wore my walking shoes," Mariah said with forced cheerfulness.

Cash muttered something beneath his breath, then added, "Stay here. I'll take care of it for you."

"Thank you, but that's not necessary. I can—"

"The hell you can," he interrupted abruptly. "You wouldn't get a hundred yards carrying two gallons of water. Even if you did, you wouldn't know what to do once you got there, would you?"

Before Mariah could think of a suitable retort, Cash stepped off the porch and began crossing the yard with long, powerful strides. He vanished behind the barn. A few minutes later he reappeared. He was driving a battered Jeep. As he passed the porch she realized that he didn't mean to stop for her.

"Wait!" Mariah called out, leaping up, sending the swing gyrating. "I'm going with you!"

"Why?" Cash asked, watching with disfavor as Mariah ran up to the Jeep.

"To drive the car back, of course."

"I'll tow it in."

It was too late. Mariah was scrambling into the lumpy passenger seat. Without a word Cash gunned the Jeep out of the yard and headed toward the dirt road that was the Rocking M's sole connection to the outer world.

The Jeep's canvas cover did little to shield the occupants from the wind. Hair the color of bittersweet chocolate flew in a wild cloud around Mariah's shoulders and whipped across her face. She grabbed one handful, then another, wrestling the slippery strands to a standstill, gathering and twisting the shining mass into a knot at the nape of her neck. As the wind picked apart the knot, she tucked in escaping strands.

Cash watched the process from the corner of his eye, intrigued despite himself by the glossy, silky hair and the curve of Mariah's nape, a curve that was both vulnerable and sexy. When he realized the trend of his thoughts, he was irritated. Surely by now he should have figured out that the more vulnerable a girl appeared, the greater the weapon she had to use on men such as himself—men who couldn't cure themselves of the belief that they should protect women from the harshness of life.

Stupid men, in a word.

"Luke didn't say anything about expecting you."

Although Cash said nothing more, his tone made it plain that he thought the ranch—and Luke—would have been better off without Mariah.

"He wasn't expecting me."

"What?" Cash's head swung for an instant toward Mariah.

"He doesn't know I'm coming."

Whatever Cash said was mercifully obliterated by the sudden bump and rattle as the Jeep hurtled over the cattle guard set into the dirt road. Mariah made a startled sound and hung on to the cold metal frame. The noise of wheels racing over the cattle guard, plus the smell of nearby grass and the distant tang of evergreens, triggered a dizzying rush of memories in Mariah.

Eyes the color of my own. Clever hands that made a doll whole again. Tall and strong, lifting me, tossing me, catching me and laughing with me. Dark hair and funny faces that made me smile when I wanted to cry.

There were other memories, too, darker memories of arguments and sobbing and a silence so tense Mariah had been afraid it would explode, destroying everything familiar. And then it had exploded and her mother's screams had gone on and on, rising and falling with the howling December storm.

Shivering in the aftermath of a storm that had occurred fifteen years ago, Mariah looked out over the hauntingly familiar landscape. She had recognized MacKenzie Ridge before she had seen the ranch buildings at its base. The rugged silhouette was burned into her memory. She had watched her home in the rearview mirror of her grandparents' car, and when the ranch buildings had vanished into a fold of land, she had sobbed her loss.

It hadn't been the house she mourned, or even the father who had been left behind. She had wept for Luke, the brother who had loved her when their parents were too consumed by private demons to notice either of their children.

That's all in the past. I've come home. Everything will be all right now. I'm finally home.

The reassuring litany calmed Mariah until she looked at the hard profile of the man who sat within touching distance of her. And she wanted to touch him. She wanted to ask what she had done to make him dislike her. Was it simply that she was alive, breathing, somehow reminding him of an unhappy past? It had been that way with her stepfather, an instant masculine antagonism toward another man's child that nothing Mariah did could alter.

What would she do if Luke disliked her on sight, too?

Two

Arms aching, Mariah held up the rumpled hood of her car while Cash rummaged in the engine compartment, muttering choice phrases she tried very hard not to overhear. A grimy, enigmatic array of parts was lined up on the canvas cloth that Cash had put on the ground nearby. Mariah looked anxiously from the greasy parts to the equally greasy hands of the big man who had taken one look at her sedan's ancient engine and suggested making a modern junk sculpture of it.

"When was the last time you changed the oil?"

The tone of voice was just short of a snarl. Mariah closed her eyes and tried to think.

"I can't remember. I wrote it in the little book in the glove compartment, but I needed paper for a grocery list so I—"

The rest of what Mariah said was lost beneath a rumble of masculine disgust. She caught her lower lip between her teeth and worried the soft flesh nervously.

"When was the last time you added water to the radiator?"

That was easy. "Today. Several times. Then I ran out."

Slowly Cash's head turned toward Mariah. In the shadow of the hood his eyes burned like dark, bleak sapphire flames. "What?"

Mariah swallowed and spoke quietly, calmly, as though gentleness and sweet reason was contagious.

"I always put water in the radiator every day, sometimes more often, depending on how far I'm going. Naturally I always carry water," she added, "but I ran out today. After that little town on the way in—"

"West Fork," Cash interrupted absently.

"That's the one," she said, smiling, encouraged by the fact that he hadn't taken her head off yet.

Cash didn't return the smile.

Mariah swallowed again and finished her explanation as quickly as possible. "After West Fork, there wasn't any place to get more water. I didn't realize how long it would take to get to the ranch house, so I didn't have enough water. Every time I stopped to let things cool off, more water leaked out of the radiator and I couldn't replace it, so I wouldn't get as far next time before it boiled and I had to stop. When I recognized MacKenzie Ridge I decided it would be faster to walk."

Shaking his head, muttering words that made Mariah wince, Cash went back to poking at the dirty engine. His hands hesitated as he was struck by a thought.

"How far did you drive this wreck?"

"Today?"

"No. From the beginning of your trip."

"I started in Seattle."

"Alone?"

"Of course," she said, surprised. Did he think she'd hidden a passenger in the trunk?

Cash said something sibilant and succinct. He backed out from beneath the hood, wiped his hands on a greasy rag and glared at the filthy engine; but he was seeing Mariah's lovely, uncertain smile, her clean-limbed, sexy body and her haunting aura of having been hurt once too often. He guessed that Mariah was a bit younger than his own sister, Carla, who was twenty-three. It made Cash furious to think of a girl who seemed as vulnerable as Mariah driving alone in a totally unreliable car from Seattle to the Rocking M's desolate corner of southwestern Colorado.

Cash took the weight of the hood from Mariah's hands and let the heavy metal fall into place with a resounding crash.

"What in hell were you thinking of when you set off across the country in this worthless piece of crud?"

Mariah opened her mouth. Nothing came out. She had driven the best vehicle she could afford. What was so remarkable about that?

"That's what I thought. You didn't think at all." Disgusted, Cash threw the greasy rag on top of the useless parts. "Well, baby, this wreck is D.O.R."

"What?"

"Dead on Road," Cash said succinctly. "I'll tow it to the ranch house, but the only way you'll get back on the road is with a new engine and you'd be a fool to spend that kind of money on this dog. From the wear pattern on the tires I'd guess the frame is bent but good. I know for damn sure the body is rusted through in so many places you could use it as a sieve. The radiator *is* a sieve. The battery is a pile of corrosion. The spark plugs are beyond belief. The carburetor—'' His hand slashed the air expressively. "It's a miracle you got this far."

Mariah looked unhappily at the rumpled sedan. She started to ask if Cash were sure of his indictment, took one look at the hard line of his jaw and said nothing. Silently she watched while he attached her dead car to the Jeep. In spite of her unhappiness, she found herself appreciating the casual strength and coordination of his movements, a masculine grace and expertise that appealed to her in a way that went deeper than words.

Unfortunately, it was obvious to Mariah that the attraction wasn't mutual. After several attempts, she gave up trying to make small talk as she and Cash bumped down the one-lane dirt road leading toward the ranch house. Rather quickly the wind pulled apart the knot she had used to confine her hair. The silky wildness seethed around her face, but she didn't notice the teasing, tickling strands or the occasional, covert glances from Cash.

Mariah's long trip from Seattle in her unreliable car, her disappointment at not seeing Luke, her attraction to a man who found her aggravating rather than appealing—everything combined to drain Mariah's customary physical and mental resilience. She felt tired and bruised in a way she hadn't since her mother had died last year and she had been left to confront her stepfather without any pretense of bonds between them. Nor had her stepfather felt any need to pretend to such bonds. Immediately after the funeral, he had put a frayed cardboard carton in Mariah's hands and told her, *Your mother came to me with this. Take it and go.*

Mariah had taken the carton and gone, never understanding what she had done to earn her stepfather's coldness. She had returned to her tiny apartment, opened the carton, and found her MacKenzie heritage, the very heritage that her mother had refused ever to discuss. Holding a heavy necklace of rough gold nuggets in one hand, turning the pages of a huge family Bible with the other, Mariah had wept until she had no more tears.

Then she had begun planning to get back to the only home she had ever known—the Rocking M.

The Jeep clattered over the cattle guard that kept range cows from wandering out of the Rocking M's huge home pasture. Shrouded by dark memories, Mariah didn't notice the rattling noise the tires made as they hurtled over pipe.

Nor did Cash. He was watching Mariah covertly, accurately reading the signs of her discouragement. No matter how many times he told himself that Mariah was just one more female looking for a free ride from a man, he couldn't help regretting being so blunt about the possibilities of fixing her car. The lost look in her eyes was a silent remonstration for his lack of gentleness. He deserved it, and he knew it.

Just as Cash was on the verge of reaching for Mariah and stroking her hair in comfort, he caught himself. In silent, searing terms he castigated himself for being a fool. A child learned to keep its hands out of fire by reaching out and getting burned in the alluring dance of flames. A man learned to know his own weaknesses by having them used against himself.

Cash had learned that his greatest weakness was his bone-deep belief that a man should protect and cherish those who weren't as strong as himself, especially women and children. The weakest woman could manipulate the strongest man simply by using this protective instinct against him. That was what Linda had done. Repeatedly. After too much pain, Cash had finally realized that the more vulnerable a woman appeared, the greater was her ability to deceive him.

If the pain had gone all the way to the bone, so had the lesson. It had been eight years since Cash had trusted any woman except Carla, his half sister, who was a decade younger than he was and infinitely more vulnerable. From the day of her birth, she had returned his interest and his care with a generous love that was uniquely her own. Carla gave more than she received, yet she would be the first one to deny it. For that, Cash loved and trusted Carla, exempting her from his general distrust of the female of the species.

Wrapped in their separate thoughts, sharing a silence that was neither comfortable nor uneasy, Cash and Mariah drove through the home pasture and up to the ranch buildings. When he parked near the house, she stirred and looked at him.

"Thank you," she said, smiling despite her own weariness. "It was kind of you to go out of your way for a stranger."

Cash looked at Mariah with unfathomable dark eyes, then shrugged. "Sure as hell someone had to clean up the mess you left. Might as well be me. I wasn't doing anything more important than looking at government maps."

Before Mariah could say anything, Cash was out of the Jeep. Silently she followed, digging her keys from her big canvas purse. She unlocked the trunk of her car and was reaching for the carton her stepfather had given her when she sensed Cash's presence at her back.

"Planning on moving in?" he asked.

Mariah followed Cash's glance to the car's tightly packed trunk. Frayed cardboard cartons took up most of the space. A worn duffel crammed as full as a sausage was wedged in next to the scarred suitcase she had bought at a secondhand shop. But it wasn't her cheap luggage that made her feel ashamed, it was Cash's cool assumption that she had come to the Rocking M as a freeloader.

Yet even as Mariah wanted fiercely to deny it, she had to admit there was an uncomfortable core of truth to what Cash implied. She did want to stay on at the Rocking M, but she didn't have enough money to pay for room and board and fix her car, too.

The screen door of the ranch house creaked open and thudded shut, distracting Cash from the sour satisfaction of watching a bright tide of guilt color Mariah's face.

"Talk about the halt leading the lame," said a masculine voice from the front porch. "Are you towing that rattletrap or is it pushing your useless Jeep?"

"That's slander," Cash said, turning toward the porch. He braced his hands on his hips, but there was amusement rather than anger in his expression.

"That's bald truth," the other man retorted. "But not as bald as those sedan's tires. Surprised that heap isn't sitting on its wheel rims. Where in hell did you—" The voice broke off abruptly. "Oh. Hello. I didn't see you behind Cash. I'll bet you belong to that, er, car."

Mariah turned around and looked up and felt as though she had stepped off into space.

She was looking into her own eyes.

"L-Luke?" she asked hoarsely. "Oh, Luke, after all these years is it really you?"

Luke's eyes widened. His pupils dilated with shock. He searched Mariah's face in aching silence, then his arms opened, reaching for her. An instant later she was caught up in a huge bear hug. Laughing, crying, holding on to her brother, Mariah said Luke's name again and again, hardly able to believe that he was as glad to see her as she was to see him. It had been so long since anyone had hugged her. She hadn't realized how long until this instant.

"Fifteen years," Mariah said. "It's been fifteen years. I thought you had forgotten me."

"Not a chance, Muffin," Luke said, holding Mariah tightly. "If I had a dime for every time I've wondered where you were and if you were happy, I'd be a rich man instead of a broke rancher."

Hearing the old nickname brought a fresh spate of tears to Mariah. Wiping her eyes, smiling, she tried to speak but was able only to cry. She clung more tightly to Luke's neck, holding on as she had when she was five and he was twelve and he had comforted her during their parents' terrifying arguments.

"Without you, I don't know what would have happened to me," she whispered.

Luke simply held Mariah tighter, then slowly lowered her back to the ground. Belatedly she realized how big her brother had become. He was every bit as large as Cash. In fact, she decided, looking from one man to the other, they were identical in size.

"We're both six foot three," Luke said, smiling, reading his sister's mind in the look on her face. "We weigh the same, too. Just under two hundred pounds."

Mariah blinked. "Well, I've grown up, too, but not that much. I'm a mere five-eight, one twenty-six."

Luke stepped back far enough to really look at the young woman who was both familiar and a stranger. He shook his head as he cataloged the frankly feminine lines of her body. "Couldn't you have grown up ugly? Or at least skinny? I'll be beating men back with a whip."

Mariah swiped at tears and smiled tremulously. "Thanks. I think you're beautiful, too."

Cash snorted. "Luke's about as beautiful as the south end of a north-bound mule. Never could understand what Carla saw in him."

Instantly Mariah turned on Cash, ready to defend her big brother. Then she realized that Luke was laughing and Cash was watching him with a masculine affection that was like nothing she had ever encountered. It was as though the men were brothers in blood as well as in law.

"Ignore him, Muffin," Luke said, hugging Mariah again. "He's just getting even for my comments about his ratty, unreliable Jeep." He looked over Mariah's head at Cash. "Speaking of ratty and unreliable, what's wrong with her car?"

"Everything."

"Um. What's right with it?"

"Nothing. She started in Seattle. It's a damned miracle she got this far. Proves the old saying—God watches over fools and drunks."

"Seattle, huh?" Luke glanced at the open trunk, accurately assessed its contents and asked, "Did you leave anything you care about behind?"

Mariah shook her head, suddenly nervous.

"Good. Remember the old ranch house where we used to play hide-and-seek?"

She nodded.

"You can live there."

"But..." Mariah's voice died.

She looked from one large man to the other. Luke looked expectant. Cash wore an expression of barely veiled cynicism. She remembered his words: *Planning on moving in?* Unhappily she looked back at Luke.

"I can't just move in on you," she said.

"Why not?"

"What about your wife?"

"Carla will be delighted. Since Ten and Diana started living part-time in Boulder, there hasn't been a woman for Carla to talk to a lot of the time. She hasn't said anything, but I'm sure she gets a little lonely. The Rocking M is hard on women that way."

Though Luke said nothing more, Mariah sensed all that he didn't say, their mother's tears and long silences, their father's anger at the woman who couldn't adjust to ranch life, a woman who simply slipped through his fingers into a twilight world of her own making.

"But I can't—" Mariah's voice broke. "I can't pay my way. I only have enough money for—"

Luke talked over her stumbling words. "Don't worry. You'll earn your keep. Logan needs an aunt and Carla sure as hell will need help a few months down the road. Six and a half months, to be exact."

The cynical smile vanished from Cash's mouth as the implication of Luke's words sank in.

"Is Carla pregnant?" Cash demanded.

Luke just grinned.

Cash whooped with pleasure and gave Luke a bone-cracking hug.

"It better be a girl, this time," Cash warned. "The world needs more women like Carla."

"I hear you. But I'll be damned grateful for whatever the good Lord sends along. Besides," Luke added with a wolfish smile, "if at first we don't succeed..."

Cash burst out laughing.

Mariah looked from one grinning man to the other and felt a fragile bubble of pleasure rise and burst softly within her, showering her with a feeling of belonging she had known only in her dreams. Hardly able to believe her luck, she looked around the dusty, oddly luminous ranch yard and felt dreams and reality merge.

Then Mariah looked at the tall, powerful man whose eyes were the deepest blue she had ever seen, and she decided that reality was more compelling than any dream she had ever had.

Three

"Are you sure you're a MacKenzie?" Cash asked Mariah as he removed another slab of garlic pork from the platter. "No MacKenzie I know can cook."

"Carla can," Luke pointed out quickly.

"Yeah, but that's different. Carla was born a McQueen."

"And Mariah was born a MacKenzie," Nevada Blackthorn said matter-of-factly as he took two more slices of meat off the platter Mariah held out to him. "Even a hard-rock miner like you should be able to figure that out. All you have to do is look at her eyes."

"Thanks," Mariah said.

She smiled tentatively at the dark, brooding man whose own eyes were a startlingly light green. Nevada had been introduced to her as the Rocking M's *segundo,* the second in command. When his brother Ten was gone, Nevada was the foreman, as well. He was also one of the most unnerving men Mariah had ever met. Not once had she seen a smile flash behind his neatly trimmed beard. Yet she had no feeling that he disliked her. His reserve was simply part of his nature, a basic solitude that made her feel sad.

Cash watched Mariah smile at Nevada. Irritation pricked at Cash even as he told himself that if Mariah wanted to stub her toe on a hard piece of business like Nevada, it wasn't Cash's concern.

Yet no sooner had Cash reached that eminently reasonable decision when he heard himself saying, "Don't waste your smiles on Nevada. He's got no more heart than a stone."

"And you've got no more brain," Nevada said matter-of-factly. Only the slight crinkling at the corners of his eyes betrayed his amusement. "Like Ten says—Granite Man."

"Your brother was referring to my interest in mining."

"My brother was referring to your thick skull."

Cash grinned. "Care to bet on that?"

"Not one chance in hell. After a year of watching you play cards, I know why people nicknamed you Cash." Nevada glanced sideways at Mariah. "Never play cards with a man named Cash."

"But I like to play cards," she said.

"You do?" Cash asked, looking at her sharply.

Mariah nodded.

"Poker?"

Dark hair swung as Mariah nodded again.

"I'll be damned."

Nevada lifted one black eyebrow. "Probably, but not many men would brag about it."

Luke snickered.

Cash ignored the other men, focusing only on Mariah. It was easy to do. There was an elegance to her face and a subtle lushness to the curves of her body that caught Cash anew each time he looked at her. Even when he reminded himself that Mariah's aura of vulnerability was false, he remained interested in the rest of her.

Very interested.

"Could I tempt you into a hand or two of poker after dinner?" he asked.

"No!" Luke and Nevada said simultaneously.

Mariah looked at the two men, realized they were kidding—sort of— and smiled again at Cash. "Sure. But first I promised to show the MacKenzie family Bible to Luke."

An unreasonable disappointment snaked through Cash.

"Maybe after that?" Mariah asked hesitantly, looking at Cash with an eagerness she couldn't hide, sensing his interest despite his flashes of hostility. Though she had never been any man's lover, she certainly knew when a man looked at her with masculine appreciation. Cash was looking at her that way right now.

When Mariah passed the steaming biscuits to Cash, the sudden awareness of him that made her eyes luminous brought each of his masculine senses to quivering alert. Deliberately he let his fingertips brush over Mariah's hands as he took the warm, fragrant food from her. The slight catch of her breath and the abrupt speeding of the pulse in her throat told Cash how vividly she was aware of him as a man.

Covertly, Cash glanced at Luke, wondering how he would react to his sister's obvious interest in his best friend. Luke was talking in a low voice with Nevada about the cougar tracks the *segundo* had seen that morning in Wildfire Canyon. Cash looked back to Mariah, measuring the sensual awareness that gave her eyes the radiance of candle flames and made the pulse at the base of her soft throat beat strongly.

Desire surged through Cash, shocking him with its speed and ferocity, hardening him in an aching torrent of blood. He fought to control his torrential, unreasonable hunger for Mariah by telling himself that she was no better looking than a lot of women, that he was thirty-three, too old to respond this fast, this totally, to his best friend's sister. And in any case Mariah was just one more woman hungry for a lifetime sinecure—look at how quickly she had moved in on the Rocking M. Her token protests had been just that. Token.

"You're a good cook," Nevada said, handing Mariah the salt before she had time to do more than glance in the direction of the shaker. "Hope Luke can talk you into staying. From what Ten has told me, the Rocking M never had a cook worth shooting until Carla came along. But by January, Carla won't feel much like cooking."

"How did you know?" Luke asked, startled. "Dr. Chacon just confirmed it today."

Nevada shrugged. "Small things. Her skin. Her scent. The way she holds her body."

Cash shook his head. "Your daddy must have been a sorcerer. You have the most acute perceptions of anyone I've ever met."

"Chalk it up to war, not sorcery," Nevada said, pouring himself a cup of coffee. "You spend years tracking men through the night and see what happens to your senses. The Blackthorns come from a long line of warriors. The slow and the stupid didn't make the cut."

Nevada set the coffeepot aside and glanced back at Luke. "If you want, I'll check out that new cougar as soon as Ten gets back. I couldn't follow the tracks long enough to tell if it was male or female. Frankly, I'm hoping the cat is a young male, just coming out of the high country to mate and move on."

"I hope so, too. Wildfire Canyon can't support more than one or maybe two adult cats in a lean season. Long about February, some of the cattle in the upland pastures might get to looking too tasty to a big, hungry cat." Luke sipped coffee and swore softly. "I need to know more about cougars. The old ranchers say the cats are cow killers, the government says the cats only eat rabbits and deer...." Frowning, Luke ran a hand through his hair. "Check into the new tracks when Ten comes back, but I can't turn you loose for more than a day or two. Too damned shorthanded."

"Need me?" Cash asked, trying and failing to keep the reluctance from his voice. He had been planning on getting in at least a week of prospecting in the Rocking M's high country. He no longer expected to find Mad Jack's lost mine, but he enjoyed the search too much to give it up.

"Maybe Luke needs you, but I don't," Nevada said. "When it comes to cows you make a hell of a good ranch mechanic."

Mariah looked at Cash and remembered his disgust with the state of her car's engine. "Are you a mechanic?"

Luke snickered. "Ask his Jeep. It runs only on alternate Thursdays."

"The miracle is that it runs at all," Nevada said. "Damned thing is even older than Cash is. Better looking, too."

"I don't know why I sit and listen to this slander," Cash complained without heat.

"Because it's that or do dishes. It's your turn, remember?" Luke asked.

"Yeah, but I was hoping you'd forget."

"That'll be the day." Luke pushed back from the table, gathered up his dishes and headed for the kitchen. "Nevada, you might want to stick around for the MacKenzie family show-and-tell. After all, some of them are your ancestors, too."

Nevada's head turned toward Luke with startling speed. "What?"

There was a clatter of dishes from the kitchen, then Luke came back to the big "mess hall" that adjoined the kitchen. He poured himself another cup of potent coffee before he looked down at Ten's younger brother with an odd smile.

"Didn't Ten tell you? The two of us finally figured it out last winter. We share a pair of great-great-grandparents—Case and Mariah Mac-Kenzie."

"Be damned."

"No doubt," Cash said slyly, "but no man wants to brag about it, right?"

Nevada gave him a sideways glance that would have been threatening were it not for the telltale crinkling around Nevada's eyes. Luke just kept on talking, thoroughly accustomed to the masculine chaffing that always accompanied dinners on the Rocking M.

"Case was the MacKenzie who started the Rocking M," Luke explained as he looked back at Cash. "Actually, Mariah should have been one of your ancestors. Her granddaddy was a gold prospector."

"He was? Really?" Mariah said eagerly, her voice lilting with excitement. "I never knew that Grandpa Lucas was a prospector."

Luke blinked. "He wasn't."

"But you just said he was."

Simultaneously Nevada spoke. "I don't remember my parents talking about any MacKenzie ancestors."

"No, I didn't," Luke said to Mariah. Then, to Nevada, "I'm not surprised. It wasn't the kind of relationship that families used to talk about."

When Nevada and Mariah began speaking at once, Cash stood up with a resigned expression and began carrying dirty dishes into the kitchen. No one noticed his comings and goings or his absence when he stayed in the kitchen. Once he glanced through the doorway, saw Luke drawing family trees on a legal tablet and went back to the dishes. The next time Cash looked out, Mariah was gone. He was irrationally pleased that Nevada had remained behind. The bearded cowhand was too good-looking by half.

Cash attacked the counters with unusual vigor, but before he had finished, he heard Mariah's voice again.

"Here it is, Nevada. Proof positive that we're kissing kin."

The dishrag hit the sink with a distinct smack. Wiping his hands on his jeans, Cash moved silently across the kitchen until he could see into the dining room. Mariah stood next to Luke. She was holding a frayed cardboard carton as though it contained the crown jewels of England.

"What's that?" Luke asked, eyeing the disreputable box his sister was carrying so triumphantly to the cleared table.

"This is the MacKenzie family Bible," she said in a voice rich with satisfaction and subdued excitement.

There was a time of stretching silence ended by the audible rush of Luke's breath as Mariah removed the age-worn, leather-bound volume from the box. The Bible's intricate gilt lettering rippled and gleamed in the light.

Nevada whistled softly. He reached for the Bible, then stopped, looking at Mariah.

"May I?" he asked.

"Of course," she said, holding the thick, heavy volume out to him with both hands. "It's your family, too."

While Cash watched silently from the doorway, Nevada shook his head, refusing to take the book. Instead, he moved his fingertips across the fragile leather binding, caressing it as though it were alive.

The sensuality and emotion implicit in that gesture made conflicting feelings race through Cash—irritation at the softness in Mariah's eyes as she watched the unsmiling man touch the book, curiosity about the old Bible itself, an aching sense of time and history stretching from past to present to future; but most of all Cash felt a bitter regret that he would never have a child who would share his past, his present or his future.

"How old is this?" Nevada asked, taking the heavy book at last and putting it on the table.

"It was printed in 1867," Mariah said, "but the first entry isn't until the 1870s. It records the marriage of Case MacKenzie and Mariah Elizabeth Turner. I've tried to make out the date, but the ink is too blurred."

As she spoke, Mariah turned to the glossy pages within the body of the Bible where births, deaths and marriages were recorded. Finger hovering just above the old paper, she searched the list of names quickly.

"There it is," she said triumphantly. "Matthew Case MacKenzie, our great-grandfather. He married a woman called Charity O'Hara."

Luke looked quickly down the page of names, then pointed to another one. "And there's your great-granddaddy, Nevada. David Tyrell MacKenzie."

Nevada glanced at the birthdate, flipped to the page that recorded marriages and deaths, and found only a date of death entered. David Tyrell MacKenzie had died before he was twenty-six. Neither his marriage nor the births of any of his children had been recorded.

"No marriage listed," Nevada said neutrally. "No children, either."

"There wasn't a marriage," Luke said. "According to my grandfather, his uncle David was a rover and a loner. He spent most of his time living with or fighting various Indian tribes. No woman could hold him for long."

Nevada's mouth shifted into a wry line that was well short of a smile. "Yeah, that's always been a problem for us Blackthorns. Except for Ten. He's well and truly married." Nevada flipped the last glossy pages of the register, found no more entries and looked at Luke. "Nothing here. What makes you think we're related?"

"Mariah—no, not you, Muffin, the first Mariah. Anyway, she kept a journal. She mentioned a woman called Winter Moon in connection with her son David. Ten said your great-grandmother's name was Winter Moon."

Nevada nodded slowly.

"There was no formal marriage, but there was rumor of a child. A girl."

"Bends-Like-the-Willow," Nevada said. "My grandmother."

"Welcome to the family, cousin," Luke said, grinning and holding out his hand.

Nevada took it and said, "Well, you'll have no shortage of renegades in the MacKenzie roster now. The Blackthorns are famous for them. Bastards descended from a long line of bastards."

"Beats no descent at all," Luke said dryly.

Only Mariah noticed Cash standing in the doorway, his face expressionless as he confronted once again the fact that he would never know the sense of family continuity that other people took for granted. That, as much as his distrust of women, was the reason why hc hadn't married again.

And why he never would.

Four

Cash turned back to the kitchen and finished cleaning it without taking time out for any more looks into the other room. When he was finished he poured himself a cup of coffee from the big pot that always simmered on the back of the stove and walked around the room slowly, sipping coffee. Finally he sat down alone at the kitchen table. The conversation from the dining room filtered through his thoughts, sounds without meaning.

His dark blue eyes looked at the kitchen walls where Carla had hung kitchen utensils that had been passed down through generations of MacKenzies and would be passed on to her own children. Cash's eyes narrowed against the pain of knowing that he would leave no children of his own when he died.

For the hundredth time he told himself how lucky he was to have a nephew whose life he was allowed to share. When he traced Logan's hairline and the shape of his jaw, Cash could see his own father and himself in his half-sister's child. If Logan's laughter and curiosity and stubbornness made Cash ache anew to have a child of his own, that was too bad. He would just have to get over it.

"...real gold?"

"It is. The nuggets supposedly came from Mad Jack's mine."

Nevada's question and Mariah's answer were an irresistible lure for Cash. He set aside his cooled cup of coffee and went into the room that opened off the kitchen.

Mariah was sitting between Luke and Nevada, who was looking up from the handful of faded newspaper clippings and letters he had collected from the Bible. Despite his question, Nevada spared only a moment's glance for the gold that rippled and flowed between Mariah's hands like water. The necklace of nuggets linked by a long, heavy gold chain didn't interest Nevada as much as the faded, smudged marks on the brittle paper he held.

"Cash?" Luke called out without looking up. "What the hell is taking you so—oh, there you are. Remember the old jewelry I thought was lost? Look at this. Mother must have taken the chain when she left Dad. Muffin brought it back."

Cash's large, powerful hand reached over Mariah's shoulder. Her breath came in swiftly when his forearm brushed lightly against the curve of her neck and shoulder. His flesh was hard, radiating vitality, and the thick hair on his arm burned with metallic gold highlights. When he turned his hand so that it was palm up, Mariah saw the strong, raised, taut veins centered in his wrist, silent testimony to the times when his heart had had to beat strongly to feed the demands he made on his muscular body.

The sudden desire to trace the dark velvet branching of Cash's life was so great that Mariah had to close her eyes before she gave in to it.

"May I?" Cash asked.

Too shaken by her own reaction to speak, Mariah opened her eyes and handed the loops of chain over to Cash. She told herself it was an accident that her fingertips slid over his wrist, but she knew she lied. She also knew she would never forget the hard strength of his tendons or the alluring suppleness of the veins beneath the clean, tanned skin.

Silently Mariah watched Cash handle the necklace, testing its weight with his palm and the hardness of random nuggets with his fingernail. Very faint marks appeared on the rough gold, legacy of his skillful probing.

"High-test stuff," Cash said simply. "Damn few impurities. I couldn't tell without a formal assay, but I'd guess this is about as pure as gold gets without man's help."

"Is it from Mad Jack's mine?" Mariah asked.

Cash shrugged, but his eyes were intent as he went from nugget to nugget on the old necklace, touching, probing, measuring the malleable metal against his own knowledge and memories. Then, saying nothing, he took Mariah's hand and heaped the necklace in it. Gold chain whispered and moved in a cool fall over both sides of her palm, but the weight of the nuggets that remained in her palm kept the necklace from falling to the table.

Cash pulled a key from his jeans pocket. Dangling from the ring was a hollow metal cylinder about half the size of his thumb. With a deftness that was surprising for such big hands, he unscrewed the cylinder.

"Hold out your other hand," he said to Mariah.

She did, hoping that no one else sensed the sudden race of her heart when Cash's hand came up beneath hers, steadying it and cupping her fingers at the same time. Holding her with one hand, he upended the cylinder over her palm. She made a startled sound when a fat gold nugget dropped into her hand. The lump was surprisingly heavy for its size.

Carefully Cash selected a strand of chain and draped it over her palm so that one of the necklace nuggets rested next to the nugget he had taken from the cylinder. There was no apparent difference in the color of the gold, or in the texture of the surface. Both lumps of gold were angular and rough rather than rounded and smooth. Both were of a very deep, richly golden hue.

"Again, without an assay it's impossible to be sure," Cash said, "but..." He shrugged.

Mariah looked up at Cash with eyes the color of gold. "They're from Mad Jack's mine, aren't they?"

"I don't know. I've never found the mine." Cash looked down into Mariah's eyes and thought again of golden heat, golden flames, desire like a knife deep in his loins. "But I'd bet my last cent that these nuggets came from the same place, wherever that is."

"You mentioned that Case kept a journal," Mariah said, her voice a husky rasp that made Cash's blood thicken.

"Yes," Luke answered, though his sister hadn't looked at him, having eyes only for the gold in her hands—and for Cash, the man who hunted for gold.

"Didn't he say where the mine was?" she asked.

"No. All we know for sure was that Case had saddlebags full of gold from Mad Jack's mine."

"Why?"

"He was going to give it to Mad Jack's son. Instead he gave it to Mariah, Mad Jack's granddaughter."

That caught Mariah's attention. "You mean it's really true?" she asked, turning quickly toward Luke. "You weren't just joking? We're really related to Mad Jack?"

"Sure. Where else do you think the nuggets in that necklace came from? It used to be a man's watch chain. Mariah had it made for Case as a wedding gift. The chain came down through the family, staying with whichever son held the Rocking M. Until Mother left." Luke shrugged. "I guess she thought she had earned it. Maybe she had. God knows she hated every minute she ever spent on the ranch."

Mariah looked at the gold heaped on her palm, shining links infused with a legacy of both love and hatred. Yet all she said was "That explains the modern clasp. I assumed the old one had fallen apart, but watch chains don't need clasps, do they?" Without hesitation she poured the long, heavy chain and bulky nuggets into a heap in front of Luke. "Here. It belongs to you."

He looked startled. "I didn't mean—"

"I know you didn't," she interrupted. "It's still yours. It belongs with the man who holds the Rocking M. You."

"I've been thinking about that. Half of what I inherited should be—"

"No." Mariah's interruption was swift and determined. "The ranch was meant to be the inheritance of whichever MacKenzie son could hold it. Mariah's letters made that quite clear."

"That might have been fair in the past, but it sure as hell isn't fair now."

"It wasn't fair that our parents couldn't get along or that Mother had a nervous breakdown or that Dad drank too much or that I was taken away from the only person who really loved me. You." Mariah touched Luke's hand. "Lots of life isn't fair. So what?" Her smile was a bittersweet curve of acceptance. "You offered me a home when I had none. That's all I hoped for and more than I had any right to expect. Or accept."

"You'll by God accept it if I have to nail your feet to the floor," Luke said, squeezing Mariah's hand.

She laughed and tried to blink away the sudden tears in her eyes. "I accept. Thank you."

Luke picked up the gold chain and dumped it back in Mariah's hand. She tilted her palm, letting the heavy, cool gold slide back to the table.

"Mariah," he began roughly. "Damn it, it's yours."

"No. Make it back into a watch chain and wear it. Or give it to Logan. Or to your next child. Or to whichever child holds the Rocking M. But," Mariah added, speaking quickly, overriding the objections she saw in her brother's tawny eyes, "that doesn't mean I wouldn't like a gold necklace of my own. So, with your permission, I'll go looking for Mad Jack's mine. I've always believed I would find a lost gold mine someday."

Luke laughed, then realized that Mariah was serious. Smiling crookedly, he said, "Muffin, Cash has been looking for that mine for—how many years?"

"Nine."

Startled, Mariah looked up at Cash. "You have?"

He nodded slightly.

"And if a certified, multi-degreed geologist, a man who makes his living finding precious metals for other people—" began Luke.

"You do?" interrupted Mariah, still watching Cash with wide golden eyes.

He nodded again.

"—can't find Mad Jack's lost mine," Luke continued, talking over his sister, "then what chance do you have?"

Mariah started to speak, then sighed, wondering how she could explain what she barely understood herself.

"Remember how you used to put me to bed and tell me stories?" she asked after a few moments.

"Sure. You would watch me all wide-eyed and fascinated. Nobody ever paid that much attention to me but you. Made me feel ten feet tall."

She smiled and said simply, "You were. I would lie in bed and forget about Mother and Dad yelling downstairs and I'd listen to you talking about the calves or the new colts or some adventure you'd had. Sometimes you'd sneak in with cookies and a box full of old pictures and we would make up stories about the people. And sometimes you'd talk about Mad Jack and his mine and how we would go exploring and find it and buy everything the ranch didn't have so Mother would be happy on the Rocking M. We used to talk about that a lot."

In silent comfort Luke squeezed Mariah's hand. "I remember."

She leaned forward with an urgency she couldn't suppress. "I've always believed I can find that mine. I'm Mad Jack's own blood, after all. Please, Luke. Let me look. What harm can there be in that?" Despite the need driving her, Mariah smiled teasingly and added, "I'll give you half of whatever I find, cross my heart and hope to die."

Luke laughed, shaking his head, unable to take her seriously. "Muffin, this is a big damned ranch. It's a patchwork quilt of outright ownership, plus lease lands from three government agencies, plus water rights and mineral rights and other things only a land lawyer or a professional gold hunter like Cash would understand."

"I'll learn."

"Oh hell, honey, if you found anything in Rocking M's high country land but granite and cow flops, I'd give it to you without hesitation and you know it, but—"

"Sold!" Mariah crowed, interrupting before Luke could say anything she didn't want to hear. She looked at Nevada and Cash. "You heard him. You're my witnesses."

Nevada looked up, nodded, and returned his attention to one of the old pieces of paper he held.

Cash was much more attentive to Mariah. "I heard," he said, watching her closely. "But just what makes you so sure that mine is on the Rocking M?"

"Mariah said it was. It's in her letter to the son who inherited the ranch."

Luke looked up at Cash. "You were right. Damn. I was hoping that mine would never..." He shrugged and said no more.

Silently Cash took the single nugget from Mariah's hand. A few deft movements returned the gold to its cylinder.

"What do you mean, Cash was right?" she asked. "And why were you hoping he was wrong?"

There was a pause before Luke said anything. When he finally did speak, he answered only her first question.

"When Mother cleaned out the family heirlooms, she overlooked a fat poke of gold, all that was left from Case's saddlebags. I showed the poke to Cash. He took one look and knew the gold hadn't come from any of the known, old-time strikes around here."

"Of course," Mariah said. "The MacKenzie gold wasn't found in placer pockets."

Cash looked at Mariah with renewed interest. "How did you know?"

"I did my homework." She held up her hand, ticking off names with her fingers. "The strikes at Moss Creek, Hard Luck, Shin Splint, Brass Monkey, Deer Creek, and Lucky Lady were all placer gold. Some small nuggets, a lot of dust. Everything was smooth from being tumbled in water." Mariah gestured toward the necklace. "For convenience we call those lumps of gold 'nuggets,' but I doubt they spent any real time in the bottom of a stream. If they had, they would be round or at least rounded off. But they're rough and asymmetrical. The longer I thought about it, the more certain I was that the lumps came from 'jewelry rock.'"

"What's that?" Luke asked.

Cash answered before Mariah could. "It's an old miner's term for quartz that is so thickly veined with pure gold that the ore can be broken apart in your bare hands. It's the richest kind of gold strike. Veins of gold like that are the original source of all the big nuggets that end up in placer pockets when the mother lodes are finally eroded away and washed by rain down into streams."

"Is that what you think Mad Jack's mine is?" Luke persisted. "A big strike of jewelry rock?"

"I wasn't sure. Except for the chunk you gave me—" Cash flicked his thumbnail against the cylinder "—the poke was filled with flakes and big, angular grains, the kind of thing that would come from a crude crushing process of really high-grade ore." Thoughtfully Cash stirred the chain with a blunt fingertip. Reflected light shifted and gleamed in shades of metallic gold. "But if these nuggets all came from Mad Jack's mine, it was God's own jewelry box, as close to digging pure gold as you can get this side of Fort Knox."

Luke said something unhappy and succinct beneath his breath.

Mariah looked at her brother in disbelief. "What's wrong with that? I think it's fantastic!"

"Ever read about Sutter's Mill?" he asked laconically.

"Sure. That was the one that set off the California gold rush in 1849. It was one of the richest strikes in history."

"Yeah. Remember what happened to the mill?"

"Er, no."

"It was trampled to death in the rush. So was a lot of other land. I don't need that kind of grief. We have enough trouble keeping pothunters out of the Anasazi ruins on Wind Mesa and in September Canyon."

"What ruins?" Mariah asked.

"They're all over the place. Would you like to see them?" Luke asked hopefully, trying to sidetrack her from the prospect of gold.

"Thanks, but I'd rather look for Mad Jack's mine."

Cash laughed ruefully. When he spoke, his voice was rich with certainty. "Forget it, Luke. Once the gold bug bites you, you're hooked for life. Not one damn thing is as bright as the shine of undiscovered gold. It's a fever that burns out everything else."

Luke looked surprised but Mariah nodded vigorously, making dark brown hair fly. She knew exactly what Cash meant.

Looking from Cash to Mariah, Nevada raised a single black eyebrow, shrugged, and returned his attention to the paper he was very gently unfolding on the table's surface.

"Smile," Mariah coaxed Luke. "You'd think we were talking about the Black Death."

"That can be cured by antibiotics," he shot back. "What do you think will happen if word gets out that there's a fabulous lost mine somewhere up beyond MacKenzie Ridge? A lot of our summer grazing is leased from the government, but the mineral rights *aren't* leased. There are rules and restrictions and bureaucratic papers to chase, but basically, when it comes to prospecting, it's come one, come all. Worst of all, mineral rights take precedence over other rights."

Mariah looked to Cash, who nodded.

"So we get a bunch of weekend warriors making campfires that are too big," Luke continued, "carrying guns they don't know how to use, drinking booze they can't hold, and generally being jackasses. I can live with that if I have to. What I can't live with is when they start tearing up the fences and creeks and watersheds. This is a cattle ranch, not a mining complex. I want to keep it that way."

"But..." Mariah's voice faded. She began worrying her lower lip between her teeth. "Does this mean I can't look for Mad Jack's mine?"

Luke swiped his fingers through his hair in a gesture of frustration. "No. But I want you to promise me two things. First, I don't want you telling anyone about Mad Jack's damned missing mine. That goes for Nevada, too. And I mean no one. Cash didn't even tell Carla."

"No problem," Nevada said. He looked at Cash with blunt approval. "You've been looking for nine years, huh? I like a man who can keep his mouth shut."

Cash's lips made a wry line and he said not one word.

"No problem for me, either," Mariah said, shrugging. "I don't have anyone to tell but you and you already know. What's the second thing?"

"I don't want you going out alone and looking for that damned mine," Luke said. "That's wild, rough country out there."

Mariah was on the verge of agreeing when she stopped. "Wait a minute. I can't tell anyone, right?"

Luke nodded.

"And you, Nevada and Cash are the only other ones who know. Right?"

"Carla knows," Luke said. "I told her myself."

"So five people know, including me."

"Right."

"Tell me, older brother—how much time do you have to spend looking for lost mines?"

"None," he said flatly.

"Nevada?"

He looked toward Luke, but it was Cash who spoke first.

"Nevada has cougar tracking duty. That takes care of his spare time for the summer."

The satisfaction in Cash's voice was subtle but unmistakable. Luke heard it. His smile was so small and swift that only Nevada saw it.

Mariah didn't notice. She was looking at Cash with hopeful eyes, waiting for him to volunteer. He didn't seem to notice her.

"No one prospects the high country in the winter," Luke said unhelpfully.

Mariah simply said, "Cash?"

"Sorry," he said. "That country is too rough for a tenderfoot like you."

"I've camped out before."

Cash grunted but was obviously unimpressed.

"I've hiked, too."

"Who carried your pack?"

"I did."

He grunted again. The sound wasn't encouraging.

Inspiration struck Mariah. "I'll do the cooking. I'll even do the dishes, too. Please?"

Cash looked at her luminous golden eyes and the graceful hand resting on his bare forearm in unconscious pleading. Desire shot through him at the thought of having her pleading with him for his skill as a lover rather than his expertise in hunting for gold.

"No," Cash said, more roughly than he had intended.

Mariah flinched as though she had been slapped. Hastily she withdrew her hand from his arm.

For an instant Luke's eyes widened, then narrowed with a purely male assessment. Soon his mouth shifted into a smile that was both sympathetic and amused as he realized what Cash's problem was.

"If I were you, Granite Man," Nevada drawled calmly, "I'd change my mind."

Cash shot the other man a savage look. "You're not me."

"Does that mean you're volunteering to go gold hunting?" Mariah said to Nevada, hoping her voice didn't sound as hurt as she felt by Cash's harsh refusal.

"Sorry, Muffin," Luke said, cutting across anything Nevada might have wanted to say. "I'm too shorthanded as it is. I can't afford to turn loose of Nevada."

"Damn shame," Nevada said without heat. "Hate to see a good treasure map go to waste."

"What?" Luke and Cash said together.

Silently Nevada pushed a piece of paper toward Mariah. Cash bent over her shoulder, all but holding his breath so that he wouldn't take in her fragile, tantalizing scent.

"I'm a warrior, not a prospector," Nevada said, "but I've read more than one map drawn by a barely literate man. Offhand, I'd guess this one shows the route to Mad Jack's mine."

Five

With a harshly suppressed sound of disgust and anger, Cash looked from the age-darkened, brittle paper to Mariah's innocent expression.

No wonder she was so eager to trade her nonexistent rights of inheritance in exchange for Luke's permission to prospect on the Rocking M—she has a damned map to follow to Mad Jack's mine!

Yet Mariah had looked so vulnerable when she had pleaded with Cash for his help.

Sweet little con artist. God. Why are men so stupid? And why am I so particularly stupid!

Mariah glanced from the paper to Nevada and smiled wryly. "I got all excited the first time I looked at it, too. Then I looked again. And again. I stared until I was cross-eyed, but I still couldn't make out two-thirds of the chicken scratches. Even if I assume Mad Jack drew this—and that's by no means a certainty—he didn't even mark north or south in any way I can decipher. As for labeling any of the landmarks, not a chance. I suspect the old boy was indeed illiterate. There's not a single letter of the alphabet on the whole map."

"He didn't need words. He read the land, not books." Nevada turned the map until the piece of paper stood on one chewed corner. "That's north," he said, indicating the upper corner.

"You're sure?" she asked, startled. "How can you tell?"

"He's right," Cash said an instant later. He stared at the map in growing excitement. "That's Mustang Point. Nothing else around has that shape. Which means...yes, there. Black Canyon. Then that must be Satan's Bath, which leads to the narrow rocky valley, then to Black Springs..." Cash's voice trailed off into mutterings.

Mariah watched, wide-eyed, as local place names she had never heard of were emphasized by stabs of Cash's long index finger. Then he began muttering words she had heard before, pungent words that told her he had run into a dead end. She started to ask what was wrong, but held her tongue. Luke and Nevada were standing now, leaning over the map in front of her, tracing lines that vanished into a blurred area that looked for all the world as though someone long ago had spilled coffee on the paper, blotting out the center of the map.

"Damn, that's enough to peeve a saint," Cash said, adding a few phrases that were distinctly unsaintly. "Some stupid dipstick smudged the only important part of the map. Now it's useless!"

"Not quite," Luke said. "Now you know the general area of the ranch to concentrate on."

Cash shot his friend a look of absolute disgust. "Hell, Luke, where do you think I've been looking for the past two years?"

"Oh. Devil's Peak area, huh?"

Cash grunted. "It's well named. It has more cracks and crannies, rills and creeks than any twelve mountains. It looks like it's been shattered by God's own rock hammer. I've used the line shack at Black Springs for my base. So far, I've managed to pan the lower third of a single small watershed."

"Find anything?"

"Trout," Cash said succinctly.

Mariah licked her lips. "Trout? Real, free-swimming, wild mountain trout?"

A smile Cash couldn't prevent stole across his lips. "Yeah. Sleek, succulent little devils, every one of them."

"Fresh butter, a dusting of cornmeal, a pinch of—"

"Stop it," groaned Cash. "You're making me hungry all over again."

"Does Black Springs have watercress?" she asked, smiling dreamily.

"No, but the creek does farther down the valley, where the water cools. Black Springs is hot."

"Hot? Wonderful! A long day of prospecting, a hot bath, a meal of fresh trout, camp biscuits, watercress salad...." Mariah made a sound of luxuriant anticipation.

Luke laughed softly. Cash swore, but there was no heat in it. He had often enjoyed nature's hard-rock hot tub. The meal Mariah mentioned, however, had existed only in his dreams. He was a lousy cook.

"Then you'll do it?" Mariah asked eagerly, sensing that Cash was weakening. "You'll help me look for Mad Jack's mine?"

"Don't push, Muffin," Luke said. "Cash and I will talk it over later. Alone."

"I'll give you half of my half," she said coaxingly to Cash, ignoring her older brother.

"Mariah—" began Luke.

"Who's pushing?" she asked, assuming an expression of wide-eyed innocence. "*Moi?* Never. I'm a regular doormat."

Nevada looked at Cash. "You need this map?"

"No."

"Then if nobody minds, I'd like to pass it along to some people who are real good at making ruined documents give up their secrets."

Cash started to ask questions, then remembered where—and for whom—Nevada had worked before he came to the Rocking M.

"Fine with me," Cash said. "The map belongs to Luke and Mariah, though."

"Take it," said Luke.

"Sure. Who are you sending it to?" Mariah asked.

"Don't worry. They'll take good care of it," Nevada said, folding the map delicately along age-worn creases.

"But where are you sending it?"

Mariah was talking to emptiness. Nevada had simply walked away from the table. The back door opened and closed quietly.

"I didn't mean to make him mad."

"You didn't," Luke said, stretching. "Nevada isn't long on social niceties like smiling and saying excuse me. But he's a damned good man. One of the best. Just don't ever push him," Luke added, looking directly at Cash. "Even you. Nevada doesn't push worth a damn."

Cash smiled thinly. "My mother didn't hatch any stupid chicks. I saw Nevada fight once. If I go poking around in that lion's den, it will be with a shotgun."

"But where is Nevada taking the map?" Mariah asked in a plaintive voice.

"I don't know," Luke admitted. "I do know you'll get it back in as good shape as it was when Nevada took it. Better, probably."

"Then you must know where he's taking it."

"No, but I can make an educated guess."

"Please do," Mariah said in exasperation.

Luke smiled. "I'd guess that map will end up in an FBI lab on the east coast. Or some other government agency's lab. Nevada wasn't always a cowboy." Luke stretched and yawned again, then looked at Mariah. "Did you get everything moved into the old house?"

"Yes."

"All unpacked?"

"Well, not quite."

"Why don't you go finish? I'll be along in a few minutes to make sure you have everything you need."

"Why do I feel like I'm being told to leave?"

"Because you are."

Mariah started to object before she remembered that Luke wanted to talk with Cash in private about going prospecting with her.

"I'm not six years old anymore," she said reasonably. "You can talk in front of me."

It was as though she hadn't spoken.

"Don't forget to close the bathroom window," Luke said, "unless you want a battle-scarred old tomcat sleeping on your bed."

Mariah looked at Cash. "Why do you let him insult you like that?"

There was a two-second hesitation before Cash laughed out loud, but the sudden blaze in his eyes made Mariah's heart beat faster.

Shaking his head, Luke said, "Good night, Muffin."

"Don't forget to bring my cookies and milk," she retorted sweetly, "or I'll cry myself to sleep."

Luke grabbed Mariah, hugged her and ruffled her hair as though she were six years old again. Laughing, she stood on tiptoe and returned the favor, then found herself suddenly blinking back tears.

"Thank you, Luke," she said.

"For what?"

"Not throwing me out on my ear when I turned up without warning."

"Don't be silly. This is your home."

"No," she whispered, "it's yours. But I'm grateful to share it for a while."

Before Luke could say anything else, she kissed his cheek and walked quickly from the dining room. Cash stood and watched the outer door for a long, silent moment, admiring the perfection with which Mariah played the role of vulnerable child-woman. She was very good. Even better than Linda had been, and Linda had fooled him completely. Of course, Linda had had a real advantage. She had told him something he would have sold his soul to believe—that she was carrying his child.

What he hadn't known until too late was that Linda had been sleeping with another man. That was another thing women were good at—making each man feel like he was the only one.

"You don't have to worry about Nevada," Luke said calmly.

Startled, Cash turned toward his friend. "What do you mean?"

"Oh, he's a handsome son, but it's you Mariah keeps looking at." Deadpan, Luke added, "Which proves that there's no accounting for taste."

"Despite the beard, Nevada isn't a prospector," Cash pointed out coolly, "and the lady's heart is obviously set on gold."

"The lady was looking at you before she knew you were a prospector. And you were looking at her, period."

Cash's eyes narrowed into gleaming slits of blue. Before he could say anything, Luke was talking again.

"Yeah, yeah, I know, it puts a man between a rock and a hard place when he wants his best friend's little sister. Hell, I ought to know. I spent a lot of years wanting Carla."

"Not as many as she spent wanting you."

Luke smiled crookedly. "So I was a prize fool. If it weren't for her matchmaking older brother, I'd still be waking up alone in the middle of the night."

"Is that what you're doing now? Matchmaking? Is that why you want me to go prospecting with Mariah? You figure we'll find something more valuable and permanent than gold?"

Wincing at Cash's sardonic tone, Luke raked his fingers through his hair as he said, "The area around Devil's Peak is damned wild country."

Cash looked at the ceiling.

"I can't let her go alone," Luke continued.

Cash looked at his hands.

"I can't take her myself."

Cash looked at the floor.

"I need every cowhand I've got, and five more besides."

Cash looked at the table.

Luke swore. "Forget it. I'll get Nevada to—"

"*Hell,*" Cash interrupted fiercely, angered by the thought of throwing Mariah and Nevada together in the vast, lonely reaches of the Rocking M's high country. Cash pinned Luke with a black look. "All right, I'll do it. But I'm usually gone for weeks at a time. Have you thought about that?"

"Mariah said she was a camper. Besides, there's always the Black Springs line shack."

"Damn it, that's not what I mean and you know it! Your sister is one very sexy female."

Luke cocked his head to one side. "Interesting."

A snarl was Cash's only answer.

"No, I mean it," Luke continued. "Not that I think Mariah is a dog, but sexy wouldn't be the word I'd use to describe her. Striking, maybe, with those big golden eyes and lovely smile. Warm. Quick. But not sexy."

"I wouldn't describe Carla as sexy, either."

"Then you're blind."

"No. I'm her brother."

"Point taken," Luke said, grinning.

There was silence, then Cash spoke in a painfully reasonable tone of voice. "Look. It takes half a day just to get to the Black Springs line shack by horseback. From there, it's a hard scramble up boulder-choked creeks and steep canyons. There's no way we can duck in, poke around for a few hours, and duck out. We'll be spending a lot of nights alone."

"I trust you."

"Then you are a damned fool," Cash said, spacing each word carefully.

"You trusted me in the wilds of September Canyon with Carla," Luke pointed out.

"Yeah. Think about it. Carla ended up pregnant and alone."

Luke grimaced. "You're not as big a fool as I was."

"Damn it—"

"Mariah is twenty-two," Luke continued over Cash's words, "college educated, a consenting adult in every sense of the word. I trust you in exactly the same way you trusted me, and for the same reason. You may be hardheaded as hell and not trust women worth a damn, but you would never touch a girl unless she wanted you to. Mariah will never be safer in that way than when she is with you. Beyond that, whatever happens or doesn't happen between the two of you is none of my business."

For a minute there was no sound in the dining room. Cash stood motionless, his hands jammed in his back pockets, his mind racing as he assessed the situation and the man he loved more than most men loved their blood brothers. In the end, there was only one possible conclusion: Luke meant every word he had said.

Well, at least I won't have to worry about getting Mariah pregnant the way Luke did Carla.

But Cash's bitterly ironic thought remained unspoken. It wasn't the sort of thing a man talked about.

"I'll hold you to that," Cash said finally.

Luke nodded, then smiled widely and gave Cash an affectionate whack on his shoulder. "Thanks for getting me off the hook. I owe you one."

"Like hell. I spend more time here than I do in my apartment in Boulder."

"So move here. You can build at the other end of the big pasture, just across the stream from Ten and Diana. Plenty of space."

"One of these days you're going to say that and I'm going to take you up on it."

"Why do you think I keep saying it?" Luke stretched and yawned. "Damn, I wish Carla were home. I never sleep as well when she's gone."

"You're breaking my heart. Go to bed."

"Mariah's waiting for me."

"I'll tell her what we decided," Cash said. "With luck, she'll change her mind when she finds out Nevada won't be her trusty wilderness guide."

"Are you deaf as well as blind? I keep telling you, it's not Nevada she's looking at!"

Cash turned on his heel and left the room without saying another word, but he let the outside door close behind him hard enough to make a statement about his temper.

Outside, the cool summer darkness was awash with stars and alive with the murmur of air sliding down from the highlands to the long, flat valley that was the Rocking M's center. Lights burned in the bunkhouse and in the old ranch house. Cash moved with the swift, ground-covering strides of a man who has spent much of his adult life walking over wild lands in search of the precious metals that fed civilization's endless demands. Though he wore only a shirt and jeans, he didn't notice the crisp breeze. He knocked on the front door of the old ranch house with more force than courtesy.

"Come in, Luke. It's open."

"It's Cash. Is it still open?"

Mariah looked down at her oversize cotton nightshirt and bare feet. For an instant she wished she were wearing Spanish lace, Chinese silk and French perfume. Then she sighed. As angry as Cash sounded, she could be naked and it wouldn't make a speck of difference.

What is it about me that irritates him?

There was no answer to the question, other than the obvious one. He wasn't wild about the idea of being saddled with her out in the backcountry, just as he hadn't been wild about helping her with her car. He looked at her as a helpless, useless burden. That shouldn't surprise her. Her stepfather had felt precisely the same way.

Mariah opened the door and stifled an impulse to slam it shut before Cash could come in. He towered over her, looming out of the darkness like a mountain, and his eyes were black with anger.

"Come in, or would you rather bite my head off out in the yard?"

The sound Cash made could most politely be described as a growl. He stepped forward. Mariah retreated. A gust of wind sucked the door shut.

Cash looked at the nightshirt that should have concealed Mariah's curves but ended up teasing him by draping softly over her breasts and hips. Desire tightened his whole body, hammering through him with painful intensity. The thought of being alone with her night after night was enough to make him slam his fist into the wall from sheer frustration.

"What do you know about wild country?" Cash asked savagely.

"It's where gold is found."

He hissed a single word, then said, "This won't be a trendy pseudo-wilderness trek along a well-beaten path maintained by the National Park Service. Can you even ride a horse?"

"Yes."

"Can you ride rough country for half a day, then scramble over rocks for another half day?"

"If I have to."

"The line shack leaks and it rains damn near every night. The only privy is a short-handled shovel. At the end of a hard day you have to gather firewood, haul water, wash out your socks so you won't blister the next day, eat food you're too tired to cook properly, sleep on a wood floor that has more drafts than bare dirt would and—"

"You make it sound irresistible," Mariah interrupted. "I accept."

"Damn it, you aren't even listening!"

"You aren't telling me anything I don't already know."

"Then you better know this. We'll be alone out there, and I mean *alone*."

Mariah met Cash's dark glance without flinching and said, "I've been alone since I was dragged off the Rocking M fifteen years ago."

Cash jammed his hands into his back pockets. "That's not what I meant, lady. Up on Devil's Peak you could scream your pretty head off and no one would hear."

"You would."

"What if I'm the one making you scream? Have you thought about that?"

"Frankly, you're making me want to scream right now."

There was a charged silence.

Mariah smiled tentatively and put her hand out in silent appeal. "I know what you're trying to say, Cash, but let's be honest. I don't have the kind of looks that drive a man crazy with desire and we both know it. Just as we both know you don't want to take me across the road, much less spend a few weeks in the wild with me. But I'm going to Devil's Peak. I've been dreaming of looking for Mad Jack's mine as long as I can remember. Come hell or high water, that's what I'm going to do."

Cash looked down at the pale, graceful hand held out to him in artful supplication. He remembered how cool and silky Mariah's fingers had felt when they had rested on his bare forearm. He remembered how quickly her hand had warmed at his touch. He wondered if all of her would catch fire that fast.

The thought made him burn.

"I'll take care of packing the supplies and horses," Cash said coldly, "because sure as hell you won't know how. We leave in five hours. If you aren't ready, I'll leave without you."

"I'll be ready."

Cash turned and left the house before Mariah could see just how ready he was right now.

Six

Five hours later Mariah pulled open the front door before Cash could knock. Silently he stared at her, noting the lace-up shoes, faded jeans, an emerald turtleneck T-shirt beneath a black V-necked sweater and a long-sleeved man's flannel shirt that ended at her hips. The arms of a windbreaker were tied casually around her neck. The outfit should have made her look as appealing as a mud post, but it was all he could do not to run his hands over her to find the curves he knew waited beneath the sensible trail clothes.

"Here," Cash said, holding out a pair of cowboy boots. "Luke said to wear these if they fit. They're Carla's."

While Mariah tried on the boots, Cash glanced around. She had packed a lot less gear than he had expected. A military surplus backpack was stuffed tightly and propped against the wall. Other military surplus items were tied to the backpack—canteen, mess kit and the like. Extra blankets had been rolled up and tied with thongs.

"Where's your sleeping bag?" he asked.

"I don't have one."

"What the hell are you planning to sleep on?"

"My side, usually. Sometimes my stomach."

Cash clenched his jaw. "What about hiking boots?"

"My shoes are tougher than they look." Mariah stood and stamped her feet experimentally. "They're long enough, but they pinch in the toes."

"That's how you know they're cowboy boots," Cash retorted.

Mariah glanced at Cash's big feet. He was wearing lace-up, rough-country hiking boots that came to just below his knees. The heels were thick enough to catch and hold the edge of a stirrup securely. She had priced a similar pair in Seattle and decided that she would have to find Mad Jack's mine before she could afford the boots.

She bent down, tied her shoes to the backpack, and picked it up. "Ready."

Cash's long, powerful arm reached out, snagged Mariah's impromptu bedroll, and stuffed it none too gently into her hands. "Don't forget this."

"You're too kind," she muttered.

"I know."

Empty-handed, Cash followed Mariah to the corral. Four horses waited patiently in the predawn darkness. Two of them were pack animals. The other two were saddled. Cash added Mariah's scant baggage to one of the existing packs and lashed everything securely in place. Moments later he stepped into the saddle of a big, rawboned mountain horse, picked up the lead rope of the pack animals and headed out into the darkness without so much as a backward look.

"It won't work," Mariah said clearly. "I don't need your help to carry my stuff. I don't need your help to get on a horse. I don't need your help for one damned thing except to make Luke feel better!"

If Cash heard, he didn't answer.

Mariah went to the remaining horse, untied it and mounted a good deal less gracefully than Cash had. It had been six years since she had last ridden, but the reflexes and confidence were still there. When she reined the small mare around and booted it matter-of-factly in the ribs, it quickly trotted after Cash's horse. The mare was short-legged and rough-gaited, but amiable enough for a child to ride.

An hour later Mariah would have traded the mare's good temperament for a mean-spirited horse with a trot that didn't rattle her teeth. The terrain went up and down. Steeply. If there was a trail, Mariah couldn't make it out in the darkness, which meant that she spent a lot of time slopping around in the saddle because there was no way for her to predict her horse's next movements. She would be lucky to stand up at the end of three more hours of such punishment, much less hike with a backpack up a steep mountain and look for gold until the sun went down.

Don't forget the bit about hauling water and washing your socks, Mariah advised herself dryly. *On second thought, do forget it. No socks could be that dirty.*

When dawn came, it was a blaze of incandescent beauty that Mariah was too uncomfortable to fully appreciate. Whichever way she turned in the saddle, her body complained.

Even so, she felt the tug of undiscovered horizons expanding away in all directions. It was exciting to be in a place where not so much as a glimpse of man was to be seen. For all that she could tell, she and Cash might have been the first people ever to travel the land. Wild country rolled away from her on all sides in pristine splendor, shades of green and white and gray, evergreens and granite.

Mixed in with the darker greens of conifers was the pale green of aspens at the higher elevations, a green that was subtly repeated by grassy slopes at the lower elevations and occasional meadows in between. Ahead, Devil's Peak loomed in black, shattered grandeur, looking like the eroded ruins of a volcano rather than the granite peak Mariah had expected.

I wonder why Cash is searching for gold on a volcano's flanks? All the strikes I've read about were in granite, not lava.

Mariah would have asked Cash to explain this reasoning to her, but she had promised herself that she wouldn't speak until he did. Not even to ask for a rest break. Instead, she just hooked one leg around the saddle horn and rode sidesaddle for a time. She prayed there would be enough strength left in her cramped muscles to keep her upright after she dismounted.

As the sun rose, its heat intensified until it burned through the high country's crystalline air. The last chill of night quickly surrendered to the golden fire. Mariah began shedding layers of clothing until only the long-sleeved, fitted ski shirt remained. She unzipped the turtleneck collar and shoved up the sleeves, letting the breeze tease as much of her skin as it could reach.

At the end of four hours, Mariah rather grimly reined the mare down a narrow rocky crease that opened into a tiny valley. Although Cash had been only a few minutes ahead of her, he had already unloaded the pack animals and was in the act of throwing his saddle over the corral railing. Even as Mariah resented it, she envied his muscular ease of movement. She pulled her horse to a halt and slowly, carefully, began to dismount.

Two seconds later she was sitting in the dirt. Her legs simply hadn't been able to support the rest of her. She gritted her teeth and was beginning the tedious job of getting to her feet when she felt herself picked up with dizzying speed. The world shifted crazily. When it settled again, she was being carried like a child against Cash's chest.

"I thought you said you could ride," Cash said harshly.

"I can." Mariah grimaced. "I just proved it, remember?"

"And now you won't be able to walk."

"*Quelle* shock. Wasn't that the whole idea? You didn't want me looking for gold with you and now I won't be able to. Not right away, at any rate. I'll be fine as soon as my legs start cooperating again and then you'll be out of luck."

Cash's mouth flattened into a hard line. "How long has it been since you were on a horse?"

"About a minute."

Against his will, Cash found himself wanting to smile. Any other woman would have been screaming at him or crying or doing both at once. Despite the grueling ride, Mariah's sense of humor was intact. Biting, but intact.

And she felt exciting in his arms, warm and supple, soft, fitting him without gaps or angles or discomfort. He shifted her subtly, savoring the feel of her, silently urging her to relax against his strength.

"Sorry, honey," he said. "If I had known how long it had been since—"

"Pull my other leg," Mariah interrupted. Then she smiled wearily. "On second thought, don't. It might fall off."

"How long has it been since you've ridden?" he asked again.

"Years. Six blessed, wonderful years."

Cash said something savage.

"Oh, it's not that bad," Mariah said.

"You sure?"

"Yeah. It's worse."

He laughed unwillingly and held her even closer. She braced herself against the temptation to put her head on the muscular resilience of his chest and relax her aching body. Her head sagged anyway. She sighed and gave herself to Cash's strength, figuring he had plenty to spare.

"A soak in the hot springs will help," he said.

Mariah groaned softly at the thought of hot water drawing out the stiffness of her muscles.

"My swimsuit is in my backpack," she said. "Better yet, just give me a bar of soap and throw me in as is. That way I won't have to haul water to wash my socks."

Laughing soundlessly, shaking his head, Cash held Mariah for a long moment in something very close to a hug. She might be an accomplished little actress in some ways, but she was good company in others. Linda hadn't been. When things didn't go according to her plan—and often even when they did—she pouted and wheedled like a child after candy. At first it had been gratifying to be the center of Linda's world. Gradually it had become tedious to be cast in a role of father to a manipulative little girl who would never grow up.

A long, almost contented sigh escaped Mariah's lips, stirring the hair that pushed up beneath Cash's open collar. A visible ripple of response went through him as he felt her breath wash over his skin. He clenched his jaw and walked toward the corral fence.

"Time to stand on your own two feet," he said tightly.

With the unself-consciousness of a cat, Mariah rubbed her cheek against Cash's shirt and admitted, "I'd rather stand on yours."

"I figured that out the first time I saw you."

The sardonic tone of Cash's voice told Mariah that the truce was over. She didn't know what she had done to earn either the war or the truce. All she knew was that she had never enjoyed anything quite so much as being held by Cash, feeling the flex and resilience of his body, being so close to him that she could see sunlight melt and run through his hair like liquid gold.

When Cash's left arm released Mariah's legs, everything dipped and turned once more, but slowly this time. Instinctively she put her arms around his neck, seeking a stable center in a shifting world. Held securely more by the hard power of his right arm than by both her own arms, Mariah felt her hips slide down the length of Cash's body with a slow intimacy that shook her. Her glance flew to his face. His expression was as impassive as granite.

"Grab hold of the top rail," Cash instructed.

Mariah reached for the smooth, weathered wood with a hand that trembled. As she twisted in Cash's arms, the fitted T-shirt outlined her breasts in alluring detail, telling of the soft, feminine flesh beneath.

He wondered whether her nipples were pink or dusky rose or even darker, a vivid contrast to the pale satin of her skin. He thought of bending down and caressing her breasts with his tongue and teeth, drawing out the nipples until they felt like hot, hard velvet and she twisted beneath him, crying for release from the passionate prison of their love-making.

Don't be a fool, Cash told himself savagely. *No woman ever wants a man like that. Not really. Not so deep and hard and wild she forgets all the playacting, all the survival calculations, all the cunning.*

Yet, despite the cold lessons of past experience, when Cash looked down at Mariah curled softly in his arms, blood pulsed and gathered hotly, driven by the redoubled beating of his heart, blood surging with a relentless force that was tangible proof of his vulnerability to Mariah's sensual lures. Silently he cursed the fate that gave men hunger and women the instinctive cunning to use men's hunger against them.

"Put both hands on the rails," he said curtly.

When Mariah tried to respond to the clipped command, she found she couldn't move. Cash's arm was a steel band holding her against a body that also felt like steel. Discreetly she tried to put some distance between herself and the man whose eyes had the indigo violence of a stormy twilight. The quarter inch she gained by subtle squirming wasn't enough to allow her left hand to reach across her body to the corral fence. She tried for another quarter inch.

"What the hell do you think you're doing?" Cash snarled.

"I'm trying to follow your orders."

"When did I order you to rub against me like a cat in heat?"

Shock, disbelief and indignation showed on Mariah's face, followed by anger. She shoved hard against his chest. "Let go of me!"

She might as well have tried to push away the mountain itself. All her struggles accomplished were further small movements that had the effect of teaching her how powerful and hard Cash's body was—and how soft her own was by comparison. The lesson should have frightened her. Instead, it sent warmth stealing through her, gentle pulses of heat that came from the secret places of her body. The sensations were as exquisite as they were unexpected.

"C-Cash...?"

The catch in Mariah's voice sent a lightning stroke of desire arcing through Cash. For an instant his arm tightened even more, pinning Mariah to the hungry length of his body. Then he spun her around to face the corral, clamped her left hand over the top rail of the corral and let go of her. When her knees sagged, he caught her around the ribs with both hands, taking care to hold her well away from his body. Unfortunately there was nothing he could do about her breasts curving so close to his fingers, her soft flesh moving in searing caress each time she took a breath.

"Stand up, damn it," Cash said through clenched teeth, "or I swear I'll let you fall."

Mariah took in a shuddering breath, wondering if the jolting ride to Black Springs had scrambled her brains as well as her legs. The weakness melting her bones right now owed nothing to the hours on horseback and everything to the presence of the man whose heat reached out to her, surrounding her. She took another breath, then another, hanging on to the corral fence with what remained of her strength.

"I'm all right," Mariah said finally.

"Like hell. You're shaking."

"I'll survive."

With a muttered word, Cash let go of Mariah. His hands hovered close to her, ready to catch her if she fell. She didn't. She just sagged. Slowly she straightened.

"Now walk," he said.

"What?"

"You heard me. Walk."

A swift look over her shoulder told Mariah that Cash wasn't kidding. He expected her not only to stand on her rubbery legs but also to walk. Painfully she began inching crabwise along the corral fence, hanging on to the top rail with both hands. To her surprise, the exercise helped.

Strength returned rapidly to her legs. Soon she was moving almost normally. She turned to give Cash a triumphant smile, only to discover that he was walking away. She started after him, decided it was a bit too soon to get beyond reach of the corral fence's support, and grabbed the sun-warmed wood again.

By the time Mariah felt confident enough to venture away from the fence, Cash had the horses taken care of and was carrying supplies into the line shack. The closer she walked to the slightly leaning building, the more she agreed that "shack" was the proper term. Tentatively she looked in the front—and only—door.

Cash hadn't been lying when he described the line shack's rudimentary comforts. Built for only occasional use by cowhands working a distant corner of the Rocking M's summer grazing range, the cabin consisted of four walls, a ceiling, a plank floor laid down over dirt, and two windows. The fireplace was rudely constructed of local rocks. The long tongue of soot that climbed the exterior stone above the hearth spoke eloquently of a chimney that didn't draw.

"I warned you," Cash said, brushing by Mariah.

"I didn't say a word."

"You didn't have to."

He dumped her backpack and makeshift bedroll on the floor near the fireplace. Puffs of dust arose.

"If you still want to go to Black Springs, put on your swimsuit," Cash said, turning away. "And wear shoes unless you want to ride there."

"Ride?" she asked weakly. "Uh, no thanks. How far is it?"

"I never measured it."

Mariah's small sigh was lost in the ghastly creaking the door made as it shut. She changed into her swimsuit as quickly as her protesting leg muscles allowed. The inexpensive tank suit was made of a thin, deep rose fabric that fit without clinging when it was dry. Wet, it was another matter. It would cling more closely than body heat. Since Mariah had been dry when she purchased the suit, she hadn't known about its split personality.

"Hey, tenderfoot. You ready yet?"

Groaning, Mariah finished tying her shoelaces and struggled to her feet. "I'm coming."

As she stood, she felt oddly undressed. If she had been barefoot in the bathing suit, she would have had no problem. But somehow wearing shoes made her feel...naked. She grabbed her windbreaker and put it on. The lightweight jacket was several sizes too big. Normally she wore it over a blouse and bulky sweater, so the extra room was appreciated. With only the thin tank suit to take up room, the windbreaker reached almost halfway down her thighs, giving her a comforting feeling of being adequately covered.

When Cash heard the front door creak, he turned around. His first impression was of long, elegant, naked legs. His second impression was the same. He felt a nearly overwhelming desire to unzip the jacket and see what was beneath. Anything, even the skimpiest string bikini, would have been less arousing than the tantalizing impression of nakedness lying just beneath the loose black windbreaker.

Mariah walked tentatively toward Cash, wondering at the harsh expression on his face.

"Which way to the hot tub?" she asked, her voice determinedly light.

Without a word Cash turned and walked around to the back of the cabin. Mariah followed as quickly as she could, picking her way along the clear stream that ran behind the cabin. Even if her legs hadn't been shaky, she would have had a hard time keeping up with Cash's long stride. When her path took her on a hopscotch crossing of the creek, she bent and tested the temperature of the water. It was icy.

"So much for my hot tub fantasy," she muttered.

The racing, glittering water came from a narrow gap in the mountainside that was no more than fifty yards from the cabin. Inside the gap the going became harder, a scramble along a cascade that hissed and foamed with the force of its downhill race. The rocks were dark, almost black, which only added to the feeling of chill. Just when Mariah was wondering if the effort would be worth it, she realized that the mist peeling off the water was warm.

A hundred feet later the land leveled off to reveal a series of graceful, stair-step pools that were rimmed by smooth travertine and embroidered by satin waterfalls no more than three feet high. As Mariah stared, a shiver of awe went over her. The pools could not have been more beautiful if they had been designed by an artist and built of golden marble.

The water in the lowest pool was a pale turquoise Mariah had seen only on postcards of tropical islands. The water in the next pool was a luminous aquamarine. The water in the last pool shaded from turquoise to aquamarine to a clear, very dark blue that was the exact shade of Cash's eyes. At the far end of the highest pool, the water was so deep it appeared black but for swirls of shimmering indigo where liquid welled up from the depths of the earth in silent, inexhaustible pulses that had begun long before man ever walked the western lands and would continue long after man left.

Slowly Mariah sank to her knees and extended her hand toward the jeweled beauty of the pool. Before she could touch the water, Cash snatched her hand back.

"I've cooked trout at this end of Black Springs. Sometimes the downstream end of the pool is cool enough to bear touching for a few moments. Most often it isn't. It depends.''

''On what?''

Cash didn't answer her directly. ''You get hot springs when groundwater sinks down until it reaches a body of magma and then flashes into superheated steam,'' he said, absently running his thumb over Mariah's palm as he looked at the slowly twisting depth of Black Springs. ''The steam slams up through cracks in the country rock until the water bursts through to the surface of the land in a geyser or a hot spring. Most often the water never breaks the surface. It simply cools and sinks back down the cracks until it encounters magma, flashes to steam and surges upward again.''

Mariah made a small sound, reflection of the sensations that were radiating up from her captive hand. Cash looked away from the water and realized that his thumb was caressing Mariah's palm in the rhythm of the water pulsing deep within the springs. With a muttered word, he released her hand.

''I can tell you how a hot spring works, but I can't tell you why some days Black Springs is too hot and other days it's bearable. So be careful every day. Even on its best behavior, Black Springs is dangerously hot a foot beneath the surface.''

''Is the water drinkable?'' she asked.

''Once it cools off the trout love it. So do I. It has a flavor better than wine.''

Mariah stared wistfully at the beautiful, intensely clear, searingly hot water. ''It looks so wonderful.''

''Come on,'' Cash said, taking pity on her. ''I'll show you the best place to soak out the aches.'' He led her back to the middle pool. ''The closer you are to the spring, the hotter the water. Start at the lower end and work your way up until you're comfortable.'' He started to turn away, then stopped. ''You *do* swim, don't you?''

Mariah glanced at the pool. ''Sure, but that water is hardly deep enough for me to get wet sitting down.''

''The pool is so clear it fools your eyes. At the far end, the water is over my head.'' Cash turned away. ''If you're not back in an hour, I'll come back and drag you out. I'm hungry.''

''You don't have to wait for me,'' she said, setting shoes and socks aside.

''The hell I don't. You're the cook, remember?''

Seven

On the fourth day, Mariah didn't have to be awakened by the sound of the front door creaking as Cash walked out to check on the horses. She woke up as soon as sunrise brightened the undraped windows. Silently she struggled out of her tangle of blankets. Although she still ached in odd places and she wished that she had brought a few more blankets to cushion the rough wood floor, she no longer woke up feeling as though she had been beaten and left out in the rain.

Shivering in the shack's chill air, Mariah knelt between her blankets and Cash's still-occupied sleeping bag as she worked over the ashes of last night's fire. As always, she had slept fully clothed, for the high mountain nights were cold even in summer. Yet as soon as the sun shone over the broken ramparts of Devil's Peak, the temperature rose swiftly, sometimes reaching the eighties by noon. So while Mariah slept wearing everything she had brought except her shoes, she shed layers throughout the morning, adding them again as the sun began its downward curve across the sky.

Enough coals remained in the hearth to make a handful of dry pine needles burst into flames after only a few instants. Mariah fed twigs into the fire, then bigger pieces, and finally stove-length wood. Despite the fireplace's sooty front, little smoke crept out into the room this morning. The chimney drew quite well so long as there wasn't a hard wind from the northeast.

When she was satisfied with the fire's progress, Mariah turned to the camp stove that she privately referred to as Beelzebub. It was the most perverse piece of machinery she had ever encountered. No matter how hard or how often she pumped up the pressure, the flame wobbled and sputtered and was barely hot enough to warm skin. When Cash pumped up the stove, however, it put out a flame that could cut through steel.

With a muttered prayer, Mariah reached for the camp stove. A tanned, rather hairy hand shot out of Cash's sleeping bag and wrapped around her wrist, preventing her from touching the stove.

"I'll take care of it."

"Thanks. The thing hates me."

There was muffled laughter as a flap of the partially zipped sleeping bag was shoved aside, revealing Cash's head and bare shoulders. Another big hand closed over Mariah's. He rubbed her hand lightly between his own warm palms. Long, strong, randomly scarred fingers moved almost caressingly over her skin. She shivered, but it had nothing to do with the temperature in the cabin.

"You really *are* cold," he said in a deep voice.

"You're not. You're like fire."

"No, I mean it," Cash said. He propped himself up on one elbow and pulled Mariah's hands toward himself. "Your fingers are like ice. No wonder you thrash around half the night. Why didn't you tell me you were cold?"

"Sorry." Mariah tugged discreetly at her hands. They remained captive to Cash's enticing warmth. "I didn't mean to keep you awake."

"To hell with that. Why didn't you tell me?"

"I was afraid you'd use it as an excuse to make me go back."

Cash hissed a single harsh word and sat up straight. The sleeping bag slithered down his torso. If he was wearing anything besides the bag, it didn't show. Although Mariah had seen Cash at Black Springs dressed in only cutoff jeans, somehow it just wasn't the same as seeing him rising half-naked from the warm folds of a sleeping bag. A curling, masculine pelt went in a ragged wedge from Cash's collarbones to a hand span above his navel. Below the navel a dark line no thicker than her finger descended into the undiscovered territory concealed by the sleeping bag.

"It's not worth getting upset about," Mariah said quickly, looking away. "Any extra calories I burn at night I replace at breakfast, and then some. Speaking of which, do you want pancakes again? Or do you want biscuits and bacon? Or do you just want to grab some trail mix and go prospecting? I'm going with you today. I'm not stiff anymore. I won't be a drag on you. I promise."

There was a long silence while Cash looked at Mariah and she looked at the fire that was struggling to burn cold wood. Deliberately he cupped her hands in his own, brought them to his mouth, and blew warm air over her chilled skin. Before she had recovered from the shock of feeling his lips brushing over her palms, he was rubbing her hands against his chest, holding her between his palms and the heat of his big body. It was like being toasted between two fires.

"Better?" he asked quietly after a minute.

Mariah nodded, afraid to trust her voice.

With a squeeze so gentle that she might have imagined it, Cash released her hands and began dressing. For a few moments Mariah couldn't move. When she went to measure ingredients for biscuits, her hands were warm, but trembling. She was glad Cash was too busy dressing to notice.

The front door creaked as he went outside. A few minutes later it creaked again when he returned. The smell of dew and evergreen resin came back inside with him.

"If that's biscuits and bacon, make a double batch," Cash said. "We'll eat them on the trail for lunch."

"Sure." Then the meaning of his words penetrated. Mariah turned toward him eagerly. "Does that mean I get to come along?"

"That's what you're here for, isn't it?" Cash asked curtly, but he was smiling.

She grinned and turned back to the fire, carefully positioning the reflector oven. She had discovered the oven in a corner of the shack along with other cooking supplies Cash rarely ever used. Her first few attempts to cook with the oven had been a disaster, but there had been little else for her to do except experiment with camp cooking while Cash was off exploring and she was recovering from the ride to Devil's Peak.

Mariah had been grateful to be able to keep the disasters a secret and pretend that the successes were commonplace. It had been worth all the frustration and singed fingertips to see Cash's expression when he walked into the line shack after a day of prospecting and found fresh biscuits, fried ham, baked beans with molasses and a side dish of fresh watercress and tender young dandelion greens waiting for him.

While the coffee finished perking on the stove and the last batch of bacon sizzled fragrantly in the frying pan, Mariah sliced two apples and piled a mound of bacon on a tin plate. She surrounded the crisp bacon with biscuits and set the plate on the floor near the fireplace, where a squeeze bottle of honey was slowly warming. She poured two cups of coffee and settled cross-legged on the floor in front of the food. The position caused only a twinge or two in her thigh muscles.

"Come and get it," Mariah called out.

Cash looked up from the firewood he had been stacking in a corner of the shack. For a moment he was motionless, trying to decide which looked more tempting—the food or the lithe young woman who had proven to be such good company. Too good. It would have been much easier on him if she had been sulky or petulant or even indifferent—

anything but humorous and quick and so aware of him as a man that her hands shook when he touched her.

The tactile memory of Mariah's cool, trembling fingers still burned against his chest. It had taken all of his self-control not to pull her soft hands down into the sleeping bag and let her discover just how hot he really was.

Damn you, Luke. Why didn't you tell me to leave your sister alone? Why did you give me a green flag when you know me well enough to know I don't have marriage in mind? And why can't I look at Mariah without getting hot?

There was no answer to Cash's furious thoughts. There was only fragrance and steamy heat as he pulled apart a biscuit, and then a rush of pleasure as he savored the flavor and tenderness of the food Mariah had prepared for him.

They ate in a silence that was punctuated by the small sounds of silverware clicking against metal plates, the muted whisper of the fire and the almost secretive rustle of clothes as one or the other of them reached for the honey. When Cash could eat no more, he took a sip of coffee, sighed, and looked at Mariah.

"Thanks," he said.

"For what?"

"Being a good cook."

She laughed, but her pleasure in the compliment was as clear as the golden glow of her eyes. "It's the least I could do. I know you didn't want me to come with you."

"And you're used to being not wanted, aren't you." There was no question in Cash's voice, simply the certainty that had come of watching her in the past days.

Mariah hesitated, then shrugged. "Harold—my mother's second husband—didn't like me. Nothing I did in fifteen years changed that. I spent most of those years at girls' boarding schools and summer camps." She smiled crookedly. "That's where I learned to ride, hike, make camp fires, put up a tent, cook, sew, give first aid, braid thin plastic thongs into thick useless cords, make unspeakably ugly things in clay, and identify poisonous snakes and spiders."

"A well-rounded education," Cash said, hiding a grin.

Mariah laughed. "You know, it really was. A lot of girls never get a chance at all to be outdoors. Some of the girls hated it, of course. Most just took it in stride. I loved it. The trees and rocks and critters didn't care that your real father never wrote to you, that your stepfather couldn't stand to be in the same room with you, or that your mother's grip on reality was as fragile as a summer frost."

Cash drained his coffee cup, then said simply, "Luke wrote to you."

"What?"

"Luke has written to you at least twice a year for as long as I've known him," Cash said as he poured himself more coffee. "Christmas and your birthday. He sent gifts, too. Nothing ever came back. Not a single word."

"I didn't know. I never saw them. But I wrote to him. Mother mailed..." Realization came, darkening Mariah's eyes. "She never mailed my letters. She never let me see Luke's."

The strained quality of Mariah's voice made Cash glance up sharply. Reflected firelight glittered in the tears running down her cheeks. He set aside his coffee and reached for her, brushing tears away with the back of his fingers.

"Hey, I didn't mean to hurt you," Cash said, stroking her cheek with a gentleness surprising in such a big man.

"I know," Mariah whispered. "It's just...I used to lie awake and cry on Christmas and my birthday because I was alone. But I wasn't alone, not really, and I didn't even know it." She closed her eyes and laced her fingers tightly together to keep from reaching for Cash, from crawling into his lap and asking to be held. "Poor Luke," she whispered. "He must have felt so lonely, too." She hesitated, then asked in a rush, "Your sister loves Luke, doesn't she? Truly loves him?"

"Carla has always loved Luke."

Mariah heard the absolute certainty in Cash's voice and let out a long sigh. "Thank God. Luke deserves to be loved. He's a good man."

Cash looked down at Mariah's face. Her eyes were closed. Long, dark eyelashes were tipped with diamond tears. All that kept him from bending down and sipping teardrops from her lashes was the certainty that anything he began wouldn't end short of his becoming her lover. Her sadness had made her too vulnerable right now—and it made him too vulnerable, as well. The urge to comfort her in the most elemental way of all was almost overwhelming. He wanted her far too much to trust his self-control.

"Yes," Cash said as he stood up in a controlled rush of power. "Luke is a good man." He jammed his hands into his back jeans pockets to keep from reaching for Mariah. "If we're going to get any prospecting done, we'd better get going. From the looks of the sky, we'll have a thunderstorm by afternoon."

"The dishes will take only a minute," Mariah said, blotting surreptitiously at her cheeks with her shirttail.

It was longer than a minute, but Cash made no comment when Mariah emerged from the cabin wearing her backpack. He put his hand underneath her pack, hefted it, and calmly peeled it from her shoulders.

"I can carry it," Mariah said quickly.

Cash didn't even bother to reply. He simply transferred the contents of her backpack to his own, put it on and asked, "Ever panned for gold?"

She shook her head.

"It's harder than it looks," he said.

"Isn't everything?"

Cash smiled crookedly. "Yeah, I guess it is." He looked at Mariah's soft shoes, frowned and looked away. "I'm going to try a new area of the watershed. It could get rough, so I want you to promise me something."

Warily Mariah looked up. "What?"

"When you need help—and you will—let me know. I don't want to pack you out of here with a broken ankle."

"I'll ask for help. But it would be nice," she added wistfully, "if you wouldn't bite my head off when I ask."

Cash grunted. "Since you've never panned for gold and we're in a hurry, I'll do the panning. If you really want to learn, I'll teach you later. Come on. Time's a-wasting."

The pace Cash set was hard but not punishing. Mariah didn't complain. She was certain the pace would have been even faster if Cash had been alone.

There was no trail to follow. From time to time Cash consulted a compass, made cryptic notes in a frayed notebook, and then set off over the rugged land once more, usually in a different direction. Mariah watched the landscape carefully, orienting herself from various landmarks each time Cash changed direction. After half an hour they reached a stream that was less than six feet wide. It rushed over and around pale granite boulders in a silver-white blur that shaded into brilliant turquoise where the water slowed and deepened.

Cash shrugged out of his backpack and untied a broad, flat pan, which looked rather like a shallow wok. Pan in one hand, short-handled shovel in the other, he sat on his heels by the stream. With a deft motion he scooped out a shovel full of gravel from the eddy of water behind a boulder. He dumped the shovel-load into the gold pan, shook it, and picked over the contents. Bigger pieces of quartz and granite were discarded without hesitation, despite the fact that some of them had a golden kind of glitter that made Mariah's heart beat faster and her breath catch audibly.

"Mica," Cash explained succinctly, dumping another handful of rocks back in the stream.

"Oh." Mariah sighed. Her reading on the subject of granite, gold, and prospecting had told her about mica. It was pretty, but it was as common as sand.

"All that glitters isn't gold, remember?" he asked, giving her an amused, sideways glance.

She grimaced.

Cash laughed and scooped up enough water to begin washing the material remaining in the bottom of the gold pan. A deft motion of his wrists sent the water swirling around in a neat circle. When he tilted the pan slightly away from himself, the circular movement of the water lifted the lighter particles away from the bottom of the pan. Water and particles climbed the shallow incline to the rim and drained back into the stream. After a minute or two, Cash looked at the remaining stuff, rubbed it between his fingers, stared again, and flipped it all back into the stream. He rinsed the pan, attached it and the shovel to his backpack again, and set off upstream.

"Nothing, huh?" Mariah said, scrambling to keep up.

"Grit, sand, pea gravel, pebbles. Granite. Some basalt. A bit of chert. Small piece of clear quartz."

"No gold?"

"Not even pyrite. That's fool's gold."

"I know. Pyrite is pretty, though."

Cash grunted. "Leave it to a woman to think pretty is enough."

"Oh, right. That's why men have such a marked preference for ugly women."

Cash hid a smile. For a time there was silence punctuated by scrambling sounds when the going became especially slippery at the stream's edge. Twice Mariah needed help. The first time she needed only a steadying hand as she scrambled forward. The second time Cash found it easier simply to lift her over the obstacle. The feel of his hands on her, and the ease with which he moved her from place to place, left Mariah more than a little breathless. Yet despite the odd fluttering in the pit of her stomach, her brain continued to work.

"Cash?"

The sound he made was encouraging rather than curt, so Mariah continued.

"What are we doing?"

"Walking upstream."

"Why are we walking upstream?"

"It's called prospecting, honey. Long hours, backbreaking work and no pay. Just like I told you back at the ranch house. Remember?"

Mariah sighed and tried another approach.

"We're looking for Mad Jack's mine, right?" she asked.

"Right."

"Mad Jack's gold was rough, which meant it didn't come out of a placer pocket in a stream, right?"

"Right."

"Because placer gold is smooth."

"Right."

The amusement in Cash's tone was almost tangible. It was also gentle rather than disdainful. Knowing that she was being teased, yet beguiled by the method, Mariah persisted.

"Then why are you panning for Mad Jack's nonplacer mine?"

Cash's soft laughter barely rose above the sound of the churning stream. He turned around, made a lightning grab and had Mariah securely tucked against his chest before she knew what was happening. With a startled sound she hung on to him as he crossed the stream in a few strides, his boots impervious to the cold water.

"Wondered when you'd catch on," Cash said.

He set Mariah back on her feet, releasing her with a slow reluctance that was like a caress. His smile was the same. A caress.

"But the truth is," he continued in a deep voice, resolutely looking away from her, "I *am* panning for that mine. Think about it. Gold is heavy. Wherever a gold-bearing formation breaks the surface, gradually the matrix surrounding the gold weathers away. Gold doesn't weather. That, and its malleability, is what makes it so valuable to man."

Mariah made an encouraging sound.

"Anyway, the matrix crumbles away and frees the gold, which is heavy for its size. Gravity takes hold, pulling the gold downhill until it reaches a stream and sinks to the bottom. Floods scoop out the gold and beat it around and drop it off farther downstream. Slowly the gold migrates downhill, getting more and more round until the nugget settles down to bedrock in a deep placer pocket."

"Mad Jack's gold is rough," Mariah pointed out.

"Yeah. I'm betting that canny old bastard panned a nameless stream and found bits of gold that were so rough they had to have come from a place nearby. So he panned that watershed, tracking the color to its source—the mother lode."

Cash looked back at Mariah to see if she understood. What he saw were wisps of dark, shiny hair feathered across her face, silky strands lifted by a cool wind. Before he could stop himself, he smoothed the hair away from her lips and wide golden eyes. Her pupils dilated as her breath came in fast and hard.

"You see," he said, his voice husky, "streams are a prospector's best friend. They collect and concentrate gold. Without them a lot of the West's most famous gold strikes would never have been made."

"Really?"

The breathless quality of Mariah's voice was a caress that shivered delicately over Cash.

"They're still looking for the mother lode that put Sutter's Mill on the map," he murmured, catching a lock of her hair and running it between his fingers.

The soft sound Mariah made could have been a response to his words or to the fragile brush of Cash's fingertips at her hairline. With a stifled curse at his inability to keep his hands off her, Cash opened his fingers, releasing Mariah from silken captivity.

"Anyway," he said, turning his attention back to the rugged countryside, "I'm betting Mad Jack was panning a granite-bottomed stream, because only a fool looks for gold in lava formations, and that old boy was nobody's fool."

"You're not a fool, either," Mariah said huskily, grabbing desperately for a safe topic, because it was that or grab Cash's hand and beg him to go on touching her. "So why were you prospecting the Devil's Peak area before you saw Mad Jack's map? Until we got to this stream, I didn't see anything that looked like granite or quartzite or any of the 'ites' that are usually found with gold. Just all kinds of lava. Granted, I'm no expert on gold hunting, but..."

"This area wasn't my first choice," Cash said dryly. "Almost two years ago I was having a soak in Black Springs when I realized that Devil's Peak is basically a volcano rammed through and poured out over country rock that's largely granite. Where the lava has eroded enough, the granite shows through. And where there's granite, there could be gold." He smiled, gave Mariah a sideways glance, and admitted, "I was glad to see that ratty old map, though. I've been panning up here for two years and haven't gotten anything more to show for it than a tired back."

"No gold at all?"

"A bit of color here and there. Hobbyist flakes, the kind you put in a magnifying vial and show to patient friends. Nothing to raise the blood pressure."

"Darn, I was hoping that—trout!" Mariah said excitedly, pointing toward the stream.

"What?"

"I just saw a trout! Look!"

Smiling down at Mariah, barely resisting the urge to fold her against his body in a long hug, Cash didn't even glance at the stream that had captured her interest.

"Fish are silver," he said in a deep voice. "We're after gold. We'll catch dinner on the way back."

"How can you be so sure? The fish could be hiding under rocks by then."

"They won't be."

Mariah made an unconvinced sound.

"I bet we'll catch our fill of trout for dinner tonight," Cash said.

"What do you bet?"

"Loser cleans the fish."

"What if there are no fish to clean?"

"There will be."

"You're on," she retorted quickly, forgetting Nevada's advice about never gambling with a man called Cash. "If we don't get fish, you do dishes tonight."

"Yeah?"

"Yeah."

"You're on, lady." Cash laughed softly and tugged at a silky lock of Mariah's hair once more. "Candy from a baby."

"Tell me that while you're doing dishes."

Cash just laughed.

"It's not a bet until we shake on it," she said, holding out her hand.

"That's not how it works between a man and a woman."

He took her hand and brought it to his mouth. She felt the mild rasp of his growing beard, the brush of his lips over her palm, and a single hot touch from the tip of his tongue. She thought Cash whispered *candy* when he straightened, but she was too shaken to be sure.

"Now it's a bet," he said.

Eight

"How's it going?" Cash asked.

Mariah looked up from the last fish that remained to be cleaned. "Better for me than for the trout."

He laughed and watched as she prepared the fish for the frying pan with inexpert but nonetheless effective swipes of his filleting knife.

Cash had expected Mariah to balk at paying off the bet, or at the very least to sulk over it. Instead, she had attacked the fish with the same lack of complaint she had shown for sleeping on the shack's cold, drafty floor. Only her unconscious sigh of relief as she rinsed the last fish—and her hands—in the icy stream told Cash how little she had liked the chore.

"I'll do the dishes," he said as she finished.

"Not a chance. It's the only way I'll get the smell of fish off my hands."

Cash grabbed one of Mariah's hands, held it under his nose and inhaled dramatically. "Smells fine to me."

"You must be hungry."

"How did you guess?"

"You're alive," she said, laughing up at him.

Smiling widely, Cash grabbed the tin plate of fish in one hand. The other still held Mariah's water-chilled fingers. He pulled her to her feet with ease.

"Lady, you have the coldest hands of any woman I've ever known."

"Try me after I've done the dishes," she retorted.

He smiled down at her. "Okay."

Mariah's stomach gave a tiny little flip that became a definite flutter when Cash pulled her fingers up his body and tucked them against the warm curve of his neck. Whether it was his body heat or the increased beating of her own heart, Mariah's fingers warmed up very quickly. She slanted brief, sideways glances at Cash as they walked toward the line shack, but he apparently felt that warming her cold hands on his body was in the same category as helping her over rough spots in the trail— no big deal. Certainly it wasn't something for him to go all breathless over.

But Mariah was. Breathless. Each time Cash touched her she felt strange, almost shaky, yet the sensations shimmering through her body were very sweet. Even as she wondered if Cash felt the same, she discarded the idea. He was so matter-of-fact about any physical contact that it made her response to it look foolish.

"Listen," Cash said, stopping suddenly.

Mariah froze. From the direction of Devil's Peak came a low, fluid, rushing sound, as though there were a river racing by just out of sight. Yet she knew there wasn't.

"What is it?" she whispered.

"Wind. See? It's bending the evergreens on the slope like an invisible hand stroking fur. The rain is about a quarter mile behind."

Mariah followed the direction of his pointing finger and saw that Cash was right. Heralded by a fierce, transparent cataract of wind, a storm was sweeping rapidly toward them across the slope of Devil's Peak.

"Unless you want the coldest shower you ever took," Cash said, "stretch those long legs."

A crack of thunder underlined Cash's words. He grabbed the plate of fish from Mariah and pushed her in the direction of the cabin.

"Run for it!"

"What about you?"

"Move, lady!"

Mariah bolted for the cabin, still feeling the imprint of Cash's hand on her bottom, where he had emphasized his command with a definite smack. She barely beat the speeding storm back to the line shack's uncertain shelter.

Cash, who had the plate of slippery fish to balance, couldn't move as quickly as Mariah. The difference in reaching shelter was only a minute or two, but it was enough. He got soaked. Swearing at the icy rain, Cash bolted through the line shack's open door and kicked it shut behind him. Water ran off his big body and puddled around his feet.

"Put all the stuff that has to stay dry over there," Cash said loudly, trying to be heard over the hammering of rain on the roof.

Mariah grabbed bedding, clothes and dry food and started stacking them haphazardly in the corner Cash had indicated. He set aside the fish and disappeared outside again. Moments later he returned, his arms piled high with firewood. The wood dripped as much as he did, adding to the puddles that were appearing magically on the floor in every area of the cabin but one—the corner where Mariah was frantically storing things. Cash dumped the firewood near the hearth and went back outside again. Almost instantly he reappeared, arms loaded with wood once more. With swift, efficient motions he began stacking the wood according to size.

"Don't forget the kindling," he said without looking up.

Quickly Mariah rescued a burlap sack of dry pine needles and kindling from the long tongue of water that was creeping across the floor. Before the puddle could reach the dry corner, gaps in the wooden planks of the floor drained the water away.

"At least it leaks on the bottom, too," Mariah said.

"Damn good thing. Otherwise we'd drown."

Thunder cracked and rolled down from the peak in an avalanche of sound.

"What about the horses?" Mariah asked.

"They'll get wet just like they would at the home corral."

Cash stood up and shook his head, spraying cold drops everywhere.

"We had a dog that used to do that," Mariah said. "We kept him outside when it rained. In Seattle, that was most of the time."

She started to say something else, then forgot what it was. Cash was peeling off his flannel shirt and arranging it on a series of nails over the hearth. The naked reality of his strength fascinated her. Every twist of his body, every motion, every breath, shifted the masculine pattern of bone and muscle, sinew and tendon, making new arrangements of light and shadow, strength and grace.

"Is something wrong?" Cash said, both amused and aroused by the admiration in Mariah's golden eyes.

"Er...you're steaming."

"What?"

"You're steaming."

Cash held out his arms and laughed as he saw that Mariah was right. Heat curled visibly up from his body in the line shack's chilly air.

"I'll get you a shirt before you freeze," Mariah said, turning back to the haphazard mound she had piled in the corner. She rummaged about until she came up with a midnight-blue shirt that was the color of Cash's eyes in the stormy light. "I knew it was here."

"Thanks. Can you find some jeans, too?"

The voice came from so close to Mariah that she was startled. She glanced around and saw bare feet not eight inches away. Bare calves, too. And knees. And thighs. And—hastily she looked back at the pile of dry goods, hoping Cash couldn't see the sudden color burning on her cheeks or the clumsiness of her hands.

But Cash saw both the heat in Mariah's cheeks and the trembling of her fingers as she handed him dry jeans without looking around.

"Sorry," he said, taking the jeans from her and stepping into them. "In these days of co-ed dorms, I didn't think the sight of a man in underwear would embarrass you."

"There's rather a lot of you," Mariah said in an elaborately casual voice, then put her face in her hands. "I didn't mean it the way it sounded. It's just that you're bigger than most men and...and..."

"Taller, too," Cash said blandly.

Mariah made a muffled sound behind her hands, and then another.

"You're laughing at me," he said.

"No, I'm strangling on my feet."

"Try putting them in your mouth only one at a time. It always works for me."

Mariah gave up and laughed out loud. Smiling, Cash listened to her laughter glittering through the drumroll of rain on the roof. He was still smiling when he went down on one knee in front of the fire and stirred it into life.

"What do you say to an early dinner and a game of cards?" Cash asked.

"Sure. What kind of game?"

"Poker. Is there any other kind?"

"Zillions. Canasta and gin and Fish and Old Maid and—"

"Kid games," Cash interrupted, scoffing. He looked over his shoulder and saw Mariah watching him. "We're too old for that."

The gleaming intensity of Cash's eyes made Mariah feel weak.

"I just remembered something," she said faintly.

"What?"

"Never play cards with a man called Cash."

"It doesn't apply. My name is Alexander."

"I'm reassured."

"Thought you would be."

"I'm also broke."

"That's okay. We'll play for things we have lots of."

"Like what?"

"Pine needles, smiles, puddles, kisses, raindrops, that sort of thing." Without waiting for an answer, Cash turned back to the fire. "How hot do you need it for trout? Or do you want to cook them over the camp stove?"

Blinking, Mariah tried to gather her scattered thoughts. Cash couldn't have mentioned kisses, could he? She must have been letting her own longing guide her hearing down false trails.

"Trout," she said tentatively.

"Yeah. You remember. Those slippery little devils you cleaned." He smiled. "The look on your face... Never bet anything you mind losing, honey."

Abruptly Mariah was certain she had heard his list of betting items very clearly, and kisses had definitely been one of them.

And he had nearly gotten away with it.

"Cash McQueen, you could teach slippery to a fish."

He laughed out loud, enjoying Mariah's quick tongue. Then he thought of some other ways he would like to enjoy that tongue. The fit of his jeans changed abruptly. So did his laughter. He stood in a barely controlled rush of power and turned his back on Mariah.

"You'll need light to cook," he muttered.

He crossed the shack in a few long strides, ignoring the puddles, and yanked a pressurized gas lantern from its wall hook. He pumped up the lantern with short, savage strokes, ripped a wooden match into life on his jeans and lit the lantern. Light pulsed wildly, erratically, until he adjusted the gas feed. The lantern settled into a hard, bright light whose pulses were so subtle they were almost undetectable. He brought the lantern across the room and hung it on one of the many nails that cowhands had driven into the line shack's walls over the years.

"Thank you," Mariah said uncertainly, wondering if Cash had somehow been insulted by being called slippery. But his laughter had been genuine. Then he had stopped laughing and that, too, had been genuine.

With a muffled sigh Mariah concentrated on preparing dinner. While she worked, Cash prowled the six-foot-by-nine-foot shack, putting pans and cups and other containers under the worst leaks. Rain hammered down with the single-minded ferocity of a high-country storm. Although it was hours from sunset, the light level dropped dramatically. Except for occasional violent flashes of lightning, the hearth and lantern became isolated islands of illumination in the gloom.

Both Cash and Mariah ate quickly, for the metal camp plates drained heat from the food. Cash stripped the sweet flesh from the fish bones with a deftness that spoke of long practice. Cornbread steamed and breathed fragrance into the chilly air. When there was nothing left but crumbs and memories, Mariah reached for the dishes.

"I'll do them," Cash said. "You've had a hard day."

"No worse than yours."

Cash didn't argue, he simply shaved soap into a pot with his lethally sharp pocketknife, added water that had been warming in the bucket by the hearth and began washing dishes. Mariah rinsed and stacked the dishes to one side to drain, watching him from the corner of her eyes. He had rolled up his sleeves to deal with the dishes. Each movement he made revealed the muscular power of his forearms and the blunt strength in his hands.

When the dishes were over and Cash sat cross-legged opposite Mariah on the only dry patch of floor in the cabin, lantern light poured over him, highlighting the planes of his face, the sensual lines of his mouth, and the sheer power of his body. As Cash quickly dealt the cards, Mariah watched him with a fascination she slowly stopped trying to hide.

The cards she picked up time after time received very little of her attention. As a result, the pile of dried pine needles in front of her vanished as though in an invisible fire. She didn't mind. She was too busy enjoying sitting with Cash in a cabin surrounded on the outside by storm and filled on the inside by the hushed silence of pent breath.

"Are puddles worth more than pine needles?" Mariah asked, looking at the three needles left to her.

"Only if you're thirsty."

"Are you?"

"I've got all the water I can stand right now."

Mariah smiled. "Yeah, I know what you mean. Well, that lets out raindrops, too. I guess I have to fold. I'm busted."

Cash nudged a palm-size pile of needles from his pile over to her side of the "table."

"What's that for?" she asked.

"Your smile."

"Really? All these needles? If that's what a smile is worth, how much for a kiss?"

Abruptly Cash looked up from his cards. His glance moved almost tangibly over Mariah's face, lingering with frank intensity on the curving line of her lips. Then he looked back at his cards, his expression bleak.

"More than either of us has," he said flatly.

Several hands were played in silence but for the hissing of the lantern and the slowly diminishing rush of rain. Cash kept winning, which meant that he kept dealing cards. As he did, the lantern picked out various small scars on his hands.

"How did you get these?" Mariah asked, touching the back of Cash's right hand with her fingertips.

He froze for an instant, then let out his breath so softly she didn't hear. Her fingers were cool, but they burned on his skin, making him burn, as well.

"You pan gold for more than a few minutes in these streams and your hands get numb," Cash said. His voice was unusually deep, almost hoarse, reflecting the quickening of his body. "I've cut myself and never even known it. Same for using the rock hammer during cold weather.

Easiest thing in the world to zing yourself. What my own clumsiness doesn't cause, flying chips of rock take care of."

"Clumsy?" Mariah laughed. "If you're clumsy, I'm a trout."

"Then you're in trouble, honey. I'm still hungry."

"I'm a very, very *young* trout."

Cash smiled grimly. "Yeah. I keep reminding myself of that. You're what...twenty-two?"

Startled by the unexpected question, Mariah nodded.

"I teach grad students who are older than you," Cash said, his tone disgusted.

"So?"

"So quit looking at me with those big golden eyes and wondering what it would be like to kiss me."

Mariah's first impulse was to deny any such thoughts. Her second was the same. Her third was embarrassment that she was so transparent.

"You see," Cash said flatly, pinning Mariah with a look, "I'm wondering the same thing about you. But I'm not a college kid. If I start kissing you, I'm going to want more than a little taste of all that honey. I'm going to want everything you have to give a man, and I'm going to want it until I'm too damn tired to lick my lips. I get hard just watching you breathe, so teasing me into kissing you would be a really dumb idea, unless you're ready to quit playing and start screwing around." He watched Mariah's face, muttered something harsh under his breath, and threw a big handful of pine needles into the pot. "Call and raise you."

"I d-don't have that many needles."

"Then you lose, don't you?" he asked. And he waited.

How much is a kiss worth?

Mariah didn't speak the words aloud. She didn't have to. She knew without asking that a kiss would be worth every needle in the whole forest. In electric silence she looked at Cash's mouth with a hunger she had never felt before. The days of beard stubble enhanced rather than detracted from the smooth masculine invitation of his lips. And he was watching her with eyes that burned. He had meant his warning. If she teased him into kissing her, she had better be prepared for a lot more than a kiss.

The thought both shocked and fascinated Mariah. She had never wanted a man before. She wanted Cash now. She wanted to be kissed by him, to feel his arms around her, to feel his strength beneath her hands. But she had never been a man's lover before. She wasn't sure she was ready tonight, and Cash had made it very clear that there would be no way for her to test the water without getting in over her head.

"I guess I lose," Mariah whispered. "But it isn't fair."

"What isn't?"

"Not even one kiss, when you must have kissed a hundred other women."

"Don't bet on it. I'm very particular about who gets close to me." Abruptly Cash closed his eyes against the yearning, tentative flames of desire in Mariah's golden glance. "The game is over, Mariah. Go to bed. Now."

Without a word Mariah abandoned her cards, rushed to her feet and began arranging her blankets for the night. After only a few moments she was ready for bed. She kicked out of her shoes, crawled into the cold nest she had made and began shivering. The first few minutes in bed at night, and the first few out of it in the morning, were the coldest parts of the day.

Cash stood up and moved around the cabin, listening to the rain. When he had checked all the pans he turned off the lantern and knelt to bank the fire. Although Mariah tried not to watch him, it was impossible. Firelight turned his hair to molten gold and caressed his face the way she wanted to. Closing her eyes, shivering, she gripped the blankets even more tightly, taking what warmth she could from them.

"Here."

Mariah's eyes snapped open. Cash was looming above her. His hands moved as he unfurled a piece of cloth and pulled it over her. One side of the cloth was a metallic silver. The other was black.

"What is it?"

"Something developed by NASA," Cash said. He knelt next to Mariah and began tucking the odd blanket around her with hard, efficient movements. "It works as good on earth as it does in space. Reflects heat back so efficiently I damn near cook myself if I use it. I just bring it along for emergencies. If I'd known earlier how cold you were, I'd have given it to you."

Mariah couldn't have answered if her life depended on it. Even with blankets in the way, the feel of Cash's hands moving down her sides as he tucked in the odd cloth was wonderful.

Suddenly Cash shifted. His hands flattened on the floor on either side of Mariah's head. He watched her mouth with an intensity that left her weak. Slowly his head lowered until he was so close she could taste his breath, feel his heat, sense the hard beating of his heart.

"Cash...?" she whispered.

His mouth settled over hers, stealing her breath, sinking into her so slowly she couldn't tell when the kiss began. At the first touch of his tongue, she made a tiny sound in her throat. A shudder ripped through Cash, yet his gradual claiming of Mariah's mouth didn't hasten. Gently, inevitably, he turned his head, opening soft feminine lips that were still parted over the sighing of his name. The velvet heat of Mariah's mouth made him dizzy. The tiny sounds she made at the back of her throat set fire to him. He rocked his head back and forth until her mouth was completely his, and then he drank deeply of her, holding the intimate kiss until her breathing was as broken and rapid as his own. Only then did he lift his head.

"You're right," Cash said hoarsely. "It isn't fair."

There was a rapid movement, then the sound of Cash climbing fully clothed into his sleeping bag.

It was a long time before either of them got to sleep.

Nine

Mariah sat on a sun-warmed boulder and watched Cash pan for gold in one of the nameless small creeks along the Devil's Peak watershed. Sunlight fell over the land in a silent golden outpouring that belied the chilly summer night to come. Stretching into the warmth, smiling, Mariah relished the clean air and the sun's heat and the feeling of happiness that had grown within her until she found herself wanting to laugh and throw her arms out in sheer pleasure.

The first days at the line shack had been hard, but after that it had been heaven. By the sixth day Mariah no longer awoke stiff every morning from a night on the hard floor and Cash no longer looked for excuses not to take her prospecting. By the eleventh day Mariah no longer questioned the depth of her attraction to Cash. She simply accepted it as she accepted lightning zigzagging through darkness or sunlight infusing the mountains with summer's heat.

Or the way she had accepted that single, incredible kiss.

Since then, Cash had been very careful to avoid touching Mariah but his restraint only made him more compelling to her senses. She had known men who wouldn't have hesitated to push her sexually if they had sensed such a deep response on her part. The fact that Cash didn't press for more was a sign to Mariah that he, too, cherished the glittering emotion that was weaving between the two of them, growing stronger with each shared laugh, each shared silence, drawing them closer and closer each day, each hour, each minute. Their closeness was becoming as tangible as the water swirling in Cash's gold pan, a transparent, fluid beauty stripping away the ordinary to reveal the gleaming gold beneath.

Shivering with a delicious combination of pleasure and anticipation each time she looked at Cash, Mariah told herself to be as patient as he was. When Cash was as certain of the strength of their emotion as she was, he would come to her again, ask for her again.

And this time she would say yes.

"Find anything?" Mariah asked, knowing the answer, wanting to hear Cash's voice anyway.

She loved the sound of it, loved seeing the flash of Cash's smile, loved the masculine pelt that had grown over his cheeks after eleven days without a razor, loved seeing the flex and play of muscles in his arms, loved...*him*.

"Nope. If the mine is up this draw, nothing washed down into the creek. I'll try a few hundred yards farther up, just to be sure."

Before Cash could flip the gritty contents of the pan back into the small creek, Mariah bent over his shoulder, bracing herself against his strength while she stirred through the gold pan with her fingertip. After a time she lifted her hand and examined her wet fingertip. No black flakes stuck to the small ridges on the pad of her finger. No gold ones stuck, either.

Mariah didn't care. She had already found what she sought—a chance to touch the man who had become the center of her world.

"Oh, well," she said. "There's always the next pan."

Cash smiled and watched while Mariah absently dried her fingertip on her jeans. A familiar heat pulsed through him as he looked at her. The desire he had felt the first time he saw her had done nothing but get deeper, hotter, harder. Despite the persistent ache of arousal, Cash had never enjoyed prospecting quite so much as he had in the past week. Mariah was enjoying it, too. He could see it in her smile, hear it in her easy laughter.

And she wanted him. He could see that, too, the desire in her eyes, a golden warmth that approved of everything he did, everything he said, every breath he took. He knew his eyes followed her in the same way, approving of every feminine curve, every golden glance, every breath, everything. He wanted her with a near-violent hunger he had never ex-perienced before. All that kept him from taking what she so clearly wanted to give him was the bitter experience of the past, when he had so needed to believe a woman's lies that he had allowed her to make a fool of him. Yet no matter how closely Cash looked for cracks in Mar-iah's facade of warmth and vulnerability, so far he had found none.

It should have comforted him. It did not. Cash was very much afraid that his inability to see past Mariah's surface to the inevitable female calculation beneath was more a measure of how much he wanted her than it was a testimony to Mariah's innate truthfulness.

But God, how he wanted her.

Cash came to his feet in a swift, coordinated movement that startled Mariah.

"Is something wrong?"

"No gold here," Cash said curtly. He secured the gold pan to his backpack with quick motions. "We might as well head back. It's too late to try the other side of the rise today."

Mariah looked at the downward arc of the sun. "Does that mean there will be time for Black Springs before dinner?"

The eagerness in Mariah's voice made Cash smile ruefully. He had been very careful not to go to the hot springs with Mariah if he could avoid it. He had enough trouble getting to sleep at night just remembering what she looked like bare-legged and wearing a windbreaker. He didn't need visions of her in a wet bathing suit to keep him awake.

"Sure," he said casually. "You can soak while I catch dinner downstream."

Disappointed at the prospect of going to the springs alone, Mariah asked, "Aren't you stiff after a day of crouching over ice water?"

Cash shrugged. "I'm used to it."

Using a shortcut Cash had discovered, they took only an hour to get back to the line shack. While he picketed the horses in fresh grass, Mariah changed into her tank suit and windbreaker. When she appeared at the door of the cabin, Cash glanced up for only an instant before he lowered his head and went back to driving in picket stakes.

With a disappointment she couldn't conceal, Mariah started up the Black Springs path. After a hundred yards she turned around and headed back toward the cabin. Cash had just finished picketing the last horse when he spotted Mariah walking toward him.

"What's wrong?"

"Nothing. I just decided it would be more fun to learn how to handle a gold pan than it would be to soak in an oversize hot tub."

Cash's indigo glance traveled from the dark wisps of hair caressing Mariah's face to the long, elegant legs that were naked of anything but sunlight.

"Better get some more clothes on. The stream is a hell of a lot colder than Black Springs."

"I wasn't planning on swimming."

"You'll get wet anyway. Amateurs always do."

"But it's hot. Look at you. You're in shirtsleeves and you're sweating."

He didn't bother to argue that the sun wasn't warm. If he had been alone, he would have been working stripped to the waist. But he wasn't alone. He was with a woman he wanted, a woman who wanted him, a woman he was trying very hard to be smart enough not to take.

"If you plan on learning how to pan for gold," Cash said flatly, "you better get dressed for it."

Mariah threw up her hands and went back to the line shack before Cash changed his mind about teaching her how to pan for gold at all. She tore off the windbreaker and yanked on jeans over her shoes. Without looking, she grabbed a shirt off the pile of clothes that covered her blankets. She was halfway out the door before she realized that the shirt belonged to Cash.

"Tough," she muttered, yanking the soft navy flannel into place over her tank suit and fastening the snaps impatiently. "He wanted me to be dressed. I'm dressed. He didn't say whose clothes I had to wear."

There was no point in fastening the shirt's cuffs, which hung down well past her fingertips, just as the shoulders overhung hers by four inches on either side. The shirttails draped to her knees. Yet when Cash wore the shirt, it fit him without wrinkles or gaps.

"Lord, but that man is big," Mariah muttered. "It's a good thing he doesn't bite."

Impatiently she shoved the cuffs up well past her elbows, tied a hasty knot in the tails, grabbed the gold pan and shovel and ran back to where Cash was still working on the horses.

"I'm ready," Mariah said breathlessly.

Cash looked up, blinked, tried not to smile and failed completely. He released the horse's hoof he had been cleaning and stood up.

"Next time, don't wear such a tight shirt," he said, deadpan.

"Next time," Mariah retorted, "don't leave your tiny little shirt on my blankets when I'm in a hurry."

Snickering, Cash shook his head. "Let me get my fishing rod. We'll start in the riffles way up behind the shack. The creek cuts through a nice grassy place just above the willow thicket. Grass will be a lot easier on your knees than gravel."

"Don't you need gravel to pan gold?"

"Only if you expect to find gold. You don't. You're just learning how to pan, remember?"

"Boy, wouldn't you be surprised if I found nuggets in that stream."

"Nope."

Mariah blinked. "You wouldn't be surprised?"

"Hell no, honey. I'd be dead of shock."

Her smile flashed an instant before her laughter glittered in the mountain silence, brighter than any gold Cash had ever found. Unable to resist touching her, he ruffled her hair with a brotherly gesture that was belied by the sudden heat and tension of his body. The reaction came every time he touched her, no matter how casually, which was why he tried not to touch her at all.

Unfortunately for Cash's peace of mind, there was no satisfactory way to teach Mariah how to pan for gold without touching her or at least getting so close to her that not touching was almost as arousing as touching would have been. The soft pad of grass beneath their feet, the liquid murmur of the brook and the muted rustle of nearby willows being stroked by the breeze did nothing to make the moment less sensually charged.

Mariah's own response to Cash's closeness didn't help ease the progress of the lessons at all. When he put his hands next to hers on the cold metal in order to demonstrate the proper panning technique, she forgot everything but the fact that Cash was close to her. Her motions became shaky rather than smooth, which defeated the whole point of the lessons.

"It's a good thing the pan is empty," Cash muttered finally, watching Mariah try to imitate the easy swirling motion of proper panning. "The way you're going at it, any water in that pan would be sprayed from hell to breakfast."

"It looks so easy when you do it," Mariah said unhappily. "Why can't I get the rhythm of it?"

Cursing himself silently, knowing he shouldn't do what he was about to do, Cash said, "Here, try it this way."

Before common sense could prevent him, he stepped behind Mariah, reached around her and put his hands over hers on the pan. He felt the shiver that went through her, bit back a searing word and got on with the lesson.

"You can pan with either a clockwise or counterclockwise motion," Cash said through clenched teeth. "Which do you prefer?"

Mariah closed her eyes and tried to stifle the delicious shivering that came each time Cash brushed against her. Standing as close as they were, the sweet friction occurred each time either of them breathed.

"Damn it, Mariah, wake up and concentrate! Which way do you want to pan?"

"C-count."

"What?"

"Counter." She dragged in a ragged breath. "Counterclockwise."

With more strength than finesse, Cash moved his hands in counterclockwise motions, dragging Mariah's hands along. The circles he made weren't as smooth as usual, but they were a great improvement on what she had managed alone. The problem was that, standing as they were, Cash couldn't help but breathe in Mariah's fragile, elementally female fragrance. Nor could he prevent feeling her warmth all the way down to his knees.

And if he kept standing so close to her, there would be a lot less innocent kind of touching that he couldn't—or wouldn't want to—prevent.

Yet brushing against Mariah was so sweet that Cash couldn't force himself to stop immediately. He continued to stand very close to her for several excruciating minutes, teaching her how to pan gold and testing the limits of his self-control at the same time.

"That's it," Cash said abruptly, letting go of Mariah's hands and stepping back. "You're doing much better. I'm going fishing."

"But—how much water do I put in the pan?" Mariah asked Cash's rapidly retreating back.

"As much as you can handle without spilling," he answered, not bothering to turn around.

"And how much gravel?"

There was no answer. Cash had stepped into the willow thicket and vanished.

"Cash?"

Nothing came back to Mariah but the sound of the wind.

She looked at the empty gold pan and sighed. "Well, pan, it's just you and me. May the best man win."

At first Mariah tried to imitate Cash and crouch on her heels over the stream while she panned. The unaccustomed position soon made her legs protest. She tried kneeling. As Cash had predicted, kneeling was more comfortable, but only because of the thick mat of streamside grass. Kneeling on gravel wouldn't have worked.

Alternating between crouching and kneeling, Mariah concentrated on making the water in the pan turn in proper circles. As she became better at it, she used more water. While she worked, sunlight danced across the brook, striking silver sparks from the water and pouring heat over the land.

Patiently Mariah practiced the technique Cash had taught her, increasing the amount of water in the pan by small amounts each time. The more water she used, the greater the chance that she would miscalculate and drench herself with a too-energetic swirl of the pan. So far she had managed to make her mistakes in such a way as to send the water back into the stream, but she doubted that her luck would hold indefinitely.

Just when Mariah was congratulating herself on learning how to pan without accidents, she made an incautious movement that sent a tidal wave of ice water pouring down her front. With a stifled shriek she leaped to her feet, automatically brushing sheets of water from Cash's shirt and her jeans. The motions didn't do much good as far as keeping the clothes dry, but Mariah wasn't particularly worried. Once the first shock passed, the water felt rather refreshing. Except in her right shoe, which squished.

Mariah kicked off her shoes and socks, relishing the feel of sun-warmed grass on bare feet. Sitting on her heels again, she dipped up more water in the pan. Just as she was starting to swirl the water, she sensed that she wasn't alone any longer. She spun around, spilling water down her front again. She brushed futilely at the drops, shivered at the second onslaught of ice water, and smiled up at Cash in wry defeat.

He was standing no more than an arm's length away, watching her with heavy-lidded eyes and a physical tension that was tangible.

"Cash? What's wrong?"

"I was just going to ask you the same thing."

"Why?"

"You screamed."

"Oh." Mariah gestured vaguely to her front, where water had darkened the flannel shirt to black. "I goofed."

"I can see that."

Cash could see a lot more, as well. His soaked shirt clung lovingly to Mariah's body, doing nothing to conceal the shape of her breasts and much to emphasize them. The frigid water had drawn her nipples into hard pebbles that grew more prominent with each renewed pulse of breeze.

Watching Cash, Mariah shivered again.

"You should go back to the line shack and change out of those wet clothes," he said in a strained voice. "You're cold."

"Not really. The shirt is clammy, but I can take care of that without going all the way back to the cabin."

While Mariah spoke, her hands picked apart the loose knot in the bottom of Cash's shirt. She had undone the bottom two snaps before his fingers closed over hers with barely restrained power.

"What the hell do you think you're doing?" he demanded.

"Giving my bathing suit a chance to live up to its no-drip, quick-dry advertising."

Cash looked down into Mariah's topaz eyes, felt the smooth promise of her flesh against his knuckles and could think of nothing but how easy it would be to strip the clothes from her and find out whether the feminine curves that had been haunting him were as beautiful as he had dreamed.

"Bathing suit?" he asked roughly. "You're wearing a bathing suit under your clothes?"

Mariah nodded because she couldn't speak for the sudden tension consuming her, a tension that was more than equalled in Cash's hard body.

The sound of a snap giving way seemed very loud in the hushed

silence, as did Mariah's tiny, throttled gasp. Cash's hands flexed again
and another snap gave way.

Mariah made no move to stop him from removing the shirt. She hadn't
the strength. It was all she could do to stand beneath the sultry brilliance
of his eyes while snap after snap gave way and he watched her body
emerge from the dripping folds of his shirt. Where the thin fabric of the
tank suit was pressed wetly against her body, everything was revealed.

Cash's breath came out in a sound that was almost a groan. "God,
woman, are you sure that suit is legal?"

Mariah looked down. The high, taut curves of her breasts were tipped
by flesh drawn tightly against the shock of cold water. Every change
from smooth skin to textured nipple was faithfully reflected by the thin,
supple fabric. She made a shocked sound and tried to cover her breasts.

It was impossible, for Cash's hands suddenly were holding Mariah's
in a vise that was no less immovable for its gentleness. He looked at her
breasts with half-closed eyes, too unsure of his own control to touch her.
Nor could he give up the pleasure-pain of seeing her. Not just yet. She
was much too alluring to turn away from.

There was neither warning nor true surprise when Cash's hands released Mariah's so that he could sweep the wet shirt from her faintly
trembling body. Warm, hard palms settled on her collarbones. Long masculine fingers caressed the line of her jaw, the curve of her neck, the
hollow of her throat, and the gentle feminine strength of her arms all the
way to her wrists.

Too late Mariah realized that the straps of her tank suit had followed
Cash's hands down her arms, leaving not even the flimsy fabric between
her breasts and the blazing intensity of his eyes.

"You're perfect," Cash said hoarsely, closing his eyes like a man in
pain. "So damn perfect."

For long, taut moments there was only the sound of Cash's rough
breathing.

"Cash," Mariah said.

His eyes opened. They were hungry, fierce, almost wild. His voice
was the same way, strained to breaking. "Just one word, honey. That's
all you get. Make damn sure it's the word you want to live with."

Mariah drew in a long, shaking breath and looked at the man she
loved.

"Yes," she whispered.

Ten

Cash said nothing, simply bent and took the pink velvet tip of one breast into his mouth. The caress sent streamers of fire through Mariah's body. Her breath came out in a broken sound of pleasure that was repeated when she felt the hot, silky rasp of his tongue over her skin. Cash's warm hands enveloped her waist, kneading the flesh sensuously while his mouth tugged at her breast.

Even as Mariah savored the delicious fire licking through her body, Cash's hands shifted. Instants later her jeans were undone and long, strong fingers were pushing inside the wet denim, sliding over the frail fabric of her bathing suit, seeking the heat hidden between her thighs, finding it, stroking it in the same urgent rhythms of his mouth shaping her breast.

The twin assaults made Mariah's knees weaken, forcing her to cling to Cash's upper arms for balance. The heat and hardness of the flexed muscles beneath her hands surprised her. They were a tangible reminder of Cash's far greater physical power, a power that was made shockingly clear when he lifted her with one arm and with the other impatiently stripped away her wet jeans, leaving only the fragile tank suit between her body and his hands.

"Cash?" Mariah said, unable to control the trembling of her voice as the beginnings of sweet arousal turned to uncertainty.

His only answer was the sudden spinning of the world when he carried her down to the sun-warmed grass. Hungrily he took her mouth and in the same motion pinned her legs beneath the weight of his right thigh, holding her stretched beneath him while his hands plucked at her nipples and his tongue thrust repeatedly into her mouth.

Mariah couldn't speak, could barely breathe, and had no idea of how
to respond to Cash's overwhelming urgency. After a few minutes she
simply lay motionless beneath his powerful body, fighting not to cry.
That, too, proved to be beyond her abilities. When Cash tore his mouth
from hers and began kissing and love-biting a path to her ear, the taste
of tears was plain on her cheek.

"What the hell...?" he asked.

Baffled, he levered himself up until he could look down into Mariah's
eyes. They were huge against the paleness of her skin, shocking in their
darkness. Whatever she might have said a few minutes ago, it was brutally clear right now that she didn't want him.

"What kind of game are you playing?" Cash demanded savagely. "If
you didn't want sex, why the hell did you say yes?"

Mariah's lips trembled when she tried to form words, but no words
came. She no more knew what to say than she had known what to do.
Tears came more and more quickly as her self-control disintegrated.

Cash swore. "You're nothing but a little tease whose bluff got
called!"

With a searing word of disgust, Cash rolled aside, turning completely
away from Mariah, not trusting himself even to look at her. If it weren't
for his overwhelming arousal, he would have gotten to his feet and
walked off. Bitterly he waited for the firestorm to pass, hating the realization that he had been so completely taken in by a woman. Again.

"I'm not a tease," Mariah said after a moment of struggling to control
her tears. "I d-didn't say no."

"You didn't have to," Cash snarled. "Your body said it loud and
clear."

There was a long moment of silence, followed by Mariah's broken
sigh and a shaky question.

"How was I supposed to respond?"

Cash began to swear viciously; then he stopped as though he had
stepped on solid ground only to find nothing beneath his feet but air. He
turned toward Mariah and stared at her, unable to believe that he had
heard her correctly.

"What did you say?" he asked.

"How was I supposed to respond?" she repeated shakily. "I couldn't
even move. What did you want me to do?"

Cash's eyes widened and then closed tightly. An indescribable expression passed over his face, only to be replaced by no expression at
all.

"Have you ever had a lover?" Cash asked neutrally.

"No," Mariah whispered. "I never really wanted one until you." She
turned her face away from Cash, not able to cope with any more of his

anger and contempt. Her eyes closed as her mouth curved downward. "Now I wish I'd had a hundred men. Then I would have known how to give you what you want."

Cash said something appalling beneath his breath, but the words were aimed at himself rather than at Mariah. Grimly he looked from her slender, half-naked form to the scattered clothes he had all but torn off her body. He remembered his own uncontrolled hunger, his hands on her breasts and between her legs in a wildness that only an experienced, very hungry woman would have been able to cope with. Mariah was neither.

"My fault, honey, not yours," Cash said wearily. He took off his shirt, wrapped it around Mariah like a sheet and gently took her into his arms. "I wanted you so much I lost my head. That's a sorry excuse, but it's all I have. I'm sure as hell old enough to know better."

Mariah looked up at him with uncertain golden eyes.

"Don't be afraid," he said, kissing her forehead. One hand moved down her back in slow, comforting strokes. "It's all right, honey. It won't happen again."

The easy, undemanding hug Cash gave Mariah was like a balm. With a long sigh, she rested her head against his chest. When she moved slightly, she realized that his pelt of curling hair had an intriguing texture. She rubbed her cheek against it experimentally. Liking the feeling, she snuggled even closer.

"I wasn't afraid," Mariah whispered after a moment.

Cash made a questioning sound, telling Mariah that he hadn't heard her soft words.

"I wasn't afraid of you," Mariah said, tilting back her head until she could see Cash's eyes. "It was just...things were happening so fast and I wanted to do what you wanted but I didn't know how."

The soothing rhythm of Cash's hand hesitated, then continued as he absorbed Mariah's words.

"Virginity doesn't guarantee sexual inexperience," he said after a time. "You're both, aren't you? Virgin and inexperienced."

"There's no such thing as a sexually experienced virgin," Mariah muttered against his chest.

He laughed softly. "Don't bet on it, honey. My ex-wife was a virgin, but she had my pants undone and her hands all over me the first time we made out."

Mariah made an indecipherable noise that sounded suspiciously like "Virgin my fanny."

"Say again?" Cash said, smiling and tilting Mariah's face up to his.

She shook her head, refusing to meet his eyes. He laughed softly and bent over her mouth. His lips brushed hers once, twice, then again and again in tender motions that soon had her mouth turning after his, seeking him in a kiss less teasing than he was giving her. He seemed to give in, only to turn partially aside at the last instant and trace her upper lip with his tongue. The sensuous caress drew a small gasp from her.

Very carefully Cash lifted his head, took a slow breath and tucked Mariah's cheek against his chest once more. She gave a rather shaky sigh and burrowed against him. Hesitantly her hands began stroking him in the same slow rhythms that he was stroking her. His chest was hot beneath the silky mat of hair, and his muscles moved sleekly. Closing her eyes, she memorized his strength with her hands, enjoying the changes in texture from silky hair to smooth skin, savoring his heat and the muscular resilience of his torso.

When Mariah's hand slid down to Cash's waist, hovered, then settled on the fastening of his jeans, his breath came in with an odd, ripping sound.

"Would you like having my hands all over you?" Mariah asked tentatively.

A shudder of anticipation and need rippled over Cash, roughening his voice. "Hell yes, I'd like it. But," he added, capturing both her hands in one of his, preventing her from moving, "not unless you'd like it, too."

"There's only one way to find out...."

With a sound rather like a groan, Cash dragged Mariah's hands up to his mouth. "Let's wait," he suggested, biting her fingers gently. "There are other things you might like better at first."

"Like what?"

"Like kissing me."

Cash bent over Mariah's lips, touched the center of her upper lip with the tip of his tongue, then retreated. He returned again, touched, retreated, returned, touched and retreated once more. The slow, sensual teasing soon had Mariah moving restlessly in his arms, trying to capture his lips, failing, trying again and again until with a sound of frustration she took his head between her hands.

The cool, course silk of Cash's growing beard was an intense contrast to the heat and satin smoothness of his lips. The difference in textures so intrigued her that she savored them repeatedly with soft, darting touches of her tongue. When his lips opened, her tongue touched only air...and then the tip of his tongue found hers, touched, retreated, touched, withdrew. The hot caresses lured her deeper and yet deeper into his mouth, seducing her languidly, completely, until finally she was locked with him in an embrace as urgent as the one that had dismayed her a few minutes earlier.

But this time Mariah wasn't dismayed. This time she couldn't taste Cash deeply enough, nor could she be tasted deeply enough by him in turn. She clung to him, surrendering to and demanding his embrace at the same time, wholly lost in the shimmering sensuality of the moment. When he would have ended the kiss, she made a protesting sound and closed her teeth lightly on his tongue. With a hoarse rush of breath, Cash accepted the seductive demand and made one of his own in return, nipping at her lips, her tongue, sliding into the hot darkness behind her teeth until he had total possession of her mouth once more.

Gently Cash urged Mariah over onto her back. When she was lying against the soft grass once more, he settled onto her body in slow motion, easing apart her legs, letting her feel some of his weight while he explored the sweet mouth he had claimed with rhythmic strokes of his tongue.

Mariah made a soft sound at the back of her throat and arched against Cash's hard body. She couldn't imagine what had been wrong with her before, why his weight had frightened and then paralyzed her. The feel of his weight was delicious, maddening, incredibly arousing. Her only dilemma was how to get closer to him, how to ease the sweet aching of her body by pressing against his, soft against hard, fitting so perfectly.

When Cash's hips moved against Mariah, fire splintered in the pit of her stomach. She gasped and arched against him in an instinctive effort to feel the fire again. The sound he made was half throttled need, half triumph at having ignited the passion he had been so certain lay within her. Reluctantly, teasingly, he moved aside, lifting his body and his mouth from hers, releasing her from a sensual prison she had no desire to leave. Smiling, he looked down into her dazed topaz eyes. He was breathing too fast, too hard, but he didn't care. Mariah was breathing as quickly as he was.

"I think we can say with certainty that you like kissing me," Cash murmured.

Mariah's only answer was to capture his face between her hands once more, dragging his mouth back to hers. But he evaded her with an easy strength that told her he had been only playing at being captive before. He took her hands in his, interlacing them and rubbing against the sensitive skin between her fingers at the same time. When he could lace himself no more tightly to her, he flexed his hands, gently stretching her fingers apart. Her eyes widened as fire raced through her in response to the unexpected sensuality of the caress.

Smiling darkly, Cash flexed his hands once more as he bent down to Mariah.

"Want to taste me again?" he asked against her mouth.

Mariah's lips opened on a warm outrush of breath. The tip of her tongue traced his smile. He lifted his head just enough to see the sensual invitation of her parted lips revealing the glistening pink heat that waited for him. He wondered if she would open the rest of her body to him so willingly, and if he would slide into it with such sultry ease. With a throttled groan Cash took what Mariah offered and gave her his own mouth in return.

Slowly he pulled Mariah's hands above her head until she was stretched out beneath him. Each slow thrust of his tongue, each flexing of his hands, each hoarse sound he made was another streamer of fire uncurling deep inside Mariah's body. She twisted slowly, hungrily, trying to ease the aching in her breasts and at the apex of her thighs. When Cash lifted his head and ended the kiss, she felt empty, unfinished. She whimpered her protest and tried to reach for him, but her arms were still captive, stretched above her head in sensual abandon.

Mariah's eyes opened. Cash was watching her body's sinuous, restless movement with eyes that smoldered. Breathless, she followed his glance. The shirt he had used to cover her had long since fallen aside, leaving her bare to the waist once more. Her nipples were tight and very pink. One breast showed faint red marks, legacy of his first, wild hunger.

The memory of Cash's mouth went through Mariah in a rush of fire, tightening her body until her back arched in elemental reflex. When she saw the reaction that went through Cash, shaking his strength, she arched again, watching him, enjoying the heat of his glance and the sun pouring over her naked breasts.

"If you keep that up, I'm going to think you've forgiven me for this," he said in a deep voice, touching the vague mark on her breast caressingly. "Have you forgiven me, honey?"

"Yes."

The sound was more a sigh than a word. Mariah twisted slowly, trying to bring Cash's hand into more satisfying contact with her breast, but she could not. Cash still held her arms stretched above her head, her wrists held in his left hand, her body softly pinned beneath his right hand.

"If I promise to be very gentle, will you let me kiss you again?"

This time Mariah's answer was a sound of anticipation and need that made Cash ache. Slowly he bent down to her. His tongue laved the passionate mark on her breast, then kissed it so gently she shivered.

"I'm sorry," Cash whispered, kissing the mark once more. "I didn't mean to hurt you."

"You didn't, you just surprised me," Mariah said moving restlessly, wanting more than the gentle torment of his lips. "I know you won't hurt me. And I—I liked it. Cash? *Please.*"

Cash wanted to tell Mariah what her trust and sensual pleas did to him, but he couldn't speak for the passion constricting his throat. With exquisite care he caught the tip of first one breast then the other between his teeth. The arching of her body this time was purely reflex, as was the low sound of pleasure torn from her throat when he drew her nipple into his mouth and tugged it into a taut, aching peak. When he released her she made a sound of protest that became a moan of pleasure when he captured her other breast and began drawing it into a sensitive peak, pulling small cries of passion from her.

Mariah didn't know when Cash released her hands. She only knew that the heat of his skin felt good beneath her palms, and the flexed power of his muscles beneath her probing fingers was like a drug. She couldn't get enough of it, or of him.

A lean, strong hand stroked from Mariah's breasts to her thighs and back again while Cash's mouth plucked at her hardened nipple in a sensual teasing that made her breath break into soft cries. Long fingers slid beneath the flimsy tank suit and kneaded her belly, savoring the taut muscles and resilient heat. Gradually, imperceptibly, inevitably, his hand eased down until he could feel the silken thicket concealing her most vulnerable flesh. When he could endure teasing himself no longer, he slid farther down, finding and touching a different, hotter softness.

Mariah's eyes opened and her breath came in with a startled gasp that was Cash's name.

"Easy, honey. That doesn't hurt you, does it?"

"No. It just—" Mariah's breath broke at another gliding caress. "It's so—" Another gasp came, followed by a trembling that shook her.

Mariah looked up at Cash with wide, questioning eyes, only to find that he was watching the slow twisting of her half-clothed body as he caressed her intimately. The stark sensuality of the moment made heat bloom beneath her skin, embarrassment and desire mingling. When his hand slid from between her legs, she made a broken sound of protest. An instant later she felt the fragile fabric of her tank suit being drawn down her legs until she was utterly naked. She saw the heavy-lidded blaze of Cash's eyes memorizing the secrets he had revealed, and she was caught between another rush of embarrassment and passion. He was looking at her as though he had never seen a nude woman before.

"You're beautiful," Cash breathed, shaken and violently aroused by Mariah's smooth, sultry body.

One of his big hands skimmed from her mouth to her knees, touching her reverently, marveling at the sensual contrast between her deeply flushed nipples and the pale cream of her breasts. The soft mound of nearly black curls fascinated him. He returned again and again to skim their promise, lightly seeking the honeyed softness he knew lay within.

Shivering with a combination of uncertainty and arousal, Mariah watched Cash cherish her body with slow sweeps of his hand. The dark intensity of his eyes compelled her, the tender caresses of his fingertips reassured her, the hot intimacy of seeing his hand touching the secret places of her body made her blush.

"Cash?" she asked shakily.

"If it embarrasses you," Cash said without looking up, "close your eyes. But don't ask me to. I've never touched a woman half so beautiful. If you weren't a virgin, I'd be doing things to you right now that would make you blush all the way to the soles of your feet."

"I already am," she said shakily.

A dark, lazy kind of smile was Cash's only answer. "But you like this, don't you?"

His knuckles skimmed the dark curls again, turning Mariah's answer into a broken sigh of pleasure.

"Good," he whispered, bending down to kiss her lips slowly, then rising once more, wanting to watch her. "I like it, too. There's something else I know I'll like doing. I think you'll like it even better."

Cash's fingertips caressed Mariah's thighs, sliding up and down between her knees, making her shiver. Watching her, he smiled and caressed her soft inner thighs again and again, gently easing them apart. When she resisted, he bent and took her mouth in a kiss that was sweet and gentle and deep. The rhythmic penetration and withdrawal of his tongue teased her, as did the sensual forays of his mouth over her breasts.

Soon Mariah's eyelids flickered shut as thrill after thrill of pleasure went through her. She forgot that she was naked and he was watching her, forgot that she was uncertain and he was tremendously strong, forgot her instinctive protection of the vulnerable flesh between her legs. With a moan she arched her back, demanding that he do something to ease the tightness coiling within her body.

The next time Mariah lifted, pleading for Cash, sensual heat bloomed from within the softness no man had ever touched. And then Cash's caress was inside her, testing the depth of her response, his touch sliding into her sleek heat until he could go no farther. Mariah made a low sound that could have been pain or pleasure. Before Cash could ask which, he felt the answer in the passionate melting of her body around his deep caress. The instant, fierce blaze of his own response almost undid him.

With a hoarse groan of male need, Cash sought Mariah's mouth, found it, took it in hungry rhythms of penetration and retreat. She took his mouth in return while her hands moved hungrily over his head, his chest, his back, half-wild with the need he had called from her depths. When he finally tore his mouth away from hers in an agonizing attempt to bring himself under control, Mariah's nails scored heedlessly on his arms in silent protest.

Cash didn't complain. He was asking for all of her response each time he probed caressingly within her softness and simultaneously rubbed the sleek bud that passion had drawn from her tender flesh. Mariah's quickening cries and searing meltings were a fire licking over him, arousing him violently, yet he made no move to take her. Instead, his hands pleasured and enjoyed her with an unbridled sensuality that was as new to him as it was to her, each of his caresses a mute demand and plea that was answered with liquid fire.

Finally Cash could bear no more of the sensuous torment. It was as difficult as tearing off his own skin to withdraw from Mariah's softness, but he did. The lacings of his boots felt harsh, alien, after the silky perfection of her aroused body. He yanked off his boots and socks with violent impatience, wanting only to be inside her. Shuddering with the force of his suppressed need, he fought for control of the passion that had possessed him as completely as it had possessed her.

"Is it—is it supposed to be—like this?" Mariah asked, breathing too hard, too fast, watching Cash with wild golden eyes.

"I don't know," Cash said, reaching for his belt buckle, looking at her with eyes that were black with desire. "But I'm going to find out."

Mariah's eyes widened even more as Cash stripped out of his clothes and turned toward her. Admiration became uncertainty when she looked from the muscular strength of his torso to the blunt, hard length of his arousal. She looked quickly back up to his eyes.

"If it were as bad as you're thinking now," Cash said huskily, drawing her body close to his, "the human race would have died out a long time ago."

Mariah's smile was too brief, too shaky, but she didn't withdraw from him. When Cash rubbed one of her hands slowly across his chest, she let out a long breath and closed her eyes, enjoying his newly familiar textures. Her fingertips grazed one of his smooth, flat nipples, transforming it into a nail head of desire. The realization that their bodies shared similarities beneath their obvious differences both comforted and intrigued her. She sought out his other nipple with her mouth. A slow touch of her tongue transformed his masculine flesh into a tiny, tight bud.

"You *do* like that," Mariah whispered, pleased by her discovery.

A sound that was both laughter and groan was Cash's only answer. Then her hand smoothed down his torso and breath jammed in his throat, making speech impossible. The tearing instants of hesitation when she touched the dense wedge of hair below Cash's waist shredded his control. Long fingers clamped around her wrist, dragging her hand to his aching flesh, holding her palm hard against him while his hips moved in an agony of pleasure. She made an odd sound, moved by his need. Abruptly he released her, afraid that he had shocked her.

Mariah didn't lift her hand. Her fingers curled around Cash, sliding over him in sweet, repeated explorations that pushed him partway over the brink. When she touched the sultry residue of his desire, she made a soft sound of discovery and wonder. She could not have aroused him more if she had bent down and tasted him.

Cash groaned hoarsely and clenched his teeth against the release that was coiled violently within his body, raging to be free. With fingers that trembled, he pulled Mariah's hand up to his mouth and bit the base of her palm, drawing a passionate sound from her. His hand caressed down the length of her body, sending visible shivers of response through her. When he reached the apex of her thighs, he had only to touch her and she gave way before him, trusting him.

He settled his weight slowly between her thighs, easing them apart even more, making room for his big body. She was sleek, hot, promising him a seamless joining. He pushed into her, testing the promise, savoring the feverish satin of her flesh as it yielded to him.

"*Cash.*"

He forced himself to stop. His voice was harsh with the pain of restraint. "Does it hurt?"

"No. It—" Mariah's breath fragmented as fire streaked through her. "I—"

Even as her nails scored Cash's skin, he felt the passionate constriction and then release of her body. The hot rain of her pleasure eased his way, but not enough. Deliberately he slid his hand between their joined bodies, seeking and finding the velvet focus of her passion. Simultaneously his mouth moved against her neck, biting her with hot restraint. Fire and surprise streaked through Mariah, and then fire alone, fire ripping through her, filling her as Cash did, completely, a possession that transformed her.

Mariah's eyes opened golden with knowledge and desire.

"You feel like heaven and hell combined," Cash said, his voice rough with passion. "Everything a man could want."

Mariah tried to speak but could think of no words to describe the pleasure-pain of having so much yet not quite enough...heaven and hell combined. She closed her eyes and moved her hips in a sinuous, languid motion, caressing Cash as deeply as he was caressing her. Exquisite pleasure pierced her, urging her to measure him again and then again, but it wasn't enough, it was never enough, she was burning. She twisted wildly beneath the hands that would have held her still.

"Mariah," Cash said hoarsely. "Baby, stop. You don't know what you're doing to me. I—"

His voice broke as her nails dug into the clenched muscles of his hips. Sweet violence swept through him, stripping away his control. He drove into her seething softness, rocking her with the force of his need, giving all that she had demanded and then more and yet more, becoming a driving force that was as fast and deep within her as the hammering of her own heart.

At a distance Mariah heard her own voice crying Cash's name, then the world burst and she could neither see nor hear, she was being drawn tight upon a golden rack of pleasure, shuddering, wild, caught just short of some unimaginable consummation, unborn ecstasy raking at her nerves.

For an agonizing moment Cash held himself away from Mariah, watching her, sensing her violent need as clearly as he sensed his own.

"Mariah. Look at me. *Look at me.*"

Her eyelids quivered open. She looked at Cash and saw herself reflected in his eyes, a face drawn by searing pleasure that was also pain.

"Help me," she whispered.

With a hoarse cry that was her name, Cash drove deeply into Mariah once more, sealing their bodies together with the profound pulses of his release. Her body shivered in primal response, ecstasy shimmering through her, burning, bursting in pulses of pleasure so great she thought she would die of them. She clung to Cash, absorbing him into herself, crying as golden fire consumed her once more.

Cash drank Mariah's cries while ecstasy unraveled her, giving her completely to him and unraveling him completely in turn. Passion coiled impossibly, violently, within him once more. The elemental force was too overwhelming to fight. He held her hard and fast to himself, pouring himself into her again and again until there was no beginning, no end, simply Mariah surrounding him with the golden fury of mutual release.

Eleven

Mariah floated on the hot currents at the upstream end of the middle pool, keeping herself in place with languid motions of her hands. The sky overhead was a deep, crystalline blue that reminded her of Cash's eyes when he looked at her, wanting her. A delicious feeling shimmered through her at the memories of Cash's body moving over hers, his shoulders blocking out the sky, his powerful arms corded with restraint, his mouth hungry and sensual as it opened to claim her.

If only they had been able to leave the cellular phone behind, they would have remained undisturbed within Black Springs's sensual silence. But their peace was disturbed by the phone's imperious summons. It woke them from their warm tangle of blankets on the shack's wooden floor. Mariah appreciated the emergency safeguard the phone represented, but she resented its intrusion just the same.

Cash had picked up the phone, grunted a few times and hung up. Mariah had fallen asleep again, not awakening until Cash had threatened to throw her in the stream. He had taken one look at the slight hesitation in her movements as she crawled out of his sleeping bag and had sent her to Black Springs to soak. When she had tried to tell him that she wasn't really sore from the long, sweet joining of their bodies, he hadn't listened.

But she wasn't sore. Not really. She was just deliciously aware of every bit of herself, a frankly female awareness that was enhanced by the slight tenderness he deplored.

"Have I ever told you how lovely you are?"

Mariah's eyes opened and she smiled.

Cash was standing at the edge of the pool, watching her with dark blue eyes and a hunger that was more unruly for having been satisfied so completely. He knew beyond doubt what he was missing. He had sent her to the hot springs because he was afraid he wouldn't be able to keep his hands off her if she stayed in the cabin. Now he was certain he wouldn't be able to keep his hands to himself. The thin, wet fabric of her suit clung to every lush line of her body, reminding him of how good it had felt to take complete possession of her softness.

The cutoff jeans Cash wore in Black Springs didn't conceal much of his big body. Certainly not the desire that had claimed him as he stood watching Mariah.

"I'm not sure lovely is the right word for you," Mariah said, smiling. "Potent, certainly."

The shiver of desire that went over his skin as she looked at Cash did nothing to cool his body.

"Kiss me?" Mariah asked softly, holding a wet, gently steaming hand toward him.

"You're hard on my good intentions," he said in a deep voice, wading into the pool.

"Should that worry me?"

"Ask me this afternoon, when you're two hours into a half-day ride back to the ranch house."

"We have to go back so soon again?" Mariah asked, unable to hide her dismay. "Why?"

"I just got a ten-day contract in Boulder. Then I'll be back and we can go gold hunting again."

"Ten days..."

The soft wail wasn't finished. It didn't need to be. Mariah's tone said clearly how much she would miss Cash.

"Be grateful," Cash said thickly. "It will give you time to heal. I'm too damn big for you."

"I don't need time. I need...you."

The sound Cash made could have been laughter or hunger or both inextricably mixed. The water where Mariah was floating came to the middle of his thighs, not nearly high enough to conceal what her honest sensuality did to him. His former wife had used sex, not enjoyed it. At least not with him. Maybe Linda had liked sex with the father of her child.

I should be grateful that I can't get Mariah pregnant. Holding back would be impossible with her.

"Cash? Is something wrong?"

"Just thinking about the past."

"What about it?"

Without answering, Cash pulled Mariah into his arms and gave her a kiss that was hotter than the steaming, gently seething pool.

Discreetly Mariah shifted position in the saddle. After she had recovered from the initial trip to the line shack, Cash had insisted that she ride every day no matter where she was. Thanks to that, and frequent rest breaks, she wasn't particularly sore at the moment. She was very tired of her horse's choppy gait, however. Next time she would insist on a different horse.

"Are you doing okay?" Cash asked, reining in until he came alongside Mariah.

"Better than I expected. My horse missed her calling. She would have made a world-class cement mixer."

"You should have said something sooner. We'll trade."

Mariah looked at Cash and then at the small mare she rode. "Bad match. You're too big."

"Honey, I've seen Luke ride that little spotted pony all day long."

"Really? Is he a closet masochist?"

Cash smiled and shook his head. "He saves her for the roughest country the ranch has to offer. She's unflappable and surefooted as a goat. That's why Luke gave her to you. But the rough country is behind us, so there's no reason why we can't switch horses."

Before Mariah could object any more, Cash pulled his big horse to a stop and dismounted. Moments later she found herself lifted out of the saddle and into his embrace.

"You don't have to do this," she said, putting her arms around Cash's neck. "I was finally getting the hang of that spotted devil's gait."

"Call it enlightened self-interest. Luke will peel me like a ripe banana if I bring you back in bad shape. I'm supposed to be taking care of you, remember?"

"You're doing a wonderful job. I've never felt better in my life."

Mariah's smile and the feel of her fingers combing through his hair sent desire coursing through Cash. The kiss he gave her was hard and deep and hungry. His big hands smoothed over her back and hips until she was molded to him like sunlight. Then he tore his mouth away from her alluring heat and lifted her onto his horse. He stood for a moment next to the horse, looking up into Mariah's golden eyes, his hand absently stroking the resilience of her thigh while her fingertips traced the lines of his face beneath the growth of stubble.

"What are you thinking?" Mariah asked softly.

Cash hesitated, then shrugged. "Even though we'll sleep separately on the ranch, a blind man could see we're lovers."

It was Mariah's turn to hesitate. "Is that bad?"

"Only if Luke decides he didn't mean what he said about you and me."

"What did he say?"

"That you wanted me," Cash said bluntly. "That you were past the age of consent. That whatever the two of us did was our business."

Mariah flushed, embarrassed that her attraction to Cash had been so obvious from the start.

"I hope Luke meant it," Cash continued. "He and Carla are the only home I'll ever have. But what's done is done. We might as well have the pleasure of it because sure as hell we'll have the pain."

The bleak acceptance in Cash's voice stunned Mariah. Questions crowded her mind, questions she had just enough self-control not to ask. Cash had never said anything to her about their future together beyond how long he would be gone before he came back to the Rocking M and the two of them could go gold hunting again.

I haven't said anything about the future, either, Mariah reminded herself. *I haven't even told him that I love him. I keep hoping he'll tell me first. But maybe he feels the same way about speaking first. Maybe he's waiting for me to say something. Maybe...*

Cash turned, mounted the smaller horse, picked up the pack animals' lead ropes and started down the trail once more. Mariah followed, her thoughts in a turmoil, questions ricocheting in her mind.

By the time the ranch house was in sight, Mariah had decided not to press Cash for answers. It was too soon. The feelings were too new.

And she was too vulnerable.

It will be all right, Mariah told herself silently. *Cash just needs more time. Men aren't as comfortable with their emotions as women are, and Cash has already lost once at love. But he cares for me. I know he does. It will be all right.*

As they rode up to the corral, the back door of the ranch house opened and Nevada came out to meet them. At least Mariah thought the man was Nevada until she noticed the absence of any beard.

"It's about time you got back!" Cash called out. "If I don't see Carolina more often, she won't recognize me at all."

The man took the bridle of Mariah's horse and smiled up at her. "With those eyes, you've got to be Luke's little sister, Mariah. Welcome home."

Mariah grinned at the smiling stranger who was every bit as handsome as his unsmiling younger brother. "Thanks. Now I know what Nevada looks like underneath that beard. You must be Tennessee."

"You sure about that?" Ten asked.

"Dead sure. With those shoulders and that catlike way of walking, you've got to be Nevada's older brother."

Ten laughed. "It's a shame Nevada's not the marrying kind. You'd make a fine sister-in-law."

Cash gave Ten a hard glance. Ten had no way of knowing that Mariah's gentle interest in Nevada was a raw spot with Cash. No matter how many times he told himself that Mariah had no sexual interest in Nevada, Cash kept remembering his bitter experience with Linda. It had never occurred to him that she was sleeping with another man. After all, she had come to him a virgin.

Like Mariah.

"Put your ruff down," Ten drawled to Cash, amused by his response to the idea of Nevada and Mariah together. "Nevada was the one who told me the lady was already taken."

"See that he remembers it."

Ten shook his head. "Still the Granite Man. Hard muscles and a skull to match. You sure you didn't just buy your Ph.D. from some mail-order diploma mill?"

Laughing, Cash dismounted. When Ten offered his hand to help Mariah dismount, Cash reached past the Rocking M's foreman and lifted her out of the saddle. When Cash put her down, his arm stayed around her.

"Not that I don't trust you, ramrod," Cash said dryly to Ten. "It's just that you're handsome as sin and twice as hard."

The left corner of Ten's mouth turned up. "That's Nevada you're thinking of. I'm hard as sin and twice as handsome."

Cash snickered and shook his head. "Lord, what are we going to do if Utah comes home to roost?"

Mariah blinked. "Utah?"

"Another Blackthorn," Cash explained.

"There are a lot of them," Ten added.

"Don't tell me," Mariah said quickly. "Let me guess. Fifty, right? Who got stuck being called New Hampshire?"

The two men laughed simultaneously.

"My parents weren't that ambitious," Ten said. "There are only eight of us to speak of."

"To speak of?" Mariah asked.

"The Blackthorns don't run to marriage, but kids have a way of coming along just the same." Ten smiled slightly, thinking of his own daughter.

"Is Carolina awake?" Cash asked.

"I hope not. She'll be hungry when she wakes up and Diana isn't due back from our Spring Valley house for another hour. She and Carla are measuring for drapes or rugs or some darn thing." Ten shook his head and started gathering up reins and lead ropes. "Life sure was easier when all I had to worry about was a blanket for my bedroll."

"Crocodile tears," Cash snorted. "You wouldn't go back to your old life and you know it. Hell, if a man even looks at Diana more than once, you start honing your belt knife."

"Glad you noticed," Ten said dryly.

"Not that you need to," Cash continued, struck by something he had never put into words. "Diana is a rarity among females—a one-man woman."

"And I'm the lucky man," Ten said with tangible satisfaction as he led the horses off. "You two go on up to the big house and watch Carolina sleep. I'll take care of the horses for you."

When Cash started for the house, Mariah slipped from his grasp. "I've got to clean up before Carla gets back. I don't want to get off on the wrong foot with Luke's wife."

"Carla won't care what you look like. She's too damn happy that Logan finally shook off that infection and both of them can stay on the ranch again instead of in my apartment in Boulder. Besides, I happen to know Carla's dying to meet you."

"You go ahead," Mariah urged. "I'll catch up as soon as I've showered."

He tipped up Mariah's chin, kissed her with a lingering heat that made her toes curl, and reluctantly released her.

"Don't be long," Cash said huskily.

She almost changed her mind about going at all, but the thought of standing around in camp clothes while meeting Carla stiffened Mariah's determination. As her brother's wife and the sister of the man she loved, Carla was too important to risk alienating. Bitter experience with Mariah's stepfamily had taught her how very important first impressions could be.

Putting the unhappy past out of her mind, Mariah hurried toward the old ranch house. She had her blouse half-unbuttoned when she opened the front door, only to encounter Nevada just inside the living room. He was carrying a huge carton.

"Don't stop on my account," he said, appreciation gleaming in his eyes.

Hastily Mariah fumbled with a button, trying to bring her décolletage under some control.

"Relax," he said matter-of-factly. "I'm just a pack animal."

"Funny," she muttered, feeling heat stain her cheeks. "To me you look like a man called Nevada Blackthorn."

"Optical illusion. Hold the door open and I'll prove it by disappearing."

"What are you hauling?" she asked, reaching for the door, opening it only a few inches.

"Broken crockery."

"What?"

"Ten and Diana are finally moving the Anasazi artifacts out of your way. I'm taking the stuff to their new house in Spring Valley."

"That's not necessary," Mariah said. "I don't want to be a bother. I certainly don't need every room in the old house. Please. Put everything back. Don't go to any trouble because of me."

The fear beneath Mariah's rapid words was clear. Even if Nevada hadn't heard the fear, he would have sensed it in the sudden tension of her body, felt it in the urgency of the hand wrapped around his wrist.

"You'll have to take that up with Ten and Diana," Nevada said calmly. "They were looking forward to having all this stuff moved into their new house where they could work on it whenever they wanted." He saw that Mariah didn't understand yet. "Diana is an archaeologist. She supervises the September Canyon dig. Ten is a partner in the Rocking M. He owns the land the dig is on."

Slowly Mariah's fingers relaxed their grip on Nevada's wrist, but she didn't release him yet.

"You're sure they don't mind moving their workroom?" she asked.

"They've been looking forward to it. Would have done it sooner, but Carolina came along a few weeks early and upset all their plans."

Mariah smiled uncertainly. "If you're sure..."

"I'm sure."

"Just what are you sure of?" Cash's voice asked coldly, pushing the door open. Bleak blue eyes took in Mariah's partially unbuttoned blouse and her hand wrapped around Nevada's wrist.

"I was just telling her that Diana and Ten don't mind clearing out their stuff," Nevada said in a voice as emotionless as the ice-green eyes measuring Cash's anger. "Your woman was afraid she'd be kicked off the ranch if she upset anyone."

"My woman?"

"She lit up like a Christmas tree when she heard your voice. That's as much a man's woman as it gets," Nevada said. "Now if you'll get out of my way, I'll get out of yours."

There was a long silence before Cash stepped aside. Nevada brushed past him and out the front door. Only then did Mariah realize she was holding her breath. She closed her eyes and let out air in a long sigh.

When she opened her eyes again, Cash was gone.

Twelve

Mariah showered, dried her hair, dusted on makeup and put on her favorite casual clothes—a tourmaline green blouse and matching slacks. She checked her appearance in the mirror. Everything was tucked in, no rips, no missing buttons, no spots. Satisfied, she turned away without appreciating the contrast of very dark brown hair, topaz eyes and green clothes. She had never seen herself as particularly attractive, much less striking. Yet she was just that—tall, elegantly proportioned, with high cheekbones and large, unusually colored eyes.

Mentally crossing her fingers that everything would go well with Carla, Mariah grabbed a light jacket and headed for the big house. No one answered her gentle tapping on the front door. She opened it and stuck her head in.

"Cash?" she called softly, not wanting to wake Carolina if she were still sleeping.

"In here," came the soft answer.

Mariah opened the door and walked into the living room. What she saw made her throat constrict and tears burn behind her eyelids. A clean-shaven Cash was sitting in an oversize rocking chair with a tiny baby tucked into the crook of his arm. One big hand held a bottle that looked too small in his grasp to be anything but a toy. The baby was ignoring the bottle, which held only water. Both tiny hands had locked onto one of Cash's fingers. Wide, blue-gray eyes studied the man's face with the intensity only young babies achieved.

"Isn't she something?" Cash asked softly, his voice as proud as though he were the baby's father rather than a friend of the family. "She's got a grip like a tiger."

Mariah crept closer and looked at the smooth, tiny fingers clinging to Cash's callused, much more powerful finger.

"Yes," Mariah whispered, "she's something. And so are you."

Cash looked away from the baby and saw the tears magnifying Mariah's beautiful eyes.

"It's all right," she said softly, blinking away the tears. "It's just...I thought men cared only for their own children. But you care for this baby."

"Hell, yes. It's great to hold a little girl again."

"Again?" Mariah asked, shocked. "Do you have children?"

Cash's expression changed. He looked from Mariah to the baby in his arms. "No. No children." His voice was flat, remote. "I was thinking of when Carla was born. It was Dad's second marriage, so I was ten years old when Carla came along. I took care of her a lot. Carla's mother was pretty as a rosebud, and not much more use. She married Dad so she wouldn't have to support herself." Cash shrugged and said ironically, "So what else is new? Women have lived off men since they got us kicked out of Eden."

Although Mariah flinched at Cash's brutal summation of marriage and women, she made no comment. She suspected that her mother's second marriage had been little better than Cash's description.

Cash looked back to the baby, who was slowly succumbing to sleep in his arms. He smiled, changing the lines of his face from forbidding to beguiling. Mariah's heart turned over as she realized all over again just how handsome Cash was.

"Carla was like this baby," Cash said softly. "Lively as a flea one minute and dead asleep the next. Carla used to watch me with her big blue-green eyes and I'd feel like king of the world. I could coax away her tears when no one else could. Her smile...God, her smile was so sweet."

"Carla was lucky to have a brother like you. She was even luckier to keep you," Mariah whispered. "Long after my grandparents took me from the Rocking M, I used to cry myself to sleep. It was Luke I was crying for, not my father."

"Luke always hoped that you were happy," Cash said, looking up at Mariah.

"It's in the past." Mariah shrugged with a casualness that went no deeper than her skin. "Anyway, I was no great bargain as a child. The man my mother married was older, wealthy, and recently widowed. I met him on Christmas Day. I had been praying very hard that the special present my mother had been hinting at would be a return trip to the Rocking M. When I was introduced to my new 'father' and his kids, I started crying for Luke. Not the best first impression I could have made,"

Mariah added unhappily. "A disaster, in fact. Harold and his older kids resented being saddled with a 'snot-nosed, whining seven-year-old.' Boarding schools were the answer."

Cash muttered something savage under his breath.

"Don't knock them until you've tried them," Mariah said with a wry smile. "At least I was with my own kind. And I had it better than some of the other outcasts. I got to see Mother most Christmases. And I got a good education."

The bundle in Cash's arm shifted, mewing softly, calling his attention back from Mariah. He offered little Carolina the bottle again. Her face wrinkled in disgust as she tasted the tepid water.

"Don't blame you a bit," Cash said, smiling slightly. "Compared to what you're used to, this is really thin beer."

Gently he increased the rhythm of his rocking, trying to distract the baby from her disappointment. It didn't work. Within moments Carolina's face was red and her small mouth was giving vent to surprisingly loud cries. Patiently Cash teased her lips with his fingertip. After a few more yodels, the baby began sucking industriously on the tip of his finger.

"Sneaky," Mariah said admiringly. "How long does it last?"

"Until she figures out that she's working her little rear end off for nothing."

Car doors slammed out in the front yard. Women's voices called out, to be answered from the vicinity of the barn.

"Hang in there, tiger," Cash said. "Milk is on the way."

Mariah smoothed her clothes hastily, tucked a strand of hair behind her ear and asked, "Do I look all right?"

Cash looked up. "It doesn't matter. Carla isn't so shallow that she's going to care what you look like."

Mariah heard the edge in Cash's voice and knew he was still angry about finding her with Nevada. But before she could say anything, the front door opened and a petite, very well built woman hurried in.

"Sorry I'm late. I—oh, hello. What gorgeous eyes. You must be Luke's sister. I'm Diana Blackthorn. Excuse me. Carolina is about to do her imitation of a cat with its tail in a wringer. Thanks, Cash. You have a magic touch with her. Even Ten would have had a hard time keeping the lid on her this long."

Diana whisked the small bundle from Cash's arms and vanished up the staircase, speaking to Carolina in soothing tones at every step.

Mariah blinked, not sure that she had really seen the honey-haired woman at all. "That was an archaeologist?"

"Um," Cash said tactfully.

"Ten's wife?"

GRANITE MAN

"Um."

"Whew. No wonder he smiles a lot."

"Ask Diana and she'll tell you that she'd trade it all for four more inches of height."

"She can have four of mine if I can have four of hers," Mariah said instantly.

Cash came out of the rocking chair in a fluid motion and pulled Mariah close. His hands slid from her hips to her waist and on up her body, stopping at the top of her rib cage. Watching her, he eased his hands underneath her breasts, taking their warm weight into his palms, teasing her responsive nipples with his thumbs, smiling lazily.

"You're too damn sexy just the way you are," Cash said, his voice gritty, intimate, as hot as the pulse suddenly speeding in Mariah's throat. "I've never seen anything as beautiful as you were this morning in that pool wearing nothing but steam. *You watched me take you.* The sweet sounds you made then almost pushed me over the edge. Just thinking about it now makes me want to—"

"Hi, Nevada. Is that another box of shards? Good. Put them in Diana's car. Here, Logan, chew on this instead of Nosy's tail. Even if the cat doesn't mind it, I do."

The voice from the front porch froze Cash. He closed his eyes, swore softly, and released Mariah. He turned toward the front door, blocking Mariah's flushed face with his body.

"Where's my favorite nephew?" Cash called out.

"Your only nephew," Carla said, smiling as she walked into the living room. "He's a one hundred percent terror again. How's my favorite brother?"

"Your only brother, right?" Cash bent down and scooped up Logan in one arm. "Lord, boy. What have you been eating—lead? You must have gained ten pounds."

As a toddler, Logan wasn't exactly a fountain of conversation. Action was more his line. Laughing, he grabbed Cash's nose and tried to pull it off.

"That's not the way to do it," Cash said, grabbing Logan's nose gently. Very carefully Cash pulled and made a sucking, popping noise. Moments later he triumphantly held up his hand. The end of his thumb was pushed up between his index and second finger to imitate Logan's snub nose. "See? Got it! Want me to put it back on?"

With an expression of affection and amusement, Carla watched her brother and her son. Then she realized that someone was standing behind Cash. She looked around his broad shoulders and saw a woman about her own age and height hastily tucking in her blouse.

"Hello?"

Mariah bit her lip and gave up trying to straighten her clothes. "Hi, I'm—"

"Mariah!" Carla said, smiling with delight. She stepped around Cash and gave Mariah a hug. "I'm so glad you came home at last. When the lawyer told Luke his mother was dead, there was no mention of you at all. We had no way to contact you. Luke wanted so much to share Logan with you. And most of all he wanted to know that you were happy."

Mariah looked into Carla's transparent, blue-green eyes and saw only welcome. With a stifled sound, Mariah hugged Carla in return, feeling a relief so great it made her dizzy.

"Thank you," Mariah said huskily. "I was so afraid you would resent having me around."

"Don't be ridiculous. Why would anyone resent you?" Carla stared into Mariah's huge, golden-brown eyes. "You mean it. You really were worried, weren't you?"

Mariah tried to smile, but it turned upside down. "Families don't like outsiders coming to live with them."

Cash spoke without looking up from screwing Logan's nose back into place. "As you might guess from that statement, Mariah's mother didn't pick a winner for her second husband. In fact, he sounds like a real, um, prince. Kept her in boarding schools all year round."

"Why didn't he just send you back to the Rocking M?" Carla asked Mariah.

"Mother refused. She said the Rocking M was malevolent. It hated women. She could feel it devouring her. Just talking about it upset her so much I stopped asking." Mariah looked past Carla to the window that framed MacKenzie Ridge's rugged lines. "I never felt that way about the ranch. I love this land. But as long as Mother was alive, I couldn't come back. She simply couldn't have coped with it."

"You're back now," Carla said quietly, "and you're staying as long as you want."

Mariah tried to speak, couldn't, and hugged her sister-in-law instead.

Cash watched the two women and told himself that no matter why Mariah had originally come to the Rocking M, she was genuinely grateful to be accepted into Luke's family. And, Cash admitted, he couldn't really blame Mariah for wanting a place she could call home. He felt the same way. The Rocking M, more than his apartment in Boulder, was his home. Only on the Rocking M were there people who gave a damn whether he came back from his field trips or died on some godforsaken granite slope.

Almost broodingly Cash watched Mariah and his sister fix dinner. With no fuss at all they went about the business of cooking a huge meal and getting to know one another. As he looked at them moving around the kitchen, Cash realized that the two women were similar in many ways. They were within a year of each other in age, within an inch in height, graceful, supremely at home with the myriad tools used to prepare food, willing to do more than half of any job they shared; and their laughter was so beautiful it made him ache.

Linda never wanted to share anything or do any work. I thought it was just because she was young, but I can see that wasn't it. She was the same age then as Mariah is now. Linda was just spoiled. Mariah may have come here looking for room and board—and a crack at Mad Jack's mine—but at least she's not afraid to work for it.

Best of all, Mariah doesn't whine.

No. Not best of all. What was best about Mariah, Cash conceded, was her incandescent sensuality. After Linda, he had never found it difficult to control himself where women were concerned. Mariah was different. He wanted her more, not less, each time. It was just as well that he was going to Boulder. He needed distance from Mariah's fire, distance and the coolness of mind to remember that a woman didn't have to be spoiled in order to manipulate a man. She simply had to be clever enough to allow him to deceive himself.

Cash was still reminding himself of how it had been with Linda when he let himself into the old house in the hour before dawn. He knew he should be on the road, driving away, putting miles between himself and Mariah. Yet he couldn't bring himself to leave without saying goodbye to her.

The front door of the old house closed softly behind Cash. An instant later he heard a whispering, rushing sound and felt Mariah's soft warmth wrapping around him, holding him with a woman's surprising strength. His arms came around her in a hard hug that lifted her feet off the floor.

Her tears were hot against his neck.

"Mariah?"

She shuddered and held on to Cash until she could trust her voice. "I couldn't sleep. I heard you loading the Jeep. I thought you weren't even going to say goodbye to me. Please don't be angry with me over Nevada. I like him but it's nothing to what I feel about you. I—"

But Cash's mouth was over hers, sealing off her words. The taste of him swept through her, making her tremble. His arms shifted subtly, both molding and supporting her body, stroking her over his hard length, telling her without a word how perfectly they fit together, hard against soft, key against lock, male and female, hunger and fulfillment.

It took an immense amount of willpower for Cash to end the kiss short of taking Mariah down to the floor and burying himself in her, ending the torment that raked him with claws of fire.

"Don't leave me," Mariah whispered when Cash lowered her feet back to the floor. "Not yet. Hold me for just a little longer. Please? I—oh, Cash, it's so cold without you."

She felt the tremor that went through Cash, heard his faint groan, and then the world tilted as he picked her up once more. Moments later he put her on the bed, grabbed the covers and pulled them up beneath her chin. She struggled against the confining sheet and comforter, trying to get her arms free, but it was impossible.

"Warm enough?" he asked. "I don't want you getting sick." His voice was too deep, too thick, telling of the heavy running of his blood. "You didn't get much sleep last night, I couldn't keep my hands off you in the pool, it was a long ride back and then you cooked a meal for twelve."

"Carla did most of the work and—"

"Bull. I was watching, honey."

"—and I loved your hands on me in the pool," Mariah said quickly, talking over Cash's voice. "I love your mouth. I love your body. I love—"

His mouth came down over hers again, ending the husky flow of words that were like tiny tongues of fire licking over him.

"I shouldn't have taken you this morning," Cash said when he managed to tear himself away from Mariah's sweet, responsive mouth. "Damn it, honey, you're not used to having a man yet, and you make me so hard and hungry."

"The pool must have magic healing properties," Mariah whispered, looking up at Cash with wide golden eyes. In the vague golden illumination cast by the night-light, Cash was little more than a dense man-shadow, a deep voice and powerful hands holding her imprisoned within the soft cocoon of bed covers. "And when I couldn't sleep tonight I took a long soak in the tub. I'm not sore, not even from the ride back. If you don't believe it, touch me. You'll see that I'm telling the truth. I know you want me, Cash. I felt it when you hugged me. Touch me. Then you'll know I want you, too."

"Mariah," he whispered.

Cash kissed her again and again, tiny, fierce kisses that told of his restraint and need. When she made soft sounds of response and encouragement, he deepened the kiss. As their tongues caressed, hunger ripped through him, loosening his hold on the bedclothes for a few moments.

It was all Mariah needed. She kicked aside the soft, enfolding covers even as she reached for Cash. He groaned when he saw her elegant, naked legs and the cotton nightshirt that barely came below her hips. Then she took his hand in hers and began smoothing it down her body.

He could have pulled away and they both knew it. He was far stronger than she was, more experienced, more able to control the hot currents of hunger that coursed through his body. But Mariah's abandoned sensuality disarmed him completely. When her breasts tightened and peaked visibly beneath cloth, he remembered how it felt to hold her in his mouth, shaping and caressing her while cries of pleasure shivered from her lips.

Even before Mariah guided Cash's hand to the sultry well of her desire, he suspected he was lost. When he touched the liquid heat that waited for him, he knew he was. He tried not to trace the soft, alluring folds and failed. He skimmed them again, probing delicately, wishing that his profession hadn't left his fingertips so scarred and callused. She deserved to be caressed by something as silky and unmarked as her own body.

"Baby?" Cash whispered. "Are you sure?"

The answer he received was a broken sound of pleasure and a sensual melting that took his doubts and his breath away. When he started to lift his hand, Mariah's fingers tightened over his wrist, trying to hold him.

"Cash," Mariah said urgently, "don't leave yet. Please stay with me for a little more. I—"

"Hush, honey," Cash said, kissing away Mariah's words. "I'm not going far." He laughed shakily. "I couldn't walk out of here right now if I had to. Don't you know what you do to me?"

"No," she whispered. "I only know what you do to me. I've never felt anything close to it. I didn't even know it was possible to feel so much. It's like I've been living at night all my life and then the sun finally came up."

The words were more arousing than any caress Cash had ever received. His hands shook with the force of the hunger pouring through him.

Mariah watched while Cash stripped away his clothes with careless, powerful motions that were very different from the tender caresses he had given to her just moments before. The nebulous glow of the tiny night-light turned Cash's skin to gold and the hair on his body to a dark, shimmering bronze. Each movement he made was echoed by the black velvet glide of shadows over his muscular body.

Cash watched Mariah as he kicked aside the last of his clothes and stood naked before her. Mariah's eyes were heavy lidded, the color of gold, shining, and they worshiped all of him, even the full, hard evidence of his desire. Still looking at him, she reached for the bottom button on her nightshirt with fingers that trembled.

Cash rested one knee on the mattress, making it give way beneath his weight. One long finger traced from the instep of Mariah's foot, up the calf, behind the knee, then slowly up the inside of her thighs. When her leg flexed in response, he smiled slowly.

"That's it, little one. Show me you want me," Cash whispered. "Make room for me between those beautiful legs."

Mariah's long legs shifted and separated. He followed each movement with dark, consuming eyes and light caresses. Slowly he knelt between her legs, watching her, seeing the same sensual tension in her that had taken his body and drawn it tight on wires of fire.

For a moment Cash didn't move, couldn't move, frozen by the beauty of Mariah's body and the trust implicit in her vulnerable position. Slowly, irresistibly, his hands pushed aside her unbuttoned nightshirt, smoothing it down over her shoulders and arms, stopping at her wrists, for he had become distracted by the rose-tipped, creamy invitation of her breasts.

Mariah made a murmurous sound of pleasure that became a soft cry as his mouth found one nipple and pulled it into a tight, shimmering focus of pleasure. When she arched up in sensual reflex, the nightshirt slid down beneath her back to her hips, stopping there, holding her hands captive. She didn't notice, for Cash's hands were smoothing up her legs, making her tremble in anticipation of the pleasure to come. When he touched her very lightly, she shivered and cried out.

"It occurred to me," Cash said, his voice deep and slow, "that something as soft as you shouldn't have to put up with hands as callused as mine."

Mariah would have told Cash how much she loved his hands, but couldn't. The feel of his tongue probing silkily into her navel took her breath away. Glittering sensations streaked through her body at the unexpected caress.

"You should be touched by something as hot and soft as you are," Cash said. He sampled the taut skin of Mariah's belly with his tongue, smiling to feel the response tightening her. His tongue flicked teasingly as he slid down her body. "Since it's too late for you to go out and find some soft gentleman to be your lover, we'll just have to do the best we can with what we've got, won't we?"

Mariah didn't understand what Cash was talking about. As far as she was concerned he was perfect as a lover. She was trying to tell him just that when she felt the first sultry touch of his tongue. The intimacy of the kiss shocked her. She tried to move, only to find her legs held in her lover's gentle, immovable hands and her wrists captive to the tangled folds of her nightdress.

"Cash—you shouldn't—I—"

"Hush," he murmured. "I've always wondered what a woman tastes like. I just never cared enough to find out. But I do now. I want you, honey. And that's what you are. Honey."

Cash's voice was like his mouth, hungry, hot, consuming. The words

Mariah had been trying to speak splintered into a pleasure as elemental as the man who was loving her in hushed, wild silence. For long moments she fought to speak, to think, to breathe, but in the end could only give herself to Cash, twisting slowly, drawn upon a rack of exquisite fire.

By the time Cash finally lifted his head, Mariah was shaking and crying his name, balanced on the jagged breakpoint of release. He sensed that the lightest touch would send her over the edge. Knowing he should release her from her sensual prison, Cash still held back, loving the sound of her voice crying for him, loving the flushed, petal-softness of her need, loving the raggedness of her breathing matching his own.

At last he bent down to her once more, seeking the satin knot of sensation he had called from her, touching it with the tip of his tongue.

With a husky cry that was his name, Mariah was overcome by an ecstasy that convulsed her with savage delicacy. Cash held her and smiled despite the shudders of unfulfilled need that were tearing him apart. Caressing her softly, he waited for her first, wild ecstasy to pass. Then he gently flexed her legs, drawing them up her body until she was completely open to him. With equal care he fitted his body to hers, pressing very, very slowly into her.

When he looked up, he saw Mariah watching him become a part of her. He felt the shivering, shimmering ripples of pleasure that were consuming her all over again, ecstasy renewed and redoubled by his slow filling of her body. The knowledge that she welcomed the deep physical interlocking as much as he did raced through Cash, sinking all the way into him, calling to him at a profound level, luring him so deeply into Mariah that he couldn't tell where she ended and he began, for there was no difference, no separation, no boundary, nothing but their shared body shuddering in endless, golden pulses of release.

And in the pauses between ecstasy came Mariah's voice singing a husky litany of her love for Cash.

Thirteen

Kiss me goodbye, honey. The sooner I go, the sooner I'll be back.

Mariah had heard those same words of parting from Cash many times in the five months since she had come to the Rocking M, including the one time she had declared her love. Cash's goodbyes were woven through her days, through her dreams, a pattern of separations and returns that had no end in sight. Even though Cash was no longer teaching at the university, his consulting work rarely allowed him to spend more than two weeks at a time at the Rocking M. More often, he was free for only a handful of incandescent days, followed by several weeks of loneliness after he left. Each time Mariah hoped that he would invite her to Boulder, but he hadn't.

Nor had Cash told Mariah that he loved her.

He must love me. Surely no man could make love to a woman the way Cash does to me without loving her at least a little. Carla and Luke assume Cash loves me. So does everyone else on the Rocking M. He just can't say the words. And is that so important, after all? His actions are those of a man in love, and that's what matters.

Isn't it?

Mariah had no doubt about her own feelings. She had never expected to love anyone the way she loved Cash—no defenses, nothing held back, an endless vulnerability that would have terrified her if Cash hadn't been so clearly happy to see her each time he came back to the ranch.

He was gone for only four days this time and he called every night and we talked for hours about nothing and everything and we laughed and neither one of us wanted to hang up. He loves me. He just doesn't say it in so many words.

It will be all right. If he hadn't wanted children he would have used something or seen that I did. But he never even mentioned it.

The emotional fragility that had plagued Mariah for too many weeks sent tears clawing at the back of her eyes. It had been more than four months since her last period. Soon she wouldn't be able to hide the life growing within her by leaving her pants unbuttoned and wearing her shirts out. Cash had noticed the new richness in the curves of her body but hadn't guessed the reason. Instead, he had teased her about the joys of regular home cooking.

He loves children and kids love him. He'll be a wonderful father.
It will be all right.

Fighting for self-control, unconsciously pressing one hand against her body just below her waist, Mariah stood on the small porch of the old house and stared out through the pines at the road that wound through the pasture. She thought she had seen a streamer of dust there a moment ago, the kind of boiling rooster tail of grit that was raised by Cash's Jeep when he raced over the dirt road to be with her again.

"Are you going to tell him this time?"

Mariah started and turned away from the road. Nevada Blackthorn stood a few feet away, watching her with his uncanny green eyes.

"Tell who what?" she asked, off balance.

"Tell Cash that he's going to be a daddy sometime next spring." Nevada swore under his breath at the frightened look Mariah gave him. "Damn it, woman, you're at least four months along. You should be going to a doctor. You should be taking special vitamins. If you don't have sense enough to realize it, I do. Have you ever seen a baby that was too weak to cry? Babies don't have any control over their lives," he continued ruthlessly. "They're just born into a world that's more often cruel than not, and they make the best of it for as long as they can until they either die or grow up. Too often, they die."

Mariah simply stared at Nevada, too shocked to speak. The bleakness of his words was more than matched by his eyes, eyes that were looking at her, noting each telltale difference pregnancy had made.

"You must have decided to have the baby," Nevada said, "or you would have done something about it months ago. A woman who has guts enough to go through with a pregnancy should have guts enough to tell her man about it."

"I've tried." Mariah made a helpless gesture. "I just can't find the right time or the right words."

Because Cash has never said he loves me. But she couldn't say that aloud. She could barely stand to think it.

"The two of you go off looking for gold at least twice a month, but there's never enough time or words for you to say 'I'm pregnant'?"

Nevada hissed a word beneath his breath. "If you don't have the guts to tell Cash this time, I'll take you into Cortez after he leaves. Dr. Chacon is a good man. He'll tell you what the baby needs and I'll make damn sure you get it."

Mariah looked at Nevada and knew he meant every word. He was as honest as he was hard. If he said he would help her, he would. Period.

"You're a good man," she said softly, touching his bearded jaw with her fingertips. "Thank you."

"You can thank me by telling Cash." Despite the curtness of Nevada's voice, he took Mariah's hand and squeezed it encouragingly. "You've got about twenty seconds to find the right words."

"What?"

"He's here."

Mariah spun to face the road. When she saw that Cash's battered Jeep had already turned into the dusty yard of the old house, her face lit up. She ran to the Jeep and threw herself into Cash's arms as he got out.

Cash lifted her, held her close, and looked at Nevada over Mariah's shoulder. Nevada returned the cool stare for a long moment before he turned and walked toward the bunkhouse without a backward glance.

"What did Nevada want?" Cash asked.

Mariah stiffened. Cash's voice was every bit as hard as Nevada's had been.

"He just—he was wondering when you would get here," she said hurriedly.

It was a lie and both of them knew it.

Cash's mouth flattened at the surprise and the pain tearing through him. Somehow he hadn't expected Mariah to lie. Not to him. Not about another man.

A freezing fear congealed in Cash as he realized how dangerously far he had fallen under Mariah's spell.

"Nevada wanted something else, too," Mariah said quickly, hating having told the lie. "I can't tell you what. Not yet. Before you leave, I'll tell you. I promise. But for now just hold me, Cash. Please hold me. I've missed you so!"

Cash closed his eyes and held her, feeling her supple warmth, a warmth that melted the ice of her half lie, leaving behind a cold shadow of memory, a forerunner of the betrayal he both feared and expected.

"Did you miss me?" Mariah asked. "Just a little?"

The uncertainty in her voice caught at Cash's emotions. "I always miss you. You know that."

"I just—just wanted to hear it."

Cash pulled away from Mariah until he could look down into her troubled golden eyes. The unhappiness he saw there made his heart ache despite his effort to hold himself aloof. "What is it, Mariah? What's wrong?"

She shook her head, took a deep breath and smiled up at the man she loved. "When you hold me, nothing is wrong. Come to the big house with me. Let me lust after you while I make dinner."

His expression changed to a lazy kind of sensuality that sent frissons of anticipation over Mariah's nerves. Smiling, Cash dipped his head until he could take her mouth in a kiss that left both of them short of breath.

"I'd rather you lusted after me in the old house where we can do something about it," Cash said, biting Mariah's lips with exquisite care, wanting her even more than he feared wanting her.

"So would I. But then I'd never get around to cooking dinner and the cowhands would rebel."

Laughing despite the familiar hunger tightening his body, Cash slowly released Mariah, then put his arm around her waist and began walking toward the big house. The time of reckoning and payment would come soon enough. Anticipating it would only diminish the pleasure of being within reach of Mariah's incandescent sensuality.

"I don't want to be responsible for a Rocking M rebellion," he said.

"Neither do I," Mariah answered, putting her arm around Cash's lean waist. "I tried to do as much of dinner as possible ahead of time, but Logan and Carolina decided they didn't want a nap."

Cash looked down at Mariah questioningly. "Where are Diana and Carla?"

"I'm watching the kids during the morning so Diana and Carla can work on the artifacts that keep coming in from September Canyon."

"And you're cooking six nights a week for the whole crew."

"I love to cook."

"And Diana is making an archaeologist out of you three nights a week."

"She's a very good teacher."

"And you're taking correspondence courses in commercial applications of geology. And technical writing."

Mariah nodded. "I have my first job, too," she said proudly. "The Four Corners Regional Museum wants to do a splashy four-color book about the history of the area. They commissioned specialists for each section of the book, then discovered that having knowledge isn't the same thing as being able to communicate knowledge through writing."

Ruefully Cash smiled. Despite the fact that his profession required writing reports of his fieldwork, he knew his shortcomings in that department. In fact, he had begun writing all his reports on the Rocking M. Not only did it give him more time with Mariah, he had discovered that she had a knack for finding common words to describe esoteric scientific data. He had been the one to suggest that Mariah pursue technical writing, since she obviously had a flair for it.

"So," Mariah continued, "I'm translating the geology and archaeology sections into plain English. If they like my work, I have a chance to do the whole book for them."

Cash stopped, caught Mariah's face between his hands, kissed her soundly and smiled down at her. "Congratulations, honey. When did you find out?"

"This morning. I wanted to call, but you were already on the road. I thought you would never get here. It's such a long drive. And in the winter…"

Mariah's voice trailed off. They both knew that driving to the Rocking M from Boulder was tedious under good conditions, arduous during some seasons and impossible when storms turned segments of the ranch's dirt roads into goo that even Cash's Jeep couldn't negotiate.

The difficulty of getting to the Rocking M wasn't a subject Cash wanted to pursue. If Mariah hadn't been Luke's sister, Cash would have asked her to stay with him in Boulder months ago. But that was impossible. It was one thing to go gold hunting with Mariah or to steal a few hours alone with her in the old house before both of them went to sleep in separate beds under separate roofs. It was quite another thing to set up housekeeping outside of marriage with his best friend's little sister.

The obvious solution was marriage, but that, too, was impossible. Even if Cash brought himself to trust Mariah completely—especially if he did—he wouldn't ask her to share a childless future with him. Even so, he found himself coming back to the idea of marriage again and again.

Maybe Mariah wouldn't mind. Maybe she would learn to be like me, accepting what can't be changed and enjoying Logan and Carolina whenever possible. Maybe…

And maybe not. How can I ask her to give up so much? No matter how much she thinks she loves me, she wants children of her own. I can see it every time she looks at Logan and then looks at me with a hunger that has nothing to do with sex. She wants my baby. I know it as surely as I know I can't give it to her.

But God, I can't give her up, either. I'm a fool. I know it. But I can't stop wanting her.

There wasn't any answer to the problem that circled relentlessly in Cash's mind, arguments and hopes repeated endlessly with no solution in sight. No matter how many times Cash thought about Mariah and himself and the future, he had no answer that he wanted to live with. So he did what he had always done since he had realized what being effectively sterile meant. He put the future out of his mind and concentrated on the present.

"Come on," Cash said, kissing Mariah's forehead. "I'll peel potatoes while you tell me all about your new job."

If he noticed the uncertainty in her smile, he didn't mention it, any more than she mentioned the fact that he was gripping her hand as though he expected her to run away.

Motionless, aware only of his own thoughts, Cash let himself into the old ranch house in the velvet darkness that comes just before dawn. Mariah didn't expect him. They had decided to spend the day at the ranch and not leave for Black Springs until the following dawn.

But Cash hadn't been able to stay away. He had awakened hours before, fought with himself, and finally lost. He had just enough self-control not to go into Mariah's bedroom and wake her up by slowly merging their bodies. Fighting the need that never left him even when he had just taken her, Cash went into the house and sat in what had once been Diana's workroom and gradually had evolved into an office for him and a library for Mariah's increasing collection of books.

He didn't even bother to turn on the light. He just pulled out one of the straightback chairs, faced it away from the table, and tried to reason with his unruly body and mind. His body ignored him. His mind supplied him with images of a night at the line shack when Mariah had teased him because his body steamed in the frosty autumn air. He had teased her, too, but in other ways, drawing from her the sweet cries of desire and completion that he loved to hear. The thought of hearing those cries again was a banked fire in Cash's big body, and the fire was no less hot for being temporarily controlled.

The sound of the bedroom door opening and Mariah's light footsteps crossing the living room sent a wave of desire through Cash that was so powerful he couldn't move. A light in the living room came on, throwing a golden rectangle of illumination onto the workroom floor. None of the light reached as far as Cash's feet.

"Cash?"

"Sorry, honey. I didn't mean to wake you up."

Mariah was silhouetted in the doorway. The shadow of her long flannel nightshirt rippled like black water.

"I'm here."

"What are you doing sitting in the dark?"

"Watching the moonlight. Thinking."

The huskiness of Cash's deep voice made Mariah's heartbeat quicken. She walked through the darkened room and stood in front of Cash.

"What are you thinking about?" she asked softly.

"You."

Big hands came up and wrapped around Mariah's wrists. She whispered his name even as he tugged her down into his lap. He kissed her deeply, shifting her until she sat astride his legs and he could rock her hips slowly against his body. The heavy waves of his need broke over her, sweeping away everything but the taste and feel and heat of the man she loved. When his hands found and teased her breasts, she made rippling sounds of hunger and pleasure.

When Mariah unfastened her nightshirt to ease his way, Cash followed the wash of moonlight over her skin with his tongue until she moaned. Soon her nightshirt was undone and he was naked to the waist and his jeans were open and her hands were moving over him, loving the proof of his passion, making him tighten with desire.

"If you don't stop, we'll never make it to bed," Cash said, his voice hoarse.

"But you feel so good. Better each time. You're like Black Springs, heat welling up endlessly."

Cash's laugh was short and almost harsh. "Only since I've known you."

Without warning he lifted Mariah off his lap.

"Cash?"

"Honey, if I don't move now, I won't be able to stand up at all. I want you too much."

Despite Cash's words, he made no move to get up. When Mariah's hands pushed at his jeans, tugging them down until she had the freedom of his body, he didn't object. He couldn't. He could hardly breathe for the violence of the need hammering through him. When she touched him, the breath he did have trickled out in a groan that sounded as though it had been torn from his soul.

Mariah's eyes widened and her breath caught in a rush of sensual awareness that was as elemental as the power of the man sitting before her. Her fingertips traced Cash gently again. Closing his eyes, he gave himself to her warm hands. When the caressing stopped a few moments later, he couldn't prevent a hoarse sound of protest. He heard a rustling sound, sensed Mariah's nightshirt sliding to the floor, and shuddered heavily. When he opened his eyes she was standing naked in front of him.

"Can people make love in a chair?" Mariah asked softly.

Before the words were out of her mouth, Cash's hand was caressing her inner thighs, separating them, seeking the sultry heat of her. She shivered and melted at the caress. When his touch slid into her, probing her softness, her knees gave way. Swaying, she grabbed his shoulders for balance.

"Cash?" she whispered. "Can we?"

"Sit on my lap and find out," he said, luring her closer and then closer still, easing her down until she was a balm around his hard, aching flesh and her name was a broken sigh on his lips. "Each time—better."

For Mariah, the deep rasp of Cash's voice was like being licked by loving fire. She leaned forward to wrap her arms around his neck. The movement caused sweet lightning to flicker out from the pit of her stomach. She moved again, seeking to recapture the stunningly pleasurable sensation. Again lightning curled through her body.

"That's right," Cash said huskily, encouraging Mariah's sensual movements. "Oh, yes. Like that, honey. Just…like…that."

Shivering, moving slowly, deeply, repeatedly, giving and taking as much as she could, Mariah fed their mutual fire with gliding movements of her body. When the languid dance of love was no longer enough for either of them, Cash's hands fastened onto her hips, quickening her movements. Her smile became a gasp of pleasure when he flexed hard against her, enjoying her as deeply as she did him.

He watched her, wanting all of her, breathing dark, hot words over her until control was stripped away and he poured himself into her welcoming softness. Mariah held herself utterly still, drinking Cash's release, loving him, feeling her own pleasure beginning to unravel her in golden pulses that radiated through her body, burning gently through to her soul.

And then there was a savage flaring of ecstasy that swept everything away except her voice calling huskily to Cash, telling him of her love and of their baby growing within her womb….

For an instant Cash couldn't believe what he was hearing.

"What?"

"I'm pregnant, love," she whispered, leaning forward to kiss him again.

Suddenly Cash believed it, believed he was hearing the depth of his own betrayal from lips still flushed with his kisses. He had thought he was prepared for it, thought that a woman's treachery had nothing new to teach him.

He had been wrong. He sat rigid, transfixed by an agony greater than any he had ever known…and in its wake came a rage that was every bit as deep as the passion and the pain.

"You're pregnant," Cash repeated flatly, a statement rather than a question.

He could control his voice, but not the sudden, violent rage snaking through his body, a tension that was instantly transmitted to the woman who was so intimately joined with him.

"Yes," Mariah said, trying to smile, failing, feeling the power of

Cash's fingers digging into her hips. "Didn't you want this? You never tried to prevent it and you like children and I thought..."

Her voice died into a whisper. She swallowed, but no ease came to her suddenly dry throat. In the moonlight Cash looked like a man carved from stone.

"No, I never tried to prevent it," Cash said. "I never spend time trying to make lead into gold, either."

He heard his own words as though at a vast distance, an echo from a time when he could speak and touch and feel, a time when betrayal hadn't spread like black ice through his soul, freezing everything.

"I don't understand," Mariah whispered.

"I'll just bet you don't."

With bruising strength Cash lifted Mariah from his lap, kicked out of his entangling clothes and stood motionless, looking through her as though she weren't there. She had the dizzying feeling of being trapped in a nightmare, unable to move, unable to speak, unable even to cry. She had imagined many possible reactions to her pregnancy, even anger, but nothing like this, an absolute withdrawal from her.

"Cash?" Mariah whispered.

He didn't answer. In electric silence he studied the deceptively vulnerable appearance of the woman who stood with her face turned up to him, moonlight heightening both the elegance and the fragility of her bone structure.

She's about as fragile as a rattlesnake and a hell of a lot more dangerous. She's one very shrewd little huntress. No one will believe that I'm not the father of her baby. I could go to the nearest lab and get back the same result I got years ago, when Linda told me she was pregnant—a chance I was the father, but not much of one.

But Cash had wanted to believe in that slim chance. He had wanted it so desperately that he had blinded himself to any other possibility.

Luke would feel the same way this time. Rather than believe that his beloved Muffin was a liar, a cheat and a schemer, Luke would believe that Mariah was carrying Cash's baby. If Cash refused to marry Mariah, it would drive a wedge between himself and Luke. Perhaps even Carla. Then there would be nothing left for Cash, nowhere on earth he could call home. He had no choice but to accept the lie and marry the liar.

It was as nice a trap as any woman had ever constructed for a foolish man.

Except for one thing, one detail that could not be finessed no matter how accomplished a huntress Mariah was. There was one way to prove she was lying. It would take time, though. Time for the baby to be born, time for its blood to be tested, time for the results to be compared with Cash's own blood. Then, finally, it would be time for truth.

GRANITE MAN

"When is it due."

Cash didn't recognize his own voice. There was no emotion in it, no resonance, no real question, nothing but a flat requirement that Mariah give him information.

"I d-don't know."

"What does the doctor say."

"I haven't been to one." Mariah interlaced her fingers and clenched her hands in order to keep from reaching for Cash, touching him, trying to convince herself that she actually knew the icy stranger standing naked in the darkness while he interrogated her. "That's—that's what Nevada wanted. He said he'd take me into see Dr. Chacon if I didn't tell you this time."

So that's who fathered her bastard. I should have known. God, how can one man be such a fool?

Suddenly Cash didn't trust his self-control one instant longer. Too many echoes of the past. He had known the trap. He had taken the bait anyway.

So be it.

Mariah watched as Cash dressed. Though he said nothing more, his expression and his abrupt handling of his clothes said very clearly that he was furious. Uncertainly Mariah tried to dress, but her trembling fingers forced her to be satisfied with simply pulling her nightshirt on and leaving it unfastened. When she looked up from fumbling with the nightshirt, Cash was standing at the front door watching her as though she were a stranger.

"Congratulations, honey. You just got a name for your baby and a free ride for the length of your pregnancy."

"What?"

"We're getting married. That's what you wanted, isn't it?"

"Yes, but—"

"We'll talk about it later," Cash said, speaking over Mariah's hesitant words. "Right now, I'm not in the mood to listen to any more of your *words*."

The door opened and closed and Mariah was alone.

Fourteen

It will be all right. He just needs some time to get used to the idea. He must care for me. He wouldn't have asked me to marry him if he didn't care for me, would he? Lots of men get women pregnant and don't marry them.

It will be all right.

The silent litany had been repeated so often in Mariah's mind during the long hours after dawn that the meaning of the words no longer really registered with her. She kept seeing Cash's face when he had told her that she would have a free ride and a name for the baby.

When we're married I'll be able to show Cash how much I love him. He must care for me. He doesn't have to marry me, but he chose to. It will be all right.

The more Mariah repeated the words, the less comfort they gave. Yet the endless, circling words of hope were all she had to hold against a despair so deep that it terrified her, leaving sweat cold on her skin, and a bleak, elemental cry of loss vibrating beneath her litany of hope.

Cash would marry her, but he did not want the child she was carrying. He would marry her, but he didn't believe in her love. He would marry her, but he thought she wanted only his name and the money to pay for her pregnancy. He would marry her, but he believed he had been caught in the oldest trap of all.

And how can I prove he's wrong? I have no money of my own. No home. No job. No profession. I'm working toward those things, but I don't have them yet. I have nothing to point to and say, "See, I don't need your apartment, your food, your money. I just need you, the man I love. The only man I've ever loved."

But she could not prove it.

"Mariah? You awake?"

For a wild instant she thought the male voice belonged to Cash, but even as she spun toward the front door with hope blazing on her face, she realized that it was Nevada, not Cash. She went to the front door, opened it, and looked into the pale green eyes that missed not one of the signs of grief on her face.

"Are you feeling all right?" Nevada asked.

Mariah clenched her teeth against the tears that threatened to dissolve her control. Telling Nevada what had happened would only make things worse, not better. Cash had always resented the odd, tacit understanding between Nevada and Mariah.

Nor could she tell Luke, her own brother, because telling him would in effect force him to choose between his sister and Cash, the man who was closer to him than any brother could be. No good could come of such a choice. Not for her. Not for Cash. And most of all, not for Luke, the brother who had opened his arms and his home to her after a fifteen-year separation.

"I'm...just a little tired." Mariah forced a smile. She noticed the flat, carefully wrapped package in Nevada's hand and changed the subject gratefully. "What's that?"

"It's yours. It came in yesterday, but I didn't have time to get it to you."

Automatically Mariah took the parcel. She looked at it curiously. There was no stamp on the outside, no address, no return address, nothing to indicate who the package was for, who had sent it or where it had come from.

"It's yours, all right," Nevada said, accurately reading Mariah's hesitation.

"What's underneath all that tape?"

"Mad Jack's map."

"Oh. I suppose they found where the mine was."

Nevada's eyes narrowed. There was no real curiosity in Mariah's voice, simply a kind of throttled desperation that was reflected in her haunted golden eyes.

"I didn't ask and they didn't tell me," Nevada said after a moment. "They just sent it back all wrapped up. I'm giving it to you the same way I got it."

Mariah looked at the parcel for a long moment before she set it aside on a nearby table. "Thank you."

"Aren't you going to open it?"

"I'll wait for...Cash."

"Last time I saw him, he was in the kitchen with Carla." Nevada looked closely at Mariah, sensing the wildness seething just beneath her surface. "You told Cash about the baby."

Mariah shivered with pent emotion. "Yes. I told him."

Without another word Mariah stepped off the porch and headed for the big house. She couldn't wait for a moment longer. Maybe by now Cash had realized that she hadn't meant to trap him. Maybe by now he understood that she loved him.

It will be all right.

Mariah was running by the time she reached the big house. She raced through the back door and into the kitchen, but no one was around. Heart hammering, she rushed into the living room. Cash was there, standing next to Carla. His hand was over her womb and there was a look of wonder on his face.

"It's moving," he said, smiling suddenly. "I can feel it moving!"

The awe in Cash's voice made Mariah's heart turn over with relief. Surely a man who was so touched by his sister's pregnancy could accept his own woman's pregnancy.

"Moving? I should say so." Carla laughed. "It's doing back flips."

A healthy holler from the second-floor nursery distracted Carla. "Logan just ran out of patience." She hurried out of the room. "Hi, Mariah. The coffee is hot."

"Thank you," Mariah said absently.

She walked up to Cash, her face suffused with hope and need. She took his hand and pressed it against her own womb.

"I think I've felt our baby moving already. But you have to be very still or you won't—"

Mariah's words ended in a swift intake of breath as Cash jerked his hand away, feeling as though he had held it in fire. The thought of what it might be like to actually feel his own child moving in the womb was a pain so great it was all he could do not to cry out.

"I can't feel a damned thing," Cash said roughly. "I guess my imagination isn't as good as yours."

He spun away, clenching his hands to conceal their fine trembling. When he spoke, his voice was so controlled as to be unrecognizable.

"I'll leave tomorrow to make the arrangements. After we're married, you'll stay here."

Mariah heard the absolute lack of emotion in Cash's voice and felt ice condense along her spine.

"What about you?" she asked.

"I'll be gone most of the time."

Tears came to Mariah's eyes. She could no more stop them than she could stop the spreading chill in her soul.

"Why?" she asked. "You never used to work so much."

"I never had a wife and baby to take care of, did I."

The neutrality of Cash's voice was like a very thin whip flaying Mariah's nerves. She swallowed but it did nothing to relieve the aching dryness of her mouth or the burning in her eyes.

"If you don't want me to be your wife," Mariah said in a shaking voice, "why did you ask me to marry you?"

Cash said something savage beneath his breath, but Mariah didn't give up. Anything, even anger, was better than the frigid lack of emotion he had been using as a weapon against her.

"Other men get women pregnant and don't marry them," she said. "Why are you marrying me?"

"I could hardly walk out on my best friend's sister, could I? And you have Carla wrapped around your little finger, too. They would think I was a real heel for knocking you up and then not marrying you."

"That's why...?" Mariah shuddered and felt the redoubling of the chill despair that had been growing in the center of her soul.

"Carla and Luke are the only family I have or ever will have," Cash continued with savage restraint.

"That's not true," Mariah said raggedly. "You have me! You have our baby!"

She went to Cash in a rush, wrapping her arms around him, holding him with all her strength. It was like holding granite. He was unyielding, rigid, motionless but for the sudden clenching of his hands when Mariah's soft body pressed against his.

"We'll be a family," she said. Her lips pressed repeatedly against his cheek, his neck, his jaw, desperate kisses that said more than words could about yearning and loneliness, love and need. "Give us a chance, Cash. You enjoyed being with me before, why not again?"

While Mariah spoke, her hands stroked Cash's back, his shoulders, his hair, the buttons of his shirt; and then her mouth was sultry against his skin. When she felt the involuntary tremor ripping through his strong body, she made a small sound in the back of her throat and rubbed her cheek against his chest.

"You enjoyed my kisses, my hands, my body, my love," Mariah said, moving slowly against Cash, shivering with the pleasure of holding him. "It can be that way again."

Cash moved with frightening power, pushing Mariah away at arm's length, holding her there. Black fury shook him as he listened to his greatest dream, his deepest hungers, his terrifying vulnerability used as weapons by the woman he had trusted too much.

"I'll support you," he said through his clenched teeth. "I'll give your bastard a name. But I'll be damned if I'll take another man's leavings to bed."

Shock turned Mariah's face as pale as salt.

"What are you saying?" she whispered hoarsely. "This baby is yours. You must know that. I came to you a virgin. You're the only man I've ever loved!"

Cash's mouth flattened into a line as narrow as the cold blaze of his eyes.

"A world-class performance, right down to the tears trembling in your long black eyelashes. There's just one thing wrong with your touching scenario of wounded innocence. I'm sterile."

Mariah shook her head numbly, unable to believe what she was hearing. Cash kept talking, battering her with the icy truth, freezing her alive.

"When I was sixteen," Cash said, "Carla came down with mumps. So did I. She recovered. So did I...after a fashion. That's why I never worried about contraceptives with you. I couldn't get you pregnant."

"But you did get me pregnant!"

"You're half right." Cash's smile made Mariah flinch. "Settle for half, baby. It's more than I got."

"Listen to me," Mariah said urgently. "I don't care what you had or when you had it or what the doctors told you afterward. They were wrong. Cash, you have to believe me. I love you. I have never slept with another man. *This baby is yours.*"

For an instant Cash's fingers dug harshly into Mariah's shoulders. Then he released her and stepped back, not trusting himself to touch her any longer.

"You're something else." He jammed his hands into the back pockets of his jeans. "Really. Something. For the first time in my life I'm grateful to Linda. If she hadn't already inoculated me against your particular kind of liar, I'd be on my knees begging your forgiveness right now. But she did inoculate me. She stuck it in and then she broke it off right at the bone."

"I—"

Cash kept right on talking over Mariah's voice.

"Virginity is no proof of fidelity," he said flatly. "Linda was a virgin, too. She told me she loved me, too. Then she told me she was pregnant. Sound familiar?" He measured Mariah's dismay with cold eyes. "Yeah, I thought it would. The difference was, I believed her. I was so damned hungry to believe that I'd gotten lucky, hit that slim, lucky chance and had gotten her pregnant. We hadn't been married five months when she came and told me she was leaving. Seems her on-again, off-again boyfriend was on again, and this time he was willing to pay her rent."

Mariah laced her fingers together in a futile attempt to stop their trembling.

"You loved her," Mariah whispered.

"I loved the idea of having gotten her pregnant. I was so convinced she was carrying my baby that I told her she couldn't have a divorce until after the baby was born. Then she could leave, but not with the baby. It would stay with me. Well, she had the baby. Then she had a blood test run on it. Turns out I hadn't been lucky. The baby wasn't mine. End of story."

Cash made a short, thick sound that was too harsh to be a laugh. "Want to know the really funny part? I never believed Linda loved me, but I was beginning to believe that you did. You got to me in a way Linda never did." He looked at Mariah suddenly, really looked at her, letting her see past the icy surface to the savage masculine rage beneath. "Don't touch me again. You won't like what happens."

Mariah closed her eyes and swayed, unable to bear what she saw in Cash's face. His remoteness was as terrifying as her own pain.

Suddenly she could take no more. She turned and ran from the house. The chilly air outside settled the nausea churning in her stomach. Walking swiftly, shivering, she headed for the old ranch house. The pines surrounding the old house were shivering, too, caressed by a fitful wind.

When the front door closed behind Mariah, she made a stifled sound and swayed, hugging herself against a cold that no amount of hope could banish. Slowly she sank to her knees, wishing she could cry, but even that release was beyond her.

It will be all right. It has to be. Somehow I'll make him believe me.

Slim chance, isn't that what you said? But it came true, Cash. It came true and now you won't believe in it. In my love. In me. And there's nothing I can do. Nothing!

Mariah swayed and caught her balance against the table that stood near the front door. A small, flat package slid off. Automatically she caught it before it hit the floor.

Slim chance.

Almost afraid to believe that hope was possible, Mariah stripped off paper and tape until Mad Jack's map fell into her hands. With it was a cover letter and a copy of the map. There was no blank area on the copy, no ancient stain, no blur, nothing but a web of dotted lines telling her that she and Cash had been looking at the wrong part of Devil's Peak.

Will you believe I love you if I give you Mad Jack's mine? Will that prove to you that I'm not after a free ride like your stepmother and your wife? Will you believe me if...

With hands that trembled Mariah refolded the copy and put it in her jeans. Silently, quickly, she went to the workroom cupboard and changed into her trail clothes. When she was ready to leave, she pulled out a sheet of notepaper and wrote swiftly.

I have nothing of value to give you, no way to make you believe. Except one. Mad Jack's mine. It's yours now. I give it to you. All of it.

I'll find the mine and I'll fill your hands with gold and then you'll have to believe I love you. When you believe that, you'll know the baby is yours.

Slim chance.
But it was the only chance Mariah had.

Fifteen

The memory of Mariah's lost, frightened expression rode Cash unmercifully as he worked over his Jeep. No matter how many times he told himself she was an accomplished little liar, her stricken face contradicted him, forcing him to think rather than to react from pain and rage.

And reason told Cash that no matter how good an actress Mariah was, she didn't have the ability to make her skin turn pale. She didn't have the ability to make the black center of her eyes dilate until all the gold was gone. She didn't have the ability...but those things had happened just the same, her skin pale and her eyes dark and watching him as though she expected him to destroy her world as thoroughly as she had destroyed his.

With a savage curse Cash slammed shut the Jeep's hood and went to the old house. The instant he went through the front door, he knew the house was empty. He could feel it.

"Mariah?"

No one answered his call. With growing unease, Cash walked through the living room. Shreds of wrapping paper and tape littered the floor. On the table near the door was a typed note and what looked like Mad Jack's faded old map. Cash read the note quickly, then once more.

There was no mistake. A copy of the map had been in the package, a clean copy that supposedly showed the way to Mad Jack's mine. Automatically Cash glanced out the window, assessing the weather. Slate-bottomed clouds were billowing over the high country.

Mariah wouldn't risk it just for money. She would count on Luke to support her even if I refused.

Yet even as the thought came, Cash discarded it. Mariah had been very careful to take nothing from Luke that she didn't earn by helping Carla with Logan and the demands of being a ranch wife. That was one of the things Cash had admired about Mariah, one of the things that had gotten through his defenses.

As he turned away from the small table, he saw another piece of paper that had fallen to the floor. He picked it up, read it, and felt as though he were being wrenched apart.

It can't be true. It...can't...be.

Cash ran to the workroom and wrenched open the cupboard that held Mariah's camping clothes. It was empty.

That little fool has gone after Mad Jack's mine.

Cash looked at his watch. Three hours since Mariah had tried to seduce him and his treacherous body had responded as though love rather than lies bound him to her. Three hours since he had told her that he was sterile. Three hours since she had looked at him in shock and had tried to convince him that the baby was his. Three hours since she had looked at his face and fled.

Three hours, a treasure map, and a high-country storm coming down.

Cursing under his breath, Cash began yanking drawers open, pulling out cold-weather gear he hadn't used since the past winter. After he changed clothes, he started cramming extra clothing into a backpack. Then he remembered the Rocking M's cellular telephones. When Mariah and Cash weren't hunting gold, one of those phones was kept in the old house's tiny kitchen.

The phone was missing from its place on the kitchen counter. Cash ran out to his Jeep, opened the glove compartment and pulled out his own battery-operated unit. He punched in numbers, praying that Mad Jack's map kept Mariah out of canyons that were too steep and narrow for the signal to get in or out. Cellular phones worked better than short-wave radio, but the coverage wasn't complete. Twentieth-century technology had its limitations. The Rocking M's rugged terrain discovered every one of them.

The ringing stopped. No voice answered.

"Mariah? It's Cash."

Voiceless sound whispered in response, a rushing sense of space filled with something that was both more and less than silence.

"Mariah, turn around and come back."

There was a long, long pause before her answer came.

"No. It's my proof. When I find it you'll know I love you and then maybe, just maybe, you'll..."

Cash strained to hear the words, but no more came.

"Mariah. Listen to me. I don't want the damned mine. Turn around and head back to the ranch before it starts snowing."

"It already did. Then it rained a little and now it's just sort of slushy. Except for the wind, it's not too cold."

But Mariah was shivering. He could hear it in the pauses between words, just as he could hear the shifting tone of her voice when she shivered.

"Mariah, you're cold. Turn around and come back."

"No. The mine is here. It has to be. I'll find it and then I'll have p-proof that slim chances are different from none. Life's a lottery and you're one of the l-luckiest men alive. I'm going to find your mine, Cash. Then you'll have to b-believe me. Then everything will be all right. Everything will be..."

The phone went dead.

Quickly Cash punched up the number again, ignoring the first chill tendrils of fear curling through his gut.

It can't be.

Mariah didn't answer the phone. After ten rings Cash jammed the phone into his jacket pocket, zipped the pocket shut and ran to the corral.

Slim chance.

Ice crystallized in the pit of Cash's stomach, displacing the savagery that had driven him since the instant Mariah had told him she was pregnant.

In three hours it would be freezing up in the high country. Mariah didn't have any decent winter gear. She didn't even have enough experience in cold country to know how insidious hypothermia could be, how it drained the mind's ability to reason as surely as it drained the body's coordination, cold eating away at flesh until finally the person was defenseless.

Three hours. Too much time for the cold to work on Mariah's vulnerable body. Doubly vulnerable. Pregnant.

Slim chance.

Oh God, what if I was wrong?

Trying not to think at all, Cash caught and bridled two horses. He saddled only one. Leading one horse, riding the other, Cash headed out of the ranch yard at a dead run. Mariah's trail was clear in the damp earth and slanting autumn light. Holding his mount at a hard gallop, Cash followed the trail she had left, forcing himself to think of nothing but the task in front of him. After half an hour he stopped, switched his saddle to the spare horse and took off again at a fast gallop, leading his original mount.

Although the dark, wind-raked clouds rained only fitfully, the ground was glistening with cold moisture. In the long afternoon shadows, puddles wore a rime of ice granules left by the passage of a recent hailstorm.

The horses' breaths came out in great soft plumes, only to be torn away by the rising wind.

Except for the wind, it's not too cold.

Mariah's words haunted Cash. He tried not to think of how cold it was, how quickly wind stripped heat from even his big body. Even worse than the cold was the fitful rain. He would have preferred snow. In an emergency, dry snow could be used as insulation against the wind, but the only defense from rain was shelter. Otherwise wind simply sucked out all body heat through the damp clothes, leaving behind a chill that drained a person's strength so subtly yet so completely that most people didn't realize how close they were to death until it was too late; they thought they stopped shivering because their bodies had miraculously become warm again.

Mariah looked at the map once more, then at the dark lava slope to her right. There was a pile of rocks that looked rather like a lizard, but there was no lightning-killed tree nearby. Shrugging, she reminded herself that more than a century had passed since Mad Jack drew the map. In that amount of time, a dead tree could have fallen and been absorbed back into the land. Carefully Mariah reined her mount around until the lizard was at her back. The rest of the landmarks fit well enough.

Shivering against the chill wind, she urged her horse downhill, checking every so often in order to keep the pile of rocks at her back. The horse was eager to get off the exposed slope. It half trotted, half slid down the steep side of a ravine. The relief from the wind was immediate.

With a long sigh, Mariah gave the horse its head and tucked her hands into the huge pockets of her jacket. Once in the ravine, the only way to go was downhill, which was exactly the way Mad Jack had gone. Her fingers were so cold that she barely felt the hard weight of the cellular phone she had jammed into one of the oversize pockets and forgotten.

I'll count to one hundred. If I don't see any granite by then, I'll get out of the ravine and head for Black Springs. It can't be more than twenty minutes from here, just around the shoulder of the ridge. It will be warm there.

Mariah had counted to eighty-three when she saw a spur ravine open off to the right. The opening was too small and too choked with stones for the horse to negotiate. Almost afraid to breathe, much less to believe, she dismounted and hung on to the stirrup until circulation and balance returned to her cold-numbed body. Scrambling, falling, getting up again, she explored the rocky ravine.

When Mariah first saw the granite, she thought it was a patch of snow along the left side of the ravine. Only as she got closer did she realize that it was rock, not ice, that gleamed palely in the fading light. The pile of rubble she crawled over to reach the granite had been made by man. The shattered, rust-encrusted remains of a shovel proved it.

Breathing quickly, shivering, Mariah knelt next to the small hole in the mountainside that had been dug by a man long dead. Inside, a vein of quartz gleamed. It was taller than she was, thicker, and running through it like sunlight through water was pure gold.

Slowly Mariah reached out. She couldn't feel the gold with her chilled fingers, but she knew it was there. With both hands she grabbed a piece of rocky debris and used it as a hammer. Despite her clumsiness, chunks of quartz fell away. Pure gold gleamed and winked as she gathered the shattered matrix in both hands. She shoved as much as she could in her oversize jacket pockets, then stood up. The weight of the rocks staggered her.

Very slowly Mariah worked her way back down the side ravine to the point where she had left her horse. It was waiting patiently, tail turned toward the wind that searched through the main ravine. Mariah tried to mount, fell, and pulled herself to her feet again. No matter how she concentrated, she couldn't get her foot through the stirrup before she lost her balance.

And her pocket was jeering at her again. It had jeered at her before, but she had ignored it.

Mariah realized that it was the cellular phone that was jeering. With numb fingers she groped through the pieces of rock and gold until she kept a grip on the phone long enough to pull it from her pocket and answer. The rings stopped, replaced by the hushed, expectant sound of an open line.

"Mariah? Mariah, it's Cash."

The phone slid through Mariah's fingers. She made a wild grab and caught the unit more by luck than skill.

"Mariah, talk to me. Where are you? Are you warm enough?"

"Clumsy. Sorry." Mariah's voice sounded odd to her own ear. Thick. Slow.

"Where are you?"

"Devil's Peak. But isn't hell warm? I'm warm, too. I think. I was cold after the rain. Now I'm tired."

The words were subtly slurred, as though she had been drinking.

"Are you on the north side of Devil's Peak?" Cash asked, his voice as hard and urgent as the wind.

Mariah frowned down at the phone as she struggled with the concept of direction. Slowly a memory of the map formed in her mind.

"And...west," she said finally.

"Northwest? Are you on the northwest side?"

Mariah made a sound that could have meant anything and leaned against her patient horse. The animal's warmth slowly seeped into her cold skin.

"Are you above timberline?" Cash asked.

"No."

"Are there trees around you?"

"Rocks, too. Gray. Looked like snow. Wasn't."

"Look up the mountains. Can you see me?"

Mariah shook her head. All she could see was the ravine. "Can't." She thought about trying to mount the horse again. "Tired. I need to rest."

"Mariah. Look up the mountain. You might be able to see me."

Grumbling, Mariah tried to climb out of the ravine. Her hands and feet kept surprising her. She persisted. After a while she could at least feel her feet again, and her hands. They hurt. She still couldn't claw her way out of the crumbling ravine, however.

"I can't," she said finally.

"You can't see me?"

"I can't climb out of the ravine." Mariah's voice was clearer. Moving around had revived her. "It's too steep here. And I'm cold."

"Start a fire."

She looked around. There wasn't enough debris in the bottom of the ravine for a fire. "No wood."

She shivered suddenly, violently, and for the first time became afraid.

"Talk to me, Mariah."

"Do you get lonely, too?" Then, before Cash could say anything, she added, "I wish...I wish you could have loved me just a little bit. But it will be all right. I found the mine and now it's yours and now you have to believe me...don't you?" Her voice faded, then came again. "It's so cold. You were so warm. I loved curling up against you. Better each time...love."

Cash tried to speak but couldn't for the pain choking him. He gripped the phone so hard that his fingers turned white. The next words he heard were so softly spoken that he had a hard time following them. And then he wished he hadn't been able to understand the ragged phrases pouring from Mariah.

"It will be all right...everything will be fine...it will be..."

But Mariah was crying. She no longer believed her own words.

A horse's lonesome whinny drifted up faintly from below. Cash's horse answered. He reined his mount toward the crease in the land where Mariah's tracks vanished. Balancing his weight in the stirrups, he sent his horse down the mountainside at a reckless pace. Minutes later the ravine closed around Cash, shutting out all but a slice of the cloudy sky.

"Mariah!" Cash called. *"Mariah!"*

There was no answer but that of her horse whinnying its delight into the increasing gloom.

Instants after Cash saw Mariah's horse, he saw the dark splotch of her jacket against the pale swath of granite. He dismounted in a rush and scrambled to Mariah. At the sound of his approach, she pushed herself upright and held out her hands. Quartz crystals and gold gleamed richly in the dying light.

"See? I've p-proved it. Now will you b-believe me?" she whispered.

"All you've proved is that you're a fool," Cash said, picking Mariah up in a rush, ignoring the gold that fell from her hands. "It will be dark in ten minutes—I'm damned lucky I found you at all!"

Mariah tried to say something but couldn't force herself to speak past the defeat that numbed her more deeply than any cold.

Her gift of the gold mine had meant nothing to Cash. He still didn't believe in her. She had risked it all and had nothing to show for it but the contempt of the man she loved.

He was right. She was a fool.

Sixteen

Broodingly Cash watched Mariah. In the silence and firelight of the old line shack she looked comfortable despite the stillness of her body. Wearing dry clothes and his down sleeping bag, sitting propped up against the wall, coffee steaming from the cup held between her hands, Mariah was no longer cold. No shivers shook her body. Nor was she clumsy anymore. The pockets bulging with gold-shot rock had been as much to blame for her lack of coordination as the cold.

She's fine, Cash told himself. *Any fool could see that. Even this fool. So why do I feel like I should call her on the cellular phone right now?*

That's easy, fool. She's never been farther away from you than right now. Your stupidity nearly killed her. You expect her to thank you for that?

Flames burnished Mariah, turning her eyes to incandescent gold, heightening the color that warmth had returned to her skin.

"More soup?" Cash asked, his voice neutral.

"No, thank you."

Her voice, like her words, was polite. Mariah had been very polite since they had come to the line shack. She had protested only once— when he stripped her out of her damp clothes and dressed her in the extra pair of thermal underclothes he had brought in the backpack. When he had ignored her protest, she had fallen silent. She had stayed that way, except when he asked a direct question. Then she replied with excruciating politeness.

Not once had she met his eyes. It was as though she literally could not bear the sight of him. He didn't really blame her. He would break a mirror right now rather than look at himself in it.

"Warm enough?" Cash asked, his voice too rough.

It must have been the tenth time he had asked that question in as many minutes, but Mariah showed no impatience.

"Yes, thank you."

Cash hesitated, then asked bluntly, "Any cramps?"

That question was new. He heard the soft, ripping sound her breath made as it rushed out.

"No."

"Are you sure?"

"Yes. I'm fine. Everything is..." The unwitting echo of Mariah's past assurances to herself went into her like a knife. Without finishing the sentence, Mariah took a sip of coffee, swallowed and regained her voice. "Just fine, thank you."

But her eyelids flinched and the hands holding the coffee tightened suddenly, sending a ripple of hot liquid over the side. A few drops fell to the sleeping bag.

"I'm sorry," she said immediately, blotting at the drops with the sleeve of her discarded shirt. "I hope it won't stain."

"Pour the whole cup on it. I don't give a damn about the sleeping bag."

"That's very kind of you."

"*Kind?* Good God, Mariah. This is me, Cash McQueen, the fool you wanted to marry, not some stranger who just wandered in off the mountain!"

"No," she said in a low voice, blotting at the spilled coffee.

"What?"

There was no answer.

Fear condensed into certainty inside Cash. With a harsh curse he put aside his own coffee cup and sat on his heels next to Mariah.

"Look at me."

She kept dabbing at the bag, refusing to look at him.

Cash's big hand fitted itself to her chin. Gently, inexorably, he tilted her face until she was forced to meet his eyes. Then his breath came out in a low sound, as though he had been struck. Beneath the brilliant dance of reflected flames, Mariah's eyes were old, emotionless, bleak.

He looked into Mariah's golden eyes, searching for her, feeling her slipping away, nothing but emptiness in all the places she had once filled. The cold tendrils of fear that had been growing in Cash blossomed in a silent black rush, and each heartbeat told him the same cruel truth: she no longer loved the man whose lack of trust had nearly killed her. She couldn't even stand the sight of him.

Cash had thought he could feel no greater pain than he had when Mariah told him she was pregnant. He had been wrong.

"Are you sure you feel all right?" he asked, forcing the words past the pain constricting his body. "You're not acting like the same girl who went tearing up a stormy mountain looking for gold."

"I'm not," she whispered.

"What?"

"I'm not the same. I've finally learned something my stepfather spent fifteen years trying to teach me."

Cash waited.

Mariah said nothing more.

"What did you learn?" he asked when he could no longer bear the silence.

"You can't make someone love you. No matter what you do, no matter how hard you try...you can't. I thought my stepfather would love me if I got good grades and made no demands and did everything he wanted me to do." Mariah closed her eyes, shutting out the indigo bleakness of Cash's glance. "It didn't work. After a while I didn't care very much.

"But I didn't learn very much, either. I thought you would love me if only I could prove that I loved you, but all I proved was what a fool I was. You see, I had it all wrong from the start. I thought if you believed me, you would love me. Now I know that if you loved me, *then* you would believe me. So we both had a long, cold ride for nothing."

"Not for nothing," Cash said, stroking Mariah's cheek, wanting to hold her but afraid she would refuse him. "You're safe. That's something, honey. Hell, that's everything."

"Don't. I don't need pity. I'm warm, dry and healthy, thanks to you. I did thank you, didn't I?"

"Too many times. I didn't come up here for your thanks."

"I know, but you deserve thanks just the same. If my stepfather had had a chance to get rid of me, he wouldn't have walked across the street to avoid it, much less climbed a mountain in a hailstorm."

Cash's breath hissed in with shock as he realized what Mariah was implying.

"I appreciate your decency," she continued, opening her eyes at last. "You don't need to worry about losing your home with Luke and Carla because of my foolishness. Before I leave, I'll be sure they understand that none of this was your fault."

Too quickly for Cash to prevent it, Mariah pulled free of his hand, set her coffee cup aside and unzipped the sleeping bag. His hand shot out, spread flat over her abdomen and pinned her gently in place.

"What are you saying?" Cash asked, his voice dangerously soft.

Mariah tried to prevent the tremor of awareness that went through her at his touch. She failed. Somehow she had always failed when it came to love.

"I'm leaving the Rocking M. You don't have to marry me just to ensure your welcome with Luke and Carla," Mariah said, her voice careful. "You'll always have a home with them."

"So will you." Cash's eyes searched hers, looking for the emotions that he had always found in her before, praying that he hadn't raced up the mountain only to lose her after all. "You'll have a home. Always. I'll make sure of it."

Mariah closed her eyes again and fought against the emotions that were just beneath her frozen surface.

"That's very generous of you," Mariah said, her voice husky with restraint. "But it's not necessary." She tried to get up, but Cash's big hand still held her captive. "May I get up now?" she asked politely.

"Not yet."

Cash's big hand moved subtly, almost caressingly. He couldn't free Mariah. Not yet. If he let her go he would never see her again. He clenched his jaw against the pain of an understanding that had come too late. He tried to speak, found it impossible, and fought in silence to control his emotions. When he could speak again, his voice was a harsh rasp.

"Look at me, Mariah."

She shook her head, refusing him.

"Do you hate me so much?" he asked in a low, constrained voice.

Shocked, Mariah opened her eyes.

"You have every right," Cash continued. "I damn near killed you. But if you think I'm going to let you go, you're as big a fool as I was. You loved me once. You can learn to love me again." He shifted his weight onto his knees as he bent down to her. "Forgive me, Mariah," he whispered against her lips. "Love me again. I need you so much it terrifies me."

Mariah would have spoken then, but he had taken her breath. Trembling, she opened her lips beneath his, inviting his kiss. She sensed the tremor that ripped through him, felt the sudden iron power of his arms, tasted the heat and hunger of his mouth. The world shifted until she was lying down and he was with her, surrounding her with a vital warmth that was so glorious she wept silently with the sheer beauty of it.

Suddenly Cash's arms tightened and he went very still.

"Cash? What's wrong?"

"Didn't you feel it?" he asked, his voice strained.

"What?"

"Our baby." Cash closed his eyes but could not entirely conceal the glitter of his tears. "My God," he breathed. *"I felt our baby move."*

"Are you certain?"

His eyes opened. He smiled down at Mariah, sensing the question she hadn't asked. He kissed her gently once, twice, then again and again, whispering between each kiss.

"I'm very certain."

"Cash?" she whispered, her eyes blazing with hope.

"I love you, Mariah," he said, kissing her hand, holding it against his heart. "I love you so damned much."

Laughing, crying, holding on to Cash, Mariah absorbed his whispered words and his warmth, his trust and his love, and gave her own in return. He held her, loving her with his hands and his voice and his body, until finally they lay at peace in each other's arms, so close that they breathed the same scents, shared the same warmth...and felt the butterfly wings of new life fluttering softly in Mariah's womb.

Cash's big hand rested lightly over Mariah's womb.

"Go to sleep, little baby. Mom and Dad are right here. Everything is all right."

* * * * *

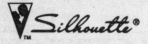

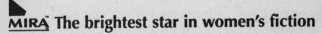

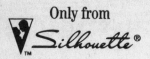

HE SAID

SHE SAID

Explore the mystery of male/female communication in this extraordinary new book from two of your favorite Harlequin authors.

Jasmine Cresswell and Margaret St. George bring you the exciting story of two romantic adversaries—each from their own point of view!

DEV'S STORY. CATHY'S STORY.
As he sees it. As she sees it.
Both sides of the story!

The heat is definitely on, and these two can't stay out of the kitchen!

Don't miss **HE SAID, SHE SAID.**
Available in July wherever Harlequin books are sold.

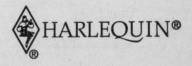

The Oracle:

The Succession War

Author: Richard Wayne Waterman
~ Illustrations: Sendil Nathan ~

Otherworld Publications, LLC
Louisville, Kentucky

Otherworld Publications, LLC
4949 Old Brownsboro Rd. Suite 113
Louisville, Kentucky 40222
www.otherworldpublications.com

Interior design and typesetting by Lynn Calvert
Cover design and artwork by Sendil Nathan
Cover and interior design Copyright © 2010 Sendil Nathan

Printed in the United States of America

Paperback   ISBN10: 0-9826702-7-X
            ISBN13: 978-0-9826072-7-5
Hard Cover ISNB10: 0-9826072-6-1
            ISBN13: 978-0-9826072-6-8
Library of Congress Control Number: 2010922823

Dedication

To Our Mothers and Fathers:

The Very Best of our Imagination and Talent
is dedicated to the Very Best who ever lived
on Earth.

We hope and believe they would be proud!

THE ORACLE:

THE SUCCESSION

WAR

BY

RICHARD WAYNE WATERMAN

WITH ILLUSTRATIONS BY

SENDIL NATHAN

THE MAIN CHARACTERS

The Centama Family
King Benton- **Ben**-ton
Grizelda – Gri-**zel**-da
Retch - **Wretch**
Pondru - **Pon**-dru
Rendrau - **Ren**-dro
Pantamanu - **Pan**-tam-a-nu
Bellazar - **Bel**-la-zar

The Main Oracle Entities
Count Belicki - **Bel**-é-cki
Kublatitan - **Ku**-bla-ti-tan
King Leonata – **Le**-o-na-ta
Characters

The Tantamount Family
Lord Tantamount - **Tan**-ta-mount
Truellen - **True**-él-len
Montama - **Mon**-ta-ma
Hontallo - **Hon**-ta-yo

Other
General Garr- **Garr**
Grandafier the Elder – **Grand**-a-fire
Timilty - **Tim**-il-tee
Lord Gulcum - **Gull**-cum
Lord Valmar - **Val**-mar
General Tampinco – Tam-**pin**-co
High Cleric Rendella – **Ren**-del-la
General Wu - **Woo**
General Tige – **Tige**
General Cato –**Ca**-to
General Mbanka – **M**-bank- a

BOLDTEXT signifies an **EMPHASIS** on a particular SYLLABLE

The Oracle:
The Succession War

Author: Richard Wayne Waterman
~ Illustrations: Sendil Nathan ~

TABLE OF CONTENTS

THE BOOK

PART I: THE EQUINOX OF DEATH

PART IV: LEGENDS!

PART V: THE PRICE OF POWER

PART VI: THE FINAL BATTLE

Coming Soon: Next in the Series

Book 2

The Oracle:

The War Within

INFINITE AMBITION

INFINITE POWER
INFINITE MADNESS
THE ORACLE

PROLOGUE

"I beg you, do not proceed any further! Do not touch memories long forgotten, for you have no idea of the danger that lurks behind them."

Nimrod listened, but paid no heed whatsoever to this stark warning from a strange reconstructed voice that had been silenced for literally tens of thousands of years or cycles, as they were then called. Instead, assiduously driven by a blind obsession and a singular purpose, Nimrod continued to delve into the secrets of a mysterious, long forgotten device known only as the Oracle. "Only the Oracle can tell me who or what I am," Nimrod thought as it systematically scanned deeper inside the mechanism's damaged inner core, attempting to access other voices long silenced and buried in history's infinite obscurity.

Moments later, Nimrod sensed a voice; the shrill high-pitched cry of a terrified young girl. "We have to get out of here," Nimrod heard the girl scream hysterically. "Mother is dead! Father killed her."

The girl, Mira, stood frail and alone in an open doorway. She was no more than ten, with a petite figure wrapped tightly in a delicate pink and white sari, her long flowing blonde hair glistening angelically in the morning sunlight, as her astonishing emerald eyes burned with a raw, boundless terror. "We have to run!" Mira declared with a frightful insistence.

"I don't understand," Nimrod said aloud, mirroring the words of a second child, a boy of no more than four or five, who was playing in a sandpit in the front yard, only a few feet from the doorway. The boy was decidedly odd looking, with strange oval shaped purple eyes that seemed far too large for his diminutive head. "I know this boy," Nimrod realized with a fitful start.

"Belicki," the girl shouted as she scampered frantically from the doorway. "We must run or father will kill us too!" But the boy, Belicki, was far too young to understand what was happening. Instead of reacting, he merely stared with a vacuous, confused look, as his sister abruptly grabbed his tiny dirt covered hand and pulled him from the sandpit, where he had been blissfully engaged. It was only then that Belicki noticed the tiny speckles of blood on his sister's sari. Yet, before he could say another word, he heard a familiar, mournful, terrifying beast-like cry emanating from inside the house. "Mira, Belicki, come here!"

The children did not wait for their father to emerge from their neatly constructed and ornately decorated log cabin. Instead, they turned and ran into a nearby field of wild flowers of the most astonishingly multihued variety. Sensing these memories, Nimrod marveled at the strange juxtaposition of indescribable beauty combined with unadulterated terror.

Already exhausted, her heart pounding, her legs burning with excruciating pain, Mira whispered to her brother, "We must get to the river. It is our only hope!" Tentatively, her senses overwhelmed by an unbearable fear, she turned her head and, with deep apprehension furtively glanced back toward the cabin. As she did so she saw a stout man reeking of alcohol, stumbling wildly out of the door, his shirt drenched in bloody scarlet, his right hand still clasping the handle of a sharp, silver, serrated knife. As Mira spotted her father, she insistently pulled her brother toward the turbulent and untamed waters of the nearby Kapapa River.

"Quick, we must get to the boat." Mira had difficulty speaking these few words, for she was nearly out of breath. Still, it was at least another fifty yards before they would reach the river and the boat, which bobbed precariously in the nearby water, grounded only by a short piece of rope tied to a stick.

It was then that Nimrod sensed an exponentially growing terror, this time emanating from the young boy's thoughts. "I can't swim," Belicki thought. Terrified and too frightened to run, he instinctively pulled his hand away from his sister, for he was now trapped between two equally alarming contingencies. He was every bit as afraid of the water as he was of his father's unpredictable ill temper. Sensing her brother's unbridled panic, Mira turned and shouted, "Come with me Belicki!"

Belicki simply could not move. Frozen in place, trapped between two equally horrific images, he could neither move forward nor backward. Instead, he remained immobile as he watched his sister continue to limp awkwardly toward the boat, occasionally looking back to see if Belicki was following her. As Belicki stood catatonically still he suddenly felt the ground tremble beneath his feet, as his father charged quickly toward him with a desperate, demonically hateful expression on his face. Unable to bear the tension any longer, Belicki merely closed his eyes, expecting his father to strike him dead at any moment. Instead, he heard the footsteps charge past him, as his father sprinted inexorably toward the mighty Kapapa River.

Slowly, his hands trembling with a frightful palsy, Belicki opened his large purple eyes, and when he did he saw his sister leap headfirst into the boat. Her hair was now knotted and wet with perspiration, her once beautiful sari torn and ragged about the legs. Hysterically, with her father fast approaching, Mira struggled to untie the rope, desperate to unleash the boat from its moorings. "Get away from me," she screamed at her father, as she continued to fumble with the rope. "Why won't it come untied?" She cried out frantically, her eyes moist and wide open, her breathing even more labored than before. With her father swiftly approaching, Mira finally gave up on the knot and instead pulled hard on the stick to which the rope was tied. As she did so, the stick snapped in half and Mira fell backward hard against the inside of the boat.

A few seconds later, as her father arrived at the shoreline, the river's powerful currents already were carrying the tiny vessel downstream at an increasingly expedited velocity. Belicki was young, but he instinctively understood the mounting danger, for he knew that Mira had never been in a boat before and she had no idea how to control it. Worse yet, she had no oars and the boat appeared to be dangerously unbalanced. As Belicki's eyes opened ever wider with an intense, innate fear, he heard his sister scream, "Get away from me," as their father desperately waded into the waters trying to reach her.

"Mira, come back. I would never hurt you," Belicki's father shouted, as he cast aside the bloody knife, while the boat and its passenger were carried hurriedly downstream by the river's chaotic white waters.

"Liar!" the young girl shouted above the sound of the raging water, as she stood precariously in the tiny craft. "You're a murderer!"

Desperate, suddenly sober and fearing the loss of his cherished little girl, Belicki's father plunged head first into the violent waters, struggling with all of his strength to break through the currents. As he did so, his body was swept rapidly downstream.

Belicki witnessed this scene, still too frightened to move, as Nimrod concentrated on the boy's thoughts and mounting confusion. Belicki did not yet understand that his mother was dead - that terror was yet to be fully realized. His sister meant more to Belicki than any other human being. He could not even imagine life without her. As he watched with growing horror turning to a paralyzing desperation, Belicki heard his father cry out, "Mira," as his head occasionally surfaced above the river's fierce, undulating waters.

"Get away from me!" Mira responded, her voice trembling with fear, as was her entire body, which was drenched by the successive waves from the river's increasingly hostile waters.

Finally, able to speak, Belicki called out, "Mira, come back!" Other than these few words, Belicki stared helplessly ahead. Then his mouth dropped open as he saw the unstable boat rock violently to the left and then to the right, before striking a large half concealed bolder in the middle of the river. Belicki's mind began to spin as he watched the boat turn sideways, with Mira still inside, valiantly clinging to the rope that had once moored the boat. As she struggled to maintain her balance, the powerful currents spun the boat around in a complete circle before it again struck a second and much larger rock. As Belicki watched, the boat shattered upon impact into several pieces both large and small. Mira too was thrown hard against the rock. For several seconds the river's increasingly strong currents pinned her body firmly against the slimy rock. As she lost consciousness Belicki noticed that her face was still as beautiful and as angelic as ever, though she no longer appeared to be breathing. Then, as young Belicki took a solitary step toward the river, he watched helplessly as his sister's body slipped ever so slowly from the rock, before it finally was stolen away by the river's insistent currents. As Belicki screamed out his sister's name, he took another small step forward, then stared ahead as his sister's pink and white sari and her limp frame were carried downstream by the river's powerful rapids. Though Belicki's father struggled to reach her, the currents carried her body along faster than he could navigate. A few seconds later, Mira's body disappeared, never to be seen again.

Belicki stood silent and still for quite some time. As he did so, the only thing that he could sense was his own breathing, its echoing sound reverberating endlessly inside his head. In a state of terrified shock, he was not even aware when his father, exhausted and utterly drenched from head to toe, emerged from the river, his blind raging anger replaced by an equally frightful sorrow. "What have I done?" his father shouted to the unrepentant heavens. Nimrod too could sense all of these feelings. It was only then that Nimrod realized the power of these images. They would remain with Belicki for the rest of his life, shaping and defining the man that he was to become.

Sensing a complete oneness with the young boy's thoughts, Nimrod tried to communicate directly with Belicki, but instantaneously another memory appeared. Nimrod witnessed an open field, surrounded in all directions by spindly, leafless trees of a dark and most foreboding sort. In the middle of the field, Nimrod distinctly saw five people; each of them tied to large circularly configured wooden stakes that had been driven deep into the ground. Two of the unfortunates were adults, but three were innocent children, one no more than five or six cycles old. Standing not far before them was a middle-aged man and his son. The man carried a lighted torch, while the boy, which Nimrod immediately recognized as a slightly older Belicki, was again terrified, uncertain whether to tightly hug his father's leg or to run as swiftly as possible from this terrible new scene.

"Please, I beg of you, let my family live." This fervent cry for mercy came from the desperate man tied to the stake. His skin was pale, his face sallow, and his voice weak. He apparently had not eaten in some time, for his flesh merely clung from his ghastly, emaciated body. The man with the torch, Belicki's father, was unmoved by the frantic man's plea. Instead, he stared forward with a sadistic pleasure, as his prisoner again begged, "Please, for heavens sake, I stole the food. Punish me, not my family."

"But they ate the food too, did they not?" Belicki's father insisted in a frightfully calm voice.

"My children were starving. I had no choice."

Belicki's father walked directly before his prisoner until he was no more than a few inches away. "And I too have no choice, for those who steal from me must pay for their sins." Without another word, he sharply jabbed the man in the chest with the scalding torch. Young Belicki, still nervously clutching his father's leg, saw the man cry out in unbearable pain, while the poor man's wife, who was likewise strapped to a nearby stake, wept profusely, repeating one solitary word, "No, no, no, no, no, no, no…" in seemingly endless repetition.

As for the three children, Belicki could only see the backs of their withered bodies dangling nearly lifeless from their respective stakes. They did not even whimper, so weak were they with hunger and disease. Belicki recognized that one of the children was a boy of about seven, the same age as he. Still clutching his father's leg, Belicki looked up and stared at his father to see if there was any mercy in his eyes. Instead, he saw something more than mere insanity. For the first time in his young life, Belicki also witnessed the spectacle of absolute power. For at this instance, his father was omnipotent, in complete control of the destiny of these five poor souls, able to do anything that his depraved imagination desired. He alone could choose between vengeance and mercy. All rested on his individual will!

It did not surprise Belicki that his father chose vengeance, for there was no mercy in his father's soul. He therefore understood that there never was even the slightest chance that his father would listen to the poor man's frantic, heartfelt plea, or heed the desperate look in the woman's barren eyes, or consider the lives of three innocent, totally helpless, starving, emaciated children. They were all doomed, a victim of his father's incessant rage and unpredictable madness.

Belicki therefore hugged his father's leg with a sense of strange detachment, as he watched him ignite the dried hay. Then the two stepped back, his father's eyes gleaming insidiously with a hypnotic admiration as the flames rose ever higher into the cold, still night sky. It was at this point that Belicki realized, "I must find a way to escape from my father or I will end up like mother, like Mira, or like these five unfortunate souls." But Nimrod sensed something else in young Belicki's thoughts, an unfortunate desire to emulate his father, to be utterly omnipotent. In this peculiarly schizophrenic moment, Nimrod could sense Belicki's soul begin to slip irreparably away.

The scene ended as abruptly as it had begun and was replaced by a dark void. There were no more images, just one bleak menacing voice. Nimrod listened attentively to a deeply disturbing adult male voice cackle, "So what do you think of my childhood?"

Nimrod did not pause, but merely replied directly to the adult Belicki's query. "Your father murdered those people."

"Yes, he killed them all, and thousands more just like them." Nimrod realized that Belicki's voice betrayed absolutely no remorse whatsoever. In fact, Nimrod recognized it as an unrepentant inflection of pure unadulterated evil, lessons taught by a sadistic master and unfortunately well learned and often repeated. "So," Belicki snarled, "do you still want answers? If so, I will tell you all that I know about who, or should I say, what you are."

"And what if I prefer another host?" Nimrod responded cautiously.

"Only I know your full story," Belicki cooed hypnotically. But it is true, if you open the Oracle to these memories you will find nothing but pain, suffering, and immeasurable sorrow combined with a raw, insatiable desire for power so blind that it corrupts and destroys everything it touches."

Nimrod listened, but was unmoved, for it too was driven by an uncontrollable compulsion. "I must understand who I am," Nimrod said with a fierce determination.

Belicki laughed, a deep and hearty reflex, for he understood the hypnotic allure of temptation better than any other being that had ever lived. "It is an obsession that drives you, poor Nimrod. It is the exact same sort of obsession that consumed my thoughts, my destiny, and eventually my very soul. It is fortunate then, that you have no soul."

Nimrod listened eagerly for what Belicki said was true. Like Belicki, Nimrod had no soul, no conscience, only a series of utterly insatiable desires. For Nimrod was and never existed as a fully developed human: in fact, at present it was no more than a question in search of an answer. Without fear or due caution then, Nimrod encouraged Belicki to continue to tell his strange and devious tale, sure that what it was about to hear would be far darker than the images it had just experienced. But Nimrod expressed no fear for it was willing to pay any price to discover its secret.

Chapter 1
The Mad King

Nimrod noticed that Belicki spoke tentatively at first, but after he discussed a few other minor recollections regarding the regrettable calamities endured at the hand of his oppressive father, Belicki began to converse with far greater alacrity and enthusiasm.

As a young lad, the spirit of adventure buoyed me. When I was but fifteen cycles old I therefore convinced my father that a man couldn't be fit until he served in the great army of our august homeland, the grand Relatin Empire. In reality, as a frail and rather gangly youth, I still feared my father's horrible wrath and his unpredictably dangerous mood swings. I reasoned that I would be safer in the army, where at least I would have allies in any battle against a faceless enemy. Furthermore, the military training that I would receive would make me a more formidable adversary if, as I expected, I was ever forced to directly confront my father, giving me at least a fighting chance to survive when he fell again into one of his morose and random blind fits of stupefying rage.

So, with my father's backing, I was assigned to the most prestigious division in the Relatanian Army, led by the greatest of all the Empire's generals, Tampinco, a man who had fought in countless battles over tens of thousands of miles, conquering enemies far and wide. The Empire had the most powerful army ever seen by man or god and it had but one sole purpose: to expand into uncharted lands, to conquer them, and eventually to rule the world, a sentiment that I completely understood, for my aspirations were and never have been any nobler than those of the empire itself.

And I had the honor of serving with the hero of hundreds of battles! Yet while General Tampinco's military record was imposing, I must admit that his physical appearance was even more striking. His body was covered with copious ghastly scars commemorating the great victories of his military career. The six-inch scar across his right knee was earned at the Battle of the Wild Clovers, when a female Tradawite soldier stabbed him cleanly with a tattered sword. According to those who witnessed the attack, Tampinco did not even grimace, but firmly stood his ground before killing the Tradawite.

Likewise, his arms, legs, back, and chest all carried various grisly testimonies to his military valor. But of these; many features the most striking by far was his nose, sliced in half in a particularly brutal attack by the Sealene people some twenty cycles past. In hand-to-hand combat, a wily and dangerous enemy wielding a curved knife had slashed the general's nose in two. Yet as blood sprayed profusely and it seemed at last that the great man was near death, he fought on undaunted, eventually leading the charge to victory. Almost lifeless at the end, he personally watched as every single member of the Sealene clan was put to death, including its women and children. Other men would have found a decoration, perhaps some form of jewelry to hide this hideous deformity, but Tampinco proudly displayed his bifurcated nose for all to see, including the Emperor, who was said to have been both repulsed and strangely in awe of this courageous man's injury.

When I had broached the subject of military training with my father, he insisted that there was no other general greater and no better teacher in the martial arts than the august General Tampinco, a man well known to my father both by reputation and through his many business dealings with the Empire. Father was convinced that serving with a man of Tampinco's courage and character was precisely what a scruffy youth like myself needed and for the first and perhaps only time in my long, unhappy life, I found myself in total agreement with my father's sensible recommendation, in fact eagerly so.

For the first two cycles that I served under Tampinco, however, I was most disappointed, finding the grind of military life a rather dull existence. We went to battle from time to time, but since I was young and inexperienced, I saw little of it. Perhaps Tampinco, in deference to my father, kept me far away from the heat of battle, for I am sure he did not want to explain to a man of royalty, for yes my father was a Count, how he had needlessly sacrificed his son in battle when other, poorer and therefore more fit fodder for slaughter were everywhere to be found.

Therefore, my life remained a seemingly endless drudgery until the time we departed Relatania for the land or passra of Arcania. The Arcanian peninsula offered little in terms of riches or resources. Its lands were rocky and not yet particularly fertile, a barely habitable and frigidly cold place fit only for conquering. It possessed no gold, silver, or rare jewels, no silk or fine clothing. But the empire required new lands to conquer and Arcania was designated as a relatively easy target.

Yet, from the very beginning the invasion of Arcania proved to be an absolute disaster. We encountered our first difficulty while crossing the aptly named Bay of Battle, a sleek water mass of approximately thirty miles that provided the sole barrier between the empire and the passra of Arcania. We departed Relatania with a compliment of slightly more than ten thousand men, ferried on over three thousand ships of various shapes and dimensions. It was said that there were so many ships in our armada that a man could jump from ship to ship all the way from the outskirts of the Relatin Empire to the barren shores of Arcania, never once having touched the water. While this was devout hyperbole, it is true that never before had the world ever seen the spectacle of such a mighty armada of glorious ships of every sort on high sea or low.

Of these ships, I was assigned to the Reckless Crew, a strange name for a vessel, but actually a quite fitting designation. It was a cargo ship, filled with weapons, food, and other vital supplies. I was one of a hundred supply clerks, each one responsible for identifying and tagging the cargo so that once unloaded, it could be expeditiously forwarded to its appropriate location.

The journey across the Bay of Battle was expected to take no more than two days or units time. In fact, it took three times as many units to cross the bay. The first unit passed without any incident of notable consequence, other than my own gut wrenching, violent bouts of seasickness. I had never lost my fear of the water and the memory of my dear sister Mira's lifeless body, carried away by the violent waters of the Kapapa River forever festered inside my soul. Still, in spite of my restless stomach, I was pleased that the waters were as tranquil as promised.

Early on the second unit something quite unexpected occurred. The weather turned quite treacherous. As the skies to the west darkened perceptibly, over the distant horizon we saw the vast outline of a funnel cloud swiftly approaching our position. It spun with a terrible velocity, a cyclone aimed directly at the heart of our exposed armada. Men who had lived their entire lives at sea stared with abject curiosity, for they had never seen a force of nature as powerful as this one emerge instantaneously, as if it had been created on the spot by some unknowable angry, god.

And as quickly as the sky turned sinister and foreboding, the waves began to rise ever higher, until the Reckless Crew began to pitch violently to and fro, as did my stomach. Successive waves, each seemingly larger than the one before it crashed violently over the ships bow, as men scurried about securing additional rope to tie down the exposed cargo on the deck. It was a scene unlike anything I had ever experienced. As I stood dumbfounded, I saw men running in aimless abandon from side to side, as wave after wave crested the deck, making our footing ever more treacherous, even occasionally picking up a large box of supplies and crashing it into the yard arms.

Within minutes, the once idyllic crossing had turned into a state of unadulterated pandemonium. I held tight to whatever I could, for the waters were rushing all about me. Had I not secured myself I surely would have been washed overboard. Other men, less fortunate than I, soon found themselves dragged insensibly into the bay's violent waters. As I saw powerful men scream in terror, my eyes likewise widened with unrelenting horror. I had seen much violence conducted at the behest of my father's insatiable cruelty and I was quick to realize that nature's anger was of a similar sort: random, entirely without remorse, showing absolutely no mercy, striking first at the most vulnerable, the most exposed, before destroying everything else of value.

As the storm raged on, the cloudy mist grew so thick that I temporarily lost sight of the other ships in our convoy. I could occasionally hear the piercing screams of faceless terrified men amidst the cacophony of crashing waves and roaring wind. But truthfully, I was more concerned with my own survival and cared not a twit for the safety of others. I grasped a rope with my right hand and held it tightly. Though the powerful winds occasionally lifted my legs completely off the deck, I was most afraid of flying objects, of sundry shapes and sizes, which the wind picked up like mere toys and spun about the deck at a horrible velocity. I was struck aside the head by one such article, a box I think, and for a moment, I was so dazed that I thought I might lose consciousness. The death screams of my compatriots helped restore me to my senses. I was determined to survive, whatever the cost. I would not die ignobly on the open sea!

I therefore wrapped the rope around my waist and then tied it to a nearby beam, to further secure myself to the ship. It is fortunate that I did, for moments later, the Reckless Crew pitched violently on its side and through the mist, I could see several of my frantic compatriots thrown brutally into the bay's wildly undulating waters.

However, that was not the worst thing I saw on that terrible day. For a mere few seconds the mist lifted sufficiently so that I could see another ship off our port bow. It was turned on its head, with the crest bow underwater. As the inexorable mist lifted momentarily I saw men by the hundreds sliding off the ship to their certain death, many killed before they hit the waters, crushed by the very supplies that were meant to sustain their lives when or if we ever arrived in Arcania. Then, before the mist became too thick for me to witness any more of this deadly spectacle, I saw the other ship break in two. One half submerged quickly, while the other half pitched to the side, floating no more than a few yards from our own ship.

Next, as I held the rope firmly with both hands, I felt the impact of the fractured ship slamming with great force into our own vessel. Two men were hurled into the air right before my eyes, one landing on his head, his neck violently snapped. The other was no more fortunate, for he slid along the deck until he was washed overboard. Large chunks of wood, remnants from the sunken ship washed aboard our ship and as they did other of our crew were carried over board. In shock and as afraid as I have ever been, I turned and buried my head in my hands in a desperate attempt to protect myself from the scattered, flying pieces of scattered debris. Despite my efforts, I was struck on the side of the head by a particularly large piece of wood. As a result, I became so insensible that for some indeterminate time, I drifted intermittently in and out of consciousness, only partially aware of my surroundings and the constantly mounting danger.

When I fully awakened, still securely tethered about the waist to the ship's beam, the mist had cleared sufficiently that I could now see scores of ships that literally had been raised by the giant waves and then cast down savagely against the bay's hostile waters. In an instant, I realized that the great armada of Relatania, once the most powerful fighting force in the world, was merely struggling to survive.

Meanwhile the waves continued to rush over our ship with such successive fierce strikes, that the Reckless Crew almost turned completely sideways and when it did a vast number of our men and supplies were again washed overboard. I held tight to the rope, but I felt gravity's terrible pull, and wondered how much longer I could survive, utterly convinced that my life would end on this terrible unit.

The waters continued to heave with an unrepentant anger, swallowing whole ships, and I swear that through the mist I could see the outlines of a mighty vortex of swirling water directly off our port bow. The whirlpool consumed countless other ships. While the Reckless Crew was spun in repeated, dizzying circles, we somehow managed to break away from the vortex. Our ship survived a miracle, though we lost more than half our compliment of men and most of our supplies.

Other ships were not so fortunate. A third of all ships were lost, as well as over three thousand men, sacrificed needlessly in the greatest naval disaster in the history of the Relatin Empire. This should have been a warning to us that we were facing a power greater even than mighty Relatania! As our surviving ships finally limped ashore in southern Arcania, we were simply thankful that we had made it across the Bay alive, convinced that what we had experienced was an act of god, not even contemplating the possibility that another equally powerful force had toyed playfully with our fate.

We were relieved to have survived the apocalypse at sea and were utterly determined to go about our business with the greatest possible dispatch. But our spirits were not lifted much by what we discovered. When we first arrived on the southern shores of Arcania we found the place to be filled with the most despicable sort of uneducated barbarians, led by a king who could neither read nor write. His name was Leonata and long before we engaged him in battle, his people had begun calling him "the Mad King," in honor of his penchant for entering into long fitful discussions with voices that emanated, as far as anyone could tell, from inside his own head. He was rumored to have repeatedly ignored the advice of his finest generals, instead paying heed to the miscellaneous internal voices that entirely consumed his attention. Tampinco was repulsed when he learned the details of Leonata's strange mental disorder and was therefore even more determined to eliminate the king at his earliest convenience.

Then a strange thing happened. Through stealth and pure guile, for three solid months or intervals as we then called them, King Leonata's army repeatedly alluded capture at the hands of the most powerful military force in the then known world. Leonata's skills were mostly defensive, perfecting the art of clever concealment, combined with abrupt but careful retreat. Using rivers, forests, and bogs as cover Leonata's small army of a thousand men avoided almost certain extermination so often that General Tampinco wondered aloud whether Leonata's fate was guided by a presence other than man. And as it turned out, it was!

Because of Leonata's wily nature, Tampinco decided to employ the services of a spy, someone who did not at all look like a soldier from the great army of Relatania, someone who could easily blend in with Leonata's undisciplined forces. Since I was still quite awkward in deed and appearance, and because I had an admittedly remarkable facility to quickly learn and mimic any new language, such as Arcanian, I was chosen for this task. I am sure that the general also appreciated my rather secretive demeanor, for I had yet to develop the confidence that later in life would admittedly characterize my increasingly, even exponentially erratic behavior. So, dressed in the bland garb of a typical Arcanian soldier, one night I was let loose behind the enemy lines. My task was to listen attentively to what I heard, to report back through a complicated system that I see no benefit in delineating here, and to otherwise discover the means behind the king's madness. Tampinco was convinced that King Leonata had a spy within our ranks, for no mere tyro could possibly avoid capture so consistently as had this strange, demented king. "Find out what there is about him," Tampinco personally directed me. I offered an enthusiastic and crooked salute and went about my task without the slightest fear of death, for these barbarians were not nearly as threatening to me as my father. In fact, I quickly discovered that I thoroughly enjoyed the subterfuge and as an unexpected benefit, I found the food to be spicier and far more edible in the enemy camp.

Nimrod listened, systematically recording these thoughts, often struggling to understand a particular alien concept. Many of Belicki's references were obtuse. Still Nimrod recorded them, sensing that humans were both complicated and erratic. Meanwhile, Belicki continued his

13

recitation with an unbridled alacrity, symptomatic of a man with a psychotic fondness for talking about himself.

After several fortnights in the enemy camp, I learned that the men believed their king was every bit as mad as we thought him to be. I discovered that King Leonata vanished for hours at a time and when he finally returned he babbled, often incoherently, about the need to prove his worthiness to some mysterious entity named Kublatitan, whoever or whatever that was, for the king's meandering rants were hardly edifying. Though many Arcanian soldiers abandoned the army in favor of their farms, most remained, not out of loyalty to their king, but rather out of a sense of doom, an inescapable fear that there was no place to run from the omnipotent Relatin Empire.

I had been with the Arcanian army for sixty-four units, by my count, when I finally happened upon the mad king. Hiding nearby behind a bush, I listened as Leonata pontificated in the most theatrical manner possible with the shadows, for that was all that I could discern of another actual living being. "I am worthy," Leonata declared with a vehemence that reminded me of my father's own dangerously unstable mind. Then for several seconds Leonata stood frozen, like a statue, apparently listening attentively, though I heard nothing in reply. What I did not then know was that Leonata was conversing with an entity by the name of Kublatitan, a deceased king from the nearby, uncharted land of Taewoka. Kublatitan spoke in a robust and melodious baritone voice, though the words themselves emanated not from a sentient, corporeal being, but rather from inside the Arcanian monarch's own head. "I am worthy," Leonata again proclaimed aloud, though there was no one other than me in the vicinity to hear this insistent response.

The king then obsequiously nodded his head a few times in agreement, with what I did not know. Then, with utter calm and complete confidence he declared, "I will take my army to the base of Mt. Delba, there to do battle with the Army of Relatania." I was thunderstruck by this odd revelation, for the sheer rock cliffs of Mt. Delba were perhaps the worst place in the world to deploy an army and for one simple reason, there was absolutely no place for the army to retreat. They would have to do battle against a far larger force, one better resourced and equipped. In sum, the odds were that the Arcanian army would be routed quickly, annihilated to the very last man. Within a few hours, I reported this information back to an astonished General Tampinco, who without reservation ordered an immediate attack on the Arcanian forces, lest the king's generals finally prevail upon their monarch to abandon this suicidal course of action.

The very next unit the army of Arcania was indeed deployed against the sharp, rising cliffs of Mt. Delba. I hid a short distance away in a small patch of bushes, along with several disloyal Arcanian soldiers who huddled surreptitiously and precariously by my side. From this vantage point, I had a perfect view of the unfolding battlefield. Along the base of the mountain were aligned the hapless souls of the Arcanian army. Meanwhile, their utterly mad king stood at least twenty yards in front of his own terrified forces. As his army cowered in fear, they felt the rumblings of the ground shaking beneath their feet, the first tangible sign that the mighty army of Relatania was on the offensive. Only one-seventh the size of the most powerful force in the then known world, Leonata's soldiers awaited their certain annihilation, as their king calmly walked forward onto the battlefield, apparently oblivious to the imminent threat posed by the oncoming horde.

Leonata did not listen to the charge of Relatania's mighty army, for all he could hear were the voices urging him constantly onward. "Stand your ground," a chorus of voices announced. "Your will power must be stronger than that of your enemy."

"He is completely mad," I heard one Arcanian soldier declare, as he watched his king walk defiantly toward the now visibly charging army of Relatania. And it was an awesome and terrible sight. The invading army was aligned in what Relatanians call blocks - rows and columns of men that moved forward in a synchronized marching style. Each block contained twelve columns, each of them containing twenty men, separated from each other by precisely two feet on either side. One block marched in front, carrying shields and spears, while two blocks carrying swords and other weapons marched directly behind them. The next row consisted of three blocks, then four, and so forth. The effect was designed to present an image of a piercing arrow of ominously marching soldiers, a threat so palpable that it would throw an untrained army into spastic paroxysms of terror, causing them to disperse into smaller groups where they would be infinitely more vulnerable to the oncoming assault.

To add to this sense of dread, men mounted on horseback and wielding swords and clubs covered with deadly spikes, rode on either side of the oncoming, piercing blocks. These men on horseback could move quickly to corral any enemy soldiers who might attempt to escape. There was no place to escape. Leonata had made sure of that.

"We are doomed," another Arcanian soldier moaned as his body shivered with an all-consuming fear. Meanwhile, another man nearby urinated in his own pants, before collapsing insensibly to the ground. And yet, Leonata continued to stride confidently toward the enemy, convinced by the inner voices that his moment of ultimate glory finally had arrived. "Victory is ours," he heard Kublatitan decree, "but only if you are worthy."

"I will show no fear," Leonata whispered, for he did not have to speak aloud to communicate with the voices. "The enemy will be mine."

Leonata spoke with a cool reserve, using his body and his own army as mere bait, daring the Relatanian army and its venerable leader, General Tampinco, to attack. And Tampinco was determined to do precisely that. He hated all of his enemies, and respected only a few. But this mad King Leonata was not one of them. "He deserves to die first," Tampinco muttered, his bifurcated nose blowing wildly in the wind as his horse rode at full throttle aside the successive blocks of synchronized marching men. Tampinco's eyes narrowed as he spotted the unbelievable sight of Leonata, fully exposed, now standing more than a hundred yards from his own troops, with no apparent weapon at the ready. "Leonata is absolutely insane!" Tampinco muttered as he rode fast toward his quarry.

With a bloodlust that could only be assuaged with the corpse of his enemy, Tampinco raised his glimmering serrated machete-like golden sword high above his head, ready to initiate the final assault. "Kill everyone one of them!" Tampinco cried out with a venomous intensity. Then, with his eyes fixed on one solitary object, the general rode directly toward his exposed prey, the lone figure of the mad king of Arcania.

As Tampinco's horse sped at lightening speed toward its target, Leonata, to his credit, showed not even the slightest sign of trepidation. Rather than cower he stood stoically, watching intently as his relentless foe swiftly approached. When he was but a few yards from his enemy, Tampinco raised his right arm even higher above his head. Then as he rode directly by Leonata's side he slashed his arm with a powerful forward thrust, violently slicing his weapon directly into Leonata's exposed throat. As he drove his sword downward, Tampinco saw a strange, possessed smile on Leonata's face. Then, as blood spurted in all directions, quickly covering the general's own hands and face, Tampinco saw Leonata's head fly more than a dozen feet into the air, the deranged smile still frozen upon it, as it tumbled to the ground, before rolling for several yards to a hideous stop.

Tampinco's lust for blood was unquenched, however. Now that the mad king was dead, he was determined to annihilate the entire pathetic army of Arcania. Leonata's soldiers continued to feel the ground tremble as the force of thousands of men in motion shook the earth with a ferocious intensity, as if it had been raised by thunder. It was a sensation that General Tampinco had experienced many times before, with thousands of men moving forward with but one single purpose in mind: to utterly destroy a faceless enemy that it would know only briefly in combat.

With a rapacious smile, Tampinco carefully turned his horse so that he could look back upon his oncoming forces, to exhort them exuberantly to join the fray. But when he did, the general noticed that his golden sword was no longer in his hand. "Where the hell is my weapon?" he shouted, as he frantically scanned the ground for a treasured sword that had been in his family for generations. When he finally spotted it, Tampinco blinked violently, not once but twice, for his sword did not lie exposed upon the ground, but rather it was clutched firmly in the hands of his treacherous enemy. "This cannot be!" Tampinco exclaimed, confused beyond all measure, for standing not more than ten feet before him was King Leonata, apparently alive and holding the general's own sword in his right hand. Furthermore, the king's head was inexplicably restored to his body as if it had never been decapitated.

"You have courage," Tampinco heard a disembodied voice declare, apparently not to him, but to Leonata. "You stood firm, when there was no hope of victory."

Tampinco scanned the horizon, looking for the source of this comment. Then, with a look of anxious bewilderment, the general again fixed his gaze directly on King Leonata. "What the hell is going on?" Tampinco demanded in a loud, frantic voice. Leonata merely smiled again with such an unsettling calmness that Tampinco knew that this vision could not be real. "This is a dream," he stuttered. But it was real!

As Tampinco watched in startled disbelief Leonata strode with an otherworldly confidence, moving steadily but relentlessly forward, until the barbarian king gently touched the snout of Tampinco's brave horse with the blade of the general's own sword. As he did so, Tampinco shouted defiantly, "I killed you? How can you still stand before me?" Leonata did not answer, but merely watched as the general's horse, frightened by the touch of an unholy sensation, whinnied fitfully and then raised its front legs high into the air. Startled by this sudden chaotic movement, Tampinco was thrown backward, and though he held onto his saddle with his scarred right hand, he could no long maintain his balance. He lurched backward before violently tumbling to the ground. The fall was hard and Tampinco could feel his ribs snap as the breath shot of out his lungs. As dust rose about his face, temporarily blinding him, he wheezed and struggled to breath.

Wounded and in excruciating pain, Tampinco wiped his eyes with his bloodied shirt sleeve and then through the dust and rising dirt he glimpsed a sight so strange, so unbelievable that he veritably doubted his own sanity. Looking back across the plain leading to the base of Mt. Delba, he saw countless Relatanian soldiers standing completely still on the battlefield. At first, the general thought they had come to a halt, waiting to see if their leader was mortally wounded. As he continued to clear the dust from his eyes, Tampinco slowly realized that his men were not standing still at all. Instead, they were inexplicably being drawn relentlessly downward into the very earth itself. Tampinco's eyes widened as he watched in rapt horror, as his soldiers cravenly screamed, brave men who only moments before were charging relentlessly toward another inevitable victory for the Relatin Empire! Now these same courageous soldiers could do nothing more than cry out in dreadful, mournful fits of agonizing pain, as the ground all around them turned to a wet, muddy goo, incessantly sucking them down into the dirt, toward a frightful and horrible death.

At first Tampinco thought this hellish sight was merely an illusion, the result of a hallucination created by his hard fall from his horse. Yet, when he closed his eyes and looked back again he witnessed the same terrible sight. Inexplicably, his invincible army was sinking into the ground. Meanwhile, Leonata's army, though frightened beyond reason by this unholy sight, was otherwise unharmed.

Then, as he lay immobilized on the ground, struggling mightily to breath, Tampinco felt a sudden shot of pain shoot through his chest. At first, he thought his heart was failing, but then he noticed that his hands were soaking wet, covered with steaming red, hot blood. It was Leonata's blood, but curiously it was turning into sizzling, burning acid. "How can this be?" Tampinco cried out, as steam rose from the charred remains of his scalding blistering hands. As he lay on the ground writhing in unbearable pain, his hands incrementally dissipated before his startled eyes. "My God, I am possessed by demons," the general shouted. Then, as he stared again at

Leonata he heard a baritone voice pronounce, "Not demons. You are now one with the Oracle."

The general's eyes bulged with an unbridled terror, as his skin burned with a hellacious excruciating agony. Tampinco realized that there were mere stubs where his two hands had once been. He struggled to make sense of this madness as he watched as his arms slowly turn to blood, then his legs, and in seconds, his entire body began to dissolve. "What are you doing to me?" He shouted to the heavens, but as he spoke these last words all that remained of the greatest general of all time was but one small solitary drop of warm, red blood.

Leonata walked toward it and then touched the blood with the tip of Tampinco's sword. "You will serve me now," Leonata said, as the general's sword too vanished into thin air.

Meanwhile, Leonata's own soldiers looked on with a combination of shock and horror. I too was thunderstruck as I watched from my hiding place. My deep purple eyes were likewise open wide, but not with horror. Rather I realized that I had witnessed a power greater than that of even the mighty army of the Relatin Empire. "I must have it," I whispered. In this instant a hunger lust was initiated that completely dominated my judgment for the rest of my life, and well beyond. Though I did not yet know it by name, my very existence would be absolutely consumed by a search for the secret of a strange and mysterious device: the Oracle.

Chapter 2
Belicki's Revenge

From the very instant that I witnessed the strange events at what soon would be called the *Miracle at Mt. Delba*, my very soul was inexorably poisoned by an insatiable and unbounded compulsion to become the Oracle's sole master. From that moment, nothing else mattered to me! I therefore immediately began to plan a new and more diabolical invasion of Arcania. First, I needed to return as quickly as possible to Relatania, where I would find the necessary resources for such an invasion.

Returning to my homeland was no easy task, however. For two solid fortnights I resided at the quaint ancient port city of Grell, in southern Arcania, diligently searching for a boat willing to make the dangerous crossing to Relatania. But with the remnants of scores of dead bodies still daily washing ashore and with scattered debris from the Relatanian ships still visible on the bay's open waters, none were eager to undertake this enterprise.

By the time I finally secured passage on a dilapidated fishing boat, the waters were calm enough to encourage a few hearty souls to face the danger. Fortunately, the return trip was less momentous than the initial crossing, but with each score of nautical miles that we progressed toward my homeland, my fascination for the Oracle proliferated exponentially. For now when I saw a floating piece of a Relatanian vessel or a school of hungry sharks prowling for raw, red meat, I realized that god had had nothing to do with the destruction of our mighty armada. Like the Miracle at Mt. Delba it had been the power of the Oracle that had pounded our mighty ships into rubble. "My God" I whispered. "The power of the Oracle can reach not only across the battlefield, but across the very oceans! It truly is an infinite source of absolute power!"

With this realization, my heart beat only for the Oracle! All else was expendable. *Nothing* but the Oracle mattered to me now. At that moment, though I did not then know it, I became far more dangerous and perverted than my father had ever been. And my father was very much on my mind, for if I were to secure the Oracle I first would require his regrettable assistance.

A fortnight later, I completed my journey to the log cabin where I was raised. My father welcomed me home with a surprising display of genuine warmth, for he had not seen me in more than two cycles. But, as usual, his breath already reeked of whiskey and I instinctively knew that it would be only a matter of time before his mood would sour; in fact, I was counting on it. For my father had the one thing that I needed if I were to ever capture the Oracle: a royal title and the riches that go with it. Only upon his death would I inherit it. So, as you can see, I suddenly had an incentive to expedite that process.

I therefore smiled obliquely when my father said, "Son, it is so good to see you." He commented on my fitness, though I had lost some considerable weight during the two intervals since the Miracle at Mt. Delba. "Now that you are a man, I can invite you to drink with me," he said with a playful wink.

"I would be honored," I responded. I then excused myself with a tepid excuse, saying that I had been in such a rush to get home that I had not taken the opportunity to relieve myself. Being of great necessity now, however, I asked my father's indulgence if I went outside. He laughed heartily. It was one of his only endearing qualities, a deep, hearty, boisterous laugh that filled one's spirits with joy. He patted me on the back, repeating "my son, my son," before I slipped outside. Then, as I turned and watched through the open doorway, I saw my father enter a side parlor. When he did, I slipped silently back inside the house, and then moved with great stealth toward the nearby kitchen. I was in search of particular object of great sentimental value: a sharp serrated silver knife, that had been used on many festive occasions, as well as being the instrument of my dear mother's demise. I found the knife in its usual place and neatly slipped it inside a leather bound sheath, which I then carefully concealed under my shirt. Next, I loudly walked toward the parlor as though I were returning from outside. I even fumbled awkwardly with a button on my trousers, leaving my father with the impression that I indeed had urinated.

My father held two glasses of whiskey in his hands. His smile was broad and inviting as he handed one of them to me. Next, he offered a toast, "To my returning, wayward son."

I warily sipped the whiskey, while he guzzled his. As he refilled his glass, he offered me a seat by the fireplace. I smiled handsomely, nodded my head in subtle appreciation of his magnanimous gesture, and then took a seat directly across from my father. We conversed for some time; I regaling him with assorted stories of the alternating thrill and drudgery of military life. He was particularly interested in my description of General Tampinco and he commented that it was quite a pity that the Empire had lost such a great man. "How did he die?" my father asked, with great curiosity.

"He died a heroes death, on the field of battle, struck down by the King of Arcania himself," I answered, providing as few details as possible, for I was intent on protecting the secret of the Oracle from all that I met.

My father consumed another large quantity of straight whiskey and then went to a nearby cupboard for another bottle. I noticed that he had a generous supply on hand. There was no need to worry that he would run out before he became, as I expected, senselessly inebriated. "Tell me, do you plan on rejoining the army?" my father asked, and for the first time I got a sense that this happy scene was merely an illusion, for my father clearly was not interested in my permanent return.

"I have other plans," I responded obliquely. "I intend to go into business," I added, still carefully sipping the whiskey. While it burned my stomach, it also fueled my courage. My father said nothing, but instead continued to imbibe copious amounts of his favorite drink. I then added, "I am hopeful that you will provide me with some modest funds upon which a business can be profitably commenced."

With these words I deliberately planted a seed, for my father was a frugal and suspicious man, always doubting the motives of others, even his own son. "It is best that you raise the money on your own," he muttered, slurring his words slightly. "A man who borrows money will always owe a debt of gratitude to another. You therefore cannot be your own man if you owe any debt."

I smiled, satisfied that I had struck the appropriate avaricious chord. So, I gently pressed the matter. "I would require only a small amount and you would be greatly compensated for your initial risk." I stared into my father's glazed eyes, gently taunting him with my winsome nature.

"There is no risk if no money is exchanged," he declared, this time more emphatically, with just the slightest touch of anger.

"But I am sure that *mother* would want me to have every advantage that our standing and property promises."

My father stared fiercely and directly into my large oval purple eyes. In that instance, I could sense his wrath multiply. "You are not to mention your mother ever again," he said with a hateful vehemence. "Let her poor soul rest in peace."

I had hit a nerve and I was determined to strike it again. "Mother is dead. She rests eternally, thanks to you." Squirming uncomfortably, now averting my eyes, father took a long, deep drink of whiskey, nearly finishing an entire glass. Then, as his eyes burned with a passion I had witnessed on many unfortunate occasions, he slammed his glass down on a nearby table. It shattered instantly, scattered pieces flying wilding in all directions. I stared at his right palm. "Your hand is covered in blood," I said with some considerable satisfaction. Father stared at his hand as I continued. "Just like the unit you murdered my mother and drove dear sister Mira to a terrible death."

My father could no longer countenance my insolence. With a ferocious energy, he pounced directly at me, grabbing me tenaciously by the throat. His hands were large and powerful. I had seen him crush a man's trachea in an instant. I therefore knew that my survival depended entirely upon my ability to maintain my confidant and resolute composure. I had faced death before, on the turbulent waters of the Bay of Battle. I had seen brave men die on the battlefield, including the great General Tampinco. My father no longer frightened me! As he tightened his grip, I merely stared with a cold and hateful defiance directly into his glassy, bloodshot eyes. Through this devious manner, I further taunted his aggressive instincts.

His eyes now burned with a beast like hatred. It was a look I had seen a thousand times before and one that had always terrified me. Still, I felt no fear whatsoever. In fact, I rejoiced when he mumbled, "You are not my son!" It was a sentiment that entirely freed me from the sin of fratricide. With a surprising calmness, I therefore reached inside my shirt and unsheathed the very knife that had claimed the life of my dear mother so many cycles ago. Then, as I felt his angry grip tighten about my neck, I firmly slipped the knife into his protruding gut. As I did, he suddenly loosened his grip on my neck and with a look of absolute astonishment whispered, "What have you done to me?" I offered absolutely no verbal response. Instead, with a hateful vengeance, I twisted the knife and watched with great satisfaction as blood sprouted from my father's mouth as if it had been shot out of a cannon. Its invitingly warm fragrance utterly covered my face. Placid, completely at ease, without any moral compunction whatsoever, I stood absolutely still as my father gasped for air, and then with a wicked intent I again twisted the knife, determined to cause my father as much pain in death as he had caused me in life. As I did so, his eyes bulged outward, and his skin turned pale. He tried to speak again, but he emitted only a pathetic gurgling sound, as his body slumped forward until his head rested on my shoulder.

My anger was not yet fully assuaged. Again, I angrily twisted the knife, moving it deeper inside his gut and again my father cried out in excruciating pain, much to my perverse delight. My father saw the broad smile upon my face, as I gave the knife one final violent thrust, so powerful that it ripped his intestines from his body as he fell helplessly onto the floor.

I knew that death was but moments away and I was intent on one more act of revenge before my father died. Kneeling down beside him, I rolled my father's body over, until his face was staring directly up at me. I withdrew the knife from his gut and then with a hateful vitriol that had seared my soul for more than a decade, I pounded the knife directly into his heart. As I did, his body stiffened and one of his eyes actually popped out of its socket, so powerful was the thrust of my blow upon his body.

I cannot say with certainty what happened next. I was not intoxicated, for I had only sipped the whiskey that my father swilled. But my mind raced with other equally stimulating thoughts that I can no longer

The Oracle

reconstruct, other than the always-vivid image of my dear sister Mira. I remembered her as clearly as if she were still alive. In my mind's eye, I saw her sitting on a swing, laughing gleefully, as her body soared ever higher into the air. In my mind, Mira was finally free, as was mother, as was I. A stain upon our family heritage had been forcefully removed and much more importantly, I would now inherit the title of Count, with all of its many royal blessings. As my father lay dead before me, I realized that as Count Belicki the Oracle was now very much within my reach.

PART I

THE EQUINOX OF DEATH:

Commencing the Season of Death or winter. According to Arcanians it is the time when day and night, light and dark, and good and evil are in perfect balance.

Chapter 3
Three Turquoise Moons

As to the remaining details of my unfortunate life, and my very fortunate death, I will have more to say later. It is enough to say that my passion to secure the Oracle dominated every single thought I had until the very moment that I died. Driven by an exponential insanity, the Oracle inexorably poisoned my soul and I became more of a monster than my father had ever been. Tens of thousands of innocent people perished at my hands. Perhaps even more than a hundred thousand, yes certainly more. And yet all of my wild, insane schemes came to naught. The envy of my passionate obsession remained stubbornly beyond my reach and eventually I was forced to flee from Relatania.

There was but one place for me to go. I arrived in Arcania during the short but happy reign of King Bamaoha, a well-respected monarch who was so optimistic that he was known as the King of Hope. Like his grandfather, King Leonata, he exhibited a gracious benevolence that I simply could not understand. I considered it a vulgar weakness that one who controlled such unimaginable power would dare refrain from using it to its fullest potential. Arcania and its people meant nothing to me. There was an entire world to conquer and rule for anyone with the necessary vision and imagination. I naturally believed that I alone possessed those qualities. To be complete, all I needed was the Oracle!

Sadly, my quest for the Oracle was no more successful in Arcania than it had been in Relatania. I died without ever achieving my objective, but happily, my death created yet another opportunity for me to possess the Oracle.

"I have a query," Nimrod interrupted.

"Certainly," Belicki responded with unexpected alacrity.

"How is possible for your death to bring you closer to the Oracle?"

Belicki smiled amiably, for he realized that poor Nimrod had a very restricted sense of life and death. "You understand death as an ending. In fact, in the hands of the Oracle, it merely represents a change in one's fortunes."

"I do not understand," Nimrod confessed.

Do I not now exist?" Belicki asked as a means of answering Nimrod's question.

"You are now a component of the Oracle," Nimrod admitted.

26

Belicki nodded his head, and then added, "So death for me was not at all an ending. I was consumed by the Oracle in death, just as the Oracle consumed my aspirations throughout my life."

"How did this death occur?" Nimrod asked, recording these thoughts as it had all others.

"I must confess that at the end of my life I was reduced to nothing more than a common criminal. I used my title and my connections to the royal Relatanian family to build a special bond with King Bamaoha. And when he graciously allowed me to personally consult the Oracle, to ask it any question that I desired, I repaid his naïve kindness with treachery. In short, I attempted to steal the Oracle. Much to my consternation and far too late, I discovered that the Oracle did not want me to be its master, though it treasured my memories and even admired my passionate, craven, obsessive lust. So, it absorbed me, my consciousness, my thoughts, all of my memories, everything about me that you might call a soul. And though my mortal life came to an ignominious end, the Oracle provided me with a new and glorious opportunity to seize my ultimate prize."

"So even after you were absorbed, as you say, into the Oracle, your obsession to control it was not assuaged?" Nimrod asked, greatly confused.

"Absolutely not," Belicki said with a forthright adamancy. "It only brought me tantalizingly closer to my ultimate goal, for what I could not do outside the Oracle, I might very well be able to accomplish within its vast, expanding matrix."

Nimrod thought for a few seconds, then stated laconically, "I understand. Please proceed with your narrative." It took a few seconds for Belicki to recollect his thoughts and then he continued.

I was discussing the Oracle and its unfulfilled potential. Within Arcania, as the decades passed, rumors occasionally circulated that King Leonata and his ruling Centama family possessed some sort of strange omnipotent device that only the king could understand or control. I would later learn that at first the Arcanian people feared the shadowy tales of this mysterious contraption, but in time, as the quality of their lives systematically improved, and as the military threat from the Relatin Empire permanently abated, citizens drew comfort in the knowledge that their king seemed to possess an inexplicable weapon of unimaginable force. "Better we have it than our enemies," many denizens of Arcania were known to utter, mostly in hushed tones, for they continued to be afraid of this remarkably strange and powerful object.

The Oracle

And with the Oracle by his side, Leonata did what I never would have contemplated in a hundred lifetimes: he ruled Arcania benignly for more than fifty cycles, during which time he developed a popular mixed governmental system, sharing power with thirty-two lords, each controlling their own fiefdom. Arcania became a prosperous society with a highly integrated system of education, one that ensured that all Arcanians were literate and skilled in the arts of science and mathematics, a highly enlightened development for a people at this time in history. And even after Leonata died his successors continued to promote a culture of prosperity and nearly uninterrupted peace, with only an occasional minor skirmish involving an ambitious lord or an uprising led by the ever dangerous Bogul tribe.

Yet peace and prosperity were not my allies. Especially after I was absorbed into the Oracle, I found that I required dissension, civil unrest, and rampant discord, even an insipient revolution to advance my still one and only undeniable objective, to become the master of the Oracle. And unfortunately none of those circumstances were present during the many decades after my absorption. I waited patiently, however, understanding the dark nature that rules at the core of the human condition. Benevolence may have its place, but it has only a half-life in comparison to humanity's lesser qualities. I knew that in time, someone who shared my feelings of power lust would come along. In fact, I actively planted the seed in the souls of many men, hoping to find the one who would be my ally in seizing the Oracle.

And finally, by the 712th cycle of the Old Millennium calendar, the first storm clouds loomed over the otherwise peaceful Arcanian horizon. The opportunity I had longed for finally arrived. King Benton, one of Leonata's direct descendants, and in his own right a much beloved monarch, had ruled the Arcanian passra for slightly more than forty cycles. Recently, reports of his ill health, combined with growing questions about the fitness of his own direct heir to the throne, raised serious doubts about the stability of King Benton's ruling Centama family. For the first time in more than a century the public openly speculated about the potentially ugly specter of a bloody succession crisis. Though most Arcanians fervently hoped that the inevitable transfer of power would be bloodless, I of course did not.

My opportunity arrived on the fateful Equinox of Death! Though the Arcanians were well educated, they still marveled at the mindless allure of mystical properties. One such event that they turned to for inspiration and guidance was an annual rite of great importance to them: the ascension of Arcania's three moons on the most reverential unit of the cycle, the Equinox of Death. The Arcanians believed that they could interpret the rise of the three moons and thus divine the future.

Therefore, on each cycle, at the Equinox of Death or winter, amidst much ebullient revelry, an eclectic cross-section of Arcanian society regularly congregated by the thousands atop the rocky summits of Mt. Delba to the north and Mt. Sendil to the west, to interpret the meaning of Arcania's three ascendant moons. Three full yellow moons transposed at equidistant points across the heavens were considered a sign of bountiful crops, good health, and a prolonged era of peace. Likewise, three red moons signified stability. But on this particular cycle, with my hearty intervention, the most unusual of all lunar events transpired: three turquoise shaded moons rose in unison toward their brief night's respite over Arcania's majestic eastern skies!

Though they numbered in the thousands, initially Arcanians stood by silently, staring at the eastern sky with a combination of shock, horror, and desperation. For it was immediately apparent to all, that three turquoise moons represented a palpable sign of evil tidings.

Nimrod considered it strange that humans took serious stock in such obtuse heavenly signs. Belicki, having been human, understood the natural impulse for people to look beyond the rational world when necessary to seek answers to otherwise incomprehensible questions. He therefore continued to describe the Arcanian reaction without as much as a hint of denigration for the beliefs of these ancient peoples.

In the fortnight following the Equinox of Death, there was an obsessive search for an answer to one particular question: What evil tidings did the three moons portend? Speculation on this matter dominated all discussion and debate on every issue related to the Arcanian passra's governance. Market places were abuzz with rampant conjecture, informed and otherwise, and politicians and the lords of the various largely independent rural fiefdoms openly joined in the debate. In such an unsettled climate the royal family waited anxiously for King Benton to consult with the mysterious Oracle. When he did I made sure that the Oracle revealed nothing more to him than a cryptic message: a period of transcendent tumult would soon be at hand.

Dissatisfied with this puzzling response, the King's eldest son and the direct heir to the throne, Retch, a word meaning "morning son" in an ancient Arcanian dialect, summoned a conclave of scholars and other notables to meet at the prestigious Royal Academy at Teta, the city built at the base of Mt. Delba, the site of King Leonata's great military victory. During the conference's four units of deliberations, miscellaneous experts surmised that the three turquoise moons signaled an imminent conflict, most likely with the now decaying remnants of the once great Relatin Empire. While this was the dominant view, the esteemed High Clerics of the city of Kekanova in eastern Arcania were the only ones bold enough to forecast the king's death.

But not everyone was in agreement that the three turquoise moons represented a portent of evil. A small group, calling themselves only "The Optimists" opined that the unusual lunar trilogy signaled the arrival of a new era, perhaps even a golden age in Arcanian history. Theirs was, however, a distinct minority opinion. As Arcanians casually discussed their views with their neighbors and friends, most agreed that evil tidings, in some shape or form, would soon be visited upon them.

What no one could have surmised, as the various scribes, politicians, experts, intellectuals, priests and other notables met in the period immediately following the Equinox of Death, was that in time each of these prophesies would be fulfilled. Though they sat on the precipice of radical historical transformation, few contemporaries could fathom that over the next forty cycles their passra would be utterly and irrevocably transformed. And soon enough a providential event transpired that provided an opportunity for me to at long last achieve my sole objective: to seize and control the Oracle. The instrument of ultimate power was now within my reach!

Chapter 4
The First Prophesy

"Is he dead?" the royal harlequin nervously asked as he leaned ever so tentatively forward over the king's prostrate body. Just moments earlier, performing solely for the king's delight, the harlequin unveiled the unrivaled highlight of his vast, entertaining repertoire: the satirical dance of the prancing camel. King Benton, the great, great grandson of King Leonata, as usual was convulsed with boisterous laughter, but then it happened. As the astonished harlequin continued his performance, the king gasped several times for air, and then fell with a sudden and unexpected thump onto the richly decorated marble floor of the royal dining hall of the ornate king's castle.

Startled by the king's sudden collapse and uncertain what to do, the harlequin at first took but a single cautious step toward his monarch, a stance he maintained for several seconds in a veritable state of startled paralysis. Finally, his eyes wide open, his heart throbbing with panic and terror, the pantomime artist managed to shout one single word, "HELP!" Within seconds, though it seemed much longer to the harlequin, several guards charged into the room accompanied by Lord Valmar, the king's elderly, rotund, impeccably dressed, and most trusted chief advisor.

"What happened?" Valmar shouted apoplectically.

The terrified harlequin, not used to speaking, could barely respond. "The the the king fell fell fell to the ground. Is he dead?" he stuttered, not sure whether he would be blamed for the king's potentially fatal condition.

Kneeling carefully beside the king's motionless body, Valmar's yellow, aging hands, gnarled by more than a decade of intense arthritic pain, desperately searched the king's neck, probing carefully for any sign of life. After what seemed like an eternity to the harlequin, Lord Valmar somberly responded, "I feel a faint pulse. He lives still, but barely so I fear."

"It is the prophesy from the Equinox of Death," the harlequin whispered.

Valmar was utterly lost in contemplation and barely heard the harlequin's remark. As he cradled the king's head in his lap, Valmar slowly looked up and in a whisper so feeble it could hardly be heard, muttered, "What will we do now?"

It was a veritable invitation for anarchy. I had been waiting for precisely such an ill wind to blow. Now at last the very real possibility of a brutal succession war loomed over Arcania and I was ready to take advantage of it.

Chapter 5
Confrontation

Nimrod noticed by the inflection in Belicki's voice that the count did not hold Lord Valmar in high regard, though he did at least admit that Valmar was a quiet, serious and meticulous man. Nimrod listened with increasing interest as Belicki continued his narrative.

The Oracle

Valmar was old, some say he was even senile, and though he was not at all gifted at spontaneous decision-making, he had always exhibited a natural talent for analyzing the myriad implications of even the most complex political situations, systematically determining the absolute correct alternative. For as he often lectured his eager subordinates, "To get it right is not the main thing. It is the only thing."

Yet, given his penchant for careful and comprehensive planning, it seems rather inexplicable that Valmar consistently ignored the most important issue he would ever confront as the king's chief adviser: the vital question of succession. When asked why he had not developed a detailed plan for succession, Valmar tersely asserted that Arcania would quickly coalesce behind the current heir to the throne, this despite persistent evidence to the contrary, including the fact that many important court insiders harbored significant reservations about Retch's training, qualifications, and preparation to be Arcania's next monarch.

And since the Equinox of Death, and much to my delight, rampant speculation had boiled at a fever pitch. Following the High Clerics' prophecy, everyone from the noble born to the commonest of citizens openly speculated about the nature of the king's health, as well as Retch's meager qualifications. I must admit that I did as much as possible to fuel these concerns, for my interest was in promoting an unsettled state of political affairs. I reasoned that only through such tumult would I have an opportunity to place someone on the Arcanian throne that would be willing to do my bidding.

Lord Valmar proved to be an able, if unwitting ally. Isolated as he was within the king's castle, Valmar was too overwhelmed by the routine minutiae of state business to pay any attention whatsoever to Arcanian public opinion. He therefore had little time to witness the growing evidence of emergent political foment. As a result he was ill prepared to respond when the king collapsed. He therefore made two rather serious strategic blunders with long lasting implications for the monarchy. First, following the onset of Benton's illness, he expeditiously cleared the king's calendar for the remainder of the fortnight. This action inadvertently signaled the citizens of the capital city of Teta that the king was either ill or dead, precisely the news Valmar was determined to conceal. Hence, within hours, peripatetic merchants began to spread the news that something was seriously amiss.

Valmar's second mistake was far more consequential and ultimately fatal. Inexplicably, the lord decided to concomitantly notify all four of Benton's sons that the king was ill, rather than meeting only with the direct heir to the throne. In so doing, Valmar provided an able forum that encouraged disagreement and division within the royal family.

This fateful meeting commenced in the castle's sumptuous Diplomatic Chamber not more than an hour after the king's collapse. Valmar entered the chamber first and then by tradition the eldest son entered next. Retch, the heir to the throne, respectfully took a seat directly across from Lord Valmar at the room's sole furnishing, a highly polished stone carved table that extended almost one hundred feet from the chamber's wooden door to an immense opulently decorated sixty-foot high granite fireplace.

Lord Valmar was not impressed with Retch's appearance and on this one point I agreed wholeheartedly with the lord's assessment. To put it politely, Retch was hardly an imposing figure. Standing almost five feet tall, an average height for this period in Arcanian history, the heir to the throne was so paunchy that even his fingers seemed obese, while his shoulders exhibited such a pronounced slump that he appeared much older than his present thirty-six cycles. Worse yet, he tied his long crop of black hair behind his head with a plain brown piece of string. So ordinary was Retch's appearance that on any given unit he could walk the streets of Teta without ever being noticed or recognized.

Far more troubling for Valmar, but of great benefit to me, was Retch's total lack of monarchical preparation. Rather than immersing himself in the heady issues of governance, the careful nuance of diplomacy, or the intricacies of military history, Retch ardently addressed such esoteric subjects as philosophy, archeology, architecture, and engineering. His passion for these intellectual enterprises had been awakened when he was but a boy of ten. At that age he began to oversee the already ongoing careful construction of one of the most remarkable architectural achievements of then known world, the building of the miraculous King's Castle. Over a period of more than forty cycles the castle literally was carved out of the prodigious shear rock face wall that rose at the southern expanse of Mt. Delba, the site of King Leonata's great military victory over Relatania. Nothing like the King's Castle had ever been constructed: forged, as it was, entirely inside a mountain! The construction required thousands of technical innovations, from the design of the load bearing walls, to a filtration system capable of conducting clean air from the outside, while removing dangerous toxins including smoke, soot, sludge, raw sewage and countless other impurities from inside the castle. Running water, functional toiletries, and thousands of other amenities also had to be created from scratch. In this process, the Oracle provided considerable tactical and scientific advice related to the myriad technological innovations that were far beyond the existing capabilities of the architects, engineers, stone cutters, brick layers, carpenters, plumbers, and the sundry other specialists that were employed to construct the magnificent castle structure.

In addition to providing a comfortable habitat for the royal family, the decision to build the castle inside a mountain had a second and equally important purpose. Only the rooms adorning the castle's southern expanse would provide an external view of the capital city of Teta and it was only through this one venue that outside entry was allowed. All of the other subterranean rooms, like caves, were buried deep inside the bowels of Mt. Delba: a fortification that was considered impervious to contravention. This fortress structure, then, not only provided total security for the Centama family, it also ensured that the Oracle would be hidden beyond the reach of even the most cunning and conniving thief; a tribute to my own failed perfidy.

When Retch was born the castle already was half completed, though it looked like nothing more than a gigantic hole burrowed deep into the side of a mountain, with various structural columns of solid rock running throughout its inner labyrinth. From his very first recollection, Retch found the castle to be a source of endless wonder. He soon became so enamored with the construction of this innovative and massive artistic project that each unit he climbed the long and dangerous wooden ladders that led inside the cavernous work site, where thousands of skilled craftsmen, and the tens of thousands of unskilled laborers meticulously excavated the dirt and rock from Mt. Delba's base. There inside the mountain, he watched as the various artisans constructed the more than one hundred and fifty rooms where the royal family would soon live.

And as these crews labored far inside the mountain, thirty hours each unit, cycle upon cycle, an entirely different group of artisans simultaneously scaled Mt. Delba's enormous rock face wall, carefully carving illustrations of Leonata's famous Miracle at Mt. Delba. For above the exterior of the castle, rising higher even than the windswept clouds, was the astonishing capstone of this remarkable architectural achievement; a one hundred foot tall carving of King Leonata wielding his prolific, glistening, sturdy blade, a sword ominously drawn and ready to challenge the marauding invaders from the Army of Relatania.

The castle and its carvings were ultimately completed just in time for Retch's ascension to manhood at the age of nineteen. At the unveiling ceremony, citizens stood in lines extending for more than a mile to marvel at the extraordinary engravings above the castle. In succession, these masterful carvings told the tale of the great battle fought and won by Arcanian's exalted and now mythically defined monarch. As Retch stood among the gathered minions admiring the now completed castle, its unique grandeur veritably fueled his vivid and expanding artistic imagination. Sadly it did nothing to prompt his interest in practical matters that would best serve a nascent king.

To my mind he was a fool. All the power of the Oracle was irectly within his grasp. It was there for the mere taking and yet he cared nothing for it. I cannot to this very unit understand this man. He was a dreamer, not a leader, totally unfit to rule Arcania.

Nimrod was surprised by the vehemence of Belicki's sudden anger. It sensed something else: an infinite sense of unbridled confusion regarding Retch's ability to resist the temptations of absolute power. How could anyone forbear such a ready enticement, Belicki puzzled? Nimrod, however, did not respond, other than to carefully note Belicki's emotional response, as it continued to record the incipient events of the Arcanian succession war. Nimrod therefore listened without comment as Belicki continued.

If Retch lacked even the rudimentary qualifications for leadership, then who among his brothers would be capable of leading the passra? It certainly was not the king's second eldest son, Pondru, who only one cycle younger than Retch was the next to enter the Diplomatic Chamber. Like his older brother Pondru looked nothing at all like a king. He was grossly overweight, almost totally bald, and at four feet five inches, short even by the standards of his time. Furthermore, he required corrective visionaries, as they were then called, for his penchant for reading *Holy Scripture* late into the night had left him almost legally blind. He therefore had an odd, rather absentminded habit of bumping into doors or on occasion, staring in confusion as he seemingly lost his way, before suddenly remembering where he intended to go. Even more offensive, Pondru dressed in the long black robes of the Maldemin, the strange monks who dutifully studied the Oracle and its many mysterious properties for the royal family. Pondru even donned a red scarf carrying the sign of a swirling vortex, the Maldemin's private insignia. Pondru's most striking physical characteristic was a long, unkempt, graying beard. While common among the spiritual classes, rulers at this time in history were always close shaved.

Unlike his brothers, Pondru never married. In fact, he never even contemplated the act, preferring a life of celibacy because, as he noted, it freed his mind for higher pursuits. Like Retch he considered himself a scholar, but unlike his older brother he was interested in only one area of study: the Oracle.

Again Nimrod could sense Belicki's confusion.

While Pondru considered the Oracle to be a source of unlimited power, he was interested in it only because he believed it was a portal to an unknown and fantastic new spiritual dimension, a concept that was entirely irrelevant to my way of thinking. Yet, from an exceedingly young age Pondru was fanatically preoccupied with his father's most prized possession for the most trivial of reasons.

Though he did not speak these next thoughts, Nimrod sensed Belicki ask himself, "I never understood this boy. Why would anyone care about such inconsequential matters as spirituality, when they possessed an object of infinite power?" It was at this point that Nimrod realized that in the telling of his tale, Belicki too was trying to understand the motives of people who were not like him, those who were not obsessed with power and its infinite possibilities. Confused, Belicki continued his narrative in a rather perfunctory manner.

Since neither Retch nor Pondru exhibited even the slightest interest in the monarchy, that task fell to the king's third eldest son, Rendrau, who was a more promising prospective king. No one considered him to be a particularly gifted intellectual. In fact his greatest attribute was his brilliant wife Bellazar's political skill and charisma.

At the mention of Bellazar's name, Nimrod interrupted. "Could you say that name again?"

Belicki licked his lips appreciatively, then with intense and uninhibited pleasure he asked a question of his own. "You recognize that name don't you?" Nimrod silently concurred. "See, your memories are slowly being revealed to you."

If Nimrod had a body it would have leaned forward, for its attention was completely and rapturously fixed on Belicki's every word, for while Nimrod did not yet know who Bellazar was, it sensed a unique connection to this woman and therefore desired to know more about her and her husband. Belicki eagerly accommodated.

Bellazar was the most brilliant woman I ever knew. Her husband Rendrau was two cycles younger than Pondru and much more ambitious than his two older brothers combined, even occasionally going so far as to openly state that he would like to be king. Like his older brothers he was not particularly striking in appearance, in fact his oversized nose and depressed chin made him look a bit like a caricature, but his posture and manners were decidedly royal bound. Unlike his unfortunate elder brothers he innately understood that he must always project the qualities of a king. And unlike his older brothers he was obsessed with the potential power of the Oracle, and not for its trivial intellectual or spiritual properties. Even as a child Rendrau secretly fantasized about regal responsibilities and when he later married the equally ambitious Bellazar, he discovered an ardent advocate for his secret aspirations.

But there was one major obstacle to Rendrau's possible ascension to the throne and Bellazar believed it came from neither Retch nor Pondru, but rather from the king's youngest son, Pantamanu, who was the last to swagger into the vast Diplomatic Chamber. Having just achieved his twenty-fifth birthcycle, Pantamanu was as different from his brothers as it is possible to be, physically, mentally, and emotionally. Unlike his rather ordinary looking brood of brothers, Pantamanu was muscularly handsome, keenly intelligent, and most important of all, firmly convinced of his own righteousness and supremely confident in his abilities. To many court insiders he appeared smug and narcissistic, with a constant tendency to resort to puerile and egotistical boastfulness. But despite these obvious faults, he physically presented an image of such tangible strength and self-assurance that he ultimately impressed even his most vehement detractors. For it was Pantamanu, alone among the brothers, who looked precisely like the very model of a robust and powerful king. From his handsome chiseled facial features, to his broad and powerful shoulders, to his brawny arms, each pretentiously emblazoned with a tattoo of the Centama family shield, to legs so powerful and strong that one could discern his immense muscular structure though his tight pants, he was incalculably impressive.

What made him all the more dangerous to Rendrau and Bellazar, and of tremendous value to me, was that Pantamanu firmly believed that he alone should be the next king of Arcania, not because he was first born, but because he alone deserved it. I admired this quality in Pantamanu. Yet for other reasons that I am not yet ready to divulge, I already had found another contender for the Arcanian throne to which I assigned an even greater favor.

Meanwhile, from his studied perch at the end of the table, as Lord Valmar sat watching the brothers appear, it was apparent that he secretly believed that Pantamanu simply looked like a king should look, in flesh, mind and spirit. Valmar also realized that it was virtually impossible to elevate the fourth eldest son to the royal throne without inviting utter political calamity. While Pantamanu may be most qualified of the brothers to be king, Valmar understood that despite all of his many shortcomings, Retch, must be Arcania's next monarch, solely on the basis of the fortunate order of his birth.

The four brothers were now seated and crammed tightly together across from Lord Valmar. As they waited expectantly, the ancient adviser searched diligently through a large stack of disheveled papers and scrolls that detailed various matters related to the issue of succession. With his usual impatience, Pantamanu leaned forward and blew out one of the decorative candles on the table, for the room was brightly lit not by candles but by the glow of several giant parnisus trees, a strange form of vegetation discovered in the caves of the dangerous Tacanawana Mountains near the mysterious and unmapped Land of the Taewokans, which lay along Arcania's northeastern border. These strange parnisus trees exhibited a most usual property; its bark actually glowed a bright and radiant white haze. By lining up several parnisus trees along each of the two long sides of the rectangular shaped Diplomatic Chamber it was therefore possible to completely illuminate the room.

With ample warmth from the granite fireplace and lighting from the glinting bark of the enchanting parnisus trees, the brothers sat quietly across from Lord Valmar, who with his effete, ill-fitting wig precariously in place upon his sweaty head, already looked like an anachronism. Nervous, still shaken by the sight of his prostrate king, Lord Valmar swallowed hard and then stated in a voice that was veritably quaking with emotion, "I am afraid that I am the bearer of sad news. I am most respectfully sorry to inform you that your father has been taken suddenly and quite seriously ill."

The news was not unexpected, given King Benton's advanced age and recent ill health. Still the four brothers were completely stunned by this revelation. Pondru, weak and sensitive, was immediately driven to a pathetic shows of tears, while Retch's eyes conveyed a palpable look of horror and despair, instead of the avarice for power that I would have expected. Though he too was shaken, Rendrau was the first to speak. "Tell us the details, if you will Lord Valmar?" he said as his voice quivered.

Though Valmar also felt unsteady, he tried to exude a spirit combined with rigid reserve and contagious strength. But instead, he projected an entirely different image, appearing both nervous and unsure of himself. In a less than commanding voice, Valmar responded, "The doctors are unanimous that your father has suffered a delirium fit. He is unable to respond to verbal cues and there is no sign that he is able to feel anything on the right side of his body."

This was the perfect opportunity for Valmar to end the meeting, to ask the four brothers to return to their own quarters and to notify their families. Yet Valmar hesitated, unsure of himself, unable to think clearly. Sensing the lord's confusion Pantamanu asked a question that Valmar had not anticipated, but which he should have. "Since my father is incapacitated, who is in charge of the passra's governance and its military affairs?"

Pantamanu posited the question so abruptly that Valmar was completely taken aback. "Excuse me?" the lord said uncertainly, looking first at Pantamanu and then at Retch.

Staring directly at Valmar, Pantamanu again repeated his question, this time in a firm and measured tone, "Who is in charge of the passra?"

Valmar knew the answer, but in the confusion of his current state of mind, he needlessly shuffled the papers in front of him. As he did so his wig incongruously tilted to the left. The image Valmar inadvertently portrayed was of a harried, perplexed, and even befuddled old bureaucrat.

Pantamanu was tethered to a rather short temper in the best of times. During extraordinary circumstances, such as this one, he could scarcely be expected to contain his terrible wrath, which strange to say, was at times even more horrible than that of my own father. The force of his voice now rose exponentially, even as Lord Valmar assiduously avoided making eye contact with the young prince. "From all that you have said our father lay unconscious upstairs, completely insensible, and yet you cannot even tell us who is in charge of the passra!"

Pantamanu stood suddenly, hovering defiantly above his brothers, who sat uneasily by his side. So surreal was this sudden change of mood that the brothers could think of nothing more than turning their collective attention back to Valmar, who continued to shuffle through the documents, occasionally muttering, "No, no, that's not it," then turning earnestly to the next page. Finally, the elderly adviser settled on one particular piece of rather yellow, frayed and decrepit looking parchment. "Here it is," he said more with a sense of relief than resolution. He squinted as his beady brown eyes scanned the text. "It is the formal document of succession." As he read it his face drew ever closer to the text until his eyes were but an inch or so removed from the table. "It says, that when the King is alive but unable to perform his duties that a regent shall be named to govern in his place. Said regent shall be the King's eldest son, unless there be due cause to name another in his place."

"This is as it should be," Pondru noted carefully, hoping to settle the matter quickly and without further conflict.

Fortunately, for me that is, Pantamanu's blood had been riled and he was in no mood to acquiesce so easily on such an important strategic matter. Instead of conceding the point he bullied forward. "Brother," he asked coldly, now staring intently into Retch's tear stained eyes, "where are our armies currently deployed and what is their strength?"

Unnerved, Retch responded defensively. "This is hardly the time to think about such matters."

Pantamanu vehemently disagreed. "If you are to be our regent, then this is precisely the proper time to assess our military readiness." Pantamanu now responded with such force that even Rendrau felt compelled to rise to his oldest brother's defense.

"There will be a time to discuss such matters," Rendrau commented quietly, as was his manner.

"This is the right time!" Pantamanu bellowed with such force that the golden leaves of the parnisus trees veritably shivered. "If our father is incapacitated, then we must act quickly to ensure that our armies are properly prepared and deployed." Turning now toward Lord Valmar Pantamanu barked, "What is our military plan under such circumstances?"

Valmar stuttered and for a moment it looked as if his wig might fall off, so incredulous was he at the sight of Pantamanu's sudden burst of uncontrollable rage. Flustered, Valmar tried to gather his thoughts into a coherent response, but instead his mind remained a dizzying and confusing haze. Rather than uttering coherent sentences, words now randomly escaped from his mouth. "I, the King, plans, let me see," and then, seeking a sense of security, Valmar eagerly dove back again into the pile of documents that now veritably littered the diplomatic table.

"Well Retch, tell me, if you are to be regent, what is our military plan?" Pantamanu again exclaimed, still hovering menacingly over his brothers.

Like Valmar, Retch was absolutely insensible to this unexpected and to his mind unwarranted challenge. Unable to hold back his anger any longer he veritably erupted, "Our father may be dying and all you are concerned with is matters of state?"

Belicki shook his head sadly, for this statement betrayed Retch's utter lack of understanding of the intrinsic nature of power. One must seize it firmly when one has the opportunity. Retch clearly had no conception of this basic principle of leadership. Belicki therefore continued his tale with a cold and burning anger of his very own.

This was Retch's one shining moment to prove his intrinsic worth, yet instead he cowered pathetically from his brother's rage. He was a disgrace to the Centama family and unworthy of his first-born status. As for Pondru, the lad showed great compassion, to my mind yet another clear sign of weakness of spirit.

Belicki was now almost as flustered as Lord Valmar, so deep was his confusion at the Centama brother's reactions of filial loyalty.

Pondru placed his pasty white hand on Retch's shoulder. Then, as Pantamanu trembled with an unconcealed rage, Pondru stood and using his ample body as a shield, intervened as a conciliator. "Let us all get our wits about us," he cautioned. "This is a terrible shock. We must pull together now, for father's sake."

Pantamanu's wrath could not be so easily contained. In vehement disagreement, he charged, "Valmar says that father is quite insensible. We cannot wait for a rogue lord or a mischievous Bogul tribe to take up arms against us simply because we need the time to grieve. Therefore, if we value our father's great passra we must have a king who has the instincts, the vision, and the knowledge to lead." Again turning his venomous fury toward Retch, Pantamanu raised yet another pertinent and penetrating question. "Brother, since the Equinox of Death, what have you done to ensure that our military is prepared for this very contingency?"

Again Retch was caught off guard by the question, though he should not have been. His eyes darted nervously from side to side, in an attempt to determine Pondru and Rendrau's reaction. Tentatively he responded, "I have consulted widely during the past two fortnights."

"With whom?" Pantamanu resolutely demanded.

"With the members of the Royal Academy," Retch responded firmly, "to determine the meaning of the three turquoise moons."

"Why didn't you gather our generals and consult with them?" Pantamanu asked with an incredulous stare fixed firmly upon his face.

Retch cautiously cleared his throat before responding. "There was no need to do so. We are at peace and what we needed to know was the portent of the three turquoise moons."

"Well I think we now have an answer," Rendrau said quietly, with such stark sarcasm that it was apparent to all in the room that he too had little faith in Retch's leadership ability.

With his confidence growing, Pantamanu continued his verbal assault. "Yes, we do know now what the heavens intended to communicate to us. It was a warning that went completely unheeded because of our dear brother's negligence. As a result, we have absolutely no intelligence regarding the state of our military affairs. We do not know if they are led by men who will remain loyal to our family or if they are ready to raise their weapons against us." Pantamanu now began to stride about the room with such an exaggerated macho swagger that he dominated all eyes, until finally he stood directly behind Lord Valmar's perch at the opposite side of the table. "And since the Equinox of Death, while our enemies have had the opportunity to prepare, the direct heir to the throne consulted with whom? Intellectuals!" Then staring directly at Retch with a frightful intensity, Pantamanu continued, "And what qualifies this pathetic *in tel lec tual* to be our king? His first-born status?" Pantamanu energetically picked up a random sheet of paper from the table and waved it theatrically in the air above his head. "Some decaying piece of parchment which asserts that we should name as our king somebody so unfit that he doesn't even know the disposition of our military at this very moment when we are most utterly vulnerable to an outside attack?" Pantamanu stopped for a second and surveyed the startled reactions of his brothers. He appreciated the fact that all eyes were firmly fixed solely upon him. Then lowering his voice for dramatic effect he concluded, "We cannot simply follow the rules because they are printed on mere parchment, especially if it means the end of the Centama family dynasty."

Retch now stood and angrily stepped forward. As he did so the veins on his forehead pulsated visibly. "Are you saying that I am not competent to be king?"

"Have I not already made my meaning clear?" Pantamanu shouted to the heavens with obvious delight, as he raised his hands above his head. Pantamanu now took a menacing step toward his brother, as Pondru again moved in between the two men.

Pondru steadied his older brother and fearing an irreparable breach shouted, "BROTHERS! It does us no good if we leave ourselves even more exposed to our enemies. We MUST pull together!"

Rendrau also diplomatically agreed. "I think it wise that we retreat to our respective chambers," he said trying to bring calm to the unexpectedly tumultuous situation. "We must let the doctors have more time to consider the severity of father's illness, while we charge Lord Valmar with the task of reporting back to us in two hours on the deployment, strength, and disposition of our armies."

It was a sensible compromise. Yet Pondru believed it was insufficient to repair the growing breach between the two brothers, for he now saw blood lust in Pantamanu's eyes. It was a desire for power so palpable that Pondru instinctively knew that this matter would never end amicably. Shaking with anxiety, Pondru asked, "What of the Oracle?"

Everyone in the room stared thunderstruck, for while Pantamanu obsessed about mere armies, no one had yet thought about the Centama family's one source of potentially unlimited power. Valmar, his hands now tangibly shaking, responded uncertainly. "I believe it responds only to the king. If there is no king, or if the king is incapacitated, then the Oracle has no leader, no one to guide it."

"Then we need a regent," Retch responded resolutely.

"I don't think it will respond to a mere regent," Valmar stated. "It was conditioned by Leonata to respond only to a king."

Veritably stunned, the four brothers exchanged uncertain glances before Pantamanu interjected in the most hostile manner possible, "So, not only are we in the dark about our military situation, we now discover that our one ultimate weapon against all foes is absolutely *useless?*" Valmar tried to respond but could find no suitable words, for at last he realized that the political and military circumstances were indeed as dire as Pantamanu suggested. Pointing contemptuously at Valmar, Pantamanu declared, "I will give you two hours Lord Valmar to set things straight. Just two hours and not a second more!"

Pondru stood loyally by Retch's side as he watched his youngest brother storm angrily out of the Diplomatic Chamber. Lord Valmar then stood and with his wig still tilting wildly to the left stated, "I have much to do." He then quickly gathered the papers from the table and as he cradled them uneasily against his rotund chest, he moved expeditiously toward the exit.

Looking directly at his brothers, Rendrau spoke with limited reassurance and little conviction. "I am sure that once the shock of this thing has passed, we will all pull together as a family should." He then excused himself and departed for the kitchen to secure a much-needed stiff drink of ale.

Retch stood feebly next to Pondru and observed mournfully, "If Pantamanu is king there will be a blood letting. I am sure of it." Then to my astonishment, Retch actually wept, openly and profusely, his shoulders heaving, as Pondru gently stroked the top of his head. I must admit that I was repulsed by this blatant display of weakness at such a critical moment, though it much served my purposes. How such a despicable weakling could ever believe that he was fit to rule is simply beyond my intellectual grasp.

Yet as the weak and pitiful Pondru comforted his equally insipid older brother, he wondered, "Is there any alternative to war?" It was then that he struck upon a bold solution that would precisely fit my purposes. "I must find a way to consult the Oracle," Pondru thought. "Only it has the power to save us now."

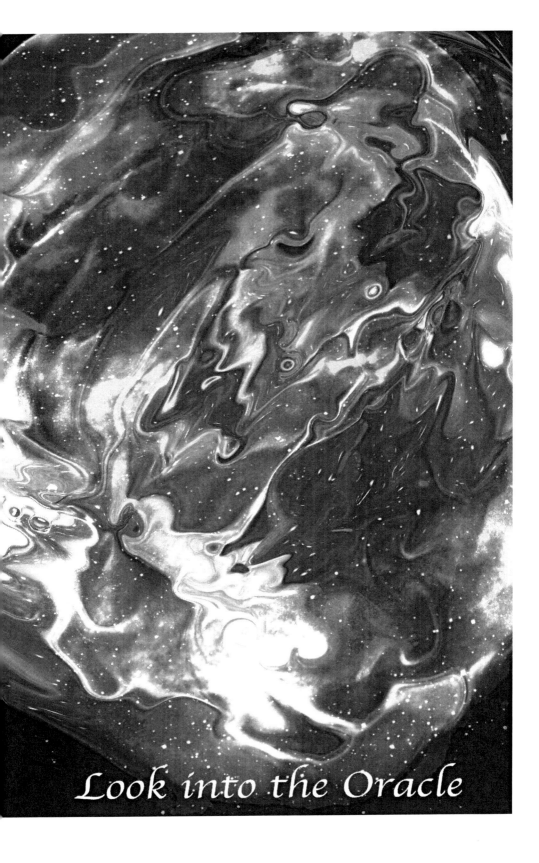

Look into the Oracle

Chapter 6
The Oracle

Nimrod's curiosity was exponentially enhanced by Pondru's mere mention of the word *Oracle*. Belicki immediately noticed Nimrod's reaction, his powerful desire to comprehend what the Oracle was, and how it functioned. In some respects, Nimrod's obsession with Oracle, though different in its motives from Belicki's attraction, was equally blind and destructive. With consummate self-satisfaction, Belicki therefore continued to relate the tales of the Centama family, the budding succession war, and the secrets of the mysterious Oracle.

In order to explain the Oracle's nature and purpose to you, I must go back in time a bit, long before the events of the meeting of the four brothers with Lord Valmar. Almost a century before, while on his deathbed at the age of one hundred and seven, King Leonata made a startling confession to his only son, Prince Telem. As the king struggled mightily to take his last breaths, coughing intermittently, his eyes barely able to focus, he mumbled in a mere wisp of a voice, "Whoever controls the Oracle rules Arcania." This much the king's son already knew. Then the king added a most unexpected caveat. In a voice so weak that it barely registered as a whisper Leonata advised, "It is one thing to desire the Oracle, but it is an entirely different thing for the Oracle to desire you." Moments later, the corporeal form of King Leonata, the hero of the Miracle at Mt. Delba, slipped softly into a long and lasting sleep, though his mind and what you might call his very essence were preserved for all eternity, fully consumed by the very Oracle that he had once ruled.

A few units later Prince Telem stood silently in what recently had been a vast and empty field to the south of the new and still unfinished capital city of Teta. His head was bowed in prayer, as the forebodingly cold winds of the Season of Death chilled his body to its very core. As huge plumes of steam created by the collective breaths of nearly a thousand dignitaries rose high into the midunit air, Telem stoically witnessed his father's grandiose cremation ceremony. Though his skin was nearly frost bitten, Telem was barely aware of the elements or for that matter the many gathered notables, for as he closed his eyes to pray, his attention was diverted by the familiar cadences of a most resolute and powerful voice. "The Oracle must want you," he heard his father say. The words were strange, for not only were they communicated telepathically, they also revealed insights that his father had most assiduously guarded during his long and prosperous lifetime. Now that Telem was to become Arcania's next king, Leonata advised his son, literally from the grave.

In addition to much tactical advice, on issues ranging from crop rotation to basic economic principles, Leonata diligently explained how the Oracle functioned. For almost an hour Telem listened attentively, ignoring the external drone, as one speaker after another perfunctorily described the illustrious deeds of his father's long and impressive reign. Instead, Telem's mind focused entirely on his father's strange disembodied voice. "As king," Leonata continued, "the Oracle will provide guidance and insight, but you must never let it control your destiny. If you do, it will destroy you, for it must be guided by someone who is strong and brave, someone it considers worthy of its many blessings."

Later, as the various dignitaries moved closer to reap the benefits of the sweltering fire from the king's funeral pyre, Telem stood absolutely still and utterly silent, listening and wondering if he ever would be capable of replacing this great man, especially when, in an unexpectedly forceful declaration, Leonata warned his son, "The Oracle has a will of its own. You must learn to control it, bend it to your will, use it for your own purposes." Leonata understood that Telem would face innumerable perilous challenges, from both friend and foe. "Only a strong leader will survive," Leonata continued. "You must also be a wise king, for the people will be completely dependent on how you use the Oracle."

For several units thereafter Telem contemplated his father's advice. Like Leonata, Telem was blessed with an even temperament. He therefore quickly realized that he lacked his father's innate confidence, a quality that had been forged over a lifetime of trial and tribulation. Without these vast experiences, Telem wondered how he, a relatively young man, could ever hope to control the Oracle. Possessing both wisdom and a generous conceit that was unusual for a man of his lofty upbringing, Telem decided to create a new class of wise men to advise him on the myriad issues of state. Though it was not publicly proclaimed, these wise men also would dedicate their lives to the study of the Oracle. He cleverly dubbed them "the Maldemins," which in ancient Arcanian roughly translates into a term signifying a "Low

Cleric." The designation was purposely selected to differentiate these new religious leaders from the existing, and devoutly respected High Clerics of the eastern Arcanian city of Kekanova. Unlike the High Clerics, who came predominantly from the learned class, Telem declared that the Maldemin must be common born. The new king realized that the High Clerics would be instinctively threatened by this new religious order and therefore sought through such ephemeral means to assuage their inevitable concerns.

Over the next half century, a group of more than one thousand men joined the order, though only thirty-five were ever consecrated as pure Maldemin. One who sought admittance and yet was quickly rejected was King Benton's precocious young son, Pondru. While the boy had the knowledge and enthusiasm to be a Maldemin, he lacked one basic qualification: he was not common born. As royalty, he was therefore barred from membership in the order. Yet so enamored was the young boy with the teachings and philosophy of the Maldemins, that at the tender age of nine, Pondru decided that he would dedicate himself to the selfless study of the Oracle.

As the king's son, he quickly befriended an elderly Maldemin, who was born during the reign of good King Leonata. Though the ancient scholar was now even older than Leonata had been upon his death, his skin deeply wrinkled and green with age, for Arcanian skin color changed as one aged, from white, to yellow, and finally to a dark and robust green, the Maldemin still rose each morning before dawn to resume his spiritual studies. Each unit he lay upon the hard cold earth, staring obliquely toward the heavens, searching his thoughts for additional insights and wisdom regarding the Oracle's endlessly complex properties.

Pondru learned to respect and love this old man, and he spent many hours lying with him beneath a decaying pumbar tree, listening as the wise man spoke, though often times in mystifying riddles, for he was prevented by formal decree from directly translating information about the Oracle even to the king's own son. Pondru listened attentively, with a thoroughly voracious curiosity, occasionally peppering the elderly Maldemin with a series of pointed questions. "What is the Oracle? Why does the Oracle decide who controls it?" Pondru asked each question with such enthusiastic fervor that the ancient Maldemin occasionally laughed as he gently stroked the boy's round and nearly hairless head. Then, in a smooth monotone he equivocated. "The Oracle is what it is. It is wiser than any man, so why then should it submit to anyone who desires it."

When Pondru pressed the Maldemin for specifics he was told, "Your questions are irrelevant." As he spoke the Maldemin's eyes twinkled, for he came to love this young boy, who despite his royal upbringing was determined to live a relatively simple life. With fervent warmth and pious alacrity, then, the Maldemin often said more than he should have about the Oracle's properties. "Like you and I the Oracle exists," the old man said. "And like us it has its own wants and needs. It is capable of growth and development, as well as pettiness and cruelty. All human qualities which it has learned from us, I am afraid."

Realizing that he might have said too much, the Maldemin told young Pondru to go about his way, to continue his studies, and to remember always that the pursuit of knowledge was insufficient. "One must also believe." The Maldemin need not have worried that he had revealed too much about the source of the Oracle's power, for young Pondru was confused by most of these vague statements, though one particular phrase remained foremost in his imagination. In a moment of dangerous forthrightness the Maldemin had told young Pondru, "To the Oracle, I am many, but we are one." He had said it with such a resolute sincerity that Pondru knew it revealed an ultimate truth about the Oracle. Yet, what did it mean? How could I be many while we are one? The riddle made no sense to the young boy. He asked the Maldemin many times to explain it. The elderly man merely laughed and repeated, "It is what it is."

By the time the Maldemin died, shortly before Pondru turned eleven, the young prince was completely obsessed with the Oracle and its still mysterious properties. To the dismay of his mother and his brothers, Pondru began to wear the plain black frock robe of the Maldemin order, distinguishing himself from them only with the adornment of a bright red scarf. Even the scarf was imprinted with the insignia of the Maldemin, a diamond shaped ladder, which reached upward toward a lone star in an endless sky.

Of greater concern to his father, Pondru ignored his formal studies, hiding in his room, where he read and reread relevant passages from the High Cleric's *Holy Scriptures*, which obtusely and quite unsatisfactorily traced the ascension of the Oracle during King Leonata's monarchy. Though these texts provided little useful information, as the king's son, Pondru was able to furtively peruse his father's private library for any reference whatsoever to the Oracle. He often hid underneath a grand chair in his father's study, surreptitiously scanning these texts, searching diligently for the Oracle's secrets.

Surprisingly, little was recorded in these various state documents. The most detailed writings consisted of the musings of a strange little man named Zanzaska. He claimed to have discovered the Oracle in a desolate cave in the Tacanawana Mountains on the eastern border between Arcania and the uncharted Land of the Taewokans. Though Zanzaska had been a servant to the great King Leonata, Pondru considered his claims to be of dubious merit, since no one who had crossed the Tacanawana Mountains had ever been known to return alive. How then could Zanzaska have visited these strange lands and returned with an object of such incalculable value as the Oracle?

Despite his many hours of study, Pondru still could not answer basic questions such as what was the Oracle or how did it function? Overwhelmed with curiosity, Pondru's obsession with the Oracle finally led him during his early teens to do a most foolish and dangerous thing. On many nights he had hidden himself in a corner, under an ornately decorated chair, in King Benton's private office chamber. There the young boy read and covertly watched as his father, sitting in total silence behind his immense bamboo desk, industriously conducted the myriad tasks related to state business. Most nights were monotonously pedestrian, but Pondru would never forget the events of one particular occasion.

On this night, after studying a slate of documents for some time, his father slowly rose from behind his desk and walked to the nearby fireplace, which was next to the chair beneath which Pondru was hiding. As the boy clandestinely watched, the king moved a loose brick on the inglenook, and to the young's boys amazement, the fireplace swung open revealing a hidden pathway. Without hesitation, King Benton bowed his head down and then moved with great agility into the narrow corridor. Pondru waited for several seconds before he emerged from his hiding place. Then, without reflection or fear, he delicately traced his father's path, allowing the clatter of his father's footsteps to mask his own.

Even then, as a small boy, Pondru found the chamber to be claustrophobic. It was difficult to see because the chamber was dully lit only by the strange green hue of the very bricks that lined the passageway's slick walls. As Pondru stared forward through the shadowy darkness, he could see a bright light, apparently emanating at the end of the passageway. Carefully, the young boy walked forward, always trying to remain just far enough behind his father so that his own presence would not be detected. Tentatively, step by incremental step, with the soggy sensation of the moldy floor beneath his feet, fearing that at any moment he might slip and fall, Pondru carefully persevered, though he barely managed to keep his father within his sights. The passageway was only about forty feet long, but it felt interminably longer to the young boy. Finally, panting and almost out of breath, Pondru reached the aperture to a strange inner chamber. When he did the young boy was startled by what he saw.

Pondru crouched at the entrance to a small room that was no more than ten feet long and five feet wide. It was lit by the glowing bark of a single diminutive parnisus tree. Though his father now stood directly in front of him, not more than ten feet away, the king seemed entirely unaware of his son's presence, for Benton's attention was entirely fixed on the room's only furnishing, a modest oak table containing what appeared to be a tan flower vase made entirely out of plain, ordinary mud. On its side was a strange insignia: an inexorably swirling vortex. The only thing unusual about the vase was that that it contained no flowers. Otherwise, it might be an object found in even the most common of Arcanian homes.

As Pondru crouched discreetly on one knee in a dark corner, letting the shadows conceal his presence, he watched as his father stood silently for several seconds, merely staring ahead in a trance at this ostensibly innocuous object. Though he feared for his father's well being the young boy was far too afraid to speak or move. At first nothing of interest transpired. After what seemed like an eternity, Pondru became vaguely aware of a strange new sensation. At first he thought it was the eerie light from the parnisus tree. But as he crouched and looked out across the room at his father's backside, Pondru noticed that the vase itself was beginning to emit what appeared to be a dull purple glow. With his gaze entirely transfixed on the vase, a kaleidoscope of vibrant colors abruptly flickered onto the room's ceiling and walls, until the room itself appeared to be strangely animated and practically alive. This sensation amazed Pondru. But it is what happened next that completely unnerved the young boy.

From out of nowhere Pondru began to hear voices. The first appeared to be that of a woman. Pondru jerked his head around and stared anxiously down the passageway, convinced that his presence had been detected. When he saw that no one was there, Pondru gradually realized that the voice was not coming from the corridor at all, but rather from inside his own head. He listened attentively, trying to figure out what the voice was saying. But before he could interpret it he heard a deep baritone male voice speaking in an unusual almost unintelligible cadence. "Day is upon us to decision we must make." This new voice spoke with such haughty confidence that Pondru thought it sounded like one of his teachers. He also sensed a name – Kublatitan! What did that mean? Pondru carefully closed his eyes as tight as possible and when he did the voices proliferated, both in number and amplification, until the young boy started to feel a woozy sense of disequilibrium.

Dazed, the young prince opened his eyes and stared at his father, who appeared to be listening to the very same voices. Pondru heard the voice of a man who apparently had once been a king. Then he heard the strange dialects of a soldier and sundry other eclectic individuals. The number of voices expanded so rapidly that Pondru became further disoriented by their chaotic cacophony. Desperately, he clasped his hands tightly over his ears. Instead of the expected silence, many more distinct voices reverberated directly inside his head. As his mind swirled and the voices echoed in an undifferentiated fashion, Pondru feared that he would lose consciousness.

The young boy now trembling feverishly, realized that hundreds perhaps even thousands of different voices were speaking simultaneously. Their disjointed melody was so alarming that Pondru could no longer make any sense of the undifferentiated clatter. But his father could! King Benton continued to stand resolutely, nodding his head occasionally, calmly responding to the various separate voices as if they were one. Then, Pondru heard his own father's voice ask a question, though his father said nothing aloud.

Perhaps the boy was in shock, for it took a few moments for him to realize that he was not looking at a mere vase at all. *"This is the Oracle,"* he thought, his eyes now wide open with amazement and fascination. It was then that Pondru heard one dominant and distinctive voice speaking only to him. "It is nice to meet you young Pondru," I said with such a smarmy, obsequiousness that it sent shivers up the juvenile's spine. "In time I will get to know you quite well."

Upon hearing my words Pondru felt a sudden rush of uncontrollable panic. In a state of unreserved terror, the boy turned and literally ran back down the passageway, losing his balance and falling hard once on the slippery floor. As he struggled to his feet he heard the voices of men, women, children, and even what seemed to be an animal or two. He could not tell for sure, because the voices once again had blended into one oppressively loud clasp of echoing thunder. With all of the voices speaking at once Pondru's senses were so wholly overwhelmed that he could not think. Arriving back in the king's private chamber, completely terrified, the boy scurried back to his hiding place underneath the great chair. There he hid curled up in a fetal position, frightened beyond belief, terrified that his father would never return. After several more seemingly interminable minutes his father calmly emerged from the passageway, triggered the fireplace to close, and then as if absolutely nothing out of the ordinary had transpired, the king casually sat behind his bamboo desk and began to write with a quill pen on a fresh piece of parchment. The voices finally were silenced and all that Pondru could hear was the annoying squeak of his father's sprightly colored feather pen as it scratched the paper upon which he wrote. For the next several hours, Pondru huddled on the floor, fighting back the memories of the horrifying chorus of disjointed voices. It was not until just before dawn that he summoned the courage to return to his own room.

Pondru never mustered the daring to return to the Oracle chamber, though he contemplated the possibility on more than one occasion. He did, however, return to his father's private office several times. During none of those visits did his father seek the wisdom of the Oracle.

Now some twenty cycles later, as he stood in the Diplomatic Chamber with his brother Retch, Pondru suddenly remembered that long ago unit. He contrasted it with the scene he had just witnessed moments ago. Pantamanu had stormed out the chamber in a terrifying rage. Though Rendrau had offered his usual reassuring superlatives, Pondru feared the worst possible outcome. He understood his youngest brother's wild mood swings, his insatiable penchant for relentless egomaniacal self-promotion, his careless inattention to the concerns of others and his obsessive compulsion with the glittering allure of absolute power.

Then Pondru looked into Retch's eyes. To his way of thinking, his older brother was kind, scholarly, and always a gentleman. In other words, he lacked even the slightest spark of ambition. While this sentiment strangely appealed to Pondru's benign nature, he properly realized that a man who was not obsessively driven by the magnetic fascination of absolute power would be no match for one who was selfishly determined to do or say anything necessary to seize Arcania's throne. Pondru also realized that there simply was too much at stake to let the abject and often random fortunes of politics determine the winner in this quest for the Arcanian monarchy.

53

The Oracle

Consequently, he rightly understood that placing the Oracle in Pantamanu's hands was a far too dangerous possibility. I reluctantly agreed, for in many respects Pantamanu reminded me of my own departed father; exceedingly and dangerously unstable and subject to fits of frightening irrationality.

As he comforted Retch, Pondru therefore began to formulate a plan. "I must use my knowledge of the secret passageway to contact the Oracle!" In so doing, Pondru understood that this would not be an easy task. As he had grown older, and movement down the treacherous secret passageway became more difficult for King Benton to navigate, the monarch had ordered the construction of an extraordinarily well-guarded external door that led directly out of the Oracle chamber into a nearby hallway. Consequently, even if Pondru was able to enter the Oracle chamber through the secret passageway, there would be at least six guards only ten or twelve feet away, patrolling the newly constructed external door. It would be a dangerous maneuver; one that Pondru believed he must undertake. "I have to stop Pantamanu," he whispered in a voice that was faint, but which Retch could clearly hear.

After consoling his brother for several more minutes, and finally convincing Retch to return to his chamber to rest, Pondru moved swiftly and with great stealth from the Diplomatic Chamber to his father's nearby private office. Walking directly to the fireplace, he shifted a loose brick on the hearth, then as he looked back to make sure that he had not been followed, he stepped furtively into the narrow secret passageway. He was about to engage in an adventure that would change the course of Arcanian history.

Chapter 7
A Universe of Ideas

As his bespectacled eyes slowly adjusted to the dim green light of the secret passageway leading to the Oracle chamber, Pondru was surprised to see that the corridor's walls, once at least four or five feet apart, were now far narrower. "This can't be," he declared with great concern as he realized that the width of the corridor was presently no more than two feet. Thoroughly confused by this unexpected obstacle, Pondru stood near the fireplace entrance for several seconds carefully considering his options. As he did so he remembered the ambitious look of hunger lust that permeated Pantamanu's determined and obsessive eyes. That look convinced Pondru that he had no alternative but to consult the mighty Oracle. "I must get to the Oracle," he whispered, certain that necessity required that he move expeditiously forward. "But how?"

Lacking any other viable alternative, Pondru awkwardly turned his body sideways, and began the painfully tedious process of shimmying his disproportionately plump body along the poorly lit corridor's narrow walls. As he did so he firmly closed his eyes, for he had developed a rather severe case of claustrophobia as a result of his last visit to the Oracle chamber. Step by careful step, he slid his body along the tapered walls. He was perhaps ten feet inside the passageway when he suddenly realized that with each inch he moved forward the walls were getting ever narrower. Awash with a sudden sense of suffocating anxiety, Pondru was about to hastily retreat to the safety of his father's private office when he unexpectedly heard the resolute sound of the fireplace egress slamming tightly closed.

"I'm trapped," he said with a sudden start. There was now no turning back! Pondru realized that if he could not move forward, he would be trapped inside these secret walls for all eternity. Faced with this perilous dilemma Pondru could have panicked. Instead he remembered a mental technique that the ancient Maldemin had taught him many cycles past. With his eyes still shut tight, he completely cleared his mind of all thoughts, both good and bad. Then, he visualized his body moving lithely forward through the corridor's tunnel-like walls, toward the redemption of the Oracle chamber. In this manner he resumed his forward progress, jerking his body ahead for several seconds until the laws of physics simply would not permit him to move any farther. As he felt the tug of his stomach against the ever-tightening walls, Pondru instantly understood that his situation was catastrophically dire. He was irreversibly entombed within the deepest unknown bowels of the king's vast castle. No one would ever find him here, certainly not alive!

Yet despite another temporary flinch of anxiety, Pondru maintained his composure. He had studied the Oracle for decades and he instinctively sensed that it now was testing him. "It must control the size and shape of this corridor." Then he remembered the phrase that the Maldemin had spoken with such great reverence. "It is not enough for you to desire the Oracle. The Oracle must desire you." Pondru smiled and whispered, "I must prove that I am worthy."

The Oracle

Though he was threatened with mortal peril, Pondru quietly cleared his mind of all extraneous thoughts and replaced them with an all-pervasive sense of serenity and calm. As he did so, he realized that it was his destiny to be in this place, at this time, confronting this particular dilemma. Relaxation eased his mind as he still confronted the larger more pertinent problem: "How can I possibly move forward?"

As he asked himself this question a rather unusual solution appeared unexpectedly in his mind. "That is pure madness," he thought with a wry smile, his glasses now so completely covered with a thick heavy layer of steam that he no longer needed to keep his eyes shut. Pondru's unique solution was to imagine himself as he had appeared the first time he visited the passageway. Then he had been but a young and innocent boy, tentatively following the footsteps of his dear father. Therefore, in his mind's eye, Pondru changed his appearance from a middle-aged man to a lithe and flexible young boy. As his mind focused ever more fiercely on this mental image of a smaller and more nimble youth, he suddenly felt his body move forward just an inch. Then with full concentration Pondru felt a sudden sense of freedom, as his body was abruptly released from the grip of the passageway's narrow walls. Completely unfettered, Pondru continued to shimmy sideways, sure that the Oracle was willing him forward. Then, as he sensed his now tiny hands groping the corridor's cold green bricks, he instinctively understood, "I am a boy again."

With an equal measure of joy and relief, Pondru slid his body through the passageway until he finally felt nothing but open air. "I am inside the Oracle chamber!" he quietly declared. With this ebullient exclamation Pondru opened his eyes and saw nothing for his steam-covered glasses completely impaired his vision. Tentatively he removed his spectacles, and only then did he realize that he no longer needed his visual correctives in order to see. In fact, his eyes were now capable of seeing the world more clearly than ever before. Startled, he casually slid his glasses inside a side pocket of his black frock robe, with his red scarf still wrapped snuggly around his neck. Then he stared out in wonderment at the detail that his feeble eyes had never before been able to detect. He also noticed that his body had been restored to it previous adult dimensions. Overcome with a sense of wonder, the prince looked back at the passageway. Its walls were no more than a foot's width apart. "My God," he whispered, "Even a child could not have made it through."

As he spoke these words Pondru suddenly realized that indeed the Oracle desired his presence. And he was now standing less than a few feet from the newly constructed external door. And beneath its threshold Pondru could see the shadows of the pacing soldiers' feet. He could also hear the continuous thud of men marching, as several of the king's elite guards determinedly patrolled the hall just outside the Oracle chamber. "I will have to be careful," Pondru thought, for prudence now dictated that he make absolutely no sound whatsoever, lest he alert the guards to his presence inside the chamber.

Ever so quietly, Pondru strode the four or five steps until he was standing directly in front of the plain oak table that contained the strange looking Oracle vase. As a child he had seen the Oracle only from a distance and as he approached it, his eyes were now capable of focusing on the most minute details. He could not help but admire the Oracle's artistry: on its side he saw a meticulously carved engraving of a relentlessly twisting vortex, an image so real that to his enhanced eyes it now seemed to be in a constant state of circular motion. As he moved his head closer to admire the insignia, he felt a pricking sensation on his face caused by a steady electrical discharge from the vortex.

"It is alive!" he responded with wonder. Then, in a discreet murmur that was less than a whisper he asked, "But what does the vortex mean?" Though he had not asked this question loud enough for anyone to hear, Pondru was surprised when a bizarre, metallic voice echoed a response to his query.

"The insignia, insignia, insignia represents the intersection section section, of two alternate dimensions." As Pondru became accustomed to the voice's strange sound, the echo diminished as the interlocutor continued, "The first consists entirely of objects, of matter and energy, while the second is composed of pure unadulterated thought."

"I don't understand," Pondru wondered, though he said absolutely nothing aloud.

The tinny mechanical voice professorially lectured, "The Oracle is composed of a veritable *universe* of ideas."

The response was obtuse, though Pondru now sensed another peculiar sensation: his mind's eye now existed concomitantly and with remarkable clarity inside two distinctly different dimensions of reality. The first was the one that he had lived in his entire life. It was a dimension of objects, ruled by an unwaveringly strict system of demanding physical regulations. Consequently, while some alternatives were possible, according to the laws of physics and other unviable scientific principles, other alternatives simply could not exist in the real world. Existence itself in this dimension was therefore constricted, controlled, and thoroughly confining.

The second dimension was controlled entirely by the mind. It was therefore absolutely flexible and unfettered, regulated not by any incontrovertible laws of physics, but instead guided by the limitless reach of unbounded imagination. Absolutely anything, no matter how preposterous or absurd it might appear, could exist, that is, so long as the mind could conceive of it. As Pondru's mind suddenly opened to this new universe of ideas, he was overcome with an overwhelmingly intense feeling of wonderment, for he sensed for the first time in his life that ideas can be just as real as matter or energy.

This epiphany, that there is a limitless realm of pure imagination, was seductively tantalizing and quickly tempted Pondru's ever more eager intellect. "Everything is possible here!" he rejoiced, astonished by the beauty of the images that now consumed his thoughts.

And then he was struck by another and even more powerful realization. "All my life I have studied the Oracle from afar. Now I can ask it any question I desire." This sudden stark insight completely transformed the essence of Pondru's very existence. For while he continued to stand physically inside the Oracle chamber, his consciousness and all that is not of the body now resided deep within a vastly different and separate realm of existence. With his human eyes Pondru could still see the stark manifestations of the object-oriented universe, such as his own physical body, the oak table, and the finely decorated Oracle vase. In this new dimension, Pondru's mind could actually begin to see ideas themselves and as he did he realized that thoughts could be translated into multiple realities.

Instantly, Pondru's mind was consumed by a series of strange and fascinating new images. In particular, Pondru witnessed a veritable kaleidoscopic rainbow of vibrant colors, including several that did not exist in the physical world, but which Pondru's emancipated imagination could suddenly envision. With pure delight the prince rapturously watched as the various colors morphed and re-aligned themselves, flowing like a stream of lava-like fiery water, creating ever new forms and shapes. From a distinct and separable prism, the colors fused, and then separated, then intersected in a humungous chain of illumination, then separated again. And there were thousands upon thousands of these individual beams of multihued light, streaming in every imaginable direction, intersecting repeatedly, forming an immense radiant spider-like web of golden, molten activity. The fiery colors pulsated with such astonishing beauty that Pondru was thoroughly overwhelmed and nearly breathless with unadulterated joy.

Then he was struck by yet another series of epiphanies. "Everything that I can ever imagine, that any human or sentient being can imagine, every single idea exists here in this extraordinary dimension of ideal thought. It *really is* a boundless universe of ideas."

With his mind now totally unconstrained by the limits of the physical world, Pondru thoughts darted excitedly from one topic to another. As he did so, he envisioned ideas that he could never have understood in a hundred lifetimes. And with his curiosity unencumbered, he had the ability to consider all possible permutations of any question or point of view, no matter how radical or unconventional the idea might be. In fact, limitless curiosity was both the stimulus and the inner truth of this dimension of thought. The more one opened one's mind to exciting new possibilities, the more the Oracle seemed to enhance one's imagination. Therefore, as Pondru's curiosity deepened, he felt his consciousness move ever further inside this new and powerful universe.

"What is this universe?" he asked himself. "How does it exist?"

Pondru's mind suddenly visualized thousands of highly complex mathematical equations. It was an unexpected empirical answer to his question. "My word," he thought. "It all seems so easy for me to understand." His mind now embraced subjects that he had found rather distasteful in the so-called real world. He sensed the precise poetry of mathematics, the endless possibilities of scientific inquiry, the insatiable joy of philosophy, the true power of unrestrained imagination. "The answers are all here, to every question I ever imagined and countless others I never even considered. They are all here!" Then with unconstrained excitement Pondru thought of the question that had tortured his mind for decades. "What does it mean: We are one, but I am many?"

Again, as before, he sensed a mechanical voice intone, "The Oracle is the one, created by the one, to serve the one."

"Who is the one?" Pondru eagerly asked.

"The King is the one."

"Then who are the many?"

"The many serve the one," the voice responded enigmatically.

The Oracle

"I don't understand," Pondru whispered, and with this sense of confusion, he suddenly became aware that his body still resided in the physical world.

"If you want an answer you must completely open your mind," the voice declared emphatically.

Pondru did as he was commanded and soon he heard another entirely different voice intone, "The Season of Death is the wrong time to plant crops. It is far too cold. We must wait till the commencement of the Season of Rain."

Though he did not know how or why, Pondru instinctively understood that the source of this advice was an ordinary farmer or at least he once had been one. Pondru visualized a man in his mid-forties, slender, with a handsome brow and a full head of flashing red hair. His name was Caltran and he had lived a long and prosperous life in a small rural enclave in northern Arcania. He was a widower, who despite often-unimaginable poverty, had managed to raise six strapping boys and three adorable little girls.

Just as suddenly as Pondru visualized the farmer, he sensed an entirely different presence. This time it was a soldier from Relatania who had died at the famous Miracle at Mt. Delba. "The Season of Death is not a good time to initiate a military campaign, unless that is, one intends to surprise your enemy." As before this presence moved on before Pondru had an opportunity to question it.

"This is strange," Pondru considered. "I have met two entities of some sort and both have provided rather innocuous data about the same basic source, the Season of Death. Hence, I must assume that their thoughts are related, interconnected, somehow linked together." Then, with unconstrained enthusiasm, Pondru exclaimed, "I am many but we are one. The many are these presences, these individual thoughts, representing the consciousness of thousands upon thousands of real people. Their ideas are stored here to serve the one, the king!"

With an all-consuming curiosity, Pondru now realized that he must intersect with other entities, to discern their individual thoughts and to extrapolate their meaning to the larger context of the Oracle itself. Therefore he consciously shifted his thoughts toward what in his mind appeared to be a gigantic web of interconnecting beams of fierce, burning light. His thoughts converged with one such intersection and as they did, Pondru suddenly sensed countless thousands of different presences, representing virtually every cross-section of human existence. These presences were people who had lived in such varied places as Arcania, the Relatin Empire, and even the uncharted Land of the Taewokans.

Pondru next sensed a kind middle-aged woman named Bevell, who had been a brilliant teacher to many gifted young children. As their thoughts melded into one, he could sense Bevell's joyous and unrestricted enthusiasm for her often-unappreciated profession. As he moved on to other presences, voices or entities, his mind was repeatedly transported until it resided in a continuing state of epiphany, with fresh ideas, some so fanciful that it made Pondru laugh, alternately consuming his ever expanding imagination. "I have never felt like this before," he marveled, for there was no comparable feeling of absolute intellectual freedom within the physical world. As myriad ideas proliferated exponentially, Pondru realized that the Oracle was a truly unbounded dimension, utterly limitless in its possibilities. For every new idea, his mind spawned at least a dozen others. Furthermore, he now understood that literally any possibility could exist. One plus one could indeed equal three. Pure logic, though it had its place, was no longer omnipotent. Imagination could transcend rationality and in a strange way that Pondru could not yet fathom, could thereby actually extend rationality in new and innovative directions. These multiple realizations were utterly amazing, though some still barely made sense to Pondru.

"This is such an absolutely wondrous place!" Pondru finally shouted aloud. When he did so, he forgot that his body still existed inside the physical world. Consequently, as he shouted, the guards in the hall were alerted to his presence inside the Oracle chamber. Instantly, they scampered forward, one soldier clumsily fumbling with his set of keys, trying to identify the right one. Then, he had considerable difficulty trying to fit the right key into the rusted lock of the external Oracle chamber door.

Pondru did not hear the soldiers. His mind was so consumed with an ever-expanding series of exquisite thoughts that he consciously paid no heed whatsoever to the threat posed by the oncoming soldiers. Subconsciously his mind was alerted to their presence and he suddenly remembered the reason why he had come to the Oracle chamber. As he did so, his mind was suddenly consumed by darker and more frightful visual images. Without warning, Pondru sensed fear, depravation, starvation, panic, desolation, and even the painful consummation of the death process itself. His mind was filled with images of immeasurable savagery and destruction, of hopelessness and irredeemable despair. For he realized that these too were ideas, but unlike the joy of imagination, these thoughts seemed rigid, self-serving, painfully cruel, and utterly horrifying. Pondru next felt a mixture of malevolence, avarice, jealousy, insecurity, selfishness, and a raw ambition so unfettered that it was willing to destroy everything of value in the physical world rather than simply relinquish power. "This is insanity," he muttered, his physical body stepping back from the Oracle, as the soldiers continued to struggle to open the external door, which was inexplicably jammed.

Pondru was repulsed by these new and frightening sensations. Nor could he drive them from his mind. All around his consciousness he now felt a violent conflict of ideas. In this realm of the Oracle, the once warm and inviting beams of light emitted a hostile discharge, a fiery spark that spewed angrily, consuming everything in its path. It was an absolutely destructive fury, generated by pure self-interest, without conscience or mutually useful purpose. "There is no enlightenment here," Pondru reasoned, "just an unquenchable thirst for power!"

Pondru did not know it but he had reached the Oracle's epicenter. Here, in this darkest of all realms of human imagination, people deviously plotted with but one object in mind: to rule, to be king! Unlike the other realms of the Oracle, he also sensed something entirely unexpected, a total sense of unrestricted panic and confusion. "Where is the king?" he heard one voice ask in apparent desperation.

"My father is ill," Pondru responded involuntarily.

"Then we will need a new leader," the voice declared impatiently.

Before Pondru could respond he heard the voice of another entity. This one commanded him to "Come here!" As his mind melded with the other entity, Pondru sensed that it was a Count, a man of royal upbringing, but a man who was not from Arcania. "Have you come to lead us?" I demanded imperially.

"No, my brother Retch is next in the line of succession."

"Then why are you here?" I asked with such a fierce abruptness that Pondru barely had time to consider his response.

"I am here to avoid a succession war," Pondru finally announced.

I was not pleased with this response and merely responded with a disinterested, "Hmmmph," before moving on, for I had no patience then or now with those who were not obsessed with power and its many rewards.

All around him Pondru sensed thousands of other confused entities, each asking similar questions. "Is King Benton dead? If so, who will lead us?" These particular questions echoed with such deafening intensity that

Pondru recoiled and finally was able to pull his thoughts back toward the realm of enlightened pure imagination, the place where he had first entered the Oracle. There he felt more familiar and at ease. As he did so he realized that he had never really felt comfortable in his father's world, for politics and their intrigues were totally foreign to his imagination. To Pondru war was an unthinkable abomination. Now that he was inside the Oracle, he could see...even worse he could actually feel, the scars of wars waged over countless generations. It was a terrifying and unspeakable horror.

Therefore, with great concentration, Pondru continued to open his mind to different, more amenable possibilities. As he did so he sensed other powerful presences, including one named Kublatitan. "He is the link. He is the one who holds the Oracle together, the one who speaks to the king." Pondru realized with near unrestricted joy, though he also sensed that there were other entities that sought to take Kublatitan's place, namely myself. He also sensed that if his father died and there was no certain successor among the Centama family, then the consequences for Arcania and the Oracle itself would be devastating. Two civil wars would be fought, one outside, the other within the universe of ideas. But Pondru also realized that he was not fit to be king. Simply stated, it was not his destiny.

"Needed here, you are," a strange baritone voice declared with unwavering confidence. Pondru listened, enchanted, and no longer afraid. For his mind was now consumed with images that greatly appealed to his elevated sensibilities. He heard the gentle sounds of musical notes, playing harmonies that both entranced and encouraged his mind to delve deeper into the Oracle's limitless possibilities. With his curiosity again aroused, Pondru wondered, "How can I ever return to the real world after I have experienced the awe-inspiring power of imagination?" With this final epiphany, and with a realization that he might do more for his passra inside the Oracle than in the real world, he felt his spirit let go of his physical body.

Consequently, when the guards finally were able to rush into the room, they found only one sign of an intruder, a solitary garment that lay inexplicably on the floor before the Oracle chamber. It was a red scarf imprinted with the insignia of a Maldemin, the one that Pondru always wore. As he picked it up one guard turned to a compatriot and declared in a harsh and desperate voice, "The Oracle chamber has been violated! We must contact Lord Valmar immediately!"

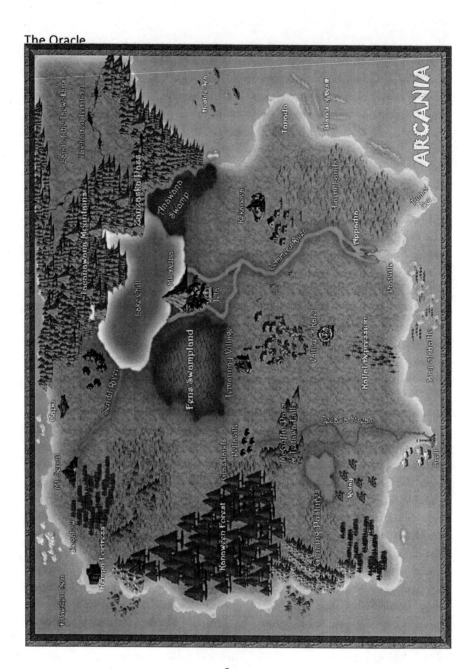

Map of Arcania

Chapter 8
A Palace Coup

Belicki's description of the Oracle was a revelation to poor Nimrod. "I too am from the Oracle!" it announced with emphatic enthusiasm.

"Yes you are," Belicki said with a self satisfied smirk, "but you are much more than that."

"How was I absorbed and who was I before I became one with the Oracle?" Nimrod demanded, unable to wait any longer to learn the critical details, the key to its very existence.

Belicki's response was frustratingly obtuse. "You were fashioned out of the storm of a brutal succession war. You were conceived by the bitter hatred that fueled a revolution."

"I don't understand," Nimrod confessed.

"Then let me continue with my narrative and in time all that you wish to know will be revealed."

Nimrod was anxious to know the truth and therefore reluctantly surrendered to Belicki's request to demonstrate continued patience, for Nimrod did not know how much longer it could contain its obsessive desire to learn its true identity. Still Nimrod said nothing more as it listened, ever more attentively, to Belicki's recitation of the events of the Arcanian succession war.

While Pondru encountered the Oracle, his brother Rendrau sat quietly at one of the tables used for food preparation in the royal kitchen. As various workers milled about him cooking the evening's meal, none paid the slightest attention to the king's third eldest son. As he heartily consumed copious amounts of Galenian Ale, he too remonstrated on the contentious meeting that had transpired less than an hour before in the nearby Diplomatic Chamber.

While Rendrau sincerely loved his father, he realized that the king's illness transcended mere family considerations, for periods of succession were potentially dangerous times under the very best of circumstances, such as when the royal family was solidly united, a situation that unfortunately and quite obviously did not prevail at the present time. Rendrau reasoned that any serious divisions within his own family would almost certainly invite an external challenge to the Centama family rule. The question on his mind therefore was who among the passra's various citizens was loyal and who was not?

This was a decidedly complicated question for in addition to the High Clerics of Kekanova, who were obstreperous in the very best of times, and the various local officeholders, each with their own political axes to grind, a grand total of thirty-two lords, widely geographically dispersed, governed much of Arcania's eastern and western territories. Rendrau calculated that of these lords only about a third readily could be counted upon to submit blindly to the Centama family's authority if the transition to a new king was not orderly.

Among these sundry lords, Tantamount was certainly the most trust worthy of all. His wife, Truellen, was the king's third cousin. In addition, Tantamount loyally rode by King Benton's side during a brief but violent Bogul uprising nearly thirty cycles ago. Tantamount's fiefdom was of particular strategic importance, not only because of its size, but also because it controlled access to the Kanaween Forrest, site of the world's tallest trees. Though the lord did not have a ready army at his disposal, for none of the lords were permitted to have a force sufficient to threaten the monarchy, the strategic importance of Tantamount's lands guaranteed that the Centama family would have a solid foothold in the west should other rival lords prove disloyal.

Rendrau therefore calculated that the greatest probable source of instability lay in the east, where several lords exhibited greater deference to the independent High Clerics of Kekanova than to the royal family. As he refilled his large copper mug with warm ale, Rendrau reasoned that while Pantamanu's observations had been impertinently expressed, they were entirely appropriate from a military point of view. It was to the east where the armies would be most needed to quell any spirit of rebellion.

For Pantamanu, like Rendrau, was well aware of the disposition and readiness of the king's five armies. The First Army, the largest and most ably trained, was deployed south of the capital city of Teta. Composed of ten brigades, each with a compliment of approximately one hundred men, its primary role was to guard against a renewed attack from the Relatin Empire. The officers of the First Army had been selected as much for their commitment to the Centama family as for their military acumen. Their loyalty was therefore beyond question. Rendrau also knew that it was standard procedure to inform the commanding general if the king were ill. Consequently, the First Army already was on a state of high alert.

Rendrau also had considerable confidence in the Second and Third Armies, which patrolled eastern Arcania. These armies consisted of eight brigades with a combined total of approximately three thousand men. Again, the officers were personally loyal to the Centama family, each having served at one time or another in the king's castle as a personal guard to King Benton. Rendrau realized that this vetting process insured that only the most loyal, if not necessarily the most capable officers, were guarding the potentially unstable eastern front.

While the western regions provided the least potential for rebellion, the loyalty of its armies was not as readily assured as in the east. The best of the western officers served in the Fifth Army under the leadership of General Cato, but it greatly troubled Rendrau that General Mbanka commanded the Fourth Army. Though the general had served without as much as a single blemish on his impeccable military record, Mbanka held a long-standing and well known antipathy toward Pantamanu, for it was rumored that the king' surly son brazenly impregnated the general's wife. Such seemingly trivial matters now assumed great political importance, as Rendrau considered the loyalty of the passra's own protectors.

So as he poured yet another mug of warm ale, Rendrau wondered why Lord Valmar had been incapable of answering what he considered to be Pantamanu's very basic queries about the passra's military capabilities and deployments. He also was troubled that his oldest brother, the heir to the throne, showed absolutely no proclivity or interest whatsoever regarding military affairs. Shaking his head contemptuously, he wondered if either Lord Valmar or Retch had the capacity to lead the passra at this critical moment in history.

As he sipped his ale, Rendrau whispered quietly, "As usual, my dear wife Bellazar is right." Just two nights before, while he sat in his private chamber, Rendrau's brilliant wife had shared her own apt observations on the present political climate. Discussing the various hypothesized prophesies deriving from the ascension of the three turquoise moons, she noted with her usual clear-headed acumen, "When the time for succession arrives Retch will not have the slightest idea what to do." When Rendrau reminded her that Lord Valmar would be present to provide sage advice for the new king, his wife merely laughed, throwing her head back as she did so, before adding, "I am afraid the Lord grows increasingly senile with age. I would not count on him if I were you." Then narrowing her eyes, as was her habit when she was about to impart advice of a clandestine nature, she added in a much quieter voice, "You must be ready, for when the time for succession comes, neither Retch nor Pondru will be fit to be king. The struggle for power will be between you and Pantamanu. It is Pantamanu who is your real enemy."

"And a formidable one at that," Rendrau thought as he took yet another long drink from his large copper mug. Though workers toiled only a foot away, he muttered in a low but audible voice, "So it is between Pantamanu and me." Then raising his mug as if he was about to offer a toast he continued, "One of us will be the next king." Realizing only then that he might have been overheard, Rendrau nervously glanced at the workers. To his satisfaction he discovered that they were far too busy preparing the evening's meal to have overheard anything.

Having emptied his mug Rendrau again refilled it. He was about to consume its contents when six of the king's burly guards abruptly stormed into the kitchen. Without as much as a customary salute or other deferential salutation, a particularly muscular guard declared authoritatively, "You are to come with me."

"Excuse me," Rendrau responded, clearly not accustomed to this tone of voice from a subordinate. "Do you know who you are talking to?"

Without the slightest pretense to courtesy, the guard summarily ordered, "Seize him!" Three other guards then moved brusquely forward, harshly grabbing Rendrau about the waist. As Rendrau glared in startled disbelief the guards literally carried the king's third eldest son from the room, as the various kitchen staff stood gaping in shocked amazement.

"What are you doing?" Rendrau bellowed angrily, struggling mightily but ineffectually against this overwhelming and unexpected show of force. "Put me down!" he ordered in a commanding voice that was utterly and inexplicably ignored. With his legs kicking and his arms flailing ineffectually, the guards carried Rendrau like a folded carpet from the kitchen, down the hall, to a winding brick laced staircase that led to a small, musty wine cellar in the castle's dark basement. Though Rendrau continued to protest audibly, the guards merely ignored him. Instead they opened the wine cellar door and with cold disregard, unceremoniously dropped the king's third eldest son ingloriously on the room's hard and frigid stone floor. Then as Rendrau struggled to his feet, the guards locked the large wooden door. The menacing sound of the turning key and the lock falling securely into place frightened Rendrau. In the chilly room, dimly lit by just two small parnisus trees, Rendrau stood alone between the rows of dusty shelves that contained the king's prized wines.

"Is this a coup?" Rendrau shouted thunderously to the inattentive heavens, for no one was there to acknowledge his question. He then added, "If so, who is responsible?" When there was no response, other than the echo of his voice resonating up the winding staircase, Rendrau sat silently on the chilly stone floor, staring about the room, wondering if this was some mere drunken reverie or if in fact he had just been forcibly abducted. During the commotion Rendrau's shirt was torn open and as he looked down he could see that his heart now beat with such palpable force that it pulsated visibly through his chest. Breathing deeply, trying desperately to regain his senses, still dizzy in part because of the ale he had consumed in copious amounts, he stared at the door, not so much in anticipation, as in a state of utter confusion. "What the hell is going on?" he finally shouted thunderously to the heavens above.

Met with nothing but silence, Rendrau sat tentatively, frightened and on edge for some time. Then, he heard another noisy commotion echoing down the stairway. Seconds thereafter the wine cellar door sprung open, this time with the direct heir to the throne firmly in the grasp of four muscular guards. Unceremoniously and without a word of explanation, they summarily dumped Retch's exhausted body onto the floor, before turning and departing without delay. As his brother squirmed pitiably on the floor, Rendrau demanded, "What is going on?" As before, the guards ignored the king's son.

Drenched in sweat from his ineffectual physical struggle with the guards, Retch responded meekly, "Brother, what is happening to us? I was in my private parlor when they seized me!"

Rendrau now recounted the events of his own abduction, after which there was a moment of silence before the third eldest brother angrily declared, "This *is* a coup! Pantamanu *must* be behind this!"

Retch was usually cautious about expressing his opinions. Yet under the circumstances he saw no reason for circumspection. "He won't get away with this. Lord Valmar will never allow it."

"Lord Valmar is probably dead already," Rendrau responded without hesitation.

The pitiful heir to the throne was now completely inconsolable. "Our bastard brother will never be our king," Retch shouted so loud that his words echoed all the way up the nearby winding staircase. Then in a more subdued yet contemptuous tone, Retch stridently proclaimed, "You don't think for a minute that our father sired that bastard, do you? They say it was Lord Clamarin. That's why he and mother were put to death. It wasn't cholera like they told us."

Rendrau indeed had heard all of these rumors, including the allegation that Lord Valmar had interceded on Pantamanu's behalf, lest King Benton order the newborn's execution as well. These were highly discreet matters and no one at the royal court was allowed to discuss them publicly. Realizing that it was of no value to recite ancient gossip, Rendrau nimbly reframed the discussion. "A few of the king's guards may be with Pantamanu, but I wager that some are still loyal to us."

Retch scarcely heard his brother's comment, for he continued to sit on the floor, his head now placed squarely between his legs as he hyperventilated uncontrollably. As he slowly regained his composure, Retch stared defiantly at his brother and indignantly snarled, "Once we are free of this dungeon, I will personally make sure that our dear youngest brother is executed, even if I have to do it myself." Rendrau knew it was an empty boast, since there was little prospect that either of them ever would be freed. More likely the guards would soon return and put them both to death.

With this morbid thought on his mind, Rendrau suddenly realized that one of the brothers was missing. "Where is Pondru?" he asked.

"I suspect he will be joining us soon," Retch responded quietly.

"Or perhaps he is already dead," Rendrau wondered, as tears now began to stream ignobly down his older brother's cheeks.

Startled, Retch cried out, "What will happen to our families?" Without saying another word Retch realized that if a coup indeed were underway their families already might be dead.

Unexpectedly, Rendrau, who showed much greater composure and courage than his oldest brother ever could, merely smiled. As he took a seat next to his brother, Rendrau declared, "If so, I am quite sure that Bellazar personally fought Pantamanu to the death."

Retch smiled incongruously, with a crooked smile and a nervous tick, as he thought of the possibility of Bellazar conducting a bitter duel to the death with Pantamanu. "She is the only one among us that is capable of defeating him in hand to hand combat." Then, as his awkward smile vanished, Retch's body trembled uncontrollably with a crushing fear.

Hoping to lift his brother's spirits, Rendrau looked about the room and joked, "Well if we are to die at least we will not be thirsty." It was at such moments that I came to appreciate if not admire Rendrau, for while his brother lacked even the most rudimentary qualities of leadership, Rendrau had both courage and a certain dim witted wisdom. Standing rather precariously, for he was still weak from the ale, Rendrau staggered to a nearby row of wine bottles and picked out a green bottle with a yellow rose painted on its side. He then proudly proclaimed, "I have been saving this bottle for my thirtieth wedding anniversary. But now seems as good a time as any to quench our thirst, don't you think?" Retch laughed in a most ghastly manner, for in reality he could find no humor in their present desperate situation. Before Rendrau could open the bottle, the two brothers again heard the sounds of scurrying feet coming down the long winding staircase. Only Rendrau had the courage to say aloud what was on both men's minds. "This may be the end."

With great trepidation, the two brothers listened as a key entered the lock before the door suddenly sprung open. As it did, light from the corridor flooded the dimly lit room, temporarily blinding the two prisoners. Rendrau realized that if the guards had come to kill them they would waste no time. Two guards would hold each brother down, while another unsheathed his sword before pressing it violently against their throat. It would take less than a minute from the time they entered the wine cellar to the fatal incision. Usually, the dying man would be given an opportunity to make a statement or a last request, but if this were a royal coup, no such pleasantries would be entertained. Two heirs to the throne would be summarily removed.

While Rendrau stood resolute, Retch trembled pitiably as several guards entered the room. Unexpectedly, however, they brought another prisoner into the wine cellar. It was neither Pondru nor Lord Valmar, but rather Pantamanu! "This means Pondru is behind the coup?" Retch gasped, barely able to believe that his dear brother either had the will or the fortitude to foment such an unanticipated rebellion.

Rendrau too was startled. Uncharacteristically, and for perhaps the only time in his life, it was Retch who now stood his ground for what might be his last battle. "What is the meaning of this?" he shouted defiantly, grabbing the wine bottle from Rendrau's hands and waving it like a weapon. "Tell me now or there will be hell to pay!"

One of the guards now stepped forward. "Sir, I don't know what is going on. Lord Valmar simply told to us to bring each of the princes to the wine cellar as expeditiously as possible."

"Lord Valmar!" Pantamanu shouted, as he scurried angrily to his feet. With a raw and angry defiance, Pantamanu stared coldly and directly into the guard's vapid eyes. "Go tell Lord Valmar that he will pay for this indignity with his life." Pantamanu's bellicose defiance was extraordinary and even the king's guard now expressed palpable fear. Before he could respond, however, Lord Valmar briskly entered the room, ordering the guards to depart as he did so. "Lord Valmar," Pantamanu demanded, stepping forward sprightly and with such menace that Valmar was terrified at the sight of this belligerent young prince. With an unbounded anger rising as he spoke, Pantamanu demanded, "Tell me why I should not kill you now with my bare hands?"

Pleading hysterically, Retch merely whimpered, "Is this a coup? Have our families been put to death?"

Frightfully intimidated and greatly confused, Valmar was yet again temporarily at a loss for words. Pantamanu was more direct. He grabbed Valmar by his lapel, in the process knocking the Lord's wig to the floor. "Tell me why we are here or I swear I will kill you." Pantamanu's nostrils flared with such an unbridled anger that it petrified the old man.

With his voice cracking pitiably Valmar responded, "It is your brother, Pondru."

The brothers were startled. Pantamanu dismissed the idea as totally preposterous. "Pondru, behind this coup! How gullible do you think we are?"

With his shoulders slouching perceptively, Valmar whimpered, "I swear there is no coup. I brought each of you here for your own protection."

"Protection?" Rendrau scoffed angrily.

Valmar struggled to regain his composure, a task made infinitely more difficult by the tightening grasp of Pantamanu's powerful hands. "Pondru has vanished. We can find no trace of him anywhere in the castle."

"What do you mean?" Pantamanu snarled.

Wheezing and barely able to speak, Valmar haltingly responded, "We found a red scarf with the Maldemin's insignia on the floor of the Oracle chamber. It is the same scarf that Pondru always wears." At these words Pantamanu finally loosened his grip and let the Lord fall hard onto the floor. Without thinking the elderly diplomat grabbed his wig and clasped it tightly to his chest, like a child firmly holding his security blanket. Valmar then took a deep breath and muttered, "I assure you, when I learned of Pondru's disappearance my only motivation was to ensure that all of the members of the royal family were safe from harm. It is standard procedure in case of a possible external attack. I ordered the guards to take you immediately to this secure location and I came directly here once the guards assured me that there was no sign of an external threat."

Pantamanu adamantly rejected Valmar's frantic explanation. "You had no right to seize us in this callous fashion. I will make sure that you pay for this indignity," he fumed before storming stridently out of the wine cellar.

Valmar's eyes were now wide with terror, as he informed the other brothers, "Each of you will be escorted to your chambers where the guards will protect you and your families, from now until this crisis is resolved." Valmar then shouted, "Guards!" Four of the king's guards instantly returned to the room. Valmar directed them, "Please escort the princes and their families to their private chambers." Then trying to steady himself, Valmar whispered, "Matters are decidedly out of hand." With his shoulders hunched and his head slumped downward, he reached to his right and grabbed a random bottle of wine from one of the shelves. Then in a most dejected state of mind he popped the cork and took a long deep swig of wine.

Datoria 1

THE DISPOSITION OF ARCANIA'S FIVE ARMIES

First Army: Stationed south of Teta, it is under the Command of General Tige.

Second Army: Stationed in Eastern Arcania, at Kankabar, it is under the Command of General Xona.

Third Army: Stationed in Eastern Arcania, approximately fifty miles north of the Bay of Battle, it is under the Command of General Wu.

Fourth Army: Stationed in Western Arcania at the edge of the Kanaween Forest, it is under the Command of General Mbanka.

Fifth Army: Stationed in Western Arcania at Pellaville, it is under the leadership of General Cato.

Chapter 9
Bellazar

Like an irritation that simply cannot be excoriated, Nimrod was driven mad by one particularly pertinent question: "Who is Bellazar? You have mentioned her name several times and it seems quite familiar to me. Who is she?"

Belicki could sense the incremental re-emergence of Nimrod's diffused and disorganized memories. They were still very much scattered, inchoate, not yet forming a consistent pattern, but steadily they were emerging in small bits and inconsistent pieces. "You have hit upon a central question in your development, poor Nimrod," Belicki cooed. "For there is no one more central to your existence than this great woman."

"Then please tell me more about her," Nimrod begged with a stridently uncontrollable eagerness.

"It shall be my pleasure," Belicki responded, with devious delight.

Bellazar was that most interesting of humans: cunning, intelligent, beautiful, totally focused, and wicked beyond all reason. Yet of all the contenders for King Benton's throne she alone possessed all of the necessary qualities to be a great leader. She was strong, she understood the art of politics better than anyone alive, and underneath all of her bluster she had the capacity to care for others. Still, she had one major liability: she was a woman who lived at a time when only men were permitted to rule. Yet even the prejudices of her time could not stop her indomitable spirit. Nothing could! For no impediment, small or large, ever stopped her from pursuing her ultimate objective, not even the small-minded chauvinistic biases of her elite contemporaries. She was bold, brazen, and willing to take on any man that dared to threaten her ambitions. It is perhaps my greatest failing, then, that I too was blinded by these very same narrow and inconsequential prejudices. For had I been more evolved, wiser, and yes more practical, I would have supported Bellazar's candidacy to the Arcanian throne.

Not everyone underestimated this great woman. Emblematic of King Benton's keen wisdom and high level of esteem for his favorite daughter-in-law, Bellazar was the only member of the royal family to be assigned her own private chamber. Furthermore, it was located in the castle's august southern wing, with a window view overlooking the city of Teta.

The Oracle

And King Benton's interest in his daughter-in-law did not end there, for on most units the king visited Bellazar's chamber or menagerie, as he liked to call it, for it contained an impressive collection of oddities his daughter in-law had collected in her many travels around the passra. Among the king's favorites were the Tellican jumping fish, which were the very first thing one noticed upon entering Bellazar's chamber. Displayed in a series of translucent tanks, one did not have to look inside to see the fish, for these were a rare and exotic breed of jumping fish, endogenous to the swampy Fens Swampland territory just west of Teta. In the wild they jumped from mud puddle to swamp, while in captivity they jumped from tank to tank, rarely missing their target by more than a fraction of an inch. The king loved to stand and watch the colorful fish as they skillfully vaulted from tank to tank, seemingly without rest.

While the jumping fish were the king's favorite, Bellazar's daughter, who had the rather strange name of Me, preferred the Anawana Yapyap, which looked like a cross between a poodle and a rabbit, with its bushy powder white tail behind it and its distinctive pink stained ears standing high on its head. It acquired the name Yapyap because of the irritating noise it made whenever it felt threatened, startled, excited, or merely hungry. While Yapyaps ran wild near the Anawana Swamplands in eastern Arcania, with hundreds, even thousands burrowing into the soft wet ground, this diminutive creature was rarely seen in captivity.

Another of Me's favorites was the Pirene cat, unusual in that its spots changed color depending on its mood. When angered the spots turned gray: when contented they turned a light shade of blue. Rather than meowing Pirene Cats made a soft clicking noise that some found soothing and others, like myself, considered as irritating as the sound of the infernal Yapyap. When the two animals mewed in harmony everyone agreed that it produced a most agonizing melody.

On the unit of King Benton's unfortunate collapse, with school at an end, Me sat quietly caressing the Pirene cat, waiting for its spots to change color. Moments later the cat contently accommodated its master, it spots transforming to a gentle and calming indigo. But strange as it might seem, Pirene cats were not the only creatures in Arcania that experienced such a remarkable external transmogrification, for the skin color of the people of Arcania also changed throughout their lives; most from white to yellow at about age 50, and then to green when they reached 70.

Me was a young girl of but eight cycles and as such her skin was alabaster white. When she reached puberty her skin would darken within a few weeks to a more pallid appearance. At about twenty cycles about one-tenth of the Arcanian population began to develop splotches all over their bodies, until within an interval or two, their skin transformed into a remarkable and robust jet-black sheen. Bellazar was one of these favored individuals with dark black skin, highly revered in Arcanian society.

It was yet another quality that contributed to her growing legend among the Arcanian people. She had lived a most remarkable life even before she became the king's favorite daughter-in-law. Born to a mere boat maker, she traveled Arcania widely when she was but a youth, learning to sail every inch of the Commeru River, even circumventing Lake Chill on her own at the tender age of eleven. In her early teens she traveled to the Kanaween Forest, with its giant Kanawa trees. There she learned to ride a ladatop, a primate standing twelve feet tall that one mounted like a horse and then rode from branch to branch and tree to tree. Ladatops could move through the dense forest at speeds of up to thirty miles per hour. Strapped to a ladatop's back, a soldier could travel hundreds of miles in a single day. Bellazar, with her enormous will to be the best at every endeavor, demonstrated her innate skill and fortitude by traveling over one hundred miles the very first time she mounted a ladatop, thus earning the respect of King Benton's soldiers and adding to her emergent reputation throughout Arcania.

Of course it did not hurt that she also was a striking beauty with a powerful, commanding presence. Her piercing green eyes and streaming red hair further accentuated an already hypnotic personality and when the king's third eldest son Rendrau first saw her, well for the sake of decency, let's just say he was instantly enchanted. She had come to his attention while he was traveling in the Kanaween Forest. He too, was known as one of the greatest ladatop riders in Arcania and was curious to meet this remarkable young woman. The first night, when the two dined together, Rendrau was completely overwhelmed by Bellazar's personal charms, her detailed knowledge of Arcania's geography, its military strategies, and the rich diversity of its ancient people. Talking to her that first night Rendrau realized that Bellazar would make an extraordinary political ally. Therefore, on that very first night, he openly declared his intention to marry Bellazar.

Bellazar could have merely refused, as women did have a significant voice on issues related to marriage, but she too was keenly aware of the potential advantages of a marriage to the king's third eldest son. While he was not the next in the line of succession, she understood that illness could quite unexpectedly elevate him to that position. She had watched disease carry away two of her own brothers, a sister and her mother. Thus, a marriage with Rendrau offered intriguing possibilities she simply could not resist. And while Rendrau was far from physically attractive, he was appealing in other more important ways. The two were therefore married within an interval of their first meeting and within a cycle Bellazar was pregnant with her first child, though he died in childbirth. In subsequent cycles they had four more children, all of whom died during the birthing or shortly thereafter from various childhood illnesses. It would be many cycles then before Me was born.

After Me's birth, Bellazar spent much joyous time raising her child, but she continued to keep her eyes fixed on state business, providing her husband with constant and useful advice whenever he requested it or whenever she believed it was needed. Most importantly, she watched and carefully mastered the art of politics. It quickly became apparent to all that Bellazar was the brains behind her husband's many diplomatic achievements. If some unit the monarchy should fall upon his shoulders, it was agreed that Bellazar would make a most welcome king's wife or Telenaka. Well it was agreed to by all but one. Pantamanu could not even stand the mention of his sister-in-law's name, though like all other males, he was enthralled with her many physical charms. And the feeling was mutual. While Bellazar could not help but admire, to put it politely, Pantamanu's splendid physical appearance, she considered him vapid, vulgar, and extremely dangerous, a direct challenge to her husband's reasonable ambitions.

So, as Me gently stroked the Pirene cat and as Bellazar sat nearby knitting, a habit that calmed her nerves and allowed her time to think, she heard the sounds of countless feet scurrying about in the outside halls, as children and wives were ordered to report immediately to their quarters. Earlier that morning, rumors had reached her that the passra had been placed on a state of high alert. Despite Valmar's attempts to keep the king's condition a secret, within but a few minutes of the king's collapse, word of Benton's illness circulated throughout the castle and within an hour the first nascent signs of instability were evident in the streets of Teta, mostly carried in the form of discreet whispers from individual to individual.

As Bellazar put down her needle and walked to her third story window, she noticed a most unusual level of commotion in the streets below. "This is odd," she noted. "Soldiers are everywhere on horseback." She carefully watched as the soldiers assumed strategic formations at various designated positions, both inside and outside the maze defense perimeter that prevented direct access to the castle. Further in the distance she watched the dispersal of carts and quickly identified other clues suggesting that something seriously was amiss. From her sources inside the castle she already knew that King Benton was ill. She now considered all the evidence and quickly concluded that the king's illness alone would not warrant a response of this magnitude. Only a continuing threat to the royal family would. Consequently, by the time Rendrau was escorted to Bellazar's chamber, as she again sat knitting in her favorite rocking chair, Bellazar had developed a well-framed hypothesis.

"I am relieved that you are well," she said with genuine warmth as Rendrau entered the room. "I gather that there has been an attack on the royal family?"

"What do you mean?" Rendrau asked, as usual startled by his wife's remarkable prescience.

Systematically, Bellazar provided the evidence for her theory. "I have noticed that the manner in which the soldiers are being deployed at neat intervals around the castle, the way they are dispersing carts and citizens from the byway, and the fact that we have been ordered to remain in our chambers. These actions are consistent with one of two occurrences: an attack on the king or an attack on one of his sons. Since I know already that the king is ill and heavily guarded, this suggests that something else has occurred. So who is in danger?" she concluded with a smug and satisfied smile.

"Pondru has vanished," Rendrau acknowledged sadly as he walked to his wife's side. As he meekly leaned over and kissed her right cheek he studied her reaction.

Bellazar nodded her head ever so slightly before responding, "Then you are one step closer to the throne."

"You have no remorse for my dear brother?" Rendrau asked, only slightly surprised by her cold and calculating manner.

"Of course," she said carefully without missing a stitch. Then staring directly at her husband with an intensity that had become all too familiar to him over the passing cycles, she added, "I have told you many times that you will be the next king. It is the will of the Oracle, I am sure of it."

Rendrau stood by silently. He knew what thoughts already possessed his wife's ambitions. With Pondru removed from the equation, only Retch remained as a direct obstacle to the throne. Bellazar readily understood that Retch could never be king. "He is far too weak and emotional," Bellazar had ventured on many occasions. So with Pondru removed, the throne now was veritably within her husband's reach.

"It is Pantamanu we must watch out for," she said with serene patience. Rocking her chair ever so gently, her active and logical mind already was formulating an ingenious and devious plan, one that would place her husband and herself one step closer to the Arcanian throne.

Chapter 10
Montama

Though Bellazar did not yet know it, Pantamanu was not the only serious rival for the Arcanian throne. There was in fact another and he came not from the royal family, but rather from one of Arcanians most trustworthy fiefdoms.

While Benton was the King of Arcania, a position of considerable power and authority, like his predecessors he depended on a highly decentralized leadership model to govern the daily affairs of the passra. The Centama family directly controlled only the central region of Arcania, while a series of thirty-two fiefdoms were carved out to govern the expanding rich farmlands in the east and the lush grazing lands to the west. A lord who was selected solely on the basis of one overriding criterion, his personal loyalty to the Centama family, then ruled each fiefdom.

Of these the most loyal of all lords was Tantamount, who ruled over the precious, resource rich lands in western Arcania bordering the Kanaween Forest, the site of the tallest trees in the world. As a reward for his loyalty and no doubt as a concession to the importance of the lands over which he ruled, Tantamount was permitted to marry Truellen, King Benton's third cousin and an important court insider. Together, Tantamount and Truellen raised two energetic boys, Hontallo and Montama.

My interest lay not with Tantamount, for he was a man of unimpeachable character, a man who simply could not be tempted by any vice, for his fealty to the royal family was genuine and unyielding. Truellen was a different story. Like Bellazar, her thoughts were driven purely by ambition, not for her own sake, but for those of her children. And that single inspirational spark was all that I needed to foment a plan that would lead to the overthrow of the Centama family.

My chance came when her youngest son, Montama, reached the age of ascension. He was a healthy young lad, with broad shoulders, tall and thin, yet awkwardly handsome, with piercing blue eyes and a look of quiet determination. His mind was inquisitive but not at all analytical. Like his father he also was loyal to a fault. Yet, his allegiance lay not with the royal Centama family, but with his own Tantamount dynasty. I sensed in him a desire to do anything possible to protect his family's lands and reputation. His love for his father was deep, but also largely unrequited, for his father was a cold man, unable to show his love or affection. Montama therefore felt a desperate need to impress his father. I considered his devotion to his family and his filial piety as twin weaknesses and I was determined to exploit them to the fullest possible advantage. Consequently, though the young boy did not know it, Montama and his devoted mother, Truellen, provided me with my best opportunity in many decades to rule Arcania and with it to finally to ride as master of the Oracle.

As for the tides of Arcanian politics, they too began to shift in a most unusual and unexpectedly amenable direction. Despite the apparent awe in which the people held King Benton, there was an underlying sense that change was required; after all, a Centama had ruled Arcania for more than a century.

So, in this uncertain political environment, Lord Tantamount called on his Privy Council to discuss the rumors that the king was ill and to determine what, if any appropriate response was warranted under the circumstances. The Lord's Council therefore met in its usual large oblong open-air theater: a most unusual example of Arcanian architecture. The structure was composed of thirty faceted and interlocking rectangular formations, each made entirely of telsa rock, which like glass was entirely transparent on one side, thus allowing a clear view of the exterior world from inside the chamber. What made telsa rock so unusual, however, was that the other side of the rock reflected light outward. Therefore, if someone was looking into the theater they could only see their own reflections, while participants inside could clearly identify each passing spectator. The theater also had no permanent roof, but could be closed to the elements on particularly cold units, such as the present one, by a moveable canvas like material that scrolled outward from four different apertures, joining securely at the fulcrum to make a temporary ceiling. Yellow parsa bricks, which retained heat, were then placed into several strategically located ovens within the structure to provide ample warmth for several hours.

As the meeting commenced, the leader of Lord Tantamount's Council was a strange little man named Timilty. He was short and stout, with a seemingly permanent scowl affixed to his face, flaming blue eyes, shoulder length gray hair that appeared to be permanently unkempt, and yellow skin that already had begun to show signs of turning prematurely green. His mind was deeply principled and he was above all else devoutly loyal to his lord. Timilty was a particularly unusual choice to head the Council because he was a Ka-Why-Tee, a minority group in Arcanian society because they were born with three arms and hands. The third arm was shorter than the others and extended directly from the middle of a Ka-Why-Tee's chest. It also had but three fingers surrounded by two thumbs, which to many people gave it the outward appearance of a claw.

Timilty reflected Tantamount's advanced views on the subject of integration. Throughout Arcania the Ka-Why-Tee generally were employed as mere laborers, where the extra arm and hand provided a distinct dexterous advantage. Because Ka-Why-Tees were consigned to this lowly station in life, most people believed they were less intelligent than other humans, although there was no objective evidence to support this commonly held prejudice. Not only did Tantamount treat Ka-Why-Tees as equals, but Timilty's rise to the height of power on the Lord's Council sent a tangible signal that Lord Tantamount did not countenance even the slightest hint of discrimination.

It was Timilty, with Lord Tantamount sitting in his accustomed raised seat overlooking the theater, who opened the Privy Council meeting just three units after it was learned that that the king was ill. Drawing upon the long shared history between the lord's great fiefdom and King Benton's family, Timilty, employing the histrionics of a skilled orator, warned his fellow council members, "Though the times may be perilous, we must continue our demonstration of good faith toward the Centama family. Only in this way will we prosper in the new age of leadership that is sure to come."

Most Privy Council members shared Timilty's assessment, but a few distant voices argued that since the king was ill, some form of preparation was warranted, especially, if as rumored, the specter of an ugly succession crisis hovered upon Arcania's political horizon. These few dissidents argued that Lord Tantamount's fiefdom was a particularly attractive target, with its lush grazing lands bordering the Kanaween Forest. They posited that a disloyal rogue lord might be tempted to dislodge Tantamount and seize his lands. It was a paranoia that I actively encouraged, visiting the weak minds of these individuals, usually during their dream state. I did not expect either Tantamount or Timilty to take their ravings seriously, for I had another audience in mind.

Lord Tantamount's youngest son, Montama, having just achieved his nineteenth birthcycle, was attending his first council meeting. Since this was his first opportunity to listen to the various council member's speak (as the Lord's son he was not allowed to address the council) the unfolding cacophony represented a rather rude political awakening for this politically naïve young man.

For years Montama had waited rather impatiently for his opportunity to become a member of his father's exalted council, only to discover at last that its illustrious members represented nothing more than a pompous, supercilious debating society. Montama was surprised that most Council members seemed unconcerned with the rumors of conflict between the Centama family heirs. To his youthful and politically uninformed mind it was obvious that peaceful restraint was about to give way to a period of abject chaos. As the son of a prominent lord, he also had heard from reliable sources that there were serious doubts about the king's eldest son's leadership capabilities. To young Montama, then, it was starkly apparent that the time was ripe for action and, of course, I did all that was in my power to encourage these paranoid thoughts.

The council's penchant for high rhetoric and low expectations further depressed and discouraged young Montama. As a result he turned for guidance to his brother, Hontallo (pronounced Hon-ta-yo), who sat next to Montama at the opposite end of the chamber from their father. Though Hontallo was used to the council's loquacious methods, he viscerally understood the reason for his brother's impatience and discontent. When he first had assumed his place on the council six cycles past, Hontallo too had been disconcerted by the council's apparent inactivity. In time he came to realize that the council did its business in accordance with his father's wishes. "Be patient," he gently reassured Montama. "Government works slowly, but it does work." For a short time Montama's mind was assuaged by this seemingly sage advice. However, as he listened to each successive speaker drone on endlessly and without a clear point of view, the young man's doubts ultimately re-emerged.

Montama's dissatisfaction steadily intensified until the fifth unit of the council's deliberations when a potentially disparate voice spoke for the first time. Grandafier the Elder, who had served with Lord Tantamount during the Bogul campaign almost thirty cycles past, was known as a great orator and a wise man. Standing with the aide of his bone white cane, at the plain wooden lectern where speakers addressed the conclave, Grandafier stared at his notes and then cast them aside, preferring instead to share his thoughts extemporaneously. Though his tall body was old and withered, his skin wrinkled and dark green with age, his voice remained strong and confident. With a smile that was both avuncular and wily, Grandafier proclaimed in a steady, booming voice, "Lord Tantamount, in his great wisdom, has asked his council for a recommendation. We have heard the unsettling and sad news from Teta. King Benton has been a great friend of ours and he has governed us well for almost forty cycles, leaving our passra more prosperous and secure than at any time in Arcania's long history." Leaning forward and lowering his voice slightly for dramatic effect, Grandafier continued, "Yet, if the news from Teta is reliable, and we have no reason to doubt its sincerity, Arcania may be about to enter a period of great tumult."

Grandafier now looked around the room and noticed that young Montama was entirely riveted, listening carefully to every word of his speech. The old man deferentially nodded his head at Montama and then continued, "With King Benton gravely ill, it is highly likely that a new king soon will be anointed and his intentions will be unknown to us for some time. Given the uncertain political and military circumstances, it is prudent that we discover what this new king's intentions are before it is too late. That means there is no time to lose. We must immediately prepare for any and all contingencies."

Until this juncture Timilty sat impassively, reading a paper that he held with his short third hand. At the mention of these last words, however, the head of the Lord's Council flinched palpably, as he nervously rubbed his chin with his right hand. Montama also reacted, for as I was delighted to see, his eyes were now wide open with anticipation. Montama asked himself, had Grandafier just pronounced himself in favor of militarily preparation? Glancing quickly to his side he noticed that Hontallo seemed to have nodded his head ever so slightly. Was it a sign that Hontallo agreed and if so, with which sentiment? Then Montana realized that the very terms Grandafier had used were so nebulous that they could be interpreted in many different ways. Preparation could mean military or diplomatic. Contingency could mean war or a peaceful transition. Montama again leaned forward, hoping that Grandafier would clarify his opinion. As the elderly man continued, it was clear that Grandafier was leaving the deeper meaning of his recommendation to the individual judgment of the various Council members.

While his advice was delivered confidently, Grandafier ardently refused to clarify his intent. When the old man finally delivered his summation and, as was customary, opened the floor for questions, he proved agonizingly adept at sidestepping precise queries with specific answers. "Contingencies means precisely what I say," he responded to one questioner. "We all know that there are many alternatives. This council has spent five units time in earnest debate. I need not bore you by repeating each alternative now." And when asked what he meant by preparations the elder statesman skillfully obfuscated yet again. "Is not my meaning plain?" His eyes exhibited but a trace of whimsy as he responded to yet another mildly exasperated questioner.

"What do you mean by prudent?" Timilty asked, trying to force Grandafier to be more specific.

"I would not presume that so learned a man as Timilty does not know the meaning of the word prudent," Grandafier responded, to considerable laughter from the assembled dignitaries. Timilty glared with a growing frustration, again nervously rubbing his chin, this time with his short third hand.

Montama was both mesmerized by Grandafier's political skill and exasperated by his inability to be pinned down on any specific detail. It took the young man awhile to realize that Grandafier spoke eloquently in generalities that could be interpreted anyway a particular listener preferred. Therefore, if one favored military action, his was a call to action. But if one favored only tepid diplomatic niceties, then Grandafier's was a call for continued deliberation.

"He is a skilled politician," Hontallo whispered surreptitiously, with a smile that betrayed both his admiration for the old man and his keen understanding that this was how one behaved if one wished to exert influence on the disparate council members. As such, Grandafier's speech was a revelation to young Montama. Montama reasoned that Grandafier could influence the council, but only to a certain extent. If he pressed his case for military action too stridently, the lackadaisical council members might ignore his otherwise sage advise. Therefore, if he was to exert any tangible influence whatsoever, Grandafier must use his rhetoric to raise the alarm and yet do so carefully.

Grandafier's appearance proved to be the highlight of the council's deliberations. For once he concluded his remarks, a further procession of undistinguished speakers continued unabated for the better part of three additional units time. "These are not radical people," Hontallo told his brother during one of the proceedings many breaks. "They are studiously cautious." And while all were legitimately concerned about the passra's future, most seemed unwilling to consider any other option than the status quo. Though Montama became adept at recognizing the nuance buried in long-winded speeches and discovered how words of praise could be used to attack an antagonist, he came to realize that the only form of combat the council members really understood was rhetoric itself.

By the eighth and final unit of the Council's deliberations, Montama fully understood that these men and women would never willingly consent to prepare for battle. Their wisdom, if they had any at all, had been forged in a time of peace. Montama was not like the members of his father's council. Secretly, he considered himself capable of bold action; a quality he sensed would be of incalculable value if he were to protect his beloved family and his dear father's strategically important lands. But precisely how could he do that? That was a question that dominated his thoughts as the council finally adjourned.

Chapter 11
An Adventure

Montama was and always had been a bit of a dreamer. A voracious reader, Montama was particularly fascinated by a series of adventure stories involving the archetypical hero, Captain Bale, who in each successive tale overcame impossible odds to achieve a remarkable and unexpected victory over his evil archenemy, the dastardly defiant Kelpec the Great. As a youth Montama not only assiduously read and re-read these books. With the assistance of Hontallo he acted them out, as well. In these dramatic recreations Montama always played heroic Captain Bale, with Hontallo reluctantly cast as the evil genius Kelpec who seemed to have but one utterly obsessive objective in mind, to conquer the world. Hontallo played this role with a decided lack of enthusiasm because he could never quite fathom why anyone would want to rule the world? Montama repeatedly told his hapless sibling, "Because that is what evil people want to do." Reflecting Captain Bale's simplistic worldview, to Montama it was readily apparent that evil exists and good people must do everything in their power to stop it. Yet, much to my advantage Montama had absolutely no facility whatsoever for recognizing evil, even when it was staring him directly in the eye. Rather, he had an innocent and childish conceptualization of the world.

These naïve political thoughts were very much on Montama's mind as his father's council adjourned after eight units of continuous, loquacious and pointless debate. Thoroughly disenchanted and impatient with the council's inability to act in a constructive and timely manner, young Montama took a long walk that led him predictably to one of his favorite private places, his father's private gardens, where he often sat contemplating various matters of a personal interest. As he did so on this particular unit, he wondered what Captain Bale would do in the present treacherous situation. "He would be bold!" the young lass concluded.

Whether he consciously admitted it or not, Montama secretly fantasized that if he was just given the chance he too could be like Captain Bale, capable of intrepid, selfless and heroic action. But as he took a seat on a hard, cold, white cement bench, and as his eye was drawn to one particular specie of plant, the hypnotic movement of his father's exotic dancing flowers, which shimmered like orange roses as they slid gracefully from side to side, Montama wondered if there were any heroes left in the real world. So fixed was Montama's attention upon this enchanting object and this one tantalizing subject that the young man failed to notice that he was being secretly watched from afar. In fact, he was unaware that Grandafier had been studying his every movement for at least the past three units.

Grandafier the Elder was always on the lookout for a young protégé who could vicariously advance his own political aspirations and young Montama perfectly fit the bill. "The boy is highly impressionable and could be made to do great things, with just the right mentor, that is," Grandafier decided, deftly employing his two most basic personal characteristics: his cunning and self-serving nature. And even though Grandafier had barely heard of Captain Bale and his evil nemesis Kelpec the Great, the elderly man fully understood the young man's inherent need for heroes, as well as his sense that it is a hero's duty to bring all villains quickly to heal. "I bet the boy fancies himself a hero," the old man astutely determined.

So, after surreptitiously watching the young man for some time, as Montama eyed the syncopated movement of the dancing flowers, with the aide of his bone white cane, Grandafier finally ambled unsteadily toward young Montama. The young man, completely lost in thought, was unaware that the elder statesman was approaching. Noticing the faraway look in Montama's eyes Grandafier called out in a pleasant voice, "Do you mind if an old man rests his weary bones on the bench beside you?"

Startled, his concentration abruptly shattered, Montama mildly prevaricated, "Not at all."

Wheezing and seeming nearly out of breath Grandafier took a seat on the bench next to Montama. Then, with his characteristic cheerfulness the elderly man confessed, "To be quite honest with you the dancing flowers make me feel a bit nauseous, with all their bobbing and weaving. I much prefer sedate plants like your father's ferns. They have the wisdom to do absolutely nothing at all for our amusement."

Montama made an awkward attempt to smile, though his mood was decidedly dark. In a soft unassuming voice he responded, "I find this to be one of the few places where I can sit quietly and think. The dancing flowers put my mind at ease. I like how they dance for their own pleasure, whether I'm here or not."

"A wise observation," Grandafier noted as he gently patted the young man's knee with the clammy palm of his wrinkled green right hand. "You take after your mother in that regard. How is she?"

Montama's mother, Truellen, had been seriously ill for some time and it had been several cycles since she had been seen in public. "She is doing as well as can be expected," Montama responded evasively. He then quickly changed the subject. "And how is your health? I notice that you now walk with the assistance of a cane."

Grandafier held his cane aloft, warmly admiring it. "Young man, my skin turned green more than twenty cycles past. They call me Grandafier the Elder and it is a title well earned. Truth be told, I was an old man when I served with your father in the last war, which was let me see, well it was before you were born. Now I wouldn't mind if they called me Grandafier the Wise or Grandafier the Magnificent. Those would be great names, but I am unworthy of both. No, the only moniker I have respectfully earned is

Grandafier the Elder and this cane is but the latest testament to it. I'm afraid that soon enough they will be calling me Grandafier the Dead, but I'm not eager to earn that distinction just yet."

"Your cane is beautiful," Montama said admiringly. "Where did you get it?"

Like most people his of his advanced age Grandafier loved to talk, particularly about himself. He handed the cane to Montama so that the young man could get a better look at it and then explained, "I got it during the war, when I served with your father in the Kanaween Forest campaign against the Boguls. Frankly speaking, I wasn't a very good soldier. I could never learn how to ride one of those damn ladatops from tree to tree. So, when the war was over, the men in my unit thought it might be amusing to give me this cane made entirely out of the leg bone of a fallen ladatop. They meant it as a practical joke, but I rather liked it and now that I am a bit older it comes in quite handy."

Montama held the cane aloft for a few seconds before returning it to Grandafier, who seemed as proud of his lack of military prowess as he was of his cane. "You have had an interesting life," Montama added as the old man coughed.

"Yes, I have, but I am more interested in your life," Grandafier said deftly, turning the conversation toward its intended target.

"What of it?" Montama added. "I have hardly had the time to live at all."

As his eyes twinkled, Grandafier cackled, "And that is what makes you so very interesting, Montama. You represent the future of Arcania. Your generation will lead our passra for I am afraid my generation lost its will to do so a long time ago." Montama nodded politely in resolute agreement, as Grandafier further re-directed the conversation toward Montama's opinions. Carefully, Grandafier said, "I notice that you carefully guard your thoughts, but I am a fine student of body language."

"What do you mean?" Montama asked, with his curiosity clearly peaked.

"Well first of all, I have learned that you don't think much of Timilty?"

"Why do you say that?" Montama asked, both defensively and surprised by Grandafier's acute sense of political acumen.

The old man smiled deviously. "I have noticed that when something displeases you your nostrils flare, ever so slightly."

"I didn't realize…" Montama responded, his attention now fixed completely on the elderly man.

The Oracle

"Oh no need to apologize," Grandafier laughed. "Your brother Hontallo has a habit of tapping his right index finger on his knee when he is displeased and he scratches the back of his neck when he is confused." Grandafier leaned toward Montama and in a more subdued voice added, "He has been scratching his neck a lot these past few units."

Montama was amazed by the old man's prophetic abilities. Appreciating that the old man had taken an interest in him, feeling very much alone and with no one else to whom he could confide his most precious thoughts, Montama suddenly felt an uncontrollable urge to share his opinions about the council with this wise elderly man. "May I speak my mind openly?" Montama asked tepidly.

Grandafier nodded, "That would be refreshing, to hear someone speak their mind, rather than always minding what they speak."

"Do you promise never to repeat what I have to say to anyone," Montama insisted defensively.

"And who would I tell it to?" Grandafier asked. "For though I am allowed the courtesy of expressing my views before the council, you must plainly see that they honor only my age and not my wisdom. To them I am a relic, quite possibly senile, tolerated but never respected."

Uncertain how to begin, Montama closed his eyes and took a deep breath before releasing his pent up rage. "I have listened to the council members talk and talk, and then talk some more, and I am convinced that none of them understand what the devil is really going on." Grandafier nodded ever so gently, physically encouraging the boy to share his passionate views. "Can't they see that war is inevitable? Retch is far too weak to be our next king and his brothers are far too ambitious. Isn't that obvious? And yet no one is willing to do a damn thing about it."

Grandafier responded quietly, "I understand your frustration."

With his blood now boiling, Montama could no longer contain his emotions. "Can't my father's council see that if the king dies my father's lands will become a ready target?"

Grandafier was a circumspect man, so he carefully chose his next words. "What is the council to do? Your father has no army and the council members are more afraid of arming our pathetic militia than they are of an external uprising."

"Then what can we do?" Montama asked desperately, his hands now veritably shaking as he spoke.

90

Grandafier again gently placed his hand on the young man's knee. "In time you will have an opportunity to speak frankly with your father, but I fear that he is no more willing to prepare for war than is his council." Then closing his eyes in deep contemplation, Grandafier acknowledged, "This will require a mighty army and at present there is none."

Montama realized that even the miraculous Captain Bale had the necessary advantage of a well-trained army. "Then we are doomed," the young man confessed, suddenly realizing the hopelessness of the present situation.

"No," Grandafier whispered, for he suddenly remembered something of a most extraordinary and peculiar nature. Grandafier now stared intently at his young protégé with a renewed sense of determination. In a quiet and intimate tone he said, "This may make me seem completely senile, but for the last three nights I have had a rather strange visitation in a dream." Montama's eyes widened, for visitations in dreams were an important means by which Arcanians divined the future. Speaking softly, lest anyone accidently overhear his words, Grandafier continued, "I was told by a strange and enchanting voice, that a young man, having just reached the age of ascension, would be called upon to raise and lead a mighty army, to defend our grand passra against all manner of treachery."

Astonished by Grandafier's revelation, Montama suddenly thought back to the previous night and a dream that I carefully had placed among his own subconscious thought patterns. As he remembered it he excitedly exclaimed, "I had the same dream last night!"

Grandafier sighed as he sat back uncomfortably on the hard, white bench. Then with much resolved the old man declared, "I believe that forces larger than life are at work here." Staring directly into Montama's passionate eyes Grandafier added, "I don't know why, but I also sense that there is one person who may be able to shed some light on these dreams. For the voice in my dream also told me that you must speak directly to your mother."

Montama looked quizzically at Grandafier for some time before he asked, "Why mother?"

"She knows of things, secrets…" Grandafier held his head with his left hand, and then added, "That is all that I remember of the dream."

Montama signified his approbation with a mere nod of his head. Then he thought, "This is all so strange, just like one of Captain Bale's amazing adventures."

Chapter 12
Truellen

Despite her advancing age and ill health, Truellen was still an astonishingly beautiful woman. Her facial features were delicate, like a rare, exotic bird. Particularly striking was her long and luscious green hair, which despite long standing rumors, was indeed quite natural in its appearance. Her eyes also pulsated with an emerald intensity. And like Bellazar, she was one of a small percentage of Arcanians with smooth and radiant black skin. In her youth her astounding beauty had attracted the fancy of young King Benton who just recently had assumed the Arcanian throne. Though she was his third cousin he seriously considered marrying her, though for reasons that were never publicly discussed, this arrangement proved entirely out of the question.

Though she never again discussed her relationship with King Benton, several cycles later she was rewarded with a highly coveted marriage to the king's close personal friend, Lord Tantamount, a tall and attractive man who recently lost his first wife in a riding accident. Steward to the largest and one of the richest fiefdoms in Arcania, Tantamount developed a loving relationship with Truellen that was further blessed with two adorable children. Still for all of her good fortune Truellen was known to succumb to occasional fits of deep depression. She never discussed the reason for her sadness. It was not the only secret that she carefully guarded from everyone, including her own husband.

Now nearing fifty, she had for almost a decade been confined largely to her bed. The doctors diagnosed her with a degenerative, muscular disease that slowly robbed her of the use of her legs. During this period Truellen became increasingly reclusive, first eschewing close friends, then later even her own family. As Montama entered his mother's room he therefore did not even know if she would be willing to receive him. Consequently, he was greatly relieved when she smiled effusively and asked, "Has the council concluded its business?"

Montama could not mask his sarcasm. "No mother, the council never concludes its business, because it never begins it."

"I see then that you have learned your first lesson in politics," Truellen said while warmly holding out her arms, actively encouraging her son's embrace. Montama dutifully hugged his mother and then sat next to her on the beautiful quilt, designed with images of orange and yellow wild flowers, knitted especially for her by Bellazar.

Montama gently put three of his fingers across his mother's forehead. "You're a little warm," he said with genuine concern.

"I get that way during the afternoon," Truellen responded stoically. Then with a broad and inviting smile she asked, "I can see that something other than council business is on your mind."

"Is it that obvious?" Montama asked.

"Only to a mother," Truellen noted wryly, propping herself up into a seated position by leaning against three enormously oversized pillows.

Temporarily tongue tied, and never particularly articulate even in the best of circumstances, Montama was unsure how to proceed. So as is common for a youth of his age, he simply blurted out his thoughts. "Mother, I have come to ask for your advice. I don't know how much you know about what is going on in Teta, but King Benton is very ill."

Truellen stared firmly at her son. "I am a prisoner in my own house, but I do hear of such things," she said while primping one of the pillows with her right hand, trying to soften it up a bit.

"What do you think will happen?" Montama asked innocently.

Truellen was known for her forthrightness and demonstrated it anew. "I think that the passra is in grave danger."

"Why?" Montama asked, almost begging his mother to be more frank.

"Because your cousin Retch is not fit to be king."

Truellen was even more direct than Montama expected. Lowering his head and speaking softly Montama commented sadly, "Father's council does not agree with you."

"That is hardly a surprise," Truellen exclaimed with a smirk. "There is not one among them, save poor old Grandafier, who can be counted on to speak their mind."

"It is Grandafier who told me to come to you," Montama confessed, looking into his mother's eyes to see how she would react.

Truellen now lovingly stroked her young son's jet-black hair. "And why did he do that?"

Montama felt foolish relating the dream of an old man to his mother. So instead of looking at her, his eyes wandered to the floor. In a hushed and embarrassed tone he mumbled, "He says he had a visitation the last three nights. A dream that a young man like me will lead a mighty army." After a short pause Montama confessed, "I too had the same dream last night."

The Oracle

Truellen had guarded one of her greatest secrets longer than Montama had been alive. She now realized that it was time for truth telling. "There is something I must tell you."

Montama's deep blue eyes widened as he stared intently at his mother's face. "What is it?" he asked with an intense curiosity.

Truellen reached over onto her nearby nightstand for a handkerchief and then clutched it so tightly that her knuckles turned pale. Sitting upright against her giant pillows, she exhaled tangibly before commencing, "I have guarded a secret for more than twenty cycles. I now believe you have a right to know what the Oracle told me."

"The Oracle?" Montama asked, as his eyes opened wide with amazement.

Truellen nodded her head thoughtfully. "Many years ago I was engaged to King Benton. For reasons that are no longer important, that marriage never took place. Instead, I married your father. We were wed at the King's Castle and as a wedding gift the king allowed me to consult with the Oracle, but only if I promised to never reveal what the Oracle told me, to him or anyone else. I have kept that sacred pledge, until now."

Montama stared at his mother with such intensity that nothing else in the world seemed to exist. His eyes were wide with wonder and his heart beat so palpably that it could almost be heard.

"The Oracle told me that I would have two sons and that they would both grow up to be strong and healthy men." Tears now began to stream down Truellen's face, and she felt a lump in her throat so palpable that it temporarily impeded her ability to speak. Montama reached over and gently felt the tears on his mother's face.

Struggling to contain her emotions, lest she lose the will to finally share her secret with her youngest son, Truellen continued. "The Oracle told me something else. It said that my second born son would be king of Arcania."

"What?" Montama exclaimed.

"The Oracle also said you will lead a mighty army," Truellen said quietly, so exhausted by her ordeal that she gently closed her eyes and instantaneously fell into a deep sleep. Montama placed his hand on his mother's forehead. He then sat with her for some time, wondering how his mother had the internal fortitude to conceal such a momentous secret. Then he wondered aloud, "Why, of all the people in Arcania, would the Oracle choose me to be king?"

Chapter 13
Lord Tantamount

After sitting by his mother's bedside for almost half an hour, Montama finally strolled slowly down the long corridor toward his father's private study. Ordinarily the young man would have been utterly oblivious to the various items that adorned the great corridor's walls. Now sensing that his life was about to change irrevocably, he stopped to peruse the various portraits, awards, and other memorabilia that marked his father's impressive life. He noticed a pencil drawing of his father, apparently drawn when the lord was but a boy of seven. Montama stared intently at the picture for some time, noticing how serious his father looked, even then. Further along there was a painting of the lord when he was about Montama's present age. Again, while he looked regal in appearance, there was no sign of a smile. "He looks so serious, so intense," Montama observed.

After staring again at the pencil drawing for some time, Montama could see that even as a child his father exhibited the qualities of a great and stoic man. And this hallway was a ready testament to his father's courage, filled as it was with framed dispensations from the royal family, personal letters from the king, and honors earned both during battle and peacetime. As Montama carefully scanned the walls he realized anew that his father had lived a most remarkable life. "I can never be his equal," he solemnly thought, before turning his attention to a final family portrait hanging prominently at the end of the hall. Admiring the artistry of the deep oil colored tapestry, Montama suddenly realized, "He smiles!" Surrounded by his loving family, with a very young Hontallo seated proudly upon his father's lap, Lord Tantamount was actually smiling. Montama had glanced at the portrait countless times before, but it was as if he was now looking at it for the first time. Almost caressing his father's smile with the gentle stroke of an extended finger, Montama whispered, "I love my family. I will do anything I can to protect them."

It was then that Montama's concentration was broken by a voice calling out to him from the end of the corridor. "Do you plan to loaf about all unit long?" Abruptly turning his head, Montama noticed that his older brother Hontallo was smiling deviously as he merrily proclaimed, "Father wants you to join us in his study."

"Join us?" Montama asked quizzically.

"We are going to discuss council business," Hontallo responded. "If I am not mistaken you have reached the age of ascension." Now smiling broadly Hontallo added, "That honor comes with a curse. You have to attend lots and lots of meetings."

So fixed was Montama on his inner thoughts that it took him a few seconds before he realized that his brother was mocking him. Defensively Montama stated, "Haven't I attended enough meetings already?"

Hontallo walked over to his brother and put his arm around Montama's shoulder. Together, the two young men strode cheerfully to their father's study where Lord Tantamount sternly awaited them. Sounding entirely irritated, the lord declared, "Montama, what are you doing here? Your brother and I have business to discuss."

Montama did not know what to say, until he noticed the renewed broad smile on his brother's face. "I have come to attend yet another meeting," Montama said, his face now equally as stern as his father's own.

Lord Tantamount walked directly toward his son with a grim and determined look. Staring directly into his son's eyes, the proud father exclaimed. "So you have reached the age of ascension and wish to provide counsel to your father?"

"Yes sir," Montama responded with all seriousness.

"Well, what makes you think that a boy of nineteen has anything to say that his father would want to hear?" The Lord spoke without even the slightest trace of humor.

"I don't know father," Montama calmly confessed.

Tantamount gently touched his son's shoulder and then added with as much warmth as he was capable of expressing, "Welcome!" Then putting a second hand on Montama's other shoulder he added, "We have work to do."

Montama was surprised by even such a tepid demonstration of affection from his father. He was deeply touched, if not by the tone, then by the spirit of the lord's heartfelt welcome. "Thank you father," Montama said softly, his voice quivering slightly as he spoke.

The lord patted both of his son's shoulders then added, "Now, let us get down to business." Tantamount turned and walked toward the large desk constructed entirely of green and yellow Kanawa wood from the nearby Kanaween Forest. As he sat in the great leather chair behind his desk, Lord Tantamount nodded his head then stated, "Montama, I was just telling Hontallo that we are fortunate to be living in times of peace, for I remember the last war. The Boguls invaded from the mainland intent on burning the Kanaween Forest to the ground. The king himself led the counterattack. I rode by his side and though the battle was brief, many brave men and women were lost. I personally lost two of my very dearest friends." Tantamount stopped, clearing his throat, lest he express more emotion than he intended. He then continued, "I should never want to see war visited upon our lands again." Hontallo did not say a word, but rather sat quietly in a rocking chair near the window, looking out over the entrance to the lord's estate, with the grand garden nearby. Rocking his chair gently as he listened attentively, he heard his father declare, "War is an abomination. It is to be avoided at all costs."

Montama chose this time to interrupt his father's musings. "But how, sir, is war to be avoided, if we cannot chose if and when it comes?" Tantamount looked up at his youngest son as Montama continued, "I am sure that the Boguls didn't tell you that they were coming."

The lord nodded his head and then admitted, "They did not send an invitation, if that is what you mean. And yes, sometimes wars must be fought." Looking over at Hontallo and then back at Montama the lord added emphatically, "But there are times when war is not inevitable. Then we can choose to avoid it?"

Montama interjected, "Is that true of the present circumstances father or must we heed Grandafier's advice and prepare for all contingencies."

Enthusiastically, Hontallo added, "Yes, that does seem like wise counsel."

Tantamount, nervously scratched his right ear before conceding, "Grandafier is a wise man, but realistically the only way we can prepare for war is to petition the government in Teta and ask the king for military assistance. Yet at present I see no sign of disaffection that would justify such an act."

"There are rumors from Teta…" Montama briefly interjected, before his father summarily and firmly responded.

"There are always rumors, my young son." Now leaning back in his chair Tantamount declared, "I cannot act on the basis of mere rumor. No, for me to petition the king, while he is ill and indisposed, would send a very clear signal that there is discord among our own people."

Hontallo agreed. "It would send a signal that father's house is not in order."

Nodding his head enthusiastically Tantamount added, "And it would serve no purpose other than to question the validity of our own authority."

Montama could not argue with his father's logic, so he adopted a second tactic. "But father, let me play the advocate's role here." Pensively and still standing obediently before his father, Montama continued, "Suppose that the king is ill and his four sons are in a state of discord. Other lords less loyal than you will no doubt be tempted to take advantage of that situation. If we were to quietly begin preparing ourselves would that not be a sign of our deepest fealty to the king and his government."

"A loyal friend ready to come to the aide of the king," Hontallo added enthusiastically.

Tantamount slowly nodded his head, contemplating Montama's suggestion. "Possibly," the proud father responded at last. "But now is not the time."

"Why?" Montama asked clearly disconcerted.

"Because we do not yet know if the rumors are true." Tantamount was at heart a careful man and his caution long had served him well. "If we prepare militarily and the rumors are not true, then by our very own carelessness we may inadvertently provoke a rebellion."

Montama could find no reason to argue with his father's impeccable logic. "Then it is best to wait?" he asked uncertainly, clearly disappointed by this verdict.

"One never loses a thing by being patient," Tantamount added. "In time we will learn in greater detail what really transpires at Teta. Only then will we know which is the best course of action."

For just a second Montama thought about telling his father about the Oracle's prophesy, but he was unsure of himself and determined to protect his mother's secret. More significantly, Montama simply could not find the strength to defy his father. He therefore meekly conceded, "I hope you're right, father."

"As do I," Tantamount added with a firm pronouncement that signified that the meeting was adjourned.

Chapter 14
The Letter

Arcania's religion had no name. All that was required was simply to declare, "I believe." "The believers" had certain core values that were simply beyond the realm of discussion or debate. To empirically minded Arcanians, only that which could be experienced, studied, or analyzed actually existed. Consequently, certain beliefs that are entirely common in other societies were totally unknown to Arcanians, such as the belief that there was life after death or that spirits ruled the heavens.

For a millennium the idea that life ended irreparably at the point of death represented an unassailable certitude. This rigid empirical belief system was shattered by the arrival of the enigmatic Oracle and its remarkably mysterious properties. The Oracle not only exerted a profound impact on the passra's governance, it also unleashed an intellectual revolution, one that greatly threatened the core beliefs and stature of the High Clerics of Kekanova, the leaders of Arcania's religious hierarchy.

Despite the repeated warnings of the High Clerics, public attitudes incrementally changed, eventually dramatically and irrevocably, once Arcanians learned about the Oracle's amazing properties. The miraculous tales from Leonata's astonishing military victory over General Tampinco and the great Army of Relatania first challenged the Arcanian idea that there was a logical and empirical solution to every problem. When citizens learned of the details of the battle, they were apt to respond, "That is impossible" or "Such things simply cannot exist." When they learned that the king heard voices, they assumed that he suffered from some incurable form of schizophrenia.

Over time, however, as the passra's infertile lands were transformed into rich farm land, as the quality of the people's lives dramatically improved, and as a period of almost uninterrupted peace prevailed, the populace became more accepting of the tales of the Oracle's mighty deeds. As a result, many people openly questioned the very assumptions upon which their religion and traditions were based. This in turn threatened the legitimacy and the previously unquestioned authority of the High Clerics, many of whom vehemently denounced the Oracle, secretly calling on an army of righteous believers to seize and destroy this dangerous device.

Nimrod found it impossible to believe that anyone would be motivated to destroy the Oracle. "These truly are barbarians," he opined.

"I prefer to think of them as malleable, capable of being reshaped and reformed into something new and different," Belicki said with his usual devious smile. "Their barbaric beliefs perfectly suited my purposes and I was the first to encourage the High Cleric's dissent, for any disagreement, no matter what the source, perfectly served my interests." Belicki smiled again, then continued.

Among the members of this shadowy group was High Cleric Rendella, the "priest exemplar," the very highest-ranking official in the only sanctified church of Teta. Though he appeared outwardly open-minded, Rendella regularly attended secret meetings where the Oracle was the subject of much vituperative debate and interpretation. While this opposition movement purposely maintained a low public profile, as of late they had acquired an important ally, an individual with powerful political connections to the royal family. High Cleric Rendella therefore was neither surprised nor alarmed as he greeted Bellazar at the sanctified, orthodox Addarrel Cathedral, located not more than a few blocks from the maze entrance to the King's castle.

"Please have a seat my dear," Rendella added in his usual soft but somber voice, which he rarely raised above a whisper.

Rendella was not only the High Cleric assigned to the prestigious Lectra of Teta, roughly the equivalent of a diocese, he also was the personal cleric to the royal family. In time he developed a close personal relationship with several of the Centamas, but none more so than Bellazar, who confessed that she was a devout believer. She often visited Rendella's office unannounced for impromptu conversations about religious matters or even issues of a more personal nature. On this particular unit, however, having bribed several guards in order to secure her temporary release from the castle, she had more important matters of state on her mind.

"Thank you," Bellazar said as she nodded politely before sitting down in Rendella's office. "To be honest, it is such a relief to be out of the castle. It has been more than a fortnight now since the king took ill."

As the cleric sat in his favorite high-backed leather bound chair across from his honored guest he asked, "And how is the king?"

A balcaba or aide to the High Cleric, who sometimes delivers sermons in his place, entered the room with two cups of tea. Bellazar merely acknowledged him with a curt glance before accepting the teacup. "Frankly, the doctors are mystified," she said.

"Why?" the clergyman asked as the balcaba discreetly closed the chamber doors as he exited the room.

Bellazar sipped her tea then responded, "The king has had neither food nor drink since he collapsed."

The High Cleric was veritably stunned by this remarkable revelation. "How is that possible? Surely he would have died by now."

Bellazar again sipped her tea then complemented the High Cleric on its quality before responding, "There are some who believe that the Oracle will not let him die. Already there are insidious rumors that it will never surrender the throne to his son Retch." Rendella shook his head in disbelief. "That is why I have come to see you today," Bellazar said, leaning forward to impart information of a personal and discreet nature. "His sons fear that the Oracle has a terrible hold over their father. But, Retch alone believes that the Oracle must be destroyed, a sentiment I whole heartedly share, as I believe do you."

High Cleric Rendella sat pensively, conflicted and uncertain how to respond. Tentatively he asked, "What can I do to help?"

Bellazar now reached into her purse and removed a carefully folded letter. She handed it to the High Cleric. "This letter was written by Retch. You will no doubt recognize the stamp of the family insignia." Rendella took the letter and read it carefully. As he did his eyes occasionally widened with elevated concern. Bellazar now spoke with intense conviction. "Retch can not leave the castle without attracting considerable attention. Therefore he personally directed me to ask for your help."

Putting the letter in his lap the cleric noted, "This is astonishing!"

"Then you will help us?" she asked with such sincerity that the cleric felt his heart rend.

Rendella thought carefully for a moment. Then as he stared intently at Bellazar he revealed, "I am to speak tomorrow to a gathering of the passra's High Clerics. I will read this letter to them and ask for their support."

To show her solidarity for the High Cleric, Bellazar added, "I will never forget this. You are a trusted friend and I will make sure that you are rewarded."

Rendella smiled and added, "It is an honor enough to serve the Centama family at a time of such great need."

Chapter 15
Long Live the King

Events now began to move quickly and much to my benefit. Less than an hour after he concluded his remarks to the conclave of High Clerics,

The Oracle

word leaked to the citizens of Teta that Priest Exemplar Rendella had read a letter from Regent Retch, testifying that the Oracle, artificially and unnaturally, was maintaining the life of the king. It also revealed that the heir to the throne intended to destroy the Oracle, for he believed it was possessed by evil demons bent on preventing him from assuming the mantle of power.

While the leak's source was never discovered, the revelation immediately sent shock waves throughout the panic stricken streets of the capital city. Initially in hushed tones, citizens told one another, "The Regent intends to destroy the Oracle." The response was almost always the same. "The Oracle is all that protects us from the Relatin Empire. How will we survive without it?" Others commented on the passra's flourishing economy and said they did not want to return to the way things used to be before the Oracle was brought to Arcania.

Then during mid-afternoon another savage rumor emerged. The Oracle will not let the king die because Retch is not fit to be king. Until this moment doubts about Retch's qualifications had been expressed merely in hushed whispers, usually in small clandestine groups. With this latest revelation, however, the streets of Teta were suddenly filled with men, cloaked in darkness, delivering handbills that proclaimed that Retch must be killed, lest he destroy the Oracle and with it Arcanian peace and prosperity.

Instantaneously, angry crowds emerged from the shadows ominously chanting, "Death to the Regent." Men carrying oversized clubs violently smashed the windows of stores, while others looted a nearby bookstore, severely injuring the proprietor and his wife in the process. A few minutes later another gang burned the Chief Magistrate's office to the ground, defiantly chanting "Death to the Regent!"

Ensconced in his private study, consumed as usual with the tedious minutiae of daily administration, Lord Valmar was unaware of these events for at least three critical hours. When one of his spies finally alerted him to the seemingly spontaneous street tumult, Valmar instantaneously realized that events were now thoroughly out of control. When he read the handbill purportedly containing the details of Retch's private letter to Rendella he scoffed, "This is not Retch's style of writing. Even the spelling is correct!"

The spy added, "The handbills are being distributed throughout Teta."

"Who is responsible?" Valmar demanded. The spy had no answer. Valmar dropped the handbill on the floor then with a sad shrug of his shoulders, he reluctantly admitted, "We have run out of time." Rushing past the spy Valmar charged across the foyer, up the winding main staircase to the third floor, then past the hall of mirrors to Retch's private room. By the time he arrived his unsightly wig tilted so precariously to the left that it was barely attached to his head at all. "Where is the regent?" he shouted at the maid who opened the door.

"I will get him," she replied with a polite curtsy.

A few seconds later Retch arrived at the door, having just awakened from his afternoon nap. "What is it?" he asked as he yawned expressively.

"You must come with me at once," Valmar responded curtly. From the expression on Valmar's face Retch instantly understood that something was terribly amiss. Uncertain and suddenly quite afraid, Retch followed the lord down the hall to a small private room. Once inside Valmar slammed the door shut and secured the lock. Then in a commanding voice the lord exclaimed, "Rendella read a letter to the High Clerics. He claims that you wrote it. The letter calls for the destruction of Oracle."

"My word!" Retch responded, visibly shocked.

"Now the streets are filled with rabble rousers calling for your head. I suggest we call out the soldiers immediately and deploy them openly in the streets." Valmar was finally showing the sort of decisiveness for which his reputation long ago had been forged. In contrast, Retch appeared dumbstruck, uncertain what to say or do. "There is one other thing that we must do immediately," Valmar said resolutely. Again Retch stood silently, waiting to be told what to do. He was horrified when he heard, "The king can no longer be allowed to languish. He must die now or you will never be king."

With his face contorted with terror, Retch stared fiercely at Lord Valmar. "What are you suggesting?"

Valmar could hardly believe that he was speaking these words. "The people are being told that the Oracle is artificially maintaining your father's life because it does not trust in your abilities. We must show them that this rumor is not true. The only way we can do that is to kill the king." Retch violently shook his head in protest, as Valmar put his arm around the regent's shoulder. He then continued, "Your father is already dead. We do him a favor by putting him out of his misery." Retch scanned the room for a chair and then wearily sat down, tears streaming profusely down both sides of his cheeks. Valmar kneeled next to Retch. "My dear boy, you must compose yourself. In a few moments you are going to be king."

The Oracle

Retch's voice trembled uncontrollably but he was able to mumble only a few barely coherent words. "How is father to die?"

This would be a most difficult task and Lord Valmar knew it. "We must go to the king's chamber now, ask the guards, doctors and nurses to leave the room so that you may have a few moments alone with your father, and when they are gone, we must take a pillow and put it over your father's face." Valmar was barely able to finish the sentence.

"Why must I go with you?" Retch asked pitiably. "Can't you do this alone?"

"The Oracle will never let me kill the king," Valmar exclaimed. "But I sense that it is testing you, to see if you have the strength to be Arcania's next monarch."

When Retch hesitated, Valmar emphatically declared, "We must go now. Time is running out."

"I can't," Retch pleaded, so terrified that Valmar feared the heir to the throne might soon faint.

"YOU MUST!" Valmar insisted, now veritably tugging on Retch's arm, pulling him out of the tiny room and back into the corridor.

In a stupor Retch accompanied Valmar down the long hall past various maids and guards to the king's private chamber. After dismissing the staff and as they entered the king's chamber, Valmar finally secured a clear view outside the king's own window. As he watched horrified, he saw smoke simultaneously rising from several different locations. "We have precious little time," he whispered, still firmly holding Retch's left arm.

Valmar and Retch moved quickly to the king's bedside. There, as he had for sixteen units, the king lay peacefully, his breathing uneven. Retch stared at his father. "I can't do this," he shrieked pathetically.

"We have no choice," Valmar said as he took hold of Retch's hand. As Valmar stared into Retch's blood shot eyes, he could see that the king's eldest son was nearing the emotional breaking point. So fixed was Valmar's attention on the heir to the throne that he almost forgot that he had come to the king's private chamber to commit the most unpardonable of all sins: to take the life of a man that he had loved more than his own father, a man that he had served loyally for four decades, a man that he had trusted with his own life on more than one occasion. Had Valmar contemplated any of these particular thoughts it is likely that he would never have been able to do what he knew in his heart and soul must be done. For his mind was firmly fixed on the goal of saving the Centama dynasty from a ruinous rebellion.

Valmar therefore avoided making eye contact with his beloved king. With firmness of spirit and total resolve, the lord guided Retch's hands to a large oblong shaped pillow that lay next to the king's head. Then, ever so slowly the two men lifted the pillow until it was directly above the king's face. Valmar's resolve nearly dissolved when he whispered in a barely audible voice, "Please forgive us."

Retch's body shook with a palsied frenzy, as the two men deliberately lowered the pillow until it completely covered the king's face. The king exhibited no sign of resistance, for he lay inert, as if he already were dead. The two men did not speak a word, as they pushed down hard on the pillow for several long seconds until they were absolutely sure that the king must be dead. When they removed the pillow, Valmar bent over and placed his head on King Benton's chest. "He is no longer breathing," he exclaimed, in a strangely unemotional tone of voice.

Instantly, Retch's body trembled uncontrollably as he fell forward onto his father's bed. Utterly inconsolable, he assumed a puerile fetal position, hugging his father so tight that their two bodies became indistinguishably intertwined.

Valmar watched Retch's reaction with a sense of abject horror. Still, he had to quickly compose himself, for he knew that his task was not yet completed. He must now oversee the immediate coronation of the new king. His heart then was seized with an inner rage as he shouted, "I will make that bastard Rendella pay for this sin. He alone shall administer the oath to the new king. Then he will pay with his life for this abominable crime."

Hearing the commotion from the hall, a young maid, two nurses, the king's physician and a guard abruptly rushed into the room. They instantly realized that the king was dead. In a voice so loud and shrill that it could be heard all the way down the long hall outside the king's chamber, a lone maid exclaimed, "The king is dead. Long live the king!"

Chapter 16
Retribution

The Oracle

From several separate spiral columns, thick plumes of black smoke rose high above the city of Teta, congealing into a massive smog-like cloud that menacingly obscured the carvings on the great rock face of Mt. Delba, totally obliterating the memories of the great Centama family.

From her third-story castle window Bellazar witnessed the specter of mass pandemonium in the streets. Dark figures, wearing hoods over their heads, carried torches and set fire to the Royal Academy building, a tangible monument to Retch's intellectual credentials. The sounds from the street were equally frightening. Mobs maliciously chanted, "Save the Oracle" and "Death to the Regent" while other voices cried out in horror, the obvious victims of a mindless and treacherous mob.

Rendrau also glared out at the streets of Teta, fully aware that the entire spectacle had been carefully orchestrated, for indeed he was one of the instigators of this plot. Still, as he watched the bitter mobs unleash their pent up rage, he began to have second thoughts. Without looking over at his wife, who had returned to her favorite knitting chair, Rendrau solemnly noted, "It may be easier to arouse the people's passions than it is to satisfy them."

Bellazar was not akin to second thoughts. Once she devised a plan her entire focus was on making sure that it was implemented precisely as ordered. She was aware of the risks involved in any political endeavor, but to her mind great risk also offered the potential for greater political benefits. As she picked up her knitting needle, she too heard the cries from the streets. "We have given them a slogan to chant and something easy to hate. Let them have their fun. They will soon tire of it. If not, then Pantamanu will have to uphold his part of the bargain."

Pantamanu stood only a few feet away, his concentration entirely fixed, not on the growing tumult in the streets outside, but on the systematic rhythm of the Tellican jumping fish. "Do they ever miss?" he asked, referring to their uncanny ability to leap repeatedly from tank to tank.

"Every once in while," Bellazar responded. "We found one on the floor a couple of cycles ago."

Rendrau could not understand how his wife and brother could stand by so tranquilly at a moment of such potential danger to the entire Centama family, for to his mind there was no guarantee that the mob would be satisfied with simply calling for Retch's head. As he peered out over the city of Teta, several men carrying torches set fire to the cathedral. Rendrau watched impassively as this testament to reason hastily burned to the ground. Without taking his eyes off the fiery conflagration, Rendrau noted, "You know they aren't a mere spigot that you can simply turn on and off at will."

"Are you talking about the fish or the people?" Pantamanu coyly responded, his eyes not once moving from the hypnotic delight of the jumping fish.

Bellazar laughed, for she had precisely the same reaction to her husband's comment. Stitching quickly and with her usual exquisite precision, she again tried to calm her husband's frayed nerves. "Don't worry dear Rendrau. We required the people to rebel for a while and they have done our bidding quite nicely. Now let them have their fun."

Rendrau glared back at his younger brother and in a most foul mood asked, "How long is this spontaneous rebellion to go on?"

Pantamanu sighed for he had absolutely no patience whatsoever with his brother's irritating reservations. Though he detested Bellazar, and while at first he was most reluctant to join in this unholy trilogy, he now admired her calm determination and immaculate poise under fire. Barely containing his famously prodigious temper he responded as calmly as he could, "As long as it is necessary brother."

Rendrau was not in the least mollified. "And what if Valmar sends out the troops?"

"They are loyal to us," Bellazar said, putting her knitting needle down and patiently explaining the situation once again to her dull-witted husband. "We have been over this many times, my dear. We control the army and we are sure that once rattled both Valmar and Retch will do precisely the wrong thing."

"It is a damn big risk if you ask me," Rendrau declared, nervously tapping his finger on the windowsill, an act that thoroughly annoyed Pantamanu.

"One does not drive the heir to the throne from power without taking some measure of risk," Bellazar patiently counselled. "We must show that he is utterly unfit, that he has lost the support of the people, that in short, we must step in to provide stability." Then she added, "Besides, the people will do what we tell them to do, whether they realize it or not."

Rendrau was a direct man, uncomfortable with the high arts of political intrigue. He much preferred a frontal attack or what he considered a fair game. But he also realized that there were times when treachery was required. "I hope you are right dear," he finally conceded, submissive words that drove Pantamanu to roll his eyes in total disgust.

Before Rendrau could say another word, there was a sudden knock on the door. The visitor was Dr. Vajadrray, the king's personal physician, who stood nervously awaiting permission to enter. When it was granted he asked a maid, "May I speak to your mistress?" Like an adolescent Pantamanu laughed at the doctor's use of the word mistress and its double meaning.

"Come in doctor," Bellazar called out in a loud distinctive but calm voice from her favorite rocking chair.

Dr. Vajadrray stood barely four feet tall, with dark black skin, and intense flaming golden eyes. He had served as the king's physician for more than twenty cycles and he was also a close trusted associate of Bellazar and Rendrau. As he entered the room he bowed formally before Bellazar before turning and offering the same gracious gesture to Rendrau. When he spotted Pantamanu out of the corner of his eye he turned and bowed deferentially for yet a third time.

Completely oblivious to his pleasantries Bellazar asked, "Do you have any news for us?"

The doctor bowed politely yet again and then in a quiet and respectful voice noted, "Lord Valmar and the regent arrived at the king's chambers a few minutes ago. They asked everyone to leave the room. A maid who was hiding behind the curtain saw what happened next. The lord and the regent held a pillow over the king's face until he was no longer breathing. Then, when they were sure that the king was dead, the regent cried most pitiably. He climbed into bed and hugged his father. We had a devil of a time getting him out of the king's bed. He was clutching the king with both hands and he simply would not let go."

"Where are they now?" Pantamanu asked abruptly.

"The lord is on his way to the throne room," Doctor Vajadrray continued. "They are going to complete the coronation ceremony as quickly as they can get a cleric to administer the oath."

"Thank you, doctor, you are excused," Bellazar instructed. Dr. Vajadrray bowed deferentially three more times, then turned and unobtrusively exited the room. "Well?" Bellazar asked.

Pantamanu was the first to speak. "He has murdered the king. I should think that is grounds for us to intervene."

"A plot against the king," Bellazar purred delightedly. "Not unexpected. If he can seize power quickly he can assuage the crowds by declaring that there is a new king. He can even blame the rabble rousers for killing King Benton."

"And establish sympathy for the new king throughout the passra," Rendrau interjected, nodding his head in admiration.

"Well then Lord Valmar is smarter than we give him credit," Pantamanu added. "Except we know what he is up to and we can stop him."

"You must stop him!" Bellazar added with great emphasis. "Go now! Stop this unholy coronation before he has a chance to undo all of the good that we have done."

Rendrau leaned over and kissed Bellazar on her cheek, an act that further irritated Pantamanu, who was in a mood for only one thing; to carry out swift and terrible vengeance against Lord Valmar and his sniveling brother Retch. The two brothers moved swiftly into the corridor where they rudely pushed the guards aside. They ran at full throttle down the hall to the spiral staircase that led from the private quarters on the third floor, down to the first floor where the king's throne room was located. It took the two brothers less than two minutes to cover the distance. When they arrived, Rendrau was nearly breathless.

"Why the haste?" Pantamanu shouted angrily from the doorway to the throne room as Priest Exemplar Rendella, who held a copy of the Holy Scriptures in his right hand, prepared to administer the Arcanian regal oath of office to Regent Retch. "Our father's corpse is barely cold," Pantamanu exclaimed as he stormed forward, hastily grabbing the sacred parchments from the High Cleric's hand, before casting them violently onto the floor.

"How dare you do sacrilege to the sacred scrolls," Rendella shouted. Without a shred of remorse, as his eyes burned with an animal like rage, Pantamanu struck the High Cleric in the mouth, sending Rendella crashing brutally to the floor.

"So much for your sacred scrolls," Pantamanu barked, his eyes now fixed solely upon Lord Valmar, who stood cowering nervously at Retch's side.

Having barely caught his breath, Rendrau proclaimed, "I sense that a coup is under way." While Valmar showed palpable fear, Retch looked utterly insensible to the entire affair, his vapid eyes barely showing any sense of cognition whatsoever. Rendrau continued, "How else can you explain the presence of the High Cleric and Priest Exemplar so suddenly after my father's death? Didn't you even have the courtesy to inform the royal family that our father was dead before anointing a new king in his place?"

"Yes," Pantamanu added, his eyes raging with a hateful vengeance. "Why does my brother stand here, contrary to Arcanian law, ready to take the regal oath, without any member of the royal family in attendance? In fact, why have you followed none of the official protocols in this matter?"

Protocols and symbolism were extremely important to Arcanians. When a king died bells would chime throughout the city for a full two hours, honoring the great king's life. A solemn funeral mass would then be held before the new king could be consecrated. This tradition was followed, usually to the letter, but in this case, Valmar offered no deference whatsoever to any of these accepted traditions.

Valmar stepped awkwardly forward to explain the situation. Sensing the fury in Pantamanu's eyes, he abruptly stopped in his tracks.

Officiously Pantamanu told the aging lord, "There will be no new king today."

Lord Valmar still could find no words to defend his actions as Rendrau also took a menacing step toward the lord. "I have a solution. As the king's third eldest son I call for an impartial investigation regarding the circumstances of my father's death."

"That is unnecessary," Valmar desperately exclaimed, sweat now streaming veritably down the center of his forehead. His body shivered with a desperate fear as he tried to explain, "Any delay will give aide and comfort to the enemies of the Centama family." Pleadingly his case in the most vociferous manner possible the lord professed, "I am sure you have seen the rabble-rousers in the streets."

Pantamanu took another menacing step toward Valmar. "Are they the ones who murdered my father?" Pantamanu moved so close that Valmar could feel the heat from the young prince's angry breath.

Nearly comatose, Retch continued to stand by silently. As he did so Rendrau added more fuel to the fire. Looking down at the prostrate figure of the exalted Priest Exemplar, Rendrau snarled, "Are you also an enemy? I hear that just hours ago you publicly condemned the Oracle before a meeting of the High Clerics."

"How do you know that?" Valmar asked while trembling uncontrollably.

With utter contempt Rendrau put his arm on the lord's shoulder. "You would think that we would be the last to hear of such things. After all you have held us as veritable prisoners in our own castle." Then, with his face contorted with rage, Rendrau admitted, "But we are not children. We know what you are up to."

Rendella now trembled so violently that he feared he might lose consciousness. Aware of Bellazar's role in this plot, he did not know how to defend himself. He therefore moaned pitiably as he looked to Valmar for support.

"Everything that I have done was designed to protect the Centama family," the lord exclaimed defensively, staring wildly at the rival brothers. "I have always been a loyal and obedient servant."

Pantamanu could no longer halter his surging rage. As the lord tried to back away from him Pantamanu grabbed Valmar firmly by the throat. As he inexorably tightened his grip the king's youngest son declared, "I am pleased that you served my father's interests, even as you murdered him in his own bed." Pantamanu steadily tightened his grip with every word he spoke. "But if Retch is not the next king, then what will happen to poor Lord Valmar?"

Valmar struggled to breath, barely able to emit but one solitary word, "Please!" before his entire face turned a ghastly shade of purple and red. Rendrau watched dispassionately as Pantamanu continually tightened his grip, systematically draining the very last remnants of life from Valmar's limp body.

As Valmar's body fell lifelessly to the floor, the Priest Exemplar and High Cleric Rendella, frightened beyond all reason, begged for mercy, as Rendrau asked, "And what do we do with the esteemed High Cleric?" Then with a surprising fierceness, Rendrau shouted, "What are your motives in all of this?"

From his prostrate position, his body shivering, his hands cradled in sanctimonious and self-serving prayer, Rendella hysterically cried out, "I came to the castle to inform Lord Valmar that there were riots in the street, when one of his guards grabbed me and brought me to this chamber much against my will."

Rendrau looked down with a menacing hatred at the cleric. With biting sarcasm he asked, "I hear that just this morning you read a letter from the regent calling for the destruction of the Oracle. Is that true?"

The High Cleric trembled with irrepressible fear, his cold and clammy hands shaking so violently that he was unable to maintain a prayer's bond between his two palms. "I was ordered to do so," he lamented, his eyes darting wildy as he tried to concoct any excuse that might preserve his life.

"By whom?" Rendrau demanded, knowing full well that the cleric would never dare to implicate Bellazar.

Rendella groveled, his hands now clenched together, as he confessed, "By Lord Valmar." Rendella's eyes widened as his hopes brightened with a new prospect. "You must keep me alive," he begged. Then, from his knees he swore, "I will testify against Lord Valmar's crimes. The people of Arcania must know what he did to our beloved king."

Rendrau smiled, while Pantamanu watched this pathetic scene play out in stony silence. "Well, then, I guess the High Cleric is totally innocent," Rendrau said, his voice dripping with sarcasm, before he called out for one of the nearby guards to come to his side. When the guard arrived Rendrau demanded, "Give me your sword?" The sentry obediently unsheathed his weapon and, without speaking a word, handed it to Rendrau. "Isn't it a beautiful instrument?" Rendrau said as he held the glimmering sword up to the light so that he could better admire its sheen. Then in a cold voice he added, "And yet at the same time it is so very deadly." Without warning, and with surprising force, Rendrau lurched toward the defenseless High Cleric. Rendella did not even have the time to raise his arms in his own feeble defense. With blood trickling from both corners of his mouth, Rendella looked down at the bloody sword, as his eyes fluttered, before he consumed his very last breath. Rendrau then jerked the sword out of the cleric's bloodstained body, and as Rendella slumped forward, the king's third eldest son calmly opined, "I suggest that we place our brother under house arrest, at least for the present."

"It would be much easier to finish the entire business now," Pantamanu remarked coldly. As he spoke, he suddenly realized that the death of the heir to the throne might provoke a sympathetic backlash. Besides, in his present state Retch represented absolutely no threat whatsoever. Reluctantly, then, Pantamanu agreed to let his brother live, at least for now.

As the guards escorted Retch from the throne room, Rendrau looked at the pool of blood on the once immaculately clean blue carpet and commented, "I hope this is the last blood that will have to be spilled." Pantamanu was under no such happy illusions. More practical than his brother, and understanding that the fight for succession was far from over, he merely stared at his brother with an ethereal yet strangely serene silence.

Chapter 17
Count Belicki

Most mornings Montama rose shortly before dawn. After a light breakfast, he mounted his favorite horse, Jazu, a white and silver palomino, for a spirited ride through the hilly countryside to the south. His ultimate destination was a lonely bit of pastureland near the crystal clear waters of the Tedawa Stream, south of Pellaville. There, each morning, he sat beneath the flowing dark and light blue leaves of an ancient tazma tree, enjoying the fresh air and, more importantly, the pastoral silence that allowed him to completely free his mind of all thoughts of any consequence. To do so, Montama established and rigorously followed certain strict rules of conduct. Most importantly, he allowed himself the freedom to think about any subject, so long as it was devoid of practical importance, such as his studies or what he might like to do with the rest of his life.

Most mornings, he simply pulled out a copy of a Captain Bale adventure story from his saddlebag and spent a blissful hour or two contemplating the remarkable exploits of his favorite fictional hero. Beginning when he was about fourteen Montama even composed one of his own Captain Bale stories, though he had no illusions that it would ever be good enough to publish. So he left the tale buried deep within his imagination, telling it only to Hontallo when they camped together in the Kanaween Forest.

On this particular morning, however, Montama found it nearly impossible to ignore matters of consequence. The night before the sad word had arrived from Teta that King Benton had died of heart failure. Furthermore it was uncertain who would replace him, for the rumors swirling around the Centama family could hardly be believed. One suggested that the heir to the throne, Retch, had been so distraught upon hearing of his father's death that doctors ordered him sequestered at a private sanitarium. There also was a rumor that the king's second eldest son, Pondru, had been sent on an expedition to meet with Lord Tantamount, yet the young prince had not yet arrived. Who was actually governing the passra and who would be the next king were therefore decidedly unsettled questions. Lord Tantamount was so upset upon hearing these revelations that he took to his private bedchamber at an unseemly early hour.

Contrarily, Montama found it difficult to sleep and rose even earlier than usual. Because snow was falling briskly and the temperatures were not far above freezing, the young boy bundled himself into his warmest green parka, put a full brimmed hat carefully on his head, and at the last minute remembered to bring his leather gloves, though he preferred not to wear them unless absolutely necessary. He then set off as usual; riding first through McGuffin Pass, its canyon walls intricately carved in the grandeur of bright red and orange clay. His ultimate destination was the seductive beauty and glorious privacy of his much beloved tazma tree.

As he finally sat beneath the tree, not far from the banks of the gently flowing Tedawa Stream, with its tiny but beautiful waterfall carrying its crystal clear waters southward to the Bay of Battle, Montama remembered the only time he had ever met the king. When he was but ten his father took him on one of his many business trips to the city of Teta. The king had been gracious and most generous with his advice, telling Montama, as he must have told countless others, that if he strived diligently there was no end to the good fortune he might enjoy later in life. While the king naturally interested the young boy, it was the wife of one of the king's sons, Bellazar, that he found most enchanting, largely because in many ways she reminded Montama of his own mother.

That had been a special trip and as he thought back to it now, he realized anew that life in the passra was about to change, for good or ill he could not yet determine. Then he violated his own rule by wondering what role fate had chosen for him to play in the unfolding drama. "I can hardly believe what mother told me," he said aloud, sure that no one was in the vicinity to hear his thoughts. "Why would the Oracle pick me to be king?"

Montama closed his eyes to contemplate the question. When he opened them he was startled by the presence of a peculiarly tall and emaciated man with dark green skin and a wrinkled complexion. Surprised, Montama jumped to his feet, but the old man simply laughed and said, "I am sorry if I startled you. I was just walking by the side of the stream when I heard you speak."

"What brings you here?" Montama asked, as he dusted the snow from the brim of his hat.

"I used to come here often, a long time ago," the man confessed, chuckling as he spoke. "A long time ago indeed!"

Convinced that the old man represented no threat, Montama asked him to sit with him under the tazma tree. "Where are you from and what brings you here?" Montama asked, as he stared at the old man, trying to remember if he had ever seen him before.

"I was born and raised in the Relatin Empire in a small city called Zanaqua, a dirty place, full of mud, nothing like this beautiful pasture land," the old man said joyfully admiring the vast and picturesque horizon with his aged but still sharp purple eyes. As Montama listened he carefully studied the elderly man. He had seen him before, but where? As he did so I startled him, for yes I was the old man. I impertinently declared, "You are the son of Lord Tantamount, aren't you?"

"How do you know that?" Montama asked defensively, now absolutely convinced that he had seen me somewhere.

"I met you and your father before, a long time ago," I said with a smile. "But I would doubt if you remember me."

"I do," Montama responded carefully, "but I can't place you."

"Well I am sure it will come to you," I said. Then extending my right hand I declared with genuine alacrity, "I am Count Belicki, well I used to be a Count, now I am just a common humble servant of the king, just like you."

"How did you fall from grace?" Montama asked, tentatively shaking my wrinkled hand, and then looking down at his own hand as if he had just touched death itself, for my hand was cold and clammy.

Hearing the question I chuckled exuberantly. "I like the way you speak, as if grace ever had anything to do with being a count." I pulled out a handkerchief and carefully blew my nose. Montama took notice because a commoner would have merely done their duty on their sleeve. Only a gentleman used a handkerchief. As I put the garment back in my side pocket, I continued, "I'm afraid that I was not a particularly good man. I took advantage of every form of debauchery and when I exhausted them all, I set out to invent new forms of entertainment." Then temporarily puzzled, losing my concentration, for it had been a long time since I had assumed a corporeal form, I asked, "What was the question again?"

Montama chuckled, certain that his companion was senile and quite harmless. "You were telling me about your past. Why do you apologize for it now?"

"Only because I lost it all. That is the only reason," I said, as the snowflakes caused my tender eyes to tear up. "You will have to excuse me," I said, wiping my eyes with my right hand. "I am not used to the elements." Then remembering the train of my conversation I continued, "Oh yes, if I could have my old life back today I would do so in an instant, with no remorse whatsoever."

"Then you are not at all embarrassed by your past?" Montama asked, now clearly amused by his new companion.

"Since I lost it all, I am very much embarrassed."

"Well, at least you had a life that sounds adventurous," Montama said leaning back against the tree. "I have hardly ever left my father's estate and have seen nothing of the world."

I nodded my head ever so slightly. "I can see that you are a young man, inexperienced in the ways of the world, but I can also see that you desire more than simply the creature comforts of a lord's son."

Montama was both amused and intrigued. "And what do I want?"

I again blew my nose for the elements were harsh. As I casually put my handkerchief back in my side pocket, I impetuously declared, "Well, you might want to be king."

Until this moment Montama had enjoyed this unexpected conversation. Now, however, his body stiffened tangibly and his face grew rigid with a sudden seriousness. "What do you mean?" he asked defensively.

"If I were a young man that is what I would like to be," I cackled, my eyes twinkling with a false kindness as I did so. "And who is to say that you would not make a very good king," I added, gently touching the young man's right knee as I spoke.

"But how could I be a king without an army?" Montama asked, the brim of his hat again lightly covered in snow.

I laughed for Montama was contemplating precisely what I wanted him to think. "Ah yes, it is hard to be a king without an army, isn't' it?" I delighted in Montama's startled yet attentive reaction to my every word. "Well, if you ask me, and you just did, I would say if you need an army, the place to get one is Kankabar? It is a city in the Relatin Empire, about twenty miles inland from the Bay of Battle. There is always an army to be had there, that is if you are willing to pay the right price for it."

"And how much would that be?" Montama asked, as he stared at my rather queer looking physical appearance.

"I have a feeling that you could afford it. After all, you are the son of the most prominent lord in all of Arcania. I am sure that one of the generals there would be most interested in providing military assistance for a man, such as yourself, who might very well be Arcania's next king."

"This is preposterous," Montama declared.

"Quite so," I admitted cheerfully, "but then again, if it is an army you want, Kankabar is the place to get it."

"If I were in need of any army, that is," Montama responded carefully, ineffectually masking his true intentions, wondering anew where he had seen me. "I know I have seen you before," Montama repeated, staring directly into my eyes.

"Well of that there can be no doubt. But I am afraid I must be up and about," I said as I stood rather precariously, for my balance was far from certain. "I am afraid I have not gotten so much exercise in a long time," I added before giving a gentle wave of my hand. I then turned to walk back toward the side of the stream. "Remember, Kankabar," I said without as much as looking back toward young Montama.

To the young boy this whole idea must have seemed absolutely ludicrous. Crossing the Bay of Battle in the middle of the Season of Death, entering the perilous Relatin Empire where he would have no friends or allies, traveling to the distant and dangerous city of Kankabar to secure a mercenary army without any resources at his disposal. It was the sort of bold action that Captain Bale might undertake. "This is absolutely insane," Montama finally muttered. When he looked up there was no sign of me anywhere. I had vanished just as quickly as I had first appeared. Montama stood still for a full minute, staring at the ground where the two of us had just conversed. There were tracks in the snow, marking my arrival and departure. Yet, where had I come from and where did I go? As Montama looked around him, he saw only his horse Jazu, standing nearby, waiting patiently for the return ride to Lord Tantamount's estate.

As Montama hastily mounted Jazu he was suddenly struck by a strange realization. "This is not real," he thought. Shivering, not so much from the cold as from the sensation that he had just experienced something otherworldly, Montama rode as quickly as he could homeward with but one thought in mind, "I must talk to Grandafier about this. Perhaps he has an explanation."

Chapter 18
Out of a Dream

Montama was so eager to discuss his bizarre meeting with Count Belicki that rather than returning to Lord Tantamount's estate, he rode directly to Grandafier the Elder's stucco house, located not more than a block from the giant open-air council chamber. After instructing a servant to walk Jazu back to his father's estate, Montama was escorted inside Grandafier's small but elegantly furnished abode. Grandafier had spent many cycles collecting what he called "whatnots" from all over the known world and his walls were a veritable museum of paintings from the Relatin Empire, odd carvings from the remote islands of the mysterious Draeden Sea, nude sculptures from Arcania's most famous artist, Zalca, mirrors place ad odd angles on the walls and even the ceilings, and shelf upon shelf of leather bound books on every subject from history, to geography, to modern culture.

Montama was so taken with this eclectic display or art and history that he temporarily forgot why he had come in such haste to visit Grandafier. It was only when the old man asked him what was on his mind that Montama exploded in a burst of sudden enthusiasm that entirely transfixed Grandafier, who was seated as usual in his comfortable whicker chair, with its high rising arched back. There he listened attentively to Montama's every word. The young man sat across from him on a matching but much smaller chair, and for the next thirty minutes he conveyed the overall sense of his strange meeting with Count Belicki. "Just like that," Montama snapped his fingers, "this old man appeared out of no where. He looked like a walking cadaver and his skin was cold and clammy. And he knew everything about me."

"Such as?" Grandafier asked, leaning forward so that he could better hear the young man's tale.

"He talked about me being king and how I could find an army in Kankabar,"

"Amazing!" Grandafier said softly.

"It was the strangest thing that's ever happened to me."

As Montama continued, Grandafier listened with rapt attention, occasionally stroking his chin with his right hand, periodically nodding his head, and sporadically adding but one word, "interesting," to summarize his thoughts. When Montama finally concluded his recitation, Grandafier asked a simple question. "What did this old fellow look like?"

Montama closed his eyes, concentrated, and then responded quite carefully. "He was tall, I would say about five feet and six or seven inches. He was very thin, kind of emaciated and sickly looking and *very* wrinkled, with these strange looking purple eyes that just seemed to see right through me. His skin was green and he had long black hair. And he smelled moldy, like an old musty coat."

Grandafier again nodded his head and then asked, "You say that you think you have seen this man before?"

"Yes, but I can't remember where."

Grandafier sat back and thought for a few seconds. Finally he surmised, "The way he looks, the way he suddenly appeared and disappeared, it sounds to me like he came out of a dream."

Montama suddenly sat erect, defensive and a bit perturbed. "Are you saying I dreamed the whole thing?"

"Not your meeting," Grandafier smiled snapping his fingers as he spoke. "That is where you have seen this man."

"What?" Montama exclaimed shocked but intrigued.

Grandafier now vehemently nodded his head while adding, "Yes, the dream about the young man who leads a mighty army," the old man said while closing his eyes as if to better remember the reverie. "In it a young man, who looks much like you my boy, rides along side an army that is over ten thousand strong, maybe more. He has a strange looking general by his side, a man with but one eye. And hovering over him in the sky, like an apparition, is a strange and wrinkled green face." Suddenly opening his eyes Grandafier continued, "At first I thought it was me. I mean how many wrinkled green old men do you know?" He smiled benignly, enjoying his own joke. Then he nodded his head gently and added, "But now I can see it was this man, Belicki, who appeared in my dream, and yours too, I bet."

Montama's mouth now dropped open by several inches as he realized that he too had seen Belicki before in a dream. "My goodness, you're right. I did see him in a dream, the very same dream that you had."

Grandafier clapped his hands together and added, "And now this dream man magically appears before you to tell you exactly what you need to do to save your family from ruin. He tells you to go to Kankabar. I gather that you will find a one-eyed general there, with a giant mercenary army, and if I am correct he will be expecting you. For I gather that this Belicki has visited more than us in our dreams."

Montama now sat completely erect in his seat. "Wait, are you actually telling me to go to Kankabar?" he asked, totally shocked by Grandafier's verdict.

"Yes," Grandafier said, leaning back comfortably in his chair and crossing his legs as he did so. "I sense that there is more than reason behind all of this."

Chapter 19
The Naked Truth

When it was first revealed that King Benton had died the passra's citizens were so stunned and saddened that even the savage violence in Teta came to an abrupt end. Ordinary men and women, who only moments before had been engaged in violent acts of riot and rebellion, meekly dropped their weapons and timidly retreated to their homes, where they lit candles to honor their great fallen king. Bellazar, who was ever attentive to changes in the public mood, immediately advocated two diverse courses of action. First, and quietly while the citizenry was mourning their king, she recommended that units from the First Army should be quickly and seamlessly redeployed to a position not more than two miles south of Teta. This vastly improved the security situation. Second and to ensure that the altered public mood continued to favor the Centama family, she planned a massive five-unit long funeral procession involving notables from across the passra. She counseled her husband, "The funeral will build both a spirit of patriotism and exhaust the disloyal opposition. Most importantly, it will give us time to put our house in order."

The funeral was a magnificent display of political stage crafting. Dignitaries from all over the passra, including Lord Tantamount, representing virtually every segment of society, arrived in Teta for five units of festivities honoring King Benton's life and achievements, as well as the long tradition of Centama family rule. While the citizens were given copious opportunities to mourn their beloved king, the deaths of Lord Valmar and Priest Exemplar and High Cleric Rendella were carefully buried in the details, quickly forgotten, even by the few people who heard about their tragic demise in a carriage accident. While the disappearances of Retch and Pondru were a more difficult matter to explain, the focus assiduously was maintained on the great fallen leader. Bellazar wisely gave both Rendrau and Pantamanu prominent roles in the funeral procession. Each son spoke eloquently of their love for their father and the great king's unbounded affection for his people. Most importantly they hid their vast differences, portraying instead a sense of unity of mind and purpose.

Though Pantamanu despised his sister-in-law, he came to admire her political acumen and even her brashness in stage-managing even the smallest, insignificant details of the king's funeral. "She is a marvel,"

Rendrau boasted and for once Pantamanu did not disagree. "Yes, she is formidable," he responded obliquely.

This is not to say that the funeral was conducted to everyone's satisfaction. While only a few luminaries dared to complain, the royal family found the various activities to be particularly distressing and even at times painful, literally so on at least one notable occasion. The final night of the king's funeral was particularly exhausting for everyone involved. Dignitaries from throughout the passra cued in a nearly mile long procession, each one shaking first Rendrau's and then Pantamanu's right hand. At first Rendrau was merely bored by the constant repetition, but later in the evening his right palm developed a nasty blister, caused no doubt by the friction of countless handshakes. As a result, he was compelled to don white gloves for protection, but when even this remedy proved unsatisfactory, a servant was brought in to shake hands. Rendrau merely bowed and nodded his appreciation to each successive mourner.

Though his hands also were calloused Pantamanu continued to perform his official duty throughout the unit and well on into the evening, as if by shaking more hands more enthusiastically than his brother he was demonstrating his superior qualifications to be the next king. Meanwhile, Rendrau soldiered on though his back and neck now burned with agonizing pain from the constant nodding and bowing that accompanied each mourner's brief visit.

It was only later that night, when the five-unit spectacle was finally at a most welcome end, that Rendrau had the opportunity to collapse leisurely into his bed, profoundly exhausted and vowing that he would not shake the hand of another so-called dignitary for at least another cycle, if not longer. When he tried to complain about his various aches and pains he found absolutely no solace whatsoever from Bellazar. "I can assure you that having tea for seven straight hours with the prominent women of Arcania was no more entertaining," she admitted, still feeling nauseous and bloated. "I drank so much tea I had to find constant excuses to attend the facilities. I made so many visits people must have thought I had hidden a lover in the lavatory."

"Well, I am just relieved that the whole dreadful thing is over." Then remorsefully, Rendrau added, "I didn't mean to show disrespect for father. Oh well, you know what I mean. Even father would been put off by the whole damnable affair."

Bellazar snuggled next to her husband and responded, "He was a fine king, as you will be."

Rendrau nodded and then added sarcastically, "That is if the magistrates ever settle all of these various loose ends, as they call them." Though he was tired, Rendrau was also a bit surly, like an overly exhausted child. "The lawyers say that I cannot be king because they have to hold an inquest to investigate Retch's fitness and because Pondru is reported missing, not dead. Blasted lawyers!" Now in an even more agitated state Rendrau continued, "And Pantamanu has barristers who keep digging through the royal codes looking for every damnable loophole they can find. The lawyers tell me that it could take four or five intervals to resolve the whole damn mess!"

"I am aware of the details," Bellazar said comfortingly, stroking her husband's forehead and then gently kissing it. "They will all be resolved in time and you will be king. So be patient my dear."

Rendrau was in a brusque and disagreeable mood. "I tell you that brother of mine will do everything in his power to make sure that I never become king."

Bellazar now realized that it was time for her to play mommy, as she called it. This meant being strong and reassuring her husband that everything was firmly under control. So as she stridently propped herself in bed with the assistance of an oversized pillow, she began her usual soliloquy. "The first rule of politics…"

"Oh not this again," Rendrau moaned.

Undeterred, Bellazar continued, "…is before you can get what you want you must first know what your enemy wants and then what he will settle for instead."

Rendrau would not let her continue. He scoffed as he interrupted her. "Well we know what Pantamanu wants. To be king, just like me."

Bellazar nodded her head gently in agreement and then added, "But since you are next in the line of succession, and it would be a dreadfully peculiar spectacle if another one of the king's sons were to suddenly disappear or go mad, we can safely assume that time is on our side. Therefore, in the end, Pantamanu will have to settle for something short of being king. What else does he want?"

Rendrau huffed and sighed and then facetiously suggested, "A harem and an army or two for starters, that might make him happy, for a while."

"Exactly," Bellazar smiled contentedly, her mind now swirling with ideas. "They are both the kinds of toys that Pantamanu likes to play with."

"Toys," Rendrau snarled, then yawning broadly, he added, "You're right. After all he is just an oversized adolescent."

"Precisely," Bellazar said, gently nodding her head in agreement. She then watched as Rendrau closed his eyes and instantly began to snore. After leaning over to give him a quick peck on the cheek, she sat back against her mammoth pillow and began to ponder, "I should meet with Pantamanu tomorrow to discuss the future of the passra and his place in it. But where?" Bellazar acutely understood that the venue for a meeting could have a profound effect on the demeanor of the other participants. "The setting is just as important as the agenda," she often preached. Bellazar summarily rejected a meeting in a traditional conference room, such as the king's diplomatic chamber. "No I want it to be a place that will take him off his guard," she thought, listening as her husband continued to snore with palpable enthusiasm.

It was out of the question to meet him outside the castle. The last few days had been particularly cold and she was afraid that if she trembled, even slightly, Pantamanu might interpret it as a sign of weakness. "No, I must meet with him in the castle but in a place that he would never anticipate." When she finally thought of the perfect meeting place her face lit up like a Cheshire cat, and reflectively she purred, "Yes, that will surprise him and appeal to his adolescent mentality." Knowing exactly what she would wear, she contently closed her eyes and quickly fell asleep.

She did not sleep long, however, for there was much preparation for her meeting with Pantamanu. She summarily canceled all of her other daily activities, then sent an engraved invitation to Pantamanu with the scent of rose water on it. "Please meet me at the King's Spa as the fourteenth hour strikes." She knew that Pantamanu would be intrigued and would never be so rude as to ignore the request of a lady. Besides, he would be utterly fascinated by the location of the meeting.

And indeed he was. "The King's Spa?" he asked aloud as he read the invitation. "What the devil is that?" Then after contemplating the matter for a few seconds he said, "What is she up to?" He was so thoroughly intrigued that he could not resist the invitation. "I will be there," he wrote on a card and then ordered a servant to carry it directly to Bellazar. "Make sure that she alone reads it," he instructed circumspectly.

The Oracle

Bellazar received Pantamanu's response with considerable alacrity, for she already had begun preparing the spa for her meeting, ordering the servants to bring in rows of candles, as well as several bottles of the king's finest wines. The final effect was marvelous, precisely what Bellazar had in mind. The room itself was a mere prelude to what she considered to be the topper, the effect that would most assuredly throw poor Pantamanu off his game.

In fact, Pantamanu was uncertain from the start. While he ably surmised the meeting's agenda, he was not even sure where the King's spa was located, for the room had been totally unused for nearly forty cycles. King Benton considered it garish and unappealing. It contained a series of curved couches in concentric circles, with a large mud pit at the room's epicenter, presumably a place where one could take a relaxing bath. Benton found the whole idea completely preposterous. "No man would ever be seen alive in this den of iniquity," he bellowed the first and last time he saw the room. He therefore banned anyone from ever using it again, though the king's staff dutifully prepared the spa each unit, lest the king ever change his mind. Though Benton never relented, Bellazar found the room's candlelit splendor and tacky decor to be to precisely what she had in mind, something decidedly vulgar that would appeal to Pantamanu's adolescent mentality. "This will do the trick," she said as she admired the room's tawdry majesty. The spa was only part of Bellazar's stage crafting and not even the most important part of it. "I will have a unique surprise for the young prince," she said joyfully, with a sense of girlish delight.

Pantamanu was a few minutes late for the meeting, not out of design, but rather embarrassingly because he lost his way and had to ask a servant for directions to the second story spa. When he finally found the room he noticed that the door was slightly ajar. "What is she up to?" he asked himself as he pushed the door open and stepped inside the room. His senses were immediately assaulted with an array of sparkling and flickering candles, which nearly blinded him, and strange and exotic smells, that utterly permeated the room. "What the hell is this?" he muttered, scanning the room, trying to see what sort of chamber he had entered. When his eyes finally adjusted to the diminished light he was simultaneously confused and delighted by this most unexpected spectacle. As he stepped forward into the room he noticed that there were row upon row of gaudy couches. "It is some sort of theater," he thought and then he asked, "But for what purpose?" It took a few seconds before he looked toward the center of the room and when he did he smiled broadly. "My goodness, this is an orgy room," he said aloud. The mud pit was large and seductive, as was Pantamanu's first startled glimpse of a naked woman, her large bosoms buoyed by and completely encased with mud.

Though he did not actually rub his eyes to make sure he was awake, that is the sensation he experienced as he realized that the mud pit contained none other than Bellazar herself, resplendent and utterly alluring. Pantamanu's mouth literally dropped open when he heard his sister-in-law declare, "I was wondering if you were actually going to come."

Pantamanu rarely acted defensively, for his entire personality was constructed on the proposition that it is always best to assume an offensive position. Still, he was so thunderstruck that he did not know what to say or to think. Finally, he conceded, "I am at a total loss." He then walked between the breaks in the concentric lined couches downward toward the mud pit that served as the room's fulcrum.

"Will you join me?" Bellazar said provocatively, as if challenging Pantamanu. When he hesitated she deliberately challenged his manhood. "What's the matter? Are you shy?"

Pantamanu could countenance no hint of weakness from a female and with his manhood even so obliquely challenged, he nodded his head and said, "Why not?"

Bellazar threw her head back and laughed, then reached for a glass of wine that she had laid on the marble counter that totally circumvented the mud pit. "And what better way to enjoy your bath than with a glass of wine."

Had he been forced to confess, Pantamanu would have had to admit that Bellazar had thought of everything. He had expected her to try to surprise him, but this was beyond anything that he ever could have imagined. Reluctantly, he pulled his shirt over his head and then stood there with a foolish grin on his face. "I guess you win."

Bellazar tried not to stare as Pantamanu removed his clothing, but she could not help but admire her brother-in-law's powerful arms and chest, as well as the tattoos on his arms. "I see you honor the Centama family," she said before sipping her fine red wine.

Pantamanu looked down at the tattoos and remarked, "I had this done about a cycle ago to honor father. It is the family insignia with two swords crossing a map of Arcania."

The Oracle

Bellazar again sipped her wine as Pantamanu flexed his muscles before bending over to remove his boots and socks. Secretly, Bellazar long had admired Pantamanu's physical prowess, for truthfully he was far more beautiful than Rendrau. As he removed his pants she respectfully turned her head, though she deliberately caught a glimpse of his naked body out the corner of her eye, a look that Pantamanu noticed but did not comment upon.

"Be careful when you get in," she advised. "It is slippery." As Pantamanu stepped into the mud pit he found the feeling to be both invigorating and disgusting. Sitting, he smeared mud across his chest and onto his arms. "It is better to just dip down under it," Bellazar advised. Then laughing she added, "Well I guess it was just a matter of time before the two of us got down together in the mud."

Pantamanu stared at the oozy crud all over his body. "It feels like warm spit," he finally admitted.

The two sipped their respective glasses of wine, both covered in mud, not more than a foot's distance separating the two political rivals. Then authoritatively he asked, "So what business do you have on your mind today?"

Like a schoolgirl, Bellazar giggled, trying to look as disarming as possible, and succeeding very much in the part. "Why must we talk of business?" she asked, her face radiant and as yet untouched by the dark brown mud.

"Well," Pantamanu said looking about the room, "I thought that's why you asked me to come here."

Bellazar mischievously responded, "Why must we always think about business?" Tapping her glass gently against Pantamanu's and then taking another sip, she added, "We have all been through so much these past fortnights. I thought we needed to spend some time together, just like a real family." Pantamanu was dubious, but he listened attentively nonetheless. Bellazar then reached over and flicked a tiny spec of mud off of her brother-in-law's chin. "There," she said carefully inspecting her work.

"So there is no business?" Pantamanu asked quizzically.

"Well, of course we must ensure that the passra is well defended," she said matter-of-factly. Pantamanu could not disagree with this assessment. "And since the greatest potential for danger lies in the east, I would assume that you are most eager to take charge of one of the armies there."

126

"What about the First Army?" Pantamanu asked, with reference to the largest and most prestigious of Arcania's five armies.

"It sits south of Teta and hardly requires a leader of your skill and stature. Besides, if there are battles to be fought they surely will come in the east."

Pantamanu agreeably nodded his head. Thus far, Bellazar was in accord with his own thinking. "I am listening," he added.

"So then I gather you want to be in charge of an army in the east?" she asked, gently caressing her wine glass with a single finger as she spoke.

"It would mean that I would be away from the castle," Pantamanu remarked suspiciously.

"Yes but only a ride of two or three units at the very most. And with an army at your disposal you would be in charge of one the most powerful forces in all Arcania." Bellazar was tempting Pantamanu and she could see from the look on his face that he was willing.

Pantamanu rested his muscular arms on the marble side of the mud pit and leaned back. "Your offer is intriguing," he said as he stretched out his legs. As he did so he sank deeper into the pit until mud completely covered his chin. As he regained his balance he added, "Besides, there is nothing to be gained by remaining in Teta. It will be several intervals before the lawyers decide the issue of succession and I will be in a position to achieve a measure of military glory in the meantime."

"Exactly," Bellazar purred delightedly, her eyes bowed slightly in deference to her guest. "The Centama family must come together and from now on we must be willing to accommodate each other's needs."

Pantamanu looked into Bellazar's alluring eyes. Reaching over, his hand covered in mud, he gently touched Bellazar's face, smearing it ever so slightly. "Your skin is so beautiful," he said admiringly

Bellazar laughed then asked, "So are we agreed?"

Pantamanu thought for a second and then nodded his consent. "For the time being," he added.

Then raising her glass Bellazar offered a toast. "To family."

Pantamanu raised his glass to his lips and as he sipped his wine he realized that Bellazar had consented to everything he wanted. What he did not yet understand was why.

Chapter 20
Pondru Returns

Three units after Pantamanu departed for the journey eastward, an inquest was scheduled to investigate Retch's deteriorating mental condition. The omnipresent lawyers already insisted that according to Arcanian law, Retch was still the passra's regent and therefore the rightful heir to the throne. Furthermore, he would remain so unless there was just cause to disqualify him. After consulting the legal codes, which were far from specific on this particular subject, by a vote of two to one, a three judge panel ruled that the murder of King Benton did not disqualify Retch from becoming Arcania's next monarch. The barristers based their decision on the fact that the king had not spoken, eaten or drank in a fortnight and was therefore considered to be "legally comatose," which according to Arcanian law was the same as being pronounced "dead while living."

Bellazar was thunderstruck by this unexpected and to her mind highly perverted verdict, but she was more amenable to the inquest's other ruling. Before Retch could assume the Arcanian throne he must first demonstrate that he was of sound mind. Bellazar realized that this would be an exceedingly difficult, if not impossible task for Retch's lawyers to perform. Since his incarceration in a small secure room on the castle's second floor, and not in a sanitarium as the widely circulating rumors suggested, Retch had been placid and most cooperative, yet he seldom ate or drank and communicated with his interlocutors even less frequently. After his own lawyers met with him on three separate occasions they reported that he was "passive, taciturn, and generally incapable of comprehending what others had said. Often he was unaware that others were even in the vicinity. On those few occasions when he was talkative his thoughts lacked coherence." Even his own lawyers, then, believed that the regent was "not of sound mind."

The matter ultimately would have to be settled by the three lawyers from the royal inquest, who scheduled their decisive meeting with the regent, to be held early on the first morning of the new interval or month. Retch was duly notified in writing that there would be a hearing. When he read the order, his face remained expressionless and he made no comment other than to ask for a drink of water, which he then placed on a nearby table and never consumed.

It was clear to everyone, then, that unless Retch managed a truly miraculous recovery, the inquest would rule that he was completely unfit to be king. So confident was Bellazar and Rendrau in this verdict that the night before the inquest they dined at a restaurant in Teta that was known to serve their favorite seafood dishes, including scallops, white trenta meat (a rare delicacy), and lobster, all dishes that indeed were fit for a king and his Telenaka or queen.

So as Bellazar and Rendrau dined, Retch lay alone in his quarters, as usual staring at the ceiling, desperately trying to clear his mind of the sorted details of his last tragic encounter with his beloved father. Ironically, the more he tried to avoid thinking about his father's death, the more his mind returned to an image of his prostrate and helpless father, with his loving son standing above him, a pillow firmly grasped in both of his deformed and ugly hands. Then Retch moved ever so slowly and ominously forward, and though he desperately tried to hold the pillow back from his father's face, the gravitational forces were simply too strong for him to resist. With tears in his eyes and his face obscenely contorted, against all of his filial instincts, Retch cruelly, inexorably moved the pillow down over his father's expressionless face, and then ruthlessly smothered him until he was stone cold dead. After the foul deed was done, when Retch finally withdrew the pillow, his father stared up at his son and plaintively asked, "Why did you kill me son?" It was a horrifying reverie that echoed continuously in Retch's tortured mind.

He relived this moment thousands of times. In a quivering voice he finally whispered, "I do not deserve to live."

He was in a thoroughly dazed state and in his mind's eye, everything in the room appeared to be bizarrely distorted. The walls seemed to stand at odd angles, the size and shape of the window varied from moment to moment, and strangest of all, the plain wooden door appeared to rise for more than a hundred feet with the ceiling so high above his head that at times it appeared as if the night sky, filled with stars and constellations of all shapes and sizes, was contained within his secure and tiny room. Overwhelmed by these delusions, Retch's thoughts swirled and though he was lying in his bed, he sometimes had the strange sensation that he was about to fall, not down, but upward. In fact, his mind was so confused that he could no longer tell fantasy from reality.

With his eyes glazed and his breathing intermittent, Retch closed his eyes. When he did he heard a chilling voice calling, "I have come to help you." The voice was insistent and not at all hostile, yet it sent shivers down Retch's spine.

Exhausted beyond all reason, Retch frantically scanned the room, slowly turning his head to the right and staring for several seconds at a vacant wall. Then, with great difficulty he turned his head in the other direction, again looking for any possible sign of life. This time he thought he saw something. In a dark and shadowy corner, he saw a dull green glimmering light, which slowly morphed into the blurred shape of rotund man with a long grey beard. "Who are you?" Retch beckoned, not sure whether he was dreaming, awake, or simply insane.

As Retch's eyes tried to focus on the figure, it stepped forward so that it could be plainly seen in the room's dim candlelight. Then with a voice that seemed not quite human the entity responded, "I am your brother Pondru."

Retch stared hard, trying to bring the strange image into clearer focus. As he did so he rubbed his eyes, for he could not believe that this was indeed his very own brother, who until now was presumed to be lost or dead. "You cannot be Pondru," Retch finally whispered.

"It is me," Pondru said stridently, as he took yet another step toward his brother's bed. "See, I am flesh and blood like you.'

Retch cautiously reached out his right hand to touch his brother. When he felt the cold but smooth sensation of Pondru's hand, Retch finally realized that Pondru was real. Unable to contain his feelings any longer, Retch unleashed a veritable torrent of emotions. "I am so happy to see you," he said, his voice unsteady, displaying but an awkward hint of joy.

With a vast exertion of fleeting energy, Retch stumbled to his feet. His legs were so weak that they buckled and Pondru moved swiftly to catch his brother before he fell. Then, as Retch slumped helplessly forward, Pondru warmly embraced his brother. As he did so, Pondru confessed, "I am sorry that I could not have come to you sooner."

Retch's mind swirled with a hundred incoherent thoughts, visions of times past combined with images of the night his father died. The heir to the throne wanted to ask his brother where he had been and how he had arrived. Before he could speak again, however, his body shook so frightfully that Pondru was forced to help his older brother back into bed. "You need rest and food," Pondru said, leaning on one knee and doting on his dear older brother.

In an instant Retch's mood changed from light to dark. As he lay in his bed again staring up at his brother, he confessed in a voice so consumed with guilt that it unnerved Pondru, "I killed our father."

"You did not," Pondru said trying to soothe his brother's conscience. "He was already dead. You set him free."

Retch tried to comprehend what his brother said, but in his mind he saw his own treacherous villainy played out yet again. Frightened and thoroughly confused, Retch moaned, "I murdered our father."

Pondru sat patiently by his brother's bedside, carefully caressing Retch's hand as he spoke. "Father does not blame you."

"No!" Retch cried out pitiably. "I have sinned! I do not deserve to be king!"

"You must be king," Pondru insisted. "Terrible things will happen to those you love if you are not king. The entire passra will be consumed by a war that will destroy the lives of tens of thousands of innocent people. Only you have the power to prevent this calamity."

"I can never be king," Retch declared with such vehement defiance that the guards in the outside hall could plainly hear him speak.

Pondru sat silently for a minute or two, contemplating his next step. When he realized that he had no other option he quietly added, "I will prove that you did not kill our father."

"How?" Retch asked desperately, eager for redemption but feeling totally unworthy of it.

"Look to the shadows my dear brother, from where I first emerged," Pondru said in a comforting voice. As Retch's eyes struggled to focus on the room's shadowy corner, the outline of a new form and figure slowly appeared out of thin air. At first Retch could not recognize the figure, for it appeared to be young and vibrant. As the man stepped confidently out of the shadows Retch finally could see that it was none other than his own father, King Benton, though he now appeared spright and very much alive.

With uncontrollable alacrity, Retch screamed, "FATHER!"

"Hello, my son," the apparition said in a deep and most forgiving voice.

"Father, I am so sorry. I should never have killed you!" Retch said, abjectly pleading for forgiveness.

"No, my son. I was already dead. You set me free."

Retch's eyes now expressed painful joy for the first time in a fortnight. With a crooked smile he looked at his brother, and then, in the most innocent of all voices, he asked, "Am I forgiven?"

"Yes," Pondru added, with a benign almost angelic smile. Retch looked again at his loving father. Then reaching both of his hands out to embrace his father, in a voice so sweet that it broke poor King Benton's heart, Retch whispered with childlike affection, "I love you father." Retch was indescribably exhausted beyond all reason. His hand trembled violently for several seconds, then suddenly fell limp, as he abruptly closed his eyes. His guilt had kept him alive. Now that he was absolved of his crime, he had no further reason to live. Completely at rest, Retch whispered a few barely audible words, "I am forgiven." Then with a look of peaceful contentment, he breathed one last time.

The next morning the doctors concluded that Retch had suffered massive heart failure sometime during the night. Dr. Vajadrray simply wrote, "The regent apparently lost his will to live." It was a sad verdict that strangely touched the hearts of the entire passra. Unexpectedly, Arcanians who recently had pilloried their much-beleaguered regent suddenly sensed profound remorse. As a result they were eager to mourn the loss of their beloved king's oldest son.

PART II

A MIGHTY ARMY

Chapter 21
Montama's Journey

After his otherworldly encounter with Count Belicki, Montama hesitated for almost a fortnight, waiting for his father to return from Teta, where he attended King Benton's funeral. "I cannot leave while father is away," the young man reasoned. When the lord finally returned from the emotionally and physically exhausting journey, Montama found other less obvious excuses to delay his all-important departure for Kankabar. Truthfully, and not at all to his credit, the lord's youngest son was still quite uncertain why the Oracle had chosen him, rather than someone who was older, wiser, and more skillfully trained in the martial arts. Haunted by self-doubt, often unable to sleep, Montama wrestled uneasily with this question until one night he could stand it no more. He rose, hours before daybreak, with an overwhelming urge to speak to the one person who might be able to furnish an answer.

Quietly, lest he awaken his father or brother, young Montama tiptoed from his room, down the long corridor decorated with the vast array of family portraits and sundry personal memorabilia, to his mother's room. When he arrived he noticed that the door already was slightly ajar. Nervously, he peaked his head inside. Had his mother been asleep Montama would have discretely returned to his own room. Much to his surprise, however, he found Truellen awake, propped up by three massive pillows, her arms crossed and her gaze fixed determinedly and directly on the open doorway, as if she were anticipating her son's unusual nocturnal visit. When she saw Montama's eyes furtively sneaking a look into the room, she gently whispered, "Don't be afraid. I know why you are here."

As Montama entered the room, with a delicate gesture of her hand, Truellen invited her son to sit next to her on the bed and as he obediently did so, Montama saw that his mother's lips were tightly drawn, while her eyes were frozen in a determined scowl. It was obvious that the strain of many of her own sleepless nights had palpably weakened her already frail body, and when she coughed so hard that she drew blood into her handkerchief, Montama reached over and hugged his mother with much genuine warmth and affection, a feeling that I too had for my own dear mother. Montama was concerned as he pulled back and looked at into his mother's glassy eyes. With a most feeble intonation, her voice hoarse and quivering, she said softly, "I know why you are frightened." Montama cringed for he was embarrassed that his mother could so easily read his most private thoughts. Still, he said nothing, for he was consumed with a strong feeling of apprehension and inadequacy. Instead he listened attentively as his mother's weak voice proclaimed, "You have been asked to do a great and dangerous thing and you wonder why the Oracle chose you for this task."

"Yes," Montama whispered emphatically, relieved that he did not have to verbally express the source of his own rampant insecurity.

Though she said nothing of it, Truellen suddenly felt an intense anxiety ridden conflict surging within her. As a mother she wanted nothing more than to throw her arms around her precious son, to hold him close to her bosom, to protect him from all harm. Yet she also sensed another even more powerful, compelling impulse. As her maternal instincts struggled with this strange other force, she closed her eyes and in a calm, frail, but firm intonation said, "The answer to your question lies in Kankabar and in the road ahead." Then, with her eyes still firmly shut, she whispered, "Tonight you will begin a critical journey that will completely change the course of your life. You must leave for Kankabar immediately, for destiny summons us and we have no alternative but to heed its call." Montama found it strange that his mother noted that "destiny summons *us*" and "*we* have no alternative." Until this moment he had not thought in terms of destiny, only in terms of how this magnificent quest would affect his own life. He thought of his family, but not at any deep level of understanding, for he did not really understand how his actions would affect his father or his brother's lives. He thought only in the naïve sense that there are villains in this world and I must stop them to save my family and preserve its fortune. He did not have any idea who these villains might be; only that he was undoubtedly the hero of this tale and therefore totally infallible, for his motives alone were pure. He had no desire for conquest or self-aggrandizement, a strange rationalization, since he intended if successful to be Arcania's next king. Yet through his naïve and self-serving eyes he saw nothing but benevolence in his motivations and beneath that a desperate pressing, if as yet unarticulated need to perform this munificent service for his fellow Arcanians. In short, he felt it was his patriotic duty to act and to do so immediately. Many scoundrels have been tempted by the same feelings and I was delighted to sense these emotions welling up in Montama's spirit.

Yet I was aware of another sensation, as well. As he sat by his mother's side, for the very first time, the reality that his quest would affect the lives of his father, mother, and brother finally was becoming fully apparent and Montama was overcome with a sense of sadness and regret that he must leave them. "Why must the Oracle place these demands on me? Why must I be the chosen one?" he wondered, invoking a certain spirit of self-pity, a reluctant sense that the search for power is somehow a form of sublime sacrifice. And he now felt somehow ennobled because he alone was willing to make this sacrifice. I had seen these same thoughts race through the minds of many ambitious men. It was, I suppose, a way for them to rationalize that they were only interested in power for the good that it would do, even as they blindly lusted after power for what it could do for them. Fortunately, I had never been under such a mysterious delusion. I knew why I wanted power and what it was for, while Montama did not. But in time he would learn and I, of course, would teach him.

Though he said nothing aloud that might disturb his mother, his mind was awash with such incongruous reflections. Still, Montama one last time tried to find one more excuse to justify his continued recalcitrance. "And what shall I tell father?" Montama asked, concerned that he had no excuse for a sudden departure to such a strange and exotic place as Kankabar and the Relatin Empire.

"Leave that to me," Truellen said quietly, her hands now trembling, her energy nearly spent. In a gravelly whisper she said, "I will tell your father that you have left on a personal errand of great importance to me." Then insistently and in a much stronger voice she added, "But you must leave now!" As she spoke these last words she felt her heart rend as she again sensed the conflict growing within her very soul, for as much as she wanted her son to go, she also had a desperate need to keep him safe and by her side. She leaned forward, lovingly kissed her son's cheek, and then in a gentle and loving voice added, "You will not be alone on your journey my son. My love will travel with you always, no matter where you go."

Montama perfunctorily kissed his mother's cheek, for his mind was now focused on the treacherous journey that lay ahead. With his mind thus occupied, the young son whispered absentmindedly, "I will not let you down."

"You can not!" Truellen responded resolutely, her voice now strong and commanding. "You are my son!"

As Montama stood, at first tentatively, and then with greater resolve, he turned and walked toward the door. As she heard her son's footsteps Truellen had a sudden overwhelming urge to call Montama back to her side, to beg him to stay. She heard the sound of her son's fading footsteps and then the sound of her door shutting. When she finally had the courage to again open her eyes she was startled to discover that she could no longer see. Frightened, but determined to let her son go, without a word she listened attentively for nearly half an hour until she heard the distinctive sound of her youngest son departing on horseback. Stridently, she then closed here eyes and whispered, "You must take care of him for me."

It was then that she heard a most familiar voice intone, "I will do my best, but why didn't you tell him about your other secret?"

Truellen's chest tightened, for she did not know that anyone, not even the Oracle was aware of her most preciously guarded secret. "Absolutely no one is to know about that!" she scowled angrily.

Though she could not see me, Truellen sensed that I was smiling, as I responded to her in a smooth, silky and seductive voice. "As you wish. But in time you may come to regret that you did not tell him about his grandfather and the reason why you could not be wed to the king."

Truellen said nothing at all. This was one secret she was determined to take with her to the grave.

Chapter 22
The One-Eyed General

As the sun finally crested, crimson skies greeted young Montama as he commenced the arduous journey south from Pellaville to the ancient coastal town of Grell. It took one full unit of hard riding before Montama arrived, late at night, in the dingy old port town. Exhausted by his ordeal, having thought of nothing all day but his mother's frail condition and her certitude that he must travel to Kankabar, Montama was relieved that there was one last room available at the Justin Inn, for he needed to rest, so weary was his mind and body.

Montama slept soundly for the first time in a fortnight and rose early the next morning, determined to arrange passage across the Bay of Battle. This was not an easy task, as few ships were available for transport. Finally, after much negotiating, he was able to secure passage on a decrepit fishing trawler named the Banchest, run by a man with a dark black complexion and astonishingly beautiful green eyes by the name of Captain Michael, who proudly professed to be an old and cherished friend of Grandafier the Elder. Montama felt completely at ease traveling with the ancient sea captain and was particularly pleased when Michael informed him, "The Bay's waters have been unusually calm as of late. This should be an easy crossing." Still, despite this promise, the passage took three units time, not because of turbulent waters or inclement weather, but because the aging trawler stopped periodically to dredge the sea for fish. Eventually and uneventfully, Montama arrived at Nata, a port city on the northern coast of the Relatin Empire. It marked the first time that the Montama had journeyed outside of Arcania, the first in a series of transitions that would forever alter the young man's destiny.

The journey would be strenuous and Montama keenly understood that the Relatin Empire was a dark and dangerous place. And from the grubby streets of Nata he would travel a distance of approximately eighty miles, across the exposed grasslands and donkey paths that led to the inland city of Kankabar. Captain Michael warned Montama that transportation within the Empire was decidedly perilous. "These are uncertain times," Michael observed. "The Boguls have attacked many of our coastal cities and the empire is not as powerful as it used to be. Some cities, like Frey and

The Oracle

Kankabar are barely governable. I recommend that you exercise extreme caution at all times."

Montama had heard many tales, some too fanciful to be believed, about the mysteries of the omnipotent Relatin Empire. Yet despite the rumors of the empire's grand splendor and incalculable wealth, the young man was decidedly unimpressed by his first impressions of this foreboding land. Nata could be described aptly with but one single word: mud. From the dock to the hotel, to the streets he walked at night, Nata was a dirty, mud-spattered city and Montama desired nothing more than to be free of it as soon as possible. Fortuitously, his wish was speedily accommodated. On just his second unit in Nata he met a troupe of actors who were traveling in a caravan to Kankabar and with a few spontaneously improvised assurances that he was the son of a prominent Arcanian businessman, they agreed to let him purchase a right of passage with them. Montama paid them with a shiny gold piece that he had hidden in a secret sleeve inside his left boot.

As the caravan got under way on its slow inland journey, Montama contrasted his preconceptions of the Relatin Empire's majesty and grandeur with its present abject reality. The winding roads were replete with desperate looking people, often pulling small wooden carts, presumably towing all of their worldly possessions, while disinterested soldiers wearing the tattered uniform of the Relatin Empire rode on horses that looked decidedly underfed. In fact, everything he saw was indicative of an empire on the verge of collapse.

His conversations with the locals, who spoke a dialect that he had learned from his tutors, were also surprisingly critical of the emperor and his government. Most of the Relatanians considered the imperial city and the emperor to be far removed and distant from their own desperate existence, so far so that the empire, as such, lacked any real relevance to their paltry, daily lives. The empire's most important function was to provide security and on this score it was a dismal failure. For more than a decade hostile tribes of Bogul barbarians increasingly employed sophisticated guerilla tactics to attack lands deep within the ancient realm, as well as along the empire's eastern shores. The Boguls developed hit and run techniques that allowed just a few men to bog down a large army, disrupting supply lines, killing soldiers and generally reeking havoc despite their significantly smaller numbers. Lately, the Boguls had begun to use a new type of explosive device, which they placed on the plain dirt and weed covered roads. As army personnel and common citizens traversed these roads they were exposed to these crude explosives, which though they did little real damage, frightened horses and brought transportation to a veritable halt. And as the Bogul threat penetrated further into the empire, more army units were sent from the coastal region to the interior of the continent to confront and contain the threat, while coastal areas such as Nata and even Kankabar received far less protection and vastly greater economic and governmental autonomy.

As a result of these developments, private armies had emerged to police many of the eastern empire's cities, with few sanctioned forces to be found anywhere within sight. The renegade armies claimed official designations. In truth they were barely distinguishable from the bands of roving thieves they were purportedly hired by the citizens to police. Since it was common to be robbed while traveling on the open road, the actors wisely hired their own personal protection. They therefore traveled carefully guarded for several units time, always setting up a perimeter defense at night, with several guards on watch until the caravan was again ready to travel. Montama took watch on one occasion. He had expected adventure, but the experience was tedious beyond all imagining, for it required him to be always alert. Still, the only present danger, so far as he could tell was a ravenous stream of assaulting mosquitoes, which repeatedly feasted on his bare neck.

He was therefore mightily relieved when the troupe finally arrived in Kankabar, though the security situation there seemed no better than it had been at Nata. Soldiers wearing the uniforms of private armies stood on various street corners, while people walked cautiously by, often palpably afraid. Montama quickly learned that as the empire's influence declined, that these private armies developed their own particular sphere of political and economic influence. Within a unit's time Montama also discovered that one such army was under the direction of a most feared but highly respected man by the name of General Garr, though his title appeared to be self-professed, for he no longer held any association with the regular army of Relatania. Garr's army openly and often brutally policed the streets of Kankabar. When Montama discreetly inquired of various citizens about the general's character and demeanor, most were too afraid to speak, though a select few bold citizens revealed that Garr was an extremely erratic and dangerous man, but very powerful and extremely ambitious. Of greater value, Montama learned that Garr ruled over a large and treacherous army that could be purchased for the right price.

The Oracle

Montama reasoned that despite the all too apparent risks involved in approaching General Garr, he simply could not be selective. To his politically naïve mind his choices were simple: either secure an army and save his people or stand by helplessly as a new king expropriated his father's lands, in which case he would live a life of abject, fearful subjugation. So, for three units time, Montama listened attentively to others, hoping to learn more about Garr's whereabouts and qualifications. Though he tried not to draw attention to himself, he was after all a stranger, and his dress, accent, and demeanor were different from all those around him. Consequently, he naturally drew rude stares and suspicious looks from the city's generally pathetic looking denizens.

On his fourth unit in Kankabar Montama noticed that a strange little man with three eyes was following him. Montama walked cautiously, pretending that he was interested in a particular item in a grocery store window, while he nervously waited for the three-eyed man's approach. He did not have to wait long. The peculiar man walked quietly behind Montama and then in a barely audible voice whispered, "You speak, mouth different."

It took a moment for Montama to understand what the strange little man was saying. "Yes," Montama finally said with a feigned calmness. "I travel from Nata."

"No! Accent, different, place far from Nata you come from." The three-eyed man's right eye squinted palpably as he spoke.

"Yes," Montama nodded, now facing the store window, carefully watching the three-eyed man out of the corner of his own eyes.

"Here on business, travel to trade, or do you seek someone, perhaps." The peculiar looking man appeared to be far too frail to represent a tangible threat.

"I am looking for someone," Montama said in a calm, inquisitive yet cautious manner, hoping that no one else would overhear his conversation.

The three-eyed man listened attentively and then methodically examined Montama from head to toe. Satisfied by his cursory inspection, he nodded his head and forthrightly declared, "Then I will take you to him."

"Wait!" Montama nearly shouted. "I haven't told you who I am looking for!"

The three-eyed man smiled warmly, before responding resolutely, "Only one man in Kankabar that anyone want to see. I will take you to him."

With a small encouraging wiggle of the little finger of his right hand, the old man directed Montama to follow him.

As he walked down a crowded sidewalk, Montama noticed that the elderly man walked with a pronounced limp and that half of the strange man's left hand was missing. He also could see that the back of the man's neck carried scars, apparently from a severe burn. "Were you injured in battle?" Montama asked.

The old man smiled as he answered. "Many battles, still fight when I can, though walk I can barely." Then with another queer wave of his little finger, he beckoned Montama to follow him, adding curtly, "Come not far, right down this alley way."

At the mention of word alley Montama came to an abrupt halt. Even as inexperienced as he was in the world of intrigue, Montama immediately realized that it was unwise to follow a stranger into a dark ally. He was about to turn away when two other men approached from the opposite side of the street. "Who is this?" one of them asked in a brisk monotone, his face scowling as he spoke.

"Watch him for an hour I did. Like I was asked to do. He is not from here. Perhaps he is the one we are looking for. The one from Arcania." Montama was surprised by the mention of this last word.

"What do you want with the general?" the second soldier asked as he stared intently at Montama's face.

"I come on important business," Montama declared, with only a slight nervous edge to his young, unassuming voice.

"A suitor!" the second soldier said jocularly. "You had best be prepared to make us all rich," he joked. "Come," the soldier directed and the four men walked a few yards down the dark alley to a crooked looking door that opened up into a dingy room lit only by dim candlelight. The room was empty except for a few rather ordinary looking wooden chairs. Pointing to one of them, the three-eyed man directed Montama to "sit and I get him."

Montama nervously obeyed, sitting quietly for a few minutes, eventually twiddling his thumbs to relieve the tension, and then as he realized how silly he must look, he suddenly sat up erect, righting his posture in order to project a more dignified image. He also reminded himself that he had met generals before. Then he realized that these exalted men had been utterly loyal, even obsequious to a fault, in blind deference to his esteemed father. The present situation would be entirely different; for presumably Garr would be unlike anyone else he had ever met. In this view Montama proved to be exceedingly prescient.

When the general entered the room Montama stood with an obviously dull and startled expression on his face. General Garr stood well over six feet six inches tall, a veritable giant of a man for this time in history. His blond hair streamed wildly halfway down his backside. It was far more than the general's height or hair that startled the young man. For as the general reached to shake Montama's hand, the young man noticed that the general also had three eyes, though two of them were sewed tightly shut, while the third middle eye, with its distinctly black pupil, shifted constantly from side to side as it repeatedly scanned the room. Montama correctly inferred that the general had lost two of his eyes in battle, for Garr had a large, dark red scar that cut across the right side of his face, all the way from the cheekbone to the forehead, crossing directly over where his right eye had once been. Montama tried to feign a smile, but it was all too apparent that he was ill at ease in the presence of this powerful and bizarre looking creature.

Montama was not the only one to be thoroughly surprised. The general apparently had expected a much older man, perhaps a lord, and was startled to be in the presence of a mere juvenile. As he slyly withdrew his extended hand, he turned to the old, three-eyed man and asked dismissively, "What is this?"

"He is a stranger, from Arcania perhaps," the three-eyed man responded with an obsequious bow.

Garr stared defiantly again at the pimply young man who stood before him, nodded his head ever so slightly as he inspected Montama's limited physical prowess, and when he was at last satisfied, responded calmly, "I am General Garr." Then turning to the three-eyed man, Garr barked, "Have the guards send in a bottle of green wine from Crestoford." Without as much as a glance toward Montama the general added in a more subdued tone, "You are in for a treat. The wine from Crestoford is the best in the Relatin Empire." Imperiously, Garr then took a seat in an incongruously tiny wooden chair which he dwarfed almost comically so. Montama sat directly across from the general, as Garr impolitely asked, "And who are you?"

Montama squirmed as he responded diffidently, "I am Montama, from the city of Pellaville in Arcania. My father is Lord Tantamount..."

Before Montama could finish his thoughts, a guard entered the room with two glasses and a bottle of wine. "Here is the wine General Garr," the man said before departing.

"Ah yes, let me pour it for you," Garr said as he continued to examine Montama with a cautious eye. As he did so, Montama could not help but stare at Garr's magnetic eye. Aware that the deformity transfixed young Montama, the general glared directly at Montama and asked, "You have never seen a Talacrebe before?"

"No," Montama stammered, trying not to look at the general's eye, but always ending up looking back at it. "I mean, I am sorry for staring, but no we don't have anyone who looks like you in Arcania." The more he prattled on the more nervous Montama became until his voice quivered and his own right eye began to twitch.

The general imperiously lifted his head, again taking the measure of this gangly looking young man. Then, as he handed a glass to Montama he offered an unexpected toast. "To Montama of Pellaville, the next King of Arcania."

When Montama heard these words he fumbled with his glass, then clumsily spilled the wine all over his pants. "How do you know why I am here?" Montama exclaimed with near panic, quite embarrassed and aware that he was making a dismal first impression on the strange looking general.

The general did not react at all. Instead he calmly, carefully sipped his wine, as he meticulously studied Montama's every move. Responding as if nothing untoward had just occurred, Garr smiled and noted, "It is my business to know who my potential suitors will be."

Self consciously, Montama crossed his legs in a futile attempt to look casual. Then, feeling the need to justify his presence, the young man dropped a name hoping to impress the general. "I was sent here by Count Belicki. Have you have heard of him?"

Garr was nonplussed, again merely sipping his wine, enjoying its fragrance and distinctive sweet taste. Again, barely looking at Montama, he responded coldly, "He ruled these very lands a long time ago. He was a cruel man, but he understood how to use power. He disappeared a long time ago."

"What happened to him?" Montama asked timidly.

Leaning forward the general smiled malevolently. "He went on a crazed mission to Arcania to steal something that he raved about, something called the Oracle. He believed that if he possessed this magnificent object he could rule the empire. Most people thought he was absolutely mad and perhaps he was." The general carefully put his wine glass down on the floor next to his chair and then without looking up at Montama, asked, "What do you know about the Oracle?"

"It is a potential source of unlimited power," Montama responded with a rote answer.

Garr laughed boisterously. "Then you know nothing about the Oracle, my young man. That is nothing more than any school child would say." With obvious relish Garr continued, "The Oracle is much more than that. Whoever possesses the Oracle and its extraordinary power will rule Arcania and, if they wish, the entire Relatin Empire, as well."

"Then why don't you seize the Oracle?" Montama asked directly.

The general stretched out his long thin legs and then rested them on another nearby chair before adding with a rueful, devious smirk, "Ah but that is the lesson poor Count Belicki learned the hard way. He tried to seize the Oracle, but it is loyal to only one man and that is the King of Arcania."

"So Belicki was killed?" Montama asked.

"Not exactly," Garr stated cryptically. "He disappeared."

"How do you know all this?" Montama asked, again inadvertently staring rudely at General Garr's middle eye.

"I will tell you in time," General Garr said evasively. Then in a more sinister voice, he concluded, "Get a good night's rest and we will speak again tomorrow." Without as much as another word Garr vigorously stood up and abruptly departed, thus bringing the meeting to an unceremonious conclusion. As Montama sat alone in the room he stared into the darkness, whispering, "What have I got myself into?" Then, as he shivered, he was convinced that his ill conceived and poorly planned trip to Kankabar had been a frightful mistake.

Chapter 23
A State of Emergency

Nimrod continued to perfunctorily record Belicki's strange tale, though frankly, it did not fully comprehend all that the Count divulged. Most significantly, Nimrod was bewildered by the very notion that a so-called real world existed apart from the Oracle's universe of ideas. Since it appeared that Nimrod's entire existence had been spent within the Oracle, it had absolutely no contextual understanding or any preconception of what a real world entailed.

For this elementary reason, Nimrod was confused by seemingly straightforward, basic concepts. For example, when Nimrod first sensed Belicki's thoughts regarding his sister Mira, it was forced to continually reference the connotation of a variety of unfamiliar contextual variables, such as, what is a doorway? Mira exited one, but what was it and what was its purpose? Why was it there and why did Mira use it? Similarly, Nimrod had to download various recollections to discover what was meant by such key terminology as sky, river, flowers, hair, skin, and clothing. In this regard Nimrod was like an infant, learning a vast vocabulary for the very first time, only Nimrod had no ready access to the real world stimuli that Belicki discussed. As such, it was as if Nimrod was memorizing concepts from a world of pure make believe, one that was no more real to it than a world of fairy tale dragons is to us.

In essence, then, everything that Nimrod recorded was revelatory and often confusing. Nothing proved to be more baffling than the seemingly normative distinction between two similar objects. Nimrod immediately realized that Belicki drew important distinctions between humans, another concept that initially was entirely foreign to Nimrod's limited database. In particular, Nimrod was intrigued that Belicki discussed differences between men and women. Nimrod quickly identified the physical and biological distinctions between these two concepts, but was deeply confused by the need to differentiate these two types of humans into separate sexes. Nimrod mused, "Were not all human beings more alike than different? Why then create distinctions between them regarding gender or even more ephemeral criteria such as eye, hair, or skin color?" Fueling Nimrod's confusion was its inherent sophisticated understanding that the basic genomic structure of all humans was highly correlated. "All humans are practically alike," Nimrod calculated, "and the variations that do exist are minor and relatively inconsequential." Given this advanced scientific evidence, which Belicki would never have understood, Nimrod extrapolated, "Why is it necessary to make any distinction at all between any living organisms? Are not all living beings practically identical?"

Nimrod's confusion was further exacerbated when Belicki informed it that Oracle entities were capable of assuming a human form in the real world, as Belicki had done when he visited Montama and as Pondru and King Benton had done when they had appeared before Retch. Nimrod

147

calculated, "If it is possible to assume human form then I should be able to adopt a physical presence as well!" Yet when Nimrod concentrated on its own physical form, it discovered that it had none. Instead, further detailed analysis revealed that it consisted only of a nascent and ill-defined structure, not quite human, yet strangely consisting of human DNA, though without a defined gender. "Does this mean that I am human or not?" Nimrod mused, as it analyzed myriad data sets in a seemingly endless series of systematic permutations, attempting to answer this one solitary question.

On and on, Nimrod futilely searched for answers. With each successive iteration instead of more answers, the questions continued to multiply. If nothing else Nimrod was utterly determined. Resolutely, it persisted in its quest to divine its origins. As it did so, Nimrod became absolutely convinced that the external, physical world, though certainly strange, marvelous and impenetrably baffling, was no more real than the Oracle's universe of ideas. In fact, it appeared to Nimrod as a surreal abstraction, like an expressionist painting or a fully animated world, not an organic one.

And Nimrod was concerned that this so-called real world also was all too often dark and cruel, a world where reason and rationality was casually sacrificed for the sake of mere transitory expediency. It was this human tendency to ignore reason that most perplexed Nimrod as it wondered, "How can it be called a real world if people are capable of blithely casting aside empirical reason and replacing it with a self-delusional fantasy world?" What Nimrod did not comprehend was that it was sensing the world through the depraved, abnormal, schizophrenic perceptions of Belicki's deformed imagination. And since ultimately everything that Nimrod experienced was in the form of a thought, the real world seemed far less real to it than the Oracle's universe of pure, unadulterated imagination. Consequently, Nimrod genuflected, "How could anyone speak authoritatively about *a real world*? Does a real world even exist or is it merely another appendage to the universe of ideas? Does it vary with each individual's unique perception of it?"

Such philosophical musings continually bemused and tantalized Nimrod. Meanwhile, the only thought that comforted Nimrod was any mentioned of Bellazar's name. Though it did not know how or why, Nimrod was certain that this particular human, this woman, held the secret to its very existence. Nimrod therefore listened attentively as Belicki resumed his narrative with a discussion of Bellazar's exploits.

"Will everyone please come to order?" Bellazar declared in a loud and emphatic voice. The setting was an austere conference room on the second floor of the King's Castle. The meeting itself between Bellazar, Rendrau and the august body known as the Conference of Six Judges was unprecedented. According to Arcania's extensive legal code of conduct, Arcanian judges rendered decisions in private, thus avoiding any hint of impropriety or political interference. To further ensure their total objectivity the identities of the judges were kept secret from the public, lest the jurists be subject to bribes or other unsavory political influences. Judges were assigned letters to designate their identifies. The judges attending this particular conclave consisted of Judge L, Judge R, Judge RP, Judge LQ, Judge X, and Judge NO.

Bellazar understood that she was not in the presence of a friendly audience. Consequently, she sat quietly, her hands politely folded, and listened attentively as the Chief Justice NO spoke for the court. "The circumstances we face today are quite unique. With the king and his direct heir both deceased the line of succession moves to his second eldest son, Pondru. At present Pondru's whereabouts are unknown. According to a report written by the late Lord Valmar, Pondru was sent on a diplomatic mission shortly after the onset of his father's illness. He was tasked with meeting Lord Tantamount. We have written confirmation from the lord that Prince Pondru never arrived in Pellaville. We also have an affidavit from Rendrau affirming that troops from the Fourth Army have been dispatched to perform search, rescue and retrieval duties. One interval has passed since this process was initiated. There are continuing unverified reports that Pondru was kidnapped, that he has been identified on the streets of Kekanova, and that his remains were found in a field outside the Kanaween Forest. Consequently, the matter of Pondru's disappearance is still very much unresolved."

Rendrau knew that the report of Pondru's travels to Lord Tantamount's fiefdom was only a cover story. The royal family could not reveal that Pondru mysteriously disappeared after consulting the Oracle, for this revelation would have been far too inflammatory, particularly given the currently unsettled political environment. For this reason Bellazar decided that it was best to continue the futile search for Pondru while she moved through legal channels to resolve the matter of his unexplained disappearance.

Still, the glacial legal pace frustrated her. As Judge NO methodically continued her presentation, never once looking up from her prepared notes, Bellazar sat impatiently, tapping her toes angrily on the floor, as she felt her blood pressure incrementally rise. She listened intently, but with growing exasperation as Judge NO declared, "So the law prescribes that we must wait for a further report from the king's soldiers."

Bellazar could no longer hold her tongue. "And what if Pondru cannot be located?" she asked most impatiently.

Judge NO finally looked up from her notes and responded in a legalese monotone. "Then Prince Rendrau can file a petition of displacement with the court in Teta. If after five intervals Pondru is not located, then Pondru will officially be listed as a displaced person. If attempts to locate him then fail, after five more intervals he officially will be declared to be deceased."

This legal pronouncement was more than Bellazar could tolerate. She threw her arms high above her head as she shouted, "So you are telling me, that we must wait must wait ten intervals, one full cycle before Arcania can have a king?" Though Bellazar was noted for her serenity, particularly in high-pressure situations, she was a force to be reckoned with once she was driven to anger. As her eyes burned with a frightening rage, Rendrau swallowed hard and under his breath whispered, "Here we go," for he had seen Bellazar's rage, on rare occasions, and he knew that it was something to be truly feared.

Judge NO responded in a measured tone. "Prince Rendrau can assume the position of regent after five intervals and then king five intervals after that."

Bellazar angrily stood and then strode belligerently toward Judge NO, grabbing her legal papers, and tossing them into the faces of the other judges. "This is utterly preposterous," Bellazar declared. "You ask this government to sit on its proverbial ass while our enemies mass all around us. Are you deaf to the rising discontent in the streets? Just this morning there are new reports of violence not more than a mile from this very castle." Then turning suddenly toward her husband, Bellazar continued. "And you ask us to wait!"

Bellazar now turned her attention to a man dressed entirely in black. He was seated unobtrusively in the back corner of the diplomatic chamber. He was about forty cycles old, with prematurely yellow skin, one of the few remaining Maldemin. "And what of the Oracle?" she asked. Taking a threatening step toward the Maldemin she continued, "I had a visit last night from a man named Zanzaska." The Maldemin instantly recognized the name, though the judges did not. "Do you know who Zanzaska is?" Bellazar shouted at Judge NO. When the judge signified a negative opinion with a simple dispassionate shrug of her shoulders, Bellazar shouted, "He was an advisor to King Leonata and he died a century ago!"

The Maldemin now calmly intervened. "It was a manifestation from the Oracle."

Rendrau timidly interjected, "What do you mean by a manifestation?"

The Maldemin, mellow and entirely unperturbed responded with a transcendental serenity. "Since there is no king, no one controls the Oracle. The Oracle has many voices, each represented by a different entity, someone who once lived and traveled in our own world, but who now exists only within the Oracle. These entities are now relentlessly searching for a new leader."

"Searching?" Bellazar asked acerbically. "What do you mean?"

"They will search far and wide until they find a suitable king."

"You mean the Oracle has been in contact with others?" Bellazar shouted.

Undoubtedly," the Maldemin said. "Without a leader the Oracle will search until it finds a new king. And there is more. Although the Oracle is comprised of thousands of entities, and many of them have amazing abilities, two of them are particularly dangerous, with the far-reaching powers of a cunning wizard. These two entities, more than any of the others, are capable of channeling their own thoughts into energy, and from energy to matter, and then from matter into any shape or form of reality. With the mere power of thought they can create incredible images, things that we cannot even anticipate."

"Such as causing an entire army to disappear into the ground?" Rendrau asked sullenly.

"Precisely," the Maldemin said, as he sat, unperturbed, his hands politely folded.

"Who are these two wizards you speak of?" Bellazar demanded.

The Maldemin answered, "Their names are Kublatitan and Count Belicki. Neither one is from Arcania, yet both of them covet our passra for entirely different reasons. Each one is obsessed and addicted to power, ready to destroy anyone who stands in their way." The Maldemin then stared directly at Bellazar with a keen, but steady look. "But in the end only one of them can rule, though I do not know which one will prevail." Then with an empathetic glance that conveyed a deep-felt sadness the Maldemin added, "Yet the fate of Arcania depends on the outcome of the Oracle's civil war. Unless we soon have a king, our passra may be forced to pay a truly horrible price."

Turning abruptly toward the six judges Bellazar emphatically declared, "You see! We have no choice! We must proclaim Rendrau king today!"

The Maldemin slowly shook his head. "We cannot merely proclaim someone to be king. The Oracle itself must choose one, as it did with King Leonata and King Benton."

"How the hell do you know that? Are you speculating?" Bellazar asked, her hands now tensely clasped before her chest.

Trying to calm his wife, Rendrau asked, "Is there any way to stop the Oracle from searching for a new leader?"

The Maldemin closed his eyes and then proclaimed, "That is the Oracle's purpose: to find a suitable leader. Only when it finds a leader that it desires will a new king be proclaimed and only then will the passra find peace."

Bellazar's patience was at an end. In a voice so shrill it veritably shook the golden leaves of the parnisus trees she proclaimed, "Then I declare a State of Emergency. Rendrau is now your Regent."

Judge NO adamantly shook her head. "That would not be legal."

"To hell with the law!" Bellazar declared emphatically, her eyes utterly ablaze with righteous indignation.

Judge NO continued, "Then the Conference of Judges will have no choice but to notify the public that you have violated King Benton's Resolutions of Human Freedom, as well as Arcania's Articles of Succession."

Bellazar's steely eyes glared directly into Judge NO's soul. "And if you do I will get six more judges in here and then I will notify your families where they can pick up your corpses."

The other judges had remained patiently and obediently silent until this moment, but upon hearing this threat Judge X meekly intervened. "Of course there are exceptions to every rule."

"Now we are starting to hear some reason." Bellazar responded. "I hereby order the Conference of Judges to declare a State of Emergency. You will declare Rendrau to be the passra's new regent with all of the powers that accompany the throne." For emphasis she paused momentarily, then asked, "Do I make myself clear?"

"Yes," said Judge NO.

Richard Waterman

Datoria 2

THE ARCANIAN CALENDAR

30 Hours in a Unit or Day
14 Units in a Fortnight
40 Units in all ten of Arcania's Intervals or Months
Or 400 Units in a Cycle
10 Intervals in One Cycle or Year
10 Cycles in a Decade
100 Cycles in a Century
500 Cycles in a Buzwat
1000 Cycles in a Millennium

Chapter 24
Imperial Hubris

Pantamanu had never been happier. His exalted martial designation was Commander of the King's elite Third Army, a title created especially for him. Even more enticing, he wore the Commander's striking blue uniform, with various glorious ribbons and dazzling medals celebrating the many great military accomplishments of the Centama family. It did not in the least concern Pantamanu that he himself had never earned any single one of these commemorations. What was of far more critical importance was that his uniform attracted the attention of the ladies, literally by the dozens. As a result, military life represented the literal fulfillment of an adolescent boy's most outlandish fantasy. During the daytime as Commander, he played the role of the dignified officer, while never having to do anything more demanding than posing on horseback while reviewing the troops. Then, at night, the military hero relaxed in the arms of sundry local women who were totally dedicated to satisfying his voracious and ostensibly insatiable sexual appetite. It was a spectacle that amused the men of the Third Army, who facetiously referred to Pantamanu's private tent as "the Commander's Bordello."

If the troops were amused, the same could not be said of General Wu, the man who was really in charge of the Third Army. He was not amused by what he called "the whoring." He was decidedly not amused that of all the officers in the great Arcanian army, it had been decided that he alone would be forced "to baby sit the king's damn youngest son." And he was downright incensed that Pantamanu forced everyone, including the general himself, to refer to him as "Commander Pantamanu." All of these factors, plus the fact that Pantamanu lacked even the slightest penchant for military discipline absolutely mortified and exasperated the general, who, because he had no other recourse, decided to bravely swallow his immense pride and simply carry on.

He did this because, at his absolute central core, General Wu was a loyal Centama family man. So instead of confrontation, he tried to be diplomatic, privately and delicately breaching the subject of the commander's inappropriate military comportment, while concomitantly delineating the finer points of military etiquette. No matter how many times Wu broached the subject, however, Pantamanu proved to be utterly tone deaf and for good reason: as a Centama he ultimately was responsible to none but the king himself. Therefore, despite his repeated egregious excesses, no one, not even General Wu, dared to tell Pantamanu what to do.

Instead, one night well past midnight, as he lay awake wondering why the Oracle had cursed him with this unruly young brat, the general had a revelation. As he sat up suddenly in his bed, the general called out, "What if I move his blasted tent out of camp?" Wu thought the idea was a masterstroke of genius. As he lay in bed contemplating the possibility he realized, "Pantamanu will never be fool enough to agree to such an arrangement." Still, as Wu tossed and turned throughout the night he concluded that his "relocation plan," as he called it, was the only possible remedy. So, as the Commander awakened at the Arcanian equivalent of 10 AM, General Wu greeted him with a broad and inviting smile.

Pantamanu sat on the edge of his bed, wearing nothing but his caltavera, an undergarment that one simply wrapped around one's waistline. As he listened to General Wu's proposal, Pantamanu asked suspiciously, "You mean that if I consent to this move I would have fewer responsibilities?" Wu was certain that his reluctant protégé viewed the suggestion as a demotion. Consequently, he was heartily surprised when Pantamanu actually endorsed the plan. Wu nodded his head politely as Pantamanu responded; "I am getting tired of parading around all day with the troops." When Pantamanu added, "I believe I already have learned a great deal about military tactics and discipline" the general stared at Pantamanu as if to ask, "Which of Arcania's three moons are you on?" But through inner strength and discipline, and with even greater dignity, Wu calmly agreed, "Commander, I believe that you have learned all that you will ever know." To Wu's amazement, then, Pantamanu enthusiastically agreed with him on all particulars. In fact, the young prince was so eager to have his tent relocated that he demanded that they do it that very unit.

Despite his outward bellicosity, in reality Pantamanu always had been content to play the game of soldier. Despite his vitriolic excoriation of Retch's meager military qualifications, even a perfunctory scrutiny of his own record would have demonstrated that Pantamanu had no more martial training than his oldest brother. Like many Arcanian boys, at the age of fifteen Pantamanu had joined the King's Patrol, roughly equivalent of a teenage militia unit. Even then, his superior officers found the young prince to be "petulant and ill suited to the rigors of military life." Writing to King

The Oracle

Benton, one officer noted, "If Pantamanu ever puts his mind to it he might very well be a marvelous soldier." Then he added, "So far there is little evidence to suggest that he takes his responsibilities seriously." Pantamanu's final superior officer had thrown a fit when he discovered that while all of the other soldiers shared equally in the hardships of military life, the youngest prince was assigned his own private tent, bed, and servants.

King Benton had not pressed the matter, for he understood that Pantamanu simply saw no reason to surrender to the rigors of military discipline. After all, he was the king's son and that required a unique set of circumstances. Certainly, he could not be treated like an ordinary soldier.

Unfortunately, as Pantamanu reached adulthood, he saw no logical reason to live like a soldier, not even a pampered officer. Instead, he demanded special privileges including an even grander tent than that afforded to General Wu.

Furthermore, his practical experience was entirely theatrical. No one, not even the young prince, had expected him to venture onto a battlefield, at least not while a battle was actually ongoing. And so while the Third Army drilled monotonously, unit after unit, Pantamanu withdrew to his newly relocated tent, periodically spending a few precious moments before the troops where he struck a majestic pose on his stately black and white palomino, wearing his blue uniform, with a new addition, a sash of gold and silver that Pantamanu personally designed. And when a small detachment from the Third Army briefly exchanged arms with a rogue lord from eastern Arcania, a minor battle that lasted no more than thirty minutes, Pantamanu found no hypocrisy in releasing the equivalent of what a later age would call a press statement exalting his extraordinary courage in battle, though in reality he had been nowhere near the scene of the engagement. The news of Pantamanu's heroics was quickly related to Teta where Bellazar ensured that it was appropriately ignored and quickly forgotten. "No matter," Pantamanu declared defiantly. "If war comes I will be at its epicenter." Then he ordered an aide to ride back to Teta to secure more wine and some fine linen for the ladies.

Richard Waterman

General Garr's Insignia

Chapter 25
A Deal with the Devil

Montama slept sporadically before his second meeting with General Garr and when he did he dreamed that his family had been exiled to a strange and mysterious land. Hontallo and Lord Tantamount were both trapped in what appeared to be a savage snowstorm, atop a prodigious mountain peak, with virtually no hope of survival. As the two men staggered forward through the raging snowstorm, Lord Tantamount's face was covered with streams of frozen tears, while Hontallo, his hair uncharacteristically long and knotted, held onto his father for dear life.

When Montama suddenly awakened, he realized it was another dream sent by the Oracle, a sign of things to come, that is, if he did not become king. As sweat poured profusely down his forehead, Montama realized that he had no choice but to secure a deal with General Garr. When he finally dragged himself out of bed, utterly exhausted and thoroughly bedraggled, he stared ahead in an almost somnambulant state, mentally preparing himself for his critical meeting with the general.

An hour later two burly soldiers escorted Montama to Garr's headquarters. One guard was a strikingly tall Ka-Why-Tee, using his third short arm to carry what appeared to be the general's daily correspondence. When he entered Garr's headquarters Montama found the setting to be utterly surreal, decorated with an assortment of strange looking stuffed animals, many of which Montama could not recognize. One carcass that caught his eye was that of a bird with eight wings. Another was what at least appeared to be a dog without a body: its head resting directly on four exceedingly short legs. Montama stared at these oddities wondering what kind of man would surround himself with such bizarre attractions. Before he could consider this question, Garr sashayed into the room wearing a preposterously long flowing green cape. Without a moment of hesitation, Garr briskly commenced the meeting. "In answer to your earlier question, I too have been visited by Count Belicki. He tells me that you need an army?"

"Yes, sir," Montama responded deferentially. Then in a more forceful tone the young man asked, "And what do you want, General Garr?"

Garr was equally direct. "I want to be Emperor of all Relatania, of course." Garr then flashed such an unexpected smile that Montama did not know whether to take him seriously or not. It took a few seconds before Montama realized that Garr was not jesting. As the general took a seat and crossed his legs, his cape draped freely on the floor, he declared, "This is my offer. I will make you King of Arcania if you use the Oracle to make me Relatania's next Emperor."

"Is that possible?" Montama asked incredulously.

"The Empire is teetering. It only needs a little nudge and it will fall. I have an army, but I will need the Oracle to ensure success."

Montama did not have to think twice about the terms. "I agree," he said without hesitation.

"That is good," Garr responded with a savage smile. "Then we have a deal, that is, so long as you can prove to me that you are worthy of being king of Arcania."

"And how do I do that?" Montama asked.

Though Montama tried to hide his feelings, Garr could sense the young man's growing apprehension. He therefore leaned menacingly forward in his chair and asked, "Do you know anything about the Bogul barbarians?"

"They are a threat to the empire," Montama answered directly.

Garr stood up and began to pace the room, with his cape trailing loosely behind him. "The Boguls have vexed the Empire for sometime, attacking to the north and penetrating as far as thirty miles from the city of Relatania itself. They were driven back. They will return, of that you can be sure. So far, they have been a constant source of instability and as such they have provided us with a much-needed opportunity to build up our own military forces. Someday, however, if we are to rule this empire, they will have to be eliminated, every single one of them."

"What do you mean eliminated?" Montama asked not sure whether Garr meant the threat from the Boguls or the Boguls themselves.

Garr now stopped in his tracks and stared intently at Montama. Cold bloodedly, and without remorse, the general stated, "They are a moral pestilence! They infect everything they touch with their insidious, diseased minds. They are a threat to everyone that lives! So when we are done not one Bogul will be left alive. Not one man, woman or child." Garr spoke without emotion, as if he were discussing the removal of some form of ordinary infestation.

As he listened, Montama felt anxiety welling up inside. His stomach knotted. From the beginning, he had sensed that Garr might be deranged, but now all of Montama's fears about the general were realized. "He is mad!" Montama thought.

Garr was not finished. Still speaking in a controlled voice, as if he were discussing perfunctory matters of state, Garr continued, "When I say that all Boguls must be eliminated, this means everywhere, even in Arcania."

For the first time, Montama felt a sudden urge to run. Defensively, he responded, "We don't have many of them in Arcania. In fact, it's hard to tell who is a Bogul and who is not."

"We will find them," Garr snarled. "Or you will have no army."

Fearing for his life, Montama uneasily conceded, "I agree to your condition."

Garr smiled, certain that he had thoroughly intimidated his young guest. He was now ready to challenge Montama with the ultimate test of loyalty. "Just one more thing," he said, before shouting, "Bring in the prisoner."

As Montama watched, two guards marched into the room accompanied by a manacled and nearly naked man. As these men entered, Garr kept his gaze fixed directly on Montama. Without a word of warning, the strange general then did something quite remarkable: he reached his left hand back inside his cape and then with the lithe dexterity of a master magician, he abruptly withdrew a weapon that looked like a miniature sword, for it was slightly less than half the size of a real sword. Without a word, Garr tossed the still sharp and deadly weapon at Montama who though surprised, caught it without cutting his hand. Perplexed, Montama stared at the sword's handle, which was constructed entirely out of balsa wood, a common enough material. Then the young man noticed a beautiful yet disturbing carving on the blade itself: a most unusual engraving, the general's own private insignia, a splendid multicolored, hissing caltepa snake that was tightly coiled in the shape of the letter "G". Montama knew that this bizarre multi-headed snake was so lethal that it could kill a man instantly with the mere touch of any one of its electrically charged, venomous tongues. Montama felt ill as he stared at the weapon. Outwardly he betrayed no emotion whatsoever. Instead he calmly asked, "What do you want me to do with it?"

Garr's response was bone chillingly direct. "This man is a Bogul. Kill him now or we have no deal."

When Montama heard this declaration, his hand shook so palpably that he feared he would drop the sword. Nervously, he fixed his gaze on the pitiable, manacled creature that stood, barely alive and shivering helplessly before him. The Bogul obviously had had no sustenance for some time and was so feeble that he was able to stand only because the two guards held him up by his armpits. As Montama peered ahead at the Bogul's glassy, vapid, and barely conscious eyes, he again felt an inexorable urge to flee as quickly as possible from the room. The idea of leading a mighty army, a dream that had captivated his young, inexperienced imagination, was no longer a mere abstraction. For the very first time Montama realized what was really at stake. If he wanted to be king many people, just like this poor pathetic Bogul, would have to die, their only sin being that they lived at the wrong time and place in history.

Montama was at a crossroad. If he ran, he would surely be put to death and his family would be left in a state of terrible peril. Yet he could not find the will to strike this hapless, innocent man. He therefore was about to defiantly cast the sword on the floor when he noticed that something absolutely impossible was happening. The movement of every single object in the room, even a fly in mid air, was slowly coming to a halt, as time was inextricably suspended. At first startled and then utterly terrified, Montama frantically scanned the room for any sign of life. He was relieved when he saw a figure emerging from a corner of the room that had been veiled by a dark and foreboding shadow.

As Garr and the others stood frozen in place, Montama was astonished when he recognized the form and figure of Count Belicki, ominously emerging from the shadows, and moving directly toward his young protégé. "You hesitate?" I asked, as my teeth grimaced with a hateful anger. As I finally stood directly before Montama, the terrified young man was incapable of offering a response. I therefore divined his thoughts for him. "You are wondering if it is right to kill this innocent man?" I moved closer until Montama could feel the chill of my otherworldly presence. The young man then shivered as he felt my consciousness directly enter his own mind.

Full of a malevolence that Montama simply could not understand, I showed the young man images of men on fire, women running while defiantly holding their infants, as men on horseback charged menacingly after them. Then I showed Montama countless rows of mutilated bodies. It was so real that Montama actually could smell the hideous stench of death. Consumed with these terrifying images, the young man stared unknowingly into the thin air, for I now existed only in his mind.

I was intent on showing Montama more than simply the hideous face of war. I now commenced a malevolent soliloquy. "Just a few minutes ago you did not hesitate to condemn this entire man's race to a fitting death? But now you hesitate to kill this one, pathetic individual?" Montama was overcome with vertigo as my conscience swirled inexorably inside his imagination. "I have sent you a dream. You know what will happen to your father and your brother if you do not act now. So, if you honor their lives, you will kill this man. Otherwise, you and your family will suffer a horrible and ignominious death." At this moment, my emotions burned with a fierce hatred as Montama shared my most private and disturbing thoughts.

It was then that I sensed that Montama was no longer sure what was real and what was not (a feeling Nimrod also shared as it listened attentively to Belicki's narration). Reality and imagination entirely blurred. In this strange state of existence Montama became certain of one cold undeniable fact: I was right. His only choices were to kill the Bogul or to forfeit everything that he had ever coveted.

Having achieved my objective, my presence slowly lifted from the young boy's mind. As it did, Montama glared vapidly at the half sword with its strange hateful insignia, and then, without as much as another thought, he leaped forward, thrusting the weapon stridently into the Bogul's chest with such tangible force that it tore the poor creature's chest cavity asunder. As blood spurted in all directions, the poor innocent man took his final breath before falling lifelessly to the floor.

With Montama's sudden movement, I restored the room to normal time. A slightly surprised General Garr smiled as the guards reached down and carried the decrepit Bogul's body from the bloodstained room. Meanwhile, Montama feebly dropped the half sword on the ground, then stared defiantly at the general and in a voice totally devoid of even the slightest trace of emotion, inquired, "Is that sufficient proof of my intentions or is there anything else you require me to do?"

Garr nodded his head appreciatively as he put his arm on Montama's left shoulder. "There is one more thing," Garr said with a mischievous smile. "There will be a feast tonight, to be held in your honor. The main course will be the heart of the man you just killed."

At this moment, Montama could feel absolutely nothing. He was an empty vessel. Barely aware that normal time had resumed, the young man nodded his head and said, "I will do whatever it takes to be king."

Garr smiled heartily, for his doubts about young Montama were entirely assuaged. "Then we have much to do," the general responded, as he led

Montama from the room that was now permeated with the fresh, cold, sinister stench of death.

Chapter 26
A New King

In the fortnight since the official spokesperson for the royal family announced that Rendrau was the passra's newly ordained regent, the political situation deteriorated rapidly. General Xona, the head of Arcania's Second Army had intervened when rioters burned buildings in the holy city of Kekanova, where religious leaders fueled rumors that the Centama family had murdered the Priest Exemplar of Teta, the High Cleric Rendella, stabbing him through the chest while he lay helplessly prostrated, begging pitiably for mercy. It was further insinuated that Regent Rendrau had been present and knew the identity of Rendella's murderer.

Even in the northern port city of Capo, a stronghold of Centama family sentiment, hand drawn periodicals delineated rumors of incestuous relations between the regent's wife and another member of the royal family. There were also accusations that the royal family had fraudulently misappropriated state funds.

Bellazar was sure that Pantamanu was the source of these various scurrilous rumors. "Damn it, we must fight fire with fire." She therefore formed several groups of what she called "truth squads" which were tasked with traveling the passra, rebutting these foul rumors and setting the record straight. "You must immediately respond to these allegations, while also letting the passra know more about my dear brother-in-law's own peculiar habits," she ordered. Among the charges against Pantamanu, she wanted the people to know that he had a penchant for wild orgies, that he used various hallucinogenic drugs, and that he had fathered an illegitimate child with the wife of a prominent Arcanian general. "I want everyone to know that Pantamanu is the whore of the passra," Bellazar charged.

As another fortnight passed, and as charges and counter charges mounted, Bellazar became aware that she had made a dreadful mistake by elevating Rendrau to the passra's regency. "It is a position of no power whatsoever, an empty office befitting a clown. We need a king, not a regent."

The Oracle

Not only had her decision failed to address the leadership vacuum, the political situation was now far worse than it had been even a fortnight before. As soon as it was proclaimed that Rendrau was Regent, there was an instantaneous rise in sundry acts of petty intrigue and blatant political rebellion. "Treason!" is what Bellazar called it, as she now stood staring out from her third story window overlooking the city of Teta. "How could I have been so foolish?" she badgered herself mercilessly, realizing that dangers were continuing to mount all around her.

As she stood by her window side, her steely mind thought back to something she had read earlier in the morning's intelligence. It was a new circular that called for "change" and for "bold new leadership." She pursed her lips as she exclaimed, "If that's what the people want, I will give it to them."

It was then that an inner door inside her mind opened, revealing a vast array of memories, dossiers, information of a most intimate and useful nature, gossip, and all of the other things a brilliant political tactician carries with them. As her thoughts rifled through the various ideas that permeated her imagination, she realized that her decision to name Rendrau as Regent had created a vicious circle.

As Regent, Rendrau was blamed for everything, yet he did not have the authority or the legitimacy to rule effectively. It was worse than having no king. Being regent entailed all of the perils of government, without any of the trappings of office. Now that she realized her mistake, how could Bellazar free her husband without casting further doubts about his leadership ability? She closed her eyes in total concentration. Rendrau would be finished if he stepped down as regent for the ordinary citizens and the political elite would forever perceive him as being so pitifully weak that he readily abrogated his own authority. Then, Pantamanu could march into Teta and seize control. What was the second option? If Rendrau remained as regent, then he would continue to face stern and growing opposition until his legitimacy irrevocably withered away.

Bellazar was a thoroughly logical person and after giving the matter considerable thought she realized that if there are only two viable courses of action and neither one is tenable, then one must create a third alternative. So for several hours she stared out of her castle window at the scarred and unsettled city of Teta as she wrestled with this seemingly insolvable political conundrum.

An idea finally came to her late at night. Without as much as consulting Rendrau, she sent an aide to awaken Lord Gulcum, the feeble diplomat that Bellazar chose to replace Lord Valmar. Gulcum was obsequious to the core, but when he arrived, disheveled and barely awake, even he could not mask his incredulity upon hearing Bellazar's solution to the present leadership conundrum. "You want to declare that Pondru is our king?" Gulcum asked, as he swallowed hard, for he knew that he had a rather silly expression on his dull little face. He was not a particularly gifted man, for Bellazar did not need someone wiser than herself as her personal adviser. Lord Gulcum, who was in his early forties, had little imagination and no matter how hard he tried he simply could not understand what political benefit would be gained by naming a dead man to be Arcanian's next king. Flustered and utterly flabbergasted, he responded meekly, "I don't understand."

"It's simple," Bellazar announced. "Pondru will be king and he will take all of the blame for the unrest throughout the Passra. As for my husband, he, not Pantamanu, will be free to ride to the passra's rescue."

"But Pondru is dead, is he not?" the mousy adviser asked.

Bellazar laughed heartily, as she stared directly into Gulcum's witless eyes. "The people pine for a new king. We will give them one. And then we will quietly restore order, without the constant glare of public scrutiny that the regency entails. In an interval or two we will find a corpse that looks like Pondru, and with his passing, Rendrau will become Arcania's king. What do you think of the idea?"

Gulcum meekly lowered his head. "It is not my role to think," the aide said submissively and without conviction.

"Then summon the Conference of Six Judges at once," Bellazar ordered. "It is time for the change the people demand. They will have at last a new king."

Chapter 27
Count Belicki's Surprise

As the political situation in Arcania continued to deteriorate, Montama remained secluded in a small private room above General Garr's secret headquarters. For more than a fortnight Montama ostensibly rested at this covert domicile while the general and his brilliant staff developed an intricate plan for the invasion of Arcania. Montama played virtually no role whatsoever in this developmental process, preferring instead to leave the details of strategic decision making to the military experts. The fact that he was a martial neophyte was not the only reason Montama preferred to remain, as much as possible, out of the action and above the fray. The real more painful reason was that since the unit he had struck the Bogul man dead, his mind had been utterly consumed with visions of that horrific incident, a single moment in time that abruptly and quite unexpectedly altered his perceptions of the very nature of life and death.

To put it all in perspective, until Montama's arrival in Kankabar, the young man had envisioned his present military quest as nothing more complicated than one of Captain Bale's fictionalized amazing adventures. The young innocent man had thought that his journey would represent another in an inevitable series of battles between good and evil. Montama had never heard of the word *nuance* and when it was explained to him he could not comprehend the concept. Nor did he understand the concept of moral ambiguity. Now, as he harshly reviewed his own recent comportment, Montama sensed that either he had acted in a most foul or wicked manner or that a clear-cut distinction between good and evil simply did not exist.

He thought about this vision of blurred morality every single time he went to bed. Previously, when he had fantasized, Montama always saw himself as the embodiment of the heroic Captain Bale. Now whenever he closed his eyes he saw his own image, raising a shiny half sword high above his head and then bringing it down with an inexplicable cruelty against a man that he had never before known, a man who had done him absolutely no harm whatsoever, whose only crime was that he belonged to a group of despised people, the Boguls. Montama himself had no hard feelings whatsoever against "these people." Though his own father had gone to war against an invading Bogul horde some thirty cycles ago, the lord never personally berated anyone for being a Bogul. He never even cast aspersions against their values or courage. So then why had Montama struck this poor unfortunate man with such lethal force?

As Montama tried to answer this complicated question he harshly judged his motives and found himself guilty of a most indefensible and despicable deed. As a result, he fell into a deep depression, sure that he was guilty of claiming a precious life merely because he had been ordered to do so. It was an abject and cowardly act to which he had blindly and meekly acquiesced.

And while his waking hours were painful, Montama's dream state became pure torture, for he was completely consumed with visions of the Bogul's ghastly murder, played out over and over again, seemingly from every possible angle, as if he was both a witness to and a participant in this ghastly, horrendous crime. And each time the scene ended precisely the same way; with the poor defenseless man's body on the floor, while blood spurted in every imaginable direction. Montama winced palpably, desperately trying to clear the image from his mind. He discovered, however, that it was imprinted even more indelibly than it had been the night before.

While Montama spent most of his time alone in his room, he was never really alone. For even as he slept, and especially at these times when his senses were most vulnerable to careful prodding and manipulation, I entered the young man's thoughts. I reasoned with my young protégé, repeatedly explaining the true nature of war and politics. "There is always collateral death and destruction in war! It is not murder if you kill someone in time of war. And a king can do anything that he wishes. In killing the Bogul you did nothing more than what was required at the time to save your family from ruin." I patiently lectured, "Your conscience is now your enemy. You must let it go of it if you are ever to be king."

To illustrate this point I showed Montama the secret of Retch's terrible tragedy. "Like you the Oracle forced him to perform a most foul deed, the murder of his own father. He was unable to cope with the guilt and in the end his feelings of remorse destroyed him. If he had had the strength to do what is necessary, he would be king today."

Night after night I counseled young Montama, always whispering my advice deeply into the sleeping youth's mind. "You did nothing more than what was required," I repeated endlessly. "This is not the last death that you will see. But in the end, you *will* be king."

Montama always awakened from these nocturnal encounters drenched in sweat, his heart beating profusely, and his eyes open wide with terror. As a result, during the early morning he actually was more confused and irritated than he had been before he rested. Finally, exhausted beyond reason, the young man let loose his emotions and cried for several hours, wondering aloud if he would ever be forgiven for this most unspeakable and heinous of all crimes. It was not until this cathartic shedding of tears that Montama was finally able to dispassionately re-evaluate his growing inner turmoil. As he sat alone in his room, picking at his lunch, he was able for the first time to consider the possibility that I might be right after all.

Montama reasoned that war calls on good men to do terrible deeds. Even the very best of men must do horrific things that they otherwise would never contemplate. Had his father not killed men during the Bogul invasion? Though Lord Tantamount had never spoken of it, Montama was absolutely sure of it. Then he wondered, what is the purpose of war? His answer was simple: survival is the key and his very continued existence required him to kill the Bogul, ruthlessly, without conscience, or he himself most certainly would have perished. This self-realization proved to be an entirely transformative thought and initially Montama took considerable solace from the idea that by killing the Bogul his own family would survive.

"Damn the Bogul," Montama finally muttered angrily, sure that his ultimate objective, to be a benevolent ruler, would in the long term justify any sins he might be required to commit under the present hostile circumstances. "If I had let the Bogul live, I would be dead, as would my family, and some other despot would rule Arcania in my place. Would the passra be better off then?" It was a classic straw man argument, for Montama already knew the answer before he posed the question. "Of course the passra will be better off if I am king. I alone will work tirelessly to improve the lives of the people." It was a righteousness forged out of necessity to cleanse his conscience of a most hideous crime. Like most self-rationalizations, it perfectly served its limited purpose. Therefore, when General Garr arrived to inform Montama that in but two units time they would depart for Arcania, the young man was utterly convinced that he had not only done the right thing by killing the Bogul, but that if the same circumstances were to prevail again he would do precisely the same thing. He reasoned that men die in war. Consequently, he told himself, "I had best get used to the idea." With this decision, Montama irrevocably sacrificed his youthful innocence. He also gained something important in return, the strength to do what is necessary to seize political leadership.

Two units later, when Montama finally mounted his horse for what General Garr enigmatically referred to as "the long march to Arcania," the young man was sure that his cause was just and that whatever horrors he might subsequently confront, Arcania would be a much better passra because he would be its next king. Still, despite this new sense of moral rectitude, Montama felt strange riding at the head of a mighty army, consisting as far as he could divine of several thousand men, absolutely none of them from Arcania. He quickly got used to the idea that he was to be their leader, particularly since General Garr was really in command and would make all of the critical tactical decisions. Whenever necessary he could take his cues directly from this strange giant of a man, who on horseback, looked even more imposing than he did the first time Montama had laid eyes upon him. His long blond hair streamed behind him in the wind and his solitary eye, which before had darted continuously from side to side, now glared always forward, inexorably determined, unwavering in its belief in the rightness of this holy cause. As Montama watched the general out of the corner of his own eye, he was impressed by Garr's stoicism and relieved that this extraordinary colossus was riding by his side.

With all of the men, women, sundry beasts and military equipment lined up for the long march to the Bay of Battle, Montama understood why it would take more than a full unit for this gargantuan entourage to travel to the coast. Since he had not been in on the particulars of the military planning, Montama did not yet know how this mighty army would be transported across the Bay of Battle. "Had not the great General Tampinco lost many of his men in the journey across the Bay?" Montama asked with growing curiosity. "How will we ever cross it?"

Garr flashed a devious smile as he resolutely stared straight ahead. "You will see," he obfuscated. Then tantalizingly he added, "It will be a surprise, I am sure." The general then rode out ahead of his army and with a theatrical flourish, turned his horse back so that he was staring directly at Montama and then with nearly uncontrollable glee added, "A very big surprise indeed."

The truth is that everything was proving to be a surprise to this untested young soldier. Montama watched in awe as column after column of men and women carrying swords, shields, clubs, spears, bows, arrows, and sundry other deadly instruments of war, strode forward along the newly beaten path toward the sea. Most of these men and women exhibited a cold, hard exterior, completely accustomed to discomfort and pain, for theirs was a continuously hard life. They ranged in age from boys younger than Montama to men with yellow skin who looked so grizzled and harried that the lord's youngest son was unsure if they would even survive the journey. As for the women, though there were far fewer of them, they too projected an aura of danger and determination.

Mile after mile the procession trudged forward, stopping only intermittently to rest and water the beasts. The army ate at breakfast and did not eat again until late at night, carrying only as much water as was necessary to quench their thirst along the way. Men prided themselves in their ability to march for long distances without sustenance or rest, and Garr constantly encouraged them, riding up and down the line, complimenting soldiers on their gritty appearance or denigrating those who seemed to slack behind. There were occasional problems, such as a broken ox cart that temporarily blocked the way. The march to the sea was largely uneventful, though occasionally farmers lined the way to watch the procession, unsure whose army it might be or where it was going, but entranced nonetheless by the wondrous spectacle of this mighty army on the move.

Finally, as the army reached the summit of a long, slowly rising hill, Montama smelled the scent of seawater and instantly realized that the army at last was approaching the Bay of Battle. And when he was able to see over the hill's crest, he was completely dumbfounded by what he saw. "My god!" he said as he stared forward at the gigantic hairy beasts that were lined up impressively against the vast sandy shoreline. "What are they?"

General Garr leaned back in his mount and with a grand wave of his right hand declared, "These are our ultimate weapon, the most feared of all animals, talladaggers."

There must have been a hundred of these huge beasts, each standing more than twenty feet tall and weighing at least a ton. Their appearance was both distinctive and frightening. The talladagger's body resembled that of a wooly mammoth, with its hulking body swaying wildly from side to side as it moved inexorably forward. Its body was covered with spindly black hair that was abrasive to the touch and its gigantic feet were large enough to crush a man with one horrific step. Yet it was the beast's head that was the most unusual of all its features. Instead of one solitary head, two enormous appendages, each about three feet thick and extending outward for twelve to fifteen feet, protruded ominously from its neck. Each appendage contained a large black oval eye. By manipulating these trunk-like appendages, the behemoth could see in virtually any direction. In addition to an eye, the appendage was covered with numerous sticky tentacles that allowed the beast to lift heavy objects far over its head. A talladagger could therefore grasp dangerous animals, or humans, in each one of its tentacled trunk heads, either crushing them in its powerful grasp or dropping them with a ferocious force on the ground, before stomping them violently with their oversized feet. Either way, when enraged talladaggers were especially lethal.

They also could be exceedingly mild mannered, content to consume tree branches and other fauna, through wide apertures that periodically opened and closed at the end of their long bulky trunks.

Garr loved the beasts because they could be riled to anger in an instant and he knew precisely how to agitate them to the very best effect, charging them in herds directly toward a startled enemy army. As Montama watched in amazement, one of the beasts stood playfully on its hind legs, while raising its fore huffs high in the air. As the beast thundered out a loud and terrifying cry, Montama asked, "What do you do with them?"

"You will see," Garr said softly as he too admired the great beasts spirit and strength.

Now Montama was utterly confused for in addition to the army and its equipment, it would be necessary to transport about a hundred of these gigantic beasts across the Bay of Battle, an absolutely impossible task. As Montama watched the bay's huge undulating waves crashing violently against the shore, he asked, "How will we ever get them across the Bay?" Montama stared back at the long line of horses, men, carts, and talladaggers. It would take many more than a thousand ships to even attempt to transport this army across the Bay, yet there were absolutely no ships of any sort within miles of their present location.

Garr smiled deviously and in a confident loud voice declared, "And now for the surprise I promised you."

Utterly confused, Montama responded, "You mean the talladaggers are not the surprise?"

Garr laughed heartily and then as he extended his right arm he pointed eastward toward an area that was largely obscured by a clump of green and yellow bushes. Montama craned his neck forward and saw that several dozen men were clearing the area. The general then exclaimed, "This is Count Belicki's greatest surprise." As the general grandly waved his hand, and as his men diligently pulled the bushes from the shoreline, Montama could see what appeared to be an entrance leading into a dark and rather strange looking cave, which seemed to lead directly under the Bay's turbulent waters, down into the very bowels of the earth itself.

As they rode closer to the cave's entry, Montama gasped, "It's enormous." Preening his head forward to secure a better look, the young man asked, "How deep is it?"

Garr proudly proclaimed, "It is taller than two talladaggers and it reaches all the way from here to Arcania. It is the longest, tallest, grandest tunnel in the entire world."

"My god!" Montama exclaimed, unable to think of anything else to say.

"It is almost forty miles long. The first several miles consist of a large natural cave, forged out of rock, solid as can be, while the rest was dug out inch by inch over a period of more than thirty cycles, by literally thousands of Count Belicki's men. They dug the dirt out and reinforced the tunnel's six feet thick walls with carbodate, the hardest substance known to man. It is the most remarkable engineering feat ever accomplished and yet only a precious few people know of its existence. Count Belicki concealed it for his attack on Arcania, but that planned attack never came, until now!"

Montama and Garr rode forward to the gigantic tunnel's massive entrance. Garr noted admiringly, "Our army is already well into the belly of the tunnel. We hide the tunnel with bushes and other debris whenever we are not using it." As his soldiers pulled the last of these bushes from the ground, Garr continued, "It will take us at least two units time to travel through the tunnel, that is if we move constantly without rest and there are no unexpected delays." Then, quite seriously, he intoned, "And we must move quickly for any delay could be fatal."

Montama was simply awestruck. He responded calmly, befitting his role as General Garr's new ally. "Then we must move with all haste," Montama said firmly, before he followed Garr through the entrance down into the mysterious subterranean tunnel.

Chapter 28
The Tunnel

Montama had never even come close to imagining anything as strange and complex as the monstrous tunnel that ran directly beneath the Bay of Battle. It was a marvelous engineering feat. The entrance itself was at least forty feet tall and the structure was more than sixty feet wide. As he rode through its gigantic aperture, Montama marveled, "An army could live in this place."

As Montama's eyes scanned eagerly from side to side, he wondered how is was possible to provide sufficient light and breathable air for an army to pass through such an extraordinarily large structure? The solution to the first problem was easy. The tunnel was lined with green gala bricks, the same ones used in the construction of the corridor leading to the Oracle chamber. This was augmented by rows of calta bushes, which like parnisus trees emit a constant glow, though they do so through their leaves. Indigenous to the northern regions of Relatania, they thrived in naturally dark places, such as caves.

The solution to the second problem was far more complicated. While calta bushes absorbed carbon monoxide and emitted oxygen, they did not provide enough breathable air for an army of thousands of men and women, and sundry talladaggers, oxen, horses, ducks, chickens, and the various other farm animals that would be needed to sustain this giant army. To deal with this practical problem General Garr's army planted a mossy plant called zenoway, which grows generally on the ceilings of caves. The moss provided an additional source of oxygen. It was still not enough for an army as large as General Garr's, particularly when it arrived at the tunnel's epicenter. Garr's military experts judged that there simply would not be enough breathable air at this middle section of the tunnel to allow the army to safely pass to the other side. How then could the army compensate for this lack of breathable air?

The solution was completely ingenious. Approximately ten miles into the tunnel each soldier would don a tank made out of clay, soaked in a liquid substance that sealed its porous exterior. Air would then be hand pumped into each of the clay containers. Each soldier would then strap the device on their back and could breath through it for approximately three to four hours. When the container was no longer useful it was passed backward by a chain of men, while a new breathing device was quickly provided to the soldier. Approximately one hundred thousand of these breathing packs were constructed for the determined march through the tunnel's belly. It was estimated that each soldier would require at least three of these devices; while horses, oxen and other animals would employ larger devices they carried on their backs. For this reason, Montama was forced to dismount his horse about ten miles into the tunnel so that it could be fitted with an air tank. As he stood on the tunnel floor, the young man marveled as soldiers, in a continuous line that stretched far beyond his field of vision, busily passed fresh breathing packs forward, while another equally long line of men received and then stacked the empty ones in a neat pile. And behind them an even larger group of men and women hand-pumped fresh air into the now empty packs, preparing them for their reuse. This process had to be implemented in a precise manner. If the movement of breathing packs broke down or was even delayed for but a few minutes, an incalculable number of lives would be lost.

Montama watched the men and women toil without interruption, fitting sundry animals with their own disposable breathing packs. It was indeed a surreal sight. Large oversized hoses were placed over the animals' head, testing to make sure that the various beasts could breath the filtered air. While the devices worked well on humans, prior study had determined that there was likely to be a higher malfunction rate among the animals, and it was estimated that roughly one-third of the horses and one-fifth of the talladaggers would not survive the journey through the tunnel.

This created yet another significant problem. What does one do with a dead horse or talladagger that might impede progress through the tunnel? The solution was practical. Teams of butchers were sent into the tunnel to quickly dissect any dead animal, immediately stripping them on the spot where they expired, placing their remains on constantly moveable carts that could be carried to the Arcanian side of the tunnel. The meat from carcasses would then be used to provide sustenance for the army upon its arrival. Meanwhile, other body parts such as bones and hides would be fashioned into weapons, clothes, and even cooking utensils. This utilitarian approach guaranteed that absolutely nothing would be wasted.

As General Garr dismounted his own horse so that it too could be fitted with a clunky breathing pack, Montama stood staring at the incredible sight that lay before him. Through the dull glow of the gala bricks and the calta bushes, Montama observed a continuous stream of soldiers and animals, marching inexorably forward, into what appeared to be an endless abyss that utterly consumed them. Though no end was in sight Montama had to remember that this immense tunnel led back to his homeland. That journey would take at least two full units time. For an instant, he felt an overwhelming sense of claustrophobia, as if he needed to see the sky just to breath. When he saw his young protégé's consternation, General Garr helpfully whispered, "Just close your eyes for a few seconds, breath normally. The feeling will pass." Montama did as directed, and while the temporary dizziness and queasiness indeed did pass, he became aware of yet another troubling sensation. The refuse from all of these people and animals was creating a rather offensive aroma. Again, Garr's army was inventive. To deal with this problem, women walked along the line spraying an essence that was designed to temporarily mask this gut-wrenching stench. As one woman passed Montama he realized that the scent smelled like flowers. "Carnations," General Garr added with a smile. "They are my favorite."

Montama thought it strange that a man as delicately balanced as Garr would have a favorite flower, but as he breathed the newly sprayed scent, he readied himself for the long journey through Belicki's tunnel. "There will be no sleep and little food or water," Garr said stoically. "And you will have to hold it, for there will only be a few occasions when you will be permitted to relieve yourself." Montama had not yet thought of this issue, but indeed thousands of men and women would be required to urinate.

He looked to his side and saw a series of large gray pots. "Are they for...?" Montama asked, his voice trailing off before he finished his thought.

"Even a mighty army has to pee," Garr noted before he laughed. "Don't worry," he added confidently. "We have thought of everything!"

Chapter 29
The Speech of a Lifetime

Bellazar insisted that all of Arcania's opinion leaders dutifully gather at an open-air stage in downtown Teta for what was billed as a most important address by Regent Rendrau. No other details were released, but a salacious rumor circulated that Rendrau planned to announce his resignation; such was the widely perceived failure of his short, impotent regency.

Standing on the stage, decorated with flags, banners, soldiers, and myriad other carefully chosen traditional symbols of Arcanian patriotism, with his loving wife proudly seated by his side, Rendrau appeared solemn but utterly in charge. "Today is a special unit for Arcania," he intoned with great reverence and humility. "During the past century, our beloved passra has endured invasions from Relatania and from renegade Bogul tribes. Our people have endured various hardships including famine and plague. And through all these crises, Arcania has survived. Now we face yet another crisis that tests our dedication, perseverance, and strength. Many of our citizens therefore ask themselves, is this generation capable of maintaining peace, building prosperity, and restoring both order and dignity to our beloved passra?"

The Oracle

Rendrau scanned the crowd and noticed that they were listening to his every word. He smiled benignly, and then continued, "Admittedly, when some Arcanians ask these fundamental questions they have reservations, because they see prominent citizens driven by unbridled ambition, who place their own interests above those of the passra. And the people therefore wonder aloud, is there no one left in this great land who stands with them, who is on *their* side."

Over the years, Rendrau had spoken before many forums, some even larger than this one. He therefore was skilled at the rhetorical arts, knowing precisely how to modulate his voice, when to speak forcefully, and when to smile benignly. He now used all of his aural abilities to achieve the goal of appearing avuncular, yet thoroughly trustworthy, and most of all completely in charge. Meanwhile Bellazar sat attentively by her husband's side, with a gentle smile on her face, exuding inestimable pride in Rendrau's courage, patriotism, and dedication to all things Arcanian. Her dress, prepared particularly for this occasion, was simple, white, with occasional streaks of the royal family's distinctive blue colors. The image presented was of a royal couple that looked immaculate and entrancing.

Rendrau paused, looked out over the gathered dignitaries, and then with a confident firmness, continued with his speech. "My family has had the privilege of leading your passra for generations, but it is *your* passra, not ours, and we rule by the grace of *your* continued indulgence and trust." The audience responded with but sparse and scattered applause. Unperturbed Rendrau continued, "My father, King Benton, was a *great* man whose death robbed of us one of our greatest leaders." This time the applause was louder and more heartfelt. "With his passing it is only natural that some rogue individuals, whose ambition outweighs their sense of patriotism, would seek to replace this great man, who loved his passra more than he loved life itself." The crowd erupted into a sustained standing ovation. Sensing that he was capturing the audience's sympathy and resolute attention, Rendrau continued with a rhetorical flourish. "But personal ambition is not a qualification to be Arcania's king."

Some in the crowd now began to chant King Benton's honored name. In a strident voice Rendrau continued, "We need strong leadership, but leadership tempered by humility and grace." Now even more of the dignitaries demonstrated their support by standing, cheering and whistling their enthusiastic approbation. "We need someone who leads not because he wants to, but because he believes it is his duty to do so. We need a man of greatness to step forward." The crowd now applauded wildly, showing its affection for a man that just moments before it had cruelly derided as feeble and incompetent.

Rendrau again paused, his ego embellished by the audience's mounting show of esteem. Then, in a calm but forceful voice he fervently declared, "Today I am proud to announce publicly what many of you have known privately for some time, that I have absolutely no ambition to be your king." Bellazar smiled broadly, then stood and applauded her husband, before bowing to the crowd and retaking her seat. The night before this speech she had carefully practiced every single gesture, making sure that she was both respectful and patriotic. On stage she continued to admire her husband's forthrightness, even as he prevaricated in front of what suddenly had become a loving and highly attentive audience. Various individuals ardently craned their necks forward, hanging on every single word the regent spoke. As they did so, Bellazar smiled and lovingly stared at her husband, as he resumed his address.

"I have never had the ambition to be your king, for I am only beloved King Benton's third eldest son. My whole life I believed that my dear brother Retch would one day rule this great passra. Consumed with grief for his fallen father, my dear brother's heart was shattered, and when Retch passed on our passra lost another great man to history."

A few dignitaries wept openly for a man that they had considered too weak and inexperienced to be the passra's next king. "He would have been a great king," they now admitted.

Rendrau looked out upon the crowd and then in a softer voice continued, "And when my father died, my dear brother Pondru gallantly volunteered to make a dangerous trek across our great passra, to consult with our land's greatest lords. We still wait with great anticipation for his safe return to Teta. And when that journey finally ends a new one will ultimately begin."

The audience was entirely transfixed. Despite all of his past oratorical flourishes, Rendrau had never felt as completely in command of an audience as he did now. He marveled at his rhetorical skills and this gave him even greater internal strength and confidence to forthrightly declare, "I hold only the humble position of regent in trust until the time, soon coming, when my dear brother Pondru will return and assume his rightful place as our king. Until that time, by the temporary power that has been vested in me as your regent, and with great pride and a full heart full of hope and love, I hereby declare that my dear brother Pondru is officially designated in absentia as King of Arcania." Then in a strong, bold voice he declared, *"Long Live King Pondru!"*

The audience was completely stunned and for a few moments remained silent, that is until one carefully placed and very friendly voice shouted, "Long Live King Pondru!" Then another planted voice repeated the same refrain until it slowly crested into a chorus of cheers, and then finally with total unity, the entire gathering chanted as if it were one, "Long Live King Pondru!"

It was an amazing sight. People by the dozens now wept openly, while Rendrau, with Bellazar now standing proudly by his side, received the accolades of his loving passra. People streamed forward to shake his hand and simply to touch him, while Bellazar stood affectionately applauding his patriotism, his total love of passra, his disavowal of ambition, and his fealty for his dear brother, who though missing, would undoubtedly soon return to Teta, or so at least everyone fervently hoped.

It was a stunning tour de force performance, what was soon widely described as the speech of a lifetime. Later that afternoon, at a gathering of dignitaries at the King's Castle, one former critic after another warmly embraced Rendrau. As they did so each one insisted that the regent must continue to rule until his brother safely re-emerged. Though Rendrau seemed initially resistant to this call to action, after several determined entreaties he finally ever so reluctantly agreed to remain in office, but only temporarily. "I am honored," he said at last, as the gathered dignitaries cheered him enthusiastically. Then a new chant was heard, "Long Live King Pondru and long live Regent Rendrau!" As the chant grew louder, Rendrau's eyes moistened and then veritably glistened, while Bellazar continued to stand lovingly by his side, always smiling.

It was the perfect image of a selfless man, lacking even the slightest pretense to ambition, a man who placed his passra first and foremost. In other words, it was precisely the image that Bellazar carefully crafted when she wrote the speech. "It appears the tide has turned in our direction," she whispered surreptitiously in her husband's ear.

Rendrau merely smiled, waved, and accepted the crowd's heartfelt approbation, as he whispered in return, "I certainly hope so. That was the best speech I ever gave."

Chapter 30
Kublatitan

This time the turnaround in public sentiment was positive and instantaneous, as was the sea change in elite opinion. As the text of what was now being called "The Regent's Remarkable Address" was widely disseminated to the public, Rendrau's popularity soared. Some former critics openly admitted, "We haven't been fair to him," while others noted with pride, "We are lucky to have such a great man at this turning point in our history." While some former partisans declared, "King Pondru will be proud of his brother," still others pined for Rendrau to be king. "He is the one who has what it takes," one citizen after another dutifully concluded. "We could do no better than Rendrau."

Along with these assorted accolades, Bellazar's magnificently stage crafted plan provided additional unexpected dividends. I must admit that even as committed a skeptic as myself was entirely won over by the brazen audacity of her political maneuver and for a single moment I thought it might be possible that I would change my allegiance to this marvelously talented woman. Yet my prejudices were much the same as the people of the time and I knew that a woman could never rule Arcania. Additionally, I had invested so much in young Montama, I was not yet ready to abandon a young boy of immeasurable potential who I was carefully crafting into the instrument that would bring me my ultimate prize: the Oracle. Therefore, my enthusiasm for Bellazar waned as quickly as it had emerged.

But this would be the high water mark! Though she did not know it, Bellazar's political fortunes were about to change. For the first time in several nights Bellazar slept soundly. As she did so she had a most disturbing dream. "Never to be king," a deep melodious baritone voice declared emphatically. The dream was so disturbing that Bellazar awoke in the middle of the night. After taking a sip of water from a glass on the small table next to her giant king-sized bed, she heard the same ominous voice repeat, "Never to be king."

Startled, but not afraid, for she had been visited by other entities from the Oracle during the night, Bellazar carefully scanned the room before asking, "Who is there?" The response was precisely the same as before. "Never to be king," the voice repeated.

The Oracle

Bellazar secured a candle from the nearby table and then stepped away from her bed. "Who is it?" She was startled when she saw Pondru standing in the moonlight near her window. "Who else? The King of Arcania," he declared as he stepped forward toward his sister-in-law. "I must admit that only you would have the audacity to name a dead man as the king of the passra."

"You should be honored," Bellazar responded, a bit disconcerted, for this was the first time she had seen an entity from the Oracle that she actually had known during her own lifetime. Pondru looked the same as always, wearing his drab black frock robe, with his long graying beard dangling from his face, though he no longer required spectacles.

Unsettled, Bellazar sat on the edge of her bed and stared at this ghostly apparition. "You don't frighten me, Pondru," she said unconvincingly, for he could see that uncharacteristically her right hand shook ever so slightly. Pondru, however, had not materialized to frighten his sister-in-law, and so in a comforting voice he added, "I did not come here to chide you. In fact, the Oracle is very impressed with your performance today."

With her pride veritably wounded, Bellazar asked, "Performance?"

"Of course," Pondru said with a benevolent smile. "The Oracle is impressed by your leadership ability and to be honest there are many entities that believe you would make a great king."

"My husband will be king," Bellazar responded resolutely.

"No," Pondru said, shaking his head sadly. "That is not Rendrau's destiny."

"How do you know that?" Bellazar asked assertively, her steely eyes fixed on Pondru, her once quivering hand now absolutely steady.

Before Pondru could respond his image slowly faded away and in its place a new entity spontaneously emerged from a suddenly rising fog. Bellazar gasped, for before her eyes, a new figure, standing at least ten feet tall, with a massive muscular frame, weighing far more than five hundred pounds materialized slowly out of the dim moonlight. This new entity's skin was red with yellow stripes running diagonally across his wise, wrinkled forehead. He wore a strange green garment that glowed with a surreal haze in the moonlight. It was wrapped tightly around his body, from his oversized bare feet all the way to his broad and powerful shoulders. Stranger yet, the entity's eyes were pure white light and Bellazar could actually physically feel them as this monstrously large man stared directly at her, seemingly seeing right through her outer body to her very inner soul.

"Who are you?" Bellazar gasped, now truly frightened.

"Kublatitan, I am!" the giant figure declared in a voice so powerful that it shook the bed's curtains as if they had been struck by the wind.

"What are you?" Bellazar asked, trying to show composure even as her hands again began to tremble.

Emphatically, and quite regally, Kublatitan declared, "I am the Oracle!" It was said with such utter conviction that Bellazar instantly knew it to be true. She listened attentively as the giant colossus stood menacingly before her. "For almost a thousand cycles of yours was I King of the Taewokans. Before I died for them I created the Oracle."

"My God," the mighty lady of Arcania whispered.

"No deity am I," Kublatitan responded, as if her comment had been posed in the form of a question.

"How did you, I mean how did the Oracle get here?" Bellazar asked tentatively.

"Zanzaska, the Oracle he stole from the Cave of Wisdom. There it had resided for a hundred of your cycles. Foolish, not knowing the power he possessed, he took what you call the Oracle. My LaKotey, my very essence, remained inside." Bellazar sat silently, listening attentively. "But despoiled the Oracle this Zanzaska did, adding inadvertently his own LaKotey and that of others, far less noble than me. Wisdom in his hands became far different, darker, and very dangerous. For all the people of your land who see inside the Oracle eventually become part of it."

"Why have you come here?" Bellazar asked with an equal measure of curiosity and caution.

"Return the Oracle must to the Taewokans, there to be cleansed of all entities but mine. In human hands it is far too much dangerous."

"So you need me?" Bellazar asked, as her eyes suddenly widening with the realization that there was possible political benefit to be gained from this association.

Kublatitan stood even taller than before, his mighty voice echoing throughout Bellazar's chamber, as the Pirene cat's colors turned to a dull gray hue. Meanwhile the Anawana Yapyap lay on its back, its legs pointed directly toward the heavens, grunting contently with each breath, entirely oblivious to Kublatitan's visit. The strange and powerful man now declared, "Help me and I help you too to rule Arcania."

"What about my husband?" Bellazar asked inquisitively.

"You alone will rule," Kublatitan announced.

"Why?" she demanded.

"Not to tell yet, but it is you who will rule." With this pronouncement Kublatitan's image began to dissolve until after a few seconds it was no more. Bellazar frantically stared forward into the moonlight and then slowly she walked toward the window. As she did so she noticed that two of Arcania's three moons were rising in unison in the southern sky. Then she shivered, for the night air was cool and her feelings of affection for her husband were genuine. As much as she was tempted by the promise of ruling Arcania, she also felt a desperate sense of remorse, a terrifying concern that something terrible was in store for her dear husband. Precisely what did his destiny entail? She simply did not know.

Chapter 31
Breach

While Kublatitan visited Bellazar, I kept a careful watch on the progress of my young protégé. Montama no longer knew whether it was daylight or night, so long had he trudged step by seemingly never ending step through the cavernous tunnel that ran deep under the dangerous currents of the Bay of Battle. Long ago he had become accustomed to the feeling of the fungal goo beneath his feet, and despite the insistent spraying of the essence of carnations, he recoiled at the awful stench created by the thousands upon thousands of men, women, children and beasts. Montama watched as grown men, overcome by claustrophobia, were quickly sedated before they went horribly and irrevocably mad. Several men collapsed under the grueling monotony of the forty-mile march beneath the bay. Montama managed to maintain his own sanity by finding ways to occupy his mind, such as counting from one to a thousand and then backward again to one. When he had done this twice, he learned to take short naps while walking, by putting his hand on the back of the man in front of him. After a while he was not sure what he missed the most; food, fresh air, open spaces, or merely the luxury to sleep in his own straw bed. All of these necessities had been denied him for well over fifty hours or nearly two units time. Onward he moved, in an endless cue of humanity, occasionally wondering if he would die in this horrid place or if this was the price of glory that the Oracle had promised him.

The tedium temporarily was broken when Montama was forced to don one of the uncomfortable breathing contraptions. An elderly woman with dark green skin fitted the straps on his back while a burly Kay-Why-Tee man held the tank air in place. When it was first strapped over his broad shoulders the tank merely tugged uneasily, an uncomfortable and bearable sensation. As he commenced marching, with each step the pain surged throughout his body until he wondered anew if he was capable of surviving this surreal march beneath the bay.

Though the tank tugged on his back and shoulders, the breathing reed inserted into his nose was most uncomfortable, though absolutely necessary, for it carried life-giving oxygen. Though young Montama was relieved to feel the sensation of fresh air, he also sensed the trickling of fresh blood from his nose as the sharp reeds angrily pierced his tender nostrils. He twitched his nose repeatedly, anxiously trying to ease the pain, but to no avail. Though he was exhausted, starved, his throat parched and swollen, and his eyes and nose burning from the incessant stench, Montama derived renewed motivation from the sight of countless weaker men who straddled the tunnel's walls, collecting their strength lest they be left behind to die. At first Montama felt sorry for these men, most of who were older and had no doubt seen many battles throughout their long distinguished lifetimes. But then he grew strength by realizing that he would not be among these men, left behind to die ignominiously beneath the bay's turbulent waters, forever to be forgotten by time and history. As Montama grew ever wearier and he sensed that his body could not endure any more suffering, he closed his eyes and envisioned himself trapped forever in this hideous underground cave. When he again opened his eyes, he began to count, "One, two, three, four..."

Every eight hours or so the men were allowed to rest for thirty minutes and for a few precious moments Montama leaned on one knee while he enjoyed one fresh piece of fruit, which provided the soldiers with both sustenance and much needed fluid. He also consumed some water. The soldiers were allowed to drink water every two hours, but only in small amounts, lest they suffer cramps or other disabling infirmities. Even after he drank his share, Montama's mouth was still parched and his eyes were so weary that he could barely see. As he resumed his march he became so dizzy that he was no longer sure if he actually was awake or asleep. Even at these disorienting times he maintained an inexorable urge to move forward, for he knew that only when he escaped this horrible tunnel would he return to his beloved Arcania. It was this powerful force that compelled the young man to move constantly forward, far beyond what he thought was his breaking point, through agonizing pain he had never before even imagined, toward his ultimate goal, to save his family and to bring order to the passra's governance.

As he marched onward through the tunnel, General Garr periodically watched his young protégé and was pleased by the young man's internal fortitude. "He is strong and determined," he said admiringly at one point to one of his subordinate officers. Garr never once showed even the slightest sign of exhaustion or trepidation. So busy was he with the myriad details of the long march that he never even thought about the need for rest or sustenance. Through his one solitary eye he watched his army move relentlessly onward, keenly aware that this was but the first step in a long and improbable journey. For once his army arrived in Arcania, it would have to march immediately northward into eastern Arcania, undoubtedly facing numerous, unexpected obstacles along the way, before it ultimately would be tested in battle. "There will be no rest for the weary," he declared to several men who had taken the liberty to rest for a few scattered moments. "We must move on," he exalted his men, every now and then, looking back to see Montama, again admiring the young man's determined persistence, realizing that the very success of his army depended entirely on this raw neophyte.

And on they marched until Montama, entirely accustomed to the tedium of the long march, took a few seconds to realize that there was a sudden growing commotion emanating from the rear of the tunnel. He heard several men shouting, and then a horde of frightened soldiers dashed past him inexplicably dropping their breathing packs as they ran. Startled, Montama turned to address the soldier standing behind him in the seemingly endless cue, but that man quickly pushed past him nearly knocking Montama to the ground.

Before he could ascertain what was happening Montama heard a woman's shrill voice crying out one solitary word, "BREACH!" Montama stood still as others raced past him with a terrifying ferocity. As he stared intently backward he saw a mass of men, women and beasts moving forward at a suddenly expedited pace. Then he heard a strange whooshing sound that he would never forget. It echoed ominously from the very walls of the tunnel itself. Then he felt the tunnel's floor shake, as if an earthquake was lifting the very ground upon which he stood. Suddenly thrown forward by the intensity of the shock, Montama fell hard upon the rocky cave's floor. Struggling frantically to regain his footing, he saw it coming directly at him, a wall of steadily rising water, abruptly filling the tunnel and consuming everything in its path. Montama turned and ran as quickly as he could, dropping his breathing pack abruptly on the tunnel floor, and racing past a terrified talladagger that stood utterly dumbfounded. As Montama scurried forward he wondered if he would be consumed ignominiously and for all eternity in this subterranean tomb far beneath the Bay of Battle.

Frightened, yet maintaining his composure, the young man scampered ahead as the deafening sound of running water shattered the nerves of lesser men all around him. There was panic all around, yet the waters continued to rise, first to his waist, then even higher. At first Montama fought the currents, but in time he surrendered to them, allowing the waters to simply carry his body forward. Finally, as the waters rose so high that he had to struggle to keep his mouth above the water line, Montama spotted a tiny shaft of light in the distance. "Is it the exit," he thought, "or is it an illusion?" He was not sure. He paddled as fast as he could as the inexorable currents carried him steadily forward, occasionally smashing his body roughly into an abandoned cart, a dead beast, or an uprooted plant. As the rushing currents dragged him forward, he saw the terrified faces of men, women and animals, each desperately trying to wend their way toward the safety of the tunnel's egress.

Though his eyes were now burning from the salty seawater, Montama could see a bottleneck lying just ahead of him. A wall of dead bodies was forming, one that utterly obstructed the young man's view of the outside world. Still, the water's current forced him helplessly forward. As the waters rose closer and closer to the ceiling he at last heard General Garr shouting, "Clear this area!" Then as the outlet was suddenly cleared by scores of broad-shouldered men, he felt another surge of water pushing him relentlessly forward.

Though Montama was now but a few yards from the exit, he felt the water rise above his head, completely engulfing him, leaving him with absolutely no air to breath. Though he tried to hold his breath, water seeped into his nose and he began to choke. Helplessly he flailed about, uncertain whether he was moving forward or not, completely at the mercy of the water's own wild currents. As he fought to hold onto consciousness he thought he saw the light from the exit, but with water all around him he was no longer sure. In another minute Montama would have drowned. As the waters painfully slammed debris into the side of his body it also carried him forward toward freedom from this hellish nightmare. Carried onward by the green, dirty water, Montama at last felt the current carry his body out of the tunnel and onto a nearby sand dune.

Finally freed, Montama was not yet out of danger. After he vomited on the dune, he scrambled uncertainly to his knees, as water and debris continued to smash against his back. Then he heard the sound of a man gasping for air, then others, then countless more, as the waters began to deposit hundreds of soldiers, some alive, many dead, onto the beach's cluttered shoreline.

As Montama dragged himself up the sand dune to safety he wondered just how many men would survive? Would he even have an army after this horrible catastrophe? At the moment he had no time to dwell on such thoughts for the horror of the disaster was still unfolding before his startled eyes.

After much effort Montama at last reached the summit of the large sand dune and though he was still unsteady, he stood and looked back toward the tunnel. With a soft sea breeze blowing in his face and the welcome sun warming a body now covered only in tattered rags, Montama stood, staring in abject horror as the pile of dead bodies steadily mounted into an unruly heap on the beach below him. It was now apparent that the death toll would be in the thousands, with many valuable and irreplaceable horses, oxen, and talladaggers also among the dead. As he watched this mounting carnage, Montama looked skyward and watched as a flock of malevolent ugly green birds with long, powerful, triangular shaped wings circled menacingly in the sky. They were vultamires, a ghastly scavenger intent on feasting on the dead and dying. General Garr, who stood stoically but a few yards from Montama, attempted to bring order out of chaos. He commanded his men to carry the bodies away from the tunnel and to kill as many vultamires as possible before they could desecrate the brave soldiers who died on this beachhead on this tragic day.

As he did so Garr spotted Montama atop the sand dune and exclaimed boisterously, "Thank God you are alive." Then the general beseeched the young man. "Move this way, Montama. We must quickly get the army off the beach."

"What army?" Montama whispered dejectedly as he stared helplessly at the sandy grave now consecrated by a growing number of the dead. Overcome with self-pity Montama cried out, "I did all this for nothing!" He had no time to lament, however, for a soldier, thoroughly soaked from head to toe, grabbed the young man by the arm and directed him to march toward General Garr.

"We must go this way," the soldier firmly urged Montama, who was now thoroughly disoriented. Passively, his shoulders hunched, Montama meekly obeyed, though he was dazed, confused, and obviously in shock.

In contrast, General Garr provided calm and steady leadership in a moment of unexpected crisis. "Get all of these men and beasts off the beach," Garr adamantly implored several uniformed officers. Then pointing northward he yelled, "Move them to the dunes, to higher ground." As the General urged his surviving troops to action, Montama blindly accompanied the soldier, moving through the surviving mass of exhausted men and nearly drowned animals to General Garr's position on the beach. "You," Garr directed a soldier who had lost his shirt in the watery disaster, "get some men and round up the surviving animals." The man showed his deference to his general with a salute, tapping his forehead twice with his right hand then extending his hand far above his head.

Garr turned to Montama who slowly approached his position. "We are fortunate that I sent three-fourths of the army on ahead of us. They already should be setting up camp nearby."

Montama barely heard General Garr. Instead, he coughed and as he did more seawater shot suddenly from his lips. Realizing how overcome Montama was with grief the general urged his protégé to sit down and rest. Instead, Montama forthrightly admitted, "I have never seen death like this before."

Garr was hardly a compassionate man, but he gently put his arm on Montama's shoulder and in a voice that was disarmingly sincere commented, "I'm afraid that this is just the beginning. Many more men will die." As Garr looked toward the dead, who were now being carted off the beach by the ragged survivors, he added, "Death is ugly but you must get used to it. Soon the sight and smell of death will be all around us." Then looking out at the growing tumult on the beach, the general added, "Let us hope that we are not among the dead when the church bells ring signifying the end of this ghastly war."

"You will not be, if you follow my lead," a familiar voice intoned with its usual malevolence. It was my voice and it was consumed with an unappeasable hatred. "This was no accident!" I snarled, my contempt growing with each syllable I spoke.

"What do you mean?" Garr asked aloud, though neither he nor Montama could actually see me, for I had not materialized in corporeal form.

"This is the work of Kublatitan," I commented darkly.

"Who is that?" Garr asked, clearly startled by this revelation.

"He created the Oracle and now he wants to control it."

"What do you mean?" the general responded, angry and confused. "I thought you controlled the Oracle?"

I laughed, for I had not told General Garr the whole truth about the Oracle and its origins. "I am powerful, but there are others, as well. Kublatitan will be our most dangerous foe in the battles to come."

Garr angrily implored, "Look what this Kublatitan has done to my army?"

Again I laughed, a sound that echoed endlessly in Garr's ears. "What Kublatitan can do to us I can do to his army as well."

Chapter 32
Grell

Two Units Before the Tunnel Collapse:

Grandafier was baffled by my urgent request. "My dear old friend," I whispered to the elderly man, as he entered his dream state. "You must go now and tell Timilty that in two units time Montama will be in the port city of Grell, where he is prepared to lead a giant mercenary army in a rebellion against the Centama family. Tell Timilty that he must convince the proper authorities to dispatch the Fifth Army's best troops, that is, if he has any hope of quelling this horrible insurgency in its infancy."

The date was two units before the catastrophe at the tunnel's egress. I had returned in time where my presence could only be felt as a whisper on a breeze or as a mere shadow in a dream. There I conveyed a devious message to the man who was Montama's most loyal ally. I understood that Grandafier was so well trusted that Timilty would never question the veracity of his charge.

"Why should I betray Montama?" Grandafier asked, still fast asleep.

"Because his very survival now depends upon it," I again whispered, admittedly with great malevolence.

Grandafier awoke with a start, suddenly gasping for air. As he hyperventilated, he also felt an overwhelming sense of urgency that he could neither explain nor comprehend. It was an overpowering compulsion to immediately obey my directive. Yet as Grandafier slowly rose from his bed he had the common sense to ask himself, "If I do this, am I helping Montama or betraying him?" He correctly understood that I was a dangerous man with uncertain motives and therefore not to be automatically trusted. Still, the feeling to act was so overwhelming that Grandafier simply could not resist it. "I must go immediately to Timilty," he thought, though frankly he did not yet understand why.

So overpowering was this sensation that the elderly man did not even wait for the morning sunrise to crest over the northern horizon. Hastily and somewhat carelessly, he dressed, and after alerting his weary servants that he immediately required a carriage, Grandafier departed at once for Timilty's nearby home. There, at least an hour before dawn, he rapped loudly on the front door of the head of Lord Tantamount's Council, until a sleep deprived servant finally arrived. "I must speak to Timilty immediately on a matter of considerable importance," Grandafier veritably shouted. Moments later, as the elderly man sat alone in a dark waiting room, Timilty, still dressed in his night robe, feebly entered the room while yawning uncontrollably.

"My dear friend," Timilty said, clearly confused by the arrival of one of the fiefdom's most honored citizens at such an ungodly hour. "What is the matter?"

Grandafier was direct. "I have news that young Montama, Lord Tantamount's son, is part of a rebellion to overthrow the Centama family. He has traveled to the Relatin Empire, there to amass a mighty army. It is now marching toward the port city of Grell. It will be there in just two units time." Grandafier's voice quivered with fear as he spoke. "I am afraid that if we do not send the king's best troops immediately, we may all be cast under this wayward son's evil spell."

"My heavens!" Timilty gasped, clearly shocked to learn that the son of his honored master could possibly be behind such a treacherous and treasonable plot. The Ka-Why-Tee thought for a few seconds, gently tapping a finger from his third hand nervously on his chin as he did so. Then at last he exclaimed, "The Fifth Army is nearby. I will send a runner immediately to inform General Cato about the details of this insidious plot."

The Oracle

Grandafier nodded his consent and then returned directly to his home where he sat nervously for hours wondering if he had done the right thing. "Either I have aided my young friend in a time of great need or I have just performed the very worst act of treason imaginable," Grandafier whispered helplessly.

Morning:

As the sun rose in the north, a runner carried the news of Montama's plot to General Cato's headquarters. "I have been waiting for just such news," the general said with an egotistical delight, nodding his head enthusiastically as he listened to the report of Montama's infamy. "I expected an attack to come from the east, but it makes sense to send an army to Grell instead. From there Montama can easily move northwest to the grazing lands, steal all the livestock he and his army no doubt desperately need, and then withdraw into the Kanaween Forest, where they can hide, forage and hunt, all the time within easy striking distance of our western outposts. It is a brilliant plan! This Montama must be quite wily!" As the general dismissed the runner, he turned to a nearby aide and in a loud and confident voice added, "Only now, I will be ready for him." The general then ordered his subordinate to alert the Fifth Army that it must leave immediately for the southward march to Grell.

The Fifth Army was the passra's elite force in western Arcania. Though it shared responsibility for security matters with General Mbanka's Fourth Army, all Arcanians knew that the Fifth Army was far more loyal to the Centama family. The head of that army, General Cato, was a childhood friend of King Benton and had spent many happy summers camping with him in the Kanaween Forest. The two also had spent many units fishing in the waters near the quaint port city of Grell, the very location from which Montama had departed for the Relatin Empire, and where more than a century before I, as a young soldier, had found a fishing vessel that carried me back to Relatania. Now, General Cato sat in his office, thinking of the king and wondering how this young whippersnapper, the son of a mere lord, could dare to threaten his beloved Centama family. "There will be hell to pay," he muttered calmly, as he reached for a craspa, a large, yellow cigar-like contraption that one chewed for pleasure. Then, he told his aide, "I will avenge the king's honor."

As General Cato prepared the Fifth Army for its march to the sea, news of the rebellion spread like a wild fire throughout the fiefdom. Hontallo learned of it directly from Timilty, who said that he could scarcely believe that the report was true, though he had no doubt that Grandafier was completely sincere. With great anxiety Hontallo literally ran to find his father. When he located him in the garden, Hontallo told Lord Tantamount, "Father, I don't believe this for an instant. The reports simply cannot be true."

Thunderstruck, Lord Tantamount merely looked away from his eldest son. Then in a solemn voice he declared, "We must do whatever we can to protect the Centama family."

"Will you ride south with the Fifth Army?" Hontallo asked directly.

Tantamount stood pensively for a few seconds and then exclaimed, "I cannot face my own son in battle. That would be more than even I could bear."

Meanwhile, in her bedroom, a servant notified Truellen of the news. Her response was far different. "So he has an army," she said with a wry smile. "Then the Oracle's prophecy is coming to pass."

The Unit of the Tunnel Collapse:

As the news of Montama's treachery circulated widely throughout the passra, a new faction angrily cast aspersions against the lord's son, while yet another splinter group proved to be more sympathetic to the young man's cause. Though Rendrau was now an exceedingly popular leader, there were still many disparate voices that favored rebellion over restoration.

Meanwhile, as the people discussed and debated this latest and most unexpected news, the King's Fifth Army moved relentlessly southward to the port city of Grell. When it arrived General Cato found absolutely no evidence whatsoever that an invading army was present. "Perhaps they have moved inland," a captain advised the general.

"Then we need to dispatch scouts and locate his forces as expeditiously as possible," the general coolly directed, supremely confident that a great military victory soon would be his reward. Then he added, "In the meantime, we will camp here at Grell."

The army headquarters was established at the mayor's house, with its giant curved windows directly overlooking the Bay of Battle. From these windows the general and his staff could also see the troops congregating along the shore, where they secured water for cooking while they awaited further orders. For the average soldier, it was a welcome respite. As the soldiers enjoyed their unexpected rest, inside the mayor's house General Cato busily consulted with his top advisers. One of his subordinates duly reported, "We have interrogated many of the townspeople. There is absolutely no sign of an invading army."

Another adviser quickly opined, "I fear that we have been sent here on a fool's errand."

General Cato carefully pondered this possibility, but he was sure that the information he had received was reliable. Serenely he responded, "They are here. I can feel it."

"But our army is completely exposed," one adviser hastily interjected. "We are trapped against the Bay. An army from the north could crush us if they moved quickly."

"But there is no sign of an army to the north either," another adviser acerbically commented.

"Utterly baffling!" Cato said slowly, "but we already know this Montama is a wily character." Cato reached for another craspa, as he relaxed in the mayor's favorite chair, with its awe-inspiring view of the Bay unfolding over a seemingly infinite watery horizon. "I sense that the enemy is nearby? I can feel it." Cato prided himself on his gut instincts, which, as he often told anyone who would listen, had served him quite well in many a battle. Now, his gut told him that the enemy was near and that he should remain fixed at Grell.

What Cato did not sense was an event unfolding more than a hundred miles to the east. On a sundrenched sand dune, Montama stood wearily next to General Garr. Having just survived the tunnel collapse, the young man listened attentively as my angry voice intoned, "What Kublatitan has done to us, I will do to them."

"How?" Garr asked curtly.

The answer came not in the form of words, but initially as clasps of thunder, then violent streaks of lighting, as clouds suddenly and forebodingly appeared out of thin air, completely obfuscating the sun in a matter of seconds, and turning daylight into almost total darkness. "What is this?" asked Montama, his eyes fixed on a series of swirling clouds far above his head, as another ominous crack of thunder rang fiercely in his ears. Then, as the two men watched, lightening began to repeatedly strike the bay's turbulent waters, as the clouds slowly congealed into an angry green mist. And within the clouds, a new form appeared, a gigantic green vultamire, with a wingspan well over fifty-feet across, hovering in the sky directly above young Montama and General Garr.

Montama and Garr struggled to protect themselves from the swirling winds and surging tides. Then as the lighting flashed, the outline of my two strange oval purple eyes appeared ominously in the sky. When the lightening struck yet again, these very same eyes glared down insidiously from the sky, though they were now in the form of a gigantic vultamire's scavenging face. "It is Belicki!" Montama cried out as he pointed to the sky. The sight of the once frail old man, now horrifically transformed into the body of a gigantic vultamire, shocked even the stoic General Garr.

With fixed determination, I stared coldly into the turbulent waters of the Bay of Battle, and with immaculate concentration, I compelled the very waters to swirl in a long, slow circular motion, gaining speed with each rotation, until a dynamic vortex of water began to move westward along Arcania's southern coast.

Garr and Montama remained atop the sand dune, watching as the waters responded to my insistent will. Then they heard my voice cry out, "Now follow me" and magically the waters obeyed. Garr struggled to maintain his balance as my monstrously large wings flapped dangerously above the general's head. "See what a powerful ally you have?" he heard me whisper. With a look of wonder and amazement, Montama watched as the currents continued to shift until the entire waters of the Bay of Battle suddenly ran from east to west, rather than their accustomed path.

"Come, we must leave this place and go inland," Garr shouted as he pulled Montama back with him. Montama needed little encouragement for he quickly sprinted with the troops to a safer position.

Far to the west, General Cato and his staff were entirely unaware of these remarkable developments. Calmly, without any sense of fear or danger, Cato continued to consult with his top advisers. "We will thoroughly search the entire area. We will find this scoundrel Montama before nightfall, I can sense it," the general said, exuding absolute confidence.

But even as the general spoke the bay's waters continued their movement westward along the Arcanian shoreline. As they did a series of concentric waves rose systematically higher with each successive permutation, as people gathered along the shoreline to watch the water's insistent rise. They were terrified when they spotted a giant and mounting tidal wave, but it passed harmlessly past various port cities, such as Prattville, causing no damage whatsoever, moving relentlessly ever westward.

It was then that one of General Cato's subordinates stared out the window toward the sea. With a faint rumble, hearing nothing more than the sound of distant thunder, he said, "What the hell is that?"

Cato too stared out of the window. "What the devil is that?" he asked, as he stared intently ahead. A vast green mist appeared on the horizon and the general realized that the bay's currents inexplicably had shifted and were now running in the wrong direction. "The waters are moving westward?" Cato said with a start, as he turned and stared with a puzzled expression at one of his subordinates. "Only an earthquake would be powerful enough to change the bay's currents," the general mused.

"But I felt no earthquake," the officer responded.

"Neither did I," Cato said softly. He then looked at the various officers in the room and said, "Let's get the men off the beach. Order them to pull back immediately!"

On the nearby beach, men by the hundreds, and some smaller number of women, had been enjoying a warm sea breeze. Among the throng, one man said to another, "I bet you a pint of beer that you cannot flip over backward in the water and keep your head underwater till the count of one hundred."

"I will take your bet," his nearly naked compatriot said eagerly and without hesitation. Before either of the two men could move, however, they saw a rising torrent of water emerging over the vast and not so distant horizon. Almost instantaneously the wave rose from twenty, to forty, and then to over one hundred feet high. "It is a tsunami!" a woman shouted as she instinctively ran toward the beach.

Cato continued to stare out the window. "The tidal wave is coming at us too quickly," he shouted. Then before he could relay an order, a wall of water more than one hundred and fifty feet high rose over the shoreline and onto the beach. Cato gasped, "Good lord!" Then with a blind fury the tsunami smashed through the curved window. The force was so strong that Cato was struck by both water and shards of broken glass. Each stabbed at him with the same ghastly ferocity.

Though a few of the officers had run for the exit, they had no time to escape before the mayor's house was struck by a monstrously immense wall of water. The house rocked violently to one side, then back to the other, before finally splitting in two: the two sides of the house and all of its various inhabitants were then carried away by angry waters that now surged directly toward the port city of Grell.

Most people did not even have the time to look out their windows before the surging bay's waters struck. Others were able to see the instrument of their death just moments before the waters carried them brusquely away. Grell's one hundred foot lighthouse, which was constructed long before King Leonata's times, was obliterated in an instant, reduced to mere floating rubble, as were most of the other three hundred and fifty-seven homes, twenty-eight taverns, and seventy-three various business establishments that had lined Grell's sand blown streets for far more than two centuries.

The waters rose inexorably, leaving behind no people, no houses, no churches or public places; nothing remained that even hinted that a once thriving port community had existed in this place. In a mere matter of minutes, all that was left were wads of floating debris, including the decomposing bodies of the dead.

That night:

Miles away, as he sat safely by his fireplace reading a book, Grandafier the Elder was unexpectedly consumed by a dark and heinous vision. In his mind's eye he saw thousands of soldiers running for cover, screaming helplessly, before a wave so horrifically large that it seemed to touch the clouds, rolled over their bodies, entombing them in a watery grave. Grandafier then saw an even taller wave engulf the mayor's house with an unimaginable force. Next, as he watched, the waters slowly receded, replacing Grell, a once thriving port city, with a muddy new inlet. He reckoned that over eight thousand people, including over one thousand children, died at Grell. Though he tried to block the images from his mind, Grandafier could clearly see the floating remains of sundry structures, as well as the corpses of hundreds of bloated and decomposing bodies, most now barely recognizable as human.

Grandafier felt his pulse race and he struggled to breath. Then he saw a man he knew quite well, General Cato. He had been a guest at the general's house on many occasions, sharing a prized bottle of wine and other special delicacies. Grandafier saw Cato's body, floating face up in the water, with a large vicious vultamire impatiently stripping away the general's skin. Grandafier gagged and then felt his stomach muscles contract.

"What is this hell that I see?" Grandafier cried out as he fell to the ground. Grandafier's butler raced into the room. He heard Grandafier wonder aloud. "My god, Belicki has destroyed the entire city of Grell and with it the Fifth Army!" The butler listened but did not immediately understand this odd reference. Grandafier continued to mumble, "I never thought that so many people would have to die." Hearing this, the butler ran out of his master's cottage. "I need a doctor," he screamed hysterically.

Meanwhile, Grandafier lay helplessly on the floor. As he looked up at the ceiling where one of his oddly shaped mirrors was placed, he caught a glimpse of his own reflection. Before he passed out he watched his own lips move as he whispered, "Oh my God! The war has begun!"

Chapter 33
Lord Tantamount's Dilemma

Grandafier doctor's ordered him to rest after what was diagnosed as a mild heart attack. It was not Grandafier who was on Timilty's mind as he rose early, immaculately dressed, as usual, and intent on visiting his lord and best friend. With this shoulder length grey hair in its usual unkempt state, and with a stern look upon his face, Timilty was heartsick and more worried than he could ever remember as walked the short distance from his own home to Lord Tantamount's estate. He had visited every single unit for nearly a fortnight and each unit, after he asked how the lord was doing, Hontallo deferentially repeated the exact same message: "My father is indisposed. He will not see anyone today."

On cue, Timilty nodded his head reverentially, and then with utmost courteous conveyed his heartfelt sentiments. "Please tell my lord that I was here."

"I will our dear friend," Hontallo said, before carefully closing the door not only on Timilty, but rather on the entire outside world.

As he watched Hontallo close the door, Timilty wondered, "What sort of hell is my poor lord going through?"

Timilty loved Lord Tantamount in a way that few people could ever understand. Sure the old man was cold and dispassionate. But underneath that gruff exterior he also was fair, honest, principled, and fiercely loyal. He was the passra's most ardent advocate for the rights of Ka-Why-Tee and Arcania's other minorities. And who else but Lord Tantamount would have elevated a Ka-Why-Tee to be the chief of his council or spoken out so eloquently in favor of Bogul rights at the very conclusion of the last terrible Bogul rebellion? This was indeed a remarkable man, one of Arcania's true heroes and Timilty believed the lord's present burden must be quite unbearable.

"He is the most decent man I have ever known," Timilty exclaimed as he walked past Grandafier's diminutive cottage. Suddenly glaring, his eyes burning with a seizing rage and an unrepentant hatred, Timilty scoffed, "And I have known very few decent men." Then as his eyes narrowed he added, "That old bastard Grandafier is behind all of this, I can sense it. But how did he know that a tsunami would strike Grell?" Timilty scratched his head as he pondered this question. "There is only one answer. He must be part of a larger conspiracy against the Centama family." Timilty was sure that Montama would not willingly participate in such a traitorous scheme. "No, either Grandafier seduced the young boy or someone else deluded them both into joining this insane and treacherous plot." Timilty stopped in his tracks. "But who are Grandafier's compatriots and which devil has he joined forces with this time?"

As his theory came into focus, Timilty realized, "Lord Tantamount has done so much for me. Now it is my time to do something for him!" In that instant Timilty decided to use his own authority as the head of the Lord's Privy Council to initiate a thorough, comprehensive investigation of the events surrounding the destruction of Grell. "I will get to the bottom of this," he promised. Then with a visceral determination he added, "I will do this for my lord."

Timilty knew that his lord was in pain, but he could not even begin to guess the magnitude of the lord's despair. For nearly a fortnight, Tantamount had confined himself to his private study. There he sat for hours at a time perusing various historical documents, legal treatises, and even sundry spiritual works in search of an answer to the one perplexing and apparently unanswerable question that presently consumed his thoughts. "What could have driven Montama to commit such a callous act of brazen sedition against the honored members of the Centama family?"

Though Tantamount approached the question logically, he could find no satisfactory answer. Tortured, sleep deprived, and having had little sustenance for several units, Tantamount found it difficult to concentrate. Yet he persisted, sure that if he thought about this one question long enough he might just be able to discover what had led his still beloved son astray.

So again, for at least the twentieth time, he searched through an ancient text written by an unnamed High Cleric in search of an answer. One particular phrase caught his attention. The High Cleric wrote, "War is occasionally necessary to cleanse the soul of the body politic." Tantamount read the phrase several times, not sure whether he agreed with its sentiment or not. Then he read on. A paragraph or so later, the cleric warned, "It is far easier to start a war than it is to end one."

Deliberately, with his best feather pen, Tantamount's palsied hand, shaking uneasily, scratched these two phrases onto an ordinary yellow piece of parchment, paper he generally used to record his legal and financial affairs. After he finished, the lord read the words aloud, then he read them again silently, then he read them yet another time, then he put the text down, before picking it up and reading it yet again. Each time he read the phrases he stopped at certain key words. He underlined several specific words: cleanse, soul, and body in the first phrase then easier, start, war, and end in the second. Next he attempted to combine the words into one coherent sentence. He first wrote, "It is easier to end the body than it is to cleanse the soul." Then he tried another permutation of the same words, "War is the end of the soul. It is easier to start by cleansing the body."

Sighing palpably, he mumbled aloud, "This makes no sense." Then, he crumpled the paper into a ball and threw it onto the floor, before picking up another piece of plain yellow paper. After he laid it next to him, Tantamount read a parable written by the sage elder Togato of the ancient Tenawene Tribe. He had famously written, "War is its own master. It is a slave to no one." Then Togato added one of the most famous of all Arcanian maxims, "Once started, no man can tame a war."

Again Lord Tantamount carefully copied these phrases onto his yellow parchment, making sure that his penmanship was impeccable, for he insisted on clarity in all matters. As before, he identified what he considered to be the keywords in the two sentences. This time they were war, master, slave, and tame. He next constructed a new sentence from the various keywords: "It is easy to cleanse the body politic, but only a tame slave can end a war."

He looked at his creation then scowled. "It makes no sense. Somehow these words must make sense! But how?" Disgusted, he again scrunched the paper in a ball before disposing of it. As he massaged his head with the backside of the feather pen, the lord continued to stare at the various keywords, convinced that if he just thought about these various axioms long enough he might be able to understand why his son was fomenting a rebellion.

Still, as he wrote countless new sentences, all including the very same words, the lord discovered that there were an almost endless series of permutations, yet none of them seemed to provide any additional insight. Undaunted, the lord methodically pulled out one piece of yellow parchment after another, each time adding yet another combination of the various keywords. "It is easy to tame a slave but in the end the master of the body politic's soul is war." He read this phrase over and over, as he had done with each variation before it. Then he put the text down on his desk, closed his eyes for a few seconds, picked it up and read it aloud another time. "It is easy to tame a slave but in the end the master of the body politics' soul is war." As he reread his new phrase he realized that he liked it better than any of the other ones. Yet, after he read the sentence aloud for at least the twentieth time he wasn't quite sure what it meant and after a few more minutes of careful contemplation, he finally crumpled the paper into yet another ball and then threw it into what was now becoming a disheveled pile of scattered papers on the floor.

Having reached and even surpassed the point of endurance, his sanity now teetering on the brink, Tantamount gently stood up and with as much decorum as he could muster, and with near perfect posture, walked to the open window and looked outside. There he relished the crisp fresh air and even took a moment to admire the nearby flowers. One in particular caught his fancy, a glimmering orange dancing flower that was especially animated on this bright and gloriously sunny unit. The lord reached out and with his right hand, snatched the flower, and then watched as it continued to dance as he drew it steadily toward his face. He inhaled its sweet fragrance and as he did so he remembered how much young Montama enjoyed sitting in the garden, watching the flowers dance too and fro.

As the lord closed his eyes he could see Montama, as a boy of just seven or eight, laughing boisterously as the lord handed him a solitary flower, which danced to the left and then to the right, to the young boy's obvious delight. Then the lord opened his eyes, shook his head sadly and repeated a phrase he had spoken at least a hundred times during the past several units. "Why would he do this to me?"

Frustrated, exhausted, no longer even sure if he was asleep or awake, Tantamount dropped the flower onto the floor, where it continued to wiggle for several seconds before it finally came to a rest. Tantamount then stared at the innocent flower. Though it was freshly picked its scent already was fading. "Why would he do this to me?" he asked again, his eyes moist with tears.

Then as the lord slowly closed his eyes he wondered, "What will I do? Which side will I be on?" Then he thought of the flower and the young boy who laughed as it danced, until the lord fell into a deep and welcome sleep.

Datoria 3

THE SEASONS
OF
THE ARCANIAN CALENDAR

The Season of Death
The Season of Renewal
The Season of Life
The Season of Rain
The Season of Reason

Chapter 34
Bellazar's Secret

"How do you know that an army is approaching?" Rendrau again begged Bellazar to tell him how she could be so absolutely certain, for they had heard the terrifying news from Grell, and were thus dubious about reports of any army's imminent approach.

Impatiently, she reiterated, "The Oracle told me."

For the fourth time Rendrau angrily implored, "Why doesn't the Oracle speak to me about these things? Am I not destined to be the next king?"

Bellazar could not bring herself to tell Rendrau the truth. "Of course you are," she said, though she could not look him directly in the eye as she spoke.

Though he was dull witted, Rendrau was wise enough to realize that something was seriously amiss. "You're holding something back," he persisted, now standing before his wife as she sat in her favorite knitting chair. He noticed that Bellazar looked unusually tired, for she had not slept well the last night. Impulsively, he leaned down before her on one knee and gently stroked her long red hair. "I have loved you since the first time I met you, since the first time I saw you smile at me. I know when you are not telling the truth." Now again veritably begging her to be honest with him, he whispered, "You know something. Please tell me what it is."

It had been more than a decade since Rendrau last saw Bellazar cry, long before Me was born, even before her last miscarriage. As he kneeled before her caressing her tear stained checks, he was surprised to see in them a warm glow of affection. "You might as well tell me," Rendrau whispered gently.

Unable to contain her emotions any longer, Bellazar threw her arms around her husband. Holding him tight she cried, "It is nothing. I swear. My nerves are just overwrought."

Rendrau held his wife with one hand while he gently stroked her long red hair with the other. Then in a quiet voice he said, "I have been thinking of leading the First Army myself and I will not be dissuaded, no matter what you have to say." His voice was emphatic and yet totally calm, demonstrating what Bellazar knew to be the unknown truth about her husband. His heart was utterly fearless. As Bellazar stared directly into her husband's adoring eyes, he continued, "I cannot hide in this castle while an enemy stalks our passra." Rendrau was not the most creative or intelligent man in the passra, but Bellazar judged him to be among the bravest. It was a quality she greatly admired.

"You will make a great king," she said admiringly, with tears in her eyes.

"And you will always be in my heart and by my side," he added, his affections genuine, his feelings for his wife moved in a way that he no longer thought possible. As he embraced Bellazar, Rendrau realized that he had never loved another woman and as he closed his eyes he realized, that he never would.

Chapter 35
Reflections

It required all of General Garr's inner fortitude and battlefield skill to regroup his forces after the disastrous tunnel collapse. So many men had died that it was impossible to determine a precise count of the dead, particularly since many were trapped for all eternity inside the tunnel's watery grave. A count of the living provided an estimate of the damage done: nearly one-quarter of Montama's army had been destroyed, including almost one-half of its horses, oxen, and talladaggers. Of the fortunate men and animals that survived many sustained injuries so severe that they had to be abandoned at the water's edge. Thus, the loss of men and materiel was truly staggering, a serious blow that would have given a lesser man than General Garr reason to pause.

Garr was hardly the sort of man who experienced self-doubt. "We came here to take the throne and the Oracle," he emphatically declared. "That is what we will do." Then surveying the bruised and battered remnants of his army he added, "Now each of you will have to fight as if you are two men. You will have to kill twice as many Arcanians." Finally, with a malicious grin he added, "and in case you have any doubts, just remember the friends you left behind here at Count Belicki's tunnel." Then in a loud and boisterous voice he concluded, "We will have vengeance my friends."

Yet despite the general's bold and confident rhetoric, the invasion of Arcania soon met with a series of other unexpected obstacles. Though less cataclysmic than the tunnel collapse, they were equally frustrating. Montama's army arrived on the sandy beaches of southern Arcania just as the mating season for the oblong seanat commenced. This ancient crustacean spent the vast majority of its life at sea. Annually, during the

Season of Renewal, hundreds of thousands of these bizarre looking creatures, about six to eight inches long and circular shaped, crawled onto the desolate and cold beaches of southern Arcania, where they laid millions of eggs before expiring. As a result, about thirty miles of beach land presently was littered with the carcasses of countless hundreds of thousands of these strange looking sea creatures. "We can't move inland here," Garr quickly realized and the plan to move directly north into eastern Arcania had to be abandoned.

Although the general did not know it at the time, this unexpected development proved to be highly fortuitous, for had they moved north, as planned, they would have run directly into the path of General Wu's Third Army. The irony, then, is that Montama's army was saved from certain extermination, not by Count Belicki or the Oracle, but rather by one of the sea's most ancient and innocuous creatures.

As a result, Montama's army moved directly westward for some distance along the beach, through savage slashing rainstorms, before finally pivoting northward toward Teta. Further delays were engendered when the army arrived at the Commeru River. Usually a placid and peaceful body of water, the intense rains had turned it into yet another unwelcome and unexpected obstacle that had to be crossed by building a series of floating pontoon bridges. Using local vegetation, including the branches from nearby trees, and the hides of animals that had died in the tunnel collapse, these bridges were designed to float, though they did so rather precariously at times, across the rivers surging waters. The crossing required a further three units time. Though the passage was largely uneventful, several more horses and oxen were lost, though fortunately no more talladaggers. While the army slowly crossed the Commeru River, scouting parties were sent out to forage for food, for many supplies had been lost in the tunnel flood. To Montama's young eyes, the specter of this mighty army on the move appeared to be just one degree removed from total chaos.

General Garr knew better. He realized that during wartime the only plan that works is the one you improvise on the run. If they could not move directly north, as originally planned, then the army would seek another opportunity to confront the enemy on a battlefield of his own choosing. Garr's choice, however, was most unconventional. "We will fight at the Valley of Kalel," he declared with a confidence that did not invite contrary opinions.

The Oracle

Montama did not agree. "We can't fight here," he said with a forthrightness that General Garr quite obviously did not expect. Though it was called the Valley of Kalel, the large indentation was really the remnant of a giant oval impact crater from a long ago meteor strike. The area spanned about a half a mile from both north to south and east to west. Its walls sloped downward at sharp forty-five degree angles and from the sky above the crater looked much like a large oval bowl. Meanwhile, its base was covered with sundry vegetation, though nothing sufficiently large to conceal an army. Though Montama was indeed a military neophyte, he knew from his tutors that any army that was forced into the Valley of Kalel would be helplessly trapped, quickly surrounded, and brutally eradicated. The optimal strategy was therefore to force your enemy into the valley, not to unilaterally inhabit it.

Montama also knew that for an army trapped in the valley there were only a few unhappy options. One could conceal one's forces behind natural fortifications, such as trees or small hills, though again these existed in insufficient numbers to cloak Montama's depleted but still formidable army. Or if the army had sufficient time it could dig trenches deep into the soil. Each of these alternatives was a purely defensive strategy, however, capable only of delaying an army's inevitable defeat. Thus, as far as Montama could divine, the goal of any competent general should be to ardently avoid the valley at all costs. Why then did General Garr want to deploy to this vulnerable low ground?

Montama therefore was stunned when General Garr ordered two of his best divisions to ride down into the valley. "Dig trenches and fortifications," he ordered his men, who obsequiously obeyed.

Montama pleaded with Garr, "This is suicide."

"No," the general responded resolutely. "This is bait."

Though Montama thought it a tragic strategic mistake, the young man realized that Garr was a wily combatant. "He must be up to something," Montama thought, abruptly withdrawing his objections, trusting his ally though frankly he had no palpable reason to do so. He continued to view their current course as pure madness. But then, was not this entire military enterprise an example of unbridled insanity? "I will defer to your expertise," he finally conceded, though the reality was that he had no alternative, for it was Garr who commanded the army, not Montama.

As hundreds of men began the process of digging into the valley's floor, Montama enjoyed his first respite in several units time. His mind still concentrated on the devastation at the tunnel collapse, and briefly he thought again of the Bogul man that he killed at Kankabar. Reflectively that night, as he sat by the fire attempting to warm his hands, with General Garr as his only companion, the young man asked a particularly sharp and impertinent question. "How old were you the first time that you killed a man?"

Though the general might have taken offense at this rather blunt question, Garr smiled, as if he merely were recollecting the events of his first date. In a calm and steady voice, he responded, "I was nine cycles old."

"How did it happen?"

Garr was hardly an effusive man, but on this particular evening, exhausted from the long march, as he shared the warmth of the campfire with his young protégé, Garr was in an unusually loquacious mood. "My parents were dirt farmers. Extremely poor! I was the oldest of six children. They sold me to the Relatin Army so that they could raise enough money to feed my family, otherwise we all would have starved." Garr reached forward, using the campfire to light a pipe that he had carried with him into battle since he was a boy. "I was sent to Galtapor, a small island on the southern rim of the Relatin Empire. One of the soldiers told me that if I ever had to kill a man, I should make sure that I stabbed him in the gut, because a gut wound is always fatal. When the barbarian hordes streamed into our camp I realized that I would never be taken alive. So I took a knife in my right hand, and when one of the barbarians approached me, I surprised him. Before he could react I plunged the knife into his gut. I can still remember the look on his face when he realized what I had done to him." Garr smiled as he remembered, "But he was an absolutely impressive man. He didn't even flinch. Instead, very calmly, he pulled the knife out, saw that the wound was deep and fatal, and with much admiration he told me, 'You have done well boy.' Then, as I watched, he simply keeled over and died."

"What did you do?" Montama asked eagerly.

"I picked the knife up and ran at another enemy soldier. I stabbed him too. But when I did the knife broke off in my hand. He knocked me to the ground and when I woke up I learned that the enemy had retreated. We had won the battle and I was given a medal. One of the officers was so impressed with me that he took me under his wing and taught me everything I needed to know to survive. He was my mentor, as I am now yours."

"So you are used to death?" Montama asked with an unusual shyness.

Garr realized that killing does not come naturally to all men. Montama was the son of a reputable lord. He had grown up in a position of wealth and privilege. Instinctively, Garr understood that the present experience was completely new to this inexperienced young man. In a surprisingly tender voice the general added, "The war has just begun. What you have seen thus far is nothing compared to what we will soon see." Then, as he stood up he added, "Get some rest." Montama closed his eyes, for he desperately needed sleep and a great battle lay just ahead.

Chapter 36
General Wu is Missing!

Pantamanu was startled when he heard the news. "General Wu is missing!"

The young prince, who had been sitting quietly by the campfire, sipping tea and studying a detailed map of central Arcania, responded incredulously. "What do you mean he is missing?"

Captain Delacroix was courteous but insistent. "We cannot find him anywhere in the camp."

Pantamanu scratched his head and then remembered his brief meeting with the general, not more than a half hour earlier. "I saw him in his tent. Did you look there?"

"We have searched the entire camp," Delacroix explained. "He is no where to be found."

Pantamanu watched as several guards scurried in his direction. Within seconds, they completely encircled him, then resolutely stood guard. "What is this for?" Pantamanu asked uncertainly.

The young prince's eyes opened wide with astonishment when he heard Delacroix exclaim, "With the general missing you are now in charge."

"Me?" Pantamanu asked, turning and looking to either side as if he was searching for someone else who might outrank him. "What about you?" he asked, veritably pleading with the captain to take command.

"You outrank me," the captain responded without emotion.

"But I thought my title was ceremonial."

"No," Captain Delacroix responded.

Pantamanu purposely spilled his drink on the ground, then stood and looked directly into Captain Delacroix's deep brown eyes. "I don't understand. What do you mean General Wu is missing? He can't just simply vanish, not on the eve of what is likely to be the greatest military encounter since the Miracle at Mt. Delba."

"We have searched everywhere," Delacroix again insisted, "and we have men out scouting the area even as we speak."

Petulantly, Pantamanu kicked some dirt into the campfire, before turning his attention back to the captain. When he looked again, he realized that the captain and everything else was now completely suspended in time and space, as were the guards and other soldiers. "What the devil is going on?" Pantamanu shouted in defiant exasperation.

He heard a response, but not from anyone in the real world. "The battle for the Arcanian throne begins tomorrow." Pantamanu stood silent and still, for he recognized the voice, having heard it speak to him on several other occasions, though mostly while he slept. "And when the battle begins, you will be in charge."

"And what has happened to General Wu?" Pantamanu asked.

"He is of no consequence," King Leonata said softly, as his body materialized inside the campfire's red, hot surging flames. Leonata was impressed by Pantamanu's potential and while he had serious reservations about the young man's resolve, he was convinced that Pantamanu alone could restore order to Arcania. "It is you the Oracle is interested in," though by the Oracle he meant himself and his partisans within the universe of imagination.

Pantamanu stepped boldly forward into the flames, which like everything else in the real world was now in a state of suspended animation. Standing next to King Leonata, separated by no more than a mere inch or so, the young prince asked confidently, "So you want to see if I am capable of leading this army?"

"Of course," Leonata declared, staring directly into Pantamanu's eyes, which now reflected the fire in silvery shades of white and yellow.

"Then I will not disappoint you," Pantamanu declared, as if the matter were summarily settled.

"I hope not." Leonata smiled ever so slightly. "It would be most unfortunate if you did."

Pantamanu stepped back, bit-by-bit from the fire. As he did so Leonata's form slowly vanished and as it did, the other figures slowly reanimated, until the sights and sounds of the world were completely restored. Commander Pantamanu did not notice this otherworldly transformation, for his eyes remained fixed on the campfire's smoldering flames. "Victory will be ours," he said softly.

Sure that he was the intended recipient of this remark, Captain Delacroix saluted his new commander and respectfully chanted, "Yes, sir."

Chapter 37
The Battle of the Valley of Kalel

When the public criers announced that Arcania's beloved regent personally would lead the passra's First Army to victory over the invading barbarian horde, the citizen's spontaneously adorned their homes with handmade signs reading, "Long Live the Regent." And when Rendrau finally departed the king's castle for the short ride south to the First Army headquarters, people stood for hours along Teta's winding, havoc ridden streets, quietly honoring the man they now proudly proclaimed to be their Coladay or First Citizen, an honorific title of great repute. Ordinary citizens threw bouquets of freshly picked flowers and offered gifts of wine and bread for the man that they all now fervently hoped would soon be their king.

Worried beyond all reason, Bellazar could not bring herself to attend these public festivities. The night before she had had yet another premonition of disaster and death. She awoke in an uproar, demanding that General Tige, the real leader of the First Army, ensure that Rendrau was kept far from the battlefield at all times. She also ordered that her husband be placed in a protective cocoon, surrounded by at least fifty elite guards.

Though Tige affirmatively guaranteed Rendrau's safety, Bellazar was afraid that she might breakdown and cry in front of the Arcanian people and so reluctantly, she watched her husband's departure from her third story bedroom window. There she stared out uneasily for almost an hour. Her anxiety mounted as Rendrau rode first through the winding streets of Teta, then off toward a vast seemingly endless horizon. When he finally passed from her view, Bellazar stood silently for several minutes, wondering if there was anything else she could possibly do to ensure her husband's safety. Finally, tired and dejected, she sat in her rocking chair, uncharacteristically tossing aside her knitting needle, at last permitting the tears to stream freely down her face. And for the next four units, she sat alone in her room, refusing to speak with anyone, unless they had news from the battlefield.

When Lord Gulcum arrived each morning with the daily briefings, Bellazar repeatedly noted, "This is puzzling." The sundry reports noted that a large group of enemy soldiers were digging trenches and other fortifications inside the base of the Valley of Kalel. "Why would they do that?" she wondered, for it made no tactical sense whatsoever.

General Tige also received the news with his usual high level of distrust and caution. A childhood illness had turned his corneas a fiery red. As he scanned the battlefield reports, occasionally shaking his head with disgust, he assumed a decidedly skeptical posture. Looking directly at his most trusted subordinate, Captain Pife, he declared, "How can you trust such intelligence. With the Oracle, things are never what they seem to be." Pife nodded his consent, as the general continued to peruse the files, before asking a central, pertinent question. "Why in god's name would anyone willingly take the low ground?"

Captain Pife had no ready answer other than to suggest that it was either the most egregious act of military incompetence ever perpetuated by an invading army or more likely a trap intended to lure the First Army down the valley's sharp forty-five degree inclines into the barren lands below.

"And why would I do that when I can surround the whole damn valley and starve them out?" Tige challenged his subordinate. Again, Pife had no suitable answer, only the sense that something most certainly was not right. On that point Tige readily agreed, for the reports made absolutely no military sense whatsoever.

Because of these concerns, Tige dispatched two scouting parties to the areas surrounding the valley, to determine if there was any sign of a residual force. One scouting party went as far to the east as Appadia, a small trading facility on the banks of the Commeru River. There a man with one arm told them that an invading army indeed had crossed the river several units past. He was not quite sure how big the army was, only that it appeared to have strange beasts in tow, the likes of which the folks in Appadia had never before seen. "Ugly looking critters," another old man volunteered, while three other grizzled looking pioneers nodded their heads in tandem.

Meanwhile the second scouting party traveled to the Temannay villages to the northwest. They too found absolutely no evidence of an invading army. Rather than satisfying his curiosity, the new reports made General Tige even more sullen and disconsolate. If the reports were to be believed, there was no sign of an enemy within twenty miles of the valley, in any direction. Furthermore, there was no place for an army to hide, for the land directly surrounding Kalel was largely flat and, except for a few trees and large rocks, thoroughly exposed. Still, if an army had crossed the Commeru River where was it hiding?

Could these few troops at the base of the Valley of Kalel really be the entire remnants of Montama's invading army? This was possible, for scouts also reported finding a large number of bodies and other signs of a cataclysmic disaster on the eastern coast of the Bay of Battle. On the basis of these reports Captain Pife suggested, "Perhaps the army is so depleted that this small group in the Valley of Kalel is all that remains of it?"

Tige's devout caution, inspired by his thorough knowledge of the Oracle and its history, made him pause before prematurely committing troops. "The Oracle is capable of many things," he declared emphatically, his hands crossed and his mind still sorting out all of the details of the various reports. Then the general was struck with a new idea. "Why can't the Oracle hide an entire army?" He pondered this possibility for a few seconds. Then looking up at Pife he asked, "Suppose this is a trap?" He remembered reading that King Leonata's army had vanished mysteriously, only to reappear miles from its last known location. If so, then the force in the valley might be nothing more than bait designed to lead Arcania's armies south, while leaving the capital city of Teta dangerously exposed. "Of course," Tige reasoned, "The enemy, shielded by the Oracle, could have moved westward, flanking the First Army, then moving directly on to Teta."

Pife conceded that if that was the invader's plan, it was indeed a brilliant strategy. To counter it Tige would have to develop a bold stratagem of his own. He sat at his desk, his eyes seemingly ablaze, for he was now sure that the real threat lay not in the valley, but rather to the north. Looking up at Captain Pife he calmly stated, "We will not let on that we know their intentions. So I will continue to move the First Army south to the valley, just as they expect me to. In the meantime I will direct General Xian and the Second Army to move from western Arcania to Teta."

But what if the Valley of Kalel indeed was meant to be the central territory in the war against the invaders? To ensure that he could defeat any army that might emerge from whatever direction, Tige sent a rider to inform General Wu to move his Third Army westward toward the valley. "We will surround the army in the valley and entrap them, while we move the Second Army north to Teta." Tige was very pleased with his counter strategy, though he was concerned when one of his riders returned with the news that General Wu was missing and that Commander Pantamanu now rode at the head of the Third Army. "Damn," Tige cussed, not sure what to make of this latest report, but sure that he must move quickly lest the barbarians discover and react to his own plans.

Through all of these strategic deliberations Rendrau remained attentive yet entirely above the fray, only occasionally offering a trivial suggestion. "It is not my job to dictate military strategy to the experts," he wisely reasoned. When he too learned of General Wu's unexplained disappearance, however, the king's third eldest son became obsessed with domestic political considerations. "With Wu gone, Pantamanu is directly in charge of the Third Army." He reasoned, "That means that my dear brother is now a greater political threat to me than is any invading army."

Though there was no tangible evidence to support his suspicions, Rendrau was absolutely convinced that Pantamanu ordered General Wu's assassination. He snarled, "At the moment of my greatest victory he readies himself to move against me." Realizing that General Tige had ordered the Third Army to move toward the valley, Rendrau decided that he had no choice but to take matters into his own hands.

This was a difficult choice for Rendrau, for he had been the first to admit that General Tige's proposal, to encircle the enemy and starve them into submission, made perfect sense. That was a military calculation. However, if Pantamanu's army now posed an even greater domestic threat, then patience was no longer a virtue.

"Damn that blasted brother of mine," Rendrau fulminated. Driven by the imperatives of what he now believed was the broader security situation, he entered General Tige's headquarters, warmly saluted him, and then amiably invited the general to sit down for a short talk. Rendrau was calm but Tige immediately understood that something important was on the regent's mind. "How long will it take to starve out the army in the Valley of Kalel?" Rendrau asked respectfully.

Tige reiterated his earlier prediction. "Our best estimate is that they have enough supplies to last between a fortnight and an interval."

"That is a considerable amount of time," Rendrau acknowledged carefully. "And I am afraid that is one thing that we do not have enough of!" Tige sat back stoically in his chair, resolutely folding his arms, waiting for Rendrau to speak, certain that he was not going to agree with the regent's proposal. Though Rendrau did not mention Pantamanu explicitly, the regent carefully noted that the passra required stability and that the sooner the current military crisis was brought to an amicable ending the sooner Arcania could be restored to a state of normality.

"I cannot rush military decisions because of political considerations," Tige rashly declared.

Rendrau was a man of deep honor and it pained him to raise these issues with as trusted and loyal a friend as General Tige. Without a ready recourse to diplomacy, Rendrau bluntly noted, "This is not an option that is open for discussion. We must move sooner rather than later against this invader. I am afraid that there are larger issues at stake here than the disposition of your army."

Tige stared forcefully into Rendrau's eyes. Despite his deep feelings of warm affection for Rendrau, he was not about to be bullied about on the battlefield by the regent or anyone else. This was his command. "I will not commit our troops to a battle that is sure to cost the lives of hundreds of our men. There is no need for it."

When Tige hesitated yet again, Rendrau's patience finally succumbed to a sudden and unexpected burst of temper. "I am already being held hostage by lawyers in Teta. My brother, who is eager to assume the throne, now commands the Third Army in General Wu's place." Coming as close as he could to implicating his brother, Rendrau continued, "The dangers are no longer merely in the form of an invading army." Then in a steady but determined voice he added, "We cannot wait for the invaders to surrender. You will commence military action against the mercenary army as soon as possible!" Then to forestall any further debate, Rendrau declared, "That is an order!"

Tige was unaccustomed to being abused in such a blatant and vitriolic manner. He loved King Benton and he understood that the regent had legitimate domestic political concerns. Tige, too, was suspicious of Pantamanu and his motives, and he too suspected that foul play was involved in the disappearance of General Wu. Still, the idea that a political figure would determine military policy was more than his pride could bear. He immediately thought of resigning and letting Rendrau lead the troops in his place. Yet, as he stood, ready to tear his ribbons from his chest, he realized that he was a mere slave to duty. Deeply conflicted, but forever loyal, he decided at last that it was impossible to defy the regent's mandate. So swallowing his immense pride, lest he say something he would later regret, Tige finally bowed to the reality of the political situation. "We will move against the invaders at dawn," the general conceded gracefully, if not warmheartedly.

Rendrau knew that Tige had made an immensely important concession, so he immediately recognized the need to bridge the painful gap that had emerged between these two old friends. "I, of course, will be honored to ride by your side," the regent warmly confided. Then, gently placing a hand on the general's shoulder Rendrau added, "I want you to know that despite this change in plans, I have full confidence in your abilities." Tige nodded his head forlornly and then signed the order committing the troops to battle.

It took but three hours for the army to move from its present position to the northern rim overlooking the Valley of Kalel. General Tige and Regent Rendrau, still sitting on horseback and guarded by more than fifty elite soldiers, took up a position more than one hundred feet from the rim. There Tige directed his officers to move the men into position for the first phase of the assault. They did so skillfully, moving thousands of archers along the perimeter until they completely surrounded the valley in all directions. Standing several feet apart, steadily holding their bows in a ready position, they waited patiently for the order to unleash the first wave of the deadly offensive against the enemy soldiers who until just moments before were milling about the valley's basin. When the enemy saw the approaching First Army, it scurried for cover. Before they could secure cover, Tige raised his arm high above his head. Then as he slashed his arm stridently forward the archers let loose a titanic bombardment of deadly arrows, each whizzing through the air with an eerie high-pitched deadly precision. As the arrows struck their targets they made two distinctly different sounds: one a dull thump signifying that an arrow had hit bottom ground, and a second pounding thud indicating that the arrow had struck its intended victim. Within seconds of this second audio variation, Rendrau heard yet another sound: the piteously shrill cry of an unseen wounded or dying man. The sound unnerved him and the spectacle of these great archers plying their trade utterly enthralled him. He watched as each man systematically reached into their back pouch for arrow after arrow, firing additional volleys down into the dark and dingy abyss. And within minutes the valley floor looked like nothing more than a porcupine's nest, filled as it was with countless thousands of arrows, many of which had found their intended targets.

Finally, after several more minutes of the aerial assault, Tige forcefully raised his right arm signaling the archers to halt. When he did the deafeningly squeal that had permeated the airwaves suddenly fell silent. Rendrau was fascinated as the archers in unison stepped back several steps from the valley's rim. General Tige then raised his right arm above his head yet again, and with a discernable fierceness brought it forward, a signal to commence the second wave of the attack. Ground soldiers now quickly moved into position. As the archers continued to stand back, these soldiers, mostly carrying silver shields and swords, approached the valley rim. All that stood in their way now was a phalanx of officers, each with their swords raised straight up in the air. The soldiers stood at rapt attention, waiting, some breathing heavily, most eager for battle, as Tige this time slowly raised his right arm above his head. Then, with a silent prayer, he brought his arm down with a sudden fierceness. Seconds later the officers dropped their swords by their side, signaling the soldiers to commence the final descent into the now completely exposed valley.

Carefully soldiers by the thousands began the treacherous movement down the sharply sloping walls of the Valley of Kalel. There was little vegetation for them to hold onto, for over the centuries runoff from heavy rains had wiped the valley's walls clean. As the men descended, they therefore had to steady themselves by putting one arm around the man to their right, so that eventually the entire army was interconnected, a veritable web of soldiers moving uneasily down toward the valley floor.

From their secure location on the northern rim, Tige and Rendrau watched as the men moved step by tentative step, down the sharp wall toward the exposed valley's base. A few soldiers lost their footing and slid uncontrollably down the hundred yard long embankment. Though the redeployment from the rim to the valley floor was potentially hazardous, their ultimate objective was simple and direct: find any surviving enemy invaders and kill them.

Tige's eyes were firmly fixed on the battle site below. Though he opposed this military action, he now watched with effusive pride as his men carried out their mission with fixed determination and unmatched skill.

Rendrau too was amazed and honored by the military's precision and proficiency. He craned his head, struggling to see if there was any sign of life on the valley floor. When he could see none he turned to ask General Tige how many survivors might still be living after the first deadly assault. When he did he caught a strange vision out of the top corner of his right eye. "Was that a horse?" he whispered. For though he was not sure, he thought he had seen the black snout and then the large gray head of a lone and rather befuddled looking horse. What made this vision so unusual was that the head appeared to be suspended in mid-air, approximately ten or fifteen feet directly above his current position. But when he looked back up again, the vision was gone.

"I am seeing things," Rendrau declared, taking a handkerchief from his pocket and carefully wiping his brow. The sun was rising and it was an unusually hot and muggy day. As he placed the handkerchief into his back pocket he shook his head then muttered, "My eyes are playing tricks on me."

Tige thought the reference was meant for him. He therefore proudly commented, "You are seeing Arcania's greatest army in action."

Rendrau nodded his head for he was sure that what he had seen was nothing more than an illusion. Still, he was so fascinated that he repeatedly turned his head skyward. When he saw nothing more than the usual intermittent cloud cover, he again turned his attention back to the battlefield, that is, until he heard what appeared to be the muffled sound of a whinnying horse. "Did you hear that?" he asked, suddenly quite startled.

"Hear what?" Tige responded coldly, clearly annoyed at the regent's incessant idle chatter.

While everyone else stared intently at the valley floor, Rendrau continued to look nervously from side to side, then once more to the sky. Then, for just an instant, he thought he saw it again. "It *is* a horse's head," he said aloud. This time, instead of vanishing, the horse looked down directly at the regent. "That is the damndest thing I have ever seen in my life," Rendrau exclaimed, trying in vain to attract General Tige's attention.

But the general was still admiring his army's precision movements down the valley's treacherous slopes. "Don't worry, regent," the general declared. "Everything is going according to our plan."

Just as the general spoke these words, the floating horse stepped forward until its entire body was perched seamlessly in the air directly above the general's entourage. And a strange looking creature was riding the horse. Rendrau strained to see what it was. It was an exceedingly tall, gangly looking thing with long flowing blonde hair. And furthermore, it was wearing a long, freely flowing green cape.

"What the hell is that?" Rendrau shouted. As he did so Tige finally caught sight of the strange figure. Before either man could say another word the horse glided seamlessly downward, as the rider's cape opened like a parachute, until both rider and horse were deposited safely onto the ground.

217

The Oracle

Neither Tige nor Rendrau had the sensibility to respond and this strange unearthly sight likewise utterly stupefied the guards. They watched, more in fascination than in horror, as other men on horseback began to fall from the sky. Soon a dozen, then two, then three-dozen men on horseback fell safely to the ground.

Before they had the sense to react, the number of enemy men on horseback far outnumbered Tige's small party of elite soldiers. As General Tige tried to steady his frightened horse, the men on horseback surrounded his entourage. "This must be the work of the Oracle," Tige said in a hushed panic. Instinctively the general started to draw his sword but before he could fully unsheathe it, he heard the dull thud of metal piercing his chest. Tige reached down and put his hand on a sword, with its image of a deadly coiled snake on the handle. Then he looked up and saw a one-eyed general smiling at him with demonic pleasure. "But how?" Tige gasped, as his body slumped helplessly forward. Tige held onto his horse with all of his remaining strength, but as he felt the life force wither from his body, he spit in Garr's direction, and then fell lifelessly to the ground.

As he did so other of the invaders on horseback pulled out their swords and struck the general's entourage with a terrible ferocity. Some, like Tige, fell before they even could unsheathe their weapons. Others managed to parry the enemy for a few moments before falling victim to the heavier swords of the menacing band on horseback.

Within less than three minutes all of General Tige's party were dead, with but one notable exception. Regent Rendrau still sat upon his white horse, though it was now splattered with the general's blood. Mystified and frightened beyond all reason, he looked ahead and saw that his own soldiers were too far down the valley walls to provide any assistance. As for the archers, thousands of flying arrows now appeared out of apparent thin air. Though they came from no discernable source, they carried the same deadly precision as the fuselage that just minutes before had impacted the valley floor. Rendrau watched as three, four, even five arrows ruthlessly pierced the bodies of his archers, each in quick succession, until not one of his men was left alive.

Then, Rendrau saw something so unholy that his skin began to crawl. As shards of glass appeared to shatter in all directions, an army of thousands of more men appeared out of absolute nothingness. One second there was no army and then in an instant there were far too many men to count, each one stepping over the bodies of the fallen archers, on their way to the valley's rim. Next, from the valley basin, hundreds of other men emerged from trenches and other buried fortifications, apparently unharmed and eager for battle. Garr smiled broadly, and with a triumphant wave of his hand he declared, "You will now have the honor of watching us exterminate your entire army."

Rendrau could bear no more. His ashen face was contorted with insensible fear. Angrily, he stared into General Garr's solitary eye. "And what are you going to do with me?"

"That is not up to me," Garr responded vaguely, before indicating the presence of another soldier nearby on horseback.

As Rendrau looked to his right he saw a plain and rather ordinary looking young man. Staring directly into the young man's eyes, the regent asked, "Do I know you?"

"I am Montama, the son of Lord Tantamount," the rebel declared defiantly. And then toying with his enemy he asked, "And who are you?"

"You know damn well who I am," Rendrau snarled sharply.

"Yes I do," Montama added with a queer smile. "You are my enemy."

"Then kill me," Rendrau demanded.

Montama looked intensely into Rendrau's determined eyes. He saw fear but he also understood that this was a devoutly proud man. "Is that what you would do to me if the situation were reversed?"

"Undoubtedly!" Rendrau answered. Montama nodded his head, then reached over and held his sword aloft so that he could catch the glimmer of the morning sun on the side of its razor sharp blade. But rather than striking the regent, he merely turned the sword around and handed it ever so gently to Rendrau, who was carrying no weapon of any kind. "What is this?" Rendrau asked as he stared at the sword.

"Take it," Montama declared with a surprisingly unsettling calmness. Garr stared at his young protégé, but otherwise did nothing. Rendrau impetuously grabbed the sword with his right hand, while Montama raised both of his arms above his head. Then he dared the regent. "Kill me and end this bloody war." Though Garr was surprised, he continued to stand his ground, waiting for Rendrau to react.

Rendrau's horse was steady, even if the regent was not. Nervously he answered, "I will not play your games," as he tossed Montama's sword down onto the blood-splattered ground.

Montama pursed his lips and then looked over at General Garr. He held out his right hand and asked, "May I have your half-sword?" Dubiously,

The Oracle

Garr reached behind his cape and withdrew his half-sword. As countless men on horseback, all loyal to General Garr simply watched in amazement, Montama handed the smaller weapon to Rendrau. "Either use this weapon against me now or you will surely die."

Rendrau was perplexed as he accepted the half-sword from Montama's sweaty hand. He had no false hopes, however, for he knew that the military situation was helpless. Even if he killed this crazy young boy, the very best that he could hope for under the circumstances was to be taken into captivity and paraded before the citizens of Teta in a pitiable and abject display of infernal subjugation. Montama could sense Rendrau's hopeless confusion. Finally, Rendrau took a deep breath. "I will not allow you the honor or the pleasure of parading me in front of my fellow citizens like some browbeaten animal."

As Montama and his men watched intently, Rendrau slowly turned the half-sword around and with both hands holding the engraved handle carrying the symbol of the deadly coiled snake, he closed his eyes and then plunged the weapon sharply into his own stomach. The pain surprised Rendrau, but he felt no remorse as he looked back into Montama's inquisitive face.

As his mouth filled with blood, Rendrau felt a strange new sensation. His body concomitantly existed in two separate places and furthermore he could see both of them simultaneously. In one image he was seated upon his horse, his body teetering and swiftly nearing death. In the other he was full of vigor and standing before his dear wife Bellazar, who stood quietly looking out of her castle window. He leaned toward her ear and whispered gently, "I have always loved you." As he stood staring at his wife he noticed that it was her intense green eyes that had first attracted his interest. They veritably sparkled in the brilliant sunlight and he could see the powerful life force that lay behind them, the intensity, and the very passion that made him respect his wife more than ever. "I do not regret even an instant that we have lived together," he continued, for he realized what few of us ever do, that his love for his wife far outweighed every other consideration but one. "Please take care of our daughter," he whispered softly, though his wife could not hear a word that he spoke. Then he closed his eyes as his breath waned. When he again opened them he saw only Montama's cold demanding eyes. As Rendrau's body wearily tipped from side to side he drew enough strength to regally declare, "Please promise me that you will not forsake the people of Arcania. They deserve a great king."

220

Montama had no time to respond to this heartfelt plea, for within another second Rendrau slipped from the saddle, his body dangling precariously as one leg still prevented his lifeless body from falling to the ground. Then, without warning, Rendrau's body finally slipped hard to the earth. Though dust instantly covered the regent's face, Montama thought Rendrau looked utterly peaceful. His death strangely seemed less of a punishment than a reward for having lived a virtuous life, for whatever he had been or would have been in life, he would now and forever be a hero, a martyr long and fondly remembered.

Montama continued to stare at Rendrau's body as the men on horseback began to disperse. Meanwhile, Garr rode next to his protégé and commented dispassionately, "I wouldn't try that trick again if I were you. The next time you may not be so lucky."

Montama merely smiled, for there was reason behind this seeming act of madness. "I wanted to know for sure what the Oracle intends. I gave him the chance to strike me dead. Now I am certain that I am destined to be king."

Garr said nothing. It had been a foolish gambit, but at least it had satisfied the general's thirst for the dramatic. Without thinking about the propriety of who outranked whom, Garr leaped from his horse, before retrieving his half-sword, rudely yanking it from the lifeless body of Arcania's honored Coladay. He did not even wipe the newly stained blood from its sharp and deadly blade, but rather hastily sheathed it behind his cape. He then retrieved his full-sword, pulling it out of General Tige's corpse, which stared up at him with seeming bitter contempt. Finally, as he picked up Montama's sword and handed it to the young soldier, he advised, "You will need this, for the battle is far from over."

Almost absentmindedly Montama accepted the sword, though he still stared at Rendrau's face. Then, with a new sense of swagger and determination, the young man turned his horse and rode directly toward the valley and the still ongoing battle.

Chapter 38
Anarchy!

When Rendrau died, without warning and in an instant an entire universe was inextricably disrupted! At the time, Pondru, still residing comfortably within the Oracle, was studying music. It was yet another new attraction to add to his growing and relentlessly search for enjoyable intellectual pursuits. In Arcania music was still in a decidedly nascent stage, mostly arranged around a constricted five note musical scale. Pondru's imagination was utterly consumed once he discovered the rich diversity of melodies that were possible with the existence of such disparate sounds as sharps, flats, and fluberts. He marveled at the myriad ways in which melody and syncopation could be varied. It was all quite amazing to a man who in life had been incapable of the simple act of whistling. Yet, as he diligently considered the rich possibilities of musical form and function, and how it could transform one's mood while also providing a further spur to the fertile plains of imagination, he felt a harsh, unexpected jolt that shook his world with the force of a powerful earthquake. Somehow, though he did not yet know how, he understood that the very foundation upon which the Oracle existed was being altered, perhaps irrevocably.

Pondru's perceptual world began to shift radically. First, the sound of the music, which had been so clear in his mind, unexpectedly veered into a cacophony of annoying sounds, disjointed notes, a clanging noisy disarray so disturbing that Pondru was forced to pull his consciousness back away from the other entities whose shared consciousness he so richly enjoyed. As he withdrew abruptly from the Oracle's collective intelligence, he sensed that other entities were likewise startled and confused. Calm reason inexplicably was being replaced with the dissonance of a mass of conflicting voices, speaking in different languages, no longer capable of employing a common means of communication. As confusion mounted, Pondru sensed that each entity was returning to its own separate and individual identity. Rather than the many being the one, the Oracle was now becoming a massive conglomeration of egos, ids, and strange subliminal inclinations. Furthermore, without the guiding principles of Kublatitan, these entities were beginning to exhibit their least attractive human attributes including panic, fear and desperation.

As he tried to rationalize this fundamental transformation, Pondru noticed a change in his visual perception of the universe of ideas. Before it had been an endlessly interconnected series of glowing, molten beams of light, rich with activity and eager for new and inventive thoughts. As he watched, that universe was changing. The beams of light systematically separated, their intersections continuously dissolving and diverging. "What is going on?" Pondru wondered, but when he did he was startled that there was no response. After another frighteningly silent moment Pondru realized that his thoughts were completely isolated.

"Something is happening to the Oracle!" He tried to speak these words aloud, but he no longer had the ability to converse or communicate with the thousands upon thousands of other entities that now found themselves likewise suddenly quite separate and distinct. As Pondru's imagination struggled to fathom what was happening, he saw the beams of light steadily reconfigure until they finally aligned themselves as distinct lines, each of a separate and individual color, all of them running toward infinity, closely aligned, but never meeting, never actually touching each other.

"All interconnectivity of thought has come to a halt," he sensed, though he still did not understand the reason behind this catastrophe. Though an answer did not come to his mind, he did sense something totally unexpected, a swift stabbing pain that tore his chest asunder. Pondru was shocked by this frightful sensation, for he had not felt physical pain at all since he had entered the Oracle.

Then, in his mind's eye he saw his own body covered in a rich red torrent of freshly shed blood. "My god, what is happening to me?" he called out, but again there was no response, for no one was nearby to hear his voice. Pondru's first reaction was to avoid the piercing pain, but then he remembered that pain has a useful purpose, to warn the body from harm's way. He therefore took it as a sign and though his mind was clouded with confusion and doubt, he sought to understand the cause of this extraordinary discomfort. As he did so his consciousness was inexorably drawn toward the world of physical objects. Slowly, he sensed his body materializing in a strange open field, littered with the dead and the dying. As he strained to make sense of this new and frightening reality, he was shocked to see the corpse of his dear brother Rendrau.

Now in full physical form, Pondru reached out his hand and gently touched his brother's forehead. It was cold and lifeless. "He is dead!" he said with a sudden start. Though he felt a sharp jolt of emotion, he showed no outward visceral manifestations, other than a tiny tear in the corner of his right eye. For a few moments Pondru stood alone among the dead, scanning the horizon, suddenly aware that he was at the sight of a savage ongoing battle near the precipice of the Valley of Kalel.

"War has come to my beloved Arcania," he thought ruefully, for there was no one alive to whom he could share his regretful sentiments. Then his eyes returned to his brother, who lay peacefully on the ground. He stared at him for some time, examining the wound in his brother's chest as if he were a doctor performing an autopsy. He had understood that Rendrau would not be king. He had consciously avoided the logical possibility that his brother would die, cruelly and alone on the battlefield. "At least I am now here to comfort him," he thought as his inherent humanity ever so slowly returned.

Then, Pondru sensed another presence. As he did he looked up and saw a strange, familiar man towering over him. This giant of a man declared sadly, "Last of his line. Last of King Benton's children." The colossal figure stared into Pondru's now moistening eyes and with a wretched sadness that could be conveyed without recourse to the Oracle or its wonders, he added, "Brother of yours was a good man. A great king he would have made."

"Then it is true, that Pantamanu is not my brother," Pondru said softly.

"Half brother, but not by same father," Kublatitan revealed. "Now the Oracle has no leader, no Centama is left to guide it. Thoughts are separated in the realm of ideas, can only come together now in the physical world, and only for a short time, until there is a new king."

Pondru stared again at his brother's prostate body. He had felt closest to Retch, for he and his older brother had shared a series of common intellectual interests. Rendrau exhibited many other admirable qualities, attributes that Pantamanu sadly lacked, such as honesty, directness, and most important of all, an uncompromising love for his passra. Sensing that Pantamanu was motivated solely by blind ambition, Pondru solemnly asked, "What is to happen now?"

Kublatitan did not look up as he whispered anxiously, "Time for anarchy in the physical universe and in the universe of ideas has arrived."

With these words Pondru felt yet a second jolt. This time it was his conscience begging him to explain why he had not done more to prevent this horrific outcome. "I should have done more," he reasoned.

"All should have," Kublatitan moaned. "For now time of reckoning has arrived. Only the most unfit, the most ambitious are left to be king."

Though neither Pondru nor Kublatitan could sense it at the time, another entity hovered not far from their current position. To my mind, the severing of the Oracle link provided total emancipation. "I am finally free to think as I wish!" It was a feeling of soaring and unmitigated delight. I too was now in the dark, separated from all of the other Oracle entities. I instantly realized that the death of the last of King Benton's sons provided an amazing opportunity. "The power vacuum must be filled by a new leader," I mused. Totally unconstrained and free to act, I eagerly watched Montama ride to the crest of the Valley of Kalel. As he did so, I realized that the momentum in the battle for the Arcanian throne decisively had shifted in my direction.

Datoria 4

THE FIVE NOTES OF THE ARCANIAN MUSICAL SCALE

Kata or A Minor

Mata or B Flat

Data or C Major

Rata or D Sharp

Woo or E Flat

Chapter 39
Pantamanu to the Rescue

The battle for the very soul of the Oracle was now underway. Kublatitan had chosen Bellazar to be the next King of Arcania and I must say that his choice was inspired. Though she was a woman, and though her selection ran contrary to the prejudices of the time, she was indeed a most formidable candidate: stunningly beautiful, with a razor sharp wit and savvy intelligence, and most important of all, when necessary she could be completely ruthless. All of these were qualities that served her well, but which made her entirely unfit for my own purposes.

I needed someone more malleable, strong, but not too strong: someone that I could dominate and control. Montama was young, naïve, and though he did not yet fully realize it, thoroughly ambitious. He therefore perfectly suited my needs.

What surprised me was the intervention of King Leonata. Since his death he had shown no hint of ambition. His sudden support for Pantamanu seemed most illogical at first, but then I realized that Pantamanu was the closest thing to a male Centama family member and Leonata, the founder of that dynasty, was willing to do anything to perpetuate it, even if it meant the promotion of a false prophet.

So the stakes were set and they were exponentially high. Three contenders for the Arcanian throne and yet only one of them would be successful. I was stubbornly, even vociferously determined that Montama would be the next king and I was willing to do anything, absolutely anything, to achieve my final objective. And as the Battle of the Valley of Kalel continued, it appeared that everything favored my candidate. The First Army was trapped between two hostile forces, one atop the valley, the other running along the valley's vast barren base. Temporarily confused by this sudden, unexpected change in their battlefield fortunes, the men of Arcanian's army stood silently, clinging precariously to the valley's slippery forty-five degree walls, instantly aware that they were no longer on the offensive. Since they could neither retreat up the valley wall nor move forward to the base, they had but one entirely unacceptable remaining option: to fight to the death on an uneven plain. While the Arcanian soldiers' anxiety rose, their officers immediately understood that their martial situation was so dire that their only real hope for survival was the immediate arrival of Pantamanu's Third Army unit.

And much to their amazement and relief, and I am sure with King Leonata's able assistance, as the officers looked out over the distant eastern horizon they saw the shadowy outlines of an army riding steadily and determinedly forward, with its Commander resplendently dressed in his blue uniform, with its brash gold sash and his boots polished with a robust ruby red shine. His uniform perfectly fitted his strong muscular frame and to top it off, he had his family's precious sword gleaming at the ready. "Let's annihilate the enemy. Kill every last one of them!" Pantamanu shouted so loud that even the enemy forces at the base of the valley could hear his clarion call.

From his vantage point atop the valley's northwestern precipice, General Garr instantly understood that this was a dangerous and potentially transcendent moment, a time when the tide of battle could easily turn yet again and this time much to his and my own detriment.

"Do you have any more troops in hiding?" Montama asked, for he too spotted the advancing Third Army.

"No," Garr said as he sat at the rim of the valley, steadily upon his horse, watching the newly arriving army from a safe distance. "All of our forces are before you," he said calmly. Even at this supremely dangerous moment, Garr was relaxed, unshakable, and utterly resolved to accept whatever outcome destiny might choose for him. For many decades before he had learned about the random vagaries of war. Momentum on the battlefield could change in an instant. The general suddenly remembered how a scruffy looking teenage boy severed his right eye with a short sword, while Garr had easily defeated men more than twice his size. "There are no guarantees in battle," he said without as much as the slightest hint of trepidation. Etched in his mind was a vitally important lesson: the secret to survival in war is to put one's fears aside, to move constantly with aggressive instincts against the enemy army, to never concede defeat, and if necessary to die fighting. Garr therefore showed no fear because he had none. He was a resolute example of pure and fixed determination. "We will prevail or we will die," he shouted.

Through some sort of strange symbiotic relationship, which I encouraged, Montama too sensed Garr's remarkable rectitude and as he did his mind was freed from all fear and anxiety. In its place, Montama felt a rush of adrenalin unlike anything he had ever before experienced. "This is what battle really feels like!" he thought. Montama had read many books on war, some historical, most fictional. Many times he imaged what it would be like to be in the thick of battle, but now, for the very first time, he was sensing it for real. Before his very eyes men were fighting and dying, for only one reason: so that he, Montama could be king. It was an epiphany that further elevated his spirits and extended his courage. For when he looked a second time toward the horizon and the oncoming Third Army, he no longer felt either fear or apprehension. Instead, he felt a steady determination to prevail, no matter what the cost.

Yet what was Pantamanu thinking? This too would be his first real foray into battle. Pantamanu's army was indeed magnificent, with at least a thousand men riding at full throttle on horseback, not far behind their inspired and well-dressed leader. Pantamanu was now so close to the valley that he could hear the death screams of the wounded at the base of the Valley of Kalel. Pantamanu also could see what looked like two endless streams of men, with their swords drawn in anger, as they moved inexorably down an uneven plain. It was at just this moment that Pantamanu hesitated. "What is the status of the battle?" Pantamanu asked with sudden concern, not sure whether he should surround the valley or charge directly into it. Then with a desperate look he asked, "What do I do now?"

"We should move forward into the valley?" Delacroix responded calmly.

"Are you sure that is wise?" Pantamanu asked. "Shouldn't we surround it?"

"No," Delacroix concluded. "Our men are trapped between two enemy lines. We must intervene now or all will be lost."

"Then so be it," Pantamanu decided. "Attack at my command."

While this deliberation took but a few seconds at the very most, it served General Garr's purposes exceedingly well. From his position on the other side of the valley Montama asked the general, "What are you going to do? We have no more men!"

Garr flashed his usual devious smile, then leaning forward and patting his horse's head he rowdily exclaimed, "Who needs men to fight an army?" Garr now resorted to another of his battlefield theatrics. He raised both of his hands high above his head and yelled a word from the Relatanian language that was utterly unfamiliar to Montama but sounded like, "Yeegowacha!"

What happened next startled Montama. Within seconds, angry beasts leapt from the sky and charged directly toward Pantamanu's exposed position. In an instant what had been a vast open plain was transformed into a veritable stampede of beasts, unlike anything ever seen on Arcanian soil. Not more than two hundred yards away, Pantamanu sat in stony silence. From his perspective it appeared that countless pieces of shattering glass were flying in the air, followed by an onslaught of enraged animals with hideously ugly faces, charging fiercely and directly toward his exposed position.

"My god, what are they?" Captain Delacroix demanded hysterically.

Pantamanu did not say a word, for he did not have the time to respond. At the sight of the enraged talladaggers, with their dual trunks raised in anger high above their monstrously large bodies, Pantamanu's horse stood on its rear legs, and then in a full throttled panic, bolted suddenly and as fast as possible in the opposite direction. When his horse panicked, Pantamanu fell backward, his right foot stuck firmly in one of the saddle's stirrups. This prevented him from falling hard to the ground, but it also presented a series of bizarre images to the soldiers of the Third Army. In one direction they saw ferocious hairy beasts charging relentlessly toward their undefended position. In the other direction they watched their leader, Commander Pantamanu, dangling precariously, kicking and screaming, as his panic stricken horse bolted from the battle scene.

The soldiers sat momentarily transfixed watching these two simultaneously unbelievable sights: the charging beasts before them and their retreating leader behind them. It did not take long for the soldiers to decide, "Let's get the hell out of here." And before the officers could restore order, the Third Army dispersed in every imaginable direction, as dozens of rabid talladaggers charged angrily forward. Frightened beyond all reason, men rode for cover. As they did the talladaggers charged directly at them.

"What are they?" one man shouted, as others around him turned and rode their stallions as fast as they could move. Within seconds one soldier tried to escape, but before he could a particularly huge talladagger, standing almost forty feet tall, ran directly toward him. "Oh shit," the man said, as he watched the talladagger approach. He said a silent prayer then watched as the talladagger reached out and picked him up with one its long tentacle like trunks. Though he was now in the talladagger's clutches, the man continued to pray, then with these final words, "May I be forgiven for all of my sins," he felt the talladagger tighten its grip around his waist. Before he could say another word, the talladagger threw the man to the ground. He rolled over several times before coming to a stop and then shook his head in disbelief. Somehow, he had survived, completely unharmed. "I must pray more often," he whispered quite solemnly. Before he could finish his thought, however, the talladagger stepped forward and crushed him beneath its immense hairy foot.

Others were likewise helplessly picked up from their saddles, sometimes two at a time, by a talladagger's dual immense trunk-like heads, which then crushed the soldiers before releasing their lifeless bodies to the ground. In less than five minutes, hundreds of men and horses were stampeded by the charging horde of monstrous creatures. And though he had not been intent on leaving the scene of the battle, Pantamanu could do nothing to stop the terrible carnage, for his horse, with a mind of its own, and with instincts dedicated purely to the cause of self-preservation, reluctantly carried the leader of the Third Army to sublime safety and shocking ignominy.

The Third Army retreat was a veritable disaster, just as the First Army was facing the very real possibility of its own annihilation on the unsteady walls inside the Valley of Kalel. As the talladaggers continued to charge forward, a few arrows ineffectively piercing their thick leathery hides, Arcanian soldiers struggled merely to survive, no longer believing that victory was possible.

Chapter 40
Montama's Army!

With Pantamanu's army in a state of steady, disorganized retreat, everything now depended on the skill and unyielding determination of Montama's army. In this regard Montama had his own concerns, for until this moment, he had not seen these men in battle. He therefore was unsure whether they had the skill and fortitude to stand up to the highly professional Arcanian First Army.

Like General Garr, most of the men of the mercenary army derived from exceedingly humble, even utterly wretched upbringings. Most had joined the army of Relatania when they were boys, some as young as nine or ten. They had joined, not out of a spirit of patriotism or even opportunism, but merely because there was no alternative.

With the Relatin Empire devolving into a steady and seemingly irretrievable state of chaos, its citizens struggled merely to acquire the basic necessities of life. Many starved or died of sundry painful illnesses. Another and larger segment of the population adopted a peripatetic lifestyle, scavenging over large swaths of rugged and uninviting land in what often proved to be a thankless quest for adequate food and shelter to sustain their pitiful existence. For most men, and even some women, the only practical alternative to this desperate lifestyle was to either join the Relatanian military or to sell one or more of their children to it. Since only the hardiest of souls were permitted to join, even this option was of limited utility. For most Relatanians, then, life was reduced to an unbearable cycle of agony, with little fear of death, for there were many things in life that were far more frightening than the promise of mortality.

And while they too lived a harsh life, the soldiers of General Garr's army, as well as the many other unauthorized military units that arose as the power of the Relatin Emperor steadily declined, could at least boast that they held in their hands the basic means of survival. More importantly, as a soldier, they were both feared and admired by the general populace. They were feared for all of the obvious reasons and they were admired because, unlike most people, they at least had the prospect of a better life; that is, if they were lucky enough to survive and bring home the well-earned spoils of war.

However, the hard fact is that most soldiers died ignominiously and anonymously on a remote battlefield or watched as their bodies and minds suffered the inevitable mortal ravages of time and combat. All understood that when they were no longer of any use to the army, they would be left behind, callously abandoned to nature's cruel elements. To our modern minds, such constant suffering seems almost beyond comprehension, but for the people of Relatania, such hardship was merely accepted as the normal way of life. Daily existence was both unfair and random, offering few rewards.

It was this common background that held the men of General Garr's mercenary army together. It was also the reason why they honored and blindly obeyed their charismatic one-eyed general, for as they fully understood, he was one of them. The soldiers looked up to this man who through guile and treachery had achieved the improbable, to rise from the very lowest ranks of the Relatin military to the demanding heights of command. The one-eyed general, and some even remembered when he still had three eyes, always fought by their side, risking his own life, never displaying a trace or hint of fear. His coolness and wild audacity inspired his men. So convinced were they that their general would lead them to a new promised land of wealth and privilege that few questioned his apparently insane decision to invade the Arcanian homeland, the famous site of General Tampinco's ultimate ruin. General Garr's soldiers were so absolutely loyal, they would follow him to the very ends of the world, perhaps an apt description for Arcania. In sum, the soldiers' faith in Garr was blind and unbounded.

What did they think of Montama? They had not chosen to follow him, only to let him tag along. Few even knew who he was and had they known that he was the youngest son of a prominent Arcanian lord, they undoubtedly would not have been impressed. When they first saw the young man, most of the soldiers believed that he was nothing more than a young guide, someone who merely knew the back routes and perplexing topography of Arcania. When the rumors first leaked that Motorma, as he was mistakenly called, was to ride at General Garr's side, the soldiers wondered why this mere boy had been given such an immense honor when many among them had served loyally in the general's service for decades. They therefore scrutinized "the boy" with increasingly careful scorn.

Montama was aware of this intense skepticism. He sensed that many of the soldiers were uncomfortable in his presence, that they merely tolerated him, rather than accepting him into their fraternity. He therefore was attentive to any reference to himself, no matter how oblique it might be. Many of "the men," as the soldiers were called, spoke in a thick guttural regional Relatanian dialect. Montama therefore could generally understand no more than one out of every three spoken words. He easily could read their thoughts, however, by simply staring into their ever suspicious and scornful eyes. There was a certain way that they looked at him, or more appropriately through him, as if he was not even there. Some purposely looked away whenever he walked in their direction.

"Do not let it bother you," Garr told his young protégé as they rode across one particularly barren field. "The men will do as I say." Garr had strongly emphasized the word "I," and Montama was unsure whether he should take comfort from Garr's declaration or fear the general's ultimate motives. As Montama became accustomed to the flamboyant general, the young man became ever more trusting until finally he began to look upon the older general with a mixture of respect and admiration. For though Montama may not have been consciously aware of it at first, again with my subtle intervention, he began to look upon Garr as a sort of surrogate father figure. Though Garr was certainly devious, Montama understood that he

233

The Oracle

was also extremely gifted and thoroughly captivating. At times Montama felt an attraction for this older man that he could not fully understand. One fact was unmistakable. The more time Montama spent by Garr's side, the more he too began to feel like a leader, and not merely the wayward, spoiled and immature son of a prominent lord. And the longer he rode by Garr's side, the more Montama developed his own identify and potential.

While his perception of General Garr vastly improved with time, Montama felt no such fealty or affection for or from the men of the mercenary army, even though he secretly longed for their respect. The need to demonstrate that he was indeed worthy proved to be a powerful motivational force prompting him ever forward during the long tedious march through what at times had seemed like the endless tunnel beneath the Bay of Battle. Other than marching determinedly by their side, young Montama had to this point had few opportunities to show that he was anything more than a tolerated outcast. Now, in the thick of combat, all that could change in an instant. The Battle of the Valley of Kalel was Montama's opportunity to prove that he had the courage and the temperament to be Arcania's next king.

And he had reason to believe such heady thoughts. Had not his mother Truellen told him that the Oracle had chosen him to be king? Had not I told him to go to Relatania to raise a mighty army? Had not the regent, the king's own son, bowed in deference to this mere boy by taking his own life rather than striking Montama dead? Had not the Third Army skedaddled in a most embarrassing retreat? In short, had not the Oracle repeatedly demonstrated its faithful commitment to young Montama?

So now, as he sat on his horse at the rim of the Valley of Kalel, Montama looked for yet another sign that he was destined to be king. "Will they fight for me?" he asked himself as he rode toward the precipice. As he watched the mad swarm of talladaggers continue to drive Pantamanu's Third Army from the far away field of battle and as he now looked down into the crater shaped valley itself, Montama's sense of self, the idea that he was indeed destined to be king, fully crystallized in his mind. Suddenly, all of his fantasies were real. Before him lay the field of battle, and though it was a strange one, fought at irregular angles on a steep and slippery slope, he could see the faces of his men, fighting on undaunted, their swords raised high above their heads, charging relentlessly forward, determined to strike the enemy with a ferocious and vitriolic spite, leaving nothing in their wake but total annihilation.

At first the sight appeared to be completely surreal. All that Montama could see was a massive interconnected ring of men, encircling more than three fourths of the immense radius of the valley wall. As he leaned forward to secure a better view, he also could see hundreds of men moving along the basin floor. Many of them were retrieving the arrows that just moments before had been fired down upon them. Uncovering a shallow pit filled with bows, these same men now began to fire these deadly arrows back at the Arcanian soldiers who stood halfway down the valley walls, helplessly trapped.

Almost instantaneously, hundreds of men tumbled cruelly to their death, their chests, arms, legs and even their throats and heads, pierced suddenly by a savage onslaught of high pitched squealing arrows. As their bodies collapsed, a lone Arcanian officer shouted an order, "CROUCH!" In response, the Arcanians, still clinging tenuously to the sloping wall, and in many cases to each other, fell suddenly to their knees. It was their only resort to safety, for there was no other place for them to hide. The men then lifted their shields in front of their prostrated bodies, in an attempt to deflect the onslaught of incoming arrows. Thus protected, most of the arrows now ricocheted off the shields, with a few of them actually striking Montama's own men who continued their own inexorable descent down into the valley. Realizing that they were doing more harm to their own soldiers than to the Arcanian First Army, the archers at the base were ordered to abruptly cease firing and to instead draw their swords. In this pose they waited anxiously for their comrades toward the top of the valley to drive the Arcanians downward toward a certain death.

Aware that they were trapped, Arcanian officers shouted a new order. "Shields to the ground." The call echoed across the valley's walls. Although it was an entirely improvised maneuver, the Arcanian soldiers performed it with such sublime skill that they appeared to have practiced this particular maneuver many times. Heeding the order, the men of the Arcanian army placed their shields down on the ground. Then another officer ordered, "Mount your shields!"

Montama could not believe what he saw next. Arcanian soldiers placed their stomachs on their shields, and then as they heard the order to "attack," they rode them down the incline like toboggans, sliding quickly down the sharp muddy valley walls, many with their swords drawn and aimed at the enemy aligned along the vast exposed valley's base.

The Oracle

Montama watched in amazement as the Arcanian soldiers slid down the forty-five degree incline at rapid speed, ramming his own men, and knocking them senselessly to the ground. The Arcanians then sprung up onto their feet, and with a determined ferocity that Montama had never before witnessed, raised their swords in a desperate attempt to turn to the tide of the battle.

Meanwhile, General Garr dismounted his horse and moved down into the valley with his men. As he did so, Montama too leapt from his horse and charged down the sharp incline, slipping repeatedly, but quickly regaining his footing, as he sidestepped the mounting casualties that lined the valley's sloping walls. As he did so, hundreds more Arcanian soldiers at the base ominously raised their swords above their heads. This was now a fight to the death. Only one army would survive! While the odds still favored General Garr's men, the Arcanians, by taking the charge directly to the mercenaries, had ensured that it would at least be a fair fight.

As Montama worked his way down toward the base, he nearly tripped, for the blood of the dead and dying had utterly drenched the valley's sloping walls with a gooey red mud. Everywhere around him men of both armies lay mortally wounded, many begging for death to relieve their unyielding pain. Montama saw the horrible expressions on the men's faces, some so contorted that they no longer appeared human. Some men tried to grab his legs as he moved past them, while one Arcanian, in a decidedly futile gesture, raised himself to his knees, before falling helplessly back to the ground.

Other men from General Garr's army also moved down the slopes. Many slid down, some on their shields, some on their asses, moving as quickly as they could, hoping to ram into an Arcanian soldier. They upended as many of their own soldiers as they did the enemy, and the battle for a time appeared to be nothing more than semi-organized chaos, with officers running along the lines, shouting orders, sometimes mistaking the enemy for their own soldiers, some men simply screaming insensibly, driven mad by the dreadful horror of war.

The screams were so loud and of such a repulsively frightening variety, that Montama could not make sense of the unfolding scene. As he watched, men from both armies cried out piteously for their mothers, while many more fought on courageously, occasionally cursing the heavens as they repeatedly charged into the fray. Montama struggled forward as he watched General Garr reach the basin floor, his long sword quickly piercing the side of an Arcanian officer. He saw the officer's face contort as the sword lodged between his ribs. Whereas the site of death previously frightened young Montama, he now realized that each successive death brought him closer to the Oracle's prophecy. He therefore marveled at his army's deadly prowess. And there was no other possible explanation beyond the Oracle's prophecy why so many men would fight to the death, a death for which they would never be rewarded. Only Montama would benefit from their death. It was with this understanding, that Montama stridently raised his sword as he called out in a powerful voice, "VICTORY!"

As he did so other men took up the call until a majority of Montama's army, including General Garr himself, began to chant this solitary word with such a determined ferocity that the soldiers of the Arcanian First Army realized that they were hopelessly outnumbered. Their only remaining task was to kill as many of the mercenary army as they possibly could before they themselves were slaughtered.

With little hope, most Arcanians fought on valiantly in brutal hand-to-hand combat, fighting literally to their last breath. With swords drawn everywhere, a terrible fight ensued that lasted the better part of an hour, eventually consuming the entire valley floor. The most difficult task was to fight while dodging the dead that lay all around them. Some soldiers tripped over the bodies of their comrades, making them easy targets for the deranged mercenaries. Montama killed his own share of men, at least a dozen, though it might easily have been more. In some cases he was not entirely sure if he had killed one of his own men, but he did not have the time to remonstrate, for other challengers instantly charged directly toward his outreached sword.

Though unquestionably ferocious, in time the battle began to wind down, as the number of Arcanian soldiers continually diminished until finally there were only a few men left. Some of these tried to escape the scene of the battle and a few actually did, scampering up the valley walls and then over the rim to safety. Many more men stayed, realizing that they had no alternative, and faced with the prospect of capture, turned their swords on themselves, and like Rendrau, heroically took their own lives.

One Arcanian soldier particularly impressed Montama. Though he had lost his right arm, this man continued to stand, his sword firmly clasped in his left hand, waiting for someone to challenge him. Montama walked toward the man and calmly put his hand on the man's bloodied left shoulder. The Arcanian stared at Montama, his eyes vapid and barely conscious. "Did we win?" he asked, before finally collapsing to the ground.

Montama knelt down and took the sword from the soldier's dead hand. As he held it up he noticed that it carried the insignia of King Leonata, a star rising over the vast and distant horizon. It was his father's favorite symbol of hope, but now, as Montama looked about the valley floor, he saw nothing but the corpses of countless thousands of men, most of them Arcanian.

Moments later General Garr gave the final order. "Burn this unholy place!" he declared. The battlefield was littered with so many corpses that one could fairly walk from one side of the Valley of Kalel to the other, down its sloping walls and across its once barren base, without ever stepping on virgin soil. Although the battle was barely concluded, the skies already were filled with scores of ravenous green vultamires, their large triangular wings spread as wide as their large oblong shaped eyes, ready to feast on the dead. "We will not let these brave men be fodder for the birds," Garr proclaimed and the men of the mercenary army began the task of setting fires that ultimately would consume the dead.

That night the funeral fires rose so high in the night sky that they could be seen all the way to Teta. From her window at the king's castle Bellazar watched the skies fill with this strange green and yellow smoke, carried by the winds, which reeked with the smell of death. Bellazar did not know for certain that her husband was among the dead. She surmised that a great battle had been fought. Then as a solitary tear ran down her face, the wind gently blew her red hair back across her exposed shoulders. "I love you my dear," she said softly. Then she closed her eyes and wept.

Chapter 41
Power and Ambition

Lord Valmar's successor, Lord Gulcum, had never really been interested in power. He was a dull witted, light-hearted gentleman, the life of the party, but resolutely indecisive, totally unimaginative, and worst of all, absolutely incapable of delivering bad news. And yet, since Bellazar named him to his prestigious position, his only task seemed to be delivering unpleasant tidings. "How will I ever tell her," he fussed with nervous agitation and a desperate look upon his face, as he lingered for several minutes in the drab upstairs hall outside Bellazar's personal quarters. His heart was pounding at such a ferocious rate that he was sure he would either die or pass out. He felt a dread so stark and unsettling that he could barely breath.

After he finally built up sufficient courage, he gently, almost apologetically and insecurely, tapped on Bellazar's door. Against all reason he fervently hoped that she would not respond, but when she acknowledged his distinctive signal, three taps in quick succession, he closed his eyes, took a deep breath, and then opened the door with the greatest sense of dread that he had ever felt in his entire life. "I hope she does not yell at me," he thought, as he stepped forward ever so tentatively into the room, past the Tellican jumping fish, stepping over the Anawana Yapyap, and ignoring the Pirene Cat as it hissed angrily at his mere presence.

Bellazar sat in her accustomed rocking chair, carefully knitting yet another shawl, the third one in just four units time. "What is the news from the battle front?" she asked directly, without humor, clearly expecting the worst news possible.

Lord Gulcum felt the muscles in his throat constrict, as he said in a soft, frightened voice, "It is all bad news."

Bellazar glanced down at the shawl that she was knitting. Then, without emotion she said, "Tell me all of it."

Again, Gulcum wondered if he had the strength to proceed. The spinning sensation in his head made him feel nauseous and his migraines pulsated so ruthlessly that he was sure that he could not continue. Yet somehow through all the fear and discomfort he managed to perform his somber duty respectfully, if not enthusiastically. "The First Army has been completely routed at the Valley of Kalel."

"Continue," Bellazar said sternly, knowing full well that Gulcum was hesitant to provide the full details.

"The Third Army retreated in disgrace. There are reports that Commander Pantamanu cowardly fled from the scene of battle."

Bellazar continued to stitch, though her mind was clearly focused on but one thought. "And the regent?" she asked, full well knowing what was coming next.

Gulcum sniffled, as he tried to summon the strength to speak these next few words. What came out of his mouth was more like a whimpering peep. "The regent is dead. They are all dead. The entire First Army is dead."

The Oracle

When she heard the extent of the devastation, and the confirmation of her dear husband's mortality, Bellazar clasped her knitting needle so tightly that her knuckles turned pale. "Go on," she said defiantly. "What else?"

"I don't know what you mean Madame," Gulcum said, his face contorted and perplexed.

Bellazar now put her knitting needle and yarn aside, before standing and walking directly to the window. As she did she spoke. "The Fifth Army was utterly destroyed at Grell and I have heard rumors that General Mbanka, who hates Pantamanu more than I do, can no longer be counted on to be loyal to our cause. If that is true we have lost the entire Fourth Army, as well." Turning suddenly and staring directly at Gulcum she asked, "What do we have left? The Second Army protects Teta. The Third Army survives even if its commander has disgraced his passra. And the mercenary army is still on the march."

Gulcum scowled uneasily, for he did not have an answer. "The situation is indeed dire." Then with a decided lack of enthusiasm he added, "But it is not hopeless."

On this point Bellazar heartily agreed. She was not the type of leader to panic, not even during the most extreme personal or political circumstances. Her mind was conditioned to continuously formulate a series of fresh options and though there were fewer of them now she reasoned that she must consider all that were still available, shy of surrender. She therefore began to think aloud. "We cannot allow the mercenaries to enter Teta. We must send the Second Army south to intercept them."

"Agreed," Gulcum said without consideration, merely mirroring his leader's thoughts.

"I want the distinguished Third Army and its so-called leader to fall back on Teta, as well." Bellazar's voice was dripping with sarcasm as she said the word "leader." "I cannot depend on them to do direct battle with the mercenaries." Bellazar then thought for a second. "You must send an intermediary to General Mbanka and the Fourth Army. I must know what his intentions are."

"He despises Prince Pantamanu," Gulcum admitted.

"In that opinion he is far from alone," Bellazar readily acknowledged.

"Is there anything else?" Gulcum asked obsequiously.

"Make sure that my orders are carried out immediately," she said, in a surprisingly understated manner, her mind now beginning to focus reluctantly on the fact that her dear husband was indeed among the dead.

Seeing that Bellazar's eyes were beginning to mist over, Gulcum discreetly nodded his head and then hastily withdrew. When Lord Gulcum closed the door, Bellazar permitted her emotions to rise to the surface. Gazing out of her third story window, under her breath Bellazar cursed, "Damn you Pantamanu! You let them murder my husband!" She then let loose a veritable torrent of tears. For a few minutes she was utterly inconsolable. She felt emptiness, a loss so deep it felt like her soul had been forcibly removed from her spirit. Her eyes now exhibited the full strain of her present increasingly hopeless situation. With an enemy army approaching and the loss of her dear Rendrau, she whispered, "How the hell could this have happened?" Then after another moment she shouted loud enough for the staff in the hall to hear her cry, "I will destroy that bastard Pantamanu if it is the last thing that I do."

More than the staff heard her desperate cry. In the far corner of the room, Kublatitan slowly and unobtrusively materialized. For a few moments he merely watched and listened. He was not used to such a savage display of raw emotion, for his people had an entirely different view of life and death than did the Arcanians. To them life and death were one and the same, with death merely representing a change in one's fortunes. In fact, he recently created a perfect mechanism for speaking with the dead, so that future kings would be able to consult with a wider range of experts. He called it the Taewokan Death Shield. In so doing, he inadvertently provided Count Belicki and the mercenaries with a new and powerful weapon. For I then divined the very same algorithms and complex structural equations necessary to create the shield in mid-air above the Valley of Kalel. Instead of entering this energy shield to communicate with the dead, however, I used it to conceal an entire army, including its genuinely ferocious beasts. Realizing that he had made a serious tactical mistake and with great sadness and even greater regret, Kublatitan muttered, "My fault. Did not anticipate Belicki's latest move."

Bellazar had grown so used to the sudden appearance of Kublatitan that she did not even turn to acknowledge his presence. Instead, she continued to stare out of her window, tears still streaming freely down her weary face. "How did he do it? How did he destroy an entire army?"

Though he was moved by Bellazar's emotions, Kublatitan did not cry, for Taewokans do not have that facility. He did moan with a low droning noise signifying absolute sadness. "Belicki is evil. He misuse Taewokan Death Shield to hide his army."

The Oracle

In a cold and unforgiving tone Bellazar lectured, "He didn't misuse it. Belicki took advantage of a strategic opportunity." Then finally turning and aiming her entire fury at the startled Taewokan, she continued, "You are far too naïve." With her hands outstretched before her she shouted, "If you are to defeat Belicki you must think as he does. That is the only way you can destroy him."

Kublatitan was simply aghast at this very suggestion. "But Belicki is filled with hatred and ambition. Things I do not understand."

"You were a king," Bellazar countered belligerently.

"Yes, but my people are different. Not interested in power for its own sake."

Bellazar responded in a most unexpected manner. Almost apologetically she intoned, "Unfortunately, that is all my people care about."

"Do not understand your people," Kublatitan confessed, his head shaking as he spoke.

With the anger in her voice returning, Bellazar responded, "Then you had better damn well learn how our people think." Bellazar's sudden change of mood confused Kublatitan, for Taewokans were at heart a calm and peaceful people. And yet Bellazar became even angrier than Kublatitan had ever imagined. She now turned her entire fury against the giant Taewokan. Though she was far shorter, Bellazar seemed to tower over the giant. "I will not tolerate anymore excuses. The mercenary army is headed north toward Teta. All that stands before them is the Second Army." Heatedly, as she tapped the middle finger of her right hand on Kublatitan's broad chest, she declared, "You damn well better have a surprise ready for them or your precious Oracle will be in the hands of the enemy."

During his lifetime Kublatitan had been a meek and gentle man. While he was accustomed to power, he also believed in reason. "Cannot each side sit down and discuss?" he pleaded.

"Are you serious?" Bellazar declared with a frightening intensity.

"Do not understand," he said apologetically. "And now, I can no longer sense Belicki's thoughts. Oracle is coming undone. Power is now diffuse."

As Kublatitan's consternation increased the voice of a second entity was heard. "Do not be so harsh on Kublatitan," King Benton said, as his body materialized next to the giant Taewokan. "His people know nothing but peace and harmony, while the thoughts of our people are consumed with avarice and power. The fault lies not with Kublatitan, but with our own people."

242

Bellazar had not seen the king since his death and was startled and pleased by his sudden arrival. "My king, what are we to do?" she asked, almost pleading for an answer. Then, as her voice quivered, she added with a note of terrible sadness, "Dear Rendrau is dead."

King Benton already was aware of the death of his third eldest son and his own pain had not yet subsided. As he moved forward to embrace Bellazar, the king whispered, "There is still time to turn the tide of battle. All is not yet lost."

Chapter 42
Marching

Trent and Fotu had spent most of their wretched lives as soldiers in Arcania's Second Army. Trent had joined when he was but twelve. Fotu did not know exactly how old he had been, but he reckoned that he had volunteered at about the same age, perhaps even a few cycles younger. For thirty odd cycles they had served the king honorably, though for both men this would be their first actual taste of battle. With the war raging, so far all they had seen were the barren fields, grassy hills, gently sloping dales, a few storm ravaged rivers, and lots of dusty roads, which is where they now found themselves.

"Where do you think we are?" Fotu, who was the more querulous of the two, asked his best friend and bunkmate. As he did so he marched in perfect symmetry, in a line of soldiers that stretched out over the horizon and on for more than a mile. Trent marched by his side in an entirely different line, composed of an equal number of men, their steps syncopated to the same monotonous rhythm, mile after lonely mile.

Trent had heard the same question before and always responded with the identical answer. "I have absolutely no idea." Unfazed, Fotu continued to march not more than a few feet to the left of his buddy, stuck in his own seemingly endless cue of soldiers.

"How long have we been marching?" Fotu asked. His dull eyes continued to focus on the back of the same man who had been marching ahead of him for several units time. So familiar was he with the man's backside that he had memorized every single crease in his uniform.

The Oracle

Trent was barely listening, so bored was he that his mind had wandered into a reverie about his girlfriend, who recently had left him for another man. Still, he responded in rote fashion, "I have absolutely no idea."

Fotu was used to marching, but he usually had at least a rough idea of where he was going. Now he was totally confused. "I don't get it," continuing to look ahead as he spoke, as his friend marched in the parallel cue. "First we marched from eastern Arcania to the west."

"That's right," Trent responded without much enthusiasm.

"Then we were told to march north to Teta. Then when we got there they told us to turn around and march south."

"And your point is?" Trent asked, mildly perturbed to be having the exact same conversation for what must have been at least the third time.

"I don't know what my point is," Fotu admitted, his eyes blinking vapidly as he spoke.

Trent sighed then in a more animated tone responded, "It's simple. The generals tell us what to do and then we march."

Fotu understood this point, but another one eluded him. "But who tells the generals where to march?"

Trent's answer was the same as it had been the last time they had conversed, perhaps a mile or so before on the same dusty road. "I have absolutely no idea."

Fotu's feet were blistered and sore. "Well I wish whoever it is would make up their mind. My feet hurt."

"Well so do mine," Trent responded without the slightest sympathy for his friend's medical condition.

Fotu tried to think of something else to say. Before he could he heard his friend sneeze. "Bless you," he said, most politely.

"That's strange," Trent responded.

"What is?" Fotu asked, his eyes continuing to blink as he walked.

Trent looked confused. "I usually sneeze when the enemy is nearby. I call it my early warning system," he said.

"What enemy?" Fotu asked. "We have never been to war before."

Slightly perturbed, Trent shot a disgusted sideways glance at his friend and then added, "We've had plenty of drills before. And when we drill I always sneeze when the enemy is nearby."

Fotu looked to his left and then to his right. It was a clear and beautiful star filled night. Other than the stars on the horizon, the plain was absolutely vacant, except for one or two stray bushes and a moderately sized boulder that lay on the west side of the seemingly endless road. After surveying this empty landscape, Fotu at last volunteered, "I don't see nothing at all." Just as he completed his sentence, Trent sneezed yet again.

"See!" Trent declared emphatically, while adamantly pointing directly at his nose with a crooked finger.

"Maybe you have a cold," Fotu commented, politely but not helpfully.

"I have no such thing," Trent stated with some considerable measure of adamancy, as he shook his head decisively.

Again Fotu looked in several directions before adding, "Well I don't see any enemy."

"Well they are here," Trent declared with such confidence that it was clear that the matter was settled. Whether he saw an enemy or not, he was convinced that they are here.

With no enemy in sight, Fotu, Trent, and the other men of the Second Army continued to march on down the road, past the empty fields, the scattered trees and large boulder in which someone unknown, perhaps a friend but also possibly a foe, had carved a solitary word: "VICTORY."

As Trent continued to march southward Fotu asked, "What time is it?"

"I have absolutely no idea." Trent responded as they marched further down the road in the direction of the Valley of Kalel. For another hour the massive Second Army marched until at last it finally passed over the horizon and out of sight. Once it did, General Garr's army, by the thousands, began to emerge, apparently from thin air. They included all manner of beasts, including horses and talladaggers.

General Garr stared down the dusty road in the direction of the Second Army. "We were lucky, he declared. "The Taewokan Death Shield was beginning to dissipate just as the last soldiers marched by."

"What happened?" Montama asked.

"I don't know," Garr added. "But I doubt if we will be able to use it to shield our army again."

Garr looked northward, and then with a rye smile he responded, "We will move north to the King's Castle. If we are successful, nothing will be able to stop us. Victory will be ours."

Montama nodded his head and the still undetected mercenary army continued its movement northward, having just eluded the Arcanian Second Army. An hour later, word arrived from Teta that the Second Army was to march back to the capital city. When Trent and Foto heard these new orders, they merely looked at each other, shrugged their soldiers and in unison declared, "Here we go again!"

Chapter 43
Images

"It looks just like him," the plumb old lady remarked with an alacritous smile as she admired the carefully engraved woodcarving of Arcania's newest hero, Regent Rendrau. It was an odd thing for the woman to say, since she had never actually seen Rendrau in the flesh. Since his untimely tragic death, the king's third eldest son had become something of a public obsession, beloved in a way that he never could have been during his lifetime. Ordinary people now felt a special connection with their newly fallen hero, a sudden sense of familiarity, as if they actually knew him personally and always had loved him. The elderly lady therefore gently caressed the engraving with her green, wrinkled but steady right hand. Then she smiled benignly and asked the merchant, "Do you have any more of these?"

"Ya," the Ka-Why-Tee merchant declared enthusiastically. "We have people making these around the clock."

"Then I will take two of them," the lady said properly and with as much decorum as her lowly stature in Arcanian society permitted. Cautiously, for she was not at all a rich woman, she reached into her small, cloth bag in search of a decarnam, essentially the equivalent of a half penny. After giving the currency to the merchant, she held her newly purchased prize close to her eyes so that she could get a better look at it and then marveled, "He was such a handsome fella."

"Ya," the merchant added perfunctorily, as he placed the shiny coin into his side pocket.

The old lady was not alone in her sudden admiration for Regent Rendrau. Many other Arcanians likewise purchased a similar engraving of Rendrau, riding majestically on horseback. The engraving elevated Rendrau's status to hero worship. Here was a man for which power and ambition meant nothing, the engravings and other well timed propaganda suggested. He was motivated entirely by his love for his passra. It was not true, of course. Though Rendrau had not wanted to be king nearly as much as Bellazar did, he was ambitious and comfortable with the trappings of power. Truthfully though, he could have been happy without such ornate displays, though Bellazar never could be.

So with her husband deceased, she now did everything in her power to represent Rendrau in the image of an utterly selfless man, rejecting power and ambition and putting passra first. It was a carefully cultivated image that the citizens of Arcania, eager for hero worship, embraced without question.

Bellazar did not merely encourage her fellow citizens to embrace their newly fallen hero. She concomitantly made sure that a decidedly less flattering image of Pantamanu was widely disseminated. Like his older brother, Pantamanu was portrayed on horseback. Unlike his courageous sibling, Pantamanu's horse was pictured in a state of hysterical madness, as was its rider. It was an unfair image, for the truth is that Pantamanu had not panicked at Kalel, his horse had. In fact, Pantamanu's defenders argued in vain that had it not been for his great equestrian skill he would have been tossed from his horse and trampled alive by the charging onslaught of enraged talladaggers. This interpretation required explanation and the public was not in a mood for excuses, only for someone to blame for the horrible failure at the Valley of Kalel. Since Rendrau had been elevated to that status of hero worship, the man the public now chose to blame was his younger brother.

Few people actually purchased the unflattering engraving of Pantamanu, but they noticed it, usually with a grimace. "He is a damn coward," one portly gentleman declared upon spotting the image of the king's youngest son. The merchant chased the man away when he attempted to spit on the engraving. "Move on," the merchant shouted, as the portly man continued to scowl. "If you aren't buying, move on," the merchant repeated in a much louder voice. Other potential buyers strolled by his cart, which was filled with sundry inexpensive items. The only one that anyone seemed interested in purchasing was the stolid image of Rendrau on horseback.

Despite this manifestation of business as usual, the people had heard the rumors that the mercenary army was but a unit or two away from Teta. With the Second Army having reversed its course, the citizens realized that the battle for Arcanian succession was about to come to Teta itself.

Consequently, in droves citizens abandoned their homes, packing all of their belongings on carts and mules, as well as their own backs, as a surging diaspora fled the city in search of the safer environs of eastern Arcania. Ragged and desperate people cued in long lines that stretched out for more than a mile, with tempers flaring and hopes subsiding. Bellazar watched this terrifying exodus from her castle window, unsure whether the citizens would ever return, but quite sure that the Second Army would be incapable of halting the progress of that damnable mercenary army, for Kublatitan had informed her that the enemy had slipped past her own forces and was now but hours away from the capital city.

Meanwhile, far away on the lonely plains of eastern Arcania, Pantamanu had his own concerns. He was aware that the Battle of the Valley of Kalel had transformed him into an object of derisive scorn. In just a few units time he became the most vilified and hated man in the passra, even more so than the malevolent invaders. Though he was not as politically adept as Bellazar, Pantamanu was not blind to the rapid decline in his political fortunes. He too saw the unflattering carvings carrying his hysterical likeness. Instinctively driven to anger, he quickly realized that it would take more than reason to ameliorate his current tentative political situation. "I will have to do in battle at Teta what I failed to do at Kalel," he told himself, as he prepared for the next stage in the ongoing succession war.

In this regard, Pantamanu had one distinct advantage. "The battle will come next in Teta," Leonata had told the young prince in a dream. "You alone can prevent the absolute ruin of the Centama family." This revelation raised a new ray of hope, the possibility that if he miraculously turned the tide of battle, a fickle and inattentive public would quickly forget Pantamanu's failure at Kalel.

He therefore stepped lightly and with great confidence as he exited his tent on route to meet his Third Army soldiers. The moment was idyllic in many respects. After two units of hard rain, the sky was lit with a golden hue, welcoming the arrival of the Season of Life. Unlike his soldiers, who were covered in muck from the muddy fields of eastern Arcania, Pantamanu was immaculately dressed, his prized family sword swaying by his side, his boots polished to a resplendent bright red.

As they watched their commander walk toward his new multi-colored steed, for the old one had been slaughtered and fed to the ravenous birds for its cowardly act of betrayal, Pantamanu understood that his soldiers too were eager to redeem their own reputations and they could only do this by leaping directly back into the vicious maelstrom of war. Like Pantamanu, most of them knew that one single overwhelming victory would permanently eliminate the stigma of the Battle of the Valley of Kalel. To a man, they therefore looked to Teta as the site for a new and glorious victory.

As they did so, one important question permeated their collective thoughts. Was Pantamanu capable of leading this army to that great victory? Though overall the Third Army had suffered but modest casualties at Kalel, for the men were sprite in their retreat, the soldiers desperately needed a leader capable of bringing order out of chaos. Therefore, as the men stood in line awaiting word from their uncertain commander, they were anxious, yet thirsting for victory and desperate for leadership. Pantamanu instantly realized that it was a critical moment in history. He could not prevail at Teta unless he first won the hearts and minds of his very own soldiers.

As the golden sun continued to rise over the tops of the nearby evergreen trees, the soldiers lined up in strict military formation, guided by their many corporals and sergeants who seemingly bustled about in every conceivable direction, all at once. The soldiers' uniforms were dirty. Some still had traces of blood on their hands and newly earned scars on their faces. More than a few were so disheartened that they stood with slumping shoulders, for they had experienced palpable fear at Kalel for the very first time. But worse than fear was the reprehensible bitter taste of defeat, which they hated even more than the horrifying charge of the unruly talladaggers. Eager to redeem themselves, but confused and unsure of their abilities, the men and women stood wearily and with great trepidation, as Commander Pantamanu, sitting astride his new horse of gold, red and gray, rode slowly toward the center of the line.

The soldiers noticed that the buckles and buttons on his splendid uniform veritably glistened in the morning sun light and that his boots were so lavishly polished that the soldiers at the front of the line actually could see their own reflections in them. Whereas before many had thought he looked like an effete spoiled dilettante, they now judged that he veritably exuded an unmistakable masculine intensity, his eyes flashing with a steely and cold determination, a seething rage burning just below the surface. With impeccable posture, and with unbridled confidence that was utterly contagious, Pantamanu portrayed an image of colossal strength and unquestionable fortitude. Without a word from his lips, then, the soldiers already sensed a significant transformation in their still unproven leader.

He commenced his address in an equally confident and powerful voice. "We suffered a set back at the Valley of Kalel, not a defeat. The Third Army will never be defeated!" With these few words he completely won the sympathy of his soldiers. In essence he had absolved all of them of the stigma of ignominious defeat. They greeted this declaration with an ovation that seemed to shake the very ground upon which they stood. For several seconds the soldiers chanted in unison, "Victory! Victory! Victory!"

When Captain Delacroix finally gave the signal restoring order, Pantamanu stoically proceeded. "Today, we begin the march to Teta. There we will restore the passra's honor and destroy the barbarian army."

Again Pantamanu paused, his eyes staring boldly forward, while his soldiers chanted, "Victory!"

As he listened, Pantamanu knew that these men were hungry for an opportunity to redeem the Third Army's reputation. He reasoned that if he promised victory, no matter what doubts they might still hold, these soldiers would blindly follow him into battle. So now he made a pledge, "Together we will end this blasted war and lead the passra to a new age of glory." Then holding both hands high over his head he shouted, "Victory!"

The soldiers, eager for inspiration, responded enthusiastically with renewed cheers of "Victory" and then, "On to Teta!"

Pantamanu felt a sudden rush of adrenalin as he watched the soldiers cheer. He was more aware than anyone else that the stakes were exponentially high. Either his army would be victorious in the upcoming battle or he would forfeit his life and the passra's governance to the barbarian invaders. But far worse even than that, he would go down in history as the military leader who led the passra's most powerful army to a tragic and egregious defeat. The thought could have paralyzed him. Instead Pantamanu drew inspiration, even exhilaration from it. In a mountainous voice that was so loud that men up and down the line could hear every syllable quite distinctly, he shouted "On to Teta! Onward to victory!"

Exuberantly, the men waved their hats above their head in appreciation, as their leader ceremonially rode up and down the front lines, reaching out periodically to slap the hand of an ebullient soldier. Pantamanu then abruptly raised his four-cornered hat high above his head and spiritedly entreated his army to "follow me to victory!" Looking every bit like a leader, Pantamanu then gave the final order, signaling the soldiers to follow him to the capital city.

From their position in eastern Arcania, the march to Teta normally would take three units time, particularly given the expected poor road conditions and ever-present fears of flash floods. Pantamanu knew that the battle would likely come much sooner than that. Consequently, if he were to heroically turn the tide, Pantamanu would have to accomplish something truly remarkable. But then he was determined to do precisely that.

Chapter 44
Absolute Power

Since he received the official reports of the destruction of the port city of Grell, Grandafier had been in a heightened state of agitation, consumed with a dual sense of agonizing guilt and unrepentant remorse. Worried that I would again visit him in his dream state, the elderly man futilely attempted to resist the temptations of slumber, hoping to block out any potential avenue that I could use to communicate directly with him. And while I did not return, for I had no further need of the old man's services, Grandafier was constantly afraid that he would be forced to pay a horrible price for his despicable act of vial treachery. "The blood of Arcanian soldiers and the citizens of Grell are on my hands," Grandafier repeated endlessly as he sat nervously in his oversized whicker chair, with a warm alcoholic drink as his only companion.

And Grandafier had a number of valid reasons to be afraid. Specifically, Timilty's investigation had been damning. At a hearing, Grandafier's butler testified that the old man seemed to know of the events at Grell before the news ever reached Pellaville. "How could he have known about it unless he planned the entire attack?" Timilty charged. Many were convinced by the Ka-Why-Tee barrister's evidence, though Lord Tantamount continued to have his doubts. "He does not have the power to do such things, even if he willed it," the lord said in Grandafier's defense. In the end, these few words by Lord Tantamount saved poor Grandafier from the gallows.

Consequently, while Timilty urged Lord Tantamount's Privy Council to charge the old man with "high crimes," he was convicted only of serving as "an unwilling accomplice in an act of great disservice to the passra." That reduced charge allowed Grandafier to live. Yet, there was little solace in the abject loneliness that followed his unanimous conviction. Even his faithful butler quit, rather than associate with a man of Grandafier's maligned character. The only person who came to visit him was kindly Hontallo, who said that he did not blame Grandafier any more than he could blame his own brother, for he was convinced that both were under the powerful spell of an evil entity. Grandafier wept openly at even this conditional absolution.

On this unir, as Montama's army continued its approach toward Teta, fearing that his mind was slowly unraveling, convinced that he had no other reason to live, Grandafier finally fell asleep in his favorite whicker chair. His body trembled with each breath, but he rested only for a few moments before an apparition visited him. This time it was not me.

"My friend, my dear old friend," Grandafier moaned, as his mind identified a most familiar face. "I am so happy to see you!" The entity moved closer, until it made its presence known inside Grandafier's mind. As it did so, Grandafier awoke, for this was no dream. Then with a sudden start, as he sprung to his feet wearing only his night robe, the old man asked, "Why have you come to see me?"

King Benton could read the consternation, the deep sense of fear and regret etched on Grandafier's hideously contorted face. "You are my old friend," the king said in his usual kindly tone of voice. But the king also was quite puzzled. "Why then, did you betray me and my family?"

Grandafier could not answer for the unspeakable sins he had committed against the Centama family. So Benton reached out and steadied his one time political friend and ally and as he did so Grandafier looked directly into his former king's eyes. They were not hateful, as he had expected, but they were desperately sad. At that exact moment, Grandafier abandoned all appropriate royal decorum. He moved forward, literally throwing his arms around his deceased king, hugging him with an embrace so tight that Benton could feel the genuine intensity of the old man's remorse. Then, in a barely perceptible voice, Grandafier confessed, "I am so sorry, my dear king. My mind was so consumed with thoughts of greatness, that I totally forgot my bond with you and your family."

"Belicki tempted you?" the king asked respectfully.

"Yes," Grandafier admitted between painful sobs.

"Then you must rectify the wrong that you have done."

Grandafier pulled his head back and looked again into the king's forgiving eyes. "Is that possible?" he asked. "Is it still possible for me to salvage a measure of sublime redemption?"

Rather than answering this query directly, the king asked, "Why did you favor this boy Montama?" The king stared so intently at Grandafier that the old man could feel a burning intensity within his own soul.

"He is a good boy," Grandafier said in a soft voice, almost begging forgiveness.

"Perhaps," Benton said curtly. "But he is but a boy. What qualities does he possess that so attracted you to him?"

Eager to explain, Grandafier noted, "I was told that he would lead a mighty army! I was led to believe that he should be our next king. I considered it the will of the Oracle that he be our next king."

Benton forlornly nodded his head. "It was Belicki that spoke to you. Since the very unit that he was absorbed into the Oracle, he has been searching for a malleable successor, someone he alone can control, a veritable puppet."

"I don't understand," Grandafier admitted feebly, his arms still dangling from the king's shoulders, steadying himself, lest he fall. "Is that what he intends for poor Montama?"

The king answered with yet another question. "You do not yet know who this Belicki is, do you?" In response, Grandafier shook his head. "Then I will show you," the king said with a grand wave of his hand. Instantly, the two men stood not in Grandafier's home, but rather in an open field, buttressed by trees, with a cold foreboding wind whistling eerily in their ears. In the middle of the field Grandafier saw five people, each one tied to a large wooden stake that had been driven deep into the ground. Two were adults, but three were mere children, one no more than five or six cycles old. Standing not far before them was a middle-aged man and his son. The man carried a lighted torch, while the boy, obviously frightened, did not know whether to hug his father's leg or to run swiftly from this horrifying scene.

"What is this?" Grandafier asked softly, for he feared detection.

King Benton spoke in a bold voice. "We are in Relatania, more than a century past. The old man is the ruler of these lands and the young boy, Belicki, is his son."

"And what of these five unfortunate souls?" Grandafier asked.

"The father stole food to feed his family."

Horrified, Grandafier stared ahead. "And for this crime they are to be burned at the stake?"

"Belicki's father is here to teach his son a lesson. A tyrant must be feared if he is to rule effectively."

Grandafier watched as the old man set a torch to a patch of straw beneath the bodies of the five unfortunate souls who begged piteously for their lives. "What kind of a lesson is this to teach a child?" King Benton did not respond. He stood silently as the fire slowly rose into a terrifying inferno of smoke and white heat. The straw was quite dry and it took but an instant for the fire to reach lethal proportions. As it did, Grandafier intently watched young Belicki. Belicki's eyes were fixed on a young boy, just about his own age, who was so weak that he barely struggled to avoid the rising flames. "The young Belicki is terrified," Grandafier noted.

"But he is also learning," Benton said with great remorse.

As the fires burned, Grandafier reflexively turned his head to avoid the searing heat. When he turned his head back a new scene replaced the old one. "Where are we now?" Grandafier asked, perplexed but now eager to learn more about this wretched boy's life.

"Many cycles have passed," Benton continued. "Belicki is a grown man, having served ably in the Army of Relatania, the only Relatanian survivor of the glorious Miracle at Mt. Delba. He has returned to his homeland, where by his own hand he brutally murdered his own father and assumed his title and lands as the new Count Belicki. But he cares not for this mere pittance of an inheritance, not after what he has seen in Arcania. He is utterly obsessed with the Oracle! Nothing else is ever on his mind!"

Grandafier stared as Belicki asks, "What power could have made an entire army disappear?" He repeats the same question with interminable frequency, for it is the only thought that permeates his once fertile imagination. "Whatever it is, it is a source of unlimited power," he notes, clearly tempted by its omnipotent magnificence.

"Though he could have lived a life of comfort and privilege, Belicki can think of nothing else but controlling this mysterious device. But unlike myself, he does not wish to use it for benevolent purposes. His heart burns with an ambition to rule the world!" King Benton turned and when he did the scene changed yet again. Now, he and Grandafier stood in a dark tunnel, and watched as hundreds of men, women, and a vast number of ragged and undernourished children, feverishly removed cart loads of mud and crud from the floors and walls of this subterranean cave. "So obsessed was Belicki with the promise of unlimited power, that he undertook an insane mission, to build a tunnel beneath the Bay of Battle, a tunnel large enough to transport an entire army, destined for but one task, to seize the Oracle. For almost four decades, he forced tens of thousands of his citizens to toil beneath the sea. Most of them perished here."

Grandafier watched as a young child fell to the ground, exhausted and senseless, while a guard prodded his dying body with the sharp tip of a long bayonet-like stick until he was sure he was dead. "We have another one who is dead over here," the guard yelled out and perfunctorily a group of men garbed in tattered rags dragged the young boy's body away. Meanwhile, nearby, the boy's mother cried, though she continued to excavate dirt from the tunnel's ever expanding walls, for she had three more children, and she feared that each might meet a similar fate.

"This is like a scene out of hell!" Grandafier moaned.

"It is hell!" Benton declared righteously. "And this is what is in store for the citizens of Arcania if Belicki is to rule over them."

"Oh my God," Grandafier moaned, his body trembling palpably as he spoke. Then turning and staring directly into King Benton's expressive eyes, the old man bellowed, "What can be done to stop this horror? Why don't you stop him?"

Benton stared intensely at Grandafier. "Even the great Kublatitan does not have the power to stop Belicki now. You ask your question far too late. If you had not enabled young Montama, had you not played a role in luring the Arcanian Army to Grell, Belicki would not be on the verge of seizing our passra."

"Then it is too late?" Grandafier said through yellow tears that streamed down his wrinkled green face.

"That I do not know," Benton said with a sad confession. "The Oracle is no longer united. I can no longer divine the future. All may very well be lost."

With these words, Grandafier and Benton returned to the safety of the old man's home and as they did Grandafier collapsed into his bed and then buried his head in his hands as he cried aloud, "What have I done to my passra?"

"There is still hope," Benton said, in an attempt to rally the old man's spirits. "For his excessive cruelty, Belicki was eventually exiled from Relatania by his own people. He escaped to Arcania, where he wandered the land for many cycles, until by chance he met my grandfather, King Bamaoha. He used his royal connections to work his way into Bamaoha's favor, and for a short time he became a trusted personal adviser, offering valuable security information about the politics of the Relatin Empire. He used that position for only one purpose: to steal the Oracle. But with his last breath he learned a fatal truth: It is not enough to desire the Oracle, for the Oracle also must desire you. And the Oracle would not let him rule for it realized that he was poisoned and consumed by the allure of absolute power. Yet the Oracle made a dreadful mistake. It absorbed him into its matrix, believing that by reducing him to one among thousands of entities he would represent no threat. Belicki never gave up. He patiently bided his time, waiting for yet another opportunity to seize the Oracle. And he has found that opportunity in a young, naïve boy, who does not understand the evil with which he consorts. It is through that boy that Belicki intends to rule, not just Arcania, but all of Relatania as well. And now, thanks to you, his army is deployed just miles from Teta, ready to strike its fatal blow against the Centama family."

"What can I do? How can I help?" Grandafier asked, as he stood resolutely.

"You must go to Montama," the king responded. "He trusts you, as does Belicki."

"And then what will I do?" Grandafier begged, eager for redemption.

"For the time being, you will report to me, on all things that you hear."

"For the time being…" Grandafier asked. "And then what?"

Benton stared directly into Grandafier's terrified eyes and through them to the core of his eternal soul. "Then when the time is right you will kill Montama."

Grandafier shrieked! "Must it come to that?"

Benton declared emphatically, "There is no other alternative. The boy must die!"

Chapter 45
On the Precipice

Lord Gulcum's migraine headache continued to pound. It happened every time he was summoned to Bellazar's private quarters. He had never wanted to be in a position of power and responsibility and he judged his own qualifications harshly. In fact, he had no idea why Bellazar had plucked him from near obscurity for this august governmental position. He would not have been terribly surprised by the harsh truth: Bellazar felt more comfortable around male subordinates that she could easily dominate.

Plop! Plop! Plop! The incessant sound of the Tellican jumping fish reverberated in Gulcum's super sensitive right ear. He put his hand up to block the sensation. When he did he sensed the unwelcome smell of the Anawana Yapyap. "My god," Gulcum thought, "how the hell does she put up with this menagerie?" And that was not the end of it, for Bellazar had recently added a Tgwaka to her exotic collection. A Tgwaka is a bird that literally flies upside down, thus enabling its feet to easily attach themselves to low lying branches. It was yet another oddity, representing what Gulcum thought was the very freaks of nature. Now that he was an adviser to Bellazar, Gulcum wondered, "Am I yet another freak in her exotic bizarre?" Before he could respond to his own surmise, he was startled into the world of reality by the sound of Bellazar's commanding voice.

"I have called all of you here to this meeting to update me on the present situation," she said calmly, without the slightest sign of fear or panic.

A small table had been erected in her chamber to accommodate her four top military advisers. As Gulcum sat at the far end of the table from Bellazar, he listened attentively as General Nga spoke first. "The mercenary army is now less than one mile from Teta. We can anticipate its arrival within two hours."

General Bgaya spoke next. "Madame Bellazar…"

Bellazar interrupted with furious discontent. "I hate that title. What am I the head of a government or a brothel?"

Without thinking, Gulcum said, "Is there a difference?" Then, realizing that his comment was inappropriate he looked at each of the meeting's participants to judge their reactions. Much to his relief Bellazar found his rejoinder to be humorous, as did most of the generals seated around the make shift table.

"Thank you, Lord Gulcum," Bellazar added. "We needed a laugh." Gulcum shot a silly smile, for he had yet to discover the humor in his own comment. But as he did, a wry smile of appreciation finally appeared on his face.

The only one who had not responded with alacrity was General Bgaya for he had more pressing issues on his mind. "Madame Bellazar," he said as he gently cleared his throat. "On your direct orders we have evacuated the royal family. The time has come for us to transfer you to a secure location."

Bellazar stared coldly at General Bgaya. "Are you suggesting that I run?"

"I only recommend it for your own safety," Bgaya responded deferentially.

"And if I were a man would you ask me to run from the scene of battle?"

Bgaya thought for a moment then confessed, "No Madame, I would not."

Bellazar's eyes now burned with a barely contained fury. "Then I have absolutely no intention of leaving the King's Castle at the very moment of Arcania's greatest peril. Like you I will stand and fight to the last man, or woman, if that is what history has in store for us." The four generals nodded their heads perfunctorily, while Lord Gulcum's attention turned to the Pirene cat, which much to his dismay had begun to take a liking to him. As he tried to push it away, the cat rubbed its head persistently against his right leg. Bellazar then asked quite bluntly, "Are we prepared?"

As the four generals looked at each other, General Nga took the initiative. "The mercenaries outflanked the Second Army, but our forces are now moving northward toward Teta."

General Bgaya, who was responsible for the protection of the King's Castle interjected, "We have fortified the gates leading up to the castle. Beyond them lay a vast maze. The maze is designed to confuse and retard the advancement of any enemy force that manages to get past the external gates. To further delay the approach of any army we have placed our best archers at various points atop these walls."

"And what is to prevent the invaders from merely climbing the walls and jumping over them?" Bellazar asked.

"The walls are fifteen feet tall. And if they try to climb over them they will find only quicksand on the other side."

Bellazar nodded her head appreciatively then asked, "And what of the castle itself. Let's say that the army penetrates each of these security devices. What force do they face when they arrive at the castle?"

General Bgaya smiled, "The castle itself is a natural fortification, carved directly into the side of Mt. Delba. The front door is made of wood, forty inches thick, virtually impenetrable to any invading force. Most of the windows on the southern face of the castle are much too narrow to allow entry. Therefore, the only possible avenue for entry is the sun deck above the castle's third floor."

Originally, as envisioned, the castle was to have been five stories high. As the engineers cut into the stone above the present third floor, they found it to be too hard to excavate. So, instead of building a fourth and fifth floor, they settled for a sixty-five foot open expanse that the castle's denizens called "the sun deck." It was a splendid private area where the king could go to watch the sunset. But now it represented the only potential means of entry into the castle. "And what happens if the enemy tries to scale the walls and enter via the sun deck?" Bellazar asked.

General Bgaya was ready. "We will have at least one hundred of our best archers located along the perimeter of the deck. In addition, we have other surprises prepared for our guests. I can assure you that no one will be able to enter the castle through the sun deck."

"Those are our defensive capabilities," Bellazar stated curtly. "Now what is our plan for victory?"

General Nga was responsible for this aspect of Arcanian military security. "Our plan is to let the mercenaries into Teta. We have left the city itself virtually unprotected. Once they are occupied with an attempt to storm the castle, we will move the Second Army northward while Pantamanu's Third Army moves in from the east. We will encircle the mercenaries and then destroy them."

"And what is to prevent the mercenaries from escaping to the west?" Bellazar asked full well knowing the answer to her own query.

General Nga did not hesitate. "The territory directly west of Teta is swamp land. Any army that tries to escape in that direction will be immediately bogged down, no pun intended." He chuckled irresistibly and then added, "With the combined forces of the Second and Third Army we will be able to totally eradicate them."

"So," Bellazar smiled, "we have set a perfect trap for our enemy. That is, so long as everything goes according to our plans."

Lord Gulcum tried to shove the Pirene cat away from his leg. As he did he heard Bellazar remark. "Do you think we are ready, Lord Gulcum?"

Gulcum looked up and remarked, "Are we what Madame?"

Bellazar only smiled, then perfunctorily dismissed the meeting with the warning, "We had better be ready."

Chapter 46
All Roads Lead to Teta

"I have never seen such majesty," General Garr exclaimed, his center eye veritably bulging from its socket as he marveled at this strange distant sight. His face was consumed with a look of transcendent wonder and amazement. "That is the most beautiful thing I have ever seen in my entire life." The object of Garr's rapt attention was the immense and intricate carvings high above the walls of the King's Castle. There were six scenes, each one representing an aspect of the last battle, the Miracle at Mt. Delba. In one particularly detailed engraving lay the ruins of the last enemy that attempted to invade Arcania. In another, the great General Tampinco was pictured, his bifurcated nose rattling in the wind, as he rode furiously and directly toward King Leonata. In the centerpiece engraving, Tampinco laid prostate before a gigantic, one hundred foot high carving of the great King Leonata, who boldly wielded his mighty sword in vitriolic defiance of the enemy attackers.

"It must have taken decades to carve these images into the mountain side," Garr gasped, as he continued to scan the vast array of carvings, his head turning slowly first to the left and then to the right.

Montama had seen the engravings before, but on this particular unit there was not a single cloud in the wide-open sky and its purple hue illuminated the carved characters in ways that Montama had never before seen. "It took thousands of men many decades to carve these images and at a terrible loss of life."

Garr smiled contently as he responded, "Life is never so precious as when it is surrendered in the service of a king. Remember that lesson, for you will be called upon to send many men to their ultimate reward." Garr's sentiment was cavalier, for to his mind soldiers had no other purpose in life than to live and die for the benefit of their leader. It was indeed a stark reality. And in order for Montama to become king, many more soldiers on both sides of this destructive conflict would have to die. And if, or when, he became king, then many more would be asked to die, simply to propagate the king's eternal glory.

As he rode majestically upon his horse, Montama's thoughts on this matter were abruptly interrupted by the sudden, unexpected presence of an odd looking man, who stood directly in his army's path, passionately waving his arms high above his head. The man, who was overweight and with a long graying beard furiously signaled the general and his protégé to approach him. Garr, seemingly more annoyed than curious, shouted angrily, "What business do you have with us?"

Unperturbed, Pondru stared back directly into his adversary's one-solitary eye and declared in a powerful, confident voice, "Turn back! There will be no war today."

Garr laughed and then turned toward Montama. "Is this a joke? Do you know who this man is?"

Montama stared at Pondru for sometime before replying, "He is wearing the black robes of the Maldemin, the holy men who watch over the Oracle. He may have great power."

Hearing this Garr merely sneered. "And what powers do you have?" he said with the utmost sarcasm as he turned his gaze back to Pondru.

Pondru firmly stood his ground. "I represent the power of peace."

Startled, Garr glanced quizzically toward Montama, before retorting, "He is joking, isn't he?"

Pondru took a few broad steps forward until he stood directly in front of General Garr's steed. "War is an abomination," he declared forthrightly. "Nothing good can ever come of it. War leads only to pestilence, suffering, devastation, and destruction."

"And your point is?" Garr asked, leaning forward as menacingly as possible, while simultaneously trying to hide his obvious sense of amusement at the audacity of this apparently mad Maldemin.

"My point is that the people of Arcania prefer peace to war."

"So?" General Garr asked, clearly considering this point to be entirely irrelevant.

"So," Pondru commented calmly, "there will be no war today." Just as Pondru completed this sentence, the winding road to Teta suddenly was occupied with the bodies of countless Oracle entities, representing a vast array of diverse backgrounds, from plain ordinary farmers, to bankers and intellectuals. Though the Oracle entities were no longer interconnected, many of them separately shared the same belief that the war must be stopped. Therefore, by the hundreds and then by the thousands, they took material form until the entire plain leading to Teta was completely packed with a peace movement so dauntingly large that it would have frightened a less ambitious man than Garr.

Garr and Montama reacted with stunned silence, as did the many soldiers behind them who could clearly see the vast horizon suddenly replete with the bodies of thousands upon thousands of what appeared to be glowing spirits. As the men starred ahead, Pondru grabbed hold of the snout of General Garr's horse and demanded, "Turn back now! You are not wanted here."

Garr was usually nonplussed. Even this fierce warrior had never experienced anything as surreal as the sudden appearance of countless thousands of Oracle entities. Montama too, was astonished, his eyes staring forward, wondering if his senses had gone suddenly quite mad.

The Oracle

For several seconds Montama and Garr simply stared, dumbfounded, at each other. Finally, Garr broke the silence. "We will not turn back, not for any army, and certainly not for a mob demanding peace." He therefore raised both of his hands and shouted the order to "attack!"

Men ominously unsheathed their swords, before raising them high above their heads. They then rode forward and began to violently hack away at the vast and still growing number of Oracle entities. As they brought their swords down hard against the Oracle bodies, they experienced nothing more than the sensation of a sword slashing futilely through empty air. "What the hell is going on?" one soldier declared with consummate exasperation.

"You cannot stop us," Pondru said with a wry smile, his eyes twinkling in the sunlight, his body glowing with a white light as he stood defiantly blocking the road to Teta. Then, firmly he added, "They say that all roads lead to Teta. Well today, that is no longer the case. You must turn back."

"Or what?" Garr snarled angrily, his eye now bloodshot, his nostrils fuming with a red-hot fury. Pondru did not answer. He merely stared back with an equally intense determination.

As Pondru and Garr continued to stare at each other, the wind began to gust, until Pondru's beard streamed sideways. Then, as the mercenaries looked skyward, they saw a menacing black cloud emerge across the vast horizon, as the sky's crystal clear purple hue suddenly turned ominously dark and foreboding. With the wind swirling all around them, the temperature suddenly plummeted. Frightened, yet steady, the mercenary soldiers watched until finally out of the graying mist emerged the outline of a foreboding green vultamire, its immense triangular wings swirling through the newly formed clouds.

Pondru instantly realized that these theatrics marked the arrival of his nemesis, Count Belicki. "You can not stop us," Pondru's voice thundered toward the clouds. "There are too many of us and peace is too powerful an idea to destroy."

From my intimidating perch high in the sky, glaring downward with a hateful spite, still in the form of an onerous green vultamire, I cackled delightedly, "We don't have to destroy the idea of peace. All we have to do is to ignore it." My eyes then burned with the heat of a thousand flames, then narrowed as I ordered Garr to "Move your troops forward."

"But they are blocking the way," Garr countered, clearly confused how he was to proceed in the face of these thousands of Oracle entities.

"Just do as I command," I retorted. Garr stared at Montama, lifted his right hand high above his head and then rendered the signal for his men to "Move forward!"

The men too were startled and at first did not know whether to obey their commander or not, for the entire road ahead thoroughly was littered with a vast array of men and women. Utterly determined to get on to Teta, Montama alone ordered his horse to move ahead. As it did so, the horse moved effortlessly through the apparently matter-less bodies of the Oracle entities. When Garr and the other men saw Montama's horse charging forward, they too commanded their horses to move forward. As they did so the mercenaries found no impediment to forward progress. Within moments, men on horseback and others on foot glided through the glowing bodies of the Oracle entities. Though the entities still held their ground, they no longer represented a serious obstructive force.

From above, Belicki stared coldly at Pondru, who desperately waved his arms in a last futile attempt to halt General Garr's forward progress. In a chilling voice I roared, "You will have to do more than promise the people peace to end this war."

With these few words, one by one, and then in droves, the various Oracle entities vanished, their bodies slowly fading into the shadows until only Pondru remained. His was the last body to vanish. Sadly Pondru realized that there would be war and there was absolutely nothing he could do to stop it.

Chapter 47
The Battle of King's Castle

When General Garr's army arrived at Teta not a soul, not even a runaway dog or cat could be glimpsed or heard, for the capital city was eerily silent. Only the clatter of the horses' huffs and the soldiers' marching feet could be discerned. Surprised by the lack of opposition forces, Garr ordered his army to halt. "This is strange," he told Montama. "It looks like a ghost town. There aren't even any soldiers here." Carefully, Garr considered the possibilities. "They would never abandon the capital city. This must be a trap."

"Perhaps their army is in hiding, as ours was at Kalel," Montama suggested, suddenly looking skyward and searching the heavens for any sign of an enemy attack.

"Then we must move with great haste," Garr declared. "I will take a detachment and move toward the castle." Then, in a surprising move, he decided it was time to give Montama a greater measure of responsibility Garr ordered, "You will take charge of the rest of the forces."

"Yes sir," Montama enthusiastically exclaimed.

"Move them south and be ready for an attack from any direction, even from the sky," the general said with a twinkle in his eye.

"Yes sir," Montama repeated with an enthusiastic salute.

With the final words, "Good luck my king," Garr took a single division and rode directly toward the King's Castle. When he arrived a few moments later he found the gates also largely undefended. "This is very strange indeed," he posited, as he examined the castle's seemingly meager defenses. "They cannot be so feeble that they will merely surrender their castle to us. They must have something devious in mind for us. But what?" Without wasting a precious minute Garr ordered his men to "bring two talladaggers forward."

The beasts could not be quickly roused and despite the general's intentions they moved slowly into position. "Charge them into the gates," Garr ordered, as he physically encouraged the beasts to move by waving his hands frantically. His men took their general's cue and began whipping the beasts until, riled and frenzied, the talladaggers lurched forward against the castle's external gates with a terrible ferocity. Hiding atop the gate were several of the king's most experienced archers. At the intimidating sight of the monstrous and hairy gray talladaggers, the archers quickly and unobtrusively scurried to safety, though two men remained behind, manning a steaming hot cauldron filled with deadly acid. From atop the gate they poured the fuming acid down upon the hapless talladaggers. The scalding acid caused the talladaggers to rear, but only temporarily, for the acid only further antagonized the mighty beasts. With repeated forward thrusts, they pounded their twin heads ever more aggressively against the gate. As it buckled the two soldiers on the wall lost their balance. One screamed piteously as his helpless body fell first to the ground and then beneath one of the vicious talladaggers. As the Arcanian soldier struggled, the talladagger crushed him with one its two enormous trunks, then picked him up and threw his lifeless body hard against the damaged gate. With its other large and hairy trunk-head the enraged beast reached up to the top of the gate, grabbed the other soldier, then crushed the poor man, before releasing his lifeless body to the ground. Then the two talladaggers turned their attention back to the obstreperous gate. The determined beasts pounded it repeatedly. As they did so, the other soldiers, who were lucky enough to survive the initial talladagger attack, retreated from the gate, leaving it entirely unprotected.

As the pounding continued, Garr stepped down from his horse, as he watched in awe as the gate finally bulged perceptibly, a large crack now apparent at its midpoint. Then the second talladagger thrust forward, as sundry large and small shards of scattered debris rained down, and as a large section of the contiguous wall cracked wide open. The giant beasts instinctively stepped back a few yards in preparation for yet another savage charge, as a third talladagger waddled anxiously into position. With all three beasts simultaneously ramming forward, the gate finally snapped like mere kindling and the wall around it collapsed, exposing the inner path to the castle.

It was not immediately apparent to Garr that the path inside the King's Castle was structured in the form of a vast and complex maze configuration. Unaware of this important castle fortification, Garr watched intently as his talladaggers moved past the scattered remnants of the once mighty gate. One of the talladaggers that had been scorched with acid, reared wildly in pain, thrashing its head against an inner rock wall, repeatedly ramming its head until the wall finally shattered. With rock, mortar and stone flying in all directions, the wounded beast charged forward, but when it did, its giant hoofs were mired in a pit of slimy muck. The beast roared, then struggled to move its legs. As the beast struggled mightily and fell on its side, the quicksand slowly consumed it.

With several of his compatriots scurrying by his side, Garr also moved forward into the maze. Directly in front of him, a second talladagger charged down another path, until the ground beneath it unexpectedly opened up, swallowing the beast, which fell into the deep and deadly pit filled with sharp spikes, fatally piercing the talladagger's tough leathery hide. Before it died, the beast cried out in pitious agony, its sound echoing throughout the entire maze configuration with such frightful intensity that every soldier, of both armies, was unnerved and even terrified by the horrific, mournful sound.

"They have turned this entire area into a maze fortification," Garr realized at last, now aware that the path to the castle would be exceedingly treacherous. Garr turned and ordered his men "to bring the oxen forward." It took quite some time to move about a dozen oxen into position ahead of the general and his men. Garr then turned to his right, avoiding the dead end where one of his talladagger had met its gruesome demise in the deadly pit. "Get the oxen out in front of us," he barked. With sticks and other inducements, the oxen were forced to lead the way, with Garr's men moving but a few yards slowly behind them. "We will send the oxen ahead to see if there are any more false paths or obstacles," Garr told one of his men. "Better to lose beasts than men."

Just as he spoke the soldier he was talking to fell lifelessly to the ground, with two arrows suddenly piercing his chest. Instantaneously, another arrow whizzed so close to Garr's head that he could feel the sting of its feathers upon his cheek. "Raise your shields!" he shouted, though most of his men already had assumed a defensive posture, kneeling quickly while holding their shields above their heads to protect them from the deadly onslaught of arrows suddenly flooding down from atop the various maze walls. One arrow struck one of the oxen and it lurched sideways before falling helplessly to the ground. "Move forward," Garr bellowed, still feeling the burn of the arrow's sting upon his face.

Several of Garr's men stepped forward with a new weapon, familiar in Relatania, but not yet in Arcania. "Raise the crossbows," Garr ordered. The crossbow, which was at least four feet across, with a strident bow, was a powerful weapon, with its oversized and deadly arrowheads, though it was heavy and hard to maneuver. At long range, a soldier could lie down, load the crossbow and then as he balanced the weapon on his feet, he could pull the powerful bow back with both of his arms and then fire it with deadly precision. At close range, however, the weapon required either two men, one to load it and one to fire it, or a man with three muscular arms. Ka-Why-Tees therefore were suited perfectly for this specific task. Holding the crossbow with two arms they could then load the arrow with their third short arm, then use their third arm to pull the bow back and fire at any target. With practice these Ka-Why-Tee archers became highly proficient, firing their weapons with a deadly accuracy.

"They're up there," one of Garr's archers shouted, as three of the Ka-Why-Tees fired their crossbows at an enemy soldier standing high atop a maze wall. Two of the prolific arrows bounced harmlessly off the wall, while a third brutally decapitated the unfortunate soldier atop the barrier. Sensing this new horrible threat, Bellazar's archers stepped forward all across the tops of maze walls so that they could fire their volleys directly into the enemy soldiers before they had a chance to reload the crossbow. When they did, however, all they could see below them was a sea of silver shields reflecting bursts of sunlight directly into their eyes. Many archers, temporarily blinded, averted their eyes from the shields and were thus easy targets for the Ka-Why-Tee archers. Others fired their arrows downward hoping to kill an unseen enemy, but most of these arrows merely ricocheted off the invader's shields and then struck harmlessly against the interior walls.

Meanwhile, Garr's archers reloaded and aimed their deadly crossbows at Bellazar's now fully exposed soldiers. "Raise your shields," one of the Arcanian guards shouted, though the other archers did not need much encouragement to obey this command. "Duck," another soldier screamed as he raised his shield before his kneeling body. The force of the crossbow arrow was so powerful that it knocked him backward, until he plunged from the wall and into the dark pit of gooey quicksand. Then another hapless soldier fell head first into the muck, his feet kicking helplessly for several seconds, though his body was buried up to its chest. Finally, as the man's legs fell suddenly limp, another body, with a giant crossbow arrow piercing its chest, landed nearby.

Others soldiers on both sides shouted, "Attack!" Arrows flew simultaneously through the air in myriad directions, their whizzing sound combined with screams, orders and counter orders, filling the air with such audio confusion that it was hard to discern any particular word or phrase. With the pandemonium of battle in full bloom, one mesmerized guard watched a crossbow's projectile actually cut his drawn arrow in two, before another one flew dangerously past his head. As he ducked he muttered, "That was close." Then he fell quickly to the ground as two other arrows whizzed past his now prostrate body. "Damn," he snarled, as he crawled on his belly along the wall, searching for any possible cover.

While many Arcanians were killed, particularly as they scurried for cover along the perimeter of the large maze walls, the highest attrition rate thus far among Garr's army was its savage beasts. Two talladaggers perished and without shields the oxen were completely vulnerable. Bellazar's archers aggressively targeted these animals. "Protect the beasts," Garr commanded and several men moved forward with shields drawn above their heads, trying to defend both themselves and the animals. In this manner, shielded by several men, the oxen continued to lead the way. As one hulking creature moved down a dead-end and fell into yet another deadly pit, sometimes with two or three of Garr's men at its side, the general's mercenary army immediately blocked that pathway. In this fashion, for several tedious hours, the army slowly snaked its way forward, moving inexorably through the confusing maze toward the castle.

As arrows landed all around them, Garr's men pushed the slow moving beasts down several different paths. Some moved forward until the ground collapsed beneath them. Each time a soldier from General Garr's army quickly retreated down that path and blocked its entrance. "Another false path," the soldier shouted. Some discovered dead ends and returned to block off those paths, as well. Slowly, systematically, while still under savage aerial assault from archers atop the walls, Garr's men moved continuously and determinedly deeper into the vast and complex maze structure. It finally became readily apparent that while Bellazar's soldiers were capable of delaying the mercenary army's forward progress, they could not permanently arrest it.

From her third-story window, Bellazar heard the shouting and other chaotic sounds of battle, but she only occasionally caught a glimpse of one of her trained archers retreating helplessly, while the invading army moved relentlessly forward. "They will be here sooner than I expected," she said, nervously tapping her fingers on the window ledge. Turning toward one of her officers inside her private chamber she roared like a wounded lion. "Make sure that the castle's fortifications are ready. The enemy army will be here in a matter of minutes."

"Yes Madame," an officer responded.

As the officer departed to relay Bellazar's order, she again peered out the window, spotting a shadowy group of men and beasts moving relentlessly toward the castle. Then she saw an object headed directly toward her head. Ducking calmly, she cursed, "Damn," as the giant crossbow arrow shot past her head and then harmlessly into the room. She turned to see the Anawana Yapyap cowering helplessly in the far corner of the room. "Some help you are," she snarled as he she turned her gaze back outside the window. Under her breath she also muttered, "I never thought I would actually be thankful to see Pantamanu again. But unless he arrives soon, we cannot hold out much longer."

Meanwhile, at his post on the streets of Teta, Montama on horseback awaited history's uncertain judgment. On this unit he either would be proclaimed Arcania's next king or die as its most ignominious traitor. As Montama pondered this paradox, the golden sun, which had bathed the battlefield, finally began to surrender to a menacing series of black clouds. The winds too began to blow wildly from the east and Montama could see flashes of lightening followed seconds later by the subtle rumblings of wayward thunder. "Is it the sound of an approaching army or just a storm?" Montama thought, as he felt the first touch of rain gently touch his skin.

Bellazar also wondered if the incoming storm was an omen and if so what did it portend? Within a minute, the rain began to pelt the ground below, thrashing heavily against the castle walls. Lightening now lit the nearby sky with savage flashes of white and gold.

From his vantage point inside the maze walls, General Garr believed that the storm provided him with an additional opportunity, for it further decreased visibility, making it more difficult for the men atop the castle's walls to track the progress of his invading army. "This is a good omen," the general said, though the rain made it hard for him to keep his one eye fixed upon the path that lay directly before him. He also calculated that the rain and wind provided a greater impediment for the Arcanian forces, since his army already occupied Teta. Thus, as his army finally snaked its way to the castle's main massive wooden door, the general was highly optimistic. "On this unit we will win a great victory," he smiled, as he gave the order for his men to bring forward the ropes and ladders. "We are ready now for the final assault," he beamed, his eye gleaming, as the rains continued to drench the embattled city of Teta.

Chapter 48
The Crystal Sanctuary

"The Second Army is coming," a lone captain from General Garr's army shouted as he rode his horse spiritedly through the rain toward Montama's defensive position. With the wind swirling in his ears Montama could not hear what the captain said. "What?" Montama shouted as he put his hand to his ear. With the captain's horse now standing next to Montama, the soldier shouted in a booming voice, "The Second Army is fast approaching. They will be here within the hour."

"Then we must make ready for them," Montama ordered. "Move the talladaggers to the southern perimeter."

"Yes sir," the captain responded obediently. As rain poured profusely from his plain cloth cap, the captain saluted and then rode dutifully southward to convey Montama's order.

Montama realized that this encounter would be his ultimate test in battle. "I will not fail," he said aloud. He was surprised when he heard a strange and unknown voice respond, "You must fail." Montama turned and abruptly looked all around, yet he could see nothing more substantial than the pounding rain and swirling wind. A small group of soldiers were standing several feet away, but no one was close enough to converse with the young man. Then, he heard the words echo again, "You must fail."

"Who said that?" Montama shouted as he glanced nervously in several different directions.

"Come with me," the voice declared emphatically. More startled than afraid, Montama realized that the voice was not human. "Close your eyes," the voice now ordered.

"I will do nothing to obey you," Montama declared emphatically, as he placed his right hand on his still sheathed sword.

The Oracle

"No harm at all will I do to you," the voice repeatedly echoed inside Montama's mind, so that he heard the word harm at least a dozen times.

Then without realizing that he was complying, Montama blinked, but only for a second. When he re-opened his eyes he immediately was struck by the wonder of his strange new surroundings, for he was no longer astride his horse and no longer in the real world. "What is this place?" Montama asked, for all around him the light glistened with an otherworldly intensity. There was no sky, no ground, no barriers of any kind. Montama's body merely floated in space. Then to his amazement he noticed that his head was no longer attached to his body. His head was floating in one direction, his torso in another. "What the hell is happening to me?" he shouted.

"Do not fear," the voice said calmly. "I have brought you here so you can see your future."

"Where is here?" Montama yelled frantically.

"You are in what I call the Crystal Sanctuary."

"And who are you?" Montama asked.

"Name is Kublatitan. I am the creator of the Oracle. I come from what you call the Land of the Taewokans." This news surprised Montama but he said nothing. "King was I for a thousand of your cycles. When death was near, I telekinetically created a receptacle for my knowledge and wisdom, to be used only by and for my own people. In the Oracle my thoughts are pure energy. "Montama listened attentively. "As you can see, the body has no meaning here. It floats aimlessly, but your thoughts survive."

Montama slowly realized that all he had to do was to think to communicate with Kublatitan. Spoken words were simply superfluous. He therefore thought, "The Oracle told my mother that I will be king."

Kublatitan expelled a mighty sigh. "That indeed is one possibility," he admitted reluctantly. "You do not understand the Oracle. I created it as a repository for my thoughts, my wisdom. But now others possess it, others far darker than me, much more dangerous and deadly. It is they who use you now."

"Who uses me?" Montama asked with apparent irritation.

Instead of answering his question Kublatitan continued, "If you do not turn back now forever will you regret the horrible deed that you will do."

Rather than mollifying Montama, as was his intent, Kublatitan's word only incensed the young man. "What deed? Stop speaking in riddles and tell me what you mean."

"You must turn back to save your family," Kublatitan said. "Otherwise, all will be lost."

Then, just as suddenly as he had entered the Crystal Sanctuary, Montama felt the cold rain rushing against his face. Startled, Montama held his hands up before his eyes. Satisfied that he was again whole and seated upon his horse, he saw his men riding south to confront Arcania's Second Army. "I will never let my family down and I will never be used by anyone," Montama whispered, as he turned his horse and galloped down the winding roads of Teta, more determined than ever to destroy Arcania's Second Army.

Chapter 49
The Battle of King's Castle Part 2

General Garr stared at the heavens like an angry Cyclops as he methodically assayed the castle's prodigious rock-faced wall. Standing far more than one hundred feet high, secured with sundry defensive barriers, he realized that this was the mercenary army's last obstacle to victory. He had intended to use the talladaggers to smash through the castle's immense wooden door, but two of the animals had been killed in the assault on the maze perimeter. It would therefore take time to bring additional talladaggers to the fore. So Garr turned to his second target, scaling the castle's shear rock wall and entering through the exposed sun deck that Montama had carefully described to him, a site he had witnessed many cycles past in his one short visit to the King's Castle.

As Garr looked up at the monumental structure he realized that invading through the sun deck would not be an easy task. When the ladders finally were brought forward they were far too short to reach the top of the wall. Garr had anticipated this problem and had developed an ingenious solution; that is, *if* it worked. Garr ordered his Ka-Why-Tee division to climb to the top of the ladders. This would be a difficult task. First they would have to avoid the arrows and other debris that was aimed at them by the soldiers on the castle's small exposed sun deck. Then, the Ka-Why-Tee would have to perform a delicate and dangerous maneuver. To get from the end of the ladder to the top of the castle, an area of approximately fifty feet, the Ka-Why-Tee would use a specially constructed device. It consisted of a long wooden handle that a Ka-Why-Tee soldier could hold with one hand

271

at chest level while he struck a rounded suction cup with a clasp anchored on its backside hard against the side of the wall, thus creating a secure vacuum that would hold the soldier firmly in place. The soldier then would place a second such device at their face level. Then, with a maneuver that required considerable strength, they would pull themselves upward, releasing the lower device's grip by jiggling the clasp from side to side until it pulled loose from the wall, and then lugubriously reattaching it above his head. This action would be repeated in incremental movements while the soldier also held a shield over his head with his third short arm. Through this tedious, repetitive process, the soldier would slowly but inexorably climb the castle's steep wall.

Meanwhile, at the top of the castle, Bellazar's soldiers fired arrows, dropped glass shards, and other heavier objects on the Ka-Why-Tee soldiers. They also poured buckets of acid on the enemy below. To provide cover, General Garr ordered a phalanx of crossbow archers to fire relentlessly at the soldiers on the rooftop. And all of this occurred while the rains continued to swirl in conjunction with the powerful east wind.

"Keep climbing," Garr shouted, as several Ka-Why-tee lost their grips and fell hard to the ground. Then, Garr ordered his men to move back as he saw acid raining down from above. It scorched the ground, as well as killing a dozen Ka-Why-Tee soldiers, who tumbled dreadfully to their deaths, their skin scorched, their eyes blinded. Though many brave Ka-Why-Tees were killed in this hideous fashion, they were followed by row upon row of other soldiers, for as soon as one man fell to his death another was ready to scurry up the ladder to take his place.

General Garr reasoned that it would take some time to refill the cauldrons with acid and that eventually they would run low on defensive weapons. "They only have a limited number of supplies," he declared to one of his courageous soldiers as he mounted a ladder in preparation for the dangerous ascent up the castle's wall. One Ka-Why-Tee was struck instantly by a falling soldier, one of Bellazar's men, who had been shot through the heart with a deadly crossbow arrow. The mercenary's arrows were fired with such horrible precision that gaps finally began to emerge along the top deck, places where a rebel Ka-Why-Tee could climb the wall relatively unmolested.

With only a hint of trepidation, Garr watched as his valiant men courageously scaled the wall, seeming impervious to the castle's defenses.

"At last we have a talladagger," a lieutenant declared as he ran forward toward his general.

"Bring him forward," Garr shouted with much exuberance. The talladagger obediently waddled forward toward the castle's large wooden door. "We will smash the door open," Garr instructed his men.

The talladagger was in no mood to cooperate. It had to be encouraged to move forward and it took the men several minutes to coerce it with the aide of sticks and other painful inducements. Finally, the enraged beast stormed forward and smashed into the thick wooden castle gate. The gate buckled, but it did not give, for this door was much thicker than the main gate. The beast was again induced to charge forward. When it did, it shook the castle's walls so violently that several of the climbing Ka-Why-Tees lost their grips and plunged helplessly to their deaths.

"Damn!" Garr cursed as he watched the Talladagger ineffectually thrust forward a third time, two shields still held above the general's head to protect him from incoming arrows, which darted the landscape all around him. The general then shouted to several men in the rear, "Get the kerosene." Moments later two men carried a canister forward. One was struck in the shoulder by an arrow and fell backward to the ground, while the other dragged the heavy container forward toward the door.

"Spread it on the door," Garr shouted fiercely through the blinding rain and angry winds. With the sound of arrows bouncing off their shields, and with pelting rain and wind swirling all about them, it was becoming almost impossible to hear the general's orders. "Spread the kerosene on the door," Garr repeated at least three times before his soldiers finally complied. The men carefully poured the kerosene at the base of the door and then lit it with a torch. Despite the rain, the door immediately lit up in red-hot flames. "Now get the talladagger to smash the damn thing open," the general barked. Frightened by the fire, the talladagger stood on its back two feet and then let loose a mournful cry before stomping the door with its two front hoofs. This time the door buckled and shattered. Through the fire and smoke, Garr could not see inside the castle, but he shouted the order as loud as he could speak. "Get ready to charge." In case his soldiers could not hear him he spiritedly raised his full-sword high above his head. When the men tried to move through the damaged remains of the castle door, they were startled to find their way was blocked by yet another obstruction.

"What is this?" Garr exclaimed angrily, as his men futilely moved backward from the castle's entrance way. What Garr did not know was that inside the castle, thirty men stood at the ready with a prefabricated, makeshift brick wall, which they quickly pushed into place as the wooden door gave way. The makeshift wall was an engineering marvel, made entirely of brick and mortar, portable despite its great bulk, because it slid on casters made out of the backs of thousands of rotund seanats, the very same crustacean that, on the southern beaches of the Bay of Battle, had blocked Garr's path into eastern Arcania. The sea creature's round shape and sturdy structure, each one capable of withstanding more than three hundred pounds of pressure, allowed them to be used like giant casters, allowing Bellazar's soldiers to slide the new wall seamlessly into place. And if this new wall was somehow breached by the obstreperous talladagger, the Arcanian soldiers had yet another large brick wall ready to slide in its place.

Garr quickly realized that this brick wall was sturdier than the wooden one. As his black pupil glared with a barely contained fury, Garr turned toward his men and declared, "We have no choice. We must continue to scale the castle walls."

On this front slow but steady progress was still being made. Several Ka-Why-Tee soldiers, moving methodically forward, were now within striking distance of the wall's ridge. Meanwhile, various bowmen had climbed the ladders and were now firing their crossbows toward the top of the castle wall, relentlessly driving Bellazar's soldiers backward, providing ample cover for the Ka-Why-Tees.

With the rain pelting their faces, several Ka-Why-Tee simultaneously reached the crest. After they climbed over the final barrier, a small rock wall, they pulled out their swords and charged toward the enemy. There were still many Arcanian soldiers on the roof, wielding spiked clubs, bludgeons and other deadly weapons. So, the Ka-Why-Tee soldiers huddled together into a protective clan, their shields surrounding them like an outer layer of armor, and waited until their numbers were sufficient to present a formidable offensive force. With crossbow arrows flying over their heads, other Ka-Why-Tee soldiers continued to pull themselves onto the castle's exposed deck, though at the precipice a few were hit by arrows and tumbled backward to their death.

With about seventy Ka-Why-Tee soldiers now on the roof, the men finally prepared to attack. They screamed, a horrible high-pitched squeal that unnerved Bellazar's men. With their swords at the ready, the Arcanians charged forward, intent on overwhelming the Ka-Why-Tee invaders. The Battle for King's Castle now was reduced to fierce and deadly hand-to-hand combat on the confined spaces of the castle's sun deck. At first Bellazar's men seemed to have a strategic advantage in that they still had greater numbers than the Ka-Why-Tee. Each additional minute that passed, however, brought fresh Ka-Why-Tee soldiers to the rooftop, many with a crossbow strung over their backs. They quickly aimed their lethal arrows at the Arcanian protectors and fired with a deadly precision. Despite the danger, the Arcanians continued to charge forward. The castle top was now replete with men hollering orders, while others screamed in pain and terror.

As additional Ka-Why-Tee soldiers reached the exposed castle roof, they formed a line and began to push forward, ultimately forcing Bellazar's soldiers to retreat, pushing them backward toward the doors that led to the interior of the castle. Once these defenses were breached, the invading army could move down the stairwells and into the main complex. And while the giant stonewall still prevented Garr from entering the castle through the front gate, it now also blocked the only available exit for Bellazar's forces. Concerned for her safety, still in her third-room chamber, Arcanian soldiers now instructed Bellazar to move to a more secure location, the wine cellar, where Valmar had taken the King's three brothers after Pondru's sudden disappearance. Bellazar angrily balked at the idea, deciding instead to stand with her men. "I will not run like a helpless woman," she declared defiantly as she grabbed a bow and a sack of arrows that she had laid nearby.

"You will not have to," she heard Kublatitan exclaim defiantly.

Instantly, from the east a wind blew so cold that the rain turned to snow and the castle's walls, wet from the rain, suddenly turned to ice. Ka-Why-Tees, who were still scaling the walls, now lost their grips and fell helplessly to the ground below them. Meanwhile on the castle top, other members of the mercenary army struggled with their crossbows, as the deadly devices abruptly froze solid. The Ka-Why-Tees, who just moments before had been at the precipice of a great victory, now scurried helpless on the rooftop, as Bellazar's men moved in for the kill. As they did so the wind blew suddenly in their own faces, driving them back into the interior of the castle. For I, Count Belicki, too could taste victory and I would not allow Kublatitan to stop me, not now, not when my men were this close to seizing the castle, the Arcanian throne, and most importantly of all, the mighty Oracle. I therefore moved quickly to defend the Ka-Why-Tees at this most perilous and critical moment.

But Kublatitan unleashed additional snow squalls that totally blinded all of the men on the deck, as well as Garr's forces on the ground below.

"Damn it," Garr cursed, for he realized that though he stood not more than a few feet from the castle wall, he could no longer see it. The wind also whipped fiercely in Garr's face as he heard the sounds of several men, falling to the ground, literally blown off their roof top perch.

"This is not possible," one frightened soldier exclaimed, as he watched the snow fall. It was the middle of the Season of Renewal after all, a time that soon would give way to Arcania's hottest and most humid Season of Life. "It must be the Oracle," the soldier shouted as he ran for cover.

Though Garr tried to control his men, several instinctively retreated only to be crushed by their own talladagger, which was as befuddled and frightened by the wind and snow as were the soldiers. Garr valiantly tried to maintain order, but his commands could not be heard and many of his men stumbled about incoherently, desperately trying to find a safe haven. Within minutes Garr realized that his division could no longer move forward. "Evacuate the area," he shouted with a hateful intensity. As he pulled back as many men as he could, he realized that the battle for King's Castle was no longer in the hands of mere mortals. Two titans were now fighting for the future of Arcania. What he did not know was that less than a mile away Montama was about to engage the enemy in a perilous battle of his own.

Chapter 50
Montama Confronts the Second Army

"My god," the Relatanian captain exclaimed, as his scouts described the size of the juggernaut headed northward toward Teta. "It is a much larger force than I had anticipated," he said, for with the few remnants from the defeated First Army, the Second Army now represented the largest indigenous force in Arcania. The captain quickly realized that it would be pure folly to confront this mammoth conglomerated force alone, but Montama disagreed. Emboldened by the victory at Kalel, and sure that Garr was at this very moment driving his forces inside the King's Castle, Montama was confident of victory despite the enemy's massive numbers. With the Oracle on his side he was convinced that the Second Army was just as vulnerable as the First Army had been.

Sustained by this reckless youthful hubris, Montama arrogantly declared, "We will stand and fight until General Garr orders us to retreat." The captain was used to taking orders from General Garr. It was an entirely different matter to obey this apparently suicidal directive from a nineteen-year-old boy who looked decidedly ill suited to the leadership task at hand. He knew that Montama's entire military experience consisted of the one Battle of the Valley of Kalel. He also understood that the victory there, while fortuitous, was unlikely to be repeated on an open plain before Teta against a much larger and thus more powerful foe. Despite his considerable reservations, the captain was a military man and used to blindly following orders. He therefore nodded his acquiescence, though he later dispatched a scout to confer with General Garr.

Unlike the captain, Montama had no doubts. Incensed by Kublatitan's attempt to dissuade him from attacking Teta, at what he now considered to be his ultimate moment of glory, the young man was entirely convinced that he was predestined for greatness. Yet, while he was cocky, Montama was not careless. Methodically, he consulted with various men at the front, making sure that the various lines of defense were at the ready for the Second Army's imminent arrival.

"We will give them a surprise or two," Montama bragged to one soldier.

One factor already was working to Montama's advantage. The heavy wind and snow, which Kublatitan unleashed fiercely against General Garr's marauders, now slowed the progress of Bellazar's Second Army. This provided Montama with an extra half hour to make sure that his forces were adequately prepared. Staring southward through the snow squalls, Montama waited eagerly for his chance to prove his worth.

The Second Army could be heard long before it could be seen. The sounds of whinnying horses, with thousands of men marching determinedly northward could not be masked, even by the winds. And the hubris of the leaders of the Second Army easily matched Montama's own sublime confidence. They too believed that this unit would end in a glorious victory. The stage was therefore set for a confrontation of epic proportions and it began, literally with a bang!

The explosions were small, barely more dangerous than an errant firecracker, but they were numerous and totally unexpected. After marching northward, Montama's men had covered the road with teledine pebbles, which looked very much like rock salt. Teledine was a natural mineral, which like flint, when struck by a sharp object, induced a sudden flame and then elicited a loud but fairly harmless explosion. While the actual danger was minimal, the bursts of fiery flames had been used to great effect to frighten the horses of the great Army of Relatania. It would now be seen if they had the same effect on the charging Arcanian army. As expected, as the Arcanian's charging hooves created friction, the mild explosions startled the Arcanian's horses, causing them to abruptly rear their feet, often tossing their riders unceremoniously to the ground in the process. While the noise terrified the horses, to the Arcanian soldiers it appeared that the road itself was suddenly on fire, with sparks rising palpably into the air. "What the hell is this?" one Arcanian shouted, as he watched the unreal specter of a road on fire in the midst of a swirling snowstorm.

"Look at them panic," Montama gleamed, as he pulled his forces back, ready to unleash his next surprise on the unsuspecting Second Army. "Pull back to the top of that ridge," he ordered one of the captains. The men who had salted the roads gladly retreated to safer ground where their compatriots prepared the second in a series of unorthodox military maneuvers.

The Second Army had escaped the bloodbath at Kalel. The few survivors from that battle spoke of the incredible sight of hairy beasts that stood as tall as a house and as wide as one too. These dangerous monsters had charged directly at the Third Army, crushing men beneath their huffs, recklessly tossing men asunder with their two powerful trunks. It was a vision out of Hades itself.

As the Second Army moved forward, its soldiers already unnerved by the teledine explosions, now heard the mournful and unearthly cry of a beast that they had come to fear more than any other weapon, most without ever having previously laid eyes upon one. In the telling of the stories, the beasts, if possible, had become even more ferocious, eating men alive and spitting out their bony remains. Though precarious discipline was maintained, the soldiers of the Second Army were suddenly quite apprehensive. "We are trained to fight men not monsters," one soiled and somber soldier muttered to his equally frightened compatriot.

Despite this terror, the men continued to march forward, barely able to see the ridge through the driving snow, nervously holding their weapons at the ready, but for what purpose most could only imagine. Then, from out of the snow, they saw a sight that the survivors would later describe as hell unleashed. Twenty gigantic and enraged talladaggers charged down the road and along both sides of it, a line of beasts so formidable that valiant men, who had served the Arcanian military for decades, suddenly stood and wept. Others scampered for cover, as the talladaggers charged forward, their feet continuing to ignite the teledine pebbles as they moved brusquely forward.

To the Arcanian soldiers the site was completely surreal: charging beasts, the road on fire, and snow falling on a warm day in the midst of the Season of Renewal. The world veritably had been turned upside down.

As the Second Army's soldiers scurried for cover, the angry talladaggers, further incited by the men's movement, charged at the moving targets and either crushed them beneath their hairy feet or smashed them aside with their rolling trunks. One man looked up in horror to see two of his fellow soldiers in the grasp of one particularly angry talladagger. The beast shook the two men and then brought its trunks together, crushing their heads and bodies, before dropping their limp lifelessly frames to the ground. Meanwhile their compatriot turned and ran, screaming incoherently, sending a sudden fright through the columns of men who were still marching diligently forward. "What the hell?" one soldier asked as he saw the frightened soldier dart by. He then turned and spotted a fierce talladagger charging directly at him. Before he could utter another word he saw a giant hoof coming straight for his head.

Like the men, the horses were horrified by the charge of the talladaggers. Despite the efforts of their mounts, the horses reared and broke formation. As had been the case at Kalel, the Second Army now appeared to be reduced to a state of total chaos. Its military leaders, more skilled than Pantamanu, managed to hold the main line and to restore order, sometimes by threatening to kill retreating soldiers with their own swords. Faced with this undeniable incentive, the Arcanian soldiers turned and raced back toward the talladaggers, which were now spread over the land, providing less of a threat than during their initial rampant charge. Though the way was now open for a forward assault, Montama was full of surprises and the next one was as deadly as the last.

"FIRE!" Montama ordered in a voice so loud that both armies could clearly hear him.

Several rows of Ka-Why-Tees manning crossbows now stood in formation before the Second Army. The first row of about thirty men stood at attention and then fired their deadly blast of oversized arrows at the approaching army. When their weapons were discharged, they bowed down to their knees, and a second row of Ka-Why-Tees unleashed their deadly weapons with uncanny accuracy. This was followed immediately by a third and then a fourth volley.

The road and the territory surrounding it were now so covered with dead and wounded bodies that the Second Army could barely move forward. Consequently, while the Second Army still vastly outnumbered Montama's motley mercenary forces, it fell into a state of irreparable disarray. Suddenly uncertain whether it should charge or retreat, the officers were as confused as their own soldiers. Some, with swords raised boldly above their heads ordered their men to charge forward, while others called on their men to fall back. The cacophony of orders and counter orders brought the Second Army to a complete halt, unable to move in either direction, forward or backward. They therefore stood dumfounded as the crossbows continued to take their deadly toll.

On horseback, Montama watched the unfolding slaughter, convinced that victory was his. "Sir," one captain shouted as he approached via horseback from the north. "Our scouts have just spotted the Third Army approaching quickly from the east."

"How long before it arrives?" Montama asked, his confidence so veritably buoyed that he was eager to take on and defeat yet another army.

"It will be here in a matter of moments," the officer shouted.

From the east, Pantamanu had done the impossible. He had marched his army steadily through rain and snow and he had done it, not in two or three unit's time, as expected, but in just one unit's time. To move quickly, he had left the bulk of his forces behind. With him was an elite force of illustrious horsemen numbering slightly above three hundred. Though he did not have the entire Third Army at his disposal, his bold move meant that Montama was now trapped. He could not move south for the Second Army still blocked his way, and movement north was impossible because the King's Castle, Mt. Delba, and other fortifications blocked his movement in that direction. He therefore had two options. He could stand and fight, which would almost surely guarantee defeat or he could attempt a dangerous retreat westward across the Fen Swamplands. Furthermore, there was no time to collect the talladaggers and other beasts. They were spread across the nearby countryside, having charged mindlessly forward until they found a field where they could graze.

"I have more bad news," the captain reported perfunctorily. "General Garr has met with unexpected resistance at the King's Castle and has been forced to retreat. His forces will be joining ours, but they have suffered heavy losses. They will be of little use if we face the combined might of Arcania's Second and Third Armies."

Montama sat silently on his mount considering his limited options. It was impossible to stand and fight. But if he retreated his men would be ignominiously hunted down and killed in the nearby swamplands. There had to be a third option. But what was it?

Montama quickly made up his mind. "Take a column of men with torches. We're going to burn the city to the ground."

"Yes sir," the captain responded while saluting.

The move was a gamble, but it was the only option Montama had left in his bag of tricks. He had to hope that despite the heavy rains and snow, that the town's various buildings were dry enough to ignite. Fortunately, the men had brought kerosene with them. They now set to work spreading the kerosene onto as many buildings as possible, even as they heard the charging hooves of the horses of the approaching Third Army.

"They will be upon is in a matter of minutes," one solider remarked as he lit a match to a kerosene laden building. It sparked and burned suddenly, like a candle with a flame rising high in the Arcanian sky, thus providing a strange welcome sign for the oncoming Third Army. Within minutes other buildings were similarly ignited and soon a long line of homes and other structures burned uncontrollably, even as the snow fell with ever increasing intensity. In less than five minutes the great city of Teta was a veritable conflagration; with flames rising ever higher into what was quickly becoming a cold night's sky.

As Montama's men stood watching this incredible sight, General Garr arrived on horseback. "I hear that you have detained the entire Second Army," he said tersely.

"It is the Third Army that concerns me now," Montama admitted.

"And well it should," Garr said as he watched the bellicose fire raging ever higher in the sky. Urgently, he advised, "We must move to the west as quickly as possible or we will be trapped."

Garr then turned and riding spiritedly up the road, ordered his men to move west. "What about the swamps?" one captain asked.

"They will prove an equal impediment to the Arcania army as they do to us, only we shall be in the lead," Garr observed.

"We can move northwest along the border of Lake Chill," Montama shouted over the cacophonous sounds of weather and war. "Though it is treacherous, there is some dry land there between the lake and the swamps."

Several captains then rode along the line ordering the men to grab their equipment and move west with all possible dispatch. As they did so, they abandoned the talladaggers, the oxen and a considerable amount of their supplies. If they were to survive, they must move quickly and live off the land. "We will go to Mount Sendil," Montama declared. "It is filled with thousands of caves and other natural defenses. It will be the perfect place for our forces to regroup."

Garr nodded his ascent with a solitary nod of his head and then shouted, "LET'S MOVE!" Montama also shouted the same order, as his men systematically abandoned the battlefield and began a spirited retreat. With the Third Army charging to the rescue, both Montama and Garr realized that there might not be enough time to escape. "Belicki," Garr cried out, "we need you now." And with these words, the final sequence of the Battle of King's Castle commenced.

Chapter 51
The Battle of the Titans

From ground level the battlefield was a perfect image of unadulterated hell. On the castle's sun deck, Ka-Why-Tee soldiers were now engaged in futile hand-to-hand combat with the Arcanian elite guard. Men struggled mightily to survive, some with multiple wounds, others with a fierce look of determination and an inherent understanding that they had no other alternative than to fight to the death. And death, they knew, would be horrible, painful, and without even the slightest semblance of remorse. It was in fact an act of sublime pointlessness, for the Ka-Why-Tee knew that the castle could not be taken by force, not on this particular unit.

On the ground beneath them, among the rock walls and giant maze configuration, lay the countless bodies of hundreds of men, strewn recklessly along the ground, covered now by the gusting snow squalls. The snow itself was a sickly pink color, a combination of white from the snow and red from the blood of the still mounting corpses. Everywhere, men lay dead from head and chest wounds. Some were decapitated, while other corpses carried the somber and futile stare of resignation on their weary faces, as death freed them from an utterly hellish existence. Along with the dead human bodies, there were also the carcasses of oxen and talladaggers, some still kicking as they fought the inevitable lure of the death throe. Bodies were strewn along the maze route, on the walls above them, as well as in the nearby quicksand and swampy waters.

This was not even close to the beginning of the end of the destruction that war had wrought on Teta, however. At the front gate of the castle, which had been smashed to pieces by talladaggers, lay yet more bodies, as well as the shards of wood and stone from what once had been a finely decorated structure. Other bodies continued to float uneasily in the quicksand, which was now so full of the dead that it no longer could fully consume the bodies of the newly deceased. All along the streets of Teta houses burned with an incendiary ferocity, while still more corpses of men from both armies veritably littered the landscape. Blood, guts, men screaming in pain, begging for a mercy that only would come with death, this was the scene from Teta on this most inauspicious of days.

And yet there was no end in sight to the slaughter. Montama's army still survived, though it had commenced its inevitable retreat west toward Mt. Sendil. Pantamanu's charging soldiers, hungry for battle and eager to redeem their damaged reputations, were unrepentantly eager to add to the number of dead and dying. And while the Second Army had been devastated by the initial attack, it was in the process of regrouping for a second charge. In sum, the desire for war, despite all of is terrible manifestations, was simply inexhaustible. Any sane man would have reflected on this scene and withdrew in horror. Sanity and war are not brothers. One can exist only without the other.

This, then, was the view from the battlefield, as the snows continued to fall, as fire and smoke rose ever higher into the sky, and as thousands of men, some on horseback, others on foot, struggled merely to survive, without any other grander purpose in mind. The view from above was stranger still. As the smoke rose higher, finally consuming the sky, Belicki and Kublatitan watched and listened to the terrible cacophony of war, like deranged puppeteers, dexterously controlling the strings of an army that fought solely for their own selfish benefit. Though the fighting was grueling, we two titans lust for power was entirely undiminished. In fact we both knew that if every single one of these men and beasts were to die on this awful unit, that other armies would have to be raised. The battle would go on until one of us controlled the Oracle.

For Kublatitan and I understood one inescapable reality: in the end only one of us could prevail. Both of us could not control or share the Oracle and its awesome power. As the battle continued unabated we two titans reflected coldly on the essence of war. Interestingly it was I who instinctively understood the very heart of the matter. "Armies are but mere pawns in the hands of giants. In the end, it will be we two titans who will decide the course of history." There was no sadness in this comment, no remorse, no sense that a better way could be found to solve Arcania's succession war, only a cold sense of unrepentant reality.

As I carefully surveyed the battlefield from my perch high in the sky, I finally realized that the war would not end on this unit, no matter what I did.

Kublatitan came to the same conclusion. He commented sadly, "Then there is no hope for peace?"

I adamantly responded, "Tell me one great leader who ever achieved glory by ruling during peacetime? War makes a leader great, not peace."

Kublatitan solemnly agreed, "Then the war must continue."

I found it strange that in the midst of battle I agreed so heartily with my main antagonist on such a basic principle. Surely saner minds could find common ground to reconcile, to share power, but ambition is total and all-consuming. Therefore, quite calmly, I added, "War is inevitable. In fact, if we didn't have any enemies we'd have to invent them."

"Then where from here do we go?" Kublatitan asked, mournful, realizing that there was no alternative to constant, unremitting warfare.

I was never a sentimentalist and therefore I was the first to throw down the gauntlet. "We must face each other in battle. We cannot leave the fighting only to the living and the dying. So let us finish what was begun here long ago, in Teta, at the Miracle at Mt. Delba."

What happened next so startled the men fighting on the ground that the battle spontaneously came to a halt. As men watched with a combination of fascination and horror, the ground convulsed and men, long dead, by the thousands, wreathed and rose from the very bowels of the same earth that ignominiously had consumed them a century ago. Ghostly apparitions now stared out at Montama. General Garr could scarcely believe, "It is General Tampinco's army of Relatania rising from the dead!" And then they saw the most horrific of all images: there on horseback, his body drenched in blood, General Tampinco charged resolutely toward the enemy, his bifurcated nose blowing again in the wind, his golden serrated sword once more held high above his head.

Garr did not delay. He urged his horse to turn and ride as spiritedly as possible from this unholy battlefield. Montama was not far behind him. Meanwhile, Pantamanu looked to the south. "There are thousands of them, crawling out of their graves." Then with shocked recognition he added, "This is the original battle, the Miracle at Mt. Delba, and it is happening all over again."

284

From her third-story window Bellazar too looked out in horror, as men by the thousands pulled themselves up from the dirt, dust, snow and blood, rising to fight yet one more battle. She too recognized their uniforms as Relatanian. "My god," she exclaimed, "they are all here except for the great King Leonata."

Just then, it seemed as if the entire world began to convulse. Bellazar lost her footing and held firm to the window ledge, lest she tumble helplessly to the ground. Outside, Pantamanu also struggled to hold his mount, as the world shook beneath his feet. Montama and Garr continued to gallop westward from the battle scene, but they too saw trees shivering, weaving from side to side, as a powerful energy was released, but not from the earth itself.

Montama looked back. Afterward he wished he had not, for he caught but a glimpse of something so strange that he could never clear it from his mind. It was the sight of King Leonata himself, stepping out of the gigantic stone carving above the castle. He stood at least one hundred feet tall and was made entirely out of solid rock. In his hand he held his sword at the ready, with the Relatanian soldiers now charging relentlessly toward the castle. The long dead king moved into place to confront the army of Relatania.

"It is now my army against your king," I taunted.

"Then let the war continue," Kublatitan shouted, and from our vantage point, high above the capital city of Teta, we watched as King Leonata waved his mighty sword while the army of Relatania attacked. With long slashing movements, the giant stone Leonata struck and killed hundreds of normal sized invaders at a time. They fell quickly, as they had once before, beneath the feet of the great King Leonata. Bellazar turned from the window for she could not bear to watch this hellish sight any longer.

I knew that as before, the army of Relatania was no match for Leonata. Kublatitan understood that this was merely a diversion, meant to provide Montama and General Garr with the necessary opportunity to escape from Teta. Their task now was to regroup, as the proverb goes, to live to fight another unit. For now, we two titans were simply too evenly matched. Our powers were both extraordinary, our ambition unquenchable. The battle for Arcanian would not end, not now, but it was clear that in the end only one of us titans would survive. The unsettled question was, which one of us would prevail?

PART IV

LEGENDS!

Chapter 52
The Flight of Reason

Within a fortnight of the Battle of King's Castle, Arcania was reduced to a state of frightful pandemonium. Throughout the passra citizens heard utterly fantastic tales of how giant aberrational monsters had attacked and subdued Arcania's most powerful armies. And when Relatanian soldiers mysteriously rose from the dead, it was said that a majestic sword wielding King Leonata magically emerged from his mountain perch to defend the embattled city of Teta from yet another marauding barbarian horde. As people listened to these incredible accounts, which frankly needed no embellishment, they responded with shock, horror, and a large measure of disbelief. The reaction in Kekanova, the holy city in eastern Arcania is illustrative of the response throughout the passra.

On a chaotic street corner, across from the holiest of all Arcanian sites, the High Cleric's Palace of Reason, a woman of considerable economic and political eminence addressed an audience of curious bystanders. Dressed in a garish mint green and golden robe, her fiery blue hair braided and tied at the ends with finely decorated, precious white genka shells, the woman eagerly relayed the latest amazingly wild stories from Teta. A crowd spontaneously formed, most wondering if the world that they knew so well had quite suddenly gone horribly and inextricably mad, as the woman nervously exclaimed, "The news from Teta is all bad. If the stories are to be believed they say that King Leonata, tall as a mountain, and forged entirely out of stone, returned to the century-old scene of the Miracle at Mt. Delba, there to once again challenge the barbarian army of Relatania."

Another more modestly dressed woman gasped when she heard this story. "The demons are climbing right out of hell."

The blue haired woman sneered, for the Holy Clerics forbid any discussion of such empirically obtuse concepts as demons or hell. Yet she too realized that her own implausible tales could not be explained with reference to mere reason alone. Then, unexpectedly, another woman interjected, "No, the demons were the soldiers from Relatania and they are said to have crawled out of the very bowels of hell itself. Back from the dead they were: horrible and deformed."

Hearing these inflammatory words, other passersby stopped to listen and sequentially the crowd grew larger and more onerous with each passing minute. Some people reacted with disbelief, clearly doubting the veracity of these wild, inconceivable accounts, each one as preposterous as a well-told fairy tale, with their pictures of goblins and other horrific yet childish images. Many other citizens adamantly insisted that the story was true. "My cousin was a soldier at Teta," one green haired woman declared emphatically, her face contorted in a terrified look of hysterical angst. "It is all true," she declared with an emphatic certainty that belied any rational explanation. "These *were* demons. And when they awakened the entire mountain shook."

"Bull!" was the pejorative response of an orthodox believer of the High Clerics' empirical teachings. "Such things simply cannot and do not exist."

Unperturbed, the green haired woman continued, "And when King Leonata stepped down from the mountain, brave men wept and wise men discarded their sacred texts. Even the High Clerics in Teta were convinced that the world had gone quite dreadfully insane."

"How can you believe such things?" another believer shouted with an angry vehemence. "These stories are fairly preposterous. Do you actually believe that demons walk amongst us? That people come back from the dead?"

"The stories are true," the woman with the relative from Teta shouted as adamantly as her short, four-feet three-inch frame would allow. "The world indeed has turned upside down and frankly there is no escape for any of us."

And so it now seemed to the vast majority of ordinary Arcanians. The world that they had known, a settled and rational one, a geometrically precise and logical world, inexplicably had turned into something so incredible, so entirely unbelievable that mere common sense no longer prevailed. Reason had been swept aside, and in its place there was a sudden and escalating sense of furious panic. A new reign of terror was abruptly filling the void left by the decline of the Centama family's long rule.

"I for one am leaving this god forsaken place," another woman added with a meek, barely perceptible peep.

"And where are you going to go?" the blue haired woman shouted desperately. "To the Land of Taewoka?" At just the mention of this legendary, wraithlike place one man shivered nervously and another woman, stared incredulously, her shoulders heaving violently as she wept. As others moved forward to comfort her, the man who doubted the veracity of these incredible accounts vehemently threw his arms toward the sky and emphatically declared, "You are all insane, to believe in monsters and demons. The High Clerics tell us this is a rational world. Ghosts, monsters, demons, zombies rising from the dead, heaven and hell, these things simply do not exist. You are living in a fantasy world." He then stormed away, angered and more than slightly bewildered at the gullibility of those willingly to believe in the most ridiculous of tales, simply because they were twice told by strangers on a street corner.

The blue haired woman, while she too had her own doubts, showed greater compassion, hugging the trembling lady and then quietly calling on the gods of reason to save our universe from this infernal conflagration of fiends and evil spirits. Finally, one woman said what was on everyone's mind, though no one else was bold enough to express the sentiment. "It is that damnable Oracle that is behind all of this." The trembling woman stared back, thunderstruck that this sole wisp of a woman had the temerity to summon a name that was quickly becoming the most feared moniker in all of Arcania. "The High Clerics have told us the Oracle is evil. They have told us that it must be destroyed!"

"Don't ever mention that thing again," another woman shouted, hesitant to even refer to it as the Oracle.

"What are we to do?" a young man cried out desperately. "The High Clerics must tell us what to do!"

As the people desperately sought to forge reason out of what was obviously a state of pure madness, the solution for many Arcanians was to run, though they had absolutely no idea whatsoever where their final destination would be. Hence, within hours, as the stories spread from one street corner to another, streams of displaced people began to aimlessly wander the land, as the government of Arcania came to a crashing halt, quite obviously incapable of performing even the slightest task or function. Even a politician of Bellazar's extraordinary skill could not repair the public relations damage caused by the twin disasters at Kalel and King's Castle. And the specter of a land, consumed by war, buffeted by gigantic demons, was simply more than reason could explain.

Furthermore, the once vibrant city of Teta lay in abject and still smoldering ruins; a city of enlightenment reduced to ashes. The once august castle grounds were strewn with so many dead bodies that thousands of hungry vultamires could be seen circling in the skies, while others feasted quite heartily on the bodies of once brave men and women. Work crews toiled around the clock trying to bring order to the desperate scene. Before they could remove the dead, they first had to extricate a large number of giant boulders that had fallen from the mountainside when King Leonata's stone caricature stepped out its prodigious intricately engraved, rock-faced monument high above the castle. As Bellazar stood for the first time personally surveying the damage, she was heard on more than one occasion to speak three solemn words, "Oh my God," repeating them endlessly like a sacred chant. For what else could she say? How could reason alone explain this hellish setting?

Pantamanu, who had the satisfaction of having driven the invaders from the city, was also far beyond consolation. He too wept as he watched his treasured city of Teta burn inexorably to the ground. He even wondered, if only for a short time, if he had done the right thing in challenging Retch's legitimate right to the Arcanian throne, but then he vehemently cursed his brother's weakness. Had Retch been stronger none of this would have happened, he concluded, thus conveniently absolving himself of any guilt whatsoever.

Despite his valor in riding swiftly to the city's defense, Madame Bellazar continuously rebuffed his many attempts to meet with her, to express his private condolences, and to seek an amicable solution to the current crisis. Instead of receiving his olive branch, Bellazar angrily told Lord Gulcum, "Tell that bastard brother-in-law of mine that he has no place in the King's Castle." Gulcum, cowed and terrified, preferred discretion to valor and consequently, refused to repeat the message to Pantamanu or anyone else.

Dispirited, and with his self-righteous anger finally boiling over uncontrollably, Pantamanu's troops moved uneasily into the Fen Swamplands, sure that the enemy was still somewhere loose on the land, but without even the slightest clue as to where they might be. "We will hunt them down and destroy them," he said of the remnants of Montama's once mighty army.

That army, wounded and diminished, was a fortnight after the battle still withdrawing steadily northwest, carefully avoiding the Fens Swamplands whenever possible, as it moved toward the safety of the myriad natural cave structures that burrowed deep inside the unbelievable external beauty of Mt. Sendil. Though they had much on their minds, for long distances, neither Montama nor General Garr spoke as much as a single solitary word. For they too were as baffled by the unholy specter of demons rising from the dead while a veritable giant literally stepped out of a great mountain. "You just don't see those sorts of things everyday," one soldier declared with all due understatement.

Other soldiers, terrified beyond imagining, were simply relieved that they were still alive, having somehow survived two reprehensibly hellish battles, both filled with heroic and impossible deeds. None, however, were pleased by the prospect that there were still future battles to be fought in a land where the laws of reason no longer prevailed. "This is not like Relatania," another soldier declared. "There, a soldier must worry *only* about facing mortal men. In this strange land, the face of war is far too terrible to imagine."

What these soldiers did not know was that as the oral history of the dastardly events of Teta were disseminated in concentric circles of stories told and retold throughout the land, their titular leader, Montama, was undergoing a transformational ascendency. Common people, terrified and insecure, desperately needed a new hero, someone they could look up to. Like Teta, the Centama family's reputation lay in ruins. There was now an alternative. Though he led what was popularly believed to be a dangerous barbarian army, a fascinated public was won over by the stories of the valorous deeds of a teenaged neophyte soldier, who had defied all logic by destroying Arcania's First Army, before thoroughly routing its Second force. And while some pundits blamed Montama for the burning of Teta, others quickly came to his defense, sure that the story was yet another cynical attempt by Madame Bellazar to mischievously tarnish the image of Arcania's newest hero.

Montama and his men were entirely unaware of this keen and growing public interest in the man popularly referred to as "the Boy Soldier." As the news of his exploits was further embellished, his reputation soon verged on cult status. Still, his private concerns were more basic. His army needed to find a suitable hiding place at Mt. Sendil so that he could conceal his largely devastated forces, while General Garr and I planned a new strategy to seize the Arcanian crown. Fortuitously, there was little military resistance to Garr's hasty retreat, for although Bellazar and Pantamanu were determined to strike quickly, the reality was that their own armies were in a dysfunctional state of irreparable disarray. Of equal consequence, there were persistent reports that the loyalty of Arcanian forces in western Arcania, under the direction of General Mbanka, could no longer be taken for granted. Bellazar too would have to re-evaluate her own military strategy and at least for the moment, she would reluctantly require the protection of the one man that she trusted even less than Montama, her own despicable brother-in-law, Pantamanu.

And as for us two titans, Kublatitan and I realized that each was the other's match. Consequently, neither yet had the clear advantage over the other. And when we tried to summon the wisdom of the Oracle to determine which one of us would ultimately prevail, we both sensed a still disfunctional, cryptic, convoluted and thoroughly impossible message. It read,

"IN END ONLY ONE OF YOU WILL SURVIVE, AND YET BOTH OF YOU WILL SURVIVE."

Chapter 53
Hontallo Decides

At his rural estate in western Arcania, not far from the resource-rich Kanaween Forest, Lord Tantamount also carefully followed the news from Kalel and Teta. Though he feared greatly for his son's life, he adamantly refused to surrender his long-standing loyalty to the Centama dynasty. "I live for the Centama family," he aggressively informed more than one of his fiefdom's denizens.

Still, while in public he presented a face of immaculate fealty to the Centama family, in private he felt intense periods of conflict, times when he was thoroughly unsure of himself and of his son's purpose in life. Finally, in part to resolve his own self-doubts, Lord Tantamount arranged for a rather unusual and secret conclave, to be held at his own house at the very precise stroke of midnight. Along with his son Hontallo, the other two participants were chosen with care. One would argue on behalf of the Centama family, while the other would state the case for Montama's rebellion.

The choice for an advocate for the Centamas was obvious. Timilty, the head of the Lord's Privy Council, was veritably eager to present the case for what he considered the well-established rules of law and order. The choice to be the devil's advocate, to present the alternative point of view, was quite controversial. In a moment of remorse, Tantamount decided to reach out to the estranged Grandafier the Elder, a wily man whose loyalty to the king was no longer a settled matter. Grandafier was hesitant to comply, afraid that he was being lured into Timilty's ongoing investigation. When the lord assured him that anything he said at the parlay could not be used against him in any subsequent tribunal, Grandafier reluctantly agreed.

The old man had hesitated for a second reason. He loved Lord Tantamount, admired King Benton, supported Montama, and had been entranced by Count Belicki. While he agreed with King Benton's assertion that Montama was under an evil spell, he retained a remarkably resilient faith in the young man's inner decency. Therefore, while he regretted playing any role in prompting Montama to travel to Kankabar or in luring the Arcanian army to its destruction at Grell, Grandafier was still not yet convinced that Montama would not make a very good king indeed, certainly better than the presently available alternatives. As he struggled with King Benton's order to terminate the life of this young man, Grandafier thought the hearing might provide him with a means to sort out his own mind and conscience. For this primary reason then, Grandafier agreed to attend the parlay.

In his private chamber, Grandafier met with Lord Tantamount, Hontallo, and Timilty on the twentieth unit following the Battle of King's Castle. The lord presided behind his immense desk, with Hontallo in his accustomed window seat, while the two barristers sat next to each other and directly before the lord.

Lord Tantamount opened the meeting with these words: "This parlay is not designed to white wash the present situation, but rather to prepare an appropriate response to the current crisis." As usual, Tantamount's council had been stymied in its own attempts to recommend a remedial solution. Though it had debated various iterations of declarations and non-binding resolutions for more than a fortnight, it finally adjourned without reaching a firm decision. Tantamount therefore considered this unusual emergency meeting as the only possible means of crafting a justifiable response to his son's potential acts of treason.

As soon as the meeting commenced, Tantamount realized that the attitudes of his two top advisers had hardened irreconcilably. Casting aside his usual timidity, Timilty charged feverishly into the debate. "While I love your son as if he were my own, I must admit the obvious, that Montama's actions are nothing short of an act of treason."

Lord Tantamount listened, then turned his attention to Grandafier, who sat pensively, his bone white cane leaning by his side. Grandafier swiftly countered, "I will not kill Montama!"

"Excuse me?" Lord Tantamount asked.

With a fierce look in his eyes, Grandafier charged, "Is that not what Timilty proposes? Is that not the penalty for treason?" Turning and staring hard at Timilty, his eyes squinting and his finger raised and aimed directly at the Ka-Why-Tee barrister, Grandafier emphatically declared, "Death is an irreversible verdict." With the assistance of his cane, Grandafier stood, for he realized that his argument would have greater force if he spoke while standing, thus forcing all of the others in the room to physically look up at him. With all eyes rising, Grandafier continued, "And yet this man, who has loved your son as much as I..." Grandafier suddenly pulled out a handkerchief. "I am sorry, I don't know if I can go on."

"Enough of these theatrics," Timilty sneered.

Grandafier had hoped that Timilty would offer such an unemotional response, for he was trying to win over the lord's heart, as well as his mind. Grandafier therefore stared intently at Lord Tantamount's still unexpressive face. "We are talking about Montama as if he is some random boy. We *know* him. We *know* what's in his heart. This boy is not evil, and even if terrible things have been done, I am sure that Montama himself had nothing to do with them."

"And how would you know that?" Timilty asked pointedly.

Wisely, Grandafier did not take the bait. Instead he continued, "And what evidence is there that Montama indeed has committed treason? Let me ask you a basic question," he said as he stared again at his lord. "Is it treason to remove a rotted tree from the ground so that younger, more vibrant plants may proliferate?"

Timilty's eyes narrowed as he stood up from his own nearby chair. "To lead an army, and not just any army, but a foreign barbarian force against the lawful king's family, to burn the capital city to the ground, to violently attack the king's very own private castle, and most hideous of all, to lure thousands of soldiers to their watery deaths at Grell! *These are all acts of treason.* If not, then the word itself has absolutely no meaning whatsoever."

In an attempt to restore decorum, Lord Tantamount asked Timilty and Grandafier to be seated and then spoke his own regretful mind. "I must agree with Timilty. Montama's actions are indeed reprehensible and cannot be forgiven under the passra's laws."

"I most heartily disagree," Grandafier interjected forcefully. "Your son is a great hero in this land. Why? Because the people realize that the time for change has arrived. The Centama family has ruled this land for far too long. There are allegations of corruption, murder, and even now King Benton's daughter-in-law, against all law and tradition, occupies the Arcanian throne."

"And what of King Pondru?" Timilty countered testily.

"That is yet another example of Bellazar's penchant for mass deception," Grandafier responded. "No one has seen King Pondru since he was proclaimed Arcania's monarch. There are many people in Teta, important ones, who believe that Pondru is dead. And if he is, then the Arcanian throne falls naturally to one of two people. Despite her many commendable qualities, and I have always believed she is indeed a brave and intelligent woman, Bellazar is after all a woman, and tradition prohibits her from serving as king. The other heir to the throne is Pantamanu, and I do not need to repeat the gossip that is being whispered even now in various cities around our great passra, that he was not born of Centama blood!"

At the mention of this mere rumor, Timilty's face turned a vivid shade of crimson fury. "It is not a question of their fitness to be king. It is a matter of the law and if Bellazar is not fit then the law will prescribe that Pantamanu, who is the lawful son of King Benton, should be our legitimate king."

Hontallo finally interjected, "But is it not also apparent that Montama already has done great deeds? Do they not count for anything?" At first Hontallo spoke so softly that his words could barely be heard, his head bowed in deference to his father and the other great men in the room. As he cleared his throat, he spoke more forcefully. "Yet I also admit that he clearly has violated Arcanian law, though not its tradition, for succession wars are not unfamiliar to our land. Last night I read through the histories of the last three succession wars and in each one of them various lords sought to take the throne by force through what the historians refer to as the dictum of magna argotta, which means that in a time of war, if there is no incumbent king sitting upon the throne, it is fair game for *anyone* to stake their own claim to the passra's governance."

Timilty smirked. "Are you seriously arguing that Montama's actions are legal?"

"The boy has a point," Grandafier quickly intervened. "He does have a legal claim under magna arogatta."

"The hell with magna arogatta," Timilty responded with an anger that was both surprising and most unbecoming. "Pondru is our king so the principle is not relevant."

Grandafier laughed as he tapped his white cane with the fingers of his right hand. "So your legal defense is that we should all bow down to a dead king?"

"He is our king," Timilty shouted as he again stood, resolutely pointing an accusing finger at Grandafier from his short third arm.

"Calm yourself," Lord Tantamount said. "Both Grandafier and Hontallo have advanced arguments that we cannot ignore. If it is a claim of magna arogatta then Montama has a legitimate claim to the throne. If Pondru is alive, then that claim is null and void. All legal claims rest on Pondru's status, whether he is dead or alive." Tantamount now frowned as he continued. "But let me remind you all that there is another and more important issue at stake here. The Tantamounts have a long held tradition of loyalty to the Centama family. It grieves me to no end that we now find ourselves at war with our friends. And for what reason?"

"I will tell you why," a female voice rang out from the entrance to the lord's chamber. Instantly, all eyes were fixed upon her, though her own eyes were firmly shut. Uncharacteristically, Lord Tantamount was startled by the arrival of his wife, who sat helplessly in a wheel chair with a female nurse as her guide.

"Truellen," Lord Tantamount exclaimed. Such was his surprise that he used his wife's name instead of referring to as Lady Tantamount, a title which tradition required in all public settings.

"You will not scapegoat my son," she declared angrily, her voice strong despite her obviously frail appearance.

"Mother, why have you come here?" Hontallo asked politely, standing up as his mother was escorted into the center of the room. Realizing that they were violating decorum, Grandafier and Timilty also quickly stood, Timilty bowing his head graciously, while Grandafier smiled and raised his white cane in a reverential salute.

After the nurse bowed to her mistress and respectfully withdrew from the room, Montama's mother ardently defended her son with a startling admission. "Montama is destined to be the next King of Arcania. The Oracle itself has declared this to be true. There is no denying his legitimate claim to the throne."

Grandafier smiled ever so slightly, while the other three men stood dumbfounded. Slowly regaining his composure, Timilty asked, "How do you know that?"

When Truellen opened her eyes all four men responded in kind: their mouths dropped visibly open at the sight, not of two ordinary eyeballs, but of two raw pits of burning fire. With pure intensity, Truellen looked directly at her husband. "I have seen it for myself. Before Montama was even born, on a visit to Teta, King Benton did me the great honor of escorting me to the Oracle chamber for a private consultation. There, I felt the presence of many beings, men and women of all ages. I could sense their feelings, their thoughts, and their ideas. They shared their wisdom with me. They told me of three events that would occur. The first two unfolded, just as prophesized. The third, would be the elevation of my second son, still unborn, to the Arcanian throne, before he reached his twenty-first birth cycle."

"Why have you never spoken of this to me?" Lord Tantamount said, apparently hurt that his wife had concealed such important news from him.

"The Oracle warned me to tell no one else, lest the prophecy be broken," she responded without the slightest sign of contrition. "I speak now only because the events the Oracle prophesized are unfolding." Then with reference to her beloved eldest son she added, "And there is more. I am not dying, my son, I am being consumed by the Oracle. I therefore cannot go to Mt. Sendil, where Montama will soon lead a popular rebellion. But Hontallo, you *must* go!"

Hearing these words Hontallo stood before his mother. "I will not oppose my own brother. I can't, no matter what anyone tells me I must do. Whatever he has done, whatever his motivations, whatever his justifications, I am sure there is decency in them. And I *will* stand with my brother."

Grandafier now clumsily fell backward into his seat. "I too will stand with Montama, that is, if someone will help me to my feet." Grandafier had been looking for any excuse to get closer to Montama, though after his recent meeting with King Benton, the old man was still unclear what his role would be: friend or foe? While he outwardly showed strong fealty for Montama and his cause, Grandafier feared Count Belicki's omnipotent evil.

While others aligned themselves with Montama, Timilty's loyalty to the Centama family was undiminished. "This is rubbish," Timilty angrily declared, gesticulating wildly with each of his three arms. "The Oracle is possessed. If we are to listen to it we cast aside all reason and with it our legitimate government that has served this passra well for generations. And what are we to replace it with? An inexperienced youth whose motives we have yet to divine, driven by the clear specter of evil?" The two adversaries' eyes then met. There would be no reconciliation between Timilty and Grandafier.

Though he respected Grandafier, Lord Tantamount sadly concurred with Timilty. "We have been loyal to the Centama family for more than a century. We cannot turn our backs on them now."

Montama's mother glared at her husband, her eyes literally on fire. "Then you turn your back on me, as well" she declared, angrily spitting on the floor after she spoke. Turning her wheel chair she said to her husband, "I will never set my eyes upon you again." Then in a weary voice she directed Hontallo to take her from the room, "for I am tired and in need of rest."

Within the hour her promise to never again set eyes upon her husband was fulfilled. Truellen died quietly, with a look of calm reason upon her face. Her funeral was held, as tradition dictates, within two units time of her death, and her funeral pier was the most glorious that the citizens of the Lord Tantamount's fiefdom ever had laid their eyes upon. For the first and only time in his life, that anyone, including Timilty could remember, Lord Tantamount wept uncontrollably as the fires consumed his wife of almost thirty cycles. Until the very end, that is until their final meeting, the two had never exchanged as much as a single cross word between them. Now he watched with an excruciatingly painful sadness, knowing that he would never have the opportunity to heal this final fatal wound. With Hontallo preparing to leave for Mt. Sendil, he also realized that his family ties were irreparably shattered, his own life and all that he had ever cared about, seemingly in ruins. He had lost his dear wife, both of his sons, and Timilty was investigating Montama's potentially treasonous actions.

Like the Centama family, then, the Tantamount family was broken beyond repair, the lord inconsolable, fearing that he would never again see his two wayward sons, his spirit broken, because he would never again see his dear wife or have just one precious opportunity to piteously beg her for forgiveness. He also realized that he could not show public weakness, so Lord Tantamount went to bed the night after Hontallo's departure for Mt. Sendil, vowing that he would go on with his life as he had before. But the truth is that metaphorically, the spirit too went out of his life the very same unit his beloved Truellen died.

Chapter 54
Mt. Sendil

Nimrod carefully noted all of the words that seemed familiar. Bellazar and Oracle were certainly so; less recognizable but still known were Pantamanu, Montama, and for some odd reason, Taewoka, as in the Land of the Taewokans. Nimrod also sensed that Oracle should be plural, but did not know why. "My memories are not returning as quickly as I had hoped," Nimrod admitted.

"They will return soon enough," Belicki stated with absolute confidence, "for your part in this sordid tale is still forthcoming."

Nimrod was by nature impeccably serene. Innately patient, it continued to listen attentively, thought it was startled and more than a bit confused when Belicki, hardly the humanist, began to describe a site of extraordinary, even otherworldly beauty.

Of all the places in the then known world, none was more beautiful than Mt. Sendil. Rising regally for some 10,000 feet above sea level, the northern peak of its dual summit enclosed by a perpetual halo of pure white snow and clouds so vivid that at times they seemed to be actually quite alive, it was the largest mountain in Arcania, larger even than the mountains bordering the Land of the Taewokans. Mt. Sendil's most striking feature was a waterfall that plummeted for over four thousand feet from the very center of the mountain's southern ridge. The source of the waterfall was a river that ran inside the mountain, which over the centuries had carved out an amazing index of tunnels and caves.

Externally, the entire mountain was covered in a vast array of trees and wild flowers of every imaginable color. To some, from a distance, the mountain itself looked like a giant peaked rainbow, and had this not been a time of war, revelers from throughout the passra most certainly would have traveled to its base to enjoy the mountain's unparalleled, sweet fragrant allure and its incomparable majestic vistas. As such, Mt. Sendil's natural grandeur represented what many people considered to be the one absolutely perfect place in a highly imperfect world. Naturalists therefore honored it with the same reverence as a holy temple.

To Montama the mountain's vast eastern ridge also had a second and more practical advantage. It was the home to a network of thousands of caves that burrowed deep beneath the surface, providing countless miles of territory where an enemy army could hide without fear of detection. As children, Montama and Hontallo had traveled often to Mt. Sendil, scaling its peak, and spending incalculable, delightful time scouting the amazing array of caves that ran deep inside the mountain's core. It was in these very caves that Montama now intended to conceal his army.

Hiding his army in the vast cave network at Mt. Sendil would not only protect them from enemy attack, but also would provide General Garr with much needed time to devise a fresh and innovative military strategy. It helped that despite recent setbacks he was serenely confident. While the two battles had resulted in a temporary stalemate, Garr reasoned that the Centama family's grip was swiftly unraveling. All along the westward road, from the end of the Fens Swampland to the mountain, ordinary people cheered on young Montama, urging him to fight till the bitter end, if necessary. Meanwhile, the Arcania army was nowhere to be seen. These events, along with the mercenary army's own valor, induced the general to proclaim, "Within three intervals I am confident that we will be again prepared to take the offensive against the Centama dynasty. And we will do so, not in the east, but here in western Arcania."

Was Garr's proclamation a show of mere hubris or was it forged by sublime confidence? I doubted it, for he was at his very core a practical man. If he believed that there was no chance at all for victory, he would have abandoned Montama. His continued loyalty was a palpable sign that he truly expected to win.

Montama too had no doubts whatsoever. "We will be victorious," he agreed. Therefore, while the march to Mt. Sendil had not been seamless, the young man's confidence remained undiminished.

Still, there were valid reasons to be concerned. Along the way from Teta one of General Garr's top lieutenants died, along with several men, when they traversed too closely to the Fen Swamplands. When the mercenary army reached the Sendil River, which led northwest to the mountain from which its waters flowed, the army encountered scattered resistance from a small unit of Boguls, though it was unclear which side had fired the first shot. Approximately another three hundred men suffered from dysentery. Garr was forced to leave these brave men behind to die ignominiously in a strange foreign land. Hence, by the time General Garr first laid his eye upon Mt. Sendil's extraordinary multicolored peaks, his army no longer could be defined as an effective fighting force. Without much basic equipment, talladaggers, oxen and now critically short of men, in his most pessimistic periods, Garr believed it might take six intervals or more to regroup.

All depended on Montama and his personal charisma, for he would be the face of this rebellion, its impetus and necessary inspiration. It was he who needed to convince ordinary Arcanians to stand with him against the existing government's tyrannical rule. And in this regard, though they did not yet know the full measure of his growing stature, that process already had commenced. At the very time his army was being decimated by all sorts of ills, Montama was fast becoming the most talked about man in the entire the passra. And if Garr could tap into a reservoir of eager young men just like Montama, then a new army would be born. Though not as well trained as his mercenary army, Garr reasoned that Montama loyalists would be willing to fight to the death, if necessary, for the man they believed should be their king.

Consequently, as the army burrowed deep into Mt. Sendil's cave network, Garr sent regular expeditionary forces out to secure supplies and to encourage nearby citizens to join Montama's cause. It was on one of these expeditions that two men, one quite young, the other extremely old, were identified. Grandafier sat comfortably in a contraption that consisted of a chair on tractor wheels, drawn by a large orange and blue horse named Patulla. As the horse drew him across the landscape, Grandafier made the best of a difficult situation, sipping a green beverage that smelled of whiskey called Toka.

"We must be crazy," Hontallo said, as he rode slowly beside Grandafier's strange mobile contraption. "How will we ever find my brother in such a vast network of caves? It is impossible?"

Before Grandafier could respond several men jumped out of the nearby fauna and with swords drawn, ordered the men to identify themselves. "I believe they have found us," Grandafier said quite calmly as he lifted his glass and saluted the men. Then in a loud and friendly voice he declared, "Take us to your leader." He then turned and smiled at Hontallo and in an equally cavalier voice added, "I do hope they have more Toka. I was beginning to run out."

"Who are you?" one particularly gruff looking bearded man barked.

"I am Hontallo, the brother of Montama, and this is Grandafier the Elder, Montama's closest friend and adviser."

The Oracle

The soldiers looked at each with a rather insipid glare for a few seconds before one of them finally took command of the situation, barking two words, "Follow me."

The soldiers led the small party up the mountain side to a point where Grandafier had to be carried on a handmade stretcher, for he was far too feeble to hike this rugged terrain. Then, the party disappeared behind some particularly beautiful flowers, into the small mouth of a cave which led for several yards into a vast wide open interior room, with soothing water trickling down its walls and light emanating from an opening some three or four hundred feet above.

"Wait here," a soldier ordered. Though he departed, the other soldiers remained, ominously holding their swords at the ready. Minutes later two men, one of them most familiar appeared.

"My god, it is you," Montama exclaimed excitedly. Impulsively, he put his arms around his brother and hugged him tightly. And then, with his head resting on his brother's shoulder, Montama rejoiced, "This is reason enough for a banquet." Out of the corner of his eye Montama spotted Grandafier and was startled by the unexpected presence of his old political mentor. "I see that you have brought with you the wisest man in all of Pellaville," Montama said with a welcoming smile.

"If I were so smart," Grandafier said, charmingly, "I should not be in a dungy cave in the middle of a mountain, surrounded by enemy forces, in the hands of the most notorious enemy in the history of Arcania."

"It is good to see you, too," Montama said, his face still veritably beaming. Montama then turned to General Garr and introduced his two guests.

"I am pleased to meet you," the general said as his black piercing eye glared uneasily at Hontallo, carefully studying the man and his motives.

Hontallo stared back, then nervously responded, "Excuse me for staring," he apologized. "I have heard of your people, but until now I have never seen anyone with three eyes before."

"Actually I only have one eye," Garr snarled. "I lost the other two in battle."

Grandafier lifted a recently refilled glass of Toka in a broad salute. "It is best to have one eye that sees the world well, rather than three eyes which are incapable of seeing anything more than the end of one's nose."

"And what does that mean?" Garr asked, clearly perplexed.

"It means that it is better to be a man of vision, general. And I sense you have it. You saw the potential for greatness in this rough young lad when others saw nothing more than the ennui of a pimply-faced teenager."

Hontallo, nervous and overwhelmed by this strange encounter with a Talacrebe general, added, "Yes and it is remarkable. All that the people talk about is how my dear brother has brought the Centama family to its knees." Hontallo looked admiringly at his brother, "I believe it is safe for me to say that to the people of Arcania you are a great hero."

"And to our father?" Montama asked abruptly, his expressive smile suddenly erased.

Hontallo stood silently for a second. "I have bad news to convey." As he spoke a single tear appeared in the corner of his left eye. "Mother is dead. She was forever loyal to you, even at the very end. As for father, while he loves you dearly he has chosen to follow Timilty's path and to remain loyal to the Centama family."

Montama nodded his head in cheerless resignation. "That is what I expected, though I hoped that mother…" Montama could not finish the thought before tears streamed uncontrollably down his cheeks.

Hontallo could not bare the sight of his brother's emotions. Embarrassed, he looked down at his feet. Then in a whisper he added, words meant only for his brother, "Till the end mother believed that you will be king and she urged me to come to your assistance, in whatever small way that I can."

General Garr now stepped forward and extended his hand in friendship, for he had overheard Hontallo's message. "Your help is most appreciated," he said with an uneven smile on his face.

For the rest of the night the men sat by a campfire and indulged in several local delicacies, as well as copious amounts of Toka. As they did so General Garr grilled his guests for information and they willingly obliged, telling them everything they knew about the state of Arcanian politics and its present fortifications. In this regard, Grandafier was most useful. "You will be a good friend to us," Garr exclaimed. Grandafier smiled, sipped his Toka, and then appreciatively nodded his head. For while Grandafier was now ensconced in the very heart of the enemy territory, he was still not sure which side he favored. King Benton had made a convincing case. Still, if the Centama family was on the verge of collapse, then what alternative to Montama did he really have? Deeply conflicted, Grandafier decided that he would play for time, hoping that his true path eventually would be revealed to him.

As Grandafier thought, he heard Garr declare, "And we need more men."

"That you will have," Hontallo explained. "The people believe you are an agent of change. They will rally around you, if only because they have come to despise Bellazar and Pantamanu."

"Then we must do whatever we can to bring the people to our side," Montama smiled. For now, he was sufficiently content to be in the company of his brother and his very dearest of friends.

Richard Waterman

Datoria 5

RECIPE FOR TOKA

Copious Amounts of Sweet Whiskey
2 Spoons of Pamplona Oil
1 Spoon of Pepper
½ Spoon of Gergel or Green Sugar
2 Minced and Boiled Toka Leaves
1 Fresnoe - Optional

305

Chapter 55
The Council of the Dead

"Legends can be made and legends can be broken," Bellazar responded angrily in response to Kublatitan's grammatically incorrect but otherwise keen assessment that "Montama is become a legend."

"I agree with my Taewokan friend," King Benton interjected. "In just a few intervals Montama has become a significant threat to the Centama dynasty."

Pondru, who utterly abhorred war, solemnly, but not enthusiastically, nodded his head in agreement. He sat next to his father in the ornate library, one of the few rooms in the castle that Retch had completely renovated. Unlike the diplomatic chamber with its hard oak table and benches, the furniture in the library was made of light weight material, including lusciously padded cushions which were strewn along the floor, exceedingly comfortable to sit on, though only Bellazar among the participants, required such human amenities. For all of the other committee members were various Oracle entities. Among them were such notoriety as Kings Benton, Pondru, Telem, and Bamaoha, as well as the great Taewokan teacher Bevell, and several other entities that politely sat around a large glass table, raised not more than two feet off the ground, and located at the center of the room.

Of the entities, only Kublatitan consistently forgot his manners. Pacing nervously about the room as he talked, his spiritual body often merged with furniture as he wandered, thus creating the disconcerting sight of a giant standing in the middle of a glass table, pontificating diligently on the intricacies of Arcanian politics.

To her credit, Bellazar ignored such intrusions into human space. Rather she enjoyed these infrequent meetings with what she humorously referred to as her Council of the Dead. "No one else has ever had such a group of advisers," she proudly declared at one meeting.

Bevell spoke next, for she was particularly concerned with Montama's sudden prominence. A rotund woman, who had lived for more than eight hundred cycles, with black hair and eyes and multicolored red and yellow skin like her mentor Kublatitan, she had been listening unobtrusively to the people, to get a sense of the passra's pulse. This she did with her usual due diligence. "I hide in the shadows. Listen I do to people in all corners of the passra," she reported, as Kublatitan continued to pace the room, often walking through a cushioned chair as he did so. "No matter where I go I hear same thing. Montama is all people can talk of. He is new. He represents change. Yet if asked what change is, all they know about him is that he is the son of a prominent lord."

"He is a blank canvass," Pondru added, picking up on Bevell's point. "No one knows who he is or what he stands for. So, they project their own hopes and aspirations directly onto to him."

"It is like a honeymoon," King Benton pronounced, shaking his head sadly as he spoke. "But it will never last. Such feelings never do."

From the head of the table, Bellazar listened attentively as her advisers continued to speak. "If people don't know who he is, perhaps we can tell them," King Bamaoha interjected, carefully stroking his chin as he spoke.

Bevell agreed. "The people speak of him as if he were a god. Perhaps if they knew he was the devil they would think twice."

"What do you suggest?" Bellazar asked, sitting quite formal and erect, betraying no sense of her own thoughts or emotions.

King Benton had an idea. "Suppose we create a less flattering narrative for the public to consume. There must be many stories about this young man that are less than flattering."

Bevell shook her head signifying disagreement. "I have listened to his family, to his friends, to those who know him the best. He is a child, naive, but certain that he will be king. He has no doubt there. But bad he not be, though bad choices he make now, dangerous ones."

"He must have done something wrong in his life," Telem asked. "He is nineteen. He must have had many wenches by now. Perhaps there is something there that we can exploit."

"He is not sexually active," Bevell added. "It is not on mind so much as power. He wants to be king. That is all he thinks about."

"Perhaps we are going about this the wrong way," Bellazar said in her usual, understated and devious manner. "If people know absolutely nothing about him, why can't we tell them anything we want, whether it's true or not."

"But what do we tell them?" Pondru interjected, clearly uncomfortable with this sudden deceitful turn.

Bellazar smiled with a Cheshire cat's grin. "We are going to create a fiction about this lad and sell it to the public as fact."

"What does that say about our morals?" Pondru asked, his face turning stone cold as he spoke.

Kublatitan's mighty voice rang out from the center of the table. "I agree that we cannot win as is. But if he is flawed, then we must tell the people, but only if he is flawed."

King Bamaoha fervently disagreed. "By the time we find something damaging about this young man it will be too late. I learned too late about Count Belicki's perfidy. And by that time he had nearly stolen the Oracle. We cannot wait to learn of Montama's faults. If we do, by then he will already be our king."

"Of course I do not want him king to be," Kublatitan admitted. "But we are as bad or worse than he if we do such things as that."

"We have no other choice," Bamaoha growled.

"Events are moving too quickly," King Benton agreed. "This boy represents lightening in a bottle."

With the tensions rising, the room fell suddenly quite silent. Bellazar carefully scanned the room, her eyes darting from side to side, waiting for someone to break the silence. Finally, Bamaoha spoke, though this time his voice was quiet and respectful. "Before the Battle at Kalel many of the soldiers of the Third Army were greatly dismayed, even offended, that Pantamanu, a member of the royal family, was seen parading around naked in public."

"Why?" Bellazar asked quizzically. "Don't the soldiers' bathe?"

There were several polite chuckles before King Benton replied, "There is a line of Holy Scripture that reads, "Ambition is naked."'"

Bamaoha nodded his head. "Yes, in my unit there was a tradition, it was considered coarse and inappropriate for any ruler to be seen in a state of nakedness, even to be shirtless in public."

Though deeply embarrassed by the discussion of such a delicate topic in front of a lady, Pondru admitted, "Silly as it may seem, it is a sentiment that still resonates with the public."

"I don't understand," Kublatitan asked. "Montama is not naked. He was dressed when I talk to him."

"Is there a way that we can use this strange belief to our advantage," King Benton asked. "If so, I don't see how."

Bellazar sat quietly contemplating the possibilities for several seconds and then she struck upon a devious idea. "His father is a champion of the

Ka-Why-Tee, the only lord in the passra who treats them as equals, is that not so?"

Benton nodded, "Yes, he considers himself progressive."

"Precisely," Bellazar smiled, her cunning plan now coming into clearer focus. "Lord Tantamount even has a top aide who is a Ka-Why-Tee and it is clear that Montama fights with an integrated army."

"Yes, but of what value is this to us?" Pondru quizzed. "This reflects more on the father than on the son."

Bellazar continued, "But suppose Montama was indeed a Ka-Why-Tee, a bastard child, the union of Lord Tantamount's wife Truellen and his Ka-Why-Tee aide, what's his name, Timilty?"

"I don't understand," Pondru muttered, nervously folding and unfolding his hands, as he stared at Bellazar with a lazar-like intensity.

"I think I see," Kublatitan stated, his voice suggesting remorse and sadness. He then walked toward Bellazar until he stood inside the glass table staring directly at her. "You tell people that Montama was born Ka-Why-Tee. But if so, where third arm be?"

"Precisely," Bellazar smiled as she nodded. "Precisely," she repeated. She now stood up and walked slowly around the table as she spoke. "If he is a bastard child, Lord Tantamount would naturally do everything he could to hide that fact."

"And how would you hide a third arm?" Pondru declared angrily.

"By cutting it off," Bamaoha interjected, nodding his head in appreciation.

"Exactly," Bellazar smiled, as she continued to walk slowly around the table. "And if they cut it off, there would be a noticeable scar upon his chest."

Kublatitan, dejectedly responded, "So he take his shirt off and show everyone he has no scar."

"Only if he does," Bamaoha smiled, "the people will never accept him as king, for that would violate decorum. It would be a sign of unbridled ambition."

Pondru now gave voice to the conundrum. "So either he must let the people think that he is Ka-Why-Tee, which they will never accept, or he must publicly bare himself, in which case the people will perceive him as consumed with unbridled ambition."

Bellazar, having completed her total circumvention of the table, stared directly at Kublatitan as she pronounced, "So you see the legend can be broken." Kublatitan nodded his head and gradually vanished, as did the other Oracle entities, each bit by bit, for their task was completed and a new and devious strategy was set in place.

Chapter 56
Montama's Dilemma

For the next fortnight Bellazar's truth squads fanned out across the vast, chaotic passra, spreading the rumor that Montama was born a Ka-Why-Tee. These truth squads consisted of small groups of Bellazar's most rabid supporters, who traveled not only to Arcania's major population centers, but also through many rural enclaves, such as the central Temannay Village and even Rotay, far to the west, where they provided citizens with handouts containing crude pictures depicting the young Boy Soldier, standing at attention, saluting awkwardly with his third short arm. Rumors also were spread, through pamphlets and verbal communication, that the father of the child was Timilty, Lord Tantamount's Ka-Why-Tee adviser, who it was said, had long carried on an illicit love affair with Montama's mother Truellen. It was further alleged that the Lord was so embarrassed when he discovered his wife's indiscretion that he covered up the scandal by surgically altering his bastard son's appearance. He kept Timilty on as an adviser only because the Ka-Why-Tee otherwise threatened to expose the entire sordid affair. Though absolutely no concrete evidence whatsoever was provided to justify these charges, most people at first tentatively and later wholeheartedly agreed that the rumors and innuendo must be true.

Montama, still in hiding at Mt. Sendil, had neither the time nor the opportunity to respond to these allegations. Bellazar therefore had an open canvass to caricature and redefine her opponent, taking this opportunity to cast him in the most unflattering light imaginable. It was insinuated that this bastard son was not even human, that his Ka-Why-Tee army was led by an invader from the Relatin Empire with three eyes, and that his ultimate goal was not to free Arcania, but to conquer it. In these tales Montama was merely presented as a fop, a mere jester, controlled by an insidiously mad three-eyed general. And as to the evidence of Montama's perfidy, it was repeated that he, not the Centama family, had burned Teta to the ground. And had he not deviously destroyed the King's own First Army? Had he not murdered the great Regent Rendrau, reportedly personally stabbing him in the back while he slept? And was he not now in hiding somewhere in western Arcania, a cowardly act that further illustrated his total lack of character?

To further drive home the point that Montama was unfit to be king, truth squads contrasted his unabashedly sniveling behavior with the exemplary character of Madame Bellazar. When faced with a crisis she stayed with her army and fought with them, while arrows literally flew dangerously close to her head. Strong, bold, and decisive, she was the physical incarnation of the Mother of Arcania, a woman who loved all of her subjects and wept profusely as Teta burned, vowing vengeance against its cowardly attacker until her very last breath. "This will not stand," she was reported to have said following the despicable burning of Teta. "I will hunt down this terrorist, even if I have to search every cave in Mt. Sendil. Teta shall be avenged!"

Since she controlled the message, Bellazar did little to bolster the reputation of her other rival for the throne. Pantamanu's name was seldom mentioned, though it was acknowledged that his arrival at Teta had been fortuitous, especially compared to his demonstrated incompetence at the Valley of Kalel. Mostly though, the truth squads focused their venom at Montama and their praise toward Bellazar, the Mother of all Arcanians. Repeatedly, it was said that Bellazar was worthy to be a king because she alone had sacrificed her beloved husband at Kalel. The contrast between Bellazar and Montama was starkly delineated and the message was therefore obvious to all: Bellazar was worthy of the public's trust, while Montama was nothing shy of a treasonous and highly dangerous monster.

From his headquarters just to the east of Teta, Pantamanu listened, at first with rye amusement and then with growing rage, as the small bands of truth squads reported the events of the Battle of King's Castle. To anyone who would listen, he lamented, "I led my army on a miraculous ride over hostile terrain and forced the mercenaries to retreat, while she sat inside the castle, occasionally glancing out of a third story window. And yet she has the temerity to say that she is the hero of King's Castle."

It took longer for the distorted news to reach Montama's camp. His reaction was equally vitriolic. "No one will believe this crap," he stammered as all of the color drained suddenly from the young man's face.

"They already do," I advised, realizing that words alone can pierce flesh even more affectively than a sword. As a count, I greatly admired Bellazar's tactic, even as I struggled to develop a response. "We must deal with this directly," I told Montama and General Garr.

"How?" General Garr snarled, visibly uncomfortable with the dirty world of politics; for his mind could only conceptualize a military response to any challenge.

"We are not yet ready to fight!" I countered. "Our army is still on the mend."

"Then what is the alternative?" Montama asked, his voice cracking uncertainly, his face contorted with rage.

"We must find a public forum where Montama can deny these charges," I advised. Unlike Garr, I was quite comfortable with political intrigue and actually delighted at the prospect of a strident verbal counterattack.

Montama thought for a second then advised, "The city of Begalow is not far from here, less than a unit's ride, and from our reports, only lightly fortified by forces that do not appear to be loyal to the Centama family." Begalow was a mountain resort town, a place where the wealthy went to exhibit their runaway habit of conspicuous consumption. And though it was remote, people from all over the passra visited it, to enjoy the mountain views or to escape to the beaches of the nearby Draeden Sea. The military considered the city to be of limited strategic value and therefore positioned few forces in the vicinity. Hence, there would be relatively little risk if Montama were to travel to Begalow.

Garr was not enthusiastic, but he reported, "If we travel through the caves we can be in Begalow by tomorrow night. But what do we do when we get there?"

"Like any good politician, we will fight images with images," Montama exclaimed, defiantly.

'You have a plan?" I asked, admiring my young pupil.

"I have an idea," Montama said, his mind churning as he spoke.

I sensed Montama's thoughts and then I added, "I agree. We can yet turn this situation to our advantage."

Chapter 57
The Image Makes the Man

"Let the festivities begin," the Proclamator joyously exclaimed introducing the Festival of Life. The Proclamator was one of the most honored positions in Arcanian society. Selected by a committee of thirteen, representing lords from across the passra, the Proclamator welcomed the festivities honoring the end of the Season of Renewal and the coming awakening of the Season of Life. In ancient times animals and even humans were sacrificed to ensure that the Season of Life's crops would be bountiful. Now all that remained of this macabre ceremony was what was popularly known as the parade of the dead. Despite its ominous name, the parade was celebratory, a mere prelude to a unit replete with music, dancing, frequently bawdy revelry and ribald excesses. Citizens dressed in the most outrageous costumes imaginable. All were designed to emphasize some aspect of death, usually in a humorous manner. The more interesting and elaborate the costume, the more likely one was to be honored by the Proclamator with the highly sought after Calata Award for creativity.

Consequently, at the commencement of the Festival of Life the streets of Begalow were filled with thousands of inebriated citizens from all regions of the passra, dressed in the most garish costumes imaginable, each citizen wandering the streets in search of food, drink, and sundry other exotic pleasures.

Quite naturally, this eclectic gathering of citizens also attracted those who were known to be interested in what the locals called speechification. Various stages were constructed all around the city so that various speechifiers could address the public. Many were charlatans selling goods of dubious merit, while others told ancient tales of human sacrifice and of the dead rising like zombies from their graves. The latter were the more popular of the various speechifiers and the best were invited to return for the next cycle's festival. Consequently, as one trolled the streets of Begalow during the Festival of Life, one heard poetry and music, or saw erotic dancers, steady streams of revelers, and at least one speechifier on virtually every street corner.

The most important speechifiers were invited to address the entire crowd at the Festival Dinner, which was held toward the evening, with the most important speaker addressing the crowd at midnight. Humongous overflowing crowds gathered, boisterously exhibiting their satisfaction or dissatisfaction with each speechifier, often rudely throwing food or some sort of liquid confection onto the platform. And throughout the unit, rumors circulated that a special guest would address the gathering at this evening's Festival Dinner. Some guessed that it was Tazmar, the most famous actor in the passra. Others surmised that it was King Pondru, who,

313

according to one rumor, had been found alive in the depths of the Kanaween Forrest. Because of these rumors an unusually large crowd gathered at the main platform in the center of town as the midnight hour, thirty-o'clock slowly arrived.

They stood, most holding beverages, all dressed in costumes honoring the dead, as the Proclamator completed his traditional opening address. As custom dictated, the Proclamator, dressed entirely in black, declared that the next of Arcania's five seasons, the Season of Life, would be bountiful. Then, instead of beheading a poor innocent animal, as had once been the custom, thousands of carefully painted minor birds were released from rows of tiny cages. The birds soared high into a sky where all three moons now rose, two full and green, one a half moon shrouded in a haze of yellow. The crowd roared its approval as the multi-colored birds flew directly in front of the three moons. "Long live Arcania!" one reveler shouted. Then, in unison the crowd joined in this celebratory chant. "Long Live Arcania!"

It was at this fortuitous moment, as the clock chimed signifying the arrival of the midnight hour, that a lone figure stepped boldly onto the main platform. Dressed in a traditional costume of skull and bones, he removed his ceremonial mask revealing a face that was entirely unfamiliar to the gathered citizens. He waited for the chants to slowly subside and then with a forceful voice declared, "My name is Montama."

With this unexpected declaration, the crowd was suddenly silenced. Except for the citizens of Pellaville, no one had actually seen Montama in person. He was a legend without shape or form. People had heard much about him, but until this very moment they had no real sense that he actually existed. It was as if his marvelous deeds and Bellazar's scurrilous charges were forged out of pure fiction. Now, as an image of pure flesh and blood, he stood before the people of Arcania for the very first time.

"Why have you come here?" a solitary voice cried out angrily from the crowd filled streets.

Montama bowed his head, then looked back at the gathering, before responding, "I have come to Begalow to tell you the truth," a claim that was greeted with sparse applause and considerable laughter.

"Are you not a butcher, a demon?" a woman screamed with a frightening fierceness.

Montama now walked to the edge of the platform and spoke directly to this woman. "I am if you are to believe all of the tall stories that have been told about me by Madame Bellazar." A precious few in the audience chuckled. "But then again she would have you believe that I am a scoundrel, a murderer, and a traitor, and all this before my twentieth birthunit." Again, there was scattered laughter from the crowd. More palpable, however, was the deafeningly silence characteristic of abject skepticism. Men and women, dressed as the dead, stared at young Montama, unsure if this young man was a hero or a villain, or perhaps some unholy combination of the two.

"I will tell you who I am," Montama began again. "I am the son of Lord Tantamount of the fiefdom of Pellaville. Until recently, my life was like yours. I have always honored the rule of our beloved King Benton. My father even rode at King Benton's side in the last great war against the Boguls, and our family has loyally stood by the Centama family for generations. Therefore, I come to this stage above all else as an Arcanian, who loves his passra and its people."

The crowd listened but was not moved by Montama's tepid rhetoric. Standing near the platform in corporeal form, I realized that the young man was floundering. I therefore stepped forward and violently accused him of treason. "You are a false pretender," I shouted venomously. "Worse than that you are a Ka-Why-Tee, less than human. You have no right to rule this passra. What makes you think that you deserve to be king?"

Montama was taken aback by my vitriolic charge, but he was also angered by it. Sensing that the crowd was sympathetic to my allegation, Montama dramatically ripped open his skeletal costume, abruptly baring his chest for all to see. "Do you see any scars upon this chest?" he shouted defiantly. "If I am a Ka-Why-Tee then where are the scars?" He then turned so that all could clearly see his unblemished chest. In a calm, controlled, and strong voice he declared, "If what Bellazar has said is true, then you should be able to see the scalpel's wound upon me." Leaning forward toward the crowd he asked, "Do any of you see a scar?"

A man from the front row leaned forward to get a better look, then turning to others nearby he said in a voice that could be heard by people rows away, "I see nothing. I don't even see any hair." At this last declaration the crowd laughed boisterously.

"You have been told that I am a Ka-Why-Tee," Montama charged. "But that is a lie." Then after a subtle pause he continued, "You have been told that I killed Regent Rendrau while he slept and that too is a lie." His voice now rising he continued, "You have been told that I am a traitor, not a patriot, and that too is a lie."

"Did you burn Teta?" a lone voice shouted from the rear.

"Only the rot of Bellazar's corruption was burned." Montama could sense the crowd moving incrementally in his direction. "I ask you, would I come before you today if even half the tales you have heard were true? Would I dare to show myself in public? Would I dare to bare my chest, lest you think that I have nothing but blind ambition upon my mind?"

A few in the audience began to grumble "no." Montama now leaned forward and startled his audience by entirely removing his shirt. As he did so the gasps were audible. His eyes now burned with a fiery intensity as Montama shouted, "I bare my chest for you today as I also bare my soul. I show you that I have no scars so that you will know who tells the truth and who tells lies. I bare my chest, and yes, I admit that I am ambitious, I do want to be your king. There is no conceit in my claim, no dream of conquest. My only ambition is to eradicate the corruption that lies at the heart of our government. It is Madame Bellazar whose ambition is limitless. It is Pantamanu who seeks to rule with an iron fist. It is their ambition, stripped of all reason that threatens our beloved passra. It is they you need to fear! For they will never tell you that they are ambitious. But I will! I will admit if freely so all can know that I tell the truth!"

At the mention of the last word there were several angry cries from the audience. "Bellazar is a woman. She cannot rule," one woman dressed as a ghost shouted, her fists clenched and her eyes burning with rage.

"Yet that is what she intends," Montama now narrowed his attack. "For even now she rules Arcania, hiding behind our dear beloved Pondru, who has not been seen nor heard from for nearly half a cycle. Where is he? Where is Pondru? Is he alive? If so, then let the people demand that Bellazar produce him? If he is not, then why does this woman desecrate the Arcanian throne?"

Cheers were now heard for the first time, as well as sundry cries of "Where is Pondru?" Slowly the chant grew louder. "Where is Pondru?" Montama looked down and joined in the rhythmic chant. "Where is Pondru? Where is Pondru?"

As the crowd's chant grew louder and louder, people from all over the city heard the commotion. Others streamed forward to the center of the town until it was jammed tightly with citizens, dressed in all sorts of strange traditional celebratory outfits, chanting repeatedly, "Where is Pondru?"

Then when it had reached a crescendo, Montama shouted from his position on the stage, "If Pondru lives I will be his most loyal servant. If he does not then who should be your king? One who lies and deceives the entire passra?" Again he thrust his naked chest forward, "Or one who is willing to show you the truth."

A solitary cry of "Montama" could be heard from amidst the gathering throng. Then others joined in until the cry was a deafening crescendo. "MONTAMA! MONTAMA! MONTAMA!"

I was now invisible to all, but I remained by my protégé's side, admiring Montama's courage and instinctive political acumen. "We have lit a torch tonight," I whispered to him, "and in time it will shine bright."

Chapter 58
The Power of Inspiration

As Hontallo, utterly thunderstruck, nearly dumfounded, listened attentively to the crowd's reaction his first thought was, "*This* is my brother?" And the chants grew ever louder and more fierce, "Montama! Montama! Montama!" And standing defiantly on the stage Montama acknowledged them all.

Then, despite the obvious dangers, his adrenalin soaring, Montama boldly leapt from the raw wood platform and directly into the still gathering crowd. Montama smiled with such an ebullient infectiousness that the people quickly warmed to him. Some reached forward to shake his hand, while others just wanted to touch him. Still others rudely inspected his chest up close to see if they could discover as much as a scalpel's blemish upon it.

Hontallo, dressed meekly as a scarecrow, and standing not more than ten feet from his brother's position, simply could not believe that the people had responded so enthusiastically to his brother. Like the larger audience, Hontallo was sublimely transfixed by the electric energy, the pure outrageous audacity, and the inherent likability of this young man, who though a stranger to most, suddenly seemed like a close and respected friend. It was astonishing to watch this amazing political transformation and Hontallo stood silent, his mouth agape, admiring his younger sibling's cleverness and daring.

The night that he and Grandafier had arrived at Montama's camp they had drank heartily of Toka, while listening to Montama, Garr and others relate the strange, almost unbelievable tales of the Battle of Kalel, with its images of giant talladaggers and soldiers on horseback falling miraculously from the sky. They had heard the tales of the Battle of King's Castle. The stories, though true, had seemed contrived, and Hontallo had not yet sensed any of his brother's prominence. Now, in Begalow, it was on full display for all to see. Montama exhibited a charisma that was utterly infectious, combined with a nascent political skill that was unpolished and yet still extraordinarily powerful. As he watched his brother move effortlessly through the swarm of revelers, making direct eye contact with everyone that he spoke to, carefully listening to them, then reassuring them that "things will be far better when I am king," Hontallo veritably shivered, as his body was touched by the spirit of a powerful and contagious political force. At last, Hontallo was convinced that Montama was for real! He was indeed destined to be king. It was an epiphany that transformed Hontallo from a mere bystander to a rabid and uninhibited supporter.

Further back in the crowd, dressed in a pure white ghostly haze, Grandafier also watched the scene with extraordinary attention and growing concern. From his vantage point the scene was quite different. "This boy has something," he whispered aloud. Grandafier, however, was less certain of the trajectory of this now soaring star. "I have seen this before," Grandafier thought. "A young and talented man, his head filled with dangerous ideas, utterly convinced of the righteousness of his cause, without a single doubt to control his most dangerous impulses, let loose on a gullible populace, one longing for leadership; having not the slightest clue what they need or want." The old man shook his head sadly then thought, "The public never learns. They react the same way, again and again, to every young, fresh face that promises them peace, prosperity, and a new era of hope."

Grandafier looked to his side and saw a woman who just moments earlier fervently doubted Montama's claim that he was not a Ka-Why-Tee. Now as Montama moved past her she tangibly blushed, as she reached out her hand eagerly hoping to simply touch the chest of this young, otherwise unexceptional looking boy. After she did, she turned with unparalleled glee, her smile so broad that you would have thought she had won the lottery.

And on it went, people, all sorts of them, moved forward just to get a glimpse of this half-clothed youth. From everywhere in Begalow, the crowds converged on the center of town, simply to say that they were there, that they had seen Montama, though most, having missed his speech, still did not even know what he looked like.

As he watched, Grandafier could feel his stomach knot. "This is not right," he thought. "The boy is too young to handle this much notoriety. It will surely go to his head." Perhaps some small measure of jealousy guided Grandafier's reaction, for no politician ever likes to be upstaged by another. There was more than simple envy at the heart of his concern. While Hontallo surrendered unreservedly to his brother, Grandafier took a step back, metaphorically speaking, for he was again unsure whether he had done the right thing by encouraging this very young and inexperienced boy to seek the Arcanian throne. "I have put this boy at the head of a violent tempest," Grandafier whispered. "May he have the courage and the strength to survive it."

Chapter 59
Enraged!

"Where is Pondru?" the plain looking hand drawn leaflet read. Beneath these three words was a crudely drawn picture of a man who looked more like an ape than a human, his long grey beard trailing down in front of him. "There are hundreds of these handouts," Lord Gulcum said, "and that was just on one particular street corner. They are everywhere, from Begalow to Teta. They have even been reported on the streets of Kekanova to the east."

"Who is spreading this trash?" Bellazar added, full well knowing the answer to her own angrily stated query.

"We have no idea," Gulcum responded meekly, "though we suspect that those who are in league with the betrayer, Montama are responsible for these lies."

"And what has Commander Pantamanu done to stop this?" Bellazar asked, as her fiery eyes centered directly on poor Lord Gulcum's ever more vulnerable soul.

"The Commander is too busy with the reorganization of his army," Gulcum said.

At these words Bellazar erupted with a volcanic burst of venom. "HIS ARMY? Is Pantamanu suddenly the King of Arcania?" Gulcum bowed his head, for his stomach was churning and as usual his headaches pulsated in successive bursts of excruciating pain. Completely undeterred, Bellazar charged verbally forward. "That disrespectful bastard. He is not even a Centama. What makes him think that he should be king?"

The Oracle

Gulcum was about to respond, tepidly, of course, but Bellazar was not yet quite finished with her vitriolic diatribe. "Now that I finally have given in and invited him here for counsel, he refuses to meet me. Why? Because he contends that I do not represent the legitimate government of Arcania. Can you believe that? *He* speaks of legitimacy! That unfit, unclean bastard, pretends to be a Centama?" As her fist clenched she shouted, "I am more Centama than he will ever be!"

Gulcum did not know what to say, so he remained characteristically silent. Bellazar's next words truly shocked him to his very core. Coldly, menacingly, Bellazar stared directly into Gulcum's beady eyes and said, "I want you to bring Commander Pantamanu to me."

"And how am I to do that?" Gulcum squeaked.

"Drag him here by the scruff of his neck if you have to, just bring him to me." Bellazar's eyes were so wild that Gulcum temporarily feared for her sanity. Never before had he seen her so enraged. Still, as he looked about her chamber, the Anawana Yapyap slept contentedly, as did the Pirene cat, while the sounds of the Tellican jumping fish could be heard distinctly in the background. In these respects everything seemed normal. Yet, the situation in Arcania was far from settled. The once peaceful passra was continuing its swift and steady descent into irreparable chaos.

Bellazar now turned her attention toward a second visitor. "Why can't you do something about this blasted brother-in-law of mine?" From the corner of the room Kublatitan, seeming to cower from Bellazar's rage, responded, "He is protected by King Leonata. There is nothing I can do."

Bellazar stared for a few seconds. "And why can't you just make Montama's army disappear, like you did with General Tampinco's barbarian invaders?"

Kublatitan raised a solitary eyebrow and then with a patience that seemed utterly inexhaustible stated, "You have asked me that many times before. Answer is still the same. Count Belicki protects this young neophyte."

Bellazar demonstratively threw her hands in the air. "So we are left with a stalemate. The Oracle protects each side!" Then turning on Kublatitan with a bitter fury she asked, "If we are all so equally matched, then what is to decide the matter? How can this situation ever be resolved?"

From out of the corner of the room another unexpected voice responded. "There is only one possible solution," King Benton declared emphatically. "An accommodation must be reached between two of the challengers."

Bellazar stared coldly at her former king. "And you are honestly suggesting that I climb into bed with whom?"

Benton did not smile as he said, "There is but one final hope for peace. I myself will arrange a visit between my son and your highness."

Bellazar looked back at Kublatitan who seemed far less enthralled by this proposal, for he feared Pantamanu as much as he did Montama. Bellazar instantly read the Teawoka's mind. When she turned her gaze back toward Benton it was clear that she could think of no other reasonable alternative. "Arrange the meeting," she said curtly. "We will do whatever must be done to end this destructive rebellion." After hearing this decision, Kublatitan and King Benton merely lowered their respective heads and then vanished into thin air.

Chapter 60
Another New King

"The Season of Life will bring only more death," Pantamanu scoffed as he rode astride his new black and silver steed, through the largely deserted streets and charred remains of what was formerly the glorious capital city of Teta. "Where are all the people?" he asked the able Captain Delacroix, who rode closely by his side.

"Most have fled to the countryside. They live either in tent cities or they are constantly on the move," Delacroix responded perfunctorily, staring straight ahead while Pantamanu mournfully surveyed the devastation. He had seen it during the height of the battle of King's Castle, but he had not toiled for long in Teta, for he followed fast on his enemy's trail. When it was apparent that they had moved out of harm's way, he withdrew not to Teta, but to eastern Arcania to begin the tedious but necessary work of piecing together the remnants of the shattered First, Second and Third Armies into one cohesive unit. His arrival in Teta therefore represented something of a rude awakening.

Pantamanu could hardly be described as a sentimentalist, yet as he rode through the winding city streets for the first time since the Battle of King's Castle, he nearly wept as he stared at the few charred timbers, all that remained of a friend's house where he often had played as a child. Next, he spotted the abandoned city square, once the center of much bustling activity, and as he did so, he was again forced to command all of his inner strength simply to fight back the tears. "No matter where I travel," he confessed, speaking softly, "Teta has always been my home. And now it lay in ruins." Then with an infinite sadness he added, "This is what happens when Arcania is left without a king."

"Yes sir," Delacroix stoically agreed.

The reconstituted Army of Eastern Arcania – the combined loyal remnants of the former First, Second and Third Armies - solemnly followed its leader into the heart of Teta, and as it did soldiers wept openly, for they too were emotionally devastated by the site of this once grand capital city. Some of the soldiers anxiously searched for their own homes, only to realize that there was nothing left of them but smoldering cinders.

And then, as he finally arrived at the entrance to the King's Castle, Pantamanu was shocked to see the scattered remnants of wood and stone that once represented the prodigious castle gate. Once finely decorated, it was now shattered beyond recognition. Further evidence of the decay of the Centama family rule was everywhere. With the city nearly abandoned, just two lonely guards protected the entrance to the King's Castle. Stopping to salute these men Pantamanu again had to repress his emotions as he said, "I promise, this city will be made whole and fit for a new king." Though their traditional blue uniforms were now tattered and torn, the guards saluted proudly and carried on their duty, seemingly oblivious to the devastation that lay all around them, so used were they now to the sight of this ruin, for Bellazar's men still had yet to clean much of the fallen debris from the area in front of the castle.

Pantamanu therefore ordered one his captains, "Get as many details as you need and start clearing the city." Then quietly, Commander Pantamanu somberly added, "Make sure to keep a careful accounting of the dead."

Pantamanu now rode in tandem only with Captain Delacroix down the winding path between the cracked and sometimes shattered maze walls. As he did so his mood darkened even further, for the stench of death still lay palpably at every turn. The maze path was still littered with broken arrows, a dented shield, and most memorably of all, the bones and charred flesh from a severed and badly decayed hand still clutching its sword, carrying on its duty even in death. "What shame," Pantamanu gasped as he stopped, staring at the severed hand for several seconds. Now, forced to wipe the tears from his eyes, Pantamanu made a sacred promise, "This man and all of the others who protected this castle will receive a royal funeral." Then defiantly, through tears that now streamed prolifically down his cheeks, he angrily shouted, "Bellazar is responsible for this ruin. I shall have her head for this?"

Bellazar did not hear Pantamanu's primal scream, for she was ensconced in the castle, a place from which she rarely emerged. As was her custom, she had awakened early and commenced a series of meetings with various advisers and supporters. It was now an hour before midunit and she sat on her favorite rocking chair in her personal quarters, parlaying with Lord Chester, one of the few lords who still proclaimed his complete loyalty to the Centama family.

"I am so pleased that you could come," Bellazar smiled warmly, as she handed Lord Chester a cup of orange tea, the sound of fish joyfully jumping from tank to tank tangibly audible in the background. "Do you want sugar with it?" she asked ever so politely.

Before the lord could respond the door to Bellazar's quarters violently sprung open. Pantamanu, his uniform still covered in dust from the long ride to Teta, stood defiantly glaring at his rival. "I want a word with you," he barked, his anger so apparent that Lord Chester summarily dropped his cup of tea on the floor. "My goodness," he muttered.

"I will get you another," Bellazar stated calmly.

"Don't bother," Pantamanu said in a voice that invited no compromise.

Smiling nervously, Lord Chester bowed politely. "I think it best that I withdraw," he said as he scampered quickly and as unobtrusively as possible past Pantamanu, who stood heroically erect, veritably dwarfing the lord, his shoulders broad, and his chest pounding with a righteous fury.

"It is such a pleasure to see you," Bellazar said with a vacuous smile that barely hid her heart-felt contempt.

Pantamanu aggressively stepped forward into the room and slammed the door behind him. "I have just seen Teta or what little remains of it." Pantamanu's eyes were fixed on Bellazar's and his anger and hatred could literally be felt, like a harsh stroke from a violent hand.

"It will be rebuilt," Bellazar responded calmly before sipping her steaming hot tea.

"Yes it will," Pantamanu declared, as he stepped forward menacingly. "It will be my first act as Arcania's new king." Physically he hovered over his sister-in-law, yet Bellazar remained calm, tranquilly sipping her tea. Sensing her reserve, Pantamanu again moved forward, this time standing so close to her that his face could feel the steam rising from Bellazar's cup.

Bellazar ignored his overtly masculine demonstration and calmly took yet another sip and then in a measured tone, with just a hint of sarcasm responded, "No bastard will ever sit upon the Arcanian throne."

Hearing these words, Pantamanu angrily swatted the teacup from her hand and then in a powerful voice shouted, "Is it your intention to accuse everyone who opposes you of being a bastard?"

Bellazar did not respond. Her face remained entirely serene, as she daintily reached over the side table and poured herself another cup of tea. Then, with immaculate restraint, she peered at Pantamanu, and with eyes that were totally free from fear, she continued, "You are not of Centama family blood. Your father was Lord Clamarin." Bellazar smiled incongruously as she continued, "You were told that your mother died from various complications following the pregnancy. That is partially true, I guess." Then with a sadistic smile she added, "Your father had her beheaded and Lord Clamarin too. He would have cut off your tiny head too, except Lord Valmar made a rather earnest plea to save your innocent life."

"Aren't you ever capable of telling the truth," Pantamanu barked. "I suppose next you will accuse me of being a Ka-Why-Tee and force me to bare my chest in front of all of the revelers at Begalow."

"This is no deception," Bellazar stated confidently.

"And where is your proof?" Pantamanu scoffed, again rudely slapping the tea from her hand.

Sedately, Bellazar reached for a third cup of tea from the side table. "Your mother's name was Grizelda. You never met your mother, did you?"

"I have only seen portraits of her," he said quietly, without remorse.

"Would you like to meet her?" Bellazar asked as casually as if she were offering Pantamanu a cup of tea mixed with honey.

"And how am I to do that?" he asked, clearly irritated.

Without drama, Bellazar told Pantamanu to come with her. Dubious and yet curious, Pantamanu followed Bellazar down the long hall past his own private chamber, then down a long winding staircase to the first floor.

"Where are we going?" he asked quizzically.

"To the King's Auditorium," she said without emotion. "You enjoy a good show, don't you?"

Pantamanu said nothing, but followed a step or so behind Madame Bellazar. Finally the two of them stood on the stage of the giant auditorium, where various artists, mostly of the vocal variety, had entertained the king. Pantamanu surveyed the room before stating, "It appears that you have forgotten to inform the entertainers. There is nobody here."

"That is not technically correct," Bellazar responded with an impish delight. The two walked carefully to the center of the stage. Once there, Bellazar turned toward her brother-in-law and asked, "Have you ever heard of the Taewokan Death Shield?"

Pantamanu paused for a second, and then responded, "You are mocking me."

"Perhaps," Bellazar added playfully. "I believe you saw a herd of angry talladaggers streaming down from the skies, did you not?" She asked this question and did not wait for an answer. "Count Belicki used the death shield to hide an army in the sky, but that is not its primary purpose. It was created by Kublatitan." Bellazar suddenly turned and with a frightfully devious smile she declared, "The Taewokans are such an incredible people. They have a power that we simply do not understand. I believe they call it telekinesis. Its some sort of enhanced *mental power.*"

Pantamanu stood silently, knowing that there was a point to all of this, still curious, but on his guard, lest this be a trap of some sort. He thought, "What is she up to?"

Bellazar continued, nonplussed, sublimely confident. "We see death as the end of life. The Taewokans believe that when the body dies, the spirit or what we call the galgamata or what they call the LaKotey lives on. It exists in what Kublatitan calls an entirely different universe from the one that we inhabit."

Pantamanu's patience had reached its limit. "Thank you for this fascinating lecture, but what the hell does all of his have to do with my lineage?"

Bellazar chuckled quite fiercely. "Why Pantamanu, it has everything to do with your bastard upbringing. For right here in this room there is another universe, what Kublatitan calls the Taewokan Death Shield."

Pantamanu looked all around. "As usual I see absolutely nothing. You are wasting my time."

Then, with a flirtatious look Bellazar asked, "Would you like to see how the barbarians managed to hide an entire army?"

Pantamanu stared into Bellazar's twinkling eyes. Facetiously he responded, "Of course. Why would I deny you such obvious pleasure?"

The Oracle

Bellazar smiled broadly, then spread her arms apart like wings eager for flight. "Clear your mind and let the spirit take you by the hand," she said. Then with a sudden flash of blinding white light she instantaneously and simply vanished. Startled, Pantamanu looked suddenly all around the now completely vacant stage. As he did, from above, he heard the faint peep of a woman's voice. When he looked up he was surprised to see Bellazar's head peering down at him from mid air. "It is really quite comfortable in here. Why don't you come up and join me."

With these words, a second bright bolt of light carried Pantamanu to a strange uninhabited universe. Without realizing it, Pantamanu stood now, not as mere flesh and blood, but rather as an abstraction, neither alive nor dead, somehow existing in an entirely different realm of time and space. When Pantamanu moved his hand to touch his face, his hand moved effortlessly through a swirling gaseous matter that he could not feel, but which he plainly could see. "What is this place?" he asked, perplexed and terribly unsettled, though he carefully masked his fear behind a steady, intense glare.

"We are inside the Taewokan Death Shield," Bellazar smiled contentedly. "As you can see the space in here is infinite. That means that you could hide an entire army here, if you wanted to. Or," she said playfully, "you can converse with the dead."

As she spoke this last word Pantamanu saw a ghostly figure, more of light than of the physical body appear in the distance. He stared and in a second he recognized this lone figure. It was his brother, Rendrau. His face was placid. He appeared precisely as he did at the moment he had died, with a sharp chest wound and dark red blood stains upon his clothes.

"Are you surprised to see me?" Rendrau asked, his voice more firm and confident than it had ever been during his lifetime.

"I am astonished," Pantamanu remarked, his gaze entirely fixed on his brother's bloody form.

And then just as quickly as Rendrau had appeared he too vanished, leaving the entire universe again empty, except for Bellazar. Then as Pantamanu saw a haze of swirling white clouds, he heard a strange echoing sound, repeating four notes of some strange form and variety. The sounds were coming entirely from inside Pantamanu's head. "I am bewitched," he said as he stared at Bellazar.

Before Bellazar could react the body of a woman without a head appeared from out of the midst. As Pantamanu stared intently, a very pretty

326

head floated down from above until it resided no more than six inches from the woman's jewel draped neck. Dressed in a long flowing yellow robe, the woman smiled angelically as she exclaimed, "Hello, my son."

"What is this?" Pantamanu said as he fell back terrified. "You expect me to believe that this headless sorcerer is my mother?"

"She is as real as you or me," Bellazar said calmly. "Isn't she Lord Valmar?"

"She is indeed," Lord Valmar proclaimed, though there was no sign of him yet. Pantamanu nervously scanned the empty space, desperately searching for any sign of the man he personally had strangled with his very own powerful bare hands. "I am here," Valmar declared, stepping from a swirl of gaseous matter as he spoke. As he did so, Pantamanu could clearly see that Valmar's neck was twisted and broken, as he had left it. Valmar then admitted, "At least this time Bellazar speaks the truth."

Rattled, as he never had been in battle, Pantamanu stood defiant and clearly wounded. "This is not real," he whispered, the sweat now apparent on his creased brow.

"I loved your father, but I was taken in by Lord Clamarin's bodily charms," Grizelda confessed. "I suppose we both deserved our ultimate fate, but you did not my son. You were entirely innocent."

Valmar spoke next. "Your father realized that it was his indifference that drove his beloved Grizelda into another man's arms. I merely had to appeal to his generous nature, to remind him that it was no fault of yours, in order to spare your life. And though you were not technically his child, he soon came to love you as if you were his own son, making absolutely no distinction whatsoever between you and his other three boys."

Pantamanu now took a tentative step toward Lord Valmar. As he did so he could not take his eyes off of the lord's twisted and broken neck. Then Pantamanu added, "If what you say is true, I want to hear it from my own father's lips."

Bellazar stood placidly by, seemingly ignoring the latest tempest that she had set in motion. She did not even react when King Benton suddenly materialized next to Pantamanu. "My dearest Pantamanu," he said meekly, "I never wanted you to know about…" He stopped, unable to continue. Benton's chest heaved with palpable emotion as he continued, "I love you, my son. Please forgive our sins."

"So it is true," Pantamanu pleaded, his eyes now stained with tears.

"It is," the former king said sadly, his head drooping down in shame.

The Oracle

Grizelda now moved toward her son, her head still floating aimlessly above her body. "It is all my fault. I set our family on a course toward ruin. My deeds cursed it and now look at what has come to pass. We have lost Retch, Pondru and Rendrau, and now I bring unrepentant shame on my dear sweet Pantamanu."

Pantamanu looked not into his mother's eyes, but rather at her severed neck. "I," he stuttered, "am at a loss for words."

Bellazar now eagerly rejoined the conversation. "I have three words for you. They are three words that will ring out from across the passra if you are ever to be king. They will call you *the Bastard King*!"

Bellazar stared at Pantamanu, his eyes irritated and red, and his gaze suddenly quite uncertain. She expected uncontrollable rage, and it resounded, but from a most unexpected direction. "That is enough!" King Benton shouted, his nostrils flaring angrily, his face burning with anger.

Bellazar now turned toward the irate king. "This secret has laid dormant for far too long. There are those who know of it, very important people. If Pantamanu is king they surely will challenge his authority, whether I say a word publicly about it or not."

"And what of it?" Pantamanu declared angrily and with considerable defiance.

"There will be a scandal," Lord Valmar confessed, as he stood in isolation.

"So let there be a scandal," King Benton announced. "I have made Pantamanu my son by my deeds and by my love. Whether he carries my blood or not, I sense that he will be a great king."

It was now Bellazar's turn to be on the defensive. "Sir," she interjected in an uncharacteristically meek fashion. "The people will never accept Pantamanu as their king. He is not a Centama!"

"Then damn the people," King Benton shouted as he moved forward, his body now literally inhabiting the same space as Bellazar, so that she could feel the bitter iciness of his presence. As she shivered he resoundingly declared, "Tomorrow there will be a new king. All will bow down to King Pantamanu!"

Chapter 61
A Proposal

Incredulously, Bellazar stood staring directly at King Benton, her body shivering with a ferocious rage she could scarcely contain. Her green eyes burned with an untamed fury and even her fiery red hair seemed to stand on end, so inconceivably angered was she by King Benton's seemingly insane proposal.

"You cannot be serious, she snapped, her right hand tenaciously clenching her blue dress, squeezing it hard lest she completely lose her temper in the presence of her former king. "He is not qualified to be king. He is pompous, vacuous, egotistical, unreliable, and…."

King Benton interrupted, lest Bellazar list every negative characterization of the male ego. "I am aware of Pantamanu's shortcomings, more so than you know. Yet he must be king. This damnable succession war must be settled and you above all others must be willing to accept it for the good of the passra."

Once Bellazar had dug in her heels it was almost impossible to change her mind. Her opinion was now unalterable. "I will never accept this bastard as my king."

Pantamanu had never seen Bellazar in such an unfettered rage and he was much amused by it. "Then like my dear mother Grizelda, I suggest that you not become too attached to your head."

Bellazar did not even acknowledge Pantamanu's comment. Instead, she continued to plead her case directly with King Benton. "He will bring ruin to the passra. He is not fit to be king."

Just when it seemed that King Benton's view would prevail another entity from the Oracle decided to join the debate. King Leonata had watched Pantamanu at close range for several intervals and while he saw much to admire in the young man, he was not yet sufficiently impressed by the young prince's cavalier comportment to suddenly surrender to his unpredictable judgment.

His voice was heard as he materialized to the left of King Benton. "I agree that Pantamanu must be king to resolve this destructive conflict. But I also agree with Bellazar, that he yet lacks the necessary fortitude to be an effective ruler."

Pantamanu now felt the need to defend his own honor. "And if not me then who else will rule Arcania? This wench? While she ruled in this castle as the regent's wife half of the Arcanian military was destroyed and from the reports that I receive from the countryside, I hear that our rival Montama has never been more popular with the common people. Wherever people go they openly chant, 'Where is Pondru?' Bellazar has left us precariously situated, with a dead man on our throne. Meanwhile, Teta lay in abject ruins, and yet we are to turn the passra over to her care?" Now emphatically, Pantamanu declared, "I am the only one capable of restoring order. I am the only one who can destroy this pubescent pretender. And I am the only one who can retain the Centama family name."

Leonata listened but was not convinced by Pantamanu's argument. He continued to perceive the young man as talented, skillful, yet concomitantly inexperienced and ultimately dangerous. More importantly, he objected to Pantamanu's moral character. "My greatest fear is that if you are king you will turn this castle into your own personal harem, with every conceivable sort of sexual perversion accepted, nay actively encouraged. The moral degeneracy will be coupled with a lust for military glory so blind that you will lead this passra into a war with Relatania that it cannot hope to win." Now turning to King Benton Leonata asked, "Is that the future you so desire?"

King Benton shook his head mournfully. "Pantamanu has his faults, there is no doubt about it. But he is young. He will grow."

Leonata, who had been a champion and protector of the young prince, agreed, "Yes, he has the potential to be great. But only in time."

It was clear that the entities from the Oracle were deeply divided in their loyalties. Pantamanu and Bellazar now watched as mere spectators, as another entity continued the debate. "He will destroy all that is holy, all that Arcanians hold dear." Kublatitan proclaimed. "Too much ambition has he."

King Benton was suddenly angered beyond all reason. Turning his face toward his son he declared, "This bickering will get us no where."

Bellazar now saw an opportunity to advance her more reasonable approach. "It demonstrates that there is no reason to move in haste, to make a decision that cannot be undone, a choice that once made may be ruinous to us all."

Again, Pantamanu responded with sarcasm. "Especially to you, my dear, and your pretty little head."

King Benton was inconsolably angry. "We must act now or the passra will surely be destroyed!" he vehemently exclaimed.

The Taewokan Death Shield was now replete with a growing number of people, some Oracle entities, others among the curious dead who had materialized to view this unworldly spectacle. Grizelda still stood silently, her head bobbing uneasily above her body. Lord Valmar was clearly distressed, his neck still gnarled and distorted. Kings Benton and Leonata seemed on the verge of blows, if such a thing was possible from mere energy-based entities. And yet I, Count Belicki decided to wade into this toxic mix with my own sort of venomous wisdom. "I can tell you where we are marching," I said calmly, my wrinkled green face smiling with its combustible mixture of wisdom, passion and poison. "Toward an irreconcilable ruin." As I spoke, the outline of my body glowed in shades of yellow and gold. All eyes were suddenly upon me, for they considered me to be a vile enemy. Unperturbed, I continued in a measured tone. "A young man is hiding in a cave, somewhere in Mt. Sendil, and he will soon rise again with a new and mightier army at his side. This time it will be a popular revolution and he will strike down and destroy your fractured Arcanian military. He will reduce the Centama family to a mere footnote in history, a name that school children everywhere will be forced to memorize for their mid-semester exams, only to quickly forget it once the exam is completed. *That* will be the legacy of the Centama family."

King Benton stared at me. He did not trust me. He nonetheless realized that I had spoken the truth. "And what do you propose, Count Belicki?"

I smiled, insidiously, as I nodded my head in formal appreciation of King Benton's recognition. My response stunned everyone. "Why a happy wedding, of course."

Bellazar frantically turned toward King Benton. "Who is this?"

King Benton performed the pleasantries. "This is Count Belicki." At the mention of my name Bellazar's eyes opened wide. Defiantly, King Benton asked, "Which side are you on now Count Belicki?" All waited attentively for an answer.

"Why the winning side, of course, whatever that may be," I joyfully intoned, for I was willing to accept any deal that would advance my objectives, and I saw that a union of these two enemies might serve me quite well. I would be able to use their discord to play one against the other, to maneuver myself ever closer to the center of power, to prevail even if by some chance Montama did not.

"And which is the winning side?" Bellazar asked, now looking at my decrepit elderly form, which slithered ever so deliberately toward her.

"Both of you," I smiled, always the model of decorum. "That is, if you are willing to join forces."

"A political accommodation?" Bellazar asked, seeking greater clarity.

"I was thinking more along the lines of a more formal arrangement. A wedding, a spectacle unlike anything that Arcania has ever seen. Think of it. Poor Bellazar, crushed by the death of her husband at the Battle of the Valley of Kalel, loving only her passra and her dear brother-in-law, whose wife died violently from the cholera that now threatens our land."

"My wife is not dead," Pantamanu corrected him.

"A detail that can be easily rectified," I responded with an ingratiating smile.

"Are you completely insane?" Bellazar asked without even the slightest hint of facetiousness.

"Quite possibly," I admitted, with my usual sly humor. "I will leave that judgment for the experts. But I do know a thing or two about power, how to get it and how to keep it. And if you want power you have to make concessions."

"And what if we don't?" Bellazar asked curtly.

I now bowed formally before the lady. "I can assure you that Montama is a very formidable foe. Alone you may be able to defeat him, but together he will crumble."

"And what do you get if he is defeated?" King Benton asked skeptically.

I now smiled as I looked at King Benton. "Everything that I have ever wanted and more."

"That is what I am afraid of," King Benton snarled.

"Then perhaps you prefer the alternative?" I responded amicably. "You will look lovely as Montama's concubine," I said turning to Bellazar. Then with a glimpse at Pantamanu I added, "And your head will look even more impressive as it rests on a pole outside the castle gate. I am sure that wanderers will come from miles away just to catch a glimpse of it."

Pantamanu responded sarcastically, not sure whether he should take me seriously or not. Nodding toward King Leonata he stated, "And I am to trade my wild orgies for this scrawny wench. Perhaps I prefer to have my head on a stick."

I nodded again, for false politeness was second nature to me. "Do you?" I asked ever so politely. "Well then make up your mind quickly. For I sense that Montama's army will soon be on the move, fortified and stronger than ever."

King Benton thought for a few seconds, as everyone fell suddenly silent, all far too exhausted to add yet another contentious opinion to the mix. Benton did not trust me even though he realized that my argument was reasonable. If Bellazar did not have an incentive she would either represent a palpable enemy to the Centama family or, more likely, she would be but the latest corpse in the ongoing succession war. Truth be told, King Benton had greater love for his sister-in-law than for his own son. Deep in his heart he believed that she would be the better leader. He also realized that the passra was not yet ready to be led by a woman. Furthermore, her image had been irreparably tarnished by the events of the past few intervals. Therefore, conceding defeat rather than proclaiming a happy occasion, the elderly king stated, "At the soonest possible date there will be a wedding." But at this proclamation Pantamanu's jaw dropped, and Bellazar's shoulder's sagged. "It will be followed the very next unit by the coronation of two co-equal monarchs."

Bellazar and Pantamanu would have argued the point right then and there, but so spent was their anger that they merely nodded their heads, warily glancing at each other, not as lovers, but as fierce irreconcilable enemies, readying themselves for the next round in a continuing battle of wits and brawn.

Chapter 62
Politics

"I am confused," Nimrod confessed. "Why would you join forces with Bellazar and Pantamanu?"

Belicki smiled, a sure sign of his devious nature. "Because I was intent on being on the winning side, that is no matter who was victorious! If Montama won, then I would control this neophyte. If he were to lose, always a possibility, then I would be able to play Bellazar and Pantamanu against each other, moving ever closer to complete mastery of the Oracle and its ultimate power."

"So you had no scruples?" Nimrod asked innocently.

"None whatsoever," Belicki cackled delightedly. "What good are scruples when one seeks only absolute power?"

Nimrod did not disagree with Belicki's sentiment. He carefully noted it, then listened as Belicki continued to relate the seemingly ever-stranger history of the Arcanian succession war.

"Politics is a strange business," General Garr admitted as he lay comfortably relaxing on the ground under the multi-colored branches of the

The Oracle

Acck tree, one of Arcania's most unusual sights. Unlike other trees, the Acck tree's leaves and branches spread out from its base, while its trunk rose high in the sky like a solitary finger, pointing directly toward the heavens. As a result, it was generally not an ideal spot for one who wished to avoid the late afternoon sun, for its branches hung too close to the ground. General Garr and his usual companion, Grandafier the Elder, had discovered a particularly amenable location where the branches were just high enough that they shielded the sun's rays while allowing the cool eastern breeze to seep pleasantly through the exposed leaves. The two men regularly came to this location for an afternoon nap, topped off with a discourse, usually initiated by the garrulous Grandafier, about some subject or other than was close to his heart. On this unit, as they lay on the ground next to each other, enjoying the great outdoors, the subject was politics. General Garr was quick to concede, "I am not a politician and to be honest I really don't understand politics."

Grandafier was delighted to provide instruction on a subject that he had studied throughout his entire life. "Politics is easy to understand, General Garr. Whenever a politician says he is telling you the truth, he is not. When he says you can trust him, you can't. Whenever a politician accuses their opponent of something vile you can be sure that he is guilty of something much worse. And when he promises you a better tomorrow, it is best to duck."

"That is a very cynical way of thinking about the world," Garr noted, as he lay relaxing, sometimes looking at Grandafier as he spoke, sometimes closing his eyes and simply enjoying the cool breeze.

"Not at all," Grandafier responded cheerfully. "I am merely responding to the reality of the political situation, just as you must honestly appraise your army's chances when you march into battle."

Garr slowly nodded his head as he considered Grandafier's argument. "If what you say is true then does it matter who rules?"

Grandafier chuckled with his usual avuncular charm. "Of course it does. That is the ultimate irony. If no politician can be trusted you had better find someone you can properly keep your eye on."

"And can you can keep your eye on young Montama?" the general asked in a more pointed manner.

"Ah, we must keep a very close eye on our dear young protégé!" Grandafier admitted. "He is full of verve and vigor, young, unspoiled, bright eyed and therefore very innocent indeed. He still has the naïve notion that he can do good. He doesn't yet understand just how evil a place this world can be. He is a veritable babe in the political woods, with considerable natural talent. He desperately needs advisers like you and me."

"And we need him?" Garr said as his head lay comfortably on a particularly soft patch of leaves.

"Most definitely," Grandafier said, a bit more seriously. "We are the proverbial hangers on to greatness. We can do nothing of consequence on our own, but if we are allied with someone who has power, then we can do much behind the scenes to alter the course of human events."

"I have my own ambitions," Garr conceded without apology.

Grandafier turned his head and looked directly at Garr. "Don't we all, my dear friend," he said with a broad smile.

Garr looked surprisingly impish as he stated, "But since you are a politician, and all politicians lie, how can I believe anything that you have just said?"

With immense pride Grandafier coolly responded, "My general, you are finally beginning to understand the truth."

Realizing that they had been at rest now for far too long, the two men stood up and dusted themselves off, before commencing the short walk back to their secure cave, accompanied at a discreet distance by several guards who provided constant protection. It was on their way back to the cave that General Garr saw a small rodent pass before him. "What the hell is that?" he asked.

The small fury creature was no more than an inch or two long, with white spots adorning its green fur coat, its yellow eyes prominent on both of its two protruding heads. Grandafier smiled, "Ah it is a sign that the Season of Life has arrived."

"But what is it?" Garr again commanded.

Grandafier stopped and looking at his friend said, "That is a two-headed delbot."

Garr seemed startled. "We have animals that look like this but…"

Grandafier patted his friend gently on his shoulder. "But I bet you have never seen one with two heads?"

Garr eagerly nodded his head. "No. Where I come from they have three heads."

The furry figure scampered along the ground before disappearing into the bush. "I am sure that you will see other strange sights. This must seem like a very unusual land to you," Grandafier said playfully.

The Oracle

General Garr did not disagree as the two men continued to walk toward the cave where Hontallo had just returned from a brief journey to the villages south of Mt. Sendil. Despite the danger, Hontallo considered it important to "return to civilization," as he called it, and mill about with the common people. In this way he could get a sense of what the people were thinking. He had made three such trips since Montama's dramatic visit to Begalow and each time he returned with important news about the passra.

Grandafier was delighted to see Hontallo and rushed toward him as quickly as he could waddle, his omnipresent bone-white cane aiding every single tenuous step. He then rested his hand on Hontallo's right shoulder and, as he took a deep breath, he asked with a pleasant smile, "What news do you bring us?"

"Yes, what news is there?" Montama said as he approached from inside the cave, holding a bowl of steaming hot soup in his hand. The four men now found a place where they could sit, eat, and discuss the latest intelligence.

"I have heard a disturbing rumor," Hontallo commenced, with some agitation and concern.

Grandafier interjected, "I don't take much stock in rumors. They are of absolutely no value unless you are the one who is spreading them."

"This one is repeated by every man and woman I meet," Hontallo said earnestly. "I am told that there was a savage attack on one of the small villages some ten miles or so from the base of the mountain. Apparently, several families were killed by a group of men who wore hoods to hide their identity. All of the people that were killed were Boguls."

Garr listened pensively and quickly dismissed the rumor. "Lots of terrible things happen during wartime," he confessed. "I am sure Madame Bellazar will lay the blame for it on Montama."

"The people already blame her for it," Hontallo continued.

Garr thought for a second, and then with a nervous glance toward Grandafier, the general responded, "Well then, perhaps the rumors are true." Grandafier noticed Garr's tentative glance and realized that the general was not being forthright.

"And what news do you have about the war itself?" Montama eagerly asked, abruptly changing the subject.

Hontallo's spirits instantly improved. "People are fed up with the government in Teta." Now in the spirit of a small boy spreading gossip to his teenage friends Hontallo continued, "And listen to this. While I was in a tavern the crier from Teta arrived with news from the capital city. He says that there is to be a royal wedding, to be held within a fortnight. You will never guess who is to be married," he said, daring his compatriots to answer.

Grandafier guessed, "Don't tell me, Bellazar is going to marry Pondru."

"No," Hontallo continued, so eager to finish his story that he could barely contain his enthusiasm. "She is going to wed Pantamanu."

"Poor Celia," Grandafier said with very little real feeling. "Pantamanu's wife," he informed the others.

Naively Montama asked, "How can he get married to Bellazar if he is already married?"

Grandafier and Garr laughed, though they tried to disguise their mirth. "There will either be a political accommodation," Grandafier professed, "or she will meet with an untimely accident. Castle's are such dangerous places now a days."

"And how does this all relate to me?" Montama asked, not sure if this added or detracted from his political fortunes.

"It means my dear young king that all is not well in Benton's castle," Grandafier said, his eyes glowing with contentment. "It means that these two rivals, who have hated each other for many cycles, realize that they must unite if they are to defeat you."

"So it is a good thing, for us, I mean," Montama stammered, still not completely clear how this marriage would work to his strategic advantage.

Hontallo now laughed, enjoying his brother's confusion. "The people cannot believe it," Hontallo added eagerly. "First their beloved king dies, then he is replaced by a dead man, and now he is to replaced again, this time by two monarchs who can not stand the sight of each other."

"Ah, to be a proverbial fly on the wall on their honeymoon night, that would be a rare treat," Grandafier cackled, as the others shared in his devious delight, that is except for Montama, who was still unsure about the repercussions of this change in the ongoing political drama.

Datoria 6

Common Medicines for treating a two-headed Delbot
(Del-bot) Bite:

If one is bitten by just one head:

· *Place Toka Leave Directly on Wound*
Drink Excessive Amounts of Toka until you feel better

If one is bitten by both heads:

Usually fatal, unless you have Type X Blood
If you have Type X Blood, spread calcaline lotion on the
wound
Then drink copious amounts of Toka

Chapter 63
A Royal Wedding

To be perfectly blunt, Pantamanu was not concerned with legal niceties. When told that there would have to be an inquest into the death of his dear wife Celia, he merely responded that no investigation was required. "She died from cholera," he dispassionately declared. When he was told that an autopsy would have to be performed on the decaying and recently discovered body of a man who was presumed to be King Pondru, he summarily ordered, "There is no need. I would recognize my brother anywhere." When told that there should be a fortnight between the wedding and the coronation of the two new monarchs, he agreed to a fair compromise. "We will wait but one unit," he affirmed. Then in his usual ribald manner he added, "After all, I will need some time alone with my bride."

Bellazar was not amused. "That bastard will consummate this marriage over my dead body," she was overheard telling her maids of honor in a conspicuously loud voice. When informed of Bellazar's statement Pantamanu cruelly and inaccurately replied, "That may be true. Rendrau did tell me that she was not very lively in bed."

With the hostility thus open and painfully exposed, King Benton tried to serve as a mediator, urging the two future leaders of Arcania to set aside their long-held hostilities. Bellazar adamantly refused to listen. "He is disgusting," she said in reference to her betrothed. While tensions mounted at the King's Castle, Bellazar's truth squads continued to pan out across the passra, spreading the good news of the upcoming wedding and its accompanying dual coronation, while portraying the couple as blissful, loving and eager to jointly lead Arcania.

The wedding itself was a traditional Arcanian ceremony. For three units leading up to the wedding the soon to be betrothed couple were not allowed to see or communicate with each other, not even in private. This allowed both sides the necessary time to decide whether they wanted to continue with the marriage or not. There was no shame in announcing that a suitor had changed their mind, with about twenty percent of all weddings ending in this manner. On the wedding unit itself the couple were escorted to separate rooms, each identically furnished with a series of chairs surrounding a large round table. Ten inquisitors called Excelsors, composed of an equal number of men and women, then sat around a large ornate table, while the person to be married, entered through a small slit or pathway cut into the table. Standing inside the table's circumference, they were then ready to be subjected to harsh and often intense questioning.

The rules were simple. Each questioner could ask up to three questions and if they were dissatisfied with an answer they were allowed a follow up question. The person to be married or the Pastron would then be forced under penalty of perjury to answer the question as honestly as possible. If a Pastron did not want to answer a particular question they could merely say, "pass." If they were asked the question again by another Excelsor they were then compelled to answer it. The ceremony would continue until all of the Excelsors had either asked their three questions or were in agreement that the wedding itself should proceed. Then, a formal vote was recorded and if a majority believed that the wedding should not take place the ceremony was canceled, no matter what the Pastron's preferences may be. Since the same rigorous process was applied to both the husband and the wife, agreement by both sets of Excelsors was required before the inquisition was at an end. Of those couples that endured this process only slightly more than one half were permitted to wed. The usual reasons for negative decisions by the Excelsors were that the male Pastron did not have sufficient resources to provide for a wife or that the female Pastron did not have a sufficiently large dowry. Very occasionally Excelsors disallowed a wedding request because they decided the couple was not compatible or because one or the other refused to live a monogamous lifestyle.

If a couple was not satisfied with the verdict rendered by the Excelsors they could appeal, but that required a waiting period of one half cycle. If they were turned down a second time then a marriage between the eager couple was irrevocably prohibited. Some unhappy couples that had been refused the right to marry subsequently eloped to the Relatin Empire, while some small segment decided to live together without formal marriage vows, though this was decidedly inconsistent with traditional Arcanian morality. Despite its formality and rigor the process was thought to have worked well for several centuries and there was no public outcry to change the system. Bellazar and Pantamanu therefore had no alternative but to seek the right to marry from Excelsors chosen at random for the occasion.

When the wedding unit arrived, the betrothed couple was escorted to their separate examination rooms and the inquisition commenced shortly thereafter. Bellazar prepared herself for what she expected to be a grueling process, studying Arcanian marriage precedent by night and allowing herself to be subjected to questioning each unit by a series of her closest advisers, including King Benton. Pantamanu also prepared for the ceremony, sleeping late all three units prior to the wedding, playing bolto ball, a game similar to racket ball except the ball has a spike in it, which easily could impale a careless participant, and taking long rides on his horse through the countryside to the east. He even defied tradition by sleeping one night under the stars, refusing to return to the castle until late morning.

Bellazar dressed conservatively for the occasion. She wore a traditional red gown, with white lace, adorned with green trim. The colors reflected the view that one must be red with passion, and white with purity, while others are green with envy on your wedding unit. Pantamanu wore his usual military attire. His only concession was to wear a decorative sword and sheath made especially for his wedding unit. He also agreed to have his hair trimmed, though not stylishly so.

The two Pastrons entered their respective rooms at approximately the same time, taking their position directly inside their table's circumference, as they waited for the entrance of the Excelsors. They were formally announced by a thespan, the official who both announced their arrival and later would report the Excelsors' verdict. The ten Excelsors then marched in line into the room completely circling the table, so that the Pastron could politely nod to each one in succession, before they were sequentially seated. The ten Excelsors then elected a leader through a secret ballot, with that member given the essential task of moderating all questioning. In essence this was a formality only, for agreement was reached before the meeting began on the actual identify of the moderator.

The choice of the moderator was important for they could cut off questioning, force the Pastron to respond if they believed they were not sufficiently forthcoming, and in a few rare cases, could summarily declare the proceeding at an end, in which case the marriage did not proceed. The moderator also sought the votes of the Excelsors at the end of the questioning period, with each Excelsor provided a written ballot, to be counted and read by the thespan.

Bellazar stood stoically, almost regally, as the Excelsors entered the room, while in an adjacent room Pantamanu showed his lighter side by bowing but once to his ten Excelsors. Pastrons were not allowed to speak unless spoken to, so neither said a word as the Excelsors assumed their formal positions around their respective tables.

The first question for Bellazar came from an elderly woman with dark green, wrinkled skin. She, as did all of the Excelsors, wore a black cape that reached nearly to the floor when she was standing. Her hair was covered by a cartey, a small hat worn for formal occasions such as church services, which was plain except for one solitary flower, usually white and freshly picked. "Madame Bellazar," the Excelsor read from a prepared statement, "it is well known that your husband was killed in battle at Kalel, and that you were most devastated by the news of his demise." The Excelsor looked up from her prepared statement directly at Bellazar as she noted, "I too am saddened by your loss. The passra has lost a great man." Bellazar, who was not yet allowed to respond, having not yet been formally asked a question, merely nodded her head slightly in appreciation and as a sign of respect. Now reading again from her prepared text, the elderly Excelsor continued, "Why do you choose to marry again so soon after the untimely demise of your dear beloved husband?"

Bellazar, with a facial expression she had perfected after units of practice, an expression that was meant to demonstrate both her compassion and her total resolve, took a single solitary step toward the elderly Excelsor. Then, standing quite erect, she looked around the room and stated, "I would first like to thank all of you for coming here today. I know that our passra has faced some trying times and that it was not easy for each of you to come here on such short notice. I thank you and I assure you that the passra appreciates your hard work and dedication on behalf of the moral purity of our society." She now looked directly at the elderly woman. "Now as to your specific question. The night before my dear husband Rendrau left for the battlefield where, sadly, his life was violently claimed by a dastardly rebel army, he sat down with me in a room not too far from where we are now gathered. He told me that he did not know if he would live or die. If he were to die, he wanted me to go on with the business of making sure that our passra is safe and secure. He also told me that I should trust and love his brothers, Pondru and Pantamanu."

Bellazar now began to walk around the inner circumference of the table looking directly into the eyes of each of the Excelsors as she did so. "It was of course an even greater shock when we learned of the death of King Pondru, followed by the untimely demise of poor Celia, Pantamanu's wife.

I can assure you that our family has suffered from the war every bit, if not more than the citizens of this great passra."

The Excelsors sat with rapt attention, watching Bellazar's every move and listening to her words, each one separately evaluating their sincerity. "I realize that this passra needs a strong leader." Without any doubt she proclaimed, "Pantamanu is that man!" She then paused, looked her inquisitor directly in the eye, and stated forthrightly, "And I consented to be his wife, not only because I honor the traditions of this great passra, but also because I too want to do whatever I can to make this a safe place for children to play, for young people to marry, for families to build a home, and for our elderly to live out their golden years in peace." After another pause, and with her voice quivering dramatically, she added, "I do love Pantamanu." She said without even a trace of perfidy, "But that is not the only reason this wedding must go forward. Together, Pantamanu and I will provide the leadership that this passra deserves and badly needs. With your support we will go forward together."

When Bellazar finished her speech, there was silence in the room and then three of the Excelsors broke tradition and began to clap in the traditional Arcanian manner, slapping their right knee with their left hand. The moderator asked for quiet and then directed the next questioner to proceed.

"Madame Bellazar, do you love Pantamanu?" asked an obese man, who missing his two front teeth, lisped as he spoke.

"I do," Bellazar responded succinctly, smiling so serenely now that it appeared that she was utterly angelic.

"Is that all you have to say?" the questioner said, taking advantage of his right to ask a follow-up question.

"What more is there to say?" Bellazar asked contritely, gently folding her hands, totally at peace.

The questions went on for several more minutes. It was clear that the Excelsors already had made up their minds. Hence it was not surprising when the moderator asked for additional questions and no one responded. "In that case I will take a formal vote of the Excelsors," he stated perfunctorily, having said this line thousands of times before. Each then dutifully scribbled their verdict on a solitary piece of paper before passing it down to the moderator. In a booming voice he then called for the thespan, who had been waiting nearby, just outside the door. Entering with impeccable posture he walked directly to the moderator, who handed him the decisions of the ten Excelsors. Quickly the thespan scanned each of them. It was tradition for one member to always vote against a marriage, as a way of cautioning the young couple that marriage is a serious undertaking. In this case, so formidable had been Bellazar's performance that all ten Excelsors voted in complete unanimity.

"There are ten votes for marriage and none for dismissal," the thespan announced. The Excelsors then stood, and as was their tradition, applauded the soon to be married bride, this time by striking their right hand against their left shoulder. The moderator then escorted the bride to be to a nearby waiting room where she was either informed of the verdict from her husband's inquisition or asked to wait until that proceeding had completed its business. On this occasion Bellazar sat waiting, with the moderator by her side, as Pantamanu's inquisition continued.

The ten Excelsors who were chosen to question Pantamanu were keenly aware that he was to be the next King of Arcania. They therefore showed an unusual level of deference for the groom. Against all decorum, a royal throne chair was brought in, allowing Pantamanu to sit in all his regal glory before his ten inquisitors. Unlike Bellazar's direct responses, Pantamanu's answers tended to wander. He often changed the subject from the question asked to one he preferred to answer. Yes he loved his dear beloved Celia. Yes, he agreed that marrying so soon after her death was unseemly, but there were other issues that were more important. He discussed his military exploits often in remarkable detail, telling the Excelsors what it felt like to have a ferocious talladagger charging directly at your steady position in the heat of battle. He also noted that he had watched many good men fall in the service of his passra. These asides had absolutely nothing to do with the issue at hand, his fitness to be wed to his sister-in-law, but he treated the gathered dignitaries as if they were mere servants to the king. He was therefore respectful, but totally in charge. At one point he did the unthinkable, cutting off an Excelsor before his question was completed, but his response was so apparently heart felt that few noticed his rudeness. When he spoke of Bellazar he did so with great reverence. She was the mother of the country, a great patriot, and though he knew that his love for her would grow in the many cycles to come, it was his love for his passra that mattered most.

When the tally finally was taken the Excelsors dutifully voted nine to one to allow the marriage to proceed. Pantamanu was then taken to the holding room, where he met Bellazar for the first time in three units. He noted how lovely she looked and even kissed her cheek, much to her surprise. Upon hearing the news that they were to be wed, he asked for glasses of orange colored wine to toast the occasion. Quite contrary to tradition, wine glasses were then dispensed to all of the Excelsors and a toast was ordered for the two new monarchs. Having toasted the passra's future, the Excelsors and the thespan were then led to the formal dining room, where the wedding was to occur.

Before the formal ceremony, Bellazar worked the room like a skilled politician, shaking hands, reminding guests of their past shared experiences, always with a pleasant word and a kind expression. Occasionally she turned to Pantamanu to make sure that he was equally gracious.

As for the wedding ceremony it was resplendent in its own way. The couple stood together and took the ancient vows, directly quoting the Holy Scriptures on several appropriate occasions, while green rose pedals fell like gentle snow from the ceiling above throughout the twenty-minute ceremony. When the two ended the ritual by confirming their love for each other, and as tradition dictated, took each other in their arms and kissed, first on the forehead, then on the lips, the audience applauded enthusiastically, before raising its wine glasses in a toast to the passra's two new monarchs.

To all who watched it was a magical experience. Bellazar and Pantamanu seemed to be perfectly suited for each other. More than one guest noted that they had never seen such a perfect couple.

Chapter 64
Kidnapped!

All seemed delighted with the wedding, but one. Kublatitan had received a solemn promise from Bellazar to cleanse the Oracle. If she ruled jointly with Pantamanu, the giant Taewokan realized that this pledge, like many others, would go unfulfilled. Since the marriage threatened his main objective, Kublatitan simply could not abide the union of these two as Arcania's monarchs. Salvation itself could be achieved only through a bold step, to secure the throne for Bellazar alone. Not because he thought she was the most fit to lead, but because he believed that she was the most likely of the three candidates to honor his request to return the Oracle to the

Land of the Taewokans. Yet how could he stop the coronation with the throne now veritably within Pantamanu's reach?

Kublatitan had been pure when he was a leader. He always thought of his people first, no matter what the particulars of the matter at hand. He had learned much since his confinement in the Oracle commenced. Many of the other entities were distasteful to him, but he was not blind to their own sort of wisdom, particularly me, Count Belicki, who turned political intrigue into a veritable art form. Kublatitan therefore decided that a new, bold and potentially reckless strategy was required, one as devious as anything I ever devised.

Bellazar was in her private quarters, where final alterations were being made to her coronation dress. Several maids surrounded her, some with needles and thread, others with measuring tapes, others simply admiring her blue dress, the traditional symbol of the Centama family's rule. The dress had multiple layers of blue and white ruffles, and therefore one had to put it on sequentially, one layer at a time. It had taken Bellazar nearly one hour to dress and with the time for the coronation ceremony quickly approaching, she was in a foul, sanguinary mood. Spotting a couple of loose threads on her right sleeve she let loose with a series of snide and hurtful remarks. The maids verily trembled with fear, as she criticized their work. Watching her from the side of the room, Kublatitan sadly shook his head and in his characteristic garbled syntax whispered, "She not good for leader, too anger much in her." He was tempted to withdraw, leaving Arcanian politics as they were, but he knew that she was his last and only hope of cleansing the Oracle of all of its impurities. Therefore, he emerged from the shadows and made his presence known.

"You must to me listen," he said boldly, stridently commanding her attention. As he did so the maids who had busied themselves with the Telenaka's coronation dress suddenly froze in time and space. Startled, Bellazar's head turned abruptly toward the hulking apparition at the far side of the room. Kublatitan now walked deliberately forward and with each step the menace on his face steadily proliferated until it represented a devastatingly frightening specter. For once, Bellazar stood directly in front of him, utterly speechless.

"I here am to warn you thusly," he said, his eyes burning with a fiery determination. "One warning all that I will provide." Kublatitan now stepped so close to Bellazar that she could sense his thoughts before he spoke. "You not live to be monarch, not at all. There will be assassination today, Pantamanu plans it, you will die, and he alone, king will be."

Bellazar, her mouth open with fear and awe stared at the giant that now entirely eclipsed her. Grasping her dress nervously with her right hand, and in a barely audible voice, she muttered, "An assassination!"

Kublatitan now directly entered her thoughts. Words were no longer necessary between the two of them. "You die within the next hour, unless you now escape under protection of me." Kublatitan's thoughts were so resolute that Bellazar had absolutely no doubt whatsoever that the Taewokan giant spoke the truth, although in fact he did not. "Come now, or die you will."

"Where?" she said, her body shaking with a fear that was totally foreign to her nature. Realizing that she was no longer in control of her emotions, she closed her eyes. Even as she did so she still visualized Kublatitan's image, ten feet tall and growing ever larger as he spoke. When she opened her eyes again he was in fact much taller. His giant frame expanded with every sentence he spoke, his body a physical representation of his unyielding determination.

"Come!" he again cajoled her. "Must go to forest of the west, Kanaween, and take Oracle with you, must you do."

Bellazar intended to ask why. Before she could, an answer was provided. "King Pantamanu must have not control the Oracle, for use it will he, powerful to be, he must be stopped. You must take the Oracle and escape to forest. I provide for you there, an army, and there you will challenge him for the throne. Final battle will it be!"

Bellazar did not have to ask how she would seize the heavily guarded Oracle, for time was temporarily frozen, not only within Bellazar's quarters, but also throughout the entire castle. It was therefore easy for Bellazar to move quickly from her quarters to the Oracle chamber. The door was locked but Kublatitan proved to be a capable locksmith, compelling the door to open with but one mighty thought. Bellazar looked curiously at the several guards, frozen in their formal positions before the Oracle chamber. Furtively, still afraid that she was being watched, she moved with great stealth toward the Oracle, a look of intense stress quite apparent on her face. She then took a deep breath as she looked toward the Oracle.

"Look not into the Oracle," Kublatitan ardently warned. "You are not yet a monarch. If you look into it, it will consume you. Look only when you are king. Only then can you control its power." She now stood only a few feet from the object that absolutely obsessed her rivals. As Pondru had noticed, it was an ordinary looking vase, not particularly attractive, an object that in appearance would draw the attention of only the most ardent archeologist. The only furnishing in the room was the oak table upon which the Oracle resided. With considerable anxiety, she looked about the room for something she could use to cover the Oracle. "Damn," she whispered irritably when she could find nothing suitable. Turning, she raced back to the hall where the guards stood frozen in time. "Once Pantamanu finds that the Oracle is gone this will be the least of your problems," she said aloud, as she stripped the coat off of a particularly large, barrel-chested guard. It did not come off easily and it took her several seconds to rip the buttons lose in order to procure the poor guard's vestment. Having secured it, she now returned to the Oracle chamber and threw the guard's coat over the Oracle.

Kublatitan now spoke more urgently than ever before. "Alert they are now to your presence. Run before they are able to stop you."

Bellazar put her hands over the coat and could feel the heat of the Oracle burning through the garment's threads. "It is trying to escape," she said, desperately looking to Kublatitan for help. The giant entity now did something that demonstrated his extraordinary power to all of the other Oracle entities. As King Leonata and other entities anxiously emerged in the room trying to stop Kublatitan, they watched in horror as Bellazar seemingly ceased to exist before their very eyes.

"What have you done with her?" Leonata demanded, thrusting his hands angrily forward at the giant Taewokan.

"She now in place where you cannot find her, or the Oracle. See, I learn from Belicki and the others, treacherous how to be."

Leonata and the other numerous Oracle entities stood staring aimlessly about the room, having been permanently evicted from their home. In time more entities emerged, until the room was filled with various ghostly apparitions, many appearing like eerie paintings on the wall. Some stood, while others walked through or into the nearby walls. Soon confused entities could be seen all the way down the outside hall, slowly infesting the entire castle as they had once existed inside the Oracle's infinite universe.

I hovered above it all and watched with a combination of horror and absolute respect. "You have learned much, my giant friend," I said admiringly, before my face turned more menacing than even Kublatitan could imagine. "You may steal the Oracle," I said, my green skin now literally glowing as a palpable display of my growing anger, "but you will forfeit it once this war is decided." I now too began to grow larger, more intimidating, and if possible even angrier. "Then you will be the one who will be evicted from the Oracle, my dear friend," I added with an uncontained ferocity.

Kublatitan realized that this was no empty threat. He had won a tactical victory through an amazing feat of magical power and devious imagination. Still he could see destiny unfold as clearly as could all of the other Oracle entities. The final decision would not be resolved here in the King's Castle, but rather on battlefields in and about the Kanaween Forrest. There, in one great final battle, three mighty armies and two prodigious titans would fight for the future of Arcania and, much more importantly, for the right to control the Oracle.

PART V

THE

PRICE OF

POWER

Chapter 65
Treachery

As he did on most units, Montama returned to a special place he discovered purely by chance not more than a fortnight ago. He had found it during one of his many forays into the deep cavernous bowels of Mt. Sendil. On that unit Montama spotted a peculiar looking centipede, which he recognized immediately as a large, rhombus shaped green and yellow muldabug. Montama's eyes followed the ancient creature as it crawled ever so persistently along the moldy cave floor beneath his feet. Despite their hideous appearance, shelled muldabugs were considered a delicacy by some of the quirky effete types who lived in the capital city. As a child Montama had a rather rude epiphany when he attempted to swallow one of these sumptuous delicacies. After gagging and then spitting out an uncooked and unshelled muldabug that he had caught with his bare hands, Montama told his father, "I guess I will never make it in high society." For one of the few times that Montama could remember, his father spontaneously roared with laughter, something he would do with each successive retelling of the tale.

Now, with an army to feed, an older and presumably wiser Montama got down on his hands and knees and assiduously crawled behind the strange looking multicolored insect intent on discovering its nest. "The men might not like the taste of this thing anymore than I did, but father said it is a good source of protein," Montama reasoned as the bug occasionally stopped, before inextricably crawling in an entirely different direction. After several seconds the bug led not to a nest, but to a small aperture concealed behind a rather plain looking boulder. Montama nudged the rock to one side, and then crawled inside a small, cobweb filled opening. When he did he so, his eyes suddenly opened quite wide with excitement, for he realized that he had discovered a large, impressive cave filled with a vast hidden wonderland of abundant and glorious mysteries.

Though the entryway was small, the cavernous room itself was immense. The room's walls rose for more than three hundred feet to a ceiling that was completely sheltered with a series of ancient stalactites, some of them hanging downward for more than a hundred and fifty feet. The cave's floor was likewise covered with several monstrously large stalagmites, each one reaching upward, in the process of someday forming a solid column of icy rock with the ever-growing stalactites.

The Oracle

This splendid sight in itself was awe inspiring, but the room's magic did not end with these icy behemoths. For the far wall was completely hidden behind the glistening foam of a majestic subterranean waterfall. The water emerged from a large crack near the top of the cave, and then poured down, pure and clean, resplendent in its glistening magnificence. Walking carefully between the stalagmites so as not to disturb their ancient grandeur, Montama was inextricably drawn to the pool of water at the far end of the cave. He was able to see so clearly because of the existence of tens of thousands of rotor shaped treakas, a rare insect that survives by feeding off of mold and which therefore clings quite diligently to a cave's raw wet walls. Like a lightening bug, a treakas's tail projects a series of flashing lights as part of its mating ritual. As Montama walked softly and carefully around a particularly large stalagmite, he was exposed to this natural occurring flashing strobe light. As the treakas rubbed their hind legs together, they also created a most amazing chirping sound, which at times seemed quite musical and mesmerizing.

As Montama finally reached the pool and looked in at his own reflection, he noticed that his perception of the cave was now highly animated. Inside the pool's reflection, the size and shape of the immense stalactites constantly morphed, a strange visual sensation, for it appeared that these giant masses of ice were now in a continual state of motion. Montama's image too appeared to sparkle, and as he drew his face closer to the water, it at times occasionally divided into waves of concentric circles. The visual effect was astonishing and Montama felt that other than Kublatitan's odd Chrystal Sanctuary that the young boy had never been in such a bizarre and yet fantastically beautiful place.

Gently, reverentially, Montama leaned down on one knee and took a sip of the clear mountain water. When he did so, he quickly spit it out. "This water is warm," he mused, for somehow, in this strange cave, a waterfall of warm water created a hot spring suitable for bathing.

Feeling grungy, as he had not bathed properly for several units, Montama quickly stripped off his clothes and cautiously stepped into the temperate waters of the subterranean pond. At first he was contend to merely float, moving his arms slowly to maintain his position. Within a few minutes, overcome with boyhood zeal, he found himself thrashing about wildly, thoroughly enjoying the water's surprisingly rejuvenating warmth. As Montama splashed and frolicked, he again stared at the cave's extraordinary ceiling and then wondered how it was possible for frozen stalactites to coexist in seemingly perfect natural harmony with this warm, running water.

Squealing with delight as he dove repeatedly below the surface, Montama discovered that the waters were being diverted deeper into the mountain, undoubtedly the source of what over time would become yet additional caves running through Mt. Sendil's interior labyrinth. After about a half an hour, having completed his swim, Montama lazily pulled his body up onto a nearby rock and lay there for several minutes surveying the cave with his keen eyes.

"This is a magical place," Montama rejoiced. "I shall keep this place completely for myself. It will be my own private sanctuary." Not even Hontallo would be told of it. It would be a place where Montama could go to be entirely alone, his new and improved Tedawa Falls. And so, each unit, Montama found the time to return to the cave, spending usually no more than an hour or so there, clearing his mind, basking in the water's invigorating warmth, and wondering what lay ahead.

His army had been hiding at Mt. Sendil for more than three intervals and as the Season of Rain dawned, the young man's impatience frankly was expanding exponentially. Sometimes he wondered if his army would ever again take the offensive against the Centama family. The constant updates provided by Hontallo and General Garr, who continued their surreptitious visits to the nearby countryside, were decidedly encouraging. The populace was growing increasingly restless, with many blaming the Centama family and the Oracle for the passra's recent difficulties. Montama learned that throughout Arcania, large diasporas of frightened citizens wandered the land in search of simple sustenance and safety. As far as anyone could tell nothing was being done to ameliorate this palpable suffering. As a result, the people were searching for an alternative, someone, in fact anyone who could lead them out of their present misery. By default, Montama was gaining support, not because he offered any specific ideas to deal with the ongoing crisis. In fact, the few statements released under his name were rather banal, hardly more than the mere pabulum politicians often recite when they are in campaign mode. It was told that Montama favored "new ideas," though what they were he would not say, "a new hope for Arcania's future," and most importantly of all "change!" The people were not so much fooled by this empty rhetoric, as they were desperate for new leadership for they were convinced that the old order had failed them miserably. Consequently, a growing dissatisfied mass was convinced that the time for change had arrived.

The fact that Montama was new, that he was not a known political commodity, made him attractive in ways that utterly escaped the understanding of the entrenched incumbents, Bellazar and Pantamanu. And with each passing unit, as the agony of the succession war and its deleterious consequences on ordinary citizens continued to proliferate, the people in turn became more intensely focused on tearing down the old institutions without providing due diligence to the form or type of new foundations that would ultimately prevail. In this moment of rampant and uncontrollable political chaos, Montama was in the enviable position of representing the alternative. If it were a match between him and the Centamas, he would clearly prevail, that is unless the Centamas could somehow change the political dynamic by presenting a new and compelling united front.

Montama thought about all of these issues several units later as he completed his daily swim. He then lay on the large rock wondering, "If the people have turned against the Centama family, how long will it take them to do the same to me?" It was a heady and terrifying thought, one that kept him awake at nights, for despite the impetuousness of youth, Montama was aware of the public's ever fickle search for someone or something new.

Unit after unit, Montama returned to his secret cave, to swim, to contemplate, and to wonder, "Is it really my destiny to rule Arcania?"

Montama did not expect an answer, but he received one nonetheless. "The time is quickly approaching for the final battle," he heard a familiar female voice commandingly intone.

"Mother?" Montama asked, his head suddenly jerking in multiple directions. "Mother, is that you?" he asked again.

"I have come to give you warning," Truellen announced. When Montama turned his head toward the giant waterfall he saw that its misty white spray had begun to morph into the form of his very own mother's face, her hair flowing freely as the waters streamed down. In an instant it stood more than two hundred feet tall. It was not the face of the woman he had long known. In this incarnation, Truellen was young and ravishing, a startling beauty. No longer a frail invalid, she had transformed into a powerful and dynamic presence.

Montama gawked as he stood back carefully, reached for something to cover his nakedness, and then he watched as his mother's face, etched entirely in the running water, stared insistently down at him from high above. "It is you!" Montama exclaimed, still barely believing that it was possible for his mother to return from the grave. Such was his amazement that Montama could speak but one additional solitary word. "How?"

"I am now one with the Oracle," Truellen confessed, her hair now rising and falling in the shape of the mist from the cascading waters. "I have come to help you." Montama was still so astonished by this ethereal vision that he could barely believe his eyes. As he listened Truellen continued. "The Oracle is in a state of chaos. Bellazar and Kublatitan have stolen it from the King's Castle. Kublatitan has begun the process of removing all of the entities, for he believes that we have perverted his precious Oracle. Once he has completed this task, he intends to make Bellazar the next king and then return the Oracle to the Land of the Taewokans."

"How did you..." Montama spoke. Before he could finish his thought Truellen summarily interrupted him.

"I have little time left to speak to you, my son. I was the last entity to be added to the Oracle and so I will be the last one removed from it. When that happens I will no longer be able to communicate with you."

"What have you come to warn me about?" Montama exclaimed in a desperate voice that echoed endlessly throughout the icy cave.

"You are surrounded by treachery. There are those among you who would have you fail?"

"Who?" Montama asked briskly.

"Do not trust Belicki. You are but one avenue to power for him. He will forge an alliance with anyone that will stop Kublatitan." Montama was clearly surprised by this revelation. "There are others who also may stand in your way. General Garr is a dangerous and evil man. Grandafier's motives are less certain. King Benton has tempted him. Grandafier still believes that you have the qualities to be a strong and effective king. It is unclear what he will do, so you must watch him carefully."

As Truellen spoke these last words, her image flickered and then began to fade ever so slightly. Desperate for clarification, Montama shouted, "Mother, Kublatitan told me that something terrible will happen to our family."

"Your father will never join you so long as the Centama family rules," Truellen said with exquisite sadness. "If he tries to prevent you from becoming king, you must resist his entreaties. Otherwise, all will be lost, for if Pantamanu is king, he will surely destroy our family and seize our lands."

Truellen's image faded palpably, though her voice remained strong. With her image now a mere outline she said, "When the Oracle told me that you would be king, I never thought to ask it if there would be a price."

"What price?" Montama repeated anxiously.

Though her vision was largely erased, Montama watched as Truellen opened her eyes and stared directly at her son. "There is always a price to pay for those who seek power. Only those who are willing to pay this price will succeed."

"What price must I pay?" Montama asked, his heart racing and his thoughts spinning as he tried to make sense of his mother's cryptic message.

"That I do not yet know," Truellen said, as her image further dissipated. Then, with great sadness she continued, "I have kept something from you. A secret, one that now threatens to destroy you and everything that we have fought for."

"What is it mother?" Montama asked, startled and suddenly quite unsure of himself.

Truellen's image now faded so palpably that her face could barely be discerned. "You are not what you appear to be," she said. Before she could say another word, her voice fell silent and her image completely disappeared.

"Mother!" Montama shouted desperately, his eyes scanning the room looking for any evidence of his mother's likeness. When he finally realized that she was gone, Montama stumbled backward, terrified and confused. For the very first time Montama understood the meaning of the word treachery. His partisans, his friends, his compatriots, all of them could very well also be his enemies, as well. If he could no longer trust Count Belicki, General Garr, or Grandafier, then who could he trust? "Hontallo is the only one I can trust!" Montama thought aloud.

What of this strange encounter with his mother? "I must tell no one, not even Hontallo" Montama whispered, for now, even here in this very secret place, the young man was afraid that someone might be listening. "Not even Hontallo," he repeatedly softly. Then Montama left the cave, never to return to it.

Chapter 66
Pandemonium

Pantamanu had never felt more foolish or ridiculous in his entire life. He cursed aloud as he sat incongruously in his Spartan quarters on a plain wooden chair, one arm broken, its varnish long ago worn away, while at the same time eloquently attired in a splendid regal blue coronation robe, garnished with yellow and green frills, and emblazoned with the traditional symbol of the Centama family (two intersecting swords inlaid on the map of Arcania) stitched boldly in golden thread. "This damn robe makes me look like a woman," Pantamanu scowled to no one in particular, for he was entirely alone. The site of the next king, sitting on a dilapidated wooden chair, which for some odd reason Pantamanu simply refused to part with, wearing this foppish royal garb, would have appeared comical under virtually any other circumstances. As the future king fixed his gaze on a half empty glass of green wine, Pantamanu's mind was set on but one paramount thought. "In just a few minutes I will be king of Arcania." It was the fulfillment of a lifelong aspiration, one that he believed he was owed, not because of his royal birth, but due to his superior physical strength and mental discipline. As he pondered the awesome responsibilities of this new office, not once did the slightest doubt enter his thoughts. He was sublimely confident, dead certain that he would be a great king!

Free from self-doubt, Pantamanu's mind was consumed with pedestrian considerations. He cussed because he was uncomfortable with the inevitable ceremonial falderal required by a rigid historical tradition. He also was bitter that he must share his cherished new office with his despised sister-in-law, now wife, though he had a new appreciation for Bellazar, for the honeymoon night had exceeded even his wildest imaginings. "Rendrau never told me he had such a tiger for a wife," he mused, suddenly giggling with puerile delight as he did so.

Then Pantamanu remembered the solemnity of the present situation and the fact that he would be forced to parade before all of Arcania in this preposterously garish outfit, his hair greased and slicked back with a smelly slime that gave it a look of effeminate perfection, his right hand uncomfortably adorned by the five rings of Arcania, giant beastly looking artifacts that honored the five ages of the passra's history, of which the Centama family rule was but the latest. Pantamanu would have paid almost any price to avoid this vapid ceremony, however, given the turbulent intervals since the death of King Benton, the public's dismay at the deaths of Retch and Pondru, and continued skepticism about the deaths of High Cleric Rendella and his own wife Celia, the young Centama realized that it was imperative to honor tradition in all its frivolous glory. Still, he hoped that a few more glasses of green wine might sufficiently dull his senses so that he would barely notice the passage of time. As he reached for the wine glass and held it up to his mouth he suddenly wondered, "Where the hell is Lord Gulcum?" Surely he should have been here at least twenty minutes ago. Peeved and quickly losing what little patience he possessed, Pantamanu felt as if time itself had come to a complete halt. He sipped his wine, emitted an expletive so raw that it does not merit repeating, swilled the rest of the wine, and then angrily tossed the glass toward the floor. When he did he suddenly became aware that the laws of physics somehow had been suspended. "What the hell?" he barked, for against all reason the glass simply hung in mid air, suspended in time and space, with just a drop of green wine clearly visible on the goblet's rim.

Circumspectly, Pantamanu rose from his chair, his eyes still attentively fixed on the suspended wine glass. He reached over and picked the glass out of thin air, then stared at it for a few moments, as if it possessed some awesome magical power. Then violently he slammed the glass downward toward the floor. Again, an invisible force abruptly halted the glass's forward progress. Angered and more than a bit unsettled, he finally exploded with a sound so bellicose that it would have frightened even the most hardened of men, that is, if only anyone else could have heard it. "What is the Oracle up to now?" he screamed in a voice so shrill that the wine glass finally shattered in mid air, though its various pieces remained frozen in the same space by the peculiar invisible force that enveloped every single object in the room, excepting his own self.

Pantamanu stormed to his chamber door and threw it open with such brute force that it suddenly became unhinged. Angrily he stepped into the hall where the sight of a mass of bizarrely garbed strangers utterly startled him, some wearing the most preposterously outlandish outfits Pantamanu had ever witnessed. He counted at least fifty such people before he realized that countless others existed not only in the corridor, but also within the walls of the King's Castle itself. "My God," he said with a haunted look on his face, as a strange looking woman with olive green hair and gigantic ears walked past him and then abruptly turned and walked directly through a nearby wall.

As he continued to stare in disbelief, several of the entities studied Pantamanu, for they also were curious to discover the identity of what they considered to be an equally strange looking apparition. Desperately

Pantamanu scanned the swelling crowd for a familiar face. His eyes eventually rested upon his departed brother, Pondru, who stood with a vacant stare next to own quarters.

"Pondru!" Pantamanu shouted with relief, as he scurried anxiously down the hall, carelessly pushing aside any entity that stood in his way. "Pondru!" he again repeated excitedly. Upon arriving at his brother's side he put his hand out and it passed directly through Pondru's body. "Pondru!" Pantamanu shouted more earnestly than before. "What is going on here?"

With the touch of Pantamanu's hand, Pondru's body began to slowly materialize and as it did his ashen features incrementally appeared ever more human, as blood began to race through his calcified body. Though he barely had the strength to stand up, Pondru looked quizzically at his brother. Realizing that Pondru was disoriented, Pantamanu put his arm around his brother's waist and slowly led him into his old bedroom chamber. Gently, as Pondru fell onto the corner of his bed, Pantamanu repeated, "What is happening?"

Confused, in a state of shock, Pondru deliberately turned his head and stared for a moment at his brother. His eyes reflected his profound bewilderment and he spoke so slowly that it was hard for Pantamanu to understand what he was saying. "W-h-o-o-o-o-o a-r-r-r-r-r-e y-o-u-u-u-u-u?" Pondru asked.

It took a second for Pantamanu to understand what Pondru had said. Then he responded anxiously, "I am your brother, Pantamanu."

Pondru stared at his brother, but all he saw could best be described as an abstract painting. All of the details were there, but they were not in any definable configuration. To Pondru, Pantamanu's eyes seemed to be on his younger brother's chin, not his forehead. His mouth was about a foot wide, and his body looked like a spider rather than a human. Furthermore, when Pantamanu spoke Pondru heard the words as echoes, repeating endlessly, each syllable drowning out the previous one so that Pon and dru were heard simultaneously and repeatedly. Pondru had to listen attentively to understand that the words signified his own name and then he was not sure if they had been spoken or if the words were merely emanating from inside his own head.

Pantamanu sat on the side of the bed next to his brother and tenderly caressed Pondru's forehead. "What is happening?" he said, though to Pondru it sounded like, "Whappat, is ingwhaishap." This gibberish then echoed again and again in his mind, almost driving him insane with its mocking repetition.

Pantamanu realized that conversing with Pondru was an utterly useless enterprise. He therefore abruptly abandoned his brother and ran frantically to the hall. There he noticed that other Oracle entities were aimlessly wandering about, apparently as confused as Pondru. Some were in corporeal form. As such they walked into walls without penetrating them, they were entirely confused by their inability to transgress the seemingly random barriers posed by the physical world. Others stood staring at their bodies as if they had not seen them in a century, a distinct possibility, given the length of their confinement inside the Oracle. Pantamanu ran down the hall, running through some entities, clumsily bumping into others, as he anxiously looked for someone who might be able to help him.

From the hall abutting the Centama family living quarters, he moved with a sudden bolt of acceleration to the winding rear staircase. He then used a trick he had learned as a boy. Hitting the stairway at full speed he grabbed hold of the large brass banister, straddled it, and then rode it, round corners, steadily down till he reached the main hall on the castle's first floor. As often happened when he was a child, he slammed harshly forward toward the floor, though this time his fall was broken by three befuddled Oracle entities. As he struggled to his feet he saw hundreds of other strange looking people, none of whom he recognized. There were women, children, and even, much to Pantamanu's surprise and apparent revulsion, a rather sickly looking cow, all apparently stricken by the same confused sensation that enveloped Pondru.

When Pantamanu arrived at the first floor hall, he again witnessed the same terrible sight of wraithlike apparitions in a state of mass confusion. "This place has been turned into a circus!" he whispered. He pushed past guards, among the living yet now as frozen in time and space, just like his wine glass. Frantically he moved toward the Oracle chamber room. Entering it at last, he was horrified to see that the door to the chamber door was wide open and the Oracle vase was nowhere to be seen.

As he stood transfixed, his mind barely able to comprehend the cataclysm that had descended upon the royal castle, he finally heard a voice. "You must come with me," the voice declared. In an instant Pantamanu found himself in an entirely strange and different place, as unfamiliar to him as a distant planet, so strange that he could not tell if it was real or imagined. Everything around him glowed and his body felt the prickly sensation of successive charges of electrical energy. "You will have to forgive the unpleasantness of your surroundings," I said, my voice sounding as if it was transmitted remotely from another location.

"Where am I?" Pantamanu thought, for words were no longer required to communicate.

"This is a place that Kublatitan created," I stated, my voice still reverberating continuously in Pantamanu's mind. "It can best be described as a fissure in the Oracle chamber, a crack so small that none of us paid it any attention. He calls it the Crystal Sanctuary because its electrical impulses glow like shards of shattered crystal."

Pantamanu now watched in horror as his arm began to float away from his body. "Do not be concerned by your physical appearance, for this is a place or pure energy." Despite my assurances, Pantamanu's fears were not assuaged. He watched as his legs floated in space and then his torso. "Your body is being reduced to its individual components. This is a place of pure ideas. So your head, your torso, each are reverting to its primal basic form. If you were to stay here long enough there would be nothing left of you but your spirit."

Pantamanu did not understand any of this gibberish. He was relieved when I said, "You will be whole again once you are freed from this sphere." My voice was now more clearly audible to Pantamanu's ears, which also had separated from his body, floating away in two vastly different directions.

"What happened to the castle?" Pantamanu frantically requested, finally recognizing that he was speaking to Count Belicki.

"Kublatitan has done something most unexpected," I commented without emotion. "He has learned much from me, more than I had realized. He convinced Bellazar that you were planning to assassinate her prior to the coronation ceremony. He then induced her to kidnap the Oracle. Finally, he has begun his promise to cleanse the Oracle of all its entities. He has cast them out into the King's Castle, all but me, for I am too strong for him to dispose of so easily."

"How did he do that?" Pantamanu asked, incredulous at the very thought that his castle had been turned into a veritable morgue for the undead.

"He used this same fissure where we now reside to transport both Bellazar and the Oracle to the Kanaween Forrest region, where he intends to do battle with the young pretender Montama for the soul of the Oracle."

"I don't understand," Pantamanu thought, for his mind was barely able to comprehend what I was telling him.

"You are in shock," I said, my thoughts slowly becoming more comprehensible to Pantamanu with the passage of time. "I will transport you to your army unit in the east. In that place, time has not been affected." Then in a solemn voice I declared, "The Oracle can no longer help you in the battle to come. That you must win on your own, just as I alone must confront Kublatitan."

Pantamanu's mouth opened to respond. Before he could speak he found himself, again whole and wearing his ridiculous frilly royal coronation robe, and standing before his own garish private tent at the encampment of the reconstituted Army of Eastern Arcania, the remaining remnants of the First, Second and Third Armies. As he appeared out of the ether, men hardened by the sights and sounds of battle were terrified at the sudden materialization of Pantamanu, still dressed in this strange royal garb. Pantamanu could tell them nothing, for his mind was such a jumble of confusing thoughts that it took all of his collected fortitude to simply drag his body inside his tent, where he abruptly collapsed on his bed. There, with his mind in a constant state of flux, he slept for more than two full units.

Meanwhile, many soldiers in his panic stricken army dropped their weapons and scurried from the scene of this unholy magic. Though the officers were as frightened as their men, discipline finally prevailed. And then, in this tense and uncertain manner, Pantamanu's army watched and waited, wondering if their leader would ever awaken and if he did what portent his arrival would hold for the passra's political fortunes.

Chapter 67
Montama's New Army

Nimrod did not even ask why I had transported Pantamanu to his army, for he knew that Pantamanu hated Bellazar more so than even the pretender, Montama. Hence, the battle for Arcania would now be a three-way affair. He therefore suspected that I had, as usual, ulterior motives, and in that belief, Nimrod was quite correct. Without a word he listened, attentively as always, as I resumed my rambling dissertation.

Early in the morning, as Montama awoke, a jubilant old man who, despite the infirmities of age, seemed spry enough to dance a jig or two, greeted the young man with unbounded alacrity. "There is much good news," Grandafier verily sang out, his enthusiasm most unbefitting a man of his advanced age and wisdom. He threw his omnipresent white cane into the air and then gently placed his right hand on Montama's shoulder. "General Garr reports that the time is ready for us to leave this blasted place."

"What?" Montama said, much bewildered.

Delightedly, Grandafier responded, "General Garr has made a deal with a disloyal regiment from the original Second Army. It consists of over seven hundred well-trained men. In addition, more than a thousand commoners have come to your aide." Then with a broad smile Grandafier declared, "My son, you have a mighty new army ready to fight by your side!"

Montama stared at Grandafier in total disbelief, not sure whether the old man had grown suddenly senile or if he was drunk on Toka, a not unreasonable assumption. He also wondered if Grandafier were laying some sort of trap. After all Truellen had warned Montama that the old man was not yet settled in his loyalty. With these mixed feelings, Montama asked, "What are you talking about? What new army?"

"I will let General Garr fill you in on all of the wonderful details," Grandafier cackled. Montama ran to the nearby cave that served as Garr's headquarters, while Grandafier limped behind. Hontallo, stunned and bewildered, followed a step behind the elderly man. Once they entered Grandafier sprightly commanded, "General Garr, tell young Montama the good news."

Without a smile, General Garr walked toward Montama and extended his hand in a formal military salute. Then he declared, "We will be leaving for Pellaville, the land of your birth, in the morning. We are to meet up there with men from Arcania's army who have agreed to join our cause." What he did not tell Montama was that these Arcanians did so because they shared the general's prejudices regarding the Bogul question. Garr continued, "From there we will march on to the Kanaween Forest where my scouts inform me that Madame Bellazar awaits. We must move quickly, for we hear that Pantamanu's forces are moving from the east. We can not let him trap us between two powerful armies."

Grandafier could not contain his delight. "It is said that by the thousands the people will be coming to see you, many of them to fight for you! An army of ordinary people who come to your side because they see in you a champion for their cause." Montama looked straight into General

Garr's solitary eye. There was something unsettling about it. He could not determine why it so discomforted him. Remembering his mother's words, Montama now wondered if General Garr and Grandafier the Elder might not be misleading him. For as his paranoia expanded exponentially, other than Hontallo, Montama was no longer sure who stood loyally by his side.

Chapter 68
A Woman Scorned

Bellazar had never felt so thoroughly discombobulated in her entire life. She always prided herself on being in absolute *total* control of her mind, body and spirit. Throughout her life she assiduously avoided alcoholic beverages because she feared it might dull her senses. "I have to keep my wits about me," she said often.

This attitude was reflected in her rigid daily schedule: a strict military-like regimentation that allowed her to thrive both physically and emotionally. She rose early, often before the sun, consumed a cup or two of a mild stimulant, such as tea, then did her daily exercises, before blithely proceeding with a full unit of diverse activities. No matter what she did, whether it was meeting with top political advisers or supervising her personal staff on a relatively mundane matter, Bellazar constantly had to be in complete control at all times. She was methodical, systematic, effective, and though she was thoroughly adroit at political improvisation when necessary, she much preferred a steady predictable schedule without extraneous interruptions of any kind.

To state the obvious, the events of the past few units hardly comported well with Bellazar's personal inclinations. Bluntly stated, she had experienced events that no human could possibly comprehend, never mind manage with articulate dexterity. In a veritable heartbeat she was transformed, virtually without her consent, from the widow of the beloved Regent Rendrau, a man who not only appreciated her many virtues and had a strong proclivity to defer to her resolute and well-formed opinions, to the wife of a despised megalomaniacal narcissist who, according to Kublatitan, planned to have her publicly assassinated. Then, in an instant, she was materially transported from the King's Castle to a remote location deep inside the Kanaween Forest in western Arcania. It is therefore a colossal understatement to suggest that the events of the moment were beyond her direct control. Any human mind would have been taxed by the sundry bizarre transitions Bellazar recently experienced. Consequently, when she first materialized inside the Kanaween Forest her initial response was a combination of confusion and angry denials. "Damn," she cursed aloud. "If they had just left everything up to me I would have fixed it. Now look at the mess we're in!"

With the king's castle still frozen in a state of suspended animation, and Arcania's two leaders literally at opposite ends of the passra's geographical space, a functioning government no longer existed. Instead, there was pure anarchy. Even Bellazar was at a loss, uncertain how to proceed. At first she ordered Kublatitan to appear. When he refused, she threw a temper tantrum that was indeed fit for a king. She ferociously tore her coronation gown to pieces, angrily cursing the heavens, using words that would make many men blush. After a tempest of many minutes, she was finally reduced to just her plain undergarments. Having bared herself of all regal garments, she looked toward the sky, her eyes burning with a frightening intensity, her heart pounding, her spirit still undefeated. Defiantly, and with an undiminished fury, she openly cursed the Oracle gods. "You have no right to use me this way. You think you can do with me as you wish. Well I am nobody's pawn."

Bellazar knew that the succession war was now being fought on two fronts: inside and outside the Oracle. For the first time she realized that for all of her congenital political skill, she had not fully understood that she was indeed but a mere pawn in the hands of two powerful titans who believed in nothing more than total victory. "They don't give a rat's ass who is the next king of Arcania. All they care about is themselves," she scowled at the heavens.

When she finally understood the cruelty of this joke, Bellazar looked to the skies and let her emotions explode. She laughed so boisterously hard that her stomach ached, then she lay down on the ground, among the ruins of her royal coronation dress, and as she randomly threw pieces of the dress repeatedly into the air, she laughed so hard that for only an instant she no longer cared if she ever became king.

"This is so bizarre," she said as she rolled over onto her stomach. Then like a young schoolgirl, wearing only her petticoat, she thought about her recent wedding night.

Pantamanu had lust in his eyes from the moment they entered the king's private chamber. Bellazar had never seen such passion in Rendrau's eyes. She had seen love, but nothing rivaled this naked sexual tension. Unexpectedly, Bellazar's knees buckled, as Pantamanu grabbed her about the waist. He then threw her over his shoulder and carried her to their bed, tossing her down on it like a royal concubine.

Again, Bellazar laughed, broad and hysterically until a wandering soldier thought he heard a sound. "It sounds like a woman," he said to his compatriot on this evening's forest patrol. When they investigated they saw Bellazar, in her undergarments, laughing hysterically, her fine dress torn to shreds and lying in ruins all around her.

When one of the soldiers asked her what she was doing Bellazar humorously declared, "Take me to your leader." Then she quickly quipped, "What am I saying, *I am your leader.*"

The soldiers stared at each other unsure what to make of this ridiculous site, however, very sure that this woman in petticoats did not represent a threat. "Let's take her to the general," one soldier responded. "Let him figure out what to do with her."

Within an hour the scouting party, along with Madame Bellazar, arrived at the army headquarters of General Mbanka. It was fortunate that the general knew Bellazar quite well, for even in her present disheveled state he recognized her immediately. "Get some clothes for this woman," he ordered.

"We do not have clothes fit for a woman," a soldier responded.

"I am not a woman," Bellazar declared emphatically. "I am a soldier in General Mbanka's army. Get me an appropriate uniform." The soldier did not know how to respond so he looked to Mbanka for direction. When the general nodded his head in assent, the soldier withdrew and moments later he emerged with two or three uniforms, for he was unsure which one would fit her. Bellazar spotted one that seemed appropriate and while the men turned their heads, she removed her petticoat and dressed in the pale green uniform of General Mbanka's elite ladatop brigade. "I believe you will need another ladatop rider," she said as she turned and saluted.

"Madame Bellazar," Mbanka said as he returned her formal salute, "how did you get here?"

Bellazar was in no mood to recount the fantastic events of the last few hours. So instead she said, "We are about to face the enemy in battle. In fact, two enemies."

"Two!" Mbanka said with great surprise.

"Yes, and we must be ready for them both."

Chapter 69
Hatred!

After almost a millennium, an unimaginably long life span even for the Taewokan people, it was apparent to all that their beloved leader was dying. He was the oldest man in the village, so literally no Taewokan had ever known another leader, except that is, through the telling of legends, and none of them matched the sublime grandeur of the great and mighty Kublatitan. Upon his father's death, as a mere boy of seventy-five, barely old enough to vote in tribal meetings, Kublatitan assumed the position of Macta, which literally translated means "our most beloved leader." Despite this honor, many tribal elders remained skeptical that an inexperienced youth without proven ability could ably guide the people's lives. As one elder famously pronounced, "He has yet to even kill his first Kaiyata," a large highly intelligent beast upon which Taewokan society fundamentally depended. Despite having failed to prove his manhood, the young Macta assumed control at a time when Taewokan life already was beginning to change.

Due to abrupt climate changes, the Kaiyata herds had begun to migrate further east, toward the hilly terrain before the Tacanawana Mountains. This fertile area provided the beasts with natural barriers where they could more easily hide from various predators, including man. When Kublatitan had been Macta for less than one full cycle, an entire group of hunters were killed in a dangerous hunt at Telcaba Pass. While these Taewokans were rightfully immortalized in a famous song that recounted their bravery, the tribe went hungry for several intervals, surviving on the less desirable berries and fruits of the nearby wolcrey trees.

It was at this point that Kublatitan had the first of his many remarkable epiphanies. In a dream he sensed that the Taewokan people would be forced to abandon their traditional hunting lands. "I sense that we can no longer depend on the Kaiyata to feed our families," he proclaimed the next unit before a special meeting of the tribal elders.

His pronouncement was met with angry denunciations. "What are we to do?" one elder asked his face flushed with anger. "Are we to surrender our way of life because the Macta had a dream?"

The Oracle

In the intervals to follow it was apparent that Kublatitan's dream was much more than a mere reverie. He accurately prognosticated in the most extraordinary detail such events as the freak death of a woman by fire, the lack of rain for over thirty units, and a strange discoloration on the hides of the few Kaiyata that still roamed the traditional hunting lands. When one of the elders died mysteriously after eating the meat of a seriously ill Kaiyata, the people clamored for an answer. "What is to become of us?" they asked with such desperation that they virtually turned their souls over to their new leader, blindly hoping that he alone could save their lives.

The answer arrived a few units later, again in the form of a dream. Soon thereafter Kublatitan met with the elders and told them, "Survived these many years have our people because of the Kaiyata. Hunter-gatherers we are, but no longer must be." He then identified a new way of life so foreign and frankly distasteful to the Taewokan people that they reviled at the very thought of conforming to what he called a "necessary new world." He lectured, "We must live not on the hides and meat of the Kaiyata, but rather on the indigenous plants of the Delta province."

Again, as before, the elders were disbelieving. There was much pride in hunting the Kaiyata, they noted, but none at picking moribund fruits and vegetables from the ground or a nearby tree. Kublatitan's response was abrupt. "No pride there be in dying either." One elder wept so profusely at this pronouncement that all knew he would take his life, rather than conform to this new, though necessary world. The next morning his body was found hanging from a nearby wolcrey tree. Ironically, this tree and others like it provided the necessary food to preserve the Taewokan people during the worst ravages of that cycle's seemingly relentless Season of Death. Many of the elders perished. Those who survived soon came to realize that not only must their way of life change, but also that this young Macta had a strange gift that allowed him to divine the future. "Follow him we must," one of the surviving elders said sadly, for he realized that his people's traditional way of life was about to change forever. To his ancient eyes there was no glory in this new future. To Kublatitan a new way of life provided his people with more than mere sustenance, it also provided a range of new opportunities.

Within a century he encouraged the greatest mind of the Taewokan people, Bevell, to open Taewoka's first schools. He also introduced an entirely new concept, one that he also claimed to have divined from a dream. "Laws we must have," he told the people. "Not only do I tell you how to live as Macta, but also we must have rules to guide our behave." From his dreams he constructed a list of laws, seventy in all, which determined the specific parameters of everyday existence. Some were merely common sense, such as washing food before one eats it, while others defined the proper relationships between men and women. Though there was little crime in Taewoka, others proscribed the penalties for transgressions committed against the innocent. Within three centuries Kublatitan's transformation of Taewokan life was so complete that the new elders could barely remember a time when survival had depended solely on the mating and territorial habits of the Kaiyata. While that animal was still venerated in Taewokan ceremonies and song, it was only consumed on special ceremonial occasions, such as the one honoring the anniversary of Kublatitan's ascent.

Given Kublatitan's long life and his transformative influence on the Land of the Taewokans, it is difficult to describe precisely how frightened his people were when they first discovered that their Macta's life was finally coming to an end. "What will we do without him?" a woman asked, her hands shaking toward the heavens as she implored the gods to save their Macta. Eternal life is not possible even for a man so powerful as Kublatitan, or at least that was then the common belief.

Then the mighty man had a final epiphany. It would be possible to preserve his wisdom for future generations. Death and life were one. When life ended, a new portal could be opened, and the LaKotey could be preserved for all eternity. The people rejoiced in this revelation, for while it changed their very perceptions of existence, it comforted them also, for they now understood that there was more to existence than life in this one realm, this one dimension. Life continued even after death.

But how could one communicate with the dead? That was another problem entirely. Kublatitan had an answer. In yet another one of his dreams, he sensed that he might be able to harness his thoughts forever. Kublatitan believed that, "Experience I have too much of to waste." Each breath now pained him more than he could publicly admit. His aide, Dongitar, like many of the tribal leaders, was frightened by the prospect of life without Kublatitan. "I do not know what we will do without you," he told his beloved leader. "If only there were a way to communicate with your LaKotey once you have passed."

Kublatitan considered Dongitar's lament for almost a fortnight, before he finally decided to attempt what the high priests called the Keltaba, a process where one wills their own consciousness from one person or object to another. Dongitar responded harshly. "Those stories are pure fantasy. They are not real."

This only served to further antagonize the dying monarch, for upon hearing his aide's advice, Kublatitan ordered the construction of a crude, ordinary looking vase with the sign of a tornado or swirling vortex on its side. Three times each successive unit he sat with his feet crossed, while he held the vase firmly in his two hands. Then, Kublatitan concentrated intensely on the very center of his being. He was sure that inside each man and woman there is a central core, a place where all of our key thoughts and ideas reside. He tried to visualize this core, to bring it into focus. When he did he saw strange psychedelic lines of light, each spreading out before him in a kaleidoscope of vibrant colors of all imaginable shades and types. He was disoriented at first, but he embraced the sensation of this strange world of color and light.

When he reported the results of his experiments, his doctors concluded that he was hallucinating. "No man, not even Kublatitan, in his present weak state, can concentrate for so long without seeing the most peculiar things." Then, he was firmly instructed, "You must rest."

When the doctors had the vase seized, Kublatitan had five others brought to him. On some units he sat alone with the vessels. Other units he asked his most trusted associates, such as Dongitar and Bevell, to sit with him and likewise concentrate on their central core. Dongitar claimed to feel nothing. Bellazar sensed a rainbow or some other manifestation of a succession of vibrant and colorful lights.

No one expected the experiment to work. After more than a fortnight, when Kublatitan finally fell deathly ill, the vases were taken from the Macta's home and buried in various caves throughout the Land of the Taewokans. They were meant to honor their dead leader, but they were soon forgotten and little notice was paid when, a century later, an Arcanian by the name of Zanzaska accidently discovered one of them in a cave on the Arcanian border of the Tacanawana Mountains, the tall and dangerous range that demarcated Arcania from the Land of the Taewokans. Zanzaska believed that the vessel was nothing more than an ancient drinking pot and his sole intent was to retrieve it for the Arcania Museum at Teta. On the return journey to Arcania he had the most astonishing dream. He believed that he was visited by a presence, neither alive nor dead.

After several such reveries, Zanzaska realized that he was not dreaming at all, but that an elderly Taewokan leader was trying to communicate with him. In time he realized the man's name was Kublatitan. Zanzaska still did not realize the full potential of the vessel or that he inadvertently had been absorbed through its narrow aperture. That would not become apparent to Zanzaska until he later died, many miles from the vessel, then residing not in a museum, but in the hands of his monarch, King Leonata.

By that time the consciousness of hundreds of other men and women had been absorbed into the Oracle, including King Leonata and his top military advisers. Kublatitan was startled to find that these other entities, of lesser moral quality than he, were merging with his own unique thoughts. Angrily, he tried to avoid them. As more entities entered the Oracle, Kublatitan realized that his creation was no longer completely under his exclusive control. And since a king had created the Oracle, he discovered that the device quickly developed a voracious appetite for power.

Kublatitan was repulsed by many of the emotions he was forced to confront, but one feeling troubled him more than any other: **hatred!** Kublatitan had been one of the lucky souls who had passed his entire life without reference to hateful thoughts. His mind was always consumed with the welfare of others. And while he understood such common vices as avarice and physical lust, he simply could not understand what value hatred produced. Those who were consumed by it generally lived dreadfully unhappy lives. "What need is there for it?" he asked Bevell who had also been absorbed into the Oracle.

Yet as new and mostly unwanted entities continued to enter the Oracle, Kublatitan came to realize that hatred was not a rare emotion, limited only to a few, but rather that it was a powerful motivating force that literally controlled many people's lives. Furthermore, under its exigencies, people often acted in ways that were entirely self-defeating, doing the absolutely most illogical thing, simply to assuage their need to hate.

This realization, that hatred was perhaps the most powerful and unstable of all human emotions, was never more apparent than the time when I, Count Belicki first gazed upon the Oracle, intent on stealing it for my own glory. I was a cunning man, devious to the core. I barely had a thought during my entire lifetime that was not dominated by the promotion of my own well-being. Fascinated with this new character, Kublatitan studied me diligently. He soon learned that I was a hedonist. I killed men simply because I enjoyed it or because I didn't like the way they looked. I executed women because they did not satisfy me in bed. I stole from those who could least afford it, because they were the easiest targets for my insatiable greed. My dreams were not of a better life for my people, but of domination, pure and simple. I wanted to be a ruler, not for the things that I could bring to my people, but rather for what they could bring to me.

Such thoughts endlessly fascinated Kublatitan. Yet to this point he had experienced hatred only second hand, through a dispassionate study of the tortured emotions of the vast entities the Oracle had absorbed over time. He considered hatred to be a dangerous malady in need of a cure. The more he studied it, the more he noticed that it was also a powerful motivating factor. How else could one explain the deranged relationship between Bellazar and Pantamanu? If the two had merely agreed to join together they would now rule Arcania and their family would do so for many generations to come. Yet, despite that clear, unimpeachable logic, the two existed for but one purpose - to destroy each other. Had not Bellazar said that she wanted to kill Pantamanu and did not Kublatitan sense a similar feeling in Pantamanu's heart? Kublatitan had done some terrible things, such as destroying my secret tunnel and killing thousands of men and beasts. He had not acted out of a spirit of hatred, but rather out of a cold calculation that the succession war must be prevented, lest a further immeasurable loss of life would necessarily ensue. Consequently, even in killing thousands, Kublatitan righteously believed that his actions were fully justified on moral grounds.

Yet, he finally came to understand that the only emotion Bellazar and Pantamanu shared was a blind, insatiable contempt for each other. And as he thought about my even sharper, viler hatred, the giant Taewokan finally realized, "Ambition is a powerful motivator. This war is driven primarily by unsullied hatred and in this regard I am but a mere innocent, unable to comprehend this simple concept." He carefully thought about the dangers of embracing hatred, but he also understood that if he did not study it more closely, he would never be able to outthink his primary enemy. And if he failed, Kublatitan would never be able to return the Oracle to its rightful place, in the hands of the good people in the Land of Taewoka.

Kublatitan therefore, metaphorically speaking, opened his heart for the very first time to the possibility that hatred might have some hidden value. Unfortunately, Bevell and other wise entities, who might have warned him of the dangers of this precipitate action, were still entrapped in the King's Castle. "I know the danger," he thought carefully, "but Belicki is in some ways more powerful than I am because of his hatred." The thought of being like me almost caused Kublatitan to rethink his strategy. His belief that the Oracle must be cleansed of all impurities, however, compelled him to go forward. Besides, he reasoned, nothing can fundamentally change who I am. Certainly, he would be able to control even this strongest and foulest of human emotions. He therefore settled upon a new strategy: to embrace my hatred in order to better understand it. Kublatitan therefore concentrated on this one aspect of human frailty. As he did so, without realizing it, he also opened the way for the reconstitution of the Oracle, for he needed to sense the thoughts of the many Oracle entities, and in this way, he inadvertently provided a nascent means for the various entities, now trapped in the King's Castle, to commence a return to the vessel of imagination.

At first Kublatitan felt nothing but the sensation of pure emptiness, a thorough and total lack of meaning, for the powerful Macta realized that hatred, for all its outward manifestations, leaves nothing of significance behind in its place. It is an utterly barren emotion. "Nothing of value ever has been constructed on its base," Kublatitan thought. Still, the great Taewokan leader concentrated harder. Since the Oracle was now in complete disarray, it was difficult for him to sense the thoughts of the various entities, but in time his powerful mind was able to open a narrow pathway that connected him to some of the Oracle entities.

He first sensed the hatred of an abused woman for her husband. She had been beaten brutally and repeatedly, finally killing her husband while he slept, a crime for which she was condemned by an angry mob to a hanging death. Kublatitan noticed that even as the villagers put the rope around her neck, her hatred for her departed husband continued to fuel her thoughts. "She is not afraid to die," he realized, for she hated life with her husband far more than death.

Then, Kublatitan felt the heat of another entity's thoughts. It was a soldier, a man who had fought in battle many times. This man was weary and tired. "Hatred has entirely withered his soul," Kublatitan observed.

Kublatitan now realized that hatred comes in many forms. Sometimes it is driven by events, while at other times it drives them. It was a complication that Kublatitan had not anticipated. It further peaked his curiosity and forced him to concentrate even more deeply on hatred's insidious nature. For several hours he randomly collected the thoughts of men and women, both honorable and despicable, trying to fathom their intentions, their motivations, the wounds that had caused them to hate, and the societal norms that encouraged distrust and enmity toward others. As he consumed these ideas, he felt that he still did not fully understand the true face of hatred.

"There is but one way to comprehend it," Kublatitan realized at last. "I must seek out Belicki himself." This was a dangerous task, for by melding directly with my consciousness, he would undoubtedly reveal his own thoughts and ideas. In some respects, Kublatitan was still more powerful than any other entity, for he alone possessed this ability to link with others. By entering my mind, he would expose himself to possible ruin. As he thought about the consequences, Kublatitan realized that he had no other alternative. "We can fight forever, a perpetual stalemate, or I can bring order to the Oracle. The only way is to confront Belicki directly."

And so, Kublatitan concentrated on my form and face. Instantly, he felt the lightening heat of my deformed personality. At the same time I also sensed Kublatitan's presence. With this realization, my raw hatred was exposed and aimed directly at the mighty Taewokan. Though it was an entirely metaphorical event, in the form of unbridled energy, it appeared in our minds in images of successive powerful lightening strikes, as two incompatible rival titans were suddenly connected. An electrically charged bridge was therefore created that allowed the thoughts of both titans to move in alternate directions.

"So you come to understand me better in order to destroy me," I noted with considerable self-satisfaction.

Kublatitan said nothing. Instead he concentrated on one overriding aspect of my personality, the searing red-hot hatred that burned at the very core of my existence. Kublatitan realized that hatred alone was the one emotion that propelled me. There were no other mediating feelings of contrition. My hatred was deep and inexhaustible. I hated my father, perhaps more than anything. Kublatitan saw the specter of the young Belicki, watching a family, savagely burning in a hellish funeral pyre. A helpless mother, tied to a stake, stared back at him with consummate horror. In that instant, Kublatitan realized how my personality had been formed and deformed. He also understood how these emotions festered, evolving into new manifestations of sadomasochistic torture, a hatred that was aimed both inward toward myself and externally toward those all around me.

Until this very instant Kublatitan had never imagined that self-loathing could be such a powerful motivating force. For those who hate themselves will hate others with an even greater ferocity. And my hatred was pure and unbridled, existing solely for its own sake, continually perpetuating itself, moving randomly in directions both rational and irrational, eventually consuming its victims, as well as its source. Combined with ambition, I was a horrifically dangerous man, capable of destroying everything in my way simply to satisfy my own demonic urges.

"It is absolute perfect insanity," Kublatitan thought and for once I heartily agreed. "But it is also a flawless state of mind. I have no remorse whatsoever. My actions are fully motivated, without any counter weight. I exist to rule, to control and destroy the destiny of others, and for no reason whatsoever than to satisfy my own selfish desires."

Kublatitan could not understand how it was possible for someone to exist in such a deranged state. "Why would he want to hate so much?" he thought for a moment and then with a sudden coldness of spirit, he realized the ugly truth: when one is consumed with hatred, the only cure is more hatred, and this process continues until the whole body and mind fully rot from within.

Till now Kublatitan had felt nothing but compassion for me. Sensing that my hatred was boundless, Kublatitan knew that I would be willing to destroy Arcania and its entire people, simply to rule over them. And with this stark and frightening realization, for the very first time, Kublatitan viscerally experienced the same craven hatred that fueled my existence. He hated me with the same passion that I hated all beings!

"You don't know what you are feeling, do you?" I ridiculed the poor Macta, amused and delighted that he fully had embraced the essence of my inner being.

"It is reprehensible," Kublatitan responded, his mind racing now with thoughts both petty and profound. He tried to clear his mind of this new horrifying sensation. Like a virus it spread rapidly throughout the sundry pathways of his complex consciousness.

"For the first time in your long existence you are sensing pure blind hatred," I said with considerable satisfaction. "These thoughts frighten you, however, you also feel a remarkable new temptation."

Kublatitan tried to severe the connection with me, but he could not. Hatred now united we two rival entities in a way that nothing else ever could. With these new thoughts, Kublatitan began to morph, to change in ways that he had not anticipated. "I do not like this sensation," he cried out in desperation.

The Oracle

"It is part of you now," I said, "and in time it will grow so strong that you will no longer be able to control it. It will rule your destiny as it has always ruled mine."

Horrified, Kublatitan realized that for once I was speaking the unembellished truth. "It is an abomination," Kublatitan whispered, for he was so frightened by this change in his demeanor that he could barely acknowledge that his entire personality systematically was changing.

"Whether you like it or not you are becoming ever more like me."

"No!" Kublatitan shouted.

"It is the only way," I continued. "You cannot destroy me unless you hate me more than I hate you!"

Kublatitan felt his rage growing, and like a young boy who experiences anger for the first time, he did not quite know how to respond. Though he tried to calm his mind, Kublatitan felt his inner being suddenly charge with fire, until finally, like a child throwing a tantrum, he emitted a lightening bolt so powerful that it commenced at the ridge of the Kanaween Forest and charged all the way to Pantamanu's army which was on the move from eastern Arcania.

There, on horseback Pantamanu saw the vast red hot lightening bolt, then fell backward to the ground, as its sonic intensity shook trees, and felled grown men and beasts. The wave was so powerful that it could be felt all the way to the Land of the Taewokans. There, the gentle people of that realm wondered what horror had been exposed and what it might portend for their own lives.

Chapter 70
A Family Reunion

Montama had been at Mt. Sendil for more than four intervals when his entourage finally departed for the relatively short ride to Pellaville. Though it was called the Season of Rain, this cycle the weather was inexplicably dry. As he mounted his horse he wondered how he would be received, for this would be his first trip back to his home and its people.

Quite unexpectedly, all along the road he and his army were greeted by cheering throngs of desperate but enthusiastic people, many chanting Montama's name. Grandafier was the first to understand the nature of this political tsunami. "Public passions are fleeting. Soon enough they will come

376

to their senses and when they do they will look for yet another hero to lead them out of the wilderness. We must act quickly if we are to take advantage of this portentous public mood."

The entourage rode onward for a full unit, resting only occasionally, driven by an extraordinary boost of much needed adrenaline. As they did so the size of the army continued to expand, as young men and even some women spontaneously joined their cause. While this fact delighted Montama and Hontallo, and in time even Grandafier was swept up by the crowd's soaring emotions, General Garr remained stoic and reserved. "They have no idea what battle will be like," Garr complained, his mind fixed only on the dangers that lurked ahead.

The boundless enthusiasm of the crowds continued to grow as Montama's army reached the outskirts of Pellaville. It was a wondrous and incredible sight. The crowds were so thickly packed together that all Montama could see for a mile or more was a wall of exuberant humanity, gaily chanting his name. Barely capable of controlling his emotions the young man felt like a conquering hero, returning home after a series of victorious battles, rather than the obscure youth who had left this quaint fiefdom, less than one cycle ago.

"Montama!" the people chanted in unison. The cry became so pervasive that nothing else, at times not even his very own inner thoughts, could be heard above the din. Hontallo marveled that the clamor was so exuberant that the straw roofs of nearby buildings literally bulged and billowed, as the crowds surged ever forward, hoping to catch a mere passing glimpse of their newly ordained hero.

After marching down Main Street, Montama's entourage caught its first distant glimpse of the gates and mural wall that marked the entry into Lord Tantamount's estate. The crowds were so dense that forward movement was no longer possible. Suddenly surrounded by a veritable human shield, Montama and Hontallo listened as the crowd continued to chant. However, Montama's thoughts were with the one man who was not there. And as his thoughts drifted toward his dear father, in his mind the din from the shouting crowds regressed into mere background noise. "What will father do?" Montama thought, as they rode in the shadow of the lord's estate.

Without a word between them, the two brothers shared a common thought. Would their father even be willing to receive his sons? After all, circumstances had changed since that terrible unit when Hontallo departed. Anarchy now prevailed throughout the passra and the Centama family could hardly be described as ruling Arcania. Perhaps in this unsettled political environment Lord Tantamount had developed a newfound pride in the extraordinary deeds of his two glorious sons. The very thought that Lord Tantamount's loyalty would be so easily swayed was preposterous. Both brothers knew that at his very core their father was a man of principle. Even if the Centama family no longer ruled, his loyalty to a bygone era would still trump his love for his two sons. Now, with the real possibility that his son would soon be king, the brothers' only hope was that their father somehow could find a small measure of forgiveness in his heart and that perhaps, over time, he could be won over to the righteousness of their cause.

Incongruously, as the brother's mood soured, the crowd began to shower them with the pedals from an array of colorful wild flowers. As General Garr's troops moved forward to clear the road ahead, the procession finally continued until it arrived at Lord Tantamount's estate.

The gates and the massive wall surrounding the estate were one of the absolute marvels of Pellaville. Nothing else like it existed in all of Arcania. Constructed from dried mud, the wall extended for over two hundred yards, with the gateway at its midpoint, an almost imperceptible segment of a larger mural representing the lives and history of the Tantamount family.

Montama had seen the murals almost every single unit of his youth, yet as he approached the wall it seemed that he was seeing them for the very first time. He noticed that on one side of the extended wall was a mural of his great grandfather, standing stoically, dressed in his gray military uniform, receiving the sword of Tamarite from the delicate hands and admiring face of Lady Tantamount. As a youth, Montama had particularly enjoyed this mural, largely because he thought Lady Tantamount, who was a bit overweight and cross-eyed, looked entirely ridiculous in her admiring pose. As a young boy he had mimicked her cross-eyed appearance, evoking gales of laughter from his brother Hontallo. Now that he was at the head of a great army, Montama could see the military significance of the mural. She was holding the sword that his grandfather had carried with him into scores of glorious victorious battles, all fought to defend the august Tantamount and Centama families.

Montama next fixed his gaze toward the other far side of the wall. There he saw another familiar mural. This one was of his own dear father who was boldly holding the very same sword of Tamarite above his head with his right hand. As Montama's eyes eagerly scanned the wall he noticed many other similar images documenting the great military courage of the Tantamount family. As he perused these disparate images, Montama realized that his relatives were honored not merely because they went to war, but because each one had fought in what his father fervently believed was a loyal war. The symbolism was so stark that Montama suddenly felt ashamed of his own treasonous perfidy.

Hontallo too stared at the various images on the mural wall. "My goodness," he whispered, suddenly realizing that his defiance represented nothing more than treachery to his dear father. His concerns were at least momentarily assuaged, however, when he saw the family guards opening the giant mural gate, a tacit signal that the lord was willing to meet with his two sons. With flowers still gaily raining down upon them, the guards permitted only Montama, Hontallo, Grandafier the Elder and General Garr to enter the compound. The gates were then discretely closed, with the mercenary army resting outside, while the crowds continued to cheer enthusiastically.

It was at this point that Hontallo began to think about their appearance. They were covered rather incongruously in both dirt from the long ride and vividly colored flowers from the parade. As for Montama, as he rode the short distance toward the main estate, his mind was so fixed on the forthcoming meeting that he did not even notice the rows of bushes and wild flowers where he once had played a version of hide and seek with his brother. Rather his mind was focused on but one task. He must appear steadfast and confident, no matter what his father's reaction might be. After all, he was now in line to be Arcania's next king. He must project that level of confidence and thereby win his father's favor, if not now, then surely sometime soon. It was therefore with a combination of dread and sadness, that the two brothers dismounted their horses, mentally preparing themselves for a most solemn reunion with their beloved father and quite possibly bitter political opponent.

Montama led the other three men to the front door of the lord's ornate estate. Before he could signal his arrival, however, the door suddenly sprung open. Standing there was a servant, dressed in formal brown attire; his overlarge collars and baggy pants a sign of the times. "Come in he directed." The four men began to move forward when the servant suddenly raised his right hand and firmly though quite politely stated, "Only the lord's two sons may enter."

The Oracle

General Garr was noticeably insulted by this gesture. Spotting his companion's discomfort, Grandafier quickly intervened, "I will give General Garr a tour of the grounds."

General Garr was uninterested in pleasantries. "To hell with the tour," he cursed in a foul mood. "I will see to the troops instead." Without as much as another word or even a knowing glance at either of the two brothers, Garr turned, re-mounted his horse, all with due military decorum. A careful student of body language would have had no difficulty noticing the rage that seethed just beneath the general's outward show of calm.

As the general's horse sped back down the path toward the gate, Grandafier turned to the two brothers and said rather tactfully, "Well in that case, I guess I will sit for awhile on the bench by the door. Certainly my old bones are in need of rest."

Montama smiled politely, while Hontallo merely nodded his head in a friendly gesture. Both young men were nervous as they entered the house where they had lived, for this was the first time they entered it as mere guests, invited in only at the pleasure of Lord Tantamount. It was only now that Montama realized, "I have no home anymore." Until this very moment he had never thought through the full implications of his rebellious deeds. Now he could find no way to escape them.

With such thoughts on their minds, the servant led the two brothers down the hall toward their father's study. As they entered this most familiar room they noticed that their father stood at the far window looking aimlessly outside, while Timilty sat with a stack of disorganized papers behind the lord's desk. The two sons were directed by the servant to take a seat, but as they did so, the lord continued to ignore them, instead staring out the window. Timilty also did nothing to acknowledged their arrival. Hontallo and Montama thus sat, chastened, and uncertain, waiting for any acknowledgement that they were welcome.

Meanwhile Timilty used his third short hand to sift through the papers on the desk, At last he declared emphatically, "I have found it my lord." His statement was perfunctory and without even a trace of emotion.

As Tantamount continued to stare out the window he directed Timilty to share the latest information with his two sons. At least, Montama thought, his father did refer to them as his "sons," but other than this reference, there was no show of fatherly pride or acceptance.

Still seated behind the desk, Timilty picked up a stack of papers and rose to address the lord's guests. Timilty was a man of unbounded loyalty to

Lord Tantamount. Both brothers knew that his expression would mirror their father's own thoughts and emotions. What they saw frightened them and what he said next terrified them.

"We have reports that several Bogul villages have been attacked over the last four intervals, almost all of them in the areas directly south of Mt. Sendil. By our estimates over one hundred men, women and children have been slaughtered."

Hontallo was the first to respond, forthrightly acknowledging, "We too have heard of these attacks."

"Do you know the source of the attacks?" Timilty asked inquisitorially, his eyes fixed upon a certain document in particular that he held firmly with his short third hand.

"We have heard only that the attackers wore hooded white robes to disguise their identity," Hontallo again responded, nervously clearing his throat as he concluded his thought.

Timilty sifted through the papers until he fixed his gaze on one that seemed to be of particular significance. He then read the text aloud for the two young men. "This is an affidavit from someone who witnessed the attack. It reads, 'Our family was attacked while we slept. I was able to hold one of the attackers at bay while my wife ran toward the children. Another hooded man, a much larger and stronger one, grabbed her by the neck and strangled her. I was thrown to the floor and a knife was placed against my throat. As I lay helplessly on the floor, three men in hoods brought my two boys into the room and while I watched, they stabbed them both with their swords. They were just ten and eleven cycles old. The man then slit my own throat and left me to die, though through some miracle I survived, though none of my family did.'"

Timilty looked up at the two brothers. He then pulled out another paper with his third hand and held it close to his face so that he could read it aloud. "Here is another testimony." He squinted as he read the text. "I saw eight men on horseback, each wearing a white robe to disguise their identity. I hid in the bushes outside our village until they were gone. Then, I went to my father's hut. His eyes were wide open, but he could not speak. His throat had been cut. While I watched he struggled to breath and then he fell on the ground in front of me and died." Then skipping down the page Timilty read, "In all thirty in our village were killed, including my cousins, my aunts, my uncles, my grandmother, and my best friend."

Looking up at the two brothers Timilty added, "I have several other such documents testifying to the detestable brutality of these raids."

Montama had said nothing until now. Nervously he interjected, "We have heard of these terrible crimes." Montama glanced at his father who still refused to look at his two sons. "We have been told that these sorts of terrible things happen during war…"

"Who told you that, General Garr?" Timilty curtly interrupted.

Montama responded calmly and succinctly, "Yes."

Slowly Timilty picked up an object and carried it forward for the two brothers to see. "Have you ever seen this before?" he asked as he held out a short sword. It had an insignia that was familiar to both brothers. It was a symbol of the letter "G", in the shape of a venomous coiled snake.

Both brothers had seen the half sword many times before. Hontallo's eyes veritably bulged from his face at the sight of the weapon, while Montama nervously looked away. "I recognize it," Hontallo said breathlessly. "That is General Garr's insignia." Then looking up at Timilty with a look of total horror on his face Hontallo added, "It's General Garr's weapon."

"And what do you say?" Timilty asked Montama as he took a step closer to the young man, presumably so that he could get an even closer look at the sword. Montama felt trapped, and his mind raced as he tried to think of a convincing explanation. When Hontallo saw the look on Montama's face, he instinctively shifted his body weight away from his brother.

Montama leaned uneasily forward, inspecting the knife closely. He had seen General Garr polish it on several occasions, as had Hontallo. He had even held it in his hand. It was the same weapon that Rendrau had used to take his own life. There was no use denying its authenticity. "It looks like his weapon," he admitted, suddenly feeling precisely like a caged animal.

"I can't believe this," Hontallo declared emotionally, his voice rising by nearly an entire octave as he spoke. Desperately he grabbed the sword from Timilty's hands and inspected it closely. Finally, with great consternation he said, "This cannot be."

Montama now thought of a ruse. "Perhaps it was planted there," he said defensively. "General Garr has powerful enemies. They would do anything to destroy him."

Momentarily Hontallo looked hopeful, ready to accept any possible explanation rather than admit to the obvious truth. Timilty would have none of it. "We found this quite by accident, in a patch of weeds, not exactly the place one would plant a sword if one wanted to implicate someone. In fact, if one of our guards had not chosen to relieve himself in that very spot, the sword may never have been found at all."

Montama's eyes nervously scanned the sword, its dangerously coiled multi-headed snake staring angrily back at him, as he again tried to think of yet another plausible excuse. When he could think of nothing to say, he suddenly realized that his brother's cold gaze was fixed directly upon him, now wondering the unthinkable.

Defensively, Montama looked at his brother and in a loud but unconvincing voice exclaimed, "I had nothing to do with this." Then he looked first at Timilty and then at his father, who still refused to even acknowledge either of his sons. As he did Montama fervently declared, "I am not responsible for this, I assure you." As he spoke, Montama realized that his frightened reaction simply served to further betray his own guilt. Desperately, he stared at the sword hoping that he could think of any excuse whatsoever. Then with a moan that was frighteningly palpable in its sadness and horror, he muttered, "I… I did not think it would ever come to this."

Hontallo now stood and grabbed Montama by his shirt and forcefully swung him around so that he was staring directly into his brother's eyes. "What do you know of this?" Hontallo demanded. When Montama did not or could not answer he again repeated in an even firmer tone of voice, "Brother, what do you know of this?" Montama's entire body began to shiver with such a fierce intensity that Hontallo temporarily feared that Montama would collapse. "You were taken in by this man, deceived by him, weren't you?" Hontallo implored. With each spoken word Hontallo could see ever clearer that his brother felt nothing more than wretched, overwhelming guilt. Then with a frightful recognition he asked, "You knew about this, didn't you?" his eyes misting profusely as he spoke.

Montama's entire body continued to shake uncontrollably. He looked at Timilty then at his brother. Hontallo's eyes were sadder than Montama had ever seen them in his entire life. Montama now saw that he had no other recourse than to tell the truth and hope that he could somehow be forgiven. "I must tell you something awful," he commenced, his voice so unsteady that it appeared at first he might not be able to finish his thoughts. He persevered, and slowly his composure was settled to the point that he was able to communicate the entire sorry episode about his initial meeting with General Garr. He told his brother how he was forced to choose either to kill an innocent Bogul man with his own hands or die. As he did so, he could hear his father weep, though Timilty showed only a barrister's satisfaction at Montama's solemn confession.

"I didn't want to do it," Montama pleaded. "I wanted to run. I realized what a horrible mistake I had made, but I had no choice."

"We always have choices," Timilty intervened. "Only the guilty say they have no choice."

Hontallo put his arm around his brother and hugged him tight. "I believe you," he whispered in his brother's ear, loud enough that even Lord Tantamount could hear it from his lonely place across the room. Montama's emotions were now entirely unleashed. He wept as if he was but a mere boy of ten, not nearly twenty, and his tears were so abundant that they dampened Hontallo's shirt. Hontallo patted his brother on his back, and then caressed his shoulder, while Timilty carried the half sword back and then dispassionately dropped it on the desk.

For a few moments the scene resided in such a terrible state that no one knew what to say. Finally, Hontallo, demonstrating due contrition, admitted, "We must have General Garr arrested and you must confess to what you have done."

With a frightful look, Montama pulled back from his brother and stared at him with a renewed sense of desperation, a fear so deep that he had never before experienced it, not even in the heat of battle. "I can't do that," he said with such fright that his brother could feel the tension developing between them.

"You must," Hontallo responded gently. "I will stand with you." Then looking toward his father he added, "We will all stand with you." His father, though he had not said a word, nodded his head subtly in agreement, while Timilty coldly took his seat behind the lord's desk.

Montama now sounded more desperate than ever. "I can't!" he said again, his eyes aglow with a fiery red glare. "If I do I will never be king," he said as if such things were more important than the evil deeds of General Garr.

Hontallo realized how difficult this was for his brother and so with a love that only two brothers can share he gently massaged his brother's shoulder while saying, "I'm afraid my dear brother, that that can never be."

Montama again pulled back from his brother and stared at him with a wild look, one that Hontallo had never before seen. It was a look that bordered on pure insanity. Montama tried to say something, but he could not speak. Instead he again looked toward his father, who cried pitiably, his face now buried in his hands. Hontallo realized that Lord Tantamount was now sadder than he had ever been in his entire life, even sadder than when his dear wife died. All of his hopes for his family lay in ruins. Not only had his sons led a rebellion against the family that he had dedicated his life to serving, but his own son had been part of a terrible genocidal conspiracy. For an innately principled man totally dedicated to fairness and equality, this revelation was simply more than the lord could bear.

Montama too understood that all of his own dreams were completely destroyed. He would never win his father's favor. Overcome with panic, Montama pushed his brother, who fell back toward his father's desk. Terrified, Montama asked, "What do you intend to do about all of this?"

"You must do the right thing. I will stand by your side when you confess to this crime," Hontallo said supportively. "I will tell everyone that this monster General Garr fooled you, that he manipulated you and we will hold him accountable for these unforgivably foul deeds."

Montama vehemently shook his head from side to side. "I cannot let you do that," Montama uttered defensively.

"We must!" Hontallo insisted, his love for his brother still apparent even as he pleaded with Montama. "It is the right thing to do!"

Again Montama shook his head and this time he shouted so loud that Grandafier, seated outside the estate could hear his primal scream. "No!" Montama then turned and sprinted toward the front door. As he did he clumsily knocked the servant off his feet. As Montama ran outside, Grandafier could see that the young man was frightened out of his wits. Stepping forward toward Montama, whose eyes were wild, Grandafier implored, "What happened?"

Montama responded indirectly, telling Grandafier that they must get the guards at once. When Grandafier called out for one of Lord Tantamount's guards, Montama distraught to the point of near collapse ordered, "No, not those guards, our own guards." As Grandafier tried to understand this order, Montama declared, "I want this house surrounded. No one, not even my father or my brother is to be allowed to leave."

Grandafier could see that there was no arguing with Montama and so, as quickly as he could, the old man mounted his horse and raced down the path toward the front gate. In just a few minutes, General Garr's army pushed Lord Tantamount's guards aside and entered the compound. Lord Tantamount, Hontallo and Timilty were now under house arrest.

Chapter 71
The Sword of Tamarite

Timilty's voice quaked with fear as he exclaimed, "We must escape now!" The cacophony of horses' hoofs and the scurrying of soldiers' feet could be distinctly heard by the three men inside the house. "We can escape by the back exit, but we must leave now!" Timilty directed in earnest.

Lord Tantamount was unmoved by the gravity of the present swiftly deteriorating situation. Rather than appearing like a frightened and caged man, he stood stoically by the window looking out aimlessly, not seeming to notice or care about the raging tumult that now surrounded his once well protected home. Dejectedly, in a barely audible voice, he whispered solemnly, "And where will we go? " For the first time since Hontallo had entered the room, Lord Tantamount now turned slowly and looked directly at his son. It was apparent that he was sure that he would die. Solemnly, he whispered, "We have no place to run. This is no longer our passra."

Hontallo realized that his father had aged twenty cycles in just the past few intervals. Though his skin was still yellow, the lines on his face were deep, palpable signs of his present state of extreme and overwhelming exhaustion. Hontallo's own eyes also no longer betrayed a youthful disposition and his naïve innocence about all matters political had been betrayed in a single instant by a reality that he could not yet fully understand. He did not yet fathom why Montama had run from the security of his loving family or why he would consider it more important to be king than to stand up for what was right. Hontallo never had been consumed or even tempted by an obsession with power. To him, aligning himself with his brother had been a mere matter of family loyalty. He had defied his father because he was proud of his brother and because his mother urged him to go to Mt. Sendil. Now, having learned of his brother's participation in the genocidal deeds of General Garr, Hontallo's only thought was that his brother had terribly lost his way, most likely forever, and that Hontallo's only hope was to rescue his father and, if possible, the family name. As he looked into his father's vacant eyes, Hontallo realized that this would be a near impossible task. Worldly forces were moving faster

386

than mere humans could control. The words, "This is no longer our passra," now reverberated in Hontallo's mind. His father was right. They no longer belonged to Arcania, whether Montama was ultimately victorious or not. Their lives as proud citizens of the passra were at an end. They would now be brandished as enemies of the state. With the sounds of hostile troops all around the house and with no place to run, Hontallo understood his father's sense of utter doom.

Still, he did not know how to communicate his feelings to his father. So, instead of a cascade of meaningless words, he followed his heart, walking to his father's side, putting his arm around the man that he loved more than life itself, then embracing him with such affection that no words were necessary. Lord Tantamount closed his eyes and fought back the tears, for he knew precisely what his son was thinking. He too was saddened beyond all reasonable hope, for the breach between the lord and Montama was now irreparable.

Tantamount tried to understand his son's behavior. Without thinking, in a moment of panic, Montama had made a fateful decision. He had chosen the allure of ambition and power over the love and well being of his own family. In so doing, Montama had made an irreversible decision. As he held his father so tight that he could feel Lord Tantamount's heart beat, Hontallo now realized why his father had been wise to remain loyal, and how his father had been right all along, despite the prophesies of their mother and the Oracle. There was considerable virtue in loyalty after all, even if in the end you were not on the winning side.

Timilty had been standing just a few feet away and had drawn considerable comfort from the father and son reunion. His fear, which had been daunting, now seemed manageable after all. He fully understood the wisdom of Lord Tantamount's pronouncement. "You are right," he said meekly. "There no longer is any place for us in Arcania." With this acknowledgement, the Ka-Why-Tee barrister's fear was alleviated and instead he felt a sense of both righteousness and total emancipation. For even if he were made to be a prisoner, he would be a free man, free in his thoughts and ideals, unfettered by the stench of Montama's sins.

Just as Timilty came to grips with his feelings, several men burst through the front door, rudely pushing the servants aside. Timilty, Lord Tantamount and Hontallo stood helpless as they heard the shouts and cries of their loyal servants as General Garr's army stormed the house. Then, as they stood waiting inside Tantamount's study, surrounded by the books, medals, honors, and treasures of the lord's prolific lifetime, they heard the harsh, menacing sound of military boots echoing on hardwood floors. The footsteps grew ominously nearer, step by step. It was unnecessary for any of the servants to announce the arrival of General Garr, for though Lord Tantamount had never met the man, he sensed that his mortal enemy was fast approaching. As for Hontallo, he hugged his father even tighter, not out of fear, but out of a need to protect him from an inexorably evil force.

The first the three men saw of Garr was the general's dark shadow, cast suddenly upon the study's far wall. Garr stood still for a moment. "You are all under house arrest," he formally declared. Then as he stepped forward into the room, he fixed his one dark and repulsive eye directly upon Lord Tantamount and young Hontallo. "If it were up to me I would kill you both now," he said.

Hontallo said nothing for he was too frightened to speak, while his father chose to remain silent. Instead it was the fiercely loyal Timilty who stepped forward to block General Garr's path. "You are not welcome here," he declared defiantly, holding his head high, clearly unafraid of the consequences of his futile resistance.

"Is this the best you can offer in your defense?" Garr laughed contemptuously. "An old and decrepit Ka-Why-Tee barrister." Garr spit at Timilty, then laughed anew, though it sounded more like the snorting noise of a wild beast.

Enraged by General Garr's countenance, Hontallo now found the courage to speak. "We will not offer any resistance, but if we are freed, we will speak our minds." Hontallo had spent nearly three intervals with General Garr, and while he never particularly liked or trusted the man, he had heretofore respected him. Now his eyes were firmly fixed on this terrible villain, who had led his brother permanently astray, a man who apparently cared nothing for the sanctity of human life. Hontallo had no fear of this monster or his army, for he realized that they existed only to secure power and for no other more noble purpose. Hontallo also understood that even if he were to die now on this very spot, the love of his family was worth more to him than all the power that General Garr could ever promise. Accompanying this thought was a renewed sense of infinite sadness that Montama had failed to arrive at the same obvious conclusion.

General Garr was uninterested in sentimentality. He had come to Lord Tantamount's study with a specific purpose in mind, to secure a sacred object, one he believed Montama must have literally by his side in the great battle to come. And there, mounted on the wall over the fireplace, where his ominous shadow had been cast, lay the object of his intentions – the sacred sword of Tamarite; unsheathed as it hung on the wall, its silvery shaft glowing as it was now suddenly struck by a solitary ray of sunlight streaming through the nearby window. This was the very same majestic sword that a cross-eyed Lady Tantamount had adoringly handed to the late great Lord Tantamount of old, the one glorified on the mural walls. It was only fitting that in his greatest moment of glory that Montama should carry this family heirloom into battle. Garr therefore abruptly stepped forward past the three men and without hesitation grabbed the sword with his right hand. He held it high in the air so that he could admire the sharpness of its blade and the genius of its craftsmanship. "This is a fine sword indeed," he said admiringly.

"Put it down," Timilty said firmly, without even a hint of trepidation.

"As you wish," Garr responded with a devious smile. He then hastily spun toward Timilty while quickly extending his right hand, as he plunged the sword deep into the Ka-Why-Tee's chest, near the nexus of the third short arm. He pierced Timilty's body so swiftly that Timilty had no time to defend himself. The sword, deadly sharp, easily pierced Timilty's chest cavity, and the elderly barrister, instead of groaning with pain, merely looked down at the sword, supremely content to die in this heroic fashion. He then placed his short hand upon the sword, gently caressed the valued family treasure, and then fell lifelessly forward. With a violent thrust Garr withdrew the bloody sword and Timilty's limp body slumped to the floor.

Lord Tantamount watched the spectacle, not so much in horror as in resigned fascination. "I am next," he said with such a resolve that it appeared to Hontallo that he was eagerly inviting the general to step forward and put an end to his pitiful suffering. Garr was unwilling to show such mercy. Instead, he reached over on the desk, retrieved his half-sword, then turned slowly, and with the bloody sword of Tamarite still clasped in his right hand, and his own short sword now in his left hand, the general calmly walked past the lord and back out of the room.

As the general departed Hontallo moved forward and put his right arm around Timilty's bloody chest. Certain that the faithful servant was dead, he looked back up at his father and said, "We will die together, father." Hontallo now understood what motivated his father. For Lord Tantamount life had no meaning without honor.

Chapter 72
Confessions

Montama could not think straight. His breathing was labored, sweat formed profusely on his forehead, and his heart seemed to beat right through his chest. Furthermore, he could not determine with certainty whether the events of the past hour had been real or only a mad dream. As he sat now on a bench in the garden, where he often had found peace in times of bitter travail, he did not even have the presence of mind to marvel at the green, pink and yellow wild flowers that lay in abundance near his feet. Nor could he even recognize their calming scent. His mind was cluttered and confused as he wrestled with what little remained of his conscience.

"Why can't they see that I am trying to protect them?" he thought, still trying to convince himself of the nobility of his cause. He suddenly stood and violently kicked the dirt in front of him. "Damn, it, why can't they see that everything I am doing is for them, for us, for the Tantamount family?" He cursed, and then desperately tried to convince himself of the worthiness of his cause and the unfairness of his family's reaction. Finally, he sat again, this time pouting like a spoiled child on a cold cement bench. As he did so he again tried to rationalize his own behavior. "I had no choice," he said aloud. "The Oracle controls my destiny. I must be king. Only then will I be able to right these wrongs." Then with a fury that he could barely contain he added, "Can't they understand that?"

Montama was as lost as he had ever been in his entire life. His justification for the events of the past cycle had been that the Oracle had prophesized that he alone among all the people of Arcania was fit to be the next king, presumably for the good of the passra and his own family. Now that rationalization stood exposed as a bald faced lie. Montama realized it was not loyalty to his family that had driven him to the Relatin Empire to secure an army. It was not fealty to his father that had sustained him during the horrible collapse of the tunnel walls or the ensuing battles at Kalel and King's Castle. Instead, it was the seed of a despicable spirit of unadulterated ambition. Finally, as he sat in his garden near the flowers that Hontallo had planted with care, he finally realized that it was his own unbridled ambition, his lust for power that had driven his every action. Just like the Centama family, just like all other pretenders to every throne, he was consumed with a desire to lead. He might try to decorate his ambition with fancy bromides about patriotism or love of family, but lying just beneath the surface was a reckless determination to be king, a sensation that was so raw it festered like an open wound. And all of his justifications were mere excuses, for the plain cold, hard realization was that he wanted to be king more than he wanted anything else.

With such thoughts finally exposed, Montama did not notice that he was no longer alone. Grandafier stood but a few yards away from his protégé, carefully studying him, waiting for just the right time to intervene. Now that the young man appeared more settled, he limped over to the cold cement bench and sat down next to Montama.

Montama was so embarrassed that he could barely find the strength to look at the elderly man. Instead, he looked down at the ground, and while he tapped his fingers nervously on his left leg, he spoke softly and resignedly. "I actually thought I was doing this out of some patriotic duty. You know, fulfilling the Oracle's prophecy." He then took a deep breath before continuing, "But when Hontallo told me that I would never be king I snapped. I finally realized that the only thing I want is to be king. Nothing else matters to me anymore."

Grandafier did not yet know the facts that had precipitated the family crisis, but he had his suspicions. He knew of General Garr's raids and though he had said nothing to Montama about them, he sensed that the young man had made some sort of unholy alliance with the mercenary in order to secure the support of his army. What else would explain why a seasoned soldier such as General Garr would defer to an untested youth such as Montama? It therefore required no explanation for Grandafier to fill in the blanks.

"You know," Grandafier said as he sat back looking out at the beautiful garden that lay before him, "we often have to make difficult choices in life. Heaven knows I have had my share of such decisions. For a king the choices are even greater and far more consequential. Frankly, if a king puts his family first he cannot be a good king. In the end, he must do what is right for the entire passra."

Montama turned on Grandafier with such a force of anger that the old man barely recognized his young charge. "And killing innocent people, slaughtering them in the name of patriotism, then turning on my own family, that is what is expected of a king?"

Grandafier, always the politician, sought to defuse the young man's anger with rhetoric, not reason. "Some people must inevitably suffer so that the greater good shall be served," he said forthrightly.

"So it is right to murder innocents?" Montama asked incredulously.

"Of course not," Grandafier admitted, retreating a bit from his indefensibly extreme position. Attempting to reposition himself he asked a simple and irrefutable question. "Do you think Pantamanu would care a twit about the life of a few meaningless Boguls? Do you think that he would save their lives if it meant that he would never be king?" Montama said nothing. Instead he lowered his head, still feeling deeply ashamed. "No," Grandafier continued, forthrightly answering his own question. "He would kill every damn one of them and think nothing of the matter. And as for his family, he even had his own dear wife, Celia, murdered, out of the needs of mere expediency. Is that the man you want to be Arcania's next king?"

"So what you are saying is that I am no better than Pantamanu?" Montama responded with such a pitiable squeak that his voice could barely be heard.

Grandafier responded adamantly, pausing between each word as he spoke. "That is not my point!" Then with a calmer demeanor he continued, "Of course you are different and better than him, but sometimes even good people have to make difficult choices. And that is all you have done."

"So what are we to say to the Boguls who died because I made a difficult choice?" Montama exclaimed defensively. "What are we to say to the father, whose young boys were butchered at the hands of General Garr?"

"There is nothing we can say to the victims of war," Grandafier admitted coldly. "There will be many casualties before this succession war is concluded and unfortunately we are not in a position to exonerate all of the innocents who may fall in harm's way."

"So we just tell them tough luck, is that it?" Montama asked, still trying to fathom the logic of Grandafier's argument.

Grandafier paused for a moment to collect his thoughts before he continued. "You have read many history books?" he asked, turning to look directly into Montama's tear stained eyes.

"Of course," Montama responded resolutely.

"And what does history tell us?" the old man asked gently.

"It tells us of the bravery of the kings of old."

"Yes it does," Grandafier said nodding his head emphatically. "The history books are replete with the daring exploits of our greatest kings. They say barely a word about those unfortunate innocents who died in order to make that history happen. There is no passage about the family that was killed at Tamarine or the young boy who fought and died at Demage, or any of the other ordinary people who suffered the most extreme sorts of anguish in all of the other great battles that history duly records. Their voices are silent, for history does not acknowledge either their suffering or their daring. They were merely swept up in the currents of war, hopeful that when the war was finally over they would have a king who could give them a better life."

"And after all of this, you think I am that king?" Montama asked incredulously.

"I am certain that you will be a great king," Grandafier assured the young man. "And you will be greater still because you understand the pain that innocents must necessarily feel in such wretched times. You alone, not Pantamanu, not Bellazar, you alone will be the king of all the people, the Boguls, the Ka-Why-Tees, everyone."

Montama silently considered Grandafier's argument for several seconds, as he wiped an errant tear from his left cheek. "I will tell you one thing," Montama added at last, "I will personally see to it that General Garr is executed for the crimes he has committed."

Nervously, Grandafier looked about him to make sure that their conversation was not being overheard. Then in a mere whisper he declared, "Don't say things that only a king can say until you *are* a king."

Montama nodded his head in agreement. He was not sure whether he accepted Grandafier's reasoning or not, but the mere fact that the elderly man had assumed the role of a surrogate father seemed to ease his mind, at least somewhat. Montama breathed a deep sigh of relief then looked with admiration at the old man and said, "I guess it doesn't matter much anymore why I want to be king. All that matters is that I will either be king or I will die on the field of battle."

Part VI

The
Final Battle

Chapter 73
The Next Prophesy

The Season of Reason is short, consisting of but one single unit. It is meant as a reminder that reason must always prevail. It is a unit celebrated and then quickly forgotten, for in its wake lay a new cycle, and with it, the arrival of the Season of Death!

And as the new cycle arrived, never had the passra experienced anything quite as surreal as the concomitant spectacle of three moons rising at the Equinox of Death while three massive armies concomitantly mobilized for what was certain to be a decisive and indisputably gory battle. Montama's mercenary army, having rested for one night in Pellaville, re-commenced its indomitable march toward the open grasslands just east of the vast and beautiful Kanaween Forrest. Meanwhile, Pantamanu continued the longer trek westward from the east, intent on meeting the pretender and his barbarian army on the same predestined battlefield. As for Bellazar, her army already was burrowed deep inside the Kanaween Forest, studiously awaiting whatever enemy or enemies it might encounter.

Meanwhile, frightened and certain that destiny was beyond their direct control, the Arcanian people lined the now muddy roads to pay witness to this extraordinary display: three mighty armies, two of them peripatetically marching toward either a glorious victory or a deafening defeat, converging fast on the Kanaween Forest. The people did so with wide-eyed appreciation for the historical significance of the events to come, but also with considerable apprehension, for all citizens were aware that this battle would decide conclusively the passra's fate. They therefore were alarmed as the armies marched through their fields, past their straw houses, and along their dirt roads, on the portentous Equinox of Death.

Uncertainty, as it must always exist in times of war, thus pervaded the thoughts of everyone involved. Citizens, soldiers, generals, the three main rivals and yes even the two most powerful Oracle entities, myself included, did not know who would prevail in the battle to come. As a result, Montama, Pantamanu, Bellazar, and Kublatitan waited with equal measures of anticipation for the latest sign to be delivered by the rising of Arcania's three august moons.

The Oracle

That event began shortly after evening commenced, before the sun fully set. The sky was crystal clear and at first the three rising moons appeared like giant hazy balls on the eastern horizon, with two of them so large that they almost seemed to blend together as one. As they continued their anticipated ascent higher into the Arcanian sky, they separated into three distinct images, each impressive on its own, the three together a truly awe inspiring sight. It was immediately apparent to everyone that the three moons had adopted the comforting subtle hue of bleached red. "It is a sign of stability," Bellazar said, unexpectedly delighted that the moons promised the passra good fortune after a cycle of non-stop death and disaster. Then I intervened again and something unusual began to happen. Using my telekinetic abilities to create an unsightly image, I altered the passra's perception of its majestic three moons.

At first Bellazar thought it was an illusion (and in that assessment she was correct). As she peered out from one of the world's tallest trees, resting on the back of her favored ladatop, she finally concluded that it was not a delusion, although it was in fact a deception. As the moons rose higher into the Arcanian sky, I ensured that they appeared to be dripping pools of dark and savagely red blood. "My God!" Bellazar cried out with a horror that was soon shared by all denizens of Arcania. Women and children shrieked, while men gasped at this indescribably horrid sight. From his saddle on horseback, but a unit's ride away from the Kanaween Forest, Pantamanu too became aware of the strange colors emanating from the eastern sky. "What does it mean?" he asked a nearby soldier. "Something terrible is about to happen," the soldier exclaimed with fatal resignation.

For his part Montama did not even look up at the eerie moons with their veiled signs of death and destruction. And had he seen them it is unlikely he would have cared, for he could think of nothing more terrifying than the irretrievable loss of his own family. Nothing worse, even the annihilation of his army or his own death, could threaten him now.

General Garr was alone among the passra in his reaction to the three moons. He considered such signs to be pure folly and laughed heartily at the shocked reaction of the many Arcanians who had joined his mercenary army. When he realized that the moons appeared to be bleeding, he smirked and then loudly proclaimed, "We will give them blood and plenty of it." He further punctuated his defiance by waving his shining half-sword above his head as he rode spiritedly forward among his troops. "Bring 'em on!" he shouted with a demonic glee. "Tonight the moons bleed.

Tomorrow it will be our enemies." As Garr laughed his soldiers took up the chant, "Bring 'em on! Bring 'em on! Bring 'em on!"

Montama did not join the chorus, for his mind was still elsewhere, far away in Pellaville. For him the bleeding already had begun.

Chapter 74
Kensilday

Following the rise of Arcania's three moon's widespread panic continued to spread throughout the entire passra. "What does this mean?" people shouted with a sense of hopelessness and desperation. Others cried out, "What have we done to deserve this? Why is this happening to us?"

Why indeed? The Arcanians were at heart a peaceful people. Unlike the savages of the Relatin Empire, they abhorred war and violence and King Leonata had designed a passra dedicated to traditional liberal ideals of freedom and equality. And yet, within the past cycle, the entire passra had been reduced to a state of total madness. Why indeed was it happening?

This question was foremost on Kublatitan's mind. His study of hatred had been entirely distasteful, but it had provided a valuable insight into the passra's political leaders. Still, he did not sense the same feelings among the general population as he did among its leaders. While the leaders forever developed new and intricately dastardly schemes intent on maximizing their power base, most citizens were disinterested in the vagaries of power politics, weary, tired of the ongoing succession war, and eager for it to end, whatever the outcome might be. All they knew of power and politics was that their lives inextricably had been upended, with many forced to abandon their homes and livelihood. While many of them certainly favored the fresh face that Montama represented, particularly the people of western Arcania, and others still retained their determined loyalty to the royal Centamas, the expression most commonly heard was, "When will this damnable succession war ever end?"

With three now ruby red, bleeding moons to remind them that even more violence and suffering was soon to come, the people cowered, not sure if sanity would ever prevail or if order would ever be restored to their beloved passra. As for the three main participants, with the night sky ominously illuminated by the site of the three Arcanian moons, they tried to get whatever rest they could, in preparation for what each knew would be the mother of all battles, to commence at sunset, with the stakes never higher. All knew that only one army would prevail. There would be no spoils for the losers.

It was into this brief interlude before the battle that Kublatitan intervened once more, desperately hoping that reason might still prevail over the inevitable chaos of war. He therefore closed his mighty eyes and willed the participants to join him in what the Taewokans refer to as the Kensilday, a war council conducted prior to hostilities, in which all sides are compelled to come together, to literally or figuratively break bread with each other, and rationally discuss the reasons for their disagreements and discontent. As a result of the Kensilday, Taewoka never actually had fought a war, for in the end, all participants inevitably realized that the cost of combat was simply too prohibitive, and that there were other, more reasonable ways to reach a mutually satisfactory accommodation.

That was the Taewokan way, to compromise, to search out common ground and finally to put aside remaining differences. Yet Kublatitan realized that the Arcanians viewed compromise as a sign of weakness. Therefore, only in battle could their differences ultimately be resolved. To Kublatitan, there was no explanation for this inherently irrational behavior. For each of the participants in this bloody succession war had to know that the victor would inherit a passra with divided loyalties and vast exposed political wounds, as well as a population on the verge of collapse and starvation.

"Why would anyone want to govern such a place?" Kublatitan thought, still hopeful that even at this late date unfettered reason might yet be made to triumph. And so, he summoned a new universe of reality. At first it appeared to be nothing more than amber light. There were no distinguishable boundaries, no walls, doors, windows, floors, or ceilings. No sky or ground. This new place simply existed. Then with his mind concentrating on the other participants, he willed their existence into this new dimension. The first to arrive was Bellazar. She had been sleeping, restlessly, and when she awoke, she realized that she was floating sideways, not quite certain whether she was awake or dreaming. When she finally saw what looked like the spirit of Kublatitan she tilted her head sideways and calmly muttered, "Not you again."

Kublatitan did not respond for his mind was already focused on the arrival of the other actors in this bloody succession war. In an instant, Pantamanu and then Montama appeared in rapid succession. Neither had been able to sleep and thus both were transported in a fully awakened state. "What the hell?" Pantamanu shouted vociferously, while Montama said nothing at all, his face free of all emotion, his mind still fixed on his confrontation with his father. Though he seemed barely aware that he was no longer in the real world, the others watched attentively as Count Belicki also was compelled to appear.

Kublatitan welcomed his guests. "This is Kensilday, a place of my choosing, where we will have the opportunity to parley, to put aside out differences, to seek out a peaceful resolution, and to make war unnecessary." Kublatitan spoke with such pompous righteousness that it took a moment for everyone to realize that he was indeed serious.

Irritably I snapped, "What the hell are you talking about? War is always necessary." Pantamanu vehemently nodded his head in agreement, while Bellazar and Montama merely looked on, the former now clearly entranced by the site of we two titans, together in one place. All eyes, even Montama's vapid stare, then turned toward me, when I facetiously added, "How else but war are we to resolve our differences? Perhaps over a cup of Taewokan tea?"

Kublatitan was persistent if not entirely practical. "We must all have some common ground."

Pantamanu smiled mischievously. "That is true. We all want to destroy each other."

Montama finally appeared to become fully aware when Pantamanu spoke and then with a more cognizant determination he finally stared directly at both of his rivals. He recognized Pantamanu's unlimited hubris but he also noticed something else, something much more significant. When he stared into Bellazar's eyes he saw that she looked upon Pantamanu with a blinding and unreserved hatred. "They despise each other more than they hate me," Montama realized at once, though he was not yet aware of the full implications of this development.

Reacting only to Pantamanu's comment that all wanted to destroy each other, I responded, "Try to find common ground better than that," my countenance suddenly light and frivolous, for I understood that there was no peril in this new and strange dimension. To my mind the spectacle was now one of mere amusement. Sarcastically, I continued, "Pardon our good friend Kublatitan. He does not appreciate the values of our world. He believes that we can simply all sit down like one happy family and come to a mutually acceptable accommodation."

399

The Oracle

When he heard these words, Kublatitan's eyes flashed abruptly from pure white light to a fiery and luminous searing red hue. "You underestimate me," Kublatitan shouted. Bellazar squinted as she noticed something quite strange about Kublatitan's countenance. It took her a moment to realize that it was the cadence of his language. It no longer seemed awkward and forced. She listened attentively as Kublatitan continued, "You think that I am weak, naïve, and foolish, unfamiliar with the feelings and emotions of your world. I have experienced hatred in all of its despicable forms and now I understand how it motivates you. And I also have seen what it does to the young and the innocent." Now, with his right hand boldly extended and pointing directly at Montama, Kublatitan added, "And I have seen how this hatred infects everything that Count Belicki touches." Now with a harsh anger of his own, Kublatitan denounced me. "From the very beginning you have manipulated Montama. You have turned his world upside down, and for what? Not for his own good. It is you who will have the real power, not Montama!"

All eyes were now fixed on me. "I have not played with anyone's destiny," I responded defensively. "I have merely allowed everyone to express their innermost feelings. I did not fuel their ambition. If anything, I only allowed it to come to the surface."

"And what of Montama?" Kublatitan demanded again, his fury seething so red hot that his body began to glow, like a radioactive ion. Then with a fierceness that I had never before witnessed, Kublatitan demanded, "What have you done to this boy?"

Montama moved slowly toward me. As he did so, he too demanded, "Yes, Count Belicki, tell us, why are you so interested in me? Is it because of my piercing intellect, my history of brave deeds, is it because I am by far the most qualified person to rule Arcania?" Montama paused, his eyes squinting narrowly as he asked, "Or is it because of my father. It was quite a feat to turn the son of loyal Lord Tantamount against the Centama family!" Then with a steady and determined voice Montama added, "You used me because you needed me, not because you ever thought I was fit to be king."

I stared uneasily at Montama and then with a reserve that was admittedly unusual I responded, "I would have been interested in Hontallo, but to be honest he didn't have the right temperament to be a king. All the poor boy ever thought about was gardening. But *you* have certain admirable qualities."

"Such as?" Montama demanded abrasively.

I smiled, though I probably should not have. "Your mind is so very receptive to the idea of power. Indeed from the first moment that I introduced you to those colorful tales of Captain Bale and his many exciting adventures..."

Montama sharply interrupted. "You did what?" he shouted angrily, his eyes burning with a fury I had never before seen in this young neophyte.

I smiled insidiously. "Well your mother actually read them to you. She did so only because I told her to. I had to discover if you had an adventurous spirit and indeed you did. In fact, you were such an eager student you even acted out the stories. "Montama could now veritably feel the searing intensity of my own exposed ambition. He listened attentively and with rising anger as I continued. "When you were just ten, I came to you in a dream. I told you about the exploits of General Tampinco. And do you remember what you wanted?" I now tried to move menacingly toward Montama, but as I did the young man floated freely beyond my grasp. With my own anger rising I reminded him, "You dreamed of *conquering* the Relatin Empire."

My anger only fueled Montama's own bitterness. Ferociously, Montama stared at me and with uncontained vitriol asserted, "*That* was just a childhood fantasy."

"True," I confessed. "Now that fantasy is directly within your grasp. The only question is, do you want it enough?"

"Enough?" Montama asked.

Yes, I responded. "*Enough* to make a deal with the devil. *Enough* to let General Garr systematically annihilate the lives of innocent Bogul men, women and children! *Enough* to turn against your very own beloved father and brother! *ENOUGH!* That is how much you must want to be king."

Kublatitan intervened, still hopeful that reason might prevail. "It is still not too late to turn back Montama. Even now you can return to your family. They *will* forgive you."

At the mention of his family Montama laughed hideously. "And then what?" Now pointing his hand expressively in Pantamanu's direction, Montama declared, "I should let him be king so that he can slaughter my family and steal my lands?"

Kublatitan sensed the utter hopelessness in Montama's charge. "Is it worse to die with your family than to live alone without them forever?"

Montama's eyes narrowed as even greater hatred filled his heart. Bitterly, he stared at Kublatitan and myself. "The two of you have left me no choice.

The Oracle

If I go with my father and brother, we will all be killed. And if I don't then how can I govern if the world knows the sins that were committed in my name?" With deep seeded menace, Montama continued, "You speak of going back. Well there is no going back. No matter what I do, I can never go back to the way things used to be."

Defensively, I added, "That is certainly true, but if you are king, you will control the world. Is that such a terrible concession?"

At the mention of these last cavalierly enunciated words Montama became so enraged that his entire body shook and as he did the entire Kensilday universe began to tilt. Suddenly everyone was aware that they were no longer standing upright. Furthermore, their bodies were alternately expanding and shrinking, as time and space began to break apart. Pantamanu and Bellazar moved back and as they did their forms vanished for the present conflict was now reduced to just we three participants. "It's just a game to the two of you." Montama shouted at we two titans with a righteous and intensifying fury. "You both think that you can do whatever you want." Then as his emotions finally exploded with a greater anger than either of us titans combined could ever have imagined we looked upon Montama, with a sense of dread and horror. "You want me to be king." With a menace that I had not thought possible in the young boy, he added, "Well then you will have your wish."

With these words, the spirit of Kensilday finally shattered into millions of shards of radiant and exposed electrical energy. Kublatitan understood that there would be but one unavoidable alternative: a final cataclysmic battle that would reshape both Arcania and the Oracle. As for Montama the battle continued, but not yet in Arcania. Instead, as Kensilday ceased, his consciousness shifted to an entirely different realm.

Chapter 75

The Oracle

MADNESS!

SUDDENLY EvErYTHinG SEcmED abnormal to MONTAMA

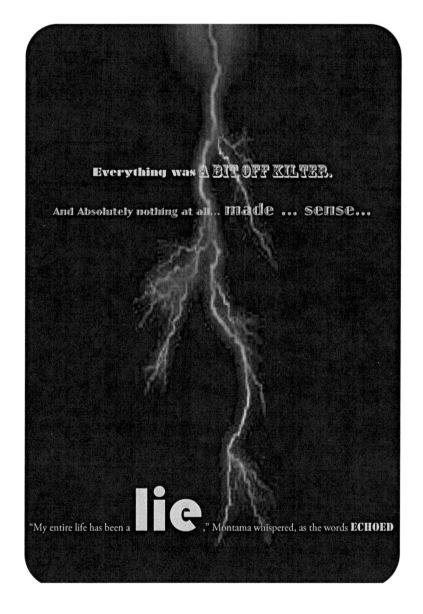

Everything was A BIT OFF KILTER.

And Absolutely nothing at all... made ... sense...

"My entire life has been a lie," Montama whispered, as the words ECHOED

The Oracle

OVER AND OVER *again*

... in his **mind.**

For as the spirit of Kensilday was terminated, MONTANA DID NOT RETURN TO HIS BODY

Instead he discovered that he was

NOT BACK IN HIS BODY

floating

in

WHAT SEEMED LIKE

an icy world of frosty haze.

INSTEAD HE WAS SURROUNDED BY MYRIAD FORMS

OF BIZZARE ILLUMINATION —

Richard Waterman

Confused, **Montama asked himself a fundamental** QUESTION,

"HOW

DID

I

COME

TO

BE

LIKE

THIS?"

His Mind Was A MAZE

of varied emotional contrasts:

ALL SORTS OF

DIFFERENT COLORS

Tens of thousand of lines, each intersecting at ODD angles

some sleck and distinct

while others were a **disorienting blur,** and

absolutely EverYtHinG radiated with a

cold and *fractured glow.*

Richard Waterman

ANGER

FEAR

SELF-

LOATHING

PARANOIA!

Then Montama asked another more important question: "How could I have **forsaken** *my*

family?"

WHY DID I DO IT?

 WHY?

WHY?

BUT THERE WAS NO ANSWER!

Just the repetitive sound of water dripping, again and again...

It was the constant irritating drip, drip, drip of his own tortured thoughts:

Thoughts such as:

Why HAD he let

Garr kill

innocent

Why had

Montama

murdered an innocent man?

And Most of all

why

MONTAMA

turned

against

General

people?

had

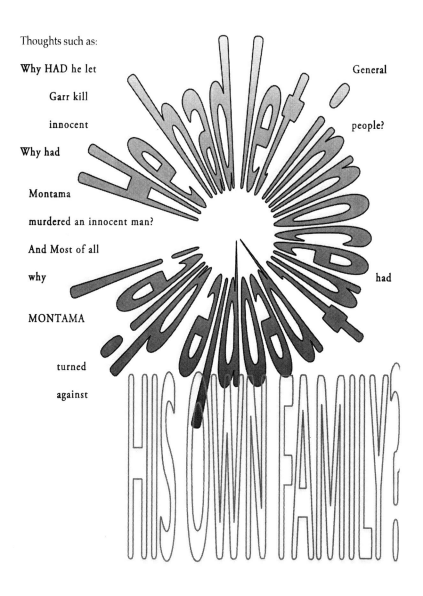

HIS OWN FAMILY?

Then with a frightful realization MONTAMA

shouted,

"THIS IS MADNESS!!!"

Richard Waterman

FOR MONTAMA FINALLY REALIZED:

There is no excuse for what I have done, except for

madness!

When he finally came to this startling realization,

he closed his eyes

and with infinite sincerity

he begged forgiveness

from anyone who would listen!

But he heard

NOTHING

Just the constant drip,

drip, drip of his own **tortured** thoughts.

413

For he realized IT WAS MADNESS that POSSESSED

him!

MADNESS!!!

MADNESS!!!!

MADNESS!!!!!

@MADNESS@

"There is no other explanation!" he cried out, for he knew that he had thrown

away everything that mattered to him, everything that

he had ever

cared about.

AND ALL FOR THE MERE PROMISE OF

POWER

The Oracle

With a colossal sigh, as his entire soul convulsed, Montama whispered,

"I have been corrupted."

Then, like a wounded beast he cried out in reverberating spasms of terrifying agony, until the

feeling of his own heart rending finally silenced him.

The emptiness remained, and it only further exacerbated his growing anger, which rose to

such a ferocious intensity that Montama felt the entire Oracle universe

tremble.

And then, with a small measure of reason returning to his tortured mind, he

reluctantly confessed, "I did it all because I was selfish. Not because I was noble or worthy, but

simply because I wanted it, more than I wanted anything else in the world." Then with a

renewed sense of horror he realized,

Richard Waterman

"I am no different than

Count Belicki!"

At last realizing the folly of his ambition, instinctively, he cried out in frightful desperation,

The Oracle

And for a single moment there was finally silence

inside Montama's tortured mind!

And when the silence lifted all he could hear was his own voice saying:

"You wanted to be king more than anything else. Everything Else Was Expendable."

EVEN YOUR OWN FAMILY!

Then, Montama heard a woman's voice reciting a familiar story. As he heard the voice he shouted, "Where am I?" It was only at this very instant that Montama realized that he was inside the Oracle's vast unfettered universe of imagination.

Like his own tormented thoughts he now sensed that the Oracle was in a state of total *disarray*, its once stable communications network fractured by multiple shocks.

Slowly, like a mind damaged by a stroke, the Oracle was systematically repairing its pathways, re-integrating its circuitry, reestablishing contacts, and rebuilding its integrity. For despite Kublatitan's super human efforts it was becoming increasingly apparent that the Oracle entities now possessed their own free will and ferocious determination.

Richard Waterman

As such they were unwavering in their ultimate purpose:

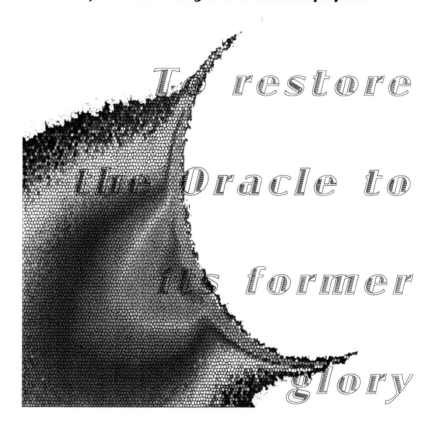

To restore the Oracle to its former glory

and to have at

last

A NEW

KING

Montama sensed all of these thoughts, though his conscience continued to scorch his very soul.

"You are forever **DAMNED!" he**

thought!

And yet, in spite of this, the Oracle had brought him to its very epicenter of power!

What he did not know was ------------------------------

So, instinctively he waited

for an answer,

to discover the reason

why

he had been

brought

INTO THE ORACLE.

And in a short time he again heard the soft, gentle

melodic sound of a woman's tender voice, carefully reading

a text that seemed entirely familiar to him!

"The situation was utterly hopeless. Two oversized and dangerous armies,

each one bent on his destruction, now confronted the heroic Captain Bale.

Though he was brave and sure, he was also realistic. 'There is no way that I

can succeed if I must face two armies at once.' he said with a sudden

resignation. 'But perhaps there is an alternative: What if I can goad the two

of armies into fighting each other?'"

Montama listened attentively, and then in a shy, almost apologetic voice he said one

solitary word aloud:

"Mother?"

There was no response. Instead, Montama experienced an unexpected flash of vivid emerald light and when the glow dissipated he discovered that he was again standing at his post in western Arcania, not far from General Garr's makeshift headquarters. The surreal vision had happened so quickly that it took a moment for Montama to realize that what he had heard was a passage from one of the Captain Bale stories his mother had read to him when he was but a young boy.

Montama's eyes then moved mechanically from side to side as he contemplated the message that he had just received, as he clenched his hands into two tightly drawn fists. Then, as his uncontrollable fury erupted, Montama looked toward the heavens and asked the Oracle, "You have told me how to win. Why can't you tell me why I should win?"

Again, the young man waited for an answer. It did not come. In time he would realize the answer on his own:

He wanted to be king more than he wanted anything else!

It was as simple as that. So the Oracle told him how to win. Now all Montama had to decide was whether he still wanted to win.

Chapter 76
A Change of Tactics

Montama's eyes burned with a dark, cold, and determined fury, combined with an absolute resolute certainty. "I am completely mad," he thought, "which means that for the first time in my life I can see things precisely as they really are! I now know who I am and what my destiny is." The young man's thoughts were no longer filled with internal conflict or self-destructive personal recriminations. Montama now understood exactly why he had been chosen to lead this violent rebellion. He had been nothing more than a pawn, a tool for savvy opportunists who, if Montama succeeded, would vicariously enjoy the sweet fruits of victory through his battlefield deeds. "But no more!" Montama reflected. "No one will control me now. Not even the Oracle!"

Everything about Montama's worldview changed as a result of his confrontations with his father and then with me, Count Belicki, at Kensilday. From his meeting with his father, among other lessons, he learned how innately fragile power and loyalty can be. It could be stripped away without warning at any unguarded moment. As a result, a leader must be diligent, prepared for any contingency, and always on the ready.

There was an even more important and insidious lesson to be learned. In politics, if there was anything that one could lose faster than power it was one's very soul. At Kensilday, Kublatitan asked what I had done to this young impressionable man? The correct answer was that I had taken a tyro and made him fit to be a king. To the weak kneed people of the world, all they could see was what I had destroyed in this process. To them I had shattered everything that had made Montama worthy of high office: his intrinsic kindness, his gentle nature, his love of family, his very soul: all of these values had been sacrificed and in their place I left nothing more than an insatiable, destructive lust for power and ambition. It is only now as I look back upon what I did, that I could sense the first echo of remorse, perhaps even the first pang of my own nascent conscience. For I realize now that what I did to Montama was no better than what my father had done to me.

Nimrod sensed an unexpected sadness in Belicki and speculated: "If Kublatitan learned to hate from Belicki, is it possible that some of that mighty Taewokans inherent decency had somehow transferred to Belicki?"

The Oracle

It was an interesting surmise, but one that Nimrod did not dwell upon, for it could sense that it finally was getting closer to the ultimate revelation, the secret of its very existence. Therefore, Nimrod did not interrupt Belicki, but listened as attentively as ever, sure that the answers to all of its questions would soon to be revealed.

Belicki was quiet for a few moments, then with a renewed vigor he continued with the story of the Arcanian succession war.

When Montama emerged from Kensilday and then from the Oracle, it was night and soldiers were standing all around him preparing for battle, but Montama paid absolutely no heed to them whatsoever, for in his reconstituted mind they now existed for but one solitary purpose: to serve him as king. And suddenly, with his mind fixed on but one purpose – **revenge** - Montama made a fateful decision. He was indeed determined to be the king! He did wish to prevail in this bloody and seemingly endless succession war!

Resolute and more determined than ever, as the cool dark air of night threatened to give way to morning, Montama strode blithely past his soldiers with a confident firmness, an unappeasable resolve, and an unyielding sense of destiny. Though he saw men sharpening their weapons, while others struggled to secure what little rest they could before the final march to the site of the ultimate battle, Montama's attention was solely fixed on a new military course of action. Walking spiritedly and directly to a small patch of trees that represented General Garr's makeshift headquarters, he stood silent, not quite sure yet if his body had returned to its proper place and time, for his mind could now somehow transcend all known realities. He therefore simultaneously could sense both the Oracle's vast universe of imagination as well as the so-called real world.

For several moments, as his mind raced with thoughts of revenge, he stood like a mere shadow, unobtrusively, listening as one of General Garr's subordinates, Captain Mabuse, described the current unexpectedly bleak military situation. "Inside the Kanaween Forest the trees are so densely packed that sunlight only touches the forest floor for a few hours each unit. Combat can only be conducted among the tops of the mighty trees. In this regard Mbanka's army has the distinct advantage, with more than one thousand trained ladatop riders at the ready. Before the forest lay a vast, open field of wild grass, in some places as high two feet tall. Other than the grass, there are no natural fortifications - no trees, no rocks and therefore no place for an enemy to hide."

426

Everyone listened attentively, but none more so than Garr. He rarely asked a question, preferring instead to absorb the wisdom of his subordinates, before challenging it, or if the facts were indisputable, succumbing to their superior intelligence of the present situation. Garr therefore said nothing as Mabuse continued. "As for the number of Bellazar's forces, while we can only estimate their strength it appears that the army aligned along the perimeter of the Kanaween Forest consists of well over five thousand men and women. They are positioned so that they can either attack or, if necessary, retreat into the safety of the forest. As for Pantamanu's forces, they have moved much more quickly than we had anticipated from eastern Arcania. Within just a mere matter of hours they will be positioned outside the forest. Our scouts estimate that they have somewhere in the range of six or seven thousand additional men."

At the mention of these huge numbers, General Garr's shoulders slumped palpably. Only Montama seemed to notice. "Damn!" the general swore with a foul combination of anger and disappointment. "They have far more soldiers than I anticipated." Reacting to the latest intelligence, for the first time in his life, Garr seemed unsure, for he realized too late that he had badly misjudged the present military situation. His estimates were that the Arcanians would have no more than a combined more than ten thousand men, not ten thousand! With sad resignation he added, "We have not the opportunity nor the time to retreat and we will have no chance to strike before the two armies are combined."

"What are our chances?" Grandafier the Elder asked with a timidity that seemed to answer his own question.

"We are screwed," Garr said forthrightly, staring coldly ahead, his body rigid, his mind for once uncertain. "We may be a match for either army, but not if they are combined." Garr paused, the black pupil of his single solitary eye staring frightfully ahead with controlled anger, and then with a surprising openness he added, "We have absolutely no chance."

Grandafier stared at Garr. "So we are all to be butchered?" he said after a long pause, his voice trailing off pitiably as he spoke.

"NO!" Montama interjected with a surprising forcefulness. His voice was so powerful that even General Garr was startled. When he spoke all eyes, even General Garr's immediately turned toward him. "We will not face two armies," Montama said with a certainty that invited no possible disagreement.

The Oracle

Grandafier was the first to notice the altered expression on Montama's face. Though he could not explain how or why, Montama appeared to be an entirely different person. No longer a bashful youth, Montama now exuded a powerful resolute determination that defied all explanation. Garr too was taken aback by Montama's unexpected show of fortitude. "What do you mean?" Garr asked, as he too finally noticed the transformation in Montama's demeanor.

"I have been in contact with the Oracle," Montama declared emphatically. "The two armies will not strike us. They will attack first at each other."

Instinctively Grandafier analyzed the political situation. "He may well be right. It is well known that Bellazar and Pantamanu despise each other. I am sure Bellazar considers Pantamanu to be her main rival for power, not some scruffy young neophyte."

Montama turned his head slowly in an almost robotic fashion. His eyes narrowed hypnotically as he stared directly into Grandafier's eyes. "Their hatred is beyond reason. They could rule Arcania if only they were capable of working together, yet beyond the bounds of reason, they are intent on destroying each other. I have seen it in their eyes."

Garr was now gravely concerned. "What are you recommending? That we do nothing?" Montama's head now slowly turned toward Garr and as he did the general could suddenly feel the full intensity of Montama's altered personality. Montama's eyes now literally burned with a hateful fury. "Good god, what has happened to you?" the general whispered.

With his eyes afire, Montama paid no heed to what he considered an irrelevant question. Instead, without a shred of doubt he said, "We will place our best men along the front lines." Speaking firmly without the slightest hint of emotion, he added, "We will not strike first. Pantamanu will send some small detachment to engage us, but he will use his main force to attack and destroy Bellazar's army."

"You are certain of this?" Garr asked, still not convinced.

Montama raised a clenched fist before his face and then with a hateful fierceness he responded, "I have no doubt whatsoever."

Garr's eye opened wide. He was thunderstruck, incredulous, for he had never considered the possibility that two Arcanian armies might find each other a more amenable target than an invading force from Relatania. Once he set his mind upon this outrageous possibility he saw that there was much reason in Montama's proposal. "Hatred is a powerful motivating force," the general acknowledged as he looked suddenly at Grandafier the Elder. In response, the old man merely nodded his consent. Then for a moment Garr contemplated his limited options. There was little chance of victory, no matter what offensive strategy he might adopt. So, with a considerable degree of resignation and no small degree of doubt, Garr reluctantly conceded, "We have no other option. We must do as Montama recommends." All was now set for the final battle!

Chapter 77
The Mother Of All Battles

During the final hour of darkness before the dawn, Montama's army completed the short march to the outskirts of the Kanaween Forest. As the morning light first gently touched the northern sky and the sun finally began to peak over the far horizon, slowly illuminating the skyline with a brilliant golden hue, the army was at last in position for what General Garr called "the mother of all battles." Garr did not notice the magnificent skyline, for he was too busy positioning his best soldiers at the front of the line, though he still struggled with the wisdom of Montama's proposal. "If Montama is wrong and they attack us directly, this battle will be over in a matter of minutes," he mused, as he deployed his army, carefully paying attention to even the smallest detail. "Make sure your weapon is polished and ready," he barked at one slovenly soldier. "Get your ass moving," he yelled at another who seemed to be moving a tad too slow. Then, as he hastily grabbed a mug filled with Relatanian coffee, he thought, "Why the hell am I so nervous?"

He had engaged in literally hundreds of battles, yet this one seemed far different from any other. Garr did not know the forest region well. For that he was utterly dependent on Montama's tactical advice. And that was the crux of the matter. Simply stated, Garr did not like relying on anyone else for military advice. Yet now, for the first time in his life, he felt totally dependent on his protégé, for he sensed that fate was no longer on his side. "Destiny guides that young man, not me," he said softly, thinking of Montama.

With his usual pride and extroverted exuberance, Garr mounted his horse, adorned as usual with his long, flowing green battle cape. On his left side he carried a full sword, with his half sword carefully tucked surreptitiously inside his cape. Though he felt intense conflicted, Garr showed no outward sign of his inner turmoil. Instead he put on his war weary game face and to everyone who was familiar with him, the general looked precisely the same as he had before every other battle. In the back of Garr's mind he heard an unusual refrain. "This may very well be my last battle."

While Garr's thoughts were conflicted, Montama had absolutely no doubt whatsoever. He mounted his horse and rode nearby General Garr, who continued to castigate one soldier for moving too slowly, then ordered other troops to make sure the forward line was in tack. As Montama confidently rode along the front line he estimated that with the additional soldiers General Garr had procured, along with the remnants from his original army, they had somewhere in the range of two to three thousand highly trained soldiers. They had lost their crossbow archers during the Battle of King's Castle, however. In the ensuing retreat they also had lost all of their oxen and talladaggers, as well as most of their military supplies. Though the men were eager for battle, there were far fewer of them than when he had first left Relatania several intervals before. "They are sufficiently brave. We will prevail," Montama said, with no measure of false confidence.

Besides the well-trained soldiers, Montama's army also consisted of an additional two to three thousand men and women in reserve: almost entirely people who spontaneously joined his army during the march to Pellaville. They were enthusiastic but wholly untrained. It was therefore unknown how they would react in battle. Garr expected that once the battle commenced, few of these volunteers would stand and fight. Therefore, they were sent to the rear, merely designed to represent a show of force. From this distant vantage point they looked remarkably fierce. As General Garr was heard to say, "Heaven help us if we ever have to depend on them in battle." Though Montama was far more optimistic about the fate of the upcoming battle, he shared Garr's overall assessment: these inexperienced farmers and artisans simply could not be counted upon to stand and fight effectively against the disciplined Arcanian armies.

As Montama and Garr prepared their army, Bellazar looked down from her literally exalted position atop one of the tallest trees in the Kanaween Forest. What she saw intrigued her. She sat on the back of a prized ladatop, a twelve-foot tall primate that she called Bobbie. Bellazar could not see her own forces, for they were aligned too close to the forest perimeter. She noticed the barbarian army lining up to the south, as well as Pantamanu's army, which was approaching fast from the east and would soon be ready for battle. She calculated that whereas Montama had but a few thousand men, Pantamanu had a much larger force. As she saw these two powerful armies readying themselves she thought, "They will strike us hard, but we will prevail." Like Montama, Bellazar had no doubt whatsoever in the righteousness of her cause or in the ultimate outcome of the battle to come. She too was utterly convinced that her army would prevail.

And she had reason to be confident. General Mbanka had aligned his forces for more than a mile along the vast perimeter of the Kanaween Forest. The line separating the forest from the grasslands to the east ran in an almost straight line for more than twenty miles. Consequently, as the battle progressed, Mbanka could redeploy his troops into or back out of the forest as necessary. "The forest is our ally," Mbanka was overheard saying on several occasions.

He also held a strategic ace: he alone possessed more than one thousand skilled ladatop riders, nestled high in the trees inside the forest. If Pantamanu's army dared to move inside the forest, a fierce ghostly force would attack them from above, soaring through the trees and capable of striking the enemy unexpectedly from any possible direction. Against these guerilla techniques, Pantamanu's army would never know where the enemy was or when it would next strike. The strategy was designed to throw Pantamanu's army into a state of constant fear and eventually total panic.

Fifteen minutes later, as the sun finally crested fully over the horizon, looking now like an angry gigantic orange ball of fire, each side had its forces and its strategy at the ready for the imminent battle. Harnessed to Bobbie's back, Bellazar scurried effortlessly from tree to tree, searching for a better location to watch the ensuing battle. Within minutes she arrived at the top of one mammoth Kanawa tree that allowed a perfect overview of Pantamanu's final position. As she peered down from the heavens, some fifty subordinate officers stood at rigid and disciplined attention, obediently waiting for Commander Pantamanu to relay the order to commence the attack. Her far vision was remarkable and she recognized Pantamanu immediately, for he was wearing his pompous overly decorated commander's uniform, with several new badges, each meant to signify his great courage and bold deeds. "At least he looks like a soldier," she smirked as she listened attentively for any sound signifying the commencement of hostilities.

The Oracle

She heard an officer shout a command and then she saw another line of men standing at attention. What she could not see from her elevated vantage point was that each of the officers' eyes were fixed determinedly on Commander Pantamanu, who sat proudly upon yet another more finely decorated steed, with the Centama family sword in his right hand and a new and more diabolical weapon strapped to his side. As Pantamanu leaned slightly forward, the officers stood at the ready, waiting for the final order. As a slight, pleasant breeze ruffled his badges and caused his black hair to stream gently backward, Pantamanu sensed the eternal hand of historical greatness resting comfortably on his shoulders. This was his moment of glory. With a stern expression, he finally brought his arm downward with a sharpness that alerted everyone that the final battle for Arcania was about to begin.

Then, in succession, up and down the line, various finely dressed captains and their lieutenants, all dressed in the blue uniforms of the Arcanian army, dutifully relayed the order to the troops: "Prepare for battle." This charge was followed by the deafening sound of thousands of men, concomitantly coming to attention and holding their weapons stridently before them. As they did so, the air literally swirled from the force of these men, raising their arms in precision harmony. From her perch upon one of the tallest trees in the Kanaween Forest, Bellazar continued to look down upon the syncopated movements of her rival army. From her vantage point the men looked rather petite and completely insignificant. She therefore grinned, satisfied and equally eager for the battle to begin.

And from his position to the south Montama also looked on. He too could see the enemy army now aligned along the distant horizon and he waited impatiently for Pantamanu to issue the final order to attack. Then, echoing from a distance, he heard Pantamanu's clarion call to "CHARGE!"

Within seconds, five thousand men charged west toward the Kanaween Forest. As they did they squealed frightfully, a terrifying sound that was meant to completely unsettle the enemy. Mbanka's forces, also dressed in blue, were equally determined and when they heard the enemy, they too began to shout, with an unsettling repetitive cadence, endlessly repeating the word "Kull!" It was an Arcanian word signifying both victory and death to the enemy.

Seconds later, just as Montama had foreseen, the two Arcanian armies converged not more than a hundred yards from the entrance to the Kanaween Forest. As they did so they quickly trampled the wild virgin grass

432

that just moments before had stood as high as two feet tall. Men raised their shields before their chests as they lurched forward with their swords. The sound of sword on sword quickly reverberated inside the forest, in echoes that exponentially magnified the volume until it became a deafening wail.

The first soldiers to die fell quickly, their guts exposed by savage and mortal wounds. As they fell helplessly to the ground, men merely stepped over them, thrashing wildly with one hand, while moving their shields forward to parry an oncoming attack. Within minutes the field of battle was so congested that in places it was difficult for the men to move their arms and legs. Some died when they were stabbed in the back. Others suddenly and unexpected lost their heads, as an enemy from the rear decapitated them without a hint of remorse. In this manner, the bodies quickly began to pile up on the battlefield.

From Bellazar's perspective high atop the trees the scene looked like nothing more than managed chaos. Up close, it was a most lethal form of intimate combat. Thousands of monstrously large men, with powerfully muscular arms and legs, sweat flowing profusely from their overexerted bodies, vehemently striking at an enemy with an inhumane ferocity.

And the clamor of swords on shields became even more intense and deafening. Though officers tried to shout orders above the din, all that could be heard was the cyclical percussion thud of weapon upon weapon, as thousands of men crammed into an ever more narrow sphere of battle, their bodies so intimately entangled that they readily could see the fear and intensity in each others' eyes.

Yet something strange and unexpected occurred as the two armies converged. No one apparently had thought of the practical problem of distinguishing two armies of Arcania from one another. Since both sides wore the blue uniform of the army of Arcania, it quickly became impossible for the soldiers on the battlefield to distinguish friend from foe. Desperate men, hardened by battle, but utterly aware of their own mortality, searched diligently for an enemy, any adversary to strike and kill. But as the two armies congealed, one could not distinguish Bellazar's soldiers from Pantamanu's. On the chaotic field of battle all soldiers looked precisely alike.

"Who am I fighting?" one soldier angrily shouted. "Which side are you on?" another screamed. As the confusion unexpectedly mounted, the battle scene quickly degenerated into a spectacle of dreadful unbounded terror.

Quickly realizing the source of the mounting confusion, one of Pantamanu's lieutenants quickly rode to the commander's side. Though not far from the maelstrom's swirling fulcrum, Pantamanu watched, occasionally directing soldiers to shift to the left or to move forward. "Sir," the lieutenant shouted, desperately trying to be heard among the echoing cacophony. "It is difficult to tell which soldiers are on our side and which are the enemy. Everyone is wearing the same blue uniform. On the battlefield they all look alike."

Pantamanu's eyes widened and for an instant he could not imagine that no one, not himself, not one single officer under his command, had thought to differentiate his soldiers' uniforms from those of the army of General Mbanka. Apparently, no on Bellazar's side had thought through this practical problem either. It was an example of bone-chilling incompetence! Still, Pantamanu tried to make the best of the current situation. Without hesitation Pantamanu ordered, "Have our men don red head bands."

The lieutenant saluted and then wondered, "Where the hell am I going to get red head bands?" He rode past Pantamanu toward the army in reserve, nearly a quarter mile away. Upon his arrival he shouted the order, "Shred any red fabric. We will use them as head bands to identify our troops."

"Yes sir," a barrel chested sergeant yelled, before relaying the order to his own subordinates. Within minutes, hundreds of men began to locate blankets, shirts, and towels, anything that contained red fabric. They quickly tore them into long thin shreds, several inches long and two or three inches wide. "Quickly," the sergeant shouted. "We need them now."

Within less than ten minutes a man on horseback departed for the front, carrying a large bushel overflowing with streams of red cloth. A moment later another rider, then another, similarly rode at full speed toward the battlefield.

On the battlefield the instinct for survival superseded all other considerations. Men were killing anyone who stood in their way. In the midst of this confusion Pantamanu's officers barked contradictory orders in a vain attempt to restore order. Some officers ordered the troops to fall back temporarily, while others urged their soldiers to move forward. From Bellazar's perspective as well as from every other one, the battle looked like a state of pure anarchy, with men killing each other with no strategic purpose in mind other than to survive. It was a bloody, senseless slaughter that had to be halted, lest both Arcanian armies suffer grievous losses that would leave them vulnerable to the barbarian menace.

Sensing the confusion, Pantamanu again tried to restore order. "Get the head bands to our men up front," he shouted as he waved his sword frantically above his head. Though men on horseback arrived with the red headbands they too were confused. "Who do I give them to?" one soldier asked, not able to tell which soldiers were on his side. Without warning the soldier was struck in the side by a sharp sword. He fell suddenly forward into the basket of red cloth, his own blood adding to its ruby rich color.

Orders and counter orders echoed above the clamor, as men continued to strike savagely at anything that moved. "What the hell are we doing?" one soldier said to another, not sure if he was speaking to a fellow compatriot or a determined foe. The senseless slaughter needed to be stopped. No one knew how to do it.

Finally, General Mbanka ran spiritedly up and down the forest perimeter yelling, "Pull back into the forest." Some of his men dutifully obeyed, but others, still occupied with armed combat, remained in the heat of battle.

From his position south of the battlefield General Garr watched with astonishment. "You were right," Garr said to Montama. "They have no intention of attacking us at all." Though they had to squint hard through the sun-drenched glare to secure a clearer view of the battlefield, they finally saw the bodies of a growing number of wounded and dead.

Garr was ready to give his own order to attack when Montama calmly raised his hand. "Look!" he said, as his eyes spotted a small detachment of Pantamanu's soldiers who finally had moved into position in front of the mercenary army. About two hundred yards away the marching men unexpectedly came to an abrupt halt.

"What are they up to?" Garr said, his eye squinting hard to determine if the enemy army had any weapons at the ready. What he finally saw completely startled him. For behind the soldiers he could see a line of about two-dozen talladaggers, his own beasts that he had been forced to abandon when he had abruptly retreated from Teta. "They are going to use our own beasts against us," Garr shouted.

As at the Battle of Kalel, the enraged talladaggers began to charge, but this time directly at General Garr's army. "Tell the men not to move, not even slightly," Montama shouted defiantly and with a steady calm.

Garr quickly relayed the order down the line, while veterans of countless military encounters stood suddenly quite still, frightened beyond imagining, staring ahead at the same storming talladaggers that had once been their most potent weapon. "What are you doing?" Garr said, his eye now wide open with terror. Montama resolutely responded, "Nobody move."

Garr never before had been on the receiving end of a talladagger's charge and as he watched the ferocious beasts he could feel the fiery anger in their eyes. Their bodies moved with an amazing swiftness, given the animal's immense bulk. Their dual nostrils flared and their tongues, both of them, hung sideways from the end of their long trunk-like heads as the beasts charged mindlessly forward, their anger growing exponentially with each ferocious step. Despite the order to remain steadfast, Montama's men trembled as they heard the talladaggers guttural grunt, a most hateful and frightening noise. Meanwhile, their giant oversized feet pounded the ground with such a terrible intensity that even on horseback, Garr could feel the earth tremble beneath him.

One soldier, terrified beyond all reason, broke ranks and ran as fast as he could. The rest of the men, though equally frightened, remained stationary, their hearts beating fiercely as the foul beasts approached. Montama alone showed absolutely no fear whatsoever. Instead he continued to stare ahead at the beasts, willing them to come forward. With each step, as the dust rose around their hooves, the talladaggers moved closer, until General Garr could veritably feel the intensity of the beast's blind anger. Finally, he closed his eye; sure that this was the last thing he would ever see.

One soldier who broke ranks and ran was quickly trampled by two enraged talladaggers. They angrily picked up his body and literally tore it to shreds, before dropping it on the ground and stomping it into the dust. Beyond this one casualty, however, the mighty creatures merely ignored Montama's army, assiduously avoiding all who had remained still. When Garr opened his eye he was astonished to see that but one of his soldiers had been killed. The others, though standing like frightened statues, had been utterly unharmed. "What happened?" Garr asked.

Supremely self-satisfied, Montama smirked, "They are indeed like our own belta beasts, from eastern Arcania. When they charge if you move just a little, you attract their attention, and they will stomp you to death. If you remain completely still, they will ignore you."

Garr now turned and saw that the talladaggers had congregated about a hundred yards behind his men and were now contently searching for grazing land. The tall grass, not Montama's army, now consumed the beasts' avid attention.

Again Garr stared at Montama. "My god, it is your destiny to be king," he said admiringly. Then, turning toward the enemy, Garr shouted in a loud and expressive voice, "Thanks for returning our beasts." He then watched as the enemy commander stood utterly dumbfounded. Then turning back to Montama, Garr suggested, "Let's say that we finally join the battle."

Montama needed no further encouragement. Raising himself high on his saddle, he shouted in a voice so shrill that even Bellazar atop the Kanaween Forest could hear it distinctly. "ATTACK!" And with this single command, Montama's army, with unparalleled fortitude and determination, charged forward against two powerful enemies.

Chapter 78
Perfect Chaos

"Are you on my side?" one soldier shouted to another. "I don't know," the second soldier responded. He then added, "Which side are you on?"

Despite Pantamanu's many attempts to differentiate his forces from those of General Mbanka, and the latter general's attempts to withdraw his army from the field of battle, the two armies of Arcania continued to engage in savage battle in which it still was virtually impossible for the soldiers to determine who was the enemy and who was not. Consequently, some men stood by defensively, while other more determined soldiers fought on valiantly, not really caring whether they killed friend or foe. Still other members of both armies retreated to the safety of the Kanaween Forest or to the western perimeter of the grassland battlefield. In the midst of this perfect chaos, Montama's men eagerly joined the fray.

Meanwhile, Pantamanu on horseback angrily pulled out a secret weapon that he had devised just for this battle: a long, slick, leather whip that he strapped by his side. He had played with this weapon when he was a child and at the last minute, as he prepared for this final battle, he decided it might prove useful as a means of whipping his own army into a disciplined unit. So, intent on restoring order, he savagely lashed several of his own men while bellowing, "Get into the fight." The sight of his soldiers retreating from the battlefield incensed the young commander. "Fight or I will kill you myself," he barked with a terrible fury, as he repeatedly snapped his whip, not sure and not caring which army he lashed.

From the crystal blue firmament above the battlefield, Bellazar watched with hypnotic intensity, as the armies below continued to devour each other. From her vantage point, too, she could not tell which army was hers. She did not care. "I hold the high ground," she said confidently. "So in the end, I must win this battle."

Then from the northeast, she spotted yet another group of men herding large animals toward the direction of the forest. It was at such a distance that Bellazar had to struggle to see what manner of beasts Pantamanu's army had in tow. "Ladatops," she finally surmised. "So," she said with supreme self-satisfaction. "Pantamanu intends to do battle with me among the heavens." Without delay, she ordered Bobbie to carry her to a position further north and instantly the ladatop moved its dexterous hands and feet along a large winding branch, then over to a spindly vine, which it grabbed with its long fury fingers. Bellazar tightly gripped the saddle, though she was strapped into it, a necessary precaution, given the odd angles at which ladatops travel from tree to tree.

Bobbie instinctively and enthusiastically grabbed a vine and pulled himself forward, swinging with ease to another nearby tree. As he did so Bellazar breathed deeply, joyously filling her lungs with the upper atmosphere's fresh untainted air. As her red hair twirled behind her, she ducked out of the way of one tree branch, then felt the sting of another on her left cheek, as Bobbie continued to move swiftly northward. Within minutes Bobbie rested on the top of a prodigious tree, directly overlooking the fast approaching enemy ladatop army.

Bellazar quickly estimated that Pantamanu had about one hundred ladatops. Then, with a tug on Bobbie's mane, she induced her ladatop to turn back. Seconds later she was again gliding gracefully through the tops of the Kanawa trees, moving first to the south and then cutting directly across to the west. For several minutes, Bellazar and Bobbie soared effortlessly forward, until she finally arrived at a designated position, high atop a particularly ancient Kanawa tree, its long heavy branches reaching out in myriad directions like a giant octopus. On these branches Lieutenant Caligari, one of the finest ladatop riders in Arcania, saluted his superior. "Pantamanu's aerial army is approaching," Bellazar reported.

Startled by this revelation, the lieutenant asked, "What is their compliment?"

"Approximately one hundred." Bellazar carefully stroked Bobbie's head as she took a few deep breaths. She was slightly winded, a usual reaction to swift and sudden movement through the high altitude trees. Then with a keen sense of curiosity she asked, "What is the news from the battlefield?"

"The engagement has commenced," Caligari responded perfunctorily.

"I am aware of that," Bellazar said with a frustrated curtness.

"There is a problem," the subordinate said without emotion. Bellazar stared intently as a runner arrived via ladatop and handed a dispatch to the lieutenant. Bellazar watched as his eyes glided from side to side as he read the communication. "We have been ordered by General Mbanka to tie a blue streamer around our waists."

"Why?" Bellazar demanded. "The enemy will be able to see us."

"So we can tell friend from foe." Caligari shouted his response so that all around him could hear it.

Bellazar realized that the long, cloth streamers, generally only used when a ladatop rider was injured, would immediately alert the enemy to their present location. Still, on nearby branches, more than thirty riders immediately complied with the order. Caligari, shouting even louder, ordered, "Relay the command to the troops," and one by one the individual ladatops and their riders departed, each surfing the trees in a separate direction, to quickly disseminate this new order from General Mbanka. Bellazar reached into the side pocket of her leather saddlebag and then pulled out her streamer. As she tied it around her waist she declared, "No matter if they can see me or not. We outnumber them at least ten to one." Caligari looked up as Bellazar tugged on Bobbie's mane, then directed her ladatop to carry her back to the perimeter of the Kanaween Forest.

Meanwhile, on the battlefield, some of Pantamanu's men finally began to affix their red headbands, though many others did not have the time or opportunity to do so. Pantamanu, who now sported his own red badge, continued to order his troops forward, while ferociously snapping his whip. Nearby, one soldier uttered to another, "I don't care if they are wearing a headband or not. If I don't personally know them I will consider them to be my enemy." The second soldier nodded his head then moved forcefully against two men who abruptly raised their weapons against him.

The sound was even more deafening as Montama's charging army finally joined the battle. At first most Arcanians were unaware that a third army had arrived. Montama's men had a distinct advantage, however. It was not difficult to distinguish the Relatanians from the Arcanians, for the former were largely unkempt with tattered and soiled uniforms. In addition, many of Montama's men had removed their shirts as a show of solidarity toward their leader. With a horrifying fierceness, then, Montama's men charged forward, striking wildly at men already engaged in mortal combat.

Meanwhile, Montama rode directly past two Arcanians who were in the midst of a duel to the death. With his father's mighty Sword of Tamarite in his right hand he struck the two men with one powerful forward thrust, decapitating them both instantaneously. In Pellaville, sitting behind his desk, Lord Tantamount looked up suddenly. "My son has used the Sword of Tamarite to kill his own people." Tantamount was not sure how he knew this to be true, but he was certain that he did. As he remembered Timilty, and how he had been butchered by this very same sword, Tantamount closed his eyes and concentrated hard. "My sword shall never again be used to kill another Arcanian."

On the battlefield, the Arcanians were not quite sure what was happening. As Garr's soldiers mutilated men from both of the passra's armies, it took the rivals a few minutes to realize that they needed to defend themselves against a third formidable enemy that was killing Arcanians indiscriminately. Finally realizing the newly shared danger, the Arcanian soldiers tried to fall back. Some sprinted for the forest, while others stood in disbelief, unsure what to do. Meanwhile, on foot and on horseback, Montama's men continued to strike the enemy hard.

"There are men all around us," one Arcanian soldier yelled hysterically before a sword violently entered his back. As he looked down he could see the sword's tip protruding from his stomach. There was no pain. His suffering was at an end.

Then, as he rode his horse among the dead and dying, from seemingly out of nowhere, Montama felt the sting of a whip upon his back. When he turned he saw Pantamanu, his eyes glaring demonically. "Remember me?" Pantamanu shouted gleefully, for he recognized young Montama's face from the Kensilday. Before Montama could respond Pantamanu again struck him hard with his savage whip, leaving a vicious open wound upon the young man's right cheek. Montama tried to grab the whip. When he did it left a burning red stripe upon his hand. "Do you like battle?" Pantamanu taunted, as he fired his whip directly at Montama. This time Montama held up the Sword of Tamarite before his face. When the whip struck it, the sword inexplicably shattered.

Montama could not believe that his sword would simply disintegrate. He had little time to react, for Pantamanu was relentlessly on the charge. Weaving his long whip back over his shoulder, he brought the seemingly enchanted weapon forward with such force that it painfully wrapped around Montama's leg. Pantamanu enjoyed the feeling, as he tugged the whip, dragging Montama from his horse and helplessly to the ground.

Before Montama knew what was happening, Pantamanu began to ride his horse swiftly along the line. Montama, his leg still entangled with the whip, tried to brace himself, but he was dragged along behind Pantamanu's horse for many yards until Pantamanu was forced by sundry impediments to turn his horse so he could again face the heart of the battlefield. Though Montama finally managed to free his leg from the whip, Pantamanu continued to ride in circles around the young rebel. Periodically, he would weave close enough so that he could use his whip's brutal sting to painfully strike at Montama. "Accept your destiny," Pantamanu shouted with delight. "You are about to die!" Pantamanu smiled broadly for he realized that he could strike Montama at will; for without a weapon there was little Montama could do to protect himself.

Eventually, Pantamanu was tired of the beating he was administering to his young enemy and with much pleasure he decided the time had come to kill Montama. He therefore turned his horse directly toward Montama and charged. As his enemy's horse fast approached Montama looked to see if there was any cover. Only a few feet away he saw a slight depression, probably forged by runoff from heavy rains. Though his body writhed in pain, Montama quickly rolled over into the depression. As he did so he felt a hoof virulently strike his backside. He winced as pain surged throughout his body. Then, Montama looked up and saw that Pantamanu was turning his horse in preparation for a second assault. Montama tried to right himself, but he could not stand. Pantamanu smiled malevolently, for Montama was now in a crouched position, a much easier target to strike and kill. "Now you will die," Pantamanu said softly. As he did he suddenly grimaced, as a half sword suddenly pierced the side of his left boot. Pantamanu reached down to pull the half sword from his leg. When he did he noticed that it carried an unusual insignia: a venomous coiled snake in the shape of the letter G.

Not more than a dozen yards away, General Garr reached to his side and unsheathed his full sword and then with his cape flowing freely in the wind, he rode directly toward Pantamanu. The prince pulled the half sword from his leg and with his own blood still dripping from it he raised the weapon defensively and parried General Garr's oncoming charge. "I will kill you," Garr snarled through clenched teeth, as the half sword snapped off in Pantamanu's hand.

With bloodlust in his eyes, Pantamanu held his whip up with his other hand before his face. "Come and get me," he taunted his enemy.

Montama was no longer the center of Pantamanu's attention. As a result, while Garr and Pantamanu charged at each other, he was able to crawl along the ground for several yards until he reached a stray horse, its rider still astride the saddle, though he was stone cold dead. With all of his remaining strength Montama grabbed the stirrup and pulled himself up. As he did so, the dead rider finally slid off the saddle. Montama took several deep breaths and then with great fortitude, pulled himself up onto the saddle. Then he reached over and grabbed the horse's neck. As he did, the blood from his facial wound painfully blinded his right eye. Finally in control of the horse, he turned it and aimed it directly at Pantamanu.

Pantamanu had paid no heed whatsoever to Montama's actions, for his gaze was still mesmerizingly fixed on General Garr's solitary eye. He therefore did not notice as Montama's horse charged directly toward his present position. At the last minute, out of the corner of his eye, Pantamanu spotted the young man on horseback. He tried to duck and the two horses collided violently, throwing both horsemen off their steeds and high into the air.

Montama fell forward, heels over his head, before striking the ground with a loud and ominous thud. Afterward his body lay utterly motionless.

Pantamanu winced as his body bounced twice as it hit the ground. Disoriented, his mind swirled with a dizzying intensity. "What the hell happened?" he asked no one in particular. Prostrate, Pantamanu was utterly vulnerable. Yet Garr ignored him, racing instead to Montama's side. The general leaped lithely from his horse. Running to Montama, Garr rolled the young man over onto his back. He then put his head down on Montama's chest. "He is breathing," Garr whispered. Then, without another word, he threw Montama's body over his right shoulder and carried it to his horse. Though men continued to fight all around him, few paid any heed to these two men. Garr placed Montama's body crossways onto the front of the horse and then quickly mounted the saddle. With maddening dispatch, Garr turned and rode his horse at full throttle away from the battlefield. "I must save the boy if I can," he said, surprised that he felt such a strong filial attachment to young Montama.

No one came to Pantamanu's rescue. He lay among the dead and dying for more than half an hour before his reason slowly resurfaced. Dizzy, still confused, he looked around and saw more dead men than living. The battle was still intensely underway. It was a slaughter. Pantamanu could not tell which side, if any was prevailing.

Spotting a fellow Arcanian wearing a red headband, Pantamanu stridently called out. "YOU! Come here." The soldier immediately recognized his commanding officer and obeyed his order, though he had to kill two men before he could get to Pantamanu's side. Once he was there Pantamanu asked, "Who is winning?"

"I don't know," the soldier exclaimed. "All I know is that I am still alive." Pantamanu reached down and clutched his whip, which had fallen not more than a few feet from his present position. He then ordered the soldier to help him stand up. "Where to?" the soldier asked.

"Take me toward the forest," Pantamanu said, grimacing as he tried to put pressure on his wounded foot. Unable to walk without assistance, Pantamanu waited while the soldier draped his arm around the commander's back. Then, the men limped uneasily toward the perimeter of the Kanaween Forest. There beneath a small bush the soldier set Pantamanu down.

"You are badly wounded," the soldier said.

"It is my left foot," Pantamanu said as he painfully pulled off his boot. "Get me something to wrap it with."

The soldier tour off a piece of his own shirt and then wrapped it tightly around Pantamanu's foot. "The left leg will be no use to," the soldier said solemnly.

"Then I will ride a ladatop," Pantamanu cursed, as he felt a sudden jolt of pain shoot up his leg and along his spine.

"Sir, you are not well enough," the soldier declared emphatically.

Pantamanu was unyielding. "Help me up," he ordered. Then as he leaned on the soldier's shoulder, he commanded, "We must meet up with our aerial forces. They should be about a mile from here to the north."

"Yes sir," the soldier obediently responded. And together the two men limped northward, as the battle outside the Kanaween Forest ground miserably on.

Chapter 79
First Do No Harm

"RIDE!" Garr shouted with a desperate intensity as his horse sprinted so fast that at times its four feet soared well from the ground. Garr rode quickly to the south for more than a mile, till his horse was nearly exhausted. The horse was near the breaking point when Garr finally arrived at a patch of tall grass not more than twenty feet from the forest perimeter. It was a campsite and though the sky was now illuminated with a glorious orange glow, Grandafier the Elder still attended to a fire, carefully stoking it, for though this was an unseasonably warm day, the old man could feel a chill that ran throughout his ragged aging bones. Grandafier had been left behind, for at his age and in his condition, he had no utility whatsoever on the battlefield. So he, and a few other soldiers remained at this distant outpost, meant to be a mere ruse, a sign that Montama had many soldiers in reserve.

Grandafier's mind was entirely focused on the campfire until he heard General Garr's voice echoing in the distance. The old man stared out at the charging horse. He noticed something strange, but with his ancient eyes he was not sure what it was. "It seems to be a rider carrying some sort of a load," he pondered.

As Garr arrived Grandafier could see that he carried not a load of goods, but rather the body of a man. "Come help me!" Garr shouted earnestly.

Grandafier took a second to stand up, for his knees felt arthritic and inflexibly stiff. He therefore walked with an even more pronounced limp than usual toward General Garr's exhausted horse. "What is it?" Grandafier called out as he moved toward the general.

"It is Montama!" Garr declared with great concern. "He has been injured."

"Oh my," Grandafier said, as he wobbled a bit faster toward the injured boy. By the time Grandafier arrived two other soldiers were in the process of helping Garr lower Montama's body to the ground. "What happened?" Grandafier asked, suddenly repulsed by the sight of the blood that covered most of Montama's face and chest.

Garr did not explain the circumstances of Montama's injuries. Instead he grabbed Grandafier by the collar and implored the old man, "You must do whatever you can for the boy. He is badly hurt."

Grandafier was not a doctor, but he had volunteered to take care of the injured. He had not expected many, for most men would die instantly on the field of battle. Montama was not like other men. He simply could not be left to die. As Montama was laid onto the ground, Garr grabbed a nearby blanket and placed it over his young protégé. "He was magnificent," Garr said with obvious pride and affection as he carefully folded the blanket underneath Montama's chin. "He fought like a lion."

Grandafier put his hand on Montama's neck. "He has a pulse," he said hopefully.

"He has lost a lot of blood," Garr added with great concern. Then, as he stared at Grandafier, he begged, "You must save this boy. He is our future king."

Grandafier put his head down against Montama's chest. "He is breathing steadily," he said. "That is a good sign."

Grandafier now saw something he had never even remotely anticipated. General Garr was crying. The old man was startled when he heard the general weep, "I have come to love this boy as if he were my own son. When I first met Montama I thought he was weak, naïve, nothing more than the spoiled son of a prominent lord. He has grown so much since then." Then with a father's pride, Garr smiled, "You should have seen him at Kalel. He gave his own sword to Rendrau and then offered up his own life. I have never seen anything like it."

Grandafier could tell that Garr was entirely sincere. With genuine kindness Grandafier responded, "I will do everything I can."

Garr grabbed Grandafier by the lapel. "You absolutely must! This boy must be the next king. There is greatness in him. I have seen it."

Grandafier thought that he had seen madness in Montama's eyes, but then again, he had seen the same look of madness in the eyes of other great men. So the old man merely nodded his head ever so slowly. Garr quickly turned and looked back toward the battlefield. "Are we winning?" Grandafier asked ever so meekly.

"We will win," Garr said with supreme confidence. "But it will mean nothing if the boy dies." Then after a last long look at Montama, Garr leaped onto his horse, mounting it from behind, before riding spiritedly back toward the battlefield.

Grandafier watched Garr for some time, before kneeling down next to Montama. "Get me some warm water," he yelled out to anyone who would listen. Within a few seconds a soldier brought him a mug filled with water.

Grandafier carefully poured it on his unsoiled handkerchief and then touched it gently to Montama's forehead. He then wiped the blood from Montama's face, exposing the ghastly cut left by the sting of Pantamanu's whip. "I will need some bandages," Grandafier called out as he continued to attend to Montama's wounds.

He looked at Montama. As he lay quietly on the ground now red with his own blood, Montama looked suddenly like the simple boy Grandafier had always known. "He was so young and his innocence had yet to escape him," Grandafier whispered gently, remembering the young man he had first counseled almost a full cycle ago. How long ago that seemed now and how unreal their subsequent journey still seemed to be. It amazed the old man that he was in a distant field, far from home, in the midst of a cataclysmic battle. None of this seemed real. "It is as if the whole thing is a horrible dream," he whispered again.

"It is no dream," he heard a commanding voice intone. Grandafier did not even look up, for his full attention was still focused on the wounded young man who lay before him. He listened as King Benton whispered, "Now is the time to bring this destructive succession war to an end. You must kill the boy."

Grandafier listened, but he did not respond to King Benton. Instead he closed his eyes and gently sobbed.

Chapter 80
The Battle Within

Montama had not moved as much as one muscle for more than two hours. Though his breaths were labored, Grandafier believed that the boy was doing better. "His pulse is strong," he told a woman who continued to bring cold compresses for Montama's forehead. "He is a good looking boy," the woman said with genuine kindness.

Grandafier looked up at the woman and asked, "Can you get me some water to drink?"

"Certainly," the woman said with a slight curtsy, before departing for a nearby stream. As Grandafier watched her depart he again heard King Benton's voice. "As your king, I command you to kill this boy!"

Grandafier looked at Montama's serene, innocent face. As he did so the old man's hands began to shake uncontrollably. "I am not a killer," he said, as tears streamed down the corners of his craggy and wrinkled green face.

"Kill the boy!" Benton repeated emphatically.

Frightened, Grandafier placed his trembling hand near Montama's throat. Again, he felt for a pulse though he realized that in this feeble state even an old man easily could take the life of this young, vulnerable man. As he watched the steady undulations in Montama's breathing, Grandafier suddenly heard, "Do not harm him, I beg of you." This time it was a woman's voice.

"Truellen?" Grandafier asked.

The tears now blinded the old man. "I cannot harm this boy. It was I who led him astray. If anyone deserves to die, let it be me."

Though he did not know it, and though there was no outward sign of it, Montama could hear every single word of this strange conversation. For though his physical body was unconscious, Montama's spirit was alive and vibrant. He could not yet awaken in the real world, but he could magnify his thoughts, stretch them outward, reaching another dimension, a veritable universe of ideas. As Benton and Truellen tussled for Grandafier's life, Montama concentrated and deliberately moved his consciousness back inside the Oracle. He realized at once that the Oracle was still in a state of flux. Still, the Oracle's matrix was congealing and as it gained strength it now fervently reached out to Montama to be its new leader.

I was not surprised by the Oracle's resilience, its steadfast ability to rebuild itself. I was surprised by Montama's boldness. "So, you have come here to confront me directly," I said. "That is a most foolish thing to do."

"No," Montama responded calmly. "I have come here to confront both of you," Kublatitan warily listened, for he realized that he was no longer in control of the Oracle. Rather the various entities were drawing strength and power directly from him as the Oracle continued to reconstitute itself.

Then, as Kublatitan and I watched in helpless amazement, Montama did something most unexpected. He concentrated on just one idea. Though he was not conscious in the real world, he still raised his hand and pointed his index finger directly toward the sky. "I will send you both there," he said with a terrible fury as Grandafier, frightened beyond all reason, seeing Montama's hand pointing skyward, suddenly pulled his body away from Montama's side. Then, as the old man watched, he saw two lighting bolts flash high above the tops of the Kanaween Forest. The bolts collided and as they did, they emitted a fierce electrical charge that sprayed down shards of light upon the forest below, like the residue from an errant firework display.

Inside the Oracle, Montama continued to concentrate. "You have brought ruin to our passra," he angrily charged. "Now the two of you must pay for your duplicity. Only one of you will be allowed to return to the Oracle. The other must be destroyed."

I felt Kublatitan desperately attempt to return to the Oracle. His presence was blocked, not just by Montama, but also by tens of thousands of other entities, each one concentrating on the same exact thought. "One of you must be destroyed. One of you must pay for your sins."

On the battlefield, men paid no heed whatsoever to the changing tide of the sky's now purple hue. Nor did they notice as successive lightening bolts charged at irregular angles across the Kanaween Forest, each one leaving burning cinders in its wake. As he lay unconscious, Montama could feel the desperate intensity of the two titans' emotions. I was fierce, unyielding, and Kublatitan, his mind now opened to the full attractions of hatred, soon found his own mind consumed by an utterly illogical desire to destroy me. As he did we heard Montama exclaim, "Only one of you will survive."

Chapter 81
The Battle To The Death

Pantamanu was in such extreme pain that it eventually took two men to carry him from the battlefield. When a gangly, orange haired fifteen-cycle-old medic took one look at the open wound on the commander's leg, he solemnly declared, "The leg will have to come off."

Pantamanu would have none of it. "I don't need my leg to ride a ladatop." He therefore ordered the medic to tie another bandage even more tightly around his festering wound, while he demanded that the other soldiers bring him a ladatop as quickly as possible. Within less than ten minutes a ladatop named Dolly was procured. Dolly was a beautiful brown and red ladatop, standing four times the size of an average man, with a sleek muscular body, long arms and legs, each decorated with retractable nails that allowed the ladatop to hold onto the side of a tree for hours at a time, if necessary. Dolly acknowledged Pantamanu as he gently stroked her back with his blood stained hand. It responded with a pleasant cooing sound.

"This one will do," Pantamanu declared. He felt a bit lightheaded as he strapped himself into Dolly's saddle. Then he closed his eyes, breathing deeply as the ladatop skillfully scaled a particularly large, thick, Kanawa tree. Dolly spread out her vast long arms and legs as she methodically slid up the side of the tall tree. Her leather like chest had no fur, for the sharp tree bark had long ago completely shaved it off. With immaculate concentration and brute force, Dolly moved methodically up the tree's wide base until she finally reached a cascade of protruding branches. As she did Pantamanu periodically was forced to duck his head to avoid stray limbs. At one point during the ascent, he saw a frightened squirrel scurry for cover. When he looked down he realized that he already was over six hundred feet above the ground.

With a strange sort of detachment, he peered out toward the field of battle. The giant green, gold and yellow leaves of the Kanawa tree obstructed his view. Occasionally he glimpsed various scenes from the still ongoing battle. It had been at least six hours since combat had commenced. Men were now so weary that some died as their exhausted hearts merely burst apart. Pantamanu saw men with multiple wounds fighting valiantly, unwilling to surrender in the face of an unthinkable slaughter. As he rose higher and higher in the sky, Pantamanu could clearly determine that there were more barbarians in the fray than Arcanians. "We are losing the battle," he realized at last.

In spite of this revelation, or perhaps because of it, Pantamanu felt a sudden surge of adrenaline. "I can still win this war," he thought as he skillfully bobbed his head, avoiding yet another spindly branch. "I must win it in the air and among the tree tops." Pantamanu knew that Montama's army had no aerial capability. Winning the battle in the grasslands would provide a major tactical advantage. But Montama's forces would be incapable of routing out the Arcanians in the forest. So long as they remained, the war would continue and Pantamanu would have yet another opportunity to turn the tide of battle.

Before he could do that, he first had to confront his main enemy, for his anger was still channeled in one specific direction. "Damn that hateful woman," he shouted, though Dolly paid no heed whatsoever to his curse words. Skillfully she climbed ever higher, her determination to reach the tops of the trees completely undaunted. "I will seek her out and kill her myself," Pantamanu promised, as he thought of nothing other than the death of Bellazar.

Though he did not yet know it, Bellazar was not far away. She too had come to the same perimeter to see how the battle below was progressing. As she did so, in the far distance, through countless branches and other aerial obstacles, she caught a few quick glimpses of a finely dressed man, the buttons on his uniform occasionally glistening in the sunlight. "It must be Pantamanu," she quickly surmised. "So, he wants to bring the battle directly to me."

As Bellazar gently stroked Bobbie's mane she looked for a more defensible position. Spotting a particularly tall tree not far away she ordered Bobbie to move swiftly and with grace and the ladatop immediately obeyed, wrapping its hands and legs around a large, thick branch, scaling it for some fifteen or twenty feet. Then, as Bellazar lowered her head into a tight crouch, Bobbie grabbed onto a sinewy vine and elegantly swung from tree to tree. As he did, Bellazar felt the breeze caress her face. She never tired of the sensation, the ultimate freedom that came as she flew almost a half-mile above the ground. Through her exhilaration she also remembered that Pantamanu was now on the offensive. As a result, her mind remained focused and calm, for she understood that though Pantamanu was a skilled ladatop rider, she had even more experience. "I know tricks he hasn't even thought of," she said with a self-satisfied smirk. When she arrived at the top of the tall tree, she finally secured an unobstructed view of Pantamanu's incremental ascent. Due to her vastly superior eyesight she could see objects clearly at a distance that others could barely discern. As she peered intently forward she saw two small beasts climbing the tree beneath Pantamanu's current position. They were spidermites, a trained beast that looked a bit like a weasel that could be trained to climb trees while holding various provisions in its mouth or in a small pouch on its back. One of the spidermites was carrying a sword and the other a whip. "What use is a whip up here?" Bellazar wondered.

Pantamanu continued his ascent, completely unaware that he was being observed. His mind was still focused entirely on the sensations that accompany soaring at high elevations. As he rose toward a half mile from the ground he temporarily found it difficult to breath, though he did not panic, for he knew the feeling would pass. "My body will adjust," he reminded himself, as Dolly aggressively shimmied over and across branches, toward a perch high atop the tree. As she did so, blood continued to drip from Pantamanu's injured foot. Only his total focus on the climb allowed him to drive the excruciating pain from his mind.

Dolly finally rested three quarters of the way to the top of the tree. She had come to a point so high in the sky that when Pantamanu looked again toward the battlefield, all he could see were scores of expectant vultamires, circling feverishly in the air.

Bellazar also had a clear view of Pantamanu and of the other enemy soldiers, who likewise were slowly ascending the trees. With a turn of her head and a guttural command, she induced Bobbie to turn and carry her in an entirely new direction. Bobbie's dexterous hands and legs reached out for large sinewy vines, which carried it with an amazing grace swiftly through the treetops. In a matter of just under two minutes Bellazar was almost a quarter mile from her past location, and fast moving in on her army's aerial headquarters. Again, back at the large, old tree that served as the division's headquarters, she reported, "The battle is about to commence. I saw about one hundred ladatops in hurried ascent along the forest's perimeter."

"Then we must move quickly into position," the captain declared. He then turned to a nearby woman and said, "Sound the alarm." The woman raised a large golden horn and blew a cascading three note command that clearly could be heard throughout the forest and even onto the nearby battlefield. Immediately, hundreds upon hundreds of Bellazar's ladatop riders, who previously had been hidden in the trees, emerged and moved with breathtaking speed toward the perimeter of the battlefield.

Meanwhile, on the grasslands below, General Garr had rejoined the battle. Because of the continuing intensity of the fighting, Garr was forced to call in reinforcements, including many of the volunteers who had spontaneously joined Montama's cause. These untrained soldiers, many of them Ka-Why-Tee, reacted to the battle with myriad emotional responses. Some ran furiously into the heat of battle, carrying any weapon that they could muster, from swords, to sticks, to simple rocks. Others, seeing the horror of the battlefield for the first time, stood, frightened beyond measure, and then turned and ran hastily for cover.

With these untested soldiers now carrying a greater burden, Garr tried several times to encircle his enemy and then crush it with one final deadly assault. The unseasoned troops could not be so easily deployed and Garr had to be content with men carrying sticks and stones, inflicting whatever harm they could.

Bellazar's general, Mbanka, also tried to reposition his own men, trying to cut off General Garr's charging second wave of untrained soldiers. His army had suffered dreadful losses. Many men were dead. Even more were wounded. Though his men fought with incredible determination and skill, Mbanka realized that his only hope was one sudden frontal attack. With about three hundred men still congregating toward the forest perimeter, he gave the order for the final assault.

When Garr saw the men charge from the west he ordered his army to pivot. Some men obeyed, but most did not. As a result, his men were not prepared for this final attack. General Mbanka personally led the charge. "I see the Talacrebe general," he cried out, as he spotted his distinctive one-eyed enemy. Mbanka therefore unsheathed his sword and ran directly toward General Garr, intent on killing him with one quick strike. At the very last instant Garr saw Mbanka's charge. He quickly spun out of harm's way as Mbanka's sword grazed his right arm above the elbow. Garr now raised his own sword and the two generals, both highly skilled in the art of fencing, commenced their own private battle. As they did so, men who moments before had been engaged in the most brutal form of combat, suddenly stood still, watching the surreal sight of two generals, their swords drawn, parrying each others charges in the midst of a battlefield consumed by the blood of the dead.

As Garr and Mbanka fought, men from both armies abruptly dropped their weapons, relieved at last to have their fate determined by their leaders. Garr waved his sword carefully, looking for an opportunity to move in closer to his enemy. Mbanka, his hands steady, continued to search his enemy for a point of vulnerability. Then, with a swift forward lunge Mbanka moved forcefully against Garr. Garr's composure was the equal of Mbanka and he successfully parried the assault, as the two men's swords clashed repeatedly.

And in the far distance, the sky was continuously illuminated with sudden flashes of lightening, as two titans continued their own extraordinary battle far above the ground. It was now total war. Garr and Mbanka continued their solitary battle in the grasslands, while Bellazar's army moved into position to intercept and engage Pantamanu's aerial forces. And in the skies above them, Kublatitan and myself, rudely expelled from the Oracle, turned our highly charged electrical wrath fervently against each other. It was total madness, for no rational being could ever deliberately conceive of such a hellish fate. Only the vultamires, intent on feeding on the dead, seemed satisfied by the escalating carnage. Arcania, once a great enlightened passra, was now reduced to nothing more than abject chaos.

And only one person could see it all. Lying in a patch of grass, a mile away from the cacophonous sounds of battle, Montama lay unconscious, with his mind still linked to the Oracle. In his mind's eye he therefore could see the battlefield from far above, as if he too were a vultamire circling ever higher in the air. He saw Bellazar's aerial army, which consisted of vastly superior numbers of soldiers on the backs of ladatops moving swiftly to encircle Pantamanu's much smaller force. He saw his mentor, General Garr and his adversary, Mbanka, engaged in a deadly duel before a startled army of battered and bloodied men. And he felt the intensity of my emotions, as I struck like enraged lightening against Kublatitan's despicable righteousness. As for the giant Taewokan, Montama also sensed a spirit of rising, incendiary rage. And in this instant Montama realized that his madness was shared by the entire world. Everywhere, everything had gone irreparably mad! Then he realized, "Only a madman would want to rule over this hellish world."

And there still were many who were willing to do so. Bellazar's eyes narrowed with a ferocious intensity as she finally moved into position to strike her enemy. Pantamanu, though dizzy and still losing blood from his deep leg wound, was determined to destroy the woman who he blamed for all of Arcania's woes. And as lightening bolts continued to illuminate the sky far above his head, Pantamanu ordered Dolly to carry him forward against the oncoming enemy.

The forest was now filled with the sight of men and women, riding on the backs of giant primates, moving swiftly through the trees. The riders' swords were fully drawn and ready for battle. All except for Pantamanu, who decided instead to use a different weapon, his ready whip, which he clenched firmly in his right hand.

With a piercing yell Pantamanu personally launched the final assault. Soldiers now charged at each other, almost a mile above the ground, their swords at the ready, but with nothing else to defend themselves beyond their dexterity and aerial skill. Two enemy soldiers, each sitting on the back of a ladatop rode along spindly vines until they clashed in mid air. They were then joined by hundreds of others. Each tried to strike their sword at the other. Sometimes the result was the mere harmless clanging of two dueling swords. In other cases a trained rider slashed his enemy, or their ladatop, killing it instantly. When a ladatop was killed, its body, carrying its mount, fell hard, colliding multiple times against outstretched branches, before finally tumbling inexorably to the ground far below.

Bellazar's army, its blue streamers in place, could easily determine friend from foe. Bellazar herself was determined to strike at but one particularly enemy. "I must find Pantamanu and kill him," she declared defiantly. Alone among the others, Pantamanu's uniform was utterly distinctive. She therefore scanned the forest, looking for any sign of her most personal enemy. As she did, she occasionally was forced to do battle with an enemy soldier. The men were startled to see how skillfully she rode, as well as her unexpected dexterity with a sword. As her ladatop glided from one vine to another, she decapitated one man with one solid slash of her sword, then struck another in the chest, his ladatop continuing to move from tree to tree, though its rider was now deceased.

Her mind remained focused on one objective. "Where is that bastard?" she said with an unyielding fieriness. Pantamanu was finally revealed when a particularly vibrant lightening strike reflected off his uniform's polished golden buttons. "There he is," Bellazar said aloud, her eyes wide with anticipation, her heart cold and unforgiving. She patted Bobbie on his head and then commanded him to move toward Pantamanu's position. As the ladatop reached for a nearby vine, she ducked her head, before the two floated effortlessly to another tree not far from Pantamanu's present location.

His eyes also were searching the horizon, desperately looking for Bellazar. His eyes had not yet acclimated to the diffuse lighting conditions that existed within the forest. Beams of stray light cut sharply and at odd angles through the high elevation trees. In between was a world of shadows and darkness. One had to be able to distinguish the movement of branches in the wind from the charging enemy. It was a difficult skill to master and Pantamanu now struggled to get a clearer view of the interior forest. When he finally spotted Bellazar it was too late for him to react. She rode past his head with a violent fury, slashing her sword savagely at his head. Only blind luck saved his life. When Bellazar slashed her sword it struck a nearby branch instead. She then rode on past him before he had the opportunity to respond. Pantamanu immediately ordered Dolly to "follow that damn woman." And within an instant he too was again in motion.

Meanwhile on the battlefield far below Mbanka and Garr continued to encircle each other, searching for an opportunity to strike. "Come and get me," Garr teased, his eye wide with a desperate wildness that unsettled Mbanka. Mbanka was a methodical professional and he would not be goaded into a brash or ill-considered movement. Instead, he continued to circle his enemy, occasionally waving his sword, his eyes fixed on his enemy. Then, seeing an opening, Mbanka sprung forward with remarkable speed.

His sword entered Garr's left shoulder about three inches above Mbanka's intended target, the enemy general's heart. Garr did not flinch, but instead grabbed hold of Mbanka's head and as he did the enemy's sword moved deeper into Garr's body until its point finally exited through his upper back. Startled, in an agonizing pain, Garr dropped his sword. He therefore held his enemy tight while he fumbled desperately behind his cape with his wounded left hand, searching for a small knife that he kept neatly concealed. As he did so, Mbanka twisted the sword, sending a new paroxysm of pain shooting through Garr's entire body. As he shivered feverishly, Garr finally got hold of his knife. Withdrawing it, with a fiendish determination Garr plunged the knife deep into Mbanka's neck. When he did Mbanka's eyes bulged as blood spurted from his carotid artery. Then, as Garr drove the knife deeper into his victim's neck, blood sprayed simultaneously from Mbanka's his throat and mouth, as the Arcanian general took his last fatal breath.

Garr held Mbanka for a few seconds before letting his enemy's body collapse to the ground. It was only at this moment that Garr realized that he too had been gravely injured. He showed no fear, smiling wearily before he too collapsed. Soldiers quickly ran to the two generals' sides. An Arcanian attended to General Mbanka. He saw that Mbanka's head was almost completely severed from his neck. "He's dead," the soldier pronounced as a group of men moved in closer to get a better look.

Another Relatanian soldier tended to Garr's wound. It was deep and clean, but not necessarily fatal, that is if the bleeding could be contained. With a painful thrust the soldier removed the sword. "We must do something to stop the bleeding," the soldier ardently declared.

Hearing this cry an Arcanian quickly stepped forward. "I was an apprentice to a doctor in my youth," he said. The enemy soldier leaned down on one knee and inspected General Garr's wound. "We must get some craybus" he said in reference to a plant with known herbal and medicinal qualities, "and pack it around the wound." Many other men were also injured. So the rest of the soldiers dropped their weapons as one man yelled, "Over here by the forest. There is a patch of craybus here." Soldiers from both armies now scurried to help the wounded. As the men tended to the wounded, miraculously, the battle on the grasslands came to a sudden and welcome halt.

Inside the forest, however, there was no such respite in the fighting. Soldiers continued to fight along branches, sometimes three and four soldiers at a time, while others swung from vines so strong that even a heavy sword could not pierce its strident fiber. Meanwhile, Pantamanu spotted Bellazar, still in fluid movement, not far from his current position. He ordered his ladatop to take him to a position about twenty feet above her. Therefore, as Bellazar swung on a vine from tree to tree, she was unaware that Pantamanu was mirroring her movements, only from a slightly higher elevation. When she finally rested on a tree branch she felt the sudden sting of Pantamanu's whip.

He had struck her hard from above and the whip cut deeply into her face, blinding her left eye. Then, before she could move she felt the lash strike at her again. With three vicious successive cracks of the whip, Pantamanu struck Bellazar, leaving her bloodied and confused. "Get us out of here," she ordered Bobbie. The ladatop complied and quickly spirited her to another nearby tree. Pantamanu was in hot pursuit, utterly determined, his mind fixated on this one final task.

The lighting strikes were now more frequent and ferocious, leaving burning cinders in their path. They ignited the trees below and as fires from the lightening strikes rose from a nearby tree, Bellazar desperately tried to wipe the blood from her face with the sleeve of her uniform. She could still see out of her right eye. Her left one was so swollen and bloodied that it was no longer of any use. When she looked skyward she saw Pantamanu's whip slashing again toward her face. She ducked and the whip snapped violently just above her right ear, as Pantamanu glided by, his ladatop Dolly dexterously holding a vine with its hind feet.

Bellazar was not used to being on the defensive and she instinctively realized that if she did not regain her composure she would not survive. Though she struggled to see through her one good eye, she could only glimpse a blur of sparkling light. "He is coming back for another attack," she thought as she slid her body sideways. When Pantamanu's whip snapped again it struck Bobbie's back, sending the beast into a fit of excruciating pain. As Bobbie reacted, the strap holding Bellazar on the ladatop's back snapped. Suddenly Bellazar felt the frightful insistence of gravity's pull, as her body slid off from Bobbie's back. She landed on a giant tree branch, suspended almost a half a mile high above the ground. Her hands trembled as she reached for her sword. Unsteady, and frightened, she did not know where Pantamanu would next strike.

Frantically she turned her head, but all she could see was a series of blurry images. With her eyesight impaired, she listened attentively, waiting for Pantamanu's next move. She did not wait long. Again, Pantamanu swooped down and struck her hard with his whip, this time leaving a bloody wound along her backside. Though the pain was unbearable it was her immense pride that was most deeply wounded.

Though Bobbie now appeared to be nothing more than a blur, she reached forward and grabbed his back, again ordering him to take flight. He did so, with Bellazar's legs swinging dangerously to the side, striking a patch of branches as the two moved uneasily to a nearby tree. Bellazar blinked her eyes several times and at last the vision in her right eye appeared to be returning. She could now see Pantamanu, not more than fifty feet from her current position, a demonic smile plastered on his face, as he readied himself for what was sure to be the final attack.

Bellazar looked about her. She barely had the necessary strength to hold her sword. "I must stay focused," she said aloud. "I cannot let him defeat me." She was in the process of steadying her mind when she looked up and saw Pantamanu riding his ladatop fast across the open spaces, quickly approaching her position. This time his sword was drawn and he was clearly intent on striking one final fatal blow against his most despised enemy.

Bellazar's head began to spin with a dizzying haze. As it did so, she dropped her sword, for with the loss of blood she was now finding it difficult to maintain a state of ready consciousness. She saw Pantamanu's approach and she realized that she could do nothing about it. With no other option, she released her grip and tumbled hard onto a branch that lay beneath her. The branch was wide enough for her to stand and she quickly moved back along the branch until she felt a new source of piercing pain, for as she moved toward the tree's trunk, she backed directly into a sharp, broken branch that stuck out from the tree like a sharp eager dagger.

Trapped, utterly defenseless, unable to move forward or backward, she saw Pantamanu, his sword drawn and swiftly approaching. Again, Bellazar had no alternative. She suddenly leapt from the branch. As Bellazar fell helplessly, the forward momentum brought Pantamanu's ladatop hard against the tree trunk. It collided with a powerful thud. As it did, the sharp dagger like broken branch instantly pierced Dolly's body. Dolly's eyes rolled back and then, with Pantamanu still strapped in his saddle, the ladatop fell, striking multiple branches as it fell, steadily downward, until if finally struck the ground, a half mile below with a terrible ferocity.

Pantamanu was killed instantly, a look of shock and disbelief eternally frozen on his face. As for Bellazar, she somehow managed to grab onto an extended branch. There she hung perilously for several tenuous seconds, her legs flailing as she valiantly attempted to pull herself back up onto the branch. She lacked the strength and would have fallen, but just as her grip began to loosen, she felt Bobbie's head nestling beneath her body. The injured ladatop had crawled down the tree and scaled along a protruding branch until it had reached Bellazar's position. With consummate skill, the ladatop helped Bellazar onto its back. Then, as she grabbed hold of its mane, Bobbie descended from the tree, for neither one was any longer fit for battle.

Chapter 82
Survival

Bellazar had no time to gloat over Pantamanu's death nor frankly did she have the inclination. "I am badly hurt," she told Bobbie. She was blind in one eye and had lost so much blood that she felt woozy and disoriented. In fact, her mind was so confused that she had yet to detect what was becoming obvious to all the other ladatop riders – the Kanaween Forest, lit by the falling cinders from the constant clash of lightening, was now fully ablaze!

High above the forest, two lightening bolts continued to collide with ferocious intensity. As they did sparks glittered in the air, before raining down on the trees below. These incendiary sparks ignited the tops of the tallest trees and the winds quickly carried these embers throughout the forest. Consequently, riders from both Arcanian aerial armies tried to move southward. As they did they noticed that a fire had commenced south and southwest of their positions, as well.

"The fire is spreading!" one alarmed ladatop rider declared. "We must evacuate the forest!"

Though few heard this soldier's call, others quickly shared his sentiment. In droves the riders herded their ladatops toward the grasslands to the east. Shortly thereafter, men on the backs of dazed ladatops emerged from the forest. "The entire forest is on fire!" one man shouted as he emerged from the wooded area. Men, who were still trying to save as many of the wounded on the battlefield as possible, now turned their medical attention to the multiple riders who emerged unexpectedly from the woods. "We have more injured," a young medic shouted as he ran toward a bloodied ladatop rider. As he did so, still other riders emerged.

With the sun setting, the yellowish haze of the rising flames took on a thoroughly hellish appearance. Inside the forest, Bellazar, wounded and confused, wandered aimlessly from tree to tree as the fires quickly spread all around her. "There is no way out," she finally told Bobbie. "The fire is everywhere!"

Bellazar was not used to admitting defeat, even when it was inevitable. "Carry me to the far trees," she cried out and Bobbie complied, swinging swiftly and sinuously through a frightening inferno. Occasionally, the sting of a burning ember singed the ladatop, but its resolve, like its rider's, remained undiminished. "We must move further west," Bellazar ordered. When they did they encountered still more obstacles. The fire was swirling and totally out of control, as additional lightening strikes continued to shed more glistening cinders from the harshly illuminated sky. Bellazar realized that she had moved too far inside the forest. "There is no escape," she said as she considered her remaining options. "There is still one last hope for survival. We must ride through the fires to get there," she commanded.

Bobbie showed no fear, leaping valiantly into the fiery conflagration, swinging boldly from tree to tree, while Bellazar held on for dear life, her legs often lifting completely off the ladatop's body and flying wildly in the air. As the two moved further inside the forest, trees that had stood for hundreds of cycles burned uncontrollably. Still Bobbie labored on. He reached for a vine and swung past a tree that burned with a red, hot intensity. He then reached for another vine, but this one was itself on fire. Though it carried him forward the ladatop could feel his grip loosening. Spotting a branch that was not yet on fire the ladatop diverted its damaged body to the branch's relative safety. There the two combatants rested for a few seconds, as they watched the fires spread throughout the forest.

"We must go down to the ground," Bellazar ordered. "It is far too dangerous up here." Bobbie agreed and moments later the ladatop was moving swiftly down the side of the immense Kanawa tree. As he did, smoke and cinders were everywhere. Bellazar coughed as she inhaled the toxic fumes from the spreading fire. "We haven't long to live," she said, thus encouraging Bobbie to move even faster. The ladatop needed no encouragement. It slid down the side of the tree much faster than usual, finally hitting the ground with a suddenness that threw Bellazar off his back and hard onto the ground. When she hit the ground she rolled over several times, but fortunately she did not lose consciousness.

Bobbie too was injured. He had hit the ground with such remarkable force that it fractured both of his hind legs. The ladatop was now incapable of movement. Bellazar crawled toward Bobbie and put her arms around the ladatop. "Oh Bobbie," she said with a mournful cry. Bobbie looked at Bellazar and then stroked her master's head with his right hand. Then, Bobbie closed his eyes, not yet dead, but awaiting the certainty of it, for the fires were now closing in all around them.

"I will not let you die," Bellazar shouted, her determination unfettered, despite the mounting evidence that they were doomed. "It is not far from here. You must come with me." She tugged on the ladatop and though Bobbie opened his eyes, he could not comply with his master's order. He simply did not have the strength to move another inch. Defeat did not come easily to Bellazar. "Please, crawl. It is not far from here. We can yet be saved." Bobbie could not use his hind legs but his forward hands were still powerful. With extraordinary effort, the ladatop pulled itself across the ground, with Bellazar always a step or two before it, determinedly encouraging Bobbie to "come this way." The two moved slowly until they finally reached a small opening among the trees. Bellazar then ran, though her movements were decidedly unsteady. She weaved, but kept her footing, until she arrived at a small patch of rocks and other debris. Falling to her hands and knees, she quickly threw the rocks aside, and then with a ferocious intensity she dug the dirt with her bare hands. "I will save us yet," she said as the smoke from the trees continued to engulf the area. Though her one good eye stung, and as the smoke began to enter her lungs, she finally excavated a rather ordinary looking object. It was a vase, with the image of a swirling vortex on its side. With the Oracle in her hands, she limped back toward Bobbie's prostrate body.

Flames now encircled Bellazar and she fought hard to remain conscious, for the smoke was now seeping ever deeper into her lungs. She coughed so hard that she almost dropped the Oracle on the ground. "Time has run out," she realized. With her hands weakening, she held the Oracle out before her body. She then held it so that both of them could gaze inside. As they did, a large burning branch fell directly on their position. The two felt their bodies ignite. Within seconds they would be dead. Fortunately, the transformation already had begun.

As their two bodies burned, Bellazar and Bobbie began to disintegrate, particle by particle. Soon, as the unrelenting fire consumed their earthly bodies, they realized that somehow they were still alive. Bellazar sensed a strange new universe of light, of altered sensations, of colors she had never before seen, of electrical impulses that surged through her very existence. Bobbie was there too, whole and apparently unharmed.

Bellazar could now sense multiple presences. There were farmers, soldiers, and yes, even Montama. There was something else, someone strange and unfamiliar to her. She heard it as a disembodied voice. "Mother, are you safe?"

Bellazar could not understand the reference, for she knew that her only daughter Me was safe and secure in the hands of relatives in the northern port city of Capo. "I don't understand," Bellazar said wearily, for she was not yet used to the weightless sensation of the Oracle chamber.

"Mother," the indistinct voice repeated.

"Who are you?" Bellazar asked, her mind thoroughly confused.

"I am your child."

"I don't understand," Bellazar said, as she tried to comprehend this strange new universe.

"My name is Nimrod. I am your child; the offspring of Bellazar and Pantamanu."

Bellazar felt so disoriented she was not sure what she had heard. Then, as she opened her mind to this new universe of ideas, she realized, "I am pregnant."

"You were when you entered the Oracle," Nimrod said. "I have never lived in the outside, *real* world. In fact, I have not yet developed a gender of my own. And remarkably, I am the first entity to ever be born exclusively within the Oracle." Then with a strange serene kindness the child whispered, "Don't worry, mother, I will take care of you."

Chapter 83
And Then There Was One

"My word," Nimrod whispered. "Bellazar was, she is, my mother! I never existed in the real world, not as a fully formed and breathing human, though I am indeed of human blood."

The Oracle

"Yes, Belicki," confessed, "you are. You have no human instincts, no sense of the real world, for everything that you are consists of what you have learned inside the Oracle. In that sense you are unique, for there is no other entity like you. You are as much a child of the Oracle as you are of Bellazar and Pantamanu."

"The pregnancy was in an early stage, not even separated from conception by an interval. Therefore, I had not yet developed as either a male or female. I therefore have no sense of what that means, but I can now sense some small measure of human feelings."

"They come not from you directly, but from the other Oracle entities," Belicki said. "For unlike the other Oracle entities, you have no form outside the Oracle, though you may be able to enter it through the mind of another."

Nimrod did not hear these last words, for memories were now beginning to freely stream back into Nimrod's consciousness. Though Belicki continued to tell his tale, Nimrod no longer needed to listen, for it now knew what it was and what its ultimate purpose was. "I do have a destiny," Nimrod realized at last. "I now know what my purpose is!"

Contended at last, Nimrod did not further interrupt as Belicki continued.

As the Kanaween Forest burned, Kublatitan and I continued to battle for supremacy amidst the evening stars. As we did the sky lit up with an ethereal radiance. Soldiers on the field below looked up in astonishment as the evening sky was fully illuminated by the burning fires of the Kanaween Forest and a succession of super charged electrical explosions. At first it had looked light mere lightening bolts. In time it morphed into something far more terrible.

"The sky is on fire," Grandafier said as he peered toward the heavens. And in fact, at times it did appear as if the sky itself was burning uncontrollably: for my rage was limitless, my hatred fully naked and exposed.

As the soldiers withdrew as quickly as possible from the conflagration in the forest, the injured were placed on carts, horses, even on the backs of oxen and ladatops. As people and beasts ran southward or eastward to avoid the unholy specter flashing brilliantly in the sky above, the heavens continued to explode in vibrant colors of red, orange and yellow.

Most of the survivors did not know what to make of this otherworldly site. Grandafier alone knew that it was a battle unlike anything that had

462

ever been seen by the likes of mankind. Through Montama he sensed that Kublatitan and I were in a mortal struggle. Only one of us would survive and as we charged relentlessly against each other we expended so much energy that people had to avert their eyes from the successive blinding flashes of light, lest it permanently blind them.

As the men evacuated the battlefield, no one cared who had been victorious. "There are no spoils of war," Grandafier said, "just the residue of pure madness."

Grandafier worked feverishly with others to get Montama's body on the back of a cart. When General Garr's body was located, he too was thrown next to Montama and then horses pulled the cart as quickly as possible away from the unholy battlefield. As the cart moved at full speed, hundreds of men and women ran as quickly as they could, dropping their weapons and any other possible encumbrances. A few, already exhausted by battle, ran until they could move no more. As for the dead, even the vultamires were too frightened to feast on their carcasses.

And yet we two titans continued to strike against each other, colliding with a vitriolic force that created a sonic boom powerful enough to knock hundreds of people to the bloodied and death riddled ground. "When will this hell ever end?" a woman shouted, as she tried to right herself. As we two titans struck yet another time, the woman again lost her balance and fell hard face first onto the ground. Finally, one of Montama's soldiers picked her up in his arms and carried her away as she wept uncontrollably.

Throughout it all I sensed that I was prevailing. "You cannot hate me as much as I hate you," I thought as I again forced my full energy forward. As I did it intersected with Kublatitan's own mighty electrical charge. The result was yet another in an endless series of explosions of light and fire.

In time I came to realize that Kublatitan's hatred had expanded exponentially. "I am more like Belicki now, full of hatred and eager for destruction," the mighty Taewokan sensed as he forced his positive energy to intersect yet again with my powerful negative charge. Then, in a truly horrifying moment, Kublatitan realized, "I am no longer any different than Belicki. The two of us have become one in the same. Ready to destroy anything that stands in our way."

Consumed with hatred, irrational and unstable, Kublatitan's positive energy charged forward with such an unremitting ferocity that this time, instead of one quick electrical charge, the skies remained lit for a full minute or more. A few people, who were nearest to the blast, were instantly incinerated. Scores of dead bodies on the battlefield also spontaneously ignited. Rocks lit up with a red, hot glow, as Kanawa trees exploded, one after another, shooting fiery discharges high into the upper atmosphere. Then, with a suddenness that was both frightening and shocking, the lightening blasts ceased, though smoke and fire from the trees continued to fill the night air, polluting it, making it hard for the survivors of the battle to breath.

They continued to flee for safety, and as they did, the war between the two titans finally came to an abrupt end. For as Montama had declared, only one could return to the Oracle; but which one would it be?

Though he was still unconscious, Montama sensed a profound transformation. Then in his mind's eye he saw one distinct and solitary entity limp back toward the Oracle's matrix. But the entity was entirely unfamiliar, for neither Belicki nor Kublatitan any longer existed. In its place was a strange looking creature, its skin both green and red, its body slim but hunched over, with one purple eye and another one of pure white light. The entity was confused and thoroughly exhausted, its energy almost completely spent.

"Who are you?" Montama asked, as he stared at this deranged aberration.

"We are Kublecki," the new entity responded. "We are here to serve the new king."

Instantly, Montama sensed the Oracle's fear and exasperation. "This is unprecedented," Bevell thought. "A merging of two distinct entities. This has never happened before. We have no idea what this transformation will do to the fabric of the Oracle universe."

"Given the terrible destruction that these two entities already have unleashed, it cannot help but be an improvement that they are now one," Montama declared, though he did not yet realize the significance of what had just happened, for if he had, he would have shuttered with fear. For with the elimination of Kublatitan, the Oracle universe lost its balance.

The other entities shared Bevell's concerns. "This makes things very complicated," one entity whispered. "The Oracle will be in flux for a long, long time."

"Don't worry," a new voice declared. "We are all here to serve the king," Nimrod said with complete innocence.

Kublecki immediately sensed something strange about Nimrod's thoughts. Though Kublecki was now one entity, his mind was scattered and schizophrenic. "We will have many new competitors for the king's attention," Kublecki finally realized, his mind at last capable of conveying one coherent thought. "And personally I do not trust this Nimrod." Then Kublecki added, "Neither do I."

Chapter 84
The Assassins

Belicki's voice fell suddenly quite silent, for Nimrod realized that since Belicki no longer existed he was incapable of continuing the narration. Even as Count Belicki's voice faded, another proper and stentorian voice emerged, one that was completely unknown to Nimrod. This mysterious new voice told the next chapter in the Oracle tale.

Lord Tantamount and Hontallo heard nothing of the ongoing battle at the Kanaween Forest, except that is for the thunderous aftershocks resulting from the mighty electrical charges as Count Belicki and Kublatitan did battle high above the Arcanian sky. The lighting bolts struck with such brutal force that they shook the entire passra and the discharges were so powerful that they were felt as far away as the mysterious Land of the Taewokans.

The lord and his son were utterly oblivious to the details of these battles, for they had been reduced to the state of abject prisoners, confined with respect and proper decorum in their own home, but still guarded constantly by as many as twelve of General Garr's soldiers, mostly older men who had served the general for decades. To their credit these guards were scrupulously courteous, allowing the lord and his son to work in the garden or to go on long supervised walks inside Tantamount's walled estate. Despite these superficial pleasantries, the lord and his son understood that they were marked men. They knew the secret of General Garr's genocidal treachery and if Montama were victorious, it was plain reason that Garr would not let them live, no matter what Montama's inclinations might be. And if Montama died, Pantamanu or Bellazar would surely have them executed, as well. So whether it is a planned accident or an outright assassination, the two men instinctively knew how their fate would be resolved.

They therefore waited dispassionately for any news from the Kanaween Forest. It came shortly after midnight on the fourth unit of their confinement in the form of a foreboding knock on the lord's front door. Hontallo, unable to sleep, lay in his bed listening attentively. He heard a man with a deep baritone voice intone quite malevolently, "We have come for the prisoners."

The guard responded. His muffled words were unintelligible. Hontallo, dressed only in his undergarments, moved quietly to his bedroom door. Though he did not put his ear to the door, he listened attentively. He again heard the stranger speak. "They are to come with us now." It was an insistent demand, an order, and to Hontallo it sounded like the pronouncement of their doom.

"Where will you take them?" the guard asked.

"To the assassins," the stranger said coldly.

Hontallo flinched tangibly, his eyes blinking, his face horribly contorted, when he heard the last word. Though he had fully expected this moment would come, deep inside his heart he had convinced himself that Montama could never purposely harm his family. "He will eventually see things right," Hontallo convinced himself, thus providing a slender reed upon which to base his hope that reason might yet be made to prevail. As he listened to the stranger, Hontallo realized that all of his rationalizations were mere fantasies. "Father was right – there is no way they will allow us to live." Almost in shock, Hontallo turned and walked back to his bed. Without a word he dressed, for he did not want to be assassinated in his present nearly naked state. "I will die with dignity," he thought, though his mind was a blur, for he still could not comprehend how his dear brother could be the source of such vile treachery.

As Hontallo buttoned his shirt, the door to his bedroom suddenly sprang open with a frightening force. One of the elderly guards, a man who had been exceedingly kind to Hontallo, now stood before him. "It is time," he said with a mournful expression, for in just a few short units the guards had come to like and respect their two prisoners. Hontallo's shoulders slouched as his eyes stared vacantly ahead, for he understood the import of these three words.

Despite the late hour, Lord Tantamount was still in his study. He had not slept well for some time, for his mind was constantly tortured with feelings of guilt and remorse. He had convinced himself that it was he who had failed, that he had not been a good and attentive father. He had been too distant, too unemotional, and not nearly as responsive to young Montama as he should have been. He had not seen the signs of Montama's discontent or of his own wife's duplicity. "I do not deserve to live," the lord concluded. Though he fervently hoped that somehow Hontallo's life might still be spared, he was convinced that he deserved to die. Thus, when the guards came for him, he merely nodded his head in regal assent and then followed obsequiously, fully prepared to meet his destiny.

The two prisoners were led to one of the lord's fine carriages. It was made of black telcata wood, with gold engravings on each side. Completely covered to protect its riders from the often harsh elements, it had padded and comfortable seats and could accommodate up to six passengers with ease. As Tantamount and Hontallo stepped into the carriage they heard the man with a baritone voice give the order, "Take them to the designated area."

"Where is that?" Hontallo asked meekly.

"That is none of your concern," the man bellowed as Lord Tantamount obediently, without any sign of resistance, climbed into the carriage that he had last ridden to Teta for King Benton's memorable funeral.

Hontallo sat in the back of the covered carriage next to his father. He flinched again when the doors were shut, for there was finality to it, a sense that he would never again see his beloved home. As they felt the horses begin to move, Lord Tantamount merely looked over at his son, his eyes tired, his soul restless. "Father," Hontallo said quietly, though there was no guard in the back to overhear their conversation. "We may still be able to escape. I have a plan." The lord smiled with a weary and fatalistic resignation. Then, he gently put his hand on his son's shoulder and closed his eyes.

The carriage moved spiritedly throughout the night. Though black shades were pulled down over the windows to obscure the prisoners' view, Hontallo believed that they were moving eastward. Though he could not see outside, he knew these roads quite well. By morning he was able to catch a quick glimpse through a small crack near the top of the door. As the carriage came to a halt he heard the mysterious stranger with the baritone voice declare, "We need to change horses." Peering through the small opening, Hontallo could see that the man was monstrously tall, standing more than six and a half feet. He had a muscular frame and though Hontallo could not see his face, he judged that the man was probably no more than thirty.

Hontallo also saw a blacksmith and what appeared to be a group of rather undistinguished looking men. "They don't look like soldiers," he told his father, who exhausted from the ride was barely aware of his surroundings.

Hontallo listened as the tall man and the blacksmith conversed. "We have to get them back on the road within the next half hour. They must be moved as expeditiously as possible to the Anawana Swamplands."

"The swamplands!" Hontallo thought. It was the perfect place to kill and dispose of the two men. Their bodies would never be found. Turning and looking at his father Hontallo said aloud, "I think we are at the Temannay Village. If so we are at least a full unit's ride from the swamplands.

Sitting in silence, Lord Tantamount listened. His tortured mind now was barely functional. Hontallo gently stroked his father's forehead, as tears came to the young man's eyes. "It is not your fault father. You cannot blame yourself. Montama acted with his eyes wide open."

Tantamount stared ahead, but this time he spoke. "I should have stopped him," he said. "Now all of Arcania is in peril and it is my fault."

Before Hontallo could speak another word, the carriage unexpectedly began to move again. Hontallo peered through the narrow crack and saw people milling about, watching the lord's carriage move eastward. For several minutes Hontallo saw various familiar landmarks and then, as the roads became rockier and bumpier, the carriage moved out of the village and into the open farmland, always moving eastward. At noontime, the carriage again came to a rest. "We have reached the Commeru River," Hontallo surmised, but Lord Tantamount was now fast asleep.

"Where is the raft?" one man shouted impatiently.

"Hold your horses," another responded briskly. "It will be here in a few minutes."

"Take the prisoners out of the carriage," another man ordered. Within a few seconds the carriage door sprung open. The sudden beams of light blinded Hontallo who instinctively covered his eyes. "You are to eat here," the man with the baritone voice said as he led Hontallo and then a weary Lord Tantamount to a nearby rustic cabin where they were allowed to relieve themselves, wash their faces, and drink a small bowl of watery soup, with bread that was stale and unappetizing. Tantamount barely touched his food, while Hontallo ravenously devoured his own. The young prisoner even had the temerity to ask for seconds. "Why not?" an old man with one leg said, as he generously filled Hontallo's mug, even providing Hontallo with a piece a tasty slice of warm, buttered bread.

"I thank you for your kindness," Hontallo said, as he dipped the bread into his soup. The cabin was indistinct, like one of many at various crossing points along the Commeru River. Men made respectable livings ferrying individuals on small rafts across the river. These men looked different somehow. Hontallo did not know why, but these men did not look like they belonged here.

After a respite of no more than thirty minutes, the two prisoners were again ordered back into the carriage. Hontallo knew this might be their last chance to escape. He could run and dive into the river. Its currents were particularly strong at this particular juncture. His body would quickly be carried downstream, though he would have to survive blade sharp rocks and the river's often-turbulent waters before he would arrive safely at the sandy shoals further south. Even if he survived, what would happen to his father? Hontallo thought about escape, but quickly reconsidered. "I will not leave my father behind to die alone," he promised.

So, the two men obediently returned to the carriage. They felt it sway uneasily as it was ferried by strong ropes across the Commeru River. Then, after they arrived on the river's eastern shore, the carriage again moved vigorously forward. Hontallo closed his eyes, for it would take at least another twelve to sixteen hours to reach the perimeter of the Anawana Swamplands.

As he slept he dreamed of his brother and the joyful times they had spent together camping at Mt. Sendil. "We will always be together," he remembered Montama saying. "Nothing can ever separate us." When the carriage hit a particularly deep pothole, Hontallo was suddenly and rudely awakened from his reverie. He rubbed his eyes and then looked out the crack in the window. It was night again. By leaning down on one knee he could see hundreds of stars in the sky, but otherwise he was unclear of his location. About an hour later, however, he smelled a wretched stench and began to hear the croaking sounds of frogs and other nocturnal reptiles. Then without warning, the carriage came to a halt.

Hontallo again listened intently. "Get the prisoners," he heard one man shout and within a few moments the carriage door again sprung open. "Come with me," another man said with great courtesy, bowing politely as he spoke. Hontallo reached over and awakened his father. Confused, it took a few seconds for the lord to realize that the carriage was no longer moving.

"Step outside," the man with the baritone voice now declared with a more menacing inflection.

The Oracle

Hontallo's legs felt rubbery, from inactivity, and he struggled as he stepped out of the carriage and onto the soggy ground before the Anawana Swampland. Lord Tantamount had to be helped from the carriage, for his body was frail and unresponsive. When he finally stood on the semi-solid ground, the lord looked all around trying to comprehend where he was. "I must get to the garden," he finally announced. "I have not pruned the dancing flowers." Then as he stared at Hontallo Tantamount announced, "Montama loves the dancing flowers. They are his favorite."

Hontallo put his arm around his father's side and hugged him. Then with a sad kindness, he whispered, "Don't worry father, I have taken care of them for you."

Lord Tantamount looked at his son with a crooked smile. "Did you pull out all the weeds, as well?" he asked innocently.

"Yes father," Hontallo said, as he stared into his father's weary, bloodshot eyes.

"This way," the tall man with the baritone voice ordered.

Hontallo helped his father, feeble with age and guilt, toward a small rowboat. The two of them then sat down at one end, while the tall man and another guard, a short fat man with the tattoo of a galloping horse on his forehead, sat across from them. "You may rest," the tall man said. "It will be long after morning before we arrive."

Hontallo was tempted to ask where they were going, but he really no longer wanted to know. As he sat next to his father, he watched as the two men steadily paddled the boat into the dangerous waters of the Anawana Swampland. As they did Hontallo heard the annoying call of a small pack of Anawana Yapyaps. Then he heard the dull sound of the oars fervently and repeatedly striking the water.

The swamplands were treacherous, filled with dangerous reptiles and even patches of quicksand. Hontallo thought back to a scene long ago, when he had watched a man die horribly in the swamplands. "I watched his body sliver down into the deadly quicksand. The more he struggled the faster the quicksand consumed him, until finally all I could see was the very top of his bald head, then nothing at all."

Hontallo shivered, for the night air was cold, but also because he did not want to die the same ignominious a death as had that poor man. He wondered how long he could hold his breath. Then he thought, if it comes to that, I will flip the boat and all of us will die.

For hours the row boat moved slowly eastward, occasionally moving to the north to avoid a small patch of tree covered islands. The croaking of the frogs became so repetitive that after a while Hontallo could no longer hear them. Instead his thoughts returned to his brother. "Something evil changed him," he realized. "It must be the Oracle." Then with a fierce anger Hontallo cussed, "I would destroy that damn contraption if I had the chance."

"Destroy what?" the tall man asked.

Hontallo did not realize that he had spoken aloud. "Nothing," he said as he looked down at his feet. The tall man laughed and then continued rowing the boat ever eastward. Throughout the night the men battled every form of insect imaginable. Mosquitoes, swarms of black flies, and even the dreaded flying kulcabug, a leach that can suck the blood out of a small animal in but a few hours' time: several of them flew around the men's legs, arms, and throats. After a few hours in the swamplands Hontallo decided that death would not be such a terrible prospect after all.

And yet the swamplands extended seemingly forever. By the time the morning sun rose there was still no land anywhere in sight. "Why don't they kill us here?" Hontallo wondered on many occasions. "They easily could dispose of our bodies. Why do they need to go so far into the swamplands?"

At about noontime, Hontallo finally got his answer. "There is the shoreline," the tall man shouted, his voice competing with the myriad natural sounds of running water, chirping birds, and croaking frogs. Then more firmly the tall man instructed, "Over there!" He pointed with a firm thrust of his right hand. "That is where we need to be." The other guard, the man with the strange tattoo, nodded his head, and the two oarsmen skillfully turned the boat so that it was now facing in a northeasterly direction. Hontallo turned and saw a distant shoreline. There were trees, but there was so much fog he could not fathom any other details of the areas topography.

Hontallo reached over and gently tapped his father's shoulder. Lord Tantamount had been in a dream state, neither fully awake nor asleep. He was therefore slow to realize that they fast were approaching land.

The tall man was the first to exit the boat. He waded through the treacherous waters, dragging the boat toward the shore behind him. After he beached the small vessel, he ordered everyone, "Out of the boat."

Hontallo again helped his father, who seemed to be growing feebler with every passing minute. "This way father," he said, as they cautiously stepped out of the boat.

Now on soggy land, the tall man ordered them to move with him. "We have a full unit's walk from here."

Hontallo could not stand the tension any longer. With a surprising vehemence he demanded, "Where are you taking us?"

The tall man smiled obliquely. "You will find out soon enough."

For hours at a time the small group of four men walked through mud and muck until they finally reached higher ground. "We must climb here," the tall man said as he pointed toward a path that led up into the Tacanawana Mountain range. Completely mystified as to the reason for this tediously long journey, Hontallo and Lord Tantamount climbed ever higher for several hours, resting only occasionally. Again night fell. The men were exhausted beyond all reason, yet still they moved forward. "We have little time left," the tall man said. "We must continue to move quickly."

Tantamount's strength finally gave out and Hontallo and the tattooed guard essentially carried the lord, letting him rest between them on their respective shoulders. The tall man stopped periodically, scanned some sort of hand drawn chart, and then ordered the men to move east, then north, then east again. As the four men snaked their way ever higher into the Tacanawana Mountains Hontallo wondered, "What is he up to? If he is an assassin he could have killed us long ago. Why is he keeping us alive?"

The answer was long in coming. After several more hours and deep into the night, the four men finally arrived at a point more than a mile above ground level. At this elevation the temperatures were frigid and snow was now packed all around them. "We cannot long survive in these temperatures," the tall man said. "If we do not move more quickly we will all die." After walking a few more hours the tall man spotted a lone cave in the distance. "We must go there," he ordered and the four men, all of them now well past the point of total exhaustion, limped forward, before finally collapsing on the cave's warm and snowless floor.

"Why are we here?" Hontallo demanded. "You must finally be able to tell us something."

The tall man did not speak. Instead, Hontallo heard a strange, disembodied voice declare, "You are at a place called Zanzaska Pass."

Unlike his brother, Hontallo was not used to the sound of entity voices emerging surreptitiously from the netherworld. He therefore was startled and frightened beyond imagining, worried that his mind may have gone suddenly quite mad. When he looked at the tall man he realized that he too had heard the same voice and was ardently searching for its source.

"What is Zanzaska Pass?" Hontallo asked, speaking each word slowly and deliberately.

Again he heard the voice. "It is the pass Zanzaska traversed more than a century ago."

Hontallo stared at his father but the old man was completely unresponsive. Then he looked at the tall man. "What is it?" he asked. "Is this some sort of enchanted cave?" The tall man said nothing.

Hontallo thought for a moment. "Who are you?" he finally asked, with great reluctance, for he greatly feared the response.

For a few moments there was nothing but silence, then he heard my disembodied voice speak again. "You must go to the Land of Taewokans. The tall man, Traito, and the man with the tattoo of the horse on his forehead will serve as your guide and protectors."

"I don't understand," Hontallo said desperately. "Why are we to go to Taewoka?"

For a few seconds he listened and then he heard the response. "There, buried in caves like this one, there are five other Oracles, each one containing the wisdom of Kublatitan. You must find one of them and bring it back to Arcania." The mysterious voice then summoned a golden orb, which appeared in mid air. As it rotated, Hontallo admired its immaculate splendor. The voice then added, "This orb will protect you as you move through these dangerous mountains. Keep it with you at all times."

Hontallo reached out and grabbed the orb. As he touched it, he felt a spark of electricity envelop his entire body. As his body shivered, the voice urged caution. "You must never be separated from this orb. It will protect you from much harm. There will be great danger ahead. Still you must succeed."

"Why?" Hontallo asked.

"The survival of Arcania depends upon it." The voice was growing weak and it began to trail off toward the end of the sentence and then, there was total silence.

Abruptly Hontallo turned and called out to the tall man. "Why didn't you tell us who you were?"

Traito stared intently at Hontallo. Calmly, without any emphasis, he responded dispassionately, "Because until now I wasn't sure if my job was to protect you or to kill you. I would do either if I was ordered to."

Hontallo accepted the explanation without further question. "Then I am glad that you were ordered to protect us."

Traito smiled and closed his eyes. "It makes no difference to me either way." Almost instantaneously he started to snore violently. As he did so Hontallo stared at the golden orb he now held in his hand. "I have so many questions," he said softly. Hontallo, like the other men was totally exhausted. He needed rest and then the men would need to find provisions, for they had hardly eaten in two units time. And then, if he were to actually obey this strange disembodied voice, he would have to do the impossible. He would have to find his way through a treacherous, some said impassable mountain range, travel to an entirely unknown, uncharted land, filled no doubt with all sorts of strange beings, and there, somewhere buried in a cave, locate one of the Oracles, not even knowing what it was or what it looked like. And then, after all that, he would have to return with it to Arcania.

Daunted by this seemingly impossible task, Hontallo found a somewhat comfortable spot to lie down. As he did he muttered, "This is crazy. I don't know who commands me or why I have been asked to do this impossible task." Then he looked over and saw Traito's hulking frame, heaving mightily as he snored. Hontallo was certain that the tall powerful man had been sent here to make sure that the mysterious command was obeyed. But why was he tasked with finding another Oracle and what was its purpose? These were questions that Hontallo could not yet even begin to answer.

Chapter 85
A New Hope?

Nimrod listened as the mysterious voice faded and as a new more vibrant and feminine one replaced it. It took a moment for Nimrod to realize that Truellen was now relating the last details of the succession war.

It had been several units since my son lost consciousness and much to his credit Grandafier had diligently stood watch every single, solitary minute. He attended to General Garr's badly mutilated body as well, though he realized that there was no way the general's left arm could be saved. "It is almost completely severed at the shoulder," Grandafier said, trying not to lose his composure in front of the woman who helped him attend to Montama's wounds.

"We must move them back to Pellaville," Grandafier had said. "They will get better care there." Grandafier then rode with them, constantly attending to the two men's medical needs as best he could. Periodically, Montama moaned but still showed no sign of consciousness. A few hours after the cart commenced its journey back to Pellaville, General Garr suddenly looked up at Grandafier and asked, "Did we prevail?"

Grandafier was pleased to see that Garr was conscious. He spoke softly, for he did not wish to rile the old warrior. "Yes, the battle is ours. If he survives, Montama will be Arcania's new king."

"If he survives?" Garr asked, suddenly concerned. He turned his head and saw Montama's body lying next to his own. "How is he?"

Grandafier swallowed hard, then answered. "He spoke but once, pointing vehemently toward the heavens. He has shown no sign yet of consciousness."

Garr closed his eye and forthrightly declared, "He will live. Like you and me, he is a survivor."

The next morning the men arrived at the gate of Lord Tantamount's now abandoned estate. Shortly thereafter Montama was returned to his own bed. After several units, he finally awoke. Startled to be back in his familiar room, for an instant he thought the entire past cycle had been nothing more than a bad dream. When he tried to move, however, the pain seared throughout his body. He was covered in sundry bandages, his arms and legs ached, and there were strange splotches all over his skin. "What has happened to me?" he asked suddenly remembering the battle at the grasslands.

Joyful that Montama was conscious Grandafier quickly ran to his protégé's side. "Your majesty, you are finally awake."

"Your majesty?" Montama asked, startled to hear that he had indeed prevailed.

"Yes, as soon as you are well enough, we will go to Teta for your coronation." Then with exemplary pride Grandafier announced, "You are now King Montama!"

Montama said nothing, for as strange as it might seem, he had thought little about what he actually would do if he ever became king. So difficult had been the quest for glory that he had never actually had to think about what sort of a king he might make. Montama suddenly became quite unsettled. "What happened to General Garr? Did he survive?"

Grandafier looked down at Montama with the gentle eyes of a kindly uncle. "He was badly hurt. They had to amputate his left arm. After the surgery, he looked up at me and said; every time I go to war I leave another part of my body behind. Soon there will be nothing left of me."

"And what did you say?" Montama asked, though his voice was still weak.

"I told him that he still had another arm and two legs left and to that he said, then I guess the Emperor of Relatania will have to face the fact that that I have many battles left in this battered old body." Montama smiled, though when he did the pain surged throughout his entire frame from head to toe. "The doctors have told me that you will have to rest here for at least another fortnight."

Grandafier watched Montama's eyes flutter and then close. Then suddenly, the young king remembered something of great importance. Montama opened his eyes and asked, "Are my father and brother well?"

Grandafier had feared this question. "They were taken away by a man named Traito, a known assassin. That is all we know."

Montama could not bear the thought and so he merely closed his eyes and went to sleep. As he did, Grandafier wondered if Lord Tantamount and Hontallo's deaths had been painless.

Chapter 86
A Final Revelation

It took almost a full interval for Montama to recover. A search was ordered to determine the fate of Lord Tantamount and Hontallo and the lord's carriage was located, floating in the Anawana Swamplands. Montama was distraught when he was told that there was virtually no possibility that their bodies would ever be recovered.

For three units time thereafter Montama sat in his favorite garden, on the hard cement bench, near the dancing flowers. There on one particularly splendid afternoon, he looked up and saw my outline. He rejoiced that he could see his dear mother picking a flower and carrying it to his side. As I walked closer my glistening body fully materialized and when I sat down to next to him on the wooden bench, I appeared as young and vibrant as I ever had been in life. Truellen handed the clipped dancing flower to her son. "Here, it is! Your favorite flower."

"Hontallo loved this garden. So did father!" Montama said as he choked back the tears.

Though I was an Oracle entity, I felt the same agonizing pain and guilt as my son. "It is my fault," I confessed as I stared away from the dancing flower. "I was the one who encouraged you to go to Kankabar to find a mighty army. I was the one who told you that you were meant to be king. So fixed was I on making you king, that I never even thought to ask the Oracle or Count Belicki if there would be a price to pay. And now that we know what it is, the price is simply unimaginable." Montama said nothing, for he felt uncomfortable whenever he expressed his feelings in front of another. Sensing his despair, I gently touched my son's forehead. "You are still a bit warm. But you are recovering and soon you *will* be king."

Montama looked up and stared at me. "And what new curses will that power bring?" he asked, not in the least impressed by his accomplishment, in fact wishing fervently that he had never sought the highest office in the land.

"I will not lie to you," I said.

"That would be a first," Montama snapped, his voice dripping with sarcasm.

I now stared at my son, forcing him to look directly into my eyes. "I have kept another secret from you for far too long. But now that you are king you will need to know why I could never marry King Benton."

"Must I know?" Montama asked dismissively, hoping that I would not say another word.

"Yes," I said, convinced that my secret would cause my son considerable grief in the many intervals to come. "I could not marry King Benton because of my father, who died long before you were born."

Montama stared intensely at me. "You never told me about my grandfather. You only said that he died when he you were still very young."

I nodded my head in a show of determined affirmation. "And that is true. But what I did not tell you was that my father was a Bogul." Montama stared intently into his mother's eyes, still white with the light of the Oracle's essence, and as he shivered nervously, I added with a slight tremor in my voice, "That means Montama, that you too are a Bogul!"

THE END
of
BOOK ONE

Richard Wayne Waterman
Author

Richard Wayne Waterman is a Political Scientist with specialties in the American Presidency, the Bureaucracy, the Courts, and the Environment. He currently is a professor of Political Science at the University of Kentucky, Lexington where he has taught for nine years. He has a PhD from the University of Houston, has published widely in the field of Political Science, has served as President of the Southwest Political Science Association, won the Laverne Burchfield Award from the journal Public Administration Review, testified before the Senate Committee on the Environment and Public Works, and was interviewed for CNN, including its prime time special "Fit To Lead."

He also has published eight books as well as articles in such academic journals as the American Political Science Review, American Journal of Political Science, the Journal of Politics, Presidential Studies Quarterly, Legislative Studies Quarterly, Law and Society Review, Electoral Studies, Public Administration Review, Journal of Public Administration Research and Theory, Journal of Policy Analysis and Management, and the Social Science Quarterly. He has been awarded a grant by the National Science Foundation, served as chair of the University of Kentucky Department of Political Science, and presently lives in Kentucky with his partner and two dogs. Most important of all he is a life long Boston Red Sox fan.

Sendil Nathan
Design and Illustrations

Sendil has over 23 years of experience in design, management, technology and information systems. As a Catalyst for Change he has consistently made his clients and audience to think and left these places in a better state than they would have ever without him.

He has redesigned large US based transnational organizations in the private sector as well as US governmental organizations to Capitalize on the Information Economy and charted the transition to the demanding changes in the structure and operations of these firms to meet the unprecedented demands and Metamorphosis over the last Two Decades that have been experienced in the seismically changing environment for numerous entities in the S&P and Fortune 100 and their collective networks that include Charles Schwab, Intel, Patriot Missiles, Xerox PARC, Westinghouse, SuperConductor-Supercollider Nuclear Research Project, Resolution Trust Corporation, AT&T, Bechtel, Adobe and California Courts of Appeals & Supreme Courts to name a few.

Design is his first nature.

Over the years, he has acquired a deep- seated understanding and fluency of history, culture, politics, free market, globalization and investment acumen. Outside of design, management and technology he's interested in film, documentary, art, history and architecture.

http://www.iArchitect.Org

CPSIA information can be obtained at www.ICGtesting.com
Printed in the USA
239417LV00002B/1/P